SHADOWS OF THE MUSIC INDUSTRY

WRITTEN BY:

MICHAEL HUR

SHADOWS OF THE MUSIC INDUSTRY

I would like to thank Jesus Christ, my wife Pamela, and all true believing Christians everywhere.

Welcome to the book of Shadows of the Music Industry. This book is an account of the untold history regarding artists and events of the music industry. In this book we explore the stories of Satanism, the occult, mind control, cover-ups and the lives and the deaths of various musical artists from the 30's through the 2000's and into our time. The book takes an exploration into these aspects that surround the lives of these artists. The stories presented here are unauthorized and also based upon testimony, case-files, court and law enforcement records and actual clear facts. The book takes a Christian view point of subjects not talked about in churches, or in the media. It is a book that is a must read for fans of the music industry. It is also an important book for anyone who still believes in a higher character for all the human race.

TABLE OF CONTENTS

Chapter 1

The beginning of the influence of the modern music industry is something many people should look into. Those of a Christian faith should know the information of what was told about the start of popular music in America, and its influence around the world. It is a fact Rock n' Roll music came from Rhythm and Blues music.

Many Church groups in that time spoke about Satan being a prime influence in Rhythm and Blues music while its defenders state that; Rhythm and Blues only spoke about the real conditions of many poor people, and the kind of lives they lived. So in understanding, what the Bible says about the ways of Satan did Satan really climb all over the influence of the music Rhythm and Blues?

Major record companies in connection to the Hollywood image were willing to sign any act that could perform the kind of Blues that was popular in the underground or barn club scene. They saw the amount of money that could be made by selling these records, and making these acts famous among white and black customers. Many of these acts were already famous when they were signed but were not making a lot of money until the record companies started to promote their music and image.

As they were doing so many Church groups, and insiders on the scene began to make some very strange statements about these artists. The statements they made came from their testimony that a lot of the Rhythm and Blues artists were involved with Satanism and magic. Some stated that many of them made deals with the devil for fame and money. They stated that not all of the Blues artists did this. There were many who expressed a natural gift to play the music while others were engaged in devil worship. So is this true were their artists engaged in devil worship, and secret pacts with Satan while playing the popular form of music at the time? That is a question that many will have to decide for themselves. One thing is clear that in the teachings of the Bible, when you compare the lifestyles of the artists and the music and its understanding there is a satanic element in Rhythm and Blues music.

Rock n' Roll also has strong satanic elements in its music. Rock n' Roll is a child of Rhythm and Blues music. Rhythm and Blues music has glorified drunkenness, lust, womanizing, cheating, gambling, drugs, violence, violence against women, and depravity. Other songs sung about encounters with evil spirits, and the influence that the devil had upon them. One wonders that if the music did not promote satanic elements then why are satanic elements present in a lot of the works of these artists and their music? Could it be that the Church groups, and their ministers who spoke against the music, and stated that music should be used to honor Jesus Christ were in fact right about that statement? As Christians why would we be against that statement by defending such music that is promoting things the Bible speaks against? Could there be something wrong in the way we see what is good or bad about music today and yesterday?

Many black and white American ministers spoke about the self-destructive messages of Rhythm and Blues music. Some of them used to play the music at clubs and barn shows. One of these ministers was a man named Gary Davis who became famous in that scene of Rhythm and Blues.

Davis stated that after living an immoral life while being a Blues artist he decided to give his life to Jesus Christ. When he did so he began to tell his testimony about the evils of that lifestyle, and how other artists were involved with satanic rituals. Gary Davis believed that any style of music when used right can be used to move people for GOD. But the style of popular Blues, Davis stated, did not move people for GOD but for violence, sex, and drugs. Davis stated that the barn party scene was filled with lust and drugs. People drank hard, and throughout the night they would shoot up heroin, and artists would openly have sex with other men's wives and underage girls. The people who went to the parties were looking to do these things as well. People spoke loud and mean, and laughed at things they should not have been laughing about.

The most talked about Blues artist that many Blues artists spoke about being very involved with satanic worship was a man named Robert Johnson. Robert Johnson's guitar playing, and his music is believed to have been used as the form that would create the Rock n' Roll sound and style of lyrics. His songs are believed to have been greatly used in the development of the Rock n' Roll sound and feel.

The story behind Robert Johnson is of a person who took a dark path in life, and according to those who personally knew him, stated that he sold his soul to the devil to play better than any Blues artist out there. Robert Johnson never denied this, and sometimes to his close friends he would brag about his deal with Satan. It is stated of Robert Johnson by those in the Blues scene of that time that Robert was not a gifted musician naturally but was very drawn to the Blues scene, and wanted very badly to be part of it.

In order to be an insider in that scene you had to know how to play, and you had to be good enough to be accepted as a Blues artist. It was stated of Robert that he imaged himself as a Blues artist but it was only in his imagination that in truth he did not know how to play, and was not even trained in how to play guitar. Robert would not be denied however, and so he began to show up at the shows, and began asking people to give him a quick course in how to play some guitar licks.

After showing Robert a thing or two, Robert wanted to be part of the circle of Blues artists, and so one day Robert, in his not too bright thinking, got on stage to prove to the others what he could do with a guitar.

The artists who were there that night spoke about the fact when Robert began playing he was so horrible that people began to boo him, and wanted to rush him off stage. After Robert was forced from the stage he in bitterness left, and he began to wander around the dusty roads. These events took place in the 1930's.

One day, as he was wandering, the story is that Robert encountered a man who seemed to have been strange, and there was something fearful, and evil about him. Robert had a conversation with him telling him of his ordeals of wanting to become a Blues artist. The man told Robert that the devil could give him such skill to make his dream come true, and that all he had to do was give his soul to him.

Robert was not a Christian nor a moral man, and thought nothing wrong about such an offer. Robert asked the strange man what he had to do, and the man stated that he was to go to Dockery's Plantation at the hour of midnight, and that the devil would appear to him there.

The Plantation was located near an area called the crossroads which was four roads that meet into the shape of a cross. When Robert came there he would wait till midnight, and then Robert heard strange howling sounds. From there Satan appeared to him as the fallen angel took the form of a black man with dark glasses.

When Satan appeared to him Robert had his guitar with him, and Satan asked him if he would give his life to serve him. Robert agreed, and so Satan took his guitar, and tuned it and gave it back to Robert. Satan told him that he would be the greatest Blues guitarist walking the earth, and from there he disappeared after handing back the guitar to Robert.

When Robert walked away he felt a dark presence come over his body, and heard voices in his head of song lyrics. He then took the guitar, and he felt possessed by spirits, and began to play in such a way that it was sure to blow away the Blues artists who made fun of him.

Robert spent the next few months using his newfound gift from Satan and began to write down songs coming from the spirits in his head. He also started to pray to Satan, and began to practice any satanic ritual he could learn from those involved with voodoo and magic.

When Robert came back to the Blues scene he encountered the same group of Blues artists who laughed him off stage. Robert told him he wanted another chance to show them what he learned since he was gone. At first the Blues artists told him not to bother with it, and that there is no way he could get good enough in only a few months when it took years of practice. But Robert kept pushing them until they let him go on stage. Once they did Robert, took out his guitar and began to play and it shocked everyone in the room. He was so good that they could not believe it was the same man from before.

After that, Robert took on any Blues artist in the room to contend with him, and Robert beat them all. When the jam session was over everyone was confused, and silent about what they saw. It felt unnatural to them, and some of Robert's close friends asked him how he got that good in such a short time. After a while of bothering him, Robert told them about selling his soul to Satan. Some people could not believe that while others stated that only Satan could have made someone that good in only a short time.

Soon record companies came calling, and Robert started to record his music. His songs were haunting and disturbing. Songs about serving Satan, beating up women, drinking and cheating with men's wives, and going through demonic attacks and violent encounters in the bars and on the streets. He sang songs about using drugs and about hellhounds which were evil spirits coming to take his soul. Robert was often demonically attacked, and would even be up all night in a possessed state howling like a wolf.

Robert, during his time as a Blues artist, was the best but the most hated by his peers, and people who came to know him. His behavior was described as demonic possession. He would hurt people and beat them up. He was arrogant, and his character was filled with haughtiness and vanity. He would take other men's wives, and have sex with them, and beat up the husbands who would object to it. He often beat up his girlfriends, and sought to control other people. He often aroused a great deal of hatred from men and women he encountered.

In 1938 Robert was having very bad demonic attacks of Satan looking to send him to Hell that he often sung about it. He even recorded songs about it. During a show that year, a man came into the show looking to get even with Robert. The man's wife was cheating on him with Robert Johnson.

After the show Robert was looking for a drink, and the man said he would get him one, and when he did the man dropped poison in the drink. When Robert drank it he had a strong reaction to it and began to foam out of his mouth and was breaking into sweats.

Robert was then bedridden, and during this time he was found screaming in the room, and howling like a wolf. He would tell people that the devil was coming to collect. Soon Robert was not making any sense at all, and then he died from the poison he drank. This account was told about him from close friends, and the Blues artists who remembered him. The tracks of Roberts's songs were developed, and sold and soon used to develop the sound of Rock n' Roll.

Chapter 2

As Rock n' Roll came upon the scene it was hard to name who was the artist that created it. So many of them came out at the same time that it was clear that it was a music already in play, and the record companies wanted to bring it to the mainstream public. The question has always been however. Is Rock n' Roll really Christian music, and did those who made it popular, meaning the fans of the music, did they have Christian morals on their minds at the time?

Rock n' Roll was being played at underground clubs, and barn party houses before it went mainstream. Several investigations went into this club, and party scene of many young people from ages 14 to 25. In 1948 they were called Beatniks, and in the 50's they were called the Beat Generation. Both terms came from the scene the investigators witness, and heard from the crowds there on the scene.

In the late 40's, and early 50's the sound of Rhythm and Blues was changing into a faster and shaking melody of loose aggression and sexuality. The music being played was given a name, and the name was Rock n' Roll. The name came from sex. The slang word for sex at the time was 'to rock and roll.' It meant to take a girl, and roll her over, and have wild sex with her. This is where the name came from among this Beat Generation who fell in love with this style of music.

Soon this music would be taken out of the underground scenes, and then brought to mainstream America, and around the world. To understand the questions of the satanic nature of Rock n' Roll is to also look deeper into the culture of the underground Beat Generation. Rock n' Roll before it was America's music was the music of that culture, and so what was this culture into? Well I can tell you that it was not praying or holding to the Way of Jesus Christ.

The world of the 40's and 50's underground culture was a world of drug users. They were pot smokers, and they shot up meth and snorted cocaine. They were into homosexuality before it was open to do so, and they were heavy into having sex with whomever they wanted to. They had no regard for marriage and the Bible. They were into eastern religions, and witchcraft and had a rebellious spirit toward their parents, and authority persons especially the police. It was a world of cheaters, hustlers, drug addicts, thieves, gangs, and other unsavory people. The artists who performed for them also shared many of the beliefs of the crowds to one extent or another.

The name Beat Generation represented a slang for 'beaten down' or in other words the outsiders of polite society. They were mostly young, and they came from all classes of society rich, middle, and poor. They came from many cultures from whites, blacks, Spanish, European, Asian, from north, west, and south. They appeared to many as if they were a movement within themselves. One thing is clear, when their music went mainstream so did their culture which exploded on the scene in the 1960's.

Church groups, and ministers and even other Christian minded artists warned people of that culture. They stated that if the music went mainstream then so would the vices of those who supported it. One thing is clear, the Church groups were right. To deny that Rock n' Roll also fostered drugs, sex, and violence is to deny the events that took place in history among the youth culture.

The defenders of Rock n' Roll state that the music only spoke about what was already going on in the hearts and minds of the people. In the end everyone has to make up their own mind regarding it.

One thing is clear, messages of Rock n' Roll did not improve the spiritual conditions going on with the people of that time. No matter the argument a lot of lives were destroyed, and Jesus Christ was very hated, and people began to rebel against reading the Bible.

I would not say that Rock n' Roll was to blame for all the unfaithfulness of the generations to come, but it sure did not help this spiritual problem at all. It only made lots of money off the rage, and darkness in the people.

It is a proven fact that music can influence the mind for good or bad. So to think Rock n' Roll is totally innocent is not wise at all. The Beat Generation of the 50's were heavy on escapism, often seeking to retreat into these scenes to avoid the world around them. To do this to such a level can be bad for learning how to handle problems everyone faces in their lives.

In this world they developed a culture of slangs and attitudes. They called themselves 'hipsters' and redefined the word 'cool '. Instead of hats they wore dark sunglasses. Instead of suits it was jeans and t-shirts. Instead of American cars they wanted fast European cars and motorcycles.

Their mind-set on themselves was that they thought of themselves as being better than others. That they were special, and they took themselves way too seriously at times especially those of them with special skills, and musical or entertainment gifts.

Many of them were anti-social toward those outside of their little groups. Many of them would bum around the streets often having no place to go to during the day. They would hitch-hike, and many begged for money or food. They seemed lost in their own world having dreams to see their names in lights or to be important but yet never really looking to be more grounded in education, and what they can do. Their attitudes as a unit was known as hipsters.

The origin of this name came from a street gang formed in 1910 called the Daddy Hipsters. Before the Beat Generation wore sunglasses, and t-shirts the Daddy Hipsters were already doing so. The Daddy Hipsters were known to be a pack of thugs who controlled the neighborhoods they were in using violence and fear. They would sneer down any who crossed their path, and often robbed and jumped people. They committed crimes of stealing cars and selling drugs.

This gang had a certain style of dress that became popular in the underground club scene. The Daddy Hipsters formed other chapters of gangs in suburb areas of America, and so they had a major influence on young people living in middle class America. That influence became the look, and attitude of the Beat Generation of the 40's and 50's.

The fascination young people had with dangerous groups, and lifestyles came from the times they were in. Many of them felt alone, and fearful but hardly any of them had a strong desire to get closer to GOD as GOD was becoming a form of Bible beating in their homes, and Churches rather than a Great Councilor and friend. What they needed to fill those voids in their hearts they were not getting at home, and sadly not even at Church so these underground scenes filled it instead.

Chapter 3

There is an argument about the influence of the rock stars from the start of them when they went mainstream popular. There were also rumors of even darker things as well. Many people who had worked in the industry in some way or who had done behind the scenes investigations into their lives, spoke about satanic secret occults in the music industry. Many people find this very hard to believe while some believe that it's true. Others just out right refuse to believe this at all. One wonders what the truth is, and is there a way to see the clues behind this possible awful reality in the music industry. These rumors, and testimonies' include artists having some blood relation to powerful elite banking, and government families.

Artists being subjected to cruel sexual acts, and satanic rituals. Artists being subjected to forms of mind-control, and ritual satanic abuse. One wonders about the full truth of this, and if one day this possible truth will become a painful fact. If that ever happens, it would be one of the most shocking cover-ups in American history.

One of the main concerns Christian ministers had at the time was the promotion of the New Age religions through the artists of the music industry and its fans. Many fans of the Rock n' Roll Beat Generation would go out among the street corners, and coffee houses, nightclubs, and barn scenes and preach new age spirituality.

These hipsters preached witchcraft, Hindu practices, black magic, kabbalah, and voodoo, and even Satanism. Many of the speakers did have a strong influence over many people, and many of these preachers of the New Age faith did win over many converts. This means thousands were turning away from GOD, and believing in a faith that is anti-Christian.

Many rock stars lead lives that promoted the ideas, and faith of the New Age as well. Some would openly promote it while others practiced it in secret because they did not want their customers who were their fans to know they were not Christians.

These rock stars were indeed God-like to the people especially the youth. Many ministers stated that these artists were idols of a dark nature. That they were leading people under the wings of Satan, and were being deceived to follow rebellious and lustful lifestyles. Most stated that these rock stars were influencing millions to turn away from Jesus Christ. They believed they were teaching them to be immoral, violent, to lie and con people. That they promoted criminal behavior, and were making evil to look good.

Their arguments in accordance to what the Bible teaches did have heavy weight to it. The practices of these fans, and the rock stars they praised were condemned in the Bible. The Bible called these practices as being sins against GOD. To understand their points on this we have to look at a few of these very popular artists.

One such artist was a man named Chuck Berry. Chuck Berry is believed to have been the one who pieced together the modern Rock n' Roll sound. It was said that the white artists of Rock n' Roll including Elvis, learned their style of play by listening to him.

Some very strange things were said about Chuck Berry. Rather if these things are true I leave for you to decide. Some stated that Berry was into voodoo, and that he suffered a form of demonic possession.

Several times local police were called at a few shows Berry did where Berry, and his band mates would spend some time in their car smoking pot. They would smoke so much pot that a cloud of smoke would rise out of the car when they opened the doors.

Berry's music was a graphic description of teen lust, fast cars, and consumer culture. His major hit single Maybelline came out in 1955. The song sings about a high speed chase of a man who has just caught his woman cheating on him.

Roll over Beethoven that came out in 1956 was a teen party song, and other hits were Rock n' Roll Music that came out in 1957, and Johnny B. Goode which came out in 1958. A noted song of Chuck Berry was Sweet Little Sixteen. On the surface the song seems to sing about a girl coming of age on her birthday, but people who knew Barry said it had a darker meaning. They stated that Barry was into having sex with very young girls who were teenagers, and pre-teens.

In 1959 Chuck Berry was a high-profile star with several hit records, and he even appeared in movies. In December of 1959 Chuck's career came to a full stop due to a scandal that he was guilty of. Berry was arrested under the Mann Act for having sex with a 14 year old girl. Barry had also transported the young Native American girl across state lines, and he wanted the girl to work as a hat check girl at a club he owned.

After his arrest Berry's trial lasted two weeks, and in March of 1960 he was found guilty. Berry was sentenced to five years in prison, and a $5,000 fine. Through an appeal Berry would only serve one and a half years in prison.

Chuck Berry, when he got out of prison did manage to get back his career, and would go on to even work with other artists. He even became a successful restaurant owner. But it seems for Berry that old habits do die hard. In the late 1980's Chuck got hit with another scandal when a camera was discovered in the ladies bathroom of a restaurant he owned in Missouri. It turned out that it was Berry who had the camera installed in the women's bathroom. When the police found out about it they raided his home, and found videotapes of many women using the bathroom. One of these females was a minor. The police also found 62 grams of marijuana.

Berry was charged with felony drug possession, and child-abuse charges, and was sued by 59 women who were customers at his restaurant. The trial would cost Berry 1.2 million dollars, and he got two years' probation.

Another artist to look into was Jerry Lee Lewis where many strange rumors were said about him. It was said about Jerry Lee that he came from a Christian family background but that he turned his back on GOD for fame and money. As a child he used to sneak off, and go to barn house shows to see the loose women, and hear the sounds of Rhythm and Blues. As he became older he discovered his talent for music, and he was highly skilled at the piano.

It was also said of him that he had encounters with evil spirits, and sought a pact with the devil. One wonders if that is true, did Jerry Lee sell his soul to the devil for a record contract.

Sam Phillips was the man who signed Jerry Lee to his first record contract. Some people even said about Phillips that he was involved with the New Age faith, and he too turned his back on the teachings of Jesus Christ.

Could that be true as well? Many people stated of Jerry Lee that he suffered bouts of demonic possession, and had a certain wild energy about him that seemed to greatly influence people around him, and it even frighten people. Is there any truth to that as well?

One day Jerry Lee was in the studio with Sam Phillips, and there was a mic that was left on while the two of them were having a strange conversation. The details of this conversation was Jerry having an argument with Phillips about being demon possessed. Jerry was complaining to Phillips that he had the devil in him, and he also started to disagree with Phillips that the devil can save souls. Phillips and his people were heard telling Jerry a strange thing about a new faith for the people. But Jerry was still complaining that the Bible makes it clear that dealing with the devil will send him into Hell. Somewhere at this point the mic was discovered to still be on so they turned it off. A strange conversation indeed.

Jerry Lee's peers and friends spoke about Jerry often being worried that he was going to Hell, and told his other Rock n' Roll peers that they too were going to Hell for dealing with the devil. But they would dismiss him while Jerry Lee was very serious about it.

When Jerry Lee Lewis broke on the scene he was seen as an overnight success. His major hit singles were Whole Lot of Shaken Going On, Great Balls of Fire, and Breathless. His fame was so huge that many thought that when Elvis was drafted into the Army Jerry Lee would become the new King of Rock n' Roll. But it was not to be as an ugly scandal broke forth regarding Jerry's taste for very young women, and I mean really young.

At the height of Jerry Lee's fame he began to become sexually involved with his 12 year old first cousin named Myra. Jerry was 22 years old at the time of this relationship. When Myra turned 13 years old Jerry Lee married her. When Jerry Lee did this everyone was against it, and told him to end the relationship as quickly and quiet as possible but Jerry refused to do that. He instead took her with him when he went on tour in England. During a press interview a British reporter named Ray Berry noticed the young girl cuddling up to Jerry, and he asked the young girl who she was, and she stated that she was his wife. When Ray asked Jerry Lee about it he refused to deny it, and when asked how old she was Jerry lied and said she was 15 years old when in fact she was 13.

Ray broke the news to the British press which then leaked to the

American press, and overnight the world knew the truth. That Jerry Lee married a child and his cousin to boot. This scandal took place in 1958, and it destroyed his career. England told him to leave and never come back.

When he came back to America he was blacklisted on all the radio stations. Dick Clark dropped him from his upcoming shows that he was to appear on. His fans sent him hate mail, and burned his records. Even Sam Phillips turned his back on him, and dropped him from the label. Jerry Lee went from making $10,000 a show to $250 performing at bars.

After sometime Jerry Lee went back working for several record companies behind the scenes as a song writer. He was also still touring local concert shows. A strange rumor regarding Jerry Lee Lewis is that after his fall from fame he became a mind-control handler. No one really knows how true this claim is.

Little Richard was also an artist with a strange background. He was also one of the rare artist who spoke openly about satanic dealings in the music industry. Little Richard when he was a boy to a pre-teen was horribly abused by his father. His father was described as a Bible beater, and the Church he was part of was very strict, and also their members were very quick to beat their kids very badly.

The Bible does not teach to abuse children in such a manner. In fact, it tells parents not to be harsh with their children. The Bible states that children already belong to the Kingdom of GOD, and to spare the rod spoil the child does not mean to beat your child senseless. It actually means to educate the child to mold his character against the ways of a wicked world. Beating a child will never teach a child to not be wicked. In fact, most of the time they become more wicked through such abuse. Little Richard's father would beat him so badly that blood would spill from his back.

One time Richard got into some trouble with a Church group for simply playing the piano. Because the minister did not like the music he was playing he went to Richard's father, and made a huge deal out of it, and he told Richard's father to beat him. I must admit for a minister to tell another Church member to beat their son bloody red is a Church no one should be attending.

For Little Richard that was the last straw, and before his father could beat him again he ran away from home, and never looked back. Little Richard was blessed with musical gifts, and he was a highly gifted piano player. After running away he worked many odd jobs as a laborer where he washed dishes, and did other odd jobs. He would often find ways to play the piano, and sing where he could. He had a strong singing voice.

One day an entertainer noticed his skill, and wanted him to join his entertainment group. The kind of entertainment they provided was playing to homosexual crowds in gay nightclubs that were very underground at the time. People knew they were there but no one spoke about it. Little Richard's first act for them was as a singing drag queen. It was said of Little Richard that his time there brought him to become a bi-sexual, and he got into satanic rituals. It is hard to say out right if Little Richard was a devil worshipper but many people who worked in that scene stated that devil worship was common among the gay crowds, and entertainers in that scene.

For Little Richard it could have been just a way to make money, and be accepted as an artist until something even darker got a hold of him. Many say that dark element was demonic possession. Was Little Richard possessed by demons? When Little Richard broke into the music industry he brought his drag queen look with him but toned it down drastically.

Instead of wearing a dress he came up with a look to appeal to both gay, and straight people. He however kept on wearing women's make-up. Little Richard's first major hit single was a song called Tutti Frutti which came out in 1955. No one really knew what the song was really about. It was promoted as a dance song for young teens. But others said it had a darker element that the song was about gay sex.

His next hit single was a song called Rip it Up which was a huge hit with young teens, and it was also promoted as a dance song. Sometime later Little Richard became more open about the satanic nature of the music industry, and stated the real reason why he is in the music industry. When speaking about the rock groups in the music industry Little Richard stated that there were some rock groups who stand in a circle, and take a cup and they drink each other's blood. He stated that they also get on their knees afterwards, and pray to the devil. Clearly this act Little Richard is talking about is satanic worship.

In regards to Little Richard's purpose in the music industry he stated that he was directed, and commanded by another power. That this power was the power of darkness, the power of Satan the devil. He stated that the people need to realize that there is a force that is fighting against the people of the world. That the devil was the one controlling the minds of the people, and directing the lives of the people. These statements keep in mind are not coming from an outsider looking in but from a major artist on the inside.

Another major act was Bill Haley and the Comets who recorded the huge smash hit single titled Rock Around the Clock which was first recorded in 1953, and was released in 1955. The song was also used in the soundtrack of the film called Blackboard Jungle. Bill Haley and his band gave Rock n' Roll a safer image because of the way Bill, and his band looked. They were well dressed and they looked like the parents of many young teen fans. This wholesome image many said was only just an act that under the surface of this band, they were a very aggressive group.

It was said of them that they were one of the last band members on earth to piss off. Bill Haley and the Comets as told by those who knew them had a subversive way of starting trouble with large crowds at their concerts. The story is when they first came on the scene they were famous, and things were going their way. But soon much of the attention was turned to Elvis, and others that they felt overshadowed. When the European tour was underway the Comets were very popular there and they drew thousands of screaming crowds. This tour got started in 1957, and ended in 1958. The entire tour was dominated by riots that the Comets are believed to have incited through comments, and impressions they made on stage. London and Berlin are the two noted ones.

In London the Comets are believed to have been the ones to

encourage the fans to rush the Waterloo Station. Thousands of fans nearly destroyed the station, and fought it out with the London police. The British press dubbed it 'The Second Battle of Waterloo'.

The one in Berlin was even worse. The Comets are believed to have whipped the crowd into such a frenzy that night on purpose. The result was thousands of German fans rushed the stage, and destroyed it and the massive crowds were fist-fighting each other, and caused a large amount of destruction of property. Many other shows ended the same way.

In the 1950's there were three artists who were highly gifted, and were a major force of talent in the music industry. Their names were Buddy Holly, Ritchie Valens, and the Big Bopper, whose real name was J.P. Richardson. Each of them came from very different backgrounds but would all share a common fate in the music industry. Their names would forever be tied together as the day the music died when these three men died in a plane crash together.

Buddy Holly got inspired to play Rock n' Roll music after watching Elvis Presley perform on stage. He turned out to have a high talent for it. He was soon signed to a record deal along with his band called the Crickets. His major hit singles were That'll Be The Day, Oh Boy, and Peggy Sue. His fame first shot up in 1957. Buddy Holly had a gift for bringing people together.

In the 1950's most black Americans were not into Rock n' Roll they still held to the old Rhythm and Blues sound. There were only a few rock bands they liked to listen to. One of those bands was Buddy Holly. In fact they listened to him so much that many black Americans thought that Buddy Holly was black. This led to a tour with other popular black artists, and often when Buddy Holly and the Crickets took the stage the large African-American crowds were shocked that he was white, and his band was white. When he started to play he instantly won them over.

One major example is when Buddy Holly and the Crickets were to play the Apollo Show. The Apollo Show was known to boo the pants off of you if they did not like you. They were an all-black crowd, and when it came to music only the best will do. Many in attendance that night came to the Apollo to see the Crickets, and they too thought that Buddy Holly and his band were black. When they took the stage, and the curtain opened the Apollo crowd were stunned quiet that they were white. They then started to heckle them, and the Crickets almost were going to flee offstage but Buddy held them in place by telling them to start playing. When they did once again Buddy Holly and the Crickets won this tough crowd over, and they applauded them.

What is different about Buddy Holly and the Crickets is that white and black crowds loved them, and they both bought their music.

Ritchie Valens is the one credited for starting Latin-American rock music. He began playing in bars and nightclubs before he was even old enough to attend them. Valens grew up really quick, and he even looked older than his actually age. His rise to fame started at only 16 years of age, he began to hone his skill as a pre-teen, and he died at the age of only 17 years old.

His mother and his family were the ones who encouraged, and supported his skill and his dream of becoming a music industry star. Ritchie was an explosive guitarist. Even for his age he is called one of the greatest of all time when it came to guitar skills. There was a reason why his family supported him so much in a tough business. It was because he was that good, and everyone who heard him knew it.

Being Latin-American in the 1950's was hard on Ritchie. The music industry made him change his last name to Valens because his last name sounded too Spanish. He at first was offended of having to change his name but for success he gave into it. He and his family had to struggle with being poor. His mother worked odd jobs, and struggled to maintain their trailer home.

In high-school he met the love of his life, a girl named Donna. Donna's family who came from a high-scale middle class family rejected Ritchie outright. In truth it was not because he was poor but it was because he was poor and Latin. Ritchie would write a song about her that became a major hit.

Ritchie got discovered at a show that was put together at a

community center that his mom helped with. In attendance was a talent scout who was blown away by Ritchie's guitar playing and singing. The show came to a crashing end when Ritchie's half-brother nicknamed Bob started a rumble at the show.

Bob was a drug-runner for a biker gang who helped Ritchie's mom and his family members to settle in the trailer community they lived in. Before that they were living in wooden huts. After the show Ritchie was signed to a record company where there he recorded his first major hit single called Donna. His heartbreak was turned to success. The money he made off that single was more than enough to buy his mother her first home. His entire family would move into this home, and they now became part of the middle class.

Ritchie would go on to appear in a movie, and then he had an idea for a new song called La Bamba. La Bamba was originally an old Mexican folk song. In traditional Mexican music it was a very popular song. Ritchie knew that most of his fans were white young fans of Rock n' Roll. He wanted to bring over also young Latin-Americans to his music. He was seeking to bring two worlds together.

When Ritchie told his manager about the idea to re-record La Bamba as a rock song they were against it especially when he said he wanted to sing it in Spanish. After a back and forth argument they finally agreed to let him do it. When he did they were blown away by the guitar solo Ritchie created for it. Many said later that the guitar solo was ahead of its time. When La Bamba was released it was a huge hit with both white and Latin-American fans. The song itself lead to a rock industry in South America.

One of the strange aspects of Ritchie's life was his nightmares. He often told his close friends that he had dreams of dying in a plane crash. These dreams were so bad that it caused him to have a fear of flying. He even sought to see a Shaman about his dreams. The witch-doctor gave him a necklace of protection to prevent the dreams, but he still kept on having them, and still had a constant fear of flying. In fact he would demand to drive anywhere he went to avoid flying. When he had to board a plane it was because he had no choice, and he would break into sweats during flights.

The Big Bopper was born Jiles Perry Richardson. He was an unlikely rock star. No one is sure why he broke into the music industry to become a rock star other then he had a passion for music. The Bopper's first major hit single was a song called Chantilly Lace. The song was about dating a young pretty girl that he calls on the telephone. The Big Bopper is credited for making music history in 1958 when he filmed what many consider the first music video.

He also had a gift for bringing white and black audiences together. He too was an artist that African-American fans originally thought he was black. That was because Bopper sung like a black man with a very deep voice with much soul in his lyrics. Bopper, before breaking into the industry as an artist, was a radio disc jockey who was passionate about playing the new rock recordings. It was said that he spent so much time on the air that he would take quick showers in between songs. He started off as a song-writer, and would organize tours for other rock stars. He then broke into the business singing his own songs.

When Buddy Holly, Ritchie Valens, and the Big Bopper meant their deaths together it happened in the year 1959. The three artists came together for a mid-west tour called the Winter Dance Party. When the musicians had started the tour they had been traveling by bus for over a week. In fact during the tour the bus had broken down. When they came to Clear Lake, Iowa the three artists would perform their very last show although they did not know it would be.

On the night of the plane crash it was February 2, 1959. Buddy and Ritchie both caught colds, and Bopper came down with influenza. After the show was over their next show was in Moorhead, Minnesota, and Holly, feeling sick did not want to ride in the bus anymore. The three artists were also mad that they had not been paid yet, and they hardly had any rest, nor could they get any laundry done.

Holly decided to charter a plane that was to leave at Mason City airport. His plan was to fly to Fargo, North Dakota so that he could arrive at Moorhead early. He wanted to get some rest from his sickness, do some laundry for the guys and mainly get some rest.

When Holly secured the plane he told the other band members that only two others could go with him because it was a three passenger plane. Because Bopper was very sick he was chosen to go, and then it came down between Ritchie Valens and Tommy Allsup, the guitarist for Holly's band. It was decided that they should flip a coin to win the seat, and Ritchie won the coin toss. Ritchie was very nervous about boarding the plane but he was so sick that he felt he could not handle the long bus ride.

The three artists would board the plane at the airport, and then they sat waiting for clearance from the control tower. Snow was blowing all across the runway but the control tower stated that the skies were clear. They then gave them permission to lift off. What was odd about it was that the tower should have known that a blizzard was heading their way but still they gave them clearance to fly.

When the plane took off it got about five miles from the airport, and it was in the air for about ten minutes. But then something went wrong. The radar station could no longer track them. The plane crashed down. No one saw or heard the crash. The bodies of these artists, and the pilot were not discovered until the next morning. The bodies were laying in the blowing snow throughout the night. No one is sure what went wrong. The plane did not have anything wrong with it. Pilot error was never shown. The official story is that the plane encountered a massive blizzard which forced the plane down and crashed it.

One of the questions regarding it was why did the control tower give them clearance by telling them that the skies were clear but yet knowing a blizzard was heading their way. These three artists died very young the youngest being Ritchie who was only 17 years old. Rumors regarding this tragic event were also said. No proof was ever shown regarding them.

Some of the stories goes like this, many felt that their deaths were a ritual satanic sacrifice to Satan set up by the music industry. Could that really be true? Another theory was that certain racist families among the American elite wanted them dead because they brought cultures of people together, and they wanted to put a stop to it. So they therefore set up a plane crash for them to die in. Could that be true? One can only wonder about why this horrible event had to take place.

Eddie Cochran was a good friend of all three of these artists. Eddie gained famed when in the late 1950's he would record a major hit single that was under two minutes long. The song was called Summertime Blues. The song was about a young teenage boy not having the kind of fun he wanted to for the summer. Eddie's image was of a rugged young man with a rebellious attitude. He was adored by thousands of screaming teenage girls.

After the deaths of Buddy, Ritchie, and the Big Bopper, Eddie was having terrible nightmares. Friends of Eddie Cochran stated that he began to be haunted by morbid premonitions that he would die young. These hauntings frighten him so badly that he became anxious to give up life on the road. Friends of Eddie stated that he was constantly worried of suffering the same fate of his three close friends. It was stated that he began to have dreams of dying in a car accident. These dreams, and fears became so bad that he wanted to stop touring and leave the industry. As he tried to do so, financial responsibilities prevented him from leaving and caused him to tour in the United Kingdom.

On Saturday April 16, 1960 Eddie along with his fiancée named Sharon Sheeley, got into a taxi. The driver was named George Martin and as he was driving he began to go very fast, and was speeding down the roads. The taxi ended up blowing out a tire, and the driver lost control of the car. The car would slam head on into a lamp post. Eddie was sitting in the backseat of the car when it happened along with his fiancée Sharon. Eddie quickly shielded her but was thrown out of the car when the door flew open.

Eddie slammed into the pavement, and he died of severe head injuries. Martin, the driver, survived the crash but oddly served no jail time. Instead he was charged with speeding, and dangerous driving and was suspended from driving for a period of time. When Eddie Cochran died he was only 21 years of age.

Rumors about this death also surfaced. These rumors were never proven true. The main one was that it too was a satanic ritual hit as a sacrifice for Satan. One can only wonder if that statement is true or not.

Chapter 4

In the 1950's Rock n' Roll arose, and became mainstream music, and its fan base were teenagers mainly. Church groups began to attack the music, and they would point out the devil's influence in the music. Their arguments were centered on the sexual behavior of young teens, and the rebellious attitudes they were showing their parents. They often blamed this music for many of these problems. They pointed out the rise of teenage crimes and immorality since the music hit the record stores. They also argued that artists should sing for GOD, and not for pleasures and worldly wants. Many Christians could see the common sense of their messages and warnings.

There was no doubt that teenage immorality and crimes did sharply rise when the music came forth. There is also no doubt that music is made to influence emotional states in people. In fact the word music comes from the word muse which is to inspire.

Rock n' Roll defenders stated that the problems of teenagers was the result of bad parenting and the problems in society in general. One can only wonder which argument is true. As a Christian, if you are a Christian, there is no doubt that there is a satanic element in the messages of many rock songs and rock stars. Many people believe that many of the Church groups had a real reason to be worried about their children listening to rock music. They wanted to protect them from harmful influences that the Bible calls sins. But also there were Church groups that many said were totally evil and were total hypocrites about their protest against Rock n' Roll. They stated that the only reason why those Church groups attacked Rock n' Roll was because they did not want white children dancing with black and Spanish children. There was sadly also truth to that statement as well.

Many concerts were actually shut down when parents, and the police saw white girls dancing with black young men. There were teenage dance events in schools that were shut down when whites were dancing with blacks.

The Bible does not support racism at all. The real teachings of the Bible shows that all cultures of people are equal and equally loved in the eyes of GOD. That Jesus died for everyone's sins, and that no favorites were among him in regards to human cultures.

Jesus did not want us to sin anymore but to turn from it. It is also a sin to hate someone based on their skin color. It shows that some Church groups had the right message doing it for the right reasons, to protect children from a reckless lifestyle, while other Churches had the wrong message, doing it for the wrong reasons to keep people living in fear.

The most noted rock star that we should look into was the one called the King of Rock n' Roll. His name was Elvis Presley. There have been many rumors about Elvis. His career accomplishments are very well known. His hit songs, and movies are also known throughout the entire world.

At the rise, and height of his career in the 1950's he was loved by the young, and disliked by their parents. In the 1960's those young people became adults and parents, and they still loved his music and movies. Even in the 70's he was still beloved by these most loyal fans who would not accept the fact that he died. Many people stated that Elvis was a Christian, a godly man. They would declare him to be a saint even bringing him offerings at his grave-sight. Some fans have even gone so far to worship him, and make shrines of him in their homes. They would burn candles to it and even pray to him.

The Bible does call this idolatry but try telling these fans who do so that, and you will get an angry response from them. It is very rare that an artist is worshipped in such manner. There have been a few of them like James Dean, Bruce Lee, Tupac, and a few others. One wonders why these artists are worshipped in such a manner that they are seen as gods among these fans.

Rumors regarding Elvis' religious beliefs actually came from his close friends and family members. His circle of friends were called the Memphis Mafia which is a rather strange name for a group of friends. When Elvis died they started to speak openly about Elvis' true beliefs regarding GOD, and his drug use and sexual habits. Other rumors were also said that Elvis was managed by a man they called Col. Tom Parker.

This rumor was that Elvis was a victim of a CIA program called monarch mind-control, and that Parker was his mind-control handler which is someone who keeps him in line. There has been no evidence to prove this. This rumor was not just said once but many times it was spoken. One wonders if it's true or not. Parker it was stated did have an odd control over Elvis. But was it mind-control or was it a business dealing where if Elvis did not do what he said he could lose money. One can only wonder.

Another rumor was that Elvis was related to elite bloodline families of America and Europe who were royalty and bankers. This has never been really confirmed but there was a study done into his family tree that did show relation to a few princes in England who lived a very long time ago.

Another rumor was that Elvis' close family like his mother and uncles were into Satanism, and were not official members of a Church but only went to Church on holidays. That rumor has never been proven. But also there are no records of Elvis being baptized in any Church nor was there any records of him being a long standing member of any Church. It seems that he sometimes attended Church but was not very active in it.

Some said that Elvis was very popular in high-school but this turned out to be not true. His high-school peers stated that Elvis was seen as a strange kid, and was often made fun of. That he was alone and often withdrew from other people, and seemed creepy to other people. It was stated that he never expressed any musical talent to them, and they were shocked when one day they saw him on T.V. singing Hound Dog, and that thousands of teenagers were screaming their heads off at him.

No one really knows how Elvis got his band together and

became famous in the first place. The story of this beginning has changed so many times no one knows what the truth of it is. Many rumors about Elvis' sexual depravity is very well known. It was stated that after concerts teenage girls would line up in front of his car or a room back-stage, and Elvis would have sex with about 20 to even 30 girls a night at times. No one knows if that number is fully true but eye witnesses do recall the girls lined up by his car or room, and there was over 50 of them who were hand-picked by Elvis' people, and they were in line to have sex with him. Many of these teenagers were not even 16 years old. Many said that Elvis even had babies all across the country that even he was not aware of. These statements were back up by many people who worked with him in the music industry. I got to tell you a truly Christian minded person would not do things like that in such an open, and shameless way. In fact Elvis did not say himself in the 1950's that he was a Christian it was his P.R. people who did.

Elvis did not confess Christ until he started to make Gospel albums and his close circle of friends stated that the only reason he did was to make money from it. This statement does have truth to it. One day Elvis was riding in the backseat of a car with a camera on him, and a hidden mic was still on. At that point a Gospel album Elvis did was selling thousands of copies. While riding in the backseat Elvis began to brag about a girl he fornicated with the night before. While doing so one of his friends told him that the mic was still on. Elvis then in a joking way told his friend he was a sneaky bastard and started to put on the Christian act by singing 'What a Friend We Have in Jesus'. The Bible would call this hypocrisy.

Another statement about Elvis was that Elvis was racist. This came from a foul comment Elvis made when asked if black artists helped him to become a talented rock artist. Elvis was reported to have said these awful words, 'the only thing niggers can do for me is shine my shoes'. Bear in mind that the style of Elvis' play was first done in the mainstream by Chuck Berry who was an African-American artist.

Some witchcraft groups believed Elvis was an angel or an elf due to his name which they believed was short for Elves. Some said the name means Evils. But this I must say I leave for you to decide. Oddly Elvis did do a song called I'm Evil where he sings about himself being totally evil.

Many defenders of Elvis state that Elvis stood for righteous causes but they fail however to state what those righteous causes were. Elvis never took part in the Civil Rights movement, and the Jim Crow defenders actually loved Elvis, and even sought to give him rewards.

Another strange rumor about Elvis was that he was a member of the Theosophical Society. A society that was an occult that held to the doctrine of pantheistic ancient Gnosticism. It was believed that Elvis read, and believed in the works of Madam Helena Blavatsky who was a Russian mystic. She also openly worshipped Lucifer, and her works were greatly admired by Hitler. This membership has never been proven but Elvis did have some of her works in his vast book collection. His friends stated that Elvis was a reader but his favorite books were about eastern religions, pagan occults, and practices. In fact, the night he died he was reading a book in the bathroom called Sex and Psychic Energy. In 1956 Elvis was a national and world-wide rock star. His fame was seen as overnight success and his fans in the millions were at his beck and call.

Elvis came under fire by Church groups and parents alike. They stated that he had an unwholesome impact on young people and that he incited rebellion and lust into thousands of teenagers. Teenage girls would even admit that they became horny listening to his music and watching him on stage. Some believed he was possessed by evil spirits.

When Elvis became a Hollywood movie star he still came under attack for promoting lust, violence, and sexual immorality. Parents and Church groups greatly complained about Elvis' performances. Elvis would straddle the microphone in the most suggestive manners, and his groin would be gyrating inches from the upright stand. He would be shaking in convulsive movements in such a way that people believed he was demon possessed. Was he really demon-possessed? Or was this just bad dancing.

Many of Elvis' close friends seem to suggest that Elvis had

demonic spirits in him. One of Elvis' close friends named Larry Geller stated that Elvis told him about spirits that would talk to him inside his head. He stated that Elvis believed at first that it was the spirit of his twin brother Jesse who died at birth. But overtime Elvis came to realize that it was not the spirit of his brother but it was something else. Elvis then came to believe according to Geller that they were the spirits of dead guru masters who were worshipped by ancient people in the past. He stated that Elvis told him that these spirits helped him to become famous and that he works under their commands. He would go on to state that Elvis believed that these spirits were guiding him and had been all his life and that his fame did not just happen but it was planned out by these spirits.

Another friend of Elvis named Gary Herman stated that Elvis recognized the devil's part in his success. Another friend of Elvis who was Red West who was also a member of the Memphis Mafia also talked about strange energy that came from Elvis. Red believed that Elvis had some sort of psychic powers and that Elvis often would try to hypnotize people. Red stated that Elvis would show these powers again, and again. One strange story came from another member of the Memphis Mafia named Sonny West.

Sonny stated that Elvis was having problems with a man named Mike Stone. One day according to Sonny, Elvis sat him down, and tried to hypnotize him by giving him suggestions. Sonny stated that he was finding it hard to snap out of it, and during it Elvis reached for a gun among his vast gun collection. From there Elvis put an automatic rifle in his hands, and told Sonny that he had to kill Mike Stone. Sonny then snapped out of it for good, and told Elvis that he was not a killer. Oddly other members of the Memphis Mafia stated that Elvis had a list of people that he wanted to kill.

Another strange story came from a man named David Stanley who was a relative of Elvis, and he even lived in Elvis' famous home called Graceland. David stated that one day while driving with Elvis a terrible rainstorm came upon them. Elvis then got sick of it, and step out of the car and began to do something strange with his hands and arms. From there David saw the entire rainstorm part from the path they were driving on, and they ended up driving on dry ground with clear skies.

The actions that these men talked about regarding Elvis is called in the Bible as being sorcery. The Bible tells us that there were false-prophets, and pagan priests who were able to perform what are called wonders through demonic powers. People like Moses, Paul, Peter, and others had encounters with them, and showed the power of GOD against them.

If what these men are saying is true then Elvis was in touch with things that were very dangerous. The Memphis Mafia also spoke about what Elvis really thought regarding Jesus Christ. That he often told his friends that they were his apostles, and that he was their Christ. They also stated that Elvis believed that Jesus and Mary Magdalene had a sexual relationship, and that they often got stoned together.

They also stated that Elvis' stage customs his jump-suit look were actually designed after ancient Hindu occult masters. Elvis often read their books, and in the 60's and 70's began to copy their fashion sense. Many others also stated that Elvis had a strong belief in the New Age movement and a global system of government. He one time stated that he can't wait for it to arrive, and that all those Bible believers will get theirs one day.

A Christian pastor one time spoke with Elvis having knew him when Elvis was young. Elvis stated to him these words,' Pastor, I'm the most miserable man you've ever seen. I've got all the money I'll ever need to spend. I've got millions of fans. I got friends, but I'm doing what you taught me not to do and I'm not doing the things you taught me to do.'

Elvis' use of drugs was very well known but only known in full after his death. When Elvis was recognized by Richard Nixon for presenting a clean, and sober image in the mist of many rock stars who promoted drugs, many knew that this was a joke. The day Elvis got the reward, and did the press conference he was very high on drugs. He was so high in fact he was sweating during the interview. Many of Elvis' rock peers from the 50's and 60's recalled Elvis' use of drugs. It was said of him that he gave drugs freely to the likes of Jerry Lee Lewis, Bill Haley, and others and that he was the one who got Johnny Cash started on drugs.

His Memphis Mafia family also handled Elvis' drugs by buying the drugs for him, and picking the drugs up and serving the drugs to him. In fact David Stanley's job while living with Elvis was to serve Elvis drugs throughout the morning and night.

Elvis' sexual depravity was very well known. He liked young girls and very young girls. Also some said that Elvis was a bi-sexual as well. Stating that the song he did for a movie called Jail House Rock was a song that was actually about gay lovers in prison. Once again this has never been proven. What is known is that Elvis started having sex with a girl named Priscilla when she was only 13 years old, and he was also having sex with other men's wives.

When it became known that Elvis was involved with Priscilla he was pressured into marrying her when she was only 14 years old. When Elvis married her he was never faithful to her at all. He continued sleeping with other women sometimes two or four in the same night.

The day Elvis died was a sad day for millions of his loyal fans. David Stanley was the one who found his body in the bathroom on the night he died. Elvis woke up that night in cold sweats and called David to bring him some drugs. Elvis took the drugs, and then later he went to the bathroom and took a book with him called Sex and Psychic Energy. No one is for sure what happened to him in the bathroom. When David came down to see what was going on he found Elvis in the bathroom. Elvis' face was blue and very puffy. His tongue was pitch black and half bitten off. It looked like before he died of an overdose he was frighten by something.

Chapter 5

The Bible tells Christians that we are to flee from youthful lusts, and pursue righteousness, faith, love, and peace. That those who do this must call on the Lord with a pure heart. Many people with a Christian faith have come to ask the question does popular music intercept these teachings. It's a question everyone must decide for themselves.

Mind-control programming is a topic that comes up again, and again in regards to the music and movie industry. Some think it's just a crazy notion while others say it's a real problem in the entertainment industry. Many say there is real evidence out there that supports the reality of people being mind-controlled by industry artists, and also that many artists themselves have been mind-controlled in one form or another. Their argument is that the mainstream media is controlled, and so therefore it's never taken seriously or even reported on. These are questions that people must decide for themselves by looking into it. The United States government did admit, and even released a statement that the CIA did have a mind-control program called MK-Ultra or the Monarch Program. In fact, Canada had kicked out several U.S. officials for engaging in the programming. They filmed, and took pictures of children being tortured and abused. That extreme acts of sexual abuse, and cruelty was done to them as part of this program. Even Bill Clinton came out, and gave an apology for it on behalf of the United States government. However, there has never been any evidence to show that certain famous artists were victims of mind-control programming. There have been people however who stated that they were victims of mind-control but managed to be de-programmed. They stated that they saw famous artists being mind-controlled, and being abused in some very horrible ways. Hard evidence has never been presented in their testimony only the details of what they say they saw. Some say that even though there is no hard evidence that certain artists did drop clues that they were victims of mind-control. They stated that a person has to think outside the box, and read in-between the lines. Their reasons behind these statements is that any evidence regarding this would be quickly suppressed. That the scandal would rock the very core of government actions around the world. But once again these are questions that a person must decide for themselves.

Most Church groups never even heard of mind-control programming or that the U.S. government admitted to having such a program. Many of them never even heard the details of what others said publicly about it. They don't even know that certain self-proclaimed victims published books about their experiences. Some of them even visited doctors who were able to prove that they had been tortured in the manner they spoke of. Such a topic like this is not something you will hear about in Church on a Sunday morning.

In America, and around the world we have a craze for celebrity worship. There are fans of artists that pay more attention to their favorite star then they do the teachings of the Bible. Some fans even find their favorite celebrity more popular then Jesus Christ. Many say this is a sad condition in society that people can't be themselves but want to be someone else. They imagine these celebrities as holding the wishes, and dreams of the people. In really it's only in their imaginations. Celebrities are only people with all the flaws, and hang-ups that all people have. They are only artists and not their savior. The Bible would call celebrity worship as being idolatry. Music and entertainment if done with the intent not to corrupt people is not a sin to do. Keep in mind people are born with a gift to entertain, but worshipping an entertainer is a sin.

When it comes to the dark subjects spoken about the music industry demon possession often comes up. Other subjects are mind-control, mind-control handlers, and others. It is said of mind-control handlers that they are assigned to a certain artist to watch them, and keep them in line. They do this by forms of intimidations often using threats, blackmail, extortion, and other means. They use manipulation, abuse, and set them up for sex scandals and drug scandals. It is also said that handlers are also mind-control victims with a handler that watches them. None of this has ever been proven but it does come up again and again in the music and film industry.

Others have said that demon-possession occurs within mind-control victims and that a form of black magic is used. The statements are that mind-control programmers are also into sorcery and satanic blood rituals. That victims are given electro shock treatments, and they are raped and beaten. Many of them are forced to commit horrible deeds in satanic rituals to force a condition called altered states of consciousness. In this state it is believed that demon possession happens that will cause it's victims to have many split personalities in their head. This impulses the victim to go by different names, and talk in different accents, and so forth. Could all this be true? Is this the dark secret in the entertainment industry?

Another story was about why Hollywood stars have rooms full of mirrors. Many say that it's because they are constantly concerned about the way they look. Others say that it has do to with a mind-control program called mirror programming. The strange story behind this subject is that victims will learn how to match certain identical items to its symbolism using cards then mirrors. This is done to build mirror images of these items in their brains. Even their senses are effected and trained to also make the mirror images in their brains understandable. It is said that when they show a mirror image they will give the victim a linen fabric like silk or cotton to give the sense of touch to flow over to the understanding of the image. Memories of the victim that largely contributes to a person's personality become twisted and fractured. When the memory cortex due to the programming becomes broken then alter-personalities are born. This happening is caused by subjecting the victim to mental and physical torture during the mirror programming. When this process happens the feeling inside the brain of the victim is like taking his or her brain and smashing it into a thousand pieces like a broken mirror. It is believed that demon-possession then follows this process, and all the broken fragments of the person's brain develop into demonic spirits inside their brain. The evil spirits then develop the victims multiple personalities inside their brains. The suffering is that there is the real person still there the real core self but the prime self becomes deceived into thinking that one of the alter-personalities is the real core self. When the victim wishes to talk with one of the personalities inside their brain they will sit in their room of mirrors. There it is believed they go into a trance, and then the demonic spirit will appear in the mirror looking like the victim or even someone else. Is any of this true? Are artists victims of such a horrible program as this? One only can wonder.

Artists like Marlon Brando, Marilyn Monroe, Michael Jackson, Jimi Hendrix, and many, many others talked about rooms they had full of mirrors. In fact, royal kings, queens, princes, and princesses where known to have rooms full of mirrors. These royals had rooms that were paneled with mirrors reaching from the ceiling to the floor where the walls themselves were composed of mirrors. Some of them had the floors polished and made of silver so that it reflected every person and object inside the room. Some would say these royals were very vain about themselves, and some would say they too had early forms of mind-control and sorcery.

Many artists of today and yesterday have spoken about their rooms full of mirrors. Some of them, like Michael Jackson and Marilyn Monroe, even stated that they talk to spirits in these rooms. Jimi Hendrix one time wrote a strange song regarding this. The song was called Room Full of Mirrors. Noted lyrics from the song went like this, 'Well I took my spirit and I crashed my mirrors. Now the whole world is here for me to see. Broken glass was falling in my brain; cuttin and screaming and crying in my head'. Many will guess what Hendrix was singing about. Was it drugs, heartbreak, or demonic possession or was it mind-control mixed with demonic possession? It's a question people have to decide for themselves.

Chapter 6

Many music artists have met some horrible deaths due to some reckless lifestyles. Some wonder if these deaths really happened the way the reports of the media, and police officers said it did. Often these deaths leave more questions than answers from those who look into them. Some believe that these deaths are ritual sacrifices to Satan. There has been no proof to show this. They state that many of these deaths were covered up to look like overdoses or accidents. These claims seem to come up again and again.

The death of Brian Jones was a death that was suspected of being a satanic hit. One can wonder if that is true or not. Brian Jones was the one who formed the legendary hard rock group called the Rolling Stones. Brian was the one who hand-picked the members of the group and even named the band. He was the original bandleader of this most notorious group. Brian

Jones was a talented, and wide-ranging multi-instrumentalist. His main instruments was the guitar, harmonica, and keyboards. Brian was the one who brought in Mick Jagger and Keith Richards into the group. Jagger and Richards were childhood friends looking to become famous rock stars. They got their chance, and wish as members of the Rolling Stones. Overtime Jagger and Richards took over the leadership role of the group especially when they became the song-writing team of the group. This did not sit well with Brian, and he began to often feud with Jagger and Richards. At the same time the members of the band got heavy into drugs, and it took a bad toll on Jones. In June of 1969 the members of the Rolling Stones got sick of the fights with Brian Jones and they told him to leave the group. One month later Brian was found dead in his swimming pool at his own home called Cotchford Farm. No one can explain how this man died in his own swimming pool. The rumors regarding this is that the Rolling Stones got heavy into Satanism during their rise to fame. That hey were part of an occult called the Process Church which was an offspring witchcraft coven of the Church of Satan headed by Anton LaVey. No one can confirm if this is true but they state that someone attacked Jones, and killed him and threw him into the swimming pool to make it look like a drowning. The rumor was that the other band members wanted him gone, and allowed him to become a sacrifice for Satan. One wonders if this could be true or was it that Jones took too many drugs, and passed out in the pool. No one knows for sure.

Mama Cass whose real name was Elliot was another example of strange rumors. She became world-wide famous when she sang with a group called the Mamas and the Papas. She got her start working in a singing group called the Big 3 along with Tim Rose and Jim Hendricks. One rumor of Mama Cass Elliot was that she was related to elite banking and government families of America and Europe. That her humble beginnings were not as humble as people think. Another rumor was that she was a mind-control victim but no proof was ever shown of this. She was into drugs and often struggled with her weight. Another rumor about her is that she was into witchcraft, and occult rituals but this also has not been proven.

When the Mamas and the Papas broke up Elliot started a solo

career, and would release five albums. At the height of her solo career in 1974 Elliot was performing sold out shows at the London Palladium. After a show she did she then went to sleep at the London flat No.12 at 9 Curzon Place. She never woke up and died at the age of 32 years old. The story of her death caused by a ham sandwich came from the police. When they found her they stated they found a partially eaten sandwich, and they thought she choked on it, but the autopsy showed that no food at all was found in her windpipe. Her death was ruled as a heart attack. Others had other ideas regarding her death as they stated she was poisoned. They also stated that someone should have tested the sandwich she was eating to see if it was poisonous, but no one did. Now no one can say for sure what really happened. Oddly enough four years later at that same place in London upon that same No.12 flat the drummer of The Who named Keith Moon also died there.

His death has many rumors to it as well. Many said it was a satanic hit in fact satanic hits often come up again and again regarding these deaths, but no one knows for sure. Moon died at the same age Mama Cass Elliot did.

Another artist that met a strange fate was Janis Joplin. Janis was called the Queen of Psychedelic Soul. In her short career she had ten hit songs. Her most noted song was Me and Bobby McGee which was a number one hit song. Joplin was multi-talented. She was also a painter, dancer, and music arranger.

During her high-school days Joplin was often taunted for being different from the other teenagers, and for having her own views on life. She was called a 'pig,' 'freak,' and 'creepy' and because she made friends with black teenagers she was also called a 'nigger lover', a very horrible term from awful white teenagers.

Joplin was known to walk around barefooted, and would wear Levi jeans when all the girls wore skirts. She would carry around an autoharp with her wherever she went, and would play it and sing when she could. Joplin would make her way to the hippie scene in Haight-Ashbury. She got her start in a band called the Big Brother and the Holding Company. This band became very popular in the hippie community in Haight-Ashbury.

When she hooked up with these groups of people there she became addicted to drugs. She was smoking pot, dropping acid, and she became addicted to heroin. She also lost her faith in Christianity, and began to practice eastern religious beliefs. Joplin and her band began to promote the teachings of a Hare Krishna guru named Bhaktivedanta Swami. They would also perform with Swami on stage along with other Krishna gurus named Allen Ginsberg and Moby Grape each of them also being musical artists.

Much of the money the band made went to the San Francisco Hara Krishna temple. There were other rumors about Joplin as well. Many said that when she broke into the music industry she became a mind-control victim, and that Paul A. Rothschild was her handler who used to control her through her heroin addiction. This has never been proven. Another rumor was that she was related to elite banking families, but this to has not been proven.

After Joplin and the Big Brother band had performed at the Monterey Pop Festival they started to become very popular. She and her band would appear on the Dick Cavett Show, and soon they became very big in the industry. Joplin at this time was being praised as one of the greatest singers of leading women in rock music. Many told her she should dump the band and go solo. This advice often caused resentment with other band members.

By the recording of the second album, Joplin played a major role in the arrangement and production of the songs. This album would be called Cheap Thrills. At this point she became sole leader of the band, and the band started to be called Janis Joplin and the Big Brother and Holding Company. The band started to put out some hit songs but soon the band started to break apart due to the resentment the other band members had for Joplin.

She was then forced to leave the band, and then she formed a new band called Kozmic Blues Band. By this point Joplin was shooting up at least $200 a day of heroin. Efforts by close friends were made to keep her clean but often these efforts would not work. At the Woodstock concert Joplin was flown in by helicopter riding with a pregnant Joan Baez along with Joplin's mother. Before her performance she shot up heroin in the backstage area. She would then pull a performance together even though she was three sheets to the wind so to speak. During the performance she would talk to the crowds asking them if they were happy with all the drugs they were on.

After Woodstock Joplin gave a performance at Madison Square Garden. There she was accused of trying to start a riot. After this she began to break down, and wanted to break from the music industry. She would leave the band Kozmic Blues Band, and she went to Brazil to try and get clean and sober. For a while she did so but when she came back to the United States she was pulled back into the music industry, and she got on heroin again. She would form a new band called the Full Tilt Boogie Band.

She would end up recording her biggest album with this band called Pearl in 1970. From this album she recorded her biggest single called Me and Bobby McGee which went number one on the charts. The song was originally written by Kris Kristofferson who was Joplin's lover in the spring of 1970. At this point Joplin began to have nervous breakdowns. She often talked about being visited by U.F.O's, and she would have what sounds like demonic attacks. Joplin started to stay at the Landmark Motor Hotel because it was a place that a lot of heroin users and dealers lived at. 16 days before October 4, 1970, Jimi Hendrix was found dead at the age of 27 years old.

On October 4, 1970, Paul A. Rothschild sent John Cooke who was Joplin's road manager to the Landmark Motor Hotel. Cooke saw Joplin's Porsche 356 Cabriolet which had psychedelic paint on it parked in the parking lot. Joplin was staying in room 105. Upon entering the room John Cooke found Joplin dead on the floor as her body was lying beside the bed. The official cause of death was said to be a heroin overdose, but Cooke believes that Joplin had been given heroin that was far stronger, and more potent then what she wanted.

It was said that this was done on purpose to kill her. Joplin would die at the age of 27 years old. Oddly enough it was said that when Jim Morrison's manager found out about Joplin's death, and reflected on the deaths of both Hendrix and Joplin; it was stated that he warned Morrison that he would be next. His strange reasoning for this was because he stated that these kinds of deaths 'come in 3's'. Strange enough I did find out why such deaths come in 3's in accordance to what satanic hits mean to Satan. There are experts in Satanism who state that such deaths in 3's are done to mock the threefold character of GOD. Could this be the reason why they died? One can only decide for themselves.

Another artist to look at is Jimi Hendrix. Jimi Hendrix is called one of the greatest guitar players to ever live. Some say he was the best of the 20th century. He had a unique talent for playing the guitar with his teeth. Jimi started playing guitar at the age of 15 years old in Seattle, Washington. He had a natural gift for guitar play.

Hendrix was a troubled young man as a teenager he would often get into trouble. At 19 years old Hendrix was arrested for riding in a stolen car. He was given a chance by the authorities to either go to the Army or go to jail. Hendrix chose to go to the Army. Hendrix was seen as a skilled soldier, and he was chosen to join the 101st Airborne Division. He completed his paratrooper training in just over eight months. Major General C.W.G. Rich was so impressed with him he awarded Jimi the prestigious Screaming Eagles patch on January 11, 1962. Hendrix however still had a great love for playing music, and still played guitar in the Army. Hendrix was offered to go career but he refused, and started to express his dislike of

staying in the Army. On June 29, 1962 Hendrix was granted an honorable discharge from the Army after he constantly refused to go career.

After he came out of the Army he decided to follow his dream of making it in the music industry. He would audition for several bands, and soon he found himself playing lead and rhythm guitar for bands like the Isley Brothers, Little Richard, and Curtis Knight and the Squires, and several others. All these band members would brag about Jimi's skills to others stating how great he was.

During his time hanging out with this circle of bands it was said of Jimi that at first he was not into drugs at all but he was a clean, and sober artist starting out. Soon he got into smoking pot, dropping acid, and using cocaine. Many said that he did drugs to fit in with the other band members of the groups he played in.

Jimi found himself not going anywhere in the music industry in America, and so a friend of his told him he should try his hand in England. There Jimi played with many British rock groups, and he was hailed as being great. Also at this time he developed an addiction to LSD also called acid.

Jimi was then noticed by a man named Michael Jeffery. One of Jimi's managers had brought Michael to see him play. Michael saw money, and a vision for a new band after watching him play. Now the rumor is that Michael had ties to a group called MI6 which is the secret service of the United Kingdom. This has never been proven true. Another rumor was he had mafia ties but this too was not proven true. Oddly Michael Jeffery was seen as a dangerous man and not to be trusted. Another rumor was that Michael put Jimi through a mind-control program as a condition for fame and success in the music industry. People believed this was very true but no evidence was shown to prove this.

Jimi moved to England in 1966, and after the meeting with Jeffery it was Jeffery who came with the idea of the psychedelic hard rock band called The Experience. Jeffery also hand-picked the other two members of the band who were Noel Redding and Mitch Mitchell.

Michael Jeffery was still bitter about his last management job with the rock group called the Animals. It was said that the Animals broke away from him due to money issues and abuse at the hands of Michael Jeffery and his people. Now Michael Jeffery had a new band that he could make millions of dollars off. The band was officially named The Jimi Hendrix Experience. From their first album they became an overnight success. Soon other albums would follow that made millions of dollars. They also made millions from concert tickets as well.

The band's major hit singles were Hey Joe, Purple Haze, The Wind Cries Mary, Fire, and All Along the Watchtower. Jimi, and the Experience would give legendary performances at the

Monterey Pop Festival, and the Woodstock Festival. They would become one of the highest paid bands in history.

Many strange things were happening to Hendrix at this time. Some said that Jimi was struggling with demonic possession, that he would often hear voices in his head, and would stand in front of a mirror and pull patches of his hair out. His drug addictions became really bad. It was said that he would cut parts of his forehead, and put acid tabs on the cuts to let it dissolve into his brain. His sexual addictions were also very well known. He would have sex with 10 to 20 women a night.

He was often very hurt by what other leaders of the black power movement and the black community said about him. Most blacks in the 60's were not into hard rock only a few were by the numbers. Most of them were into Motown or Stax records. Most of Jimi's fans were white. Many black people stated that he did not care about black people or Civil Rights. Jimi was deeply hurt by this, and made it a point to go to the Dr. King memorial concert.

Jimi was also arrested several times for drug possession. In fact, it was known that Michael Jeffery had drug dealers on call to supply the band drugs. Jimi would also at times freak out on stage. He would go into strange rages, and destroy his guitar, mic, and make angry statements or sad statements on stage. Jimi began to have a lot of fights with Jeffery over missing money, and career direction. Jimi wanted to make his own kind of music, and not the music Jeffery told him to make. Soon Jimi revolted on Jeffery by refusing to show up at the studio to record their new album. At this point Jimi was hanging out with members of the black power movements. It was stated that they gave him the idea to leave the band he was in, and form an all-black band. They wanted him to use his fame to speak up for the rights of black people. So Jimi did so. He coldly dump Noel and Mitch aside, and formed an all-black band called Band of Gypsys.

Michael Jeffery was against this idea but he was still in contract with Jimi, and Jimi was still one of the highest money grossers in the music industry. It was said that Michael on the surface supported the idea but did everything he could to sabotage the band. After this new band was formed no one among Jimi's fan base liked the new music they wanted The Experience.

This would often make Jimi angry, and at times he would storm off stage or play in the face of the boos of the audience, but he was still determined to make this band work. Soon after, Hendrix was arrested for possession of LSD. Hendrix stated that this time he was innocent, and many believed him. The story was said that Michael Jeffery planted the drugs on him to set him up for an arrest. His effort was to sabotage the band. This effort, if Michael did so, worked. After the arrest the Band of Gypsys broke up.

From there Michael wanted the Experience back, and thought Jimi would come to his senses and re-join the group. Noel and Mitch were on board already to return but Jimi was bitter and angry at Michael for it was said that Jimi knew Michael had set him up.

Michael was also stealing money from him. In late 1970 when this was going on Jimi was the highest paid performer in the world. He still refused to show up at the studio he created, and then on September 18, 1970 Jimi was found dead inside a bathtub.

The official cause of death was heart-failure caused by drugs, but there was a strange thing about what was found in his body as reported in the autopsy. He had gallons, and gallons of red wine in his system that experts believed could have only been forced down his mouth. The CIA does have a name for this kind of death. They call it water-boarding, and it is a method of torture before death. One wonders what really happened to Jimi Hendrix on that night. Here are the things that were said about it.

Close friends of Jimi stated that Jimi took legal action to recover the money that Michael was stealing from him. This turns out to be proven. Another thing was said that Jimi hired friends to break into the office of Michael Jeffery to find, and steal documents that prove he was stealing from him. If this is really true the story goes on to say that they did find evidence that Michael was embezzling large amounts of money from the concerts, and record sales of Jimi Hendrix and his band members. This also cannot be confirmed.

Jimi's girlfriend who was there that night admitted to a friend in another story that she was threaten into making sure she opened the lock doors of the room that night to let the killers in. This also has not been proven. Alan Douglas who was a recording engineer for the Experience stated that two days after Jimi's death that Michael Jeffery confessed to him that he took part in the death of Hendrix, but Douglas' testimony was never taken seriously.

Other friends stated that Michael threaten Jimi when he found out he was taking him to court, and that Jimi told close friends that the next time he is in Seattle will be in a pine box. This too was not taken seriously. There are people right now at the time of me writing this who are still fighting to have the heart-failure cause of death removed, and to make it a homicide. They base this on the gallons of red wine in his system, and that it could have only been caused by someone forcing it down his mouth. So who killed Jimi Hendrix? Did Michael, and some evil hit-men enter his room, and attack him forcing gallons of red wine down his mouth to painfully choke him to death and then leave his body in the tub to make it look like an overdose? This is a question you must decide for yourself.

In the very late 1950's throughout the 1960's folk music began to change as well to a new form called rock-folk music. The two main artists who brought this change on was Joan Baez and Bob Dylan. There are some strange rumors as well regarding these two very beloved artists.
Joan Baez was born in Staten Island, New York in 1941. Her father was a man named Albert Baez who was Mexican being born in Puebla, Mexico. Albert or Alberto Baez had left Catholicism to become a minister for a Methodist Church. Albert, who came to America when he was two years old, grew up in Brooklyn, New York. There he preached to a Spanish speaking congregation. Albert would later leave the ministry, and began to study mathematics and physics. He was a brilliant man who would come to be co-inventor of the x-ray microscope. He would author one of the most widely used textbooks of physics. Her father would also work in health care, and for the

UNESCO.

Joan's mother was born in Edinburgh, Scotland. She was the daughter of an English Anglican priest. Her name was Joan Bridge, and she was blood-related to the Dukes of Chandos. The Baez family would later convert to Quakerism. The Quaker doctrine does believe in similar things with Christianity but also it is different from the Christianity of the Bible.

Joan was raised to have a strong commitment to pacifism, and social issues. Her family moved around a lot living in towns all across the United States. They also lived in England, France, Switzerland, Spain, Canada, and the Middle East, including Iraq. This moving around was because of the work her father did for the UNESCO.

Joan Baez became interested in music at a very young age, and she began to learn how to play Rhythm and Blues music. After spending years practicing the songs she began performing them publicly. Her earliest performances were done at a youth group retreat in Saratoga, California. The youth group came from Temple Beth Jacob centered in Redwood City, California. In 1958 Joan's father began working at MIT, and he moved his family to Massachusetts. Joan lived near Boston, and she was near the center of the up, and coming rock-folk music scene.

In 1958 Joan Baez came to a soon to be legendary night-club called Club 47. Club 47 was located in Cambridge, Massachusetts. There Joan gave her first full concert, and then she quickly became a regular act there. She was soon signed to a record company, and in 1960 she recorded her first album called Joan Baez. Joan Baez would first meet Bob Dylan at Club 47. After recording her second album called Joan Baez vol.2 this album would go gold. She would then perform a concert show called the Joan Baez Show, and she would introduce the crowds to a then unknown Bob Dylan. In 1962 Dylan and Baez became romantically involved, and stayed together until 1965. Joan's career would go on for over 50 years.

Bob Dylan would go on to become a legendary singer, and song-writer. His career also would go on for over 50 years. He became famous for doing civil rights, anti-war, and social unrest songs. Bob Dylan comes from a Russian Jewish family. His real name is Robert Allen Zimmerman. His grand-parents came to America after fleeing the anti-Semitic programs of the then Russian Empire. They arrived in 1902. Dylan's parents grew up in America, and were part of a small close-knit Jewish community in Minnesota.

Dylan began playing at an early age, and in the 1950's he got heavy into Rock n' Roll music as a teenager. He started a band in high-school which changed members often, and they would perform cover songs of Little Richard and Elvis Presley. After high-school Dylan went to college but he soon dropped out of college, and started to drift around the night club scenes going from city to city. In 1961 Dylan came to the city of Cambridge, and came to the Greenwich Village area. He then began to perform at Club 47, and there he would encounter Joan Baez who was already at that point in the doors of the music industry.

Dylan would write many songs for Joan Baez. In return, Baez helped Dylan to get a record contract. His first albums would sell very slowly until Dylan recorded a major hit single called Blowin in the Wind in 1963. Soon more hit singles would follow and his record sales would increase dramatically. He would go on to become a legendary figure in the music industry for singing songs about real life events regarding people like Medgar Evers, Hurricane Carter, Hattie Carroll, and others.

The rumors regarding Joan Baez and Bob Dylan are centered around mind-control and satanic worship. These claims have never been proven true. It was stated about Baez that her father was her handler, and that he sold her to the industry, and would keep her sister named Mimi around her to watch her, but there is no evidence to support this.

Bob Dylan was said by some to be involved with satanic occults, and that he too was a victim of mind-control. The rumors regarding Greenwich Village and Club 47 is that Greenwich was a haven for CIA agents who lived and retired there, and many of those agents were involved with early mind-control programs after World War 2.

Club 47 was rumored to be a haven for satanic occult members, and one rumor was that the real Boston Strangler used to go to the club. Some even said that he was an artist there. Joan one time did a song that many felt suggested that she knew more about satanic rituals then people realized. In the song she sung about demonic possession, and children worshipping the devil in what looks to be on the outside a Church building but the altar was dedicated to Satan, but no one knows if that is what she was really singing about.

The killings of the Boston Strangler took place from June 14, 1962 to January 4, 1964. 13 women were killed by this man. The ages of these women were between the ages of 19 to 85 years old. The killings took place in, and outside the Boston area, and one of the killings took place across the street from Club 47. Mostly all the victims were sexually assaulted and then strangled. The man who was arrested for it was named Albert DeSalvo. The strange story behind this is that it was said that the police had beat him into making a confession to these crimes. In 2013 DNA confirmation shows heavy doubts that DeSalvo was the killer known as the Boston Strangler. In fact, people who knew Albert often defended him as being not capable of these vicious crimes. It was said by some that the real killer has never been caught, and his presence is linked to Club 47.

Regarding Bob Dylan's involvement with satanic occults and selling his soul to the devil, there was a shocking interview he did on a show called 60 minutes. Dylan was interviewed by a man named Ed Bradley. Ed asked Dylan about how he writes songs, and Dylan told him that they were magically written. Some believe that Dylan was talking about what is called in the occult automatic hand-writing which is when a demon writes through a person who is possessed. Ed would then ask Dylan about his staying power, and why he is still performing after all these years. Dylan then stated that it was part of a deal he made long ago. Ed then asked him who he made the deal with. Dylan it is believed almost said Satan but he stops himself and said it was with the chief-commander and that he made a bargain with him long ago. Ed then asked about the chief-commander and what the bargain was all about. Dylan then explains that the chief-commander lives in a world we do not see, and that the bargain was done so that Dylan could get to the point he is now.

The Bible tells us that Satan is a host meaning an army. It states that Satan commands legions of evil spirits, and thus Satan is their chief-commander. The Bible also tells us that Satan is a spirit, and that he does live in a world that humans cannot see. The Bible also tells us that people would give their souls to Satan for the riches, and fame of the world. If Dylan is not talking about Satan as many defenders would say then really who is he talking about, because when you really look into that interview the person Dylan is mentioning is not a human being nor is he talking about Jesus.

Chapter 7

During the 1960's it was believed that a new religion was being widely promoted at the time, it was called the New Age movement, and much of its beliefs were being taught to the hearts, and minds of the people. Many messengers came out at that time preaching new doctrines of nature religions, witchcraft, eastern spirituality, and even Satanism.

They would quote the works of Aleister Crowley, Helena Blavatsky, Annie Besant, Manly P. Hall, and others. They were into promoting Hinduism, Buddhism, and Gnosticism. Christianity in that time was being attacked often and the young started to embrace the pop culture, and hippie movements that taught different religious beliefs. The drug and sex movements ensnared thousands and thousands of people. Morality came crashing down, and pleasures, and strange spiritualism started to take over in their lives. The music industry was front and center to supply the soundtrack of this time.

The Bible calls these different faiths paganism and it's worshippers are heathens. The Bible commanded GOD's people to put no other gods before GOD. The Israelites were even commanded not to practice the faith of the people outside of them. The Christian Church was also commanded to not take part in the faith of the pagan religions. In fact, most of the Apostles and followers of Christ died by torture because they refused to worship the Roman gods.

If the Apostles time travelled, and came to the 1960's I think they would say, 'Well this looks familiar.' The generation that came to exist in the 1960's were people who experimented with reckless drug use, and sexual practices. The main drugs they used was marijuana, LSD, mushrooms, heroin, and cocaine. Many of these drugs caused hallucinations and addictions that ruined thousands of lives. It even ruined the lives of the artists they idolize more than Jesus.

Many young people were also marching for righteous causes and risking their lives doing it. They would march, and work for the Civil Rights movement, the Anti-War movement, and fight causes for poor labor workers, and for people living in total poverty. Many people who took part in this were murdered, beaten, had their lives ruined by strange forces that they called the government actions done against them. Many of them even had proof that the government did sabotage, and spied on them. They had proof of wire-taps and people foreshadowing them.

These government agencies that did this to them were mainly the FBI, Military Intelligence, and local police operations. The defense of these agencies went like this. The FBI stated that they were trying to bust communists that were a threat to the U.S. government, and were working in those movements, but oddly by the numbers most of these protestors were not communists only a very few were, and they were no threat but only exercised their right to freedom of speech. Most of the people they spied on like Dr. King were not promoting a communist government. They were promoting that our government live up to the creed found in the constitution. The FBI stated that they have pictures of civil rights leaders at communist meetings but it turned out they were not there to turn communist. They were there to defend the American rights of the poor people in communist groups whose people were not getting jobs, and whose family members were starving most of the time. Military Intelligence groups said they did actions against them to bust spies, and those who would try to lead movements to overthrow the government, but the radicals they were talking about only made up a very small few of them, and most people knew who they were. Most of the protestors did not want to violently overthrow any government. They wanted a stop to war, and other corrupt things that governments was doing.

Evidence was also shown that many of these government agents tried to turn the movements violent on purpose to put a stop to them. One wonders if communists and spies was really what they were after. The police investigators stated that they went after them for causing civil riots, and for possession of drugs, and other civil disobedience, but most of the footage caught on film does not show the protestors starting the riots. It shows the police taking the first strikes. The protestors were largely unarmed and only a very few were armed. Also there has never been a case in these protests of protestors firing on police, but there are cases of police killing student protestors like in Chicago, and at Kent State where 4 students were shot to death. I could see their point on drugs but the protests were not about drugs, and the rock concerts that were about drugs were hardly ever busted up.

The 1960's showed two things. The rise of social awareness to know the truth of important issues and also the rise of the New Age culture and religions. Record sales during that time sky-rocketed into unprecedented numbers. The rumors surrounding the New Age movement was that it was centered in the hippie movement who called their followers flower children. Many said that it was anti-establishment but the rumor was that it came from the establishment. This movement was also called the counter-culture movement, and it was said that it was used as a subversion to corrupt the people who marched in righteous causes. No one knows for sure how true this is. The proof seems to be in the pudding. Many artists who supported the hippie culture also came from families that worked in the government or in large corporations, not all of them, but many did, and they were among the most popular and had a heavy influence on their fans.

Leaders of the hippie movement told young people to drop out of school and do drugs. Dropping out of school would leave them prey to being drafted into the Vietnam War which would help what was called the establishment. Doing drugs would ruin the lives of many people and it did. This would help fill the many prisons that were being built at the time as well. This would lead to a reduction of numbers of people that could get involved in righteous causes.

The leaders who marched and lead the civil rights, anti-war protests told young people to stay in school and to refrain themselves from drugs. Maybe the saying that the hippie movement was a subversion to righteous causes could be a right statement. The name Aleister Crowley comes up again, and again in regards to the teachings of hippie leaders. Crowley was a known worshipper of Satan, and very proud of it. He wrote a book called the Book of the Law that became the main doctrine for the New Age faith. His motto was 'Do what thou will' rather than do the will of GOD. This motto became 'Do your own thing' in the 1960's.

Many hippie leaders praised Crowley but Crowley was also called one of the most wicked of men to ever live. He was kicked out of Italy after a string of kidnappings occurred, and some of the bodies of the children were found. The children had been sexually assaulted, and tortured in a ritual satanic fashion before their deaths. They were never able to prove their case against him, and so they decide it was best to tell him to leave.

In England he had a castle he owned where he committed satanic rituals and abused scores of children in these horrible rituals. The man had pictures hanging on his walls of these horrible acts, and he had certain connections with the English government that kept him out of jail. It was said that he worked for the British secret service during World War 2 as a spy. That he was a close friend of Hitler, and used that friendship to supply information to the British government.

Crowley freely admitted that he was demon-possessed, and stated that Satan wrote the Book of the Law through him when he was in a trance. For so many hippie leaders to actually praise the works of this man is very twisted indeed.

In the Book of the Law Crowley spoke about killing children as a human sacrifice. He told his followers that actions like these would grant them special powers from Satan. He also spoke about eating human waste for these strange powers as well.

Crowley told his followers that the best way to get close to Satan was to do all kinds of drugs. His drug of choice was heroin. In fact before his death in the mid-1940's he was in debt, and strongly addicted to heroin. It would be clear to say that those hippie leaders who preached his doctrine left out this information.

Most of the flower children most likely never read the Book of the Law, and those that did many hated the things they read. Regarding Aleister Crowley's influence in the music industry, it was said that he was the one who gave the idea to put backward messages in songs. This has never been proven, but many artists in the industry back then and even now often praised his writings, and his outlook on the New Age doctrine.

The very popular pop-rock group called the Beatles released an album in the mid-1960's called Sgt. Pepper's Lonely Hearts Club Band. This album brought a new change in the image of the Beatles. They began to sport a psychedelic look, and began to promote the use of drugs. They would state to their millions of fans that doing drugs would open their minds more. They also started to promote the teachings of Hindu spiritualism, and began to quote the teachings of their eastern guru.

The band members, especially John Lennon, were also making negative comments about Jesus Christ. The rumor regarding this album was that the album was a tribute to Aleister Crowley. This statement has never been proven. The Beatles did put pictures of all the people they admired and respected who lived throughout history on the cover of the album. One of the pictures was a picture of Aleister Crowley. In fact, another picture they almost put there got pulled out at the last minute. This picture was going to be Hitler. In fact, the cardboard cut-out of Hitler that was going to be used for the picture was still standing at the time they made the front cover. Keep in mind the words of the Beatles. They said these were pictures of people they admired and respected.

As you can guess there was no picture of Jesus Christ. In fact, the comments that John Lennon made about Jesus Christ got them into some hot water with some of their loyal fans. When these fans found out that Lennon stated that the Beatles were bigger then Jesus, and that he called Jesus a bastard these fans became outraged. They then took their favorite Beatles' albums, and in public they burned them in a fire, and began to destroy them.

The Beatles would recover from this by stating they were misunderstood, and they gave an apology. However, when you read that interview, and look at what kind of faith they were promoting one wonders if they really were misunderstood or just sucking up so that the scandal does not cost them record sales.

Around that same time the hard rock band called the Rolling Stones would also release a new album. The album was called Her Satanic Majesty's Request. The rumor surrounding this album was that it was a tribute to Satanism, and that the Rolling Stones had become members of the Process Church which was a witchcraft offspring church of the Church of Satan headed by Anton LaVey.

LaVey in the 1960's had released his works called the Satanic Bible for general people to buy. Many people did buy it, especially people into the rock scene. No one knows if the Rolling Stones were part of this coven but many insiders who worked with them would confirm the Stones satanic involvement again, and again.

One thing that is confirmed is the friendship the Stones, especially Mick Jagger, had with a man named Kenneth Anger. Kenneth Anger was a former Hollywood child star. He said of himself that he was a disciple of Aleister Crowley, and that he was also his boy child lover. Anger would go on to state that Crowley taught him everything he knew, and that he was Crowley's real chosen successor after Crowley's death.

Anger was into preaching Satanism, and would invite people over to his home to watch his film collection. They were films called snuff films which are films of people suffering real deaths. Anger's films, it was said, featured real satanic sacrifices of babies, children, men, and women being killed. It was rumored of Anger that he was the real founder of the Church of Satan, and that he hand-picked Anton LaVey to run the church for him.

Others also declared that Kenneth Anger was the real hidden hand behind the Church of Satan in California. Kenneth became a Hollywood director, and he would film a cult classic film called Lucifer Rising. Bobby Beausoleil was his main actor in the film who played the lead role. Bobby was also Anger's homosexual lover.

After doing the film Bobby was later convicted for murder as a member of the Charles Manson family. Mick Jagger would do the soundtrack for the film. Jagger, and his girlfriend at the time named Marianne Faithfull, who also was a musical artist, went with Kenneth Anger to Egypt. There they watched Anger film a satanic black mass ritual for the film Lucifer Rising.

A noted song of the Rolling Stones was Sympathy for the Devil. A song that was about Satan himself. This was one of the most popular songs the Rolling Stones ever made. It was also one of the most evil rock songs ever done. The song mocks Jesus Christ, and praises the devil. The Stones have a lot of songs like this they recorded. One wonders if the stories of their satanic worship, and involvement is more than just stories.

The story of the origin of the Beatles is also very strange. The rumor regarding them is that they were into satanic occults, and drugs way before they were famous. None of this was ever proven. They started out performing in night-clubs in England and West Germany. The areas they performed in were noted as being dangerous. The people who hung out there were into satanic occults, drugs, criminal lifestyles, and prostitution.

Many of the clubs they performed in also had stripper acts. Girls came to the stage to dance, and strip while the bands played. In West Germany the Beatles came to the Reeperbahn district where these activities went on. Many lives were ruined in that district due to drugs, prostitution, murder, and ritual deaths. The Beatles came to this district in 1960 where it should be noted Ringo Starr was not a member of the Beatles at that time. The Beatles would play in one of the night-clubs there for very little money. As they played the girls would strip naked, and dance for the men, and even women.

The district's influence upon those who walked its streets was anything but good. Prostitutes would line the streets selling their bodies behind windows in rooms that shined with a red-light.

The ages of these prostitutes ranged from 12 to 60 years old. The prices of these prostitutes were so accommodating that sex often ran after the men. Every kind of drug was available at that time and homelessness was often a problem and the poor would drop their waste right on the street.

The Beatles in regards to their skills as a band it was said that they were not that good. The crowds were more interested in the girls on stage then they were the music. Many said that they were a second rate band who only sounded good because everyone was drunk and high, and also no one was really paying any attention to them. The people who knew them in those days often wondered how they got so famous so fast.

These same people spoke about the strange things the Beatles did on stage, and their drug habits. Some of them even went so far to state they were demon-possessed. However, no one knows for sure how true their statements were. They would state that the Beatles had a hateful disposition on stage, and they often got into fights with the German fans, and would call them, 'fucking Nazis' which is the kind of language the district people used.

They also stated that they acted very strange on stage at times which led to them thinking they were possessed. They stated the Beatles would foam at the mouth at times, and bark like dogs out of nowhere. Others believed it was not possession that made them act like that but the drugs they would use. Others also stated that the reason they fought with night-club people at those times was because they were rowdy, drunk, and would do things to make the Beatles angry at them. One wonders what was really going on. The Beatles even in that time it was said they had a hatred toward Christianity especially John Lennon.

Lennon's distaste for Church people was even shown after he was famous. One time Lennon stood on the top of a balcony, and began cursing out some Church goers when they were attending St. Joseph's which was right across the street from him. Lennon then spotted a group of nuns right below him. He then took out his male member, and began pissing on top of the heads of the nuns.

West Germany was the place the Beatles were discovered. The two main people who brought them into the mainstream music industry were Brian Epstein and George Martin. A lot of rumors surround Brian Epstein. It was said of him that he had involvement with mind-control, and that he was supported by the Rothschild banking family, that he was a homo-sexual, and also a member of a satanic elite occult. There has never been any proof to these statements.

Epstein was a powerful man in the music industry. He was in charge of EMI which was Europe's largest record company at the time. He had a fleet of classical trained musicians in every field of music working under him. It was also said of EMI that they did not just produce records but they also produced military electronics for the British secret service, but no one knows how true that is. In the 1960's EMI made annual sales of 3.19 billion dollars a year, and these profits, it was clear, were not just record sales. They also had over 74,321 employees working for them.

It was Epstein's people that put the Beatles together, and they at that time removed their original drummer, and replaced him with Ringo Starr. George Martin would be the guy set in charge of them. He was EMI's studio recording director. Martin was the one who came up with the clean cut look of the Beatles. He had their hairs cut, and styled, and came up with the outfits they were to wear and established their image. In fact, this look and image became the image of almost every pop-rock band that followed the Beatles in the 1960's.

It was also said that the Beatles at first did not write the songs for their first albums. Some even said that they did not even perform them in the studio. It was said that the Beatles were not good enough yet to record them, so other musicians played the instruments for the songs instead and the Beatles were learning from them how to play their instruments better.

It was stated that the songs from their first albums which made them world famous were written by Martin, and his people. Most of his people were black talented musicians. Much of the fame of the Beatles was also said to be at first hyped up to draw people to them. It was said that Epstein, and his people arranged for the Beatles to make their first television appearance at the London Palladium. This took place in August of 1963. The official story was thousands of young teenage fans were screaming their heads off, and that a new sensation was born in music, but people who worked for the Beatles management at the time stated something totally different.

It was said that Epstein's people had paid about 100 girls to show up there at the front rows, and scream their heads off and also there was only about 400 people or less that were actually there, and not thousands. Once the girls started screaming the other girls started to do so. It was said that Epstein's people had given the newspapers the story of thousands of screaming girls, and paid the editors to write that they were a new sensation in music. One wonders how the Beatles were really made famous. It was also said that the Kennedy Airport riot was also staged by Epstein's people, that they paid a fleet of girls to rush the barricade which caused the fans behind them to follow them toward the barricade. These statements have never been proven but they come up again and again by different people who were there at the time.

It was said that these tactics worked so well that when the Beatles appeared on the Ed Sullivan Show 75 million Americans watched it. The Beatles would go on to become a world-wide famous band. Every rock band in the industry was said to be jealous of them. In fact in October of 1965, Queen Elizabeth knighted them and gave them full membership among the British elite families.

The Rolling Stones were said to be the counterparts to the Beatles. Instead of clean cut, the image of the Rolling Stones was designed to be mean, dirty, and rebellious. The start of the notorious fame of the Rolling Stones took place in the spring of 1963. It was said that their notorious image was planned out that way on purpose. After the Rolling Stones were signed to a record contract their management team arranged for them to appear on one of England's most popular shows called Thank Your Lucky Stars.

The main audience of the show were middle-age people who clearly did not like hard rock or the image of rebellious youths. It was an odd choice for a show for them to appear on. When the Rolling Stones performed the audience members became deeply offended and the viewers were shocked and mad. Thousands of angry letters were sent to the producers of the show proclaiming that it was a disgrace that long haired men who played that kind of music were allowed to perform on their favorite show.

Andrew Oldham was the Stones' hands on manager at that time. After the negative publicity the Stones received in the press Andrew was very happy about it. The Stones at that time were worried, and asked Andrew how he could be so happy about this, and why did he book them on this show.

Andrew it was said, then explained to them that they were going to make them the opposite to the nice and clean Beatles. That the more the parents hated them the more their kids will love them, and told them to wait and see. The story is that the Rolling Stones' management put the band on the show on purpose to make people angry.

Many people said that the Rolling Stones were put in a position to be the band to promote violence, sex, and drugs among the youth. They stated that the Stones' management team wanted as the main core of their fans to be young people to inspire them into lifestyles that would cause them to revolt on their parents. No one is sure how true this is, but the Stones' did have at many times a violent influence on their fans.

In 1964 the Rolling Stones performed on the Ed Sullivan Show. The fans got so charged up that they began destroying the television studio. After the carnage stopped Sullivan made a public television address to the audience, and stated 'I promise you, they will never be back on our show'. After that performance which got so much media attention the record sales of the Rolling Stones took off to very huge sales as they sold millions.

Another story regarding the Beatles, and the Rolling Stones along with other bands was that they were putting backward messages into their songs. At first this could not be proven but later on it was proven that they did have backward messages in many of these songs. The Beatles, and the Stones both stated they knew nothing about it but many find that hard to believe. Some of these messages were very disturbing. The messages often refer to the devil, fornication, sex with children, murder, and other very twisted things.

One of them even caused people to think that Paul of the Beatles was dead and replaced with a look alike, but this was not true, the real Paul is still alive at the time of this writing.

Susan Aktins, who was a former member of the Church of Satan, and a former member of the Manson family, spoke about a strange thing Charlie used to do to her. Susan was one of the people arrested for the brutal murder of Sharon Tate which was ordered by Charles Manson. Susan stated that Charlie used to sit her down, and put her in a trance, and play the records of the Beatles. Charlie would tell her that secret messages was in the songs. Susan, while listening in the state she was in, stated that she heard another set of lyrics telling her to obey and to kill. Some believe it was just the drugs she was on, or could it have been something more sinister?

It is stated in the Bible that the abuse of drugs is witchcraft, and that witchcraft can leave people open to demonic spirits. The rock bands, the occults, and others in the 60's promoted the use of drugs freely. In accordance to what the Bible teaches this teaching would leave millions exposed to evil spirits.

One time, a former friend of the Rolling Stones who was one of their roadies, spoke about the witchcraft the Rolling Stones were into. He spoke about the girlfriends of Jagger and Richards in that time, one was Marianne Faithfull, Jagger's girlfriend, and the other was Anita Pallenburg, who was Richards' girlfriend. In fact Anita turned out to have had sex with all the members of the Stones. He one time stated that the Stones were into casting spells, and would carry charms with them. He stated that Faithfull and Pallenburg had a chest they often had brought with them.

One day the former roadie, out of wonder decided to open and look inside the chest. He stated that the chest was filled with pieces of bones, and fur skins of dead animals, and had other items related to witchcraft. No one knows how true the story is, but oddly enough in 1980 a police officer named Michael Passaro was doing his rounds, and drove near Keith Richards' estate.

He stated that when he did he heard a large group of people chanting from the woods that was near Richards' estate. Michael believed that the sounds were people worshipping Satan. Sometime after hearing this Michael got a call on the radio to respond to a homicide that took place in Richards' home. When Michael got there the body of Richards' 17 year old caretaker was found dead. She had been shot to death. Michael believed that the evidence pointed to someone Richards' knew but instead it was ruled as a home invasion robbery gone bad.

The Beatles as a band would eventually break up, and the band members would go solo. The band is believed to have broken up due to the fights that band members had with John Lennon after he married a woman named Yoko Ono. Yoko was deep into witchcraft, and sorcery, and she openly promoted that fact. Lennon through this marriage got deeper into eastern spirituality. His beliefs would be called New Age faith. He started to make even nastier statements against Jesus Christ. One of those statements when asked about Jesus Christ went like this, 'a garlic-eating, stinking little yellow, greasy fascist bastard who was a Catholic Spaniard.'

Not only are these statements evil to the core they are also racist to Italian, Asian, and Spanish people. One day while taking a walk around his expensive penthouse apartment building, John Lennon was shot and killed by a strange man who many said was sent there by Satanists to assassinate him. It was not proven that an elite satanic occult had Lennon killed but nevertheless Lennon was shot dead in cold-blood.

Chapter 8

The teachings of Aleister Crowley often seem to come up in the art work, and image of many rock artists. Bands like Led Zeppelin, The Doors, Black Sabbath, Ozzy Osbourne and many others often refer to Crowley in one form or another. Jimmy Page, who played lead guitar for Led Zeppelin, actually bought the castle Crowley used to live in, and perform his satanic rituals.

It is believed that Aleister Crowley is buried in an underground chamber underneath the castle. Page also promoted the works of Crowley even appearing in cult films where he would play himself, and summon the spirit of Crowley in a mirror. The Doors on their album called 13 one time put a cover picture of Crowley on the album. Ozzy Osbourne actually dedicated an entire album to Crowley called the Blizzard of Oz. Ozzy also wrote a song dedicated to him called Mr. Crowley.

It was also believed that these rock artists who clearly admired him also read his book, and sought to practice the rituals of the book. It is not known just which rituals they did practice because some of these rituals involve the murder of children and animals. It was said of Jim Morrison that he often quoted the works of Crowley to his band mates and close friends, that he also would practice the rituals of the Book of the Law. No one knows if he actually murdered children which is something very hard to believe, but it was known he was into the sex-magic rituals described in the book. He would have sex with women who were part of witchcraft covens, and he would share glasses with them of each other's blood, and then have sex with them on top of a drawn 5-pointed star.

These actions are describe in the Bible as being full blown satanic worship. Many people close to Jim said he was demonically possessed. There was strange footage of him at a concert where different voices of people were coming out of him in a very creepy way. Many of the voices sounded inhuman. Some said he was high on drugs, while others said Jim was into shaman practices and would summon spirits before each concert he did. There is truth to both of these statements. Jim Morrison one time spoke openly about a spiritual encounter he had when he was living as a homeless person on Venice Beach.

Jim actually came from an elite military family his father was an Admiral in the United States Navy, and was involved with the Tonkin Gulf affair that led to the most hated war in American history. Jim was at one point going to college and living off his father's money but he soon dropped out of school. It was believed that his family would later disown him and he ended up homeless. One day, according to Jim he, was walking under a canal, and encountered a spirit that Jim stated was Satan. He stated that Satan ran after him, and then several spirits showed up in the form of Native American shamans. He then stated they all ran inside him, and came to live in him. Jim would go on to tell others that ever since that day he would see whole concert images in his head, and hear songs, and see lyrics that he would write down. He went on to say that he would often go into a trance writing down songs that even he did not fully understand.

His band members stated of Jim that he was not an artist in the sense of that word. They stated he was a shaman and would tune in to spiritual planes, and sing music through it. They stated that performing with Jim was a feeling of being taken over, and often they played notes that came out of nowhere. Even they were shocked as to how well they played songs they never heard of before or had written down to think on them.

One time Jim had married a woman who was a member of a witchcraft coven. Jim married her in a witchcraft ceremony. Jim and his witch-bride got married standing in the middle of a 5-point star sharing a glass of each other's blood. Another strange story was when Jim stayed at the Chateau Marmont he had woken up not remembering what he did the night before. There was glasses all about him with blood inside of them, and a naked man in his bed.

The Bible forbids the drinking of blood. The Bible teaches that the life-force of a living human or animal is in its blood, and that it's not to be drunk but poured upon the ground when death happens to a living person or creature.

Satanists, and members of occults believe that drinking blood will give them special powers. Some said they even got high or possessed by demons when drinking blood. The Bible tells us that the practices of satanic pagans were condemned by GOD, and one of those practices was drinking blood. In fact the myth of vampires was said to come from pagans who were possessed by fallen angels, and were heavy into drinking blood.

Oddly enough Aleister Crowley also taught his followers that drinking blood would give them special powers. In the 1960's we saw the birth of open-air rock concerts on a massive scale. One of the rumors behind these concerts was that there were members of the CIA, and MI6 selling drugs at these concerts. There has been no proof to this but there is proof that the CIA, and MI6 did engage in drug running sales to increase profits for black ops missions. This got discovered when several planes had crashed belonging to these secret agencies, and barrels filled with heroin, cocaine, and marijuana were found on them. Some files that became de-classified showed that the U.S. government funded an operation to test reactions of soldiers after they were given LSD, but no proof was shown that the drugs were being sold at the concerts by these agents. One does wonder who then were the CIA and MI6 selling the drugs to?

The rumors surrounding the open-air concerts of the 60's was that it was a wide-scale drug experiment, but no proof was shown to say that the concerts were plotted by people in the government to be used for experimentation upon those in attendance. What is very proven is that large amounts of drugs were used there, and they came from somewhere, and thousands, and thousands of people were getting very high and addicted to them.

One of the groups that brought large shipments of drugs to these concerts was a group called the Merry Pranksters. They were led by a man named Ken Kesey. Kesey also had close ties to Timothy Leary, a very noted hippie leader. The rumor regarding Kesey was that some said he was an undercover CIA agent but this was never proven. What is a fact is that Kesey, and his group would drive around in their painted psychedelic vans from city to city, and would drop off thousands of acid tabs in sugar cubes, or on paper blot, and they would lace coke-cola cans.

They would sell and sometimes give away these drugs which also included marijuana and mushrooms. No one really knows how Kesey and his group were getting all these drugs, or how they managed to avoid arrest so many times. Some said Kesey knew people who made LSD, and grew marijuana, and would go to these people first when he and his group came to a city, and then they would go around the city selling the drugs and come back with the money for these dealers. Many also said for him, and his group to be able to do that so many times and be known for doing it shows that there were people in higher places of authority looking out for him. Another thing Kesey, and his group would do was pick up runaway girls who were very young, and bring them to different hippie compounds and places out West, especially dropping them off in places in California, Arizona, and New Mexico.

One of the main cities he took these runaways to was San Francisco. San Francisco in the 60's had one of the largest hippie communities in the world. Thousands of runaway teens went there to live a hippie life but they ended up living a broken drug addicted life. Many also did not make it home but died due to overdoes, found kidnapped, murdered, or they disappeared without a trace.

Timothy Leary was one of the founders of this hippie community in San Francisco, and was its main defender and speaker. Leary actually told thousands of young people to drop out of school and run away from home and come to San Francisco, and live a drug addicted lifestyle. He would paint the picture of this lifestyle in a different way and promised these young people freedom to do what they like but it ended up not being what Leary had them believing.

Most of these kids had no idea how to get or hold a job or make money, get an apartment, or support themselves. Mostly all of them ended up homeless or living in groups in small apartments or were taken into state funded shelters. I guess they decided to leave this part out when Papa Phillips wrote a song called San Francisco which encouraged thousands of teens to runaway there, and to wear flowers in their hair.

These kids were also exploited as well. Many sold their bodies for drug money, and were used in white-slavery rings. Many ended up doing porn films for food, clothing, shelter, and drugs.

One of the most legendary open-air rock concerts was the First Annual Monterey International Pop Festival. It was attended by nearly 150,000 people. The festival took place from June 16, to

June 18, 1967 at the County Fairgrounds in Monterey, California. This festival became the template for the Woodstock Festival two years later. 1967 was called by the 60's generation as the Summer of Love. The festival was remembered for the first major American appearances of the Jimi Hendrix Experience, The Who, and Ravi Shankar and it was Janis Joplin's first large scale public performance. The festival also introduced Otis Redding to a large white audience where before he only played in front of a black audience. The people who planned the event were John Phillips of the Mama and the Papas, promoter Lou Adler, producer Allan Pariser, and publicist Derek Taylor. These men had put together the festival in seven weeks.

The members of the festival's board of directors, which are people who give money and input for it, were rather famous. Some of the names were Mick Jagger, Paul McCartney, Smokey Robinson, Terry Melcher, and others. Other bands who played there was the Jefferson Airplane, the Mamas and the Papas, Buffalo Springfield, and others. Other bands were also invited but did not play for many reasons.

When The Who did their set they ended their drug-fueled performance with a song called My Generation, when Pete Townshend smashed his guitar the audience became stunned and then when smoke bombs exploded behind the amps, the frightened concert staff rushed to save the microphones because they were very expensive. At the end of the mayhem drummer Keith Moon kicked over his drum kit which ended the performance.

Jimi Hendrix ended his set with his own version of the song Wild Thing. During the performance Jimi put his guitar down, and kneeled over it and started to pour lighter fluid on it. Then he set the guitar on fire. He then smash the guitar seven times before throwing the remains to the audience. This action greatly contributed to his rising fame in the United States.

Otis Redding came to the event because his promoter named Jerry Wexler saw the festival as an opportunity to advance the career of Otis. The festival would be one of his last major performances. When he came on stage he was backed by Booker T. and the MG's. Otis would die six months later in a plane crash at only 27 years old.

The Beach Boys were supposed to play at the event but were unable due to a number of issues. Carl Wilson was feuding with the U.S. government officials for his refusal to be drafted into military service during the Vietnam War. Brian Wilson was suffering from auditory hallucinations and manic-depressive/schizoaffective disorders. In fact Brian had not performed with the group live for some time. Dennis Wilson also was having personal spiritual problems which would result in a strange relationship with the Charles Manson family in 1968.

The Beatles refused to play because their pop-rock music did not fit in with the hard rock sound. Donovan could not play because due to a drug bust the U.S. government refused to give Donovan a visa. The Rolling Stones were not able to play the event because Mick Jagger and Keith Richards were arrested for drug possession, and so the U.S. government refused to give Jagger and Richards visas.

Brian Jones of the Rolling Stones did manage to be there and he would introduce Jimi Hendrix to the stage. The Motown artists were invited but Berry Gordy refused to let any of his acts appear due to the drug image of the event.

In 1967 the Monkees were the biggest selling pop-rock group and musical act of that year. They wanted to play the event but John Phillips and Lou Adler refused to let them. They did ask Peter Tork to introduce Buffalo Springfield for their set which Peter did so.

The amount of drugs that were used, and sold at the Monterey Pop Festival made one drug dealer $10,000 in 2 hours. It was said that there was over 2,000 or more drug dealers there. One drug dealer alone stated that he sold over 5,000 tabs of acid in less than 2 hours.

This concert went on for 3 days which is 72 hours, and the dealers kept running out, and getting resupplied rather quickly which was odd. It was said that large stashes of drugs were kept near the dealers and armed criminals were guarding them. Some said that many of the dealers worked for the CIA, but there was no proof to those statements.

The next major open-air rock concert was called The Woodstock Music and Art Fair which was also billed An Aquarian Exposition. The Aquarian part of the name came from new age beliefs that the future generation will be an Aquarian people. The understanding was in this doctrine that it will do away with the age of Christianity, but it is not sure if the people who came to Woodstock fully understood the meaning of the name.

The Woodstock event took place at Max Yasgur's 600 acre dairy farm in the town of Bethel, New York which was 43 miles southwest of the town of Woodstock, New York. The event was started on August 15, 1969 and ended on August 18, 1969. The event was called one of the great moments in American history. It rained for most of those three days. 32 bands would perform there in front of a peak audience of over 400,000 people.

Michael Lang was one of the main people who initiated the event. Lang was the one who organized the Miami Pop Festival which brought about 100,000 people. The other three men who organized the Woodstock event were John Roberts, Joel Rosenman, and Artie Kornfeld. Tickets to the Woodstock Festival were sold at record stores in New York City, and other places in the State of New York. People were also able to get tickets through the mail, and at the gate. Advance tickets were $18 and at the gate they were $24. These are 1969 prices so the equivalent today would be about $114 to $124 a ticket.

So many people came to the festival that it caused a massive traffic jam that was seen for miles. The amount of people became so great in numbers that the fence for the event to contain the people, and check sales had to be cut down. This resulted in thousands of people coming to the event for free.

There were several fatalities at the festival. These deaths were caused by overdoses, trampling's, and people being run-over by cars, and even a tractor, but by the numbers of people there the deaths were very small, it could have been worse.

There were also several miscarriages that sadly took place. Many resulted from these young women dropping acid. There were also births as well of young women going into labor early due to drug use.

Nearly a half a million people came to the festival with a potential for disaster, riots, looting, and general catastrophe but instead there was a sense of rugged peace in the air, and a respect for each other among the crowds. In fact the behavior, and attitudes of the crowds helped to maintain order at the festival.

Many famous bands played there like Santana, The Grateful Dead, Creedence Clearwater Revival, Janis Joplin, The Who, Jefferson Airplane, Joe Cocker, Crosby, Stills, and Nash, Sly and the Family Stone, Richie Havens, Joan Baez, and many others.

Jimi Hendrix was the last act to perform at the festival. When Hendrix finally took the stage the audience, which peaked over 400,000 people, was now reduced to 30,000 people due to rain delays. Hendrix would perform a two hour set doing a psychedelic rendition of the U.S. national anthem called the Star-Spangled Banner after which he segued into the song Purple Haze. Hendrix's image performing this number wearing a blue-beaded white leather jacket with fringe, and a red head scarf has been regarded as a defining moment of the 1960's.

People often wonder why the Beatles did not appear there. The reason why was because promoters contacted John Lennon to ask if the Beatles would play there, and John stated they would not unless Yoko Ono, and her band called Plastic Ono Band got to perform as well. The promoters then turned him down which resulted in another fight with Lennon, and his band mates over Yoko which later on the Beatles would break-up.

The Doors were also invited but turned it down due to the thinking that it would be a second class repeat they got concerning the Monterey Pop Festival. The Doors would come to regret that decision of not playing. The band called Chicago was supposed to perform but pulled out at the last minute, and they were replaced by Santana. Roy Rogers outright refused and Joni Mitchell did not want to miss her scheduled appearance on the Dick Cavett Show. Jethro Tull refused to go because he hated hippies. Bob Dylan who lived in New York State at the time was mad about the number of hippies piling up outside his house in the nearby town of Woodstock. Dylan then packed up, and left with his family for England to avoid the festival.

Many Christians should wonder if this festival was truly a great moment in time. The festival was in honor of a generation that would come to end Christianity even though most people had no idea what Aquarian was really all about. They were told it's all about peace and love but there was more to it than that. I guess we should ask ourselves what Jesus Christ thought about the event. Would Jesus have gone to the event knowing all things like Jesus knows them? After all it was raining most of the three days of the event, and they were very heavy rains. The over 400,000 people there were isolated on farmland immersed in the mud while they pumped themselves full of drugs, and for three conscience days they were stoned, and in drug-induced trances. They were fornicating, and getting stoned, and brought little children there, and did these acts in front of them. In fact, there was reports of parents missing their children after they had gone to Woodstock.

The amount of drugs there was also in very large amounts. The FBI, and the District Attorney promised there would be no arrests made for anyone using drugs at the event. So they basically gave them permission to break the law. The people also were sitting or standing not just in the mud but also in their own waste.

The person who was in charge of selling drugs to the crowds was a man named Wavy Graver. Wavy's group called the Hog Farm had all the drug-dealers under their watch and protection. Like the Merry Pranksters, they were known to drive around city to city, and sell drugs. The New York police backed out of providing security because they refused to protect drug-dealers.

So John Roberts asked the Hog Farm hippie group if they would do security instead, and they said they would. Roberts paid for an expensive 727 at the cost of $17,000 to fly about 200 members of the Hog Farm, and their leader Wavy, to keep the crowds cool, and pumped up on drugs, and to also protect the drug dealers. Many of the dealers were part of the Hog Farm.

The main drugs of the event were LSD, marijuana, and heroin. Oddly enough John Roberts was heir of a large Pennsylvania-based pharmaceutics company that owned Sandoz Laboratories in Switzerland. That was the place where LSD was first known to be synthesized.

Rumor regarding this is that Roberts got involved in the event to make thousands, and thousands of dollars on LSD sales that he got from that company. No one knows if this is true or not, but it is very strange for Roberts to spend $17,000 in 1969 on a small group of hippies to just watch over the people. One thing about business men, they don't do things for nothing.

Woodstock also featured small kids smoking pot and getting into the music and when bad acid was floating around, Wavy got on stage and told people to take half a tab. Not stop what you're doing, but take half a tab.

The open-air rock festivals of the 60's would also end on a notorious note by the end of the 1960's. The last rock festival of the 60's was called the Altamont Speedway Free Festival. It was held on December 6, 1969 at the Altamont Speedway in Northern, California.

It was at first nicknamed the Woodstock of the West but then due to the violence of the event it was called Rock n' Roll's all-time worst day. The bands that played there that day were Santana, The Flying Burrito Brothers, Jefferson Airplane, Crosby, Stills, and Nash, and the Rolling Stones. The Rolling Stones was the final act of the show. The Grateful Dead were going to perform before the Stones but due to the increasing violence they refused to get on stage.

Over 300,000 people came to this event. The event was not remembered as a moment in time. It was instead remembered for the violence that took place there. There were several deaths caused by overdoses, a hit and run death, and a drowning in an irrigation canal where bystanders watched him die thinking it was just an acid trip. There were also several births of babies, and women going into labor early due to the drugs they took. The most noted death was of Meredith Hunter who was killed by the Hell's Angels. Thousands of people were beaten, stabbed, and had broken jaws, broken ribs, and had their heads cut open. This was mostly done by fist-fights among the crowds and by the beatings the Hell's Angels did to the crowds.

There were numerous cars that were stolen, and there was extensive property damage. The two people who initiated, and came to organize the event were Spencer Dryden and Jorma Kaukonen of Jefferson Airplane. They wanted the event to be a free-concert, and wanted to bring in the Rolling Stones who next to the Beatles were the biggest Rock n' Roll band in the world at the time.

After several places turned them down, Dick Carter offered his Altamont Speedway for them to have the event. Paul Kantner also helped to organize the event but was not happy about the location. He said by the time December 5 rolled around and they were setting up the event he knew there was no way to control it. He stated there was no supervision or order, and the vibes were bad, and he knew something real bad was going to happen. When the police refused to provide security the management of the Rolling Stones was called in asking for help. The Stones' management team would hire the criminal, and notorious motorcycle gang called the Hell's Angels to do security for the event. The Stones' management paid the Oakland chapter Hell's Angels an undisclosed sum of money, and $500 worth of beer which in today's prices would equate to $3,183 worth of beer. The other side note to this was a rumor that the Hell's Angels would also be in charge of all drug sales at the event. No one knows how true this is, but Hell's Angels were seen there among the crowds selling drugs to the people of the event.

The Hell's Angels were to surround the stage to protect the bands, and some were to mingle with the crowds to keep peace and order, however hiring the Hell's Angels was the worst mistake allowed to be made. They would guard the stage with broken off pool sticks, bike-chains, and were also armed with switch-blades. Many people believed that the Rolling Stones management team knew the violent nature of the Hell's Angels, and wanted them to bring violence to the event. No one knows how true this is. When the bands started performing numerous fights erupted between the Hell's Angels and the crowds. The crowds then started throwing beer bottles at the Hell's Angels, and the flying bottles struck members of the stage staff, and other artists.

Denise Jewkes, who was six months pregnant at the time, was hit in the head by one of the bottles. She would suffer a skull fracture. At that point when other bands were performing the crowds still had it in for the Hell's Angels and they were tripping on bad acid. The crowds then began to rush the stage, and the Hell's Angels then proceeded to arm themselves with the broken off pool cues, biker chains, and blades they had with them. In a bloody fashion the Hell's Angels beat back the crowds from the stage, and injured thousands of people. The crowds then started to kick over several motorcycles of the Hell's Angels which caused the Hell's Angels to become even more aggressive and they went from beating to stabbing.

When Marty Balin of Jefferson Airplane began to yell at the Hell's Angels to stop beating up the, crowds one of the Hell's Angels punched Marty in the head, and Marty was knocked unconscious. When the Santana drummer named Michael Shrieve told the Grateful Dead what happen to Marty they refused to take the stage. The Rolling Stones would show up late at the event which caused the crowds during the wait to become angry. During the wait fights were still breaking out, and people were still tripping on bad acid.

When the Rolling Stones finally arrived they were flown in by helicopter. When Mick Jagger came out of the helicopter within seconds he was punched in the head by an angry fan. When the Stones began looking at the crowds they became visibly intimidated, and started to tell everyone when they took the stage to cool down, and don't push around. The Rolling Stones would play about a few songs, and when they played Sympathy for the Devil a fight erupted in the front rows of the crowds. The fight took place at the foot of the stage, and this forced the Stones to stop until the Hell's Angels restored order. From there the Stones would again make another appeal for calm, and then they started singing another song. That is when it happen.

Meredith Hunter was a well-dressed black man with a good looking white woman on his arm. When one of the Hell's Angels saw him he began to make hateful remarks at him by calling Meredith a nigger. This most offensive term made Meredith very angry, and he started to fight with the Hell's Angel. This fight at first was not noticed by the Stones, and Meredith, during the rumble grabbed a gun out of the Hell's Angel's side. At this point the Stones noticed, and saw what happened next. Meredith pointed the gun at one of the Hell's Angels, and then a number of Hell's Angels quickly jumped him, and began stabbing him to death. Meredith was stabbed over 20 times mainly in the chest, back, and face. The crowds felt sorry for him, and tried to help him but the Hell's Angels pushed them all away, and said if he is going to die then let him die. The concert ended soon after.

The Hell's Angels defended their position by stating that Meredith pointed the gun at Jagger, and they came to his defense, but video evidence shows the gun was pointed at one of the Hell's Angels, and not at Jagger. Members of the crowds also said that the fighting started in the first place because the Hell's Angels were making hateful remarks toward the crowds, and had provoke the crowds to come toward them, but this had never been proven true. No one really knows why all the fights broke out in the first place. The Altamont Festival would go down in history as one of the vilest concerts to ever take place.

Chapter 9

One of the main rumors regarding famous rock stars are their connections or relations to elite banking, government, and military families. Many investigators into this subject stated that many famous people in the entertainment industry come from backgrounds that are far different from the backgrounds of their millions of fans. Some of these backgrounds are even nowhere near the image of many of these people. In the music industry this also is often shown.

In the mid 50's to early 60's the U.S. government was involved in a country called Vietnam. In early August of 1964 the story is that U.S. warships came under attack by the north communist Vietnam army. This event was called the Tonkin Gulf incident. The event would lead to open warfare, and an unofficial war called the Vietnam War. It was the most unpopular war in American history. It was also the first time that the U.S. would lose a war even though our casualty numbers were far less than the communist Vietnam army. America would lose close to 60,000 soldiers and leave behind thousands of POW's who were declared missing in action. The North Vietnam army would lose close to 1,000,000 soldiers and another 2,000,000 deaths would happen to their citizens. One of the warships that came under attack that day was commanded by Admiral George Stephen Morrison. This man is the father of rock icon Jim Morrison. The accounts of their father and son relationship was not too good. There were rumors of satanic rituals done in his family but there is no proof to those statements. There were also stories of intense abuse Jim got from his father and mother. In fact one time Jim's mother showed up to a show that her son was doing with the Doors. When Jim saw her he decided to change one of the lyrics to his songs, and looked at his mother and sang, 'mother I want to fuck you'. I hate typing these words but this is what he said. When he sang these most disturbing lyrics the owners of the venue rushed him, and the band off the stage. No one is sure why he sang these awful lyrics to his mother. Some of the rumors regarding it was that he was abused by his parents, and the other story was that he was sexually abused by members of the music industry, but no proof was ever shown in these statements.

When Jim was a child his father sometimes took him to tour the warship he was in command of. Jim was seen as a troubled child, and teenager, and when he dropped out of college his father cut him off. Mostly all of Jim's millions of fans had no idea who is father was until well after his death. Jim's death was officially called an overdose but many other people believed he was murdered. The story was that Jim was warned that after Hendrix and Joplin were found dead that he would be next, so he escaped to France hoping that they would not come for him there.

No one knows for sure who 'they' are, and the story is that his girlfriend allowed several men to enter the room while Jim was in the bathtub, and they injected him with poison, but there is no proof regarding it.

Another person of elite connections was an artist and guru named Frank Zappa. He was the leader of a band called the Mothers of Invention who got their start in an area called Laurel

Canyon. Frank never became as famous as the other rock artists of his time, but he was famous among the inner scene of his rock peers for being a spiritual leader and guru. His religion also was not Christianity. People who knew hi, and were close to him stated that Frank had a hypnotic effect on his friends, and that he was able to get them to do almost anything. Others stated that he had a way of manipulating people that only Charles Manson could relate to.

Frank's beliefs were centered on the New Age religion, and the doctrine of Aleister Crowley. He was also into Hinduism and Buddhism. Frank was also known to have a very high I.Q. and an even stranger story was that he was also into satanic rituals, but no proof was ever shown in this.

The story behind this claim was that Frank had bought in that time Tom Mix's old mansion which was called the Log Cabin. Tom Mix was an actor from the golden age of Hollywood in the early 20th century. He was famous for making silent western films, and was a friend of Wyatt Earp, and even attended Earp's funeral. There was a rumor that underneath Tom's mansion there was a massive tunnel with dozens of cave rooms and that in those rooms Tom, and his Hollywood friends would throw wild parties where drinking, and drugs were used, and he also loaded the rooms with prostitutes.

No one knows if this is really true. It was said when Frank bought the home he did so knowing about the cave rooms, and he would throw wild parties down there loaded with hippie girls, drugs, and other vices. Another thing that was said was that Frank, and his music peers performed satanic rituals down there, but no one knows how true this is.

Frank to his outside fans appeared anti-establishment but records into his family shows he came from establishment blood-lines. Openly he supported the hippie movement but close friends stated that he only pretended to and that he hated hippies. It was said that he felt no kinship to flower children, and to his close friends he would support U.S. government actions in Vietnam.

Frank's father was a chemical warfare specialist assigned to

Edgewood Arsenal. Edgewood was home to America's chemical warfare program and made advance chemical bombs. Many of these bombs were dropped in the thousands on the people of Vietnam. Frank's dad also did classified work for the Edward's Air Force base which many believed involved the bombs he helped to create.

One of Frank's hands on managers was a man named Herb Cohen. Cohen was a former U.S. Marine who was believed to have been one of the marines who helped the CIA in 1961 to overthrow Prime Minister Patrice Lumumba, and his army in the country of Congo. When the CIA captured him it was believed they tortured him, and then killed him.

Frank's wife named Gail also came from an elite blood-line of generational military officers. Her father worked on classified nuclear weapons research under the U.S. Navy. In fact, before Gail married Frank she worked as an office secretary for the U.S. Naval research department. Gail also attended kindergarten school with Jim Morrison where she one time hit him over the head with a hammer. Gail was stated to have many mental problems. Some said she was possessed by demons and others said she did too many drugs with Frank. She was often hearing voices in her head, and talking to invisible people.

John Phillips also had a strange background as well. He one time attended high-school with the Lizard King himself Jim Morrison. Phillips was one of the founders of the group called the Mamas and the Papas where he was nicknamed Papa Phillips. His circle of friends where a group of young Hollywood players, directors, and music artists who dubbed their group the Young Turks. The names in this group are very famous like Jack Nicholson, Dennis Hopper, Roman Polanski, Sharon Tate, Peter Fonda, and others. The Young Turks also would party with at times Charles Manson and his occult family.

Phillips is also very well known for bringing together the Monterey Pop Festival during the Summer of Love in 1967, and he was a close friend of Frank Zappa. The father of John Phillips was a U.S. Marine officer named Captain Claude Andrew Phillips. The story of Phillips' mother is a strange one. It was stated that she would tell people she had psychic and telekinetic powers. Many said she was demon-possessed but no one knows how true this is. Her name was Dene Phillips, and it was also said of her that she worked for the federal government on strictly classified work where many said it involved mind-control programming, but this has not been proven.

Phillips' older sister named Rosie Phillips worked for the Pentagon for 30 years straight on work that she stated was classified and John's older brother named Tommy Phillips was a former U.S. Marine who became a police officer where he developed a disciplinary record for exhibiting violence toward people of color. John Phillips growing up went to a series of elite military prep schools and even had an appointment to join the U.S. Naval Military Academy at Annapolis. It was said he had a high I.Q. but was hard to manage as a student. John however did not want a military career but he wanted a career in music where it is believed that his family helped to make that happen.

John would also marry a woman named Susie Adams who was part of an American elite blood-line family, and she was a descendant of one of the founding fathers by the name of John Adams. Susie's father named James Adams, Jr. is believed to have worked black ops missions with the CIA, and the Air Force.

John Phillips himself one time told a strange story himself that he worked for the CIA during the Bay of Pigs affair but no one knows if this is true. John Phillips had a daughter by the name of MacKenize Phillips who when she grew up wrote a book about the sexual abuse John Phillips was doing to her throughout her childhood and teenage years. She stated that John had a way of controlling her mind to go into black-outs. When she was in these blackouts John would have sex with his own daughter. MacKenize revealed this on the Oprah Winfrey Show. She stated that one day when she went into a black-out she woke up to her father having sex with her. She stated that she could not remember how it started, and that later she started to recover memories of her father doing things to her mind to cause her to black-out and not remember what happened the night before. What MacKenize described in her book was a form of mind-control.

Stephen Stills is another person of interest. His father was also involved with the military, and his family also has elite blood-lines. Stills spent most of his childhood, and teenage years in places starting from Texas to El Salvador to Costa Rica to the Panama Canal Zone, and various parts of Central America. Stills spent this time of travelling a lot with his father. His father was believed to have been working with the CIA on various covert operations. It is not sure what these operations were. Some said it was drug running, and others said it was spying, and others said it was both. When Stills was asked about it he said his father was part of a group who were 'educating the unwashed masses to democracy'. No one knew what this statement really meant.

Stills was educated at some of the best military schools, and upon military bases. The military schools he went to were attended by children of elite families. Stills was known to have a peremptory personality, and was very abrasive. Stills also told strange stories to his peers that he worked for the CIA in Vietnam before the war went full-scale in 1964. No one knows if this is really true or not.

Stills in his career became the founding member of two famous bands which was Buffalo Springfield, and then the next one was Crosby, Stills, and Nash. Stills would write one of the most legendary songs of the 60's called For What It's Worth, and wrote another hit song called Bluebird.

David Crosby has very strong elite blood-lines. He is related to the Van Cortlandt family. In fact, in David's family tree it is filled with U.S. senators, congressmen, state senators, assemblymen, governors, mayors, judges, Supreme Court justices, Revolutionary and Civil War generals, members of the continental congress, and officers in the military. David Crosby is also blood-related to royals in Europe as well.

David Crosby's father was a man named Major Floyd Delafield Crosby. Crosby's family are a military elite family with a love for guns. In fact, David used to brag that he had the largest gun collection then anyone in the entertainment industry. His image was also seen as a peace and love person, but several times David had pulled his gun out to intimidate people he felt looked at him the wrong way. Some of the stories shows the behavior of a very angry man. There were rumors that David had shot his gun at people several times and even wounded a couple of people, but no one knows how true this is, and he was never arrested for it. Oddly people close to him stated that many times the law was ignored to his favor and that he was able to get away with carrying a gun on a plane when no one was able to. He did this by mentioning or calling certain people he knew that would bend the law for him. It is believed that elite families because of their money, power, and influence are often able to live above the law. Crosby is also a big speaker for homosexuals. He often donated his seed to female homosexual couples. Some of them are even famous in the music industry. In fact, when he is not giving away his seed, the money couples or single woman spend for it to have a child is very high, close to $20,000. There are in fact many children out there whose father is David Crosby.

There are strange rumors regarding David Crosby's religious beliefs. It is known that he is not a Christian. People close to him often stated that he is into witchcraft, and has been since he was famous. No one knows how true this is but witchcraft involvement does seem to come up often regarding him.

The rock artist named Jackson Browne also comes from a military background. Jackson was born in a military hospital on a West Germany base. His father had ties to the OSS before it became the CIA. His father was assigned to post-war reconstruction work in Germany.

It was believed that he worked on classified projects involving Nazi officers, and Nazi infrastructure. It was said that he was protecting certain Nazi officers to recruit them for Project Paperclip. It is not sure how true this is but Project Paperclip was very real. It involved the CIA using the military to bring in Nazi officers, and recruit them to share information they knew, and work projects for the U.S. government. Many of these former Nazis helped to create the space program called NASA. Many of the Nazis the U.S. brought to America, and protected were guilty of horrible war crimes. Instead of justice many of them got to live the American dream.

The members of the band called America also had an elite

military background. America in their career had three major hit singles called A Horse With No Name, Ventura Highway, and The Tin Man. The name of the band members were Gerry Beckley, Dan Peek, and Dewey Bunnell. These three met at an Air Force base that Gerry's dad was in command of. The fathers of Dan and Dewey worked under Gerry's father. This base was located near London, England, and it was suspected that mind-control programming was taking place there but this was never proven.

When David Crosby left the band he started called The Byrds to form Crosby, Stills, and Nash he was replaced by Gram Parsons. Gram's mother comes from an elite blood-line, and they were the richest family in Winter Haven, Florida. Her family owned 1/3 of the citrus groves in the State of Florida. The company's name was Snively Groves. The family was worth close to 1 billion dollars. Gram's father was Major Cecil Ingram Connor the 2nd. His military friends called him 'Coon Dog'. The Major was a very skilled bomber pilot who flew over 50 combat missions. Gram when he was young his mother would make Gram the sole heir of the family fortune. How this happened was a strange and sad story. Just before Christmas of 1958 Gram's father was having a bad feeling of coming doom. He sent his entire family to their mother's family in Florida. Soon after, while home alone, intruders entered his home, and they shot the Major to death execution style. Nothing was taken, and no one knows why they killed him. So Gram instead of his father became the heir.

Gram's mother would marry another man named Robert Parsons and the family took his last name, but Robert proved to be a greedy and abusive man. In June of 1965 when Gram was making his way in the music industry his mother had died. The cause of death has never been clear. Rumor was Robert had found a way to get rid of her for her money but this was never proven. Robert had thought he was the sole heir but he found out he was not but it was Gram. This information was kept from him by his wife, and it deeply angered him. Gram would go on to have small success with the Byrds, and then he founded a new band called the Flying Burrito Brothers. During that time from the late 60's to early 70's it was believed that Robert was always demanding money from Gram. Gram refused to give him not one cent. During that time Gram was getting threatening phone calls and letters. He would tell close friends that he feels someone is trying to kill him. His fears were even worse when someone burnt down his home in Topanga Canyon.

On September 19, 1973 Gram was found dead at the Joshua Tree Inn. He was 26 years old. It was believed that Robert was involved with his death but no proof was given. Gram had been strangled to death. When Gram died Robert now believed he was the heir, but it turned out that Gram left all the money to his sister without Robert's knowledge. This had made Robert enraged, but sadly Gram's sister named Avis would be murdered in 1993.

Terry Melcher also came from elite blood-lines. He is the son of legendary actress Doris Day who at one time was the number one female box office draw. Terry lost his real father when he was three years old. Doris would then marry another abusive man named Marty Melcher. Marty demanded that Terry have his last name. Marty was one of the most ruthless men in Hollywood which is saying a lot. He was violent and abusive toward Doris Day. He would take her money and often beat her and made her son watch. Marty would embezzle about 20 million dollars from Doris Day, and he put this family through a living hell.

When Terry entered the music industry he became a producer and an artist. The first band he produced was the Byrds. Terry was also part of the industry click called the Young Turks. Even stranger was Terry's friendships with occult covens. He at times hung out with Vito and his group of hippies who were very much into witchcraft. He hung out also at times with the Charles Manson family. He was also invited to join the Church of Satan but no one knows if he actually did.

Vito was one of the early friends of Terry, and he knew him since Terry was a teenager. Vito brought Terry to the nightclub scene where many of his hippie girls would party through the night. At this point Vito brought Terry into his art school where he painted his naked hippie girls. He also had the girls perform sexual favors on Terry. In the music industry scene Terry helped to fund several open-air concerts. This helped him to be connected to powerful people in the music industry. Terry had grew up in Beverly Hills, one of the richest areas in the world. In high-school he started his love for music, and formed a band. Through this band he met Bruce Johnston, and a young Phil Spector. Spector would go on to become a powerful person in the music industry. Terry in the industry would come to make friends with the Beach Boys and became a close friend to Dennis Wilson. Through this friendship Terry hung out with the Manson occult family. Terry also became friends with Gregg Jakobson who was married to Lou Costello's daughter. Terry, Dennis, and Gregg became three close friends and they were nicknamed the 'golden penetrators' due to the amount of women they ran through. Before Roman Polanski bought the house that Sharon Tate was killed in by the Manson family, Terry had owned it before him. Terry lived in the home with his girlfriend at the time named Candace Bergen, the future star of the Murphy Brown television show.

The Manson family was familiar with this house before Sharon lived in it. Through the friendship between Dennis and Terry the Manson family also hung out at this house with Terry and Candace. Few people know that NBC, before the Manson killings took place, wanted to do a special about the Manson family. Terry offered to produce it, and so the Manson family was brought to Spahn Ranch. There NBC gave Terry a vast amount of film, and cameras to capture the lives of the Manson family. Terry filmed Charlie recording his songs, and preaching his sinister doctrine. What is said to have also been filmed was the group sex acts of the Manson family, and also satanic rituals. No one knows how true this is. After the killings, NBC locked away all the films of the family in vaults, and they would even deny dealing with them. They stated that the Manson family stole the film and the cameras from their studio but this turned out to be a lie. NBC just wanted to distance themselves from their involvement with this satanic family.

Chapter 10

A subject that gets brought up about the music industry is demonic encounters and occults. Many artists have spoken about spiritual encounters and being part of religions groups that are not Christian. Some artists have even spoken about people selling their souls in certain rituals done among members of the industry. So much of this is spoken about that it's hard at times to know the facts about it. So let us look into some of these artists.

When Carlos Santana made his comeback through an album called Supernatural released in 1999 he gave a strange interview regarding the reason why the album was made. He stated that a spiritual being had appeared to him calling itself Metatron. He would go on to state that Metatron told him that he was going to put Carlos back on the radio air wave frequency to influence teenagers and college kids to a new sound in music. The being, according to Carlos, would go on to state that he was going to put Carlos in touch with the latest music artists of that time to give the people this fresh new sound. The goal of the album seems to have been according to the interview was to preach the spiritual values of Metatron. Carlos' religious beliefs are new age beliefs. He gave up on Christianity a long time ago since his start in the 1960's. Carlos is also into black magic and shamanism.

Metatron is a being that is worshipped in Jewish, Indian, African, Latin, and Eastern magic occult groups. He is seen as an angel of enlightenment, and in other various ways. He was called a speaker of the gods, and was called the angel in the bush who spoke to Moses, and also is called one of the gods, and several other things.

The Bible tells us that Satan was a former archangel, and that Satan is a host meaning an army of fallen angels, and demons. The Bible tells us that Satan pretends to be GOD, and also he wants to be worshipped as GOD is. The Bible also states that Satan is a being of music as well, and he can transform himself into an angel of light. The meaning in this is that Satan likes to appear as a good guy to trick others into following him.

The Bible also makes it clear that Satan himself is a music artist as well, and one time he was in charge of music in Heaven. All the fallen angels have music skills. The Bible also tells us that Satan has appeared to people and entered into people to get them to do his will. According to Christian belief Carlos' encounter would be called a satanic encounter, but many people would ask 'what is the harm of Carlos' music it sounds so good'.

Carlos one time spoke that his music has the ability to raise sexual drives into people. Meaning this would lead people to sex outside of marriage and into sexual immorality and homosexual practices. Some would say this is no big deal but for Christians the Bible would call this sin, and sexual sins, the Bible tells over and over again are sins GOD hates with a passion. The artists that worked with Santana on Supernatural were Everlast, Rob Thomas, Eric Clapton, Lauryn Hill, Wyclef Jean, Cee Lo Green, Dave Matthews, and several others. Some of these artists spoke about some strange experiences they had before working on the album. Some of them heard songs in their dreams that floored them and then woke up to get a call from Santana asking them if they would work on the album. They would be shocked to find that the song they were doing was the song they heard in their dreams.

Rob Thomas, who is the lead singer of Matchbox 20, stated that he heard the song Smooth in his dreams and then heard a voice giving him a phone number. He called the number, and it was Santana's number, and Carlos asked him if he would cut a song with him. When Rob came to the studio Carlos was shocked that Rob knew the lyrics to Smooth before he told him what the lyrics were.

On February 23, 2000, Carlos Santana's album Supernatural would win a record of nine Grammys. He would beat the record held by Michael Jackson who won eight Grammys for Thriller. The album would sell 15 million copies. Carlos Santana is of Mexican heritage. He is called one of the greatest guitarists of all time. His style in his guitar leads, and music is a fusion of Latin and African rhythms with his band members providing percussion instruments such as timbales and congas.

Santana started playing music at age 5. He was first trained in the violin, and then at age 8 he was trained in the guitar. Carlos was heavily influenced by Ritchie Valens, and because of his love for Valens he dreamed about becoming a Latin rock star. Carlos grew up as a child in Tijuana, and then his family moved to San Francisco. Carlos would attend James Lick Middle School, and then he attended Mission High School where he graduated. Carlos, in the early 1960's, became part of the growing hippie movement in San Francisco. In that time he worked in a diner as a dishwasher and played guitar on the side.

He would soon decide to become a full-time musician after performing for Stan Marcum and his people. Stan became his early manager. Stan was connected to people at Bill Graham's Fillmore West. One day during a Sunday matinee show, Paul Butterfield, who was slated to perform, was unable to and Stan talked Graham into letting Santana take his place. Graham then did so. During the performance Santana's guitar playing, and solo gained the notice of both the audience and Graham.

That same year Santana formed the Santana Blues Band, and the band quickly gained an immediate following on the San Francisco club circuit. The band's early success in the 60's was on the road performing at concerts and clubs. This would lead to them appearing at the Woodstock Festival in 1969.

In the 60's Santana got heavy into the drug scene which was the main thing to do among hippies. Before Santana got on stage to perform at Woodstock he dropped an LSD tab. When he began to perform his seething leads on the guitar Santana stated that he felt a spiritual presence take him over. When this happened he looked at his guitar, and it turned into a serpent. Carlos felt that he was not holding a normal guitar but a guitar in the form of a strange looking snake. On film it looks like a normal guitar but in Carlos' vision it was a snake.

It is known that drugs can open people to the demonic spiritual realm. This realm is invisible, and it can reveal itself to those it has an interest in and remain invisible to others. The Bible does show this reality as well, and dealing with it can be dangerous as the seven sons of Sceva found out in the Book of Acts.

Santana at Woodstock would give a memorable performance, and soon in 1969 Carlos Santana, and his band was signed to Columbia Records. From 1969 into the 70's Santana would make several albums. His first three albums were his biggest sellers, and his biggest album at the time was his third album

Santana 3 which went number one on the Billboard charts, and sold 2 million copies. His major hit singles were Evil Ways, Black Magic Woman, Everybody's Everything, No One to Depend On, and a few others.

During the late 60's Santana's friend named John McLaughlin introduced Santana to his new age guru named Sri Chinmoy. Chinmoy was deep into magic rituals, spells, sorcery, and would channel forth evil spirits. His followers believed he had magic powers, and others said he was deeply demonically possessed. The Bible does teach that demon-possessed persons were able to perform supernatural feats.

Chinmoy had a well-organized compound complete with uniforms for his followers. Chinmoy promised that through his teachings his followers could become gods by working with the forces of angels and demons. That these forces would give them powers. Chinmoy had won over Santana, and Santana for a time lived in Chinmoy's compound and became one of his devout students.

Santana dived deep into occult rituals, and had to do disturbing acts to please Chinmoy, and was learning mor, and more how to channel evil spirits through him. Of course Santana did not call them evil spirits he called them angels and devils, and would state he was learning how to please them both. Chinmoy also had a thing for sex-magic rituals which resulted in a lot of abuse done against women including Carlos' own wife at the time named Deborah. Some of the abuse in the coven was even aimed at men where they were forced to do homosexual acts on each other. Carlos at first started out devout but started to get sick of Chinmoy imposing upon his life, and telling Carlos what he should do with his wife. Soon a scandal broke out against Chinmoy which was not that big but the information released told of the sexual abuse done among Chinmoy's followers. At that point anyone involved with Chinmoy the music industry owners had blacklisted for some time which resulted in Santana breaking away from Chinmoy, and speaking against him and laying low for a while.

Santana in that time became a guru himself, and started to call himself among his peers as a Shaman. Shamanism is a practice that involves a practitioner reaching altered states of consciousness in order to encounter and interact with the spirit world. The aim is to channel the energies of these spirits that the Bible would call evil spirits through you to influence people in the world you live in.

Santana's comeback did not happen until he did Supernatural. In 2002 he would release a follow up album called Shaman named after the title he gave himself.

Among the strange things regarding the entertainment industry is something called the baphomet contract. Eliphas Levi one time wrote a book about satanic occults, and ritual pacts with Satan. In 1897 he drew an image of Satan in the form called baphomet. The picture shows a form of Satan appearing as a bi-sexual creature with the head of a goat, having female breasts with a male private part sticking upward with hairy goat legs. The image is combining animalism, dark spiritualism, and the features of male and female sexual parts. The image is to represent a corruption of nature and religion. The hand postures of the being represent the words as above, so below. The meaning behind the words is to tell that Satan is an angel who once lived in Heaven the world above and fell to dark places of the earth the world below. The five-point star on his head is called the seal of the morning star which tells the former position of Satan being once an angel of light. This image is often seen among many music stars especially rock stars. It is also seen on t-shirts, posters, and occult books fans will buy. Most music fans have no idea what the image means it just looks cool to them because they see their favorite artist wearing it or sporting it. Some music fans do know what it means, and they still sport it. Often this image is seen as having an even darker meaning. That it is the image of the name one worships during a satanic ritual where they sell their souls to the devil.

The Bible does talk about people throwing their lives over to serve Satan for money, fame, and power but also throwing away their souls when they pass away from earth. The Bible does not say that such a contract means a person is lost forever. A person can repent from such actions, and seek the Way of Jesus Christ. What it shows is that people do this of their own free-will and are deceived by the lies of Satan, but is there really a secret occult baphomet contract in the entertainment industry where music stars, and even Hollywood stars have sold their souls to Satan to get into the industry, and have the kind of careers many of them do? Some say yes there is. Some say no there is not. Others say some have done this while others have not. Whatever statement you agree on, a person must always make up their own mind but this matter of selling your soul in the industry comes up again and again and even artists have spoken about it.

In the 1970's a new generation of young people came about. They were called Generation X. They were seen as the generation born from parents of the 50's and 60's. They were seen from the start as a spiritually lost generation whose culture was largely not in touch with Christian spirituality but with New Age sentiments, religions, and ideas. They were a pop culture and then later an MTV generation. They were raised under a system of government, education, and churches that many believed failed them, and wrote them off.

Many of them had to work and fight hard to make their way in a world that had become darker, and more lost from Christian values, and morals. In the 60's many new forms of music were developing. One of them was a new rock style called later Heavy Metal music.

Heavy Metal came first from the British nightclubs but no one knows which person or band had originally created it. It is clear that bands like the Rolling Stones and Jimi Hendrix had inspired it. From what is shown about it is that many bands started to play a harder sound in their music. What started in these British clubs which then came to America were bands playing a faster rhythm with dark seething guitar solo leads with a sonic drive in bass playing along with pounding drum melodies. The music had a darker feeling which caused rage in people's emotions.

These bands also had a certain image to them as well. They had a satanic image openly and bands even did rituals on stage. They were not the peace, love, drugs, and sex image. They were the fear, hate, and Satan along with drugs and sex image. In the early 70's a small market opened up for these bands that very soon became a huge market. A large fan following was growing for them and record companies jumped on the chance to make money from these bands.

At this time small record companies were turning out big profits from the records of these bands. Some of them grossing from $100,000 to $300,000 from record sales. The major companies saw this, and wanted to bring this music, and image to the mainstream public. They saw that millions of dollars could be made from this music.

From the start people pointed out some obvious things about these bands. That they appeared to be devil worshippers and to be violent and twisted. Many of their defenders said it was an act and others said that many of them were into Satanism and even demon-possession.

For some of the bands this behavior and image could have been for show, but for others in regards to their own testimony it was not an act but they were real Satan worshippers.

In the Heavy Metal scene some were about the music and image and some were about the music and worshipping Satan for real. It was not an image to them. Overall Satan was heavily promoted by Heavy Metal artists. The first Heavy Metal band that went mainstream was not Led Zeppelin or Black Sabbath, it was a band called Black Widow who first started performing in 1967. In the late 60's they were the first among their scene to go mainstream and their first album after being signed was called Sacrifice.

Black Widow had four songs that hit the radio air-waves. One was called Way to Power which was about selling your soul to Satan. The second was called Come to the Sabbat which was a song about attending a satanic mass. The third song was called Conjuration which was about calling on evil spirits and the fourth song was called Sacrifice which was about offering Satan a blood sacrifice. Black Widow also had a noted stage show they would do. On stage they had a satanic altar and would put a naked woman on top of it, and hold a black mass. Black Widow, during their mainstream career, was not able to break wide open the doors of Heavy Metal music to make millions of dollars on the market. The band that did was a band that soon debuted after them called Led Zeppelin.

Led Zeppelin is often believed that they invented Heavy Metal music but that is not true. There were Heavy Metal bands already out before them. What they did do is that they made Heavy Metal a world famous form of music, and they opened the doors for a larger Heavy Metal market that would now make millions of dollars.

Led Zeppelin's sound was not just Heavy Metal but a wide variety of influences including Rhythm and Blues and folk music. The group was formed in London in 1968. At first their style of music was not Heavy Metal but blues, and hard rock until the style of Heavy Metal was introduce to them.

From 1969 throughout the 70's their first six albums were a world-wide commercial success. The band members were Robert Plant, Jimmy Page, John Paul Jones, and John Bonham. When Led Zeppelin released their second album called Led Zeppelin 2 in late 1969 this was the album that brought Heavy Metal music to a massive audience and open wide the doors for a huge Heavy Metal market.

 On November 8, 1971 Led Zeppelin released their fourth album often called Led Zeppelin 4. This album became one of the biggest selling albums in history as it sold 37 million copies world-wide. The major hit single from this album was called Stairway to Heaven. There was a very strange, and dark subject regarding the song Stairway to Heaven. The song is very noted for having backward lyrics upon it. Some of these lyrics go like this, 'Here's to my sweet Satan' 'I want to live it backwards like the zep who's power is Satan' and 'He will give you 666'.

Led Zeppelin denied having anything to do with these lyrics, but nevertheless the lyrics are on the song. By 1972 Led Zeppelin was the biggest money making band in the world. They would sell out tour after tour and toured all across the world, and the U.S. often giving over four hour performances to thousands of people.

Jimmy Page was the founder of the band called Led Zeppelin. Jimmy brought all the members together while playing in a band called the Yardbirds. The name of the band came from a 1937 photograph of a burning zeppelin called the 129 Hindenburg which was a huge flight balloon that exploded with massive force.

Jimmy Page's love for Aleister Crowley is very well known. He had books written by Aleister Crowley that he often read and quoted to his band mates. He bought the castle that Aleister Crowley once lived in and performed horrible satanic rituals in. He appeared in a cult classic movie where he summons the spirit of Crowley through a mirror. On the album Led Zeppelin 3 Page had the record company to inscribe Crowley's motto 'Do what thou wilt' on the vinyl of the album.

Other strange stories surrounding Jimmy Page were that he was a real hardcore Satanist but this has never been proven. It was said that he would cast spells against people he did not like and he put curses on his band mates so that they would play the kind of music that would please Satan. This also has not been proven.

Lead singer Robert Plant was also into pagan mythology. Many of the lyrics he wrote were centered on Norse and Welsh mythology. Robert often sung about Valhalla, and Viking conquests and the stories of Odin and Thor. He was also into the stories of witchcraft lore where the story of Stairway to Heaven came from. Led Zeppelin also had a brutal tour manager by the name of Peter Grant. Grant had a fearful way of negotiating deals, and covering up the vices of the bands he worked for including Led Zeppelin.

Before Grant worked for Led Zeppelin he worked for Bo Diddley, the Everly Brothers, Little Richard, Chuck Berry, and a few others. Peter Grant was known in the underground scene of the U.S. and U.K. and he was feared in this scene. He would ensure that the vast bulk of ticket profits would fall into the hands of the band members and not the promoters nor booking agents. If these people undermined him Peter would beat them senseless or hire people to take care of it. Peter, through these brutal methods, would secure about 90% of the gate money from concerts which was an unprecedented feat. Peter would also visit record stores in London when he found out that they were selling bootleg recordings of Led Zeppelin's albums. He would intimidate the store owners into handing over all the records, and the money they made off of it. If they refused they were beaten up, and Peter would take all the records.

Peter protected the band members from all interference from fans, press, promoters and even people working for their record company. He also had fans beaten up by his security team who were caught getting too close to the band members. In 1977 was the Oakland Incident. This happened during a concert that Led Zeppelin was to perform at where Zeppelin's security team headed by Grant had a nasty fist-fight with Bill Graham's security team.

On that day from the start of the pre-setting of the concert the two teams were not getting along and were often undermining each other. When Zeppelin's security team was walking down the ramp they had some hard exchange of words with Graham's team. At that point John Bindon, who was part of Zeppelin's team working under Grant, had punched out stage crew chief Jim Downey who worked for Graham and knocked him unconscious. In return, when Warren Grant, Peter's 11 year old son got caught ripping down signs that Graham's team had put up a man named Jim Matzorkis who also worked for Graham had slapped Peter's 11 year old son across the face. This resulted in a huge full scale brawl backstage while Led Zeppelin was performing on stage. Bill Graham afterward had filed a 2 million dollar lawsuit against Led Zeppelin but the case was settled out of court for less money.

In the late 70's many people said that the curse that Page put on the band members was coming now to hurt them, but no proof to this was shown although some horrible things did come their way.

In 1975 in Rhodes, Greece Robert Plant, and his wife at the time named Maureen were nearly killed in a car crash. The crash left them both seriously injured. In July of 1977 Robert's son named Karac died at the age of 5 of a stomach infection while Robert was on tour with the band in the United States. This devastating loss later would lead to a divorce from Maureen.

In October of 1980 John Bonham, after working long hours of rehearsals at the studio where he showed up late due to heavy drinking decided to retire for the night. He went to stay at Jimmy Page's house called the Old Mill House in Clewer, Windsor. After midnight John fell asleep and he was taken to bed but oddly he was rolled over on his side which is not something you do to a person who has fallen asleep drunk. At 1:45 p.m. the next day John Paul Jones went to get him but Bonham did not move and they found Bonham lying dead on the bed with his face in his vomit. It was called an accidental death related to asphyxia and alcohol, but some believe he was purposefully killed although no proof was shown in those statements. When John Bonham died the band called Led Zeppelin broke up and disbanded. In combine total of all their albums Led Zeppelin has sold close to 300 million albums.

Another band that came out shortly after Led Zeppelin had debuted was a band called Black Sabbath. The origins of the start of Black Sabbath is very dark and demonic. It is said that the members of Black Sabbath were part of satanic covens in England but no one knows for sure how true this is. The satanic covens they are talking about were known to be a very violent and criminal group of mostly young people. They were known to engage in many crimes from drugs to muggings. They burglarized homes, and a few of them even murdered people in satanic rituals. Ozzy Osbourne, who became the lead singer for Black Sabbath, was said to have been a member of such a coven.

As a young man he became addicted to drugs, and started to hang out with high-school drop outs who brought him into a coven. During this time when Ozzy was said to have been a member of a coven he began working at a slaughterhouse. There he learned how to kill cows, chickens, and pigs. One time he sliced open a pig, and took a cup, and drained the pig's blood into it. From there he began to drink it, and when he did Ozzy stated that he felt a strange spirit come over him, and he felt energized by it. What Ozzy is talking about would be called demonic possession and oddly enough what Ozzy did is something satanic coven members are known to do.

At that point Ozzy was getting into criminal behavior, and one time he burglarized a home, and was caught in the act by British police officers. From there he served time in an English prison, and while doing so Ozzy spoke about being haunted by spirits in prison. This would also be called demonic attacks. When Ozzy came out of jail he was inspired by these spirits to join a rock band.

Terry Butler who was also called Geezer grew up in a troubled home. When Terry was a kid he spoke about being haunted by evil spirits. While growing up he started to read books on Satanism and witchcraft. He was trying to understand why these hauntings were happening to him, and he thought the books would explain things. He soon started to paint the walls in his room black, and would wear black gothic like clothes and upside down crosses around his neck.

He too would have a strange experience during one of his hauntings to get into music. Terry was skilled at playing the guitar. Tony Iommi and drummer Bill Ward were already in the early Heavy Metal scene among the British nightclubs. They were in a band called Mythology that had broken up in 1968, right after the disbanding of Mythology Tony and Bill were looking to start a new band. At that point Geezer was playing guitar in the British Heavy Metal scene and Tony and Bill then brought him in. From there they started to look for a vocalist. Ozzy Osbourne, had bought a PA system, and put an advertisement sheet in a local music shop which read, 'Ozzy Zig Needs Gig-has own PA'. Tony and Bill saw the ad, and decided to try him out, and after hearing him sing they hired him. At first the group called themselves the Polka Tulk Blues Band even though their style was Heavy Metal. During this time Terry began to be a close friend to Ozzy Osbourne. Terry often shared his strange spiritual encounters with Ozzy and Ozzy at this point knew a lot about such encounters. Ozzy had many books also about Satanism and witchcraft and had books by Aleister Crowley. Terry was interested in such books wanting to know more so Ozzy gave him one of his books telling Terry it would help him to understand more. The book was about magic spells and rituals. Terry then went to his place, and started to read it but then all of a sudden he started to have bad vibes from it and felt it was best to stop reading it and then he put it in a cupboard.

During the night Terry woke up with a strange feeling, and the air was cold. He would look toward the bottom of his bed, and there he was frozen with fear. Terry saw a demon in the form of a shadow looking right at him. The demon then rose in form from the floor, and took a humanoid shape. Terry stated that the demon's eyes were glowing with eyes of fire, and it smiled at Terry and pointed at him. Terry then ran out of the room, and ran to Ozzy's place. When Terry told him what happened Ozzy looked shook up, and stated to Terry he had the same experience that night. Ozzy and Terry then told Tony and Bill what happened, and Tony and Bill also looked shook up, and they spoke about a similar experience that happen to them.

When they started to play together a strange thing happened to them. They felt taken over, and started to play cords, and notes they had not written down before and Ozzy was singing lyrics he did not know for sure where they were coming from. After doing the song they felt that another presence was with them and they all felt at the same time to call the song Black Sabbath and then they decided to name the band Black Sabbath. Black Sabbath was formed that year under these very dark and strange events in 1969. Soon more songs were coming to them out of the air it seemed and they were soon playing in the underground British nightclub circuit.

At this point they got a manager, and they were offered to open for Black Widow at a few gigs, and Black Sabbath impressed the people. Soon the San Francisco underground came calling, and wanted to bring some of the Heavy Metal underground bands to come, and perform at some of their nightclubs. One of the bands that went to San Francisco was Black Sabbath.

Anton LaVey, the head high-priest of the Church of Satan at the time, took a special interest in these metal bands. After watching them play he took a special interest in the band Black Sabbath. He then came up to the band, and told them that Satan had told him that in this band were his chosen right-hand men. Anton then threw a party for them in their honor and did a satanic ceremony to bless their efforts as he put it.

When Black Sabbath came back to England they had a record

deal waiting for them. They were signed to Philips Records that year and began to get radio exposure on John Peel's Top Gear radio show.

Several Black Sabbath songs were already being played on the radio before the first album came out. Those songs were NIB, Behind the Wall of Sleep, Black Sabbath, and Sleeping Village.

When Black Sabbath went into the studio to record their first album they would make this entire album in an unheard time of 70 minutes. People who saw it said they played like they were possessed by a mystical being. They would name their first album after the band calling it Black Sabbath. The album was released on Friday the 13th in February of 1970. The album was a big commercial success.

Their second album called Paranoid would go on to sell 4 million copies. Paranoid was called the most influential Heavy Metal album of that time. This album would define the sound, and style of Heavy Metal music more than any other Heavy Metal record in history. This album came out in 1971, and it too was recorded at a creepy fast pace. The album also featured the hit single Iron Man.

At this point the band was being paid only in cash as they requested, and used this cash mainly to buy drugs. They would receive a briefcase each full of cash, and then used it to buy cocaine, heroin, and all kinds of pills. At this point they would party real hard, and their demonic attacks still continued.

One time when the band was staying at a hotel in Bel-Air, Geezer that night went to sleep. He woke up in the middle of the night with a strange feeling, and looked up, and saw several evil spirits floating in the air above him. Geezer became washed with fear, and began screaming for his other band mates. Ozzy, Bill, and Tony ran into the room, and Geezer told them what happened.

The three of them then sat down, and began telling Geezer that these hauntings were happening to them as well. By the time they released their third album called Master of Reality the band members were having major drug problems, and inner fights among each other. They were getting kicked out of hotels for the wild, and strange type of parties they threw. At these parties they would gather up a bunch of Bibles, and burn them, and commit vandalism, and other disturbing acts. They were using drugs very heavily, and they even started to abuse the women they had at these parties.

Things got so bad that the band members started to often fight with each other and they centered a lot of the trouble toward Ozzy Osbourne. Ozzy often would not listen to reason, and when he was told that the band needed to cool down Ozzy refused to do that. One night Ozzy was determined to burn some Bibles in his room, and Geezer, not wanting to get kicked out of another hotel, demanded that he stop. Ozzy refused, and so Geezer punched out Ozzy knocking him out for the night. Soon the other band members got sick of Ozzy's behavior, and then they coldly kicked him out of the band, but Ozzy's career was nowhere near done.

After Black Sabbath came into the music industry many Heavy Metal bands would follow throughout the 70's going into the 80's. Blue Oyster Cult would debut, and record a major hit song called Don't Fear the Reaper. Other bands came forth with names like Angel Witch, Venom, Pagan Altar, Warhammer, December Moon, Cradle of Filth, Hell Satan, Onslaught and others.

Much of Ozzy Osbourne's career at that time was centered on the songs he did for Black Sabbath. Songs like NIB which was a love song to Lucifer, and others.

He was known for his wild and abusive behavior. His first wife named Thelma left him after repeated abuses from Ozzy which involved Ozzy beating her, grabbing her by her hair and dragging her around the room like a rag doll.

When John 'Ozzy' Osbourne thought he was finished a woman by the name of Sharon Arden stepped in. Sharon Arden is the daughter of Don Arden who is a rich, and powerful music promoter and Rock n' Roll entrepreneur. Sharon met Ozzy at the age of 18 when she was working for her father. Her father, Don Arden, was the one who managed Black Sabbath. Don was in approval of the firing of Ozzy Osbourne and he told people he was finished.

When Ozzy was fired it was 1979. Sharon had a crush on Ozzy Osbourne, and she had smart business savoy. She knew there was still money to be made from an Ozzy Osbourne solo career and she saw her chance to make a name for herself in the music industry. Sharon then offered her services to Ozzy Osbourne and he accepted. She then took over his management from the Arden Company. During this time she also started to date Ozzy Osbourne, and she eventually married him. When she took over management her next job was to find a record company that would sign Ozzy and take a chance on him. This task would prove to be very hard even for someone with her connections and Ozzy's behavior did not make things easy.

During this time Sharon set up a meeting with CBS record executives who were still unsure about signing Ozzy Osbourne. Sharon had to come up with a way to impress them, and so she came up with this angel of light look for Ozzy. The plan was for Ozzy to walk into the room wearing a white suit as a handful of doves are seen flying before him. When the day of the meeting came Ozzy wearing the suit came in while Sharon released several doves from the cage as her plan was working. When Ozzy sat down things were going well untll one of the doves lands near Ozzy. Ozzy then picks up the dove, and then out of nowhere he bites the dove's head off, and he begins to chew on it, and then swallows it. At that point the meeting is over. When people in the music industry heard about this they did not want a sit down with Ozzy. With no one to turn to Sharon was forced to seek help from her dad. Her dad managed to get a contract for Sharon and Ozzy but if they signed they would get a record contract but 60% of all record sales would go to him. There was no better deal anywhere and so Sharon and Ozzy felt they had no choice, and really they did not so they signed.

From there Sharon would be the one who coordinated the recruitment of a technically gifted band for Ozzy Osbourne. The first album Ozzy recorded as a solo artist was called Blizzard of Oz. Soon other albums would follow, and at first they sold slow until more Heavy Metal fans liked the music of Ozzy Osbourne and then his sales picked up, selling in the millions. Ozzy would have a successful solo career that was far bigger than his Black

Sabbath career. In combine the albums of Ozzy Osbourne have sold close to 80 million copies.

From the 1980's to the mid-90's Ozzy's back-up band often had to change membership due to strange deaths of band members and other members not getting along with Sharon Arden. Other strange events also happened during Ozzy's solo career. There was a high number of suicides among young people that took place regarding Heavy Metal music and the artist they brought up the most was Ozzy Osbourne. These suicide deaths regarding Ozzy Osbourne had taken place at his concerts and some of the teens killed themselves in their homes while listening to his album.

The most noted death was of 19 year old John McCollum. John did not come from a troubled home but his home was stable and not abusive either. John's attitudes on life started to change when he got into Heavy Metal music and his favorite artist was Ozzy Osbourne. During this time John started to keep a gun in his room.

One night John had Ozzy's new album at the time, and was listening to a song called Suicide Solution while wearing a pair of head-phones. While listening to the song, out of nowhere, John took the gun he had in his room and then he shot himself. John died at 19 years old.

When his parents walked into the room they found John dead with Ozzy's music playing through the head-phones. Sometime after John's death the song Suicide Solution was taken to an institute called IBAR. IBAR then put the song under analysis and what they found was shocking. They stated that the song's musical notes, and style was purposefully depressive with a feeling of hopelessness. The song also contained hemisync tones which are sound waves that influence an individual's state of mind.

The song also had subliminal lyrics which are hidden lyrics meant to leave a certain inspired message. The lyrics were, 'Why try, Get the gun and try it, shoot! Shoot!'. Along with the subliminal lyrics hideous laughter was also found with it. These subliminal words, and laughter were recorded under such a low tone that a person would have to listen to the song at least 6 times for the message to sink into their brains.

On average a person listens to a new song at least 50 times within the year. IBAR was able to show that Ozzy's song Suicide Solution did encourage young John to kill himself. The U.S. courts did outlaw the practice of leaving subliminal messages in songs or on television ads, but yet even to this day they are still showing up on songs and ads, and hardly anyone is being charged with a crime for it.

When this scandal broke out Ozzy came under police investigation but was never arrested. Ozzy would go on several television shows defending his music and position. He said that he was being unfairly attacked by crazy religious people and that it was not his fault when some crazy person wants to shoot himself. He also stated that he had no idea the lyrics were there and he had nothing to do with it.

Everyone is entitled to defend themselves, after all this is America last time I checked. However, at the same time those crazy religious people he was talking about were not crazy and they had evidence that his music did have horrible effects on people's minds. The evidence also that IBAR showed also proved that his music can effect a person's thinking to convince themselves they need to die. It's also hard to believe that he did not know about the hidden lyrics when he was the one in the studio recording the song. The voice that made those awful lyrics was either his voice or someone he knows.

The police investigations regarding Ozzy also centered on activity done at his concerts. Several investigators stated that Ozzy would hold a satanic black mass and would do altar calls asking people if they would give their lives to serve Satan. People who defended Ozzy stated that it was just an act while others stated he was very serious. Investigators stated that people at his shows looked like they were in some kind of trance. Drug deals and drug use often went on at these shows. There were also acts of violence done among the fans and violence, and rape was done against women at certain shows. There were even deaths caused by overdoses, tramplings and stabbings.

There were also even stranger stories of people seeing demons at his concerts. There were also several cases of people turning up missing after going to an Ozzy Osbourne show.

Satanists were very well known to attend his concerts. Investigators stated that they would bring cats, chickens, frogs, bats, snakes and even puppies. Sometimes the animals were dead and sometimes they were alive. The ones that were alive the Satanists would wait until their favorite songs would start to be performed by Ozzy and then they would choke or stab the animals to death, and throw the animals toward the stage. At this point they would whip themselves into a rage and start to mosh.

One time during such a concert when this twisted display against animals was going on a fan threw a live bat on stage. Ozzy saw the bat, and picked it up, and killed it by biting it's head off. This act greatly increased his fame. After the show Ozzy began foaming out of his mouth, and spent the next two weeks getting shots for rabies.

Ozzy often spoke about fighting with demonic possession. He often stated that he could relate to the character Linda Blair played in the Exorcist. His wife Sharon often stated that Ozzy has people living inside of him and that living with Ozzy was sometimes dangerous because she never knew which person she would be dealing with.

For instance, in 1982 in San Antonio, Texas, Ozzy had performed there for the Texas fans. After the concert he went to sleep but then in the middle of the night he woke up feeling like something just took him over. He then took his clothes off, and he looked through his wife's clothes, and he put on her green dress and he slipped on his wife's high heel shoes. He then went for a walk only dressed in this, and he walked over to the Alamo which was a historical landmark.

Ozzy walked over to the wall, and pulled out his male member, and started urinating all over the wall. At that point he was tackled by San Antonio Police and arrested. Ozzy was then banned for a period of 10 years from ever performing in San Antonio.

During the tour for Diary of a Madman, Ozzy had a strange request for the promoters. He told the promoters that they must provide him with at least 25 pounds of raw cow livers and pig intestines each. The reason for this was Ozzy came up with an act at his concert called the raw meat baptism.

During the shows for the tour Ozzy hired people, and even got air-compressed tubes and the job of these tubes was to fire pounds of blood soaked raw meat at the fans while Ozzy and his people also threw the raw bloody meat at them.

Ozzy's drug use is very well known, and many people were shocked that he has lived this long. His main drugs of choice was cocaine, heroin, and pills. He also did even stranger things where he was known to drink animal blood and he would even shoot it up. In fact one time it was even known that he snorted a line of ants up his nose. He also had a thing for killing frogs on the black cross he wore, and would call the frog Jesus while he did it.

One can see he was never a fan of Christianity no matter how many times he tells his fans God bless you. One of his most twisted acts involved a pack of cats. One time Ozzy went into one of his darker moods and he went to put on a white suit, and came downstairs holding a handgun. He then sat down in front of a piano, and played a few keys. He then got up, and walked over to where the cats were huddle around, and he began to violently shoot the cats to death. He kept on blasting away at the cats until he ran out of bullets. When that happened he went to grab a knife, and rounded up the remaining cats and began to stab them to death one by one while sitting under a piano. When Sharon came home she found Ozzy still sitting under the piano holding a knife with blood all over his suit while 17 cats were shot to pieces, and their blood was all over the room.

One time Ozzy attended the Heavy Metal tour of bands when they went to Russia for the first time. In Russia Ozzy received a bottle of very potent Russian vodka. One night when Sharon and Ozzy retired for the night Sharon went to read a book and Ozzy was in the bedroom drinking the vodka. When he got drunk Ozzy stated that a very evil presence came over him.

Ozzy then walked out of his room, and went downstairs to find Sharon sitting in a chair reading a book.

When Sharon noticed him Ozzy was standing there in his underwear and Sharon became nervous because Ozzy's eyes did not look normal but they were pitch black. Ozzy then spoke to Sharon, and told her, 'We have come to a decision', and she fearfully said 'We' as if to say who's we, and Ozzy said 'You have to die'. Ozzy then jumped on top of her, and began to choke her almost to the point of death until he came back to his senses and let her go.

Sharon had Ozzy arrested, and Ozzy was charged with attempted homicide but Sharon dropped the case when Ozzy agreed to go into rehab and speak with a drug-councilor. The councilor was so disturbed by Ozzy that the doctor told Sharon to leave Ozzy after having an undisclosed sinister meeting with him. Sharon however decided to stand by him.

Ozzy's blackouts are also very well known. He would at times find himself waking up in strange people's hotel rooms with naked men and women lying next to him. Ozzy's behavior does show that he has multiple personality disorders, and some people believe he is a victim of mind-control but no proof was ever shown to this.

Church groups have often spoken against Ozzy Osbourne for some obvious reasons. The self-proclaimed Prince of Darkness has spent his career glorifying themes of satanic worship, drug abuse, demonic possession, sexual immorality, magic, doctrines of Aleister Crowley, and the occult. In fact, when Ozzy Osbourne received his star on the Hollywood Walk of Fame it was Marilyn Manson who introduced Ozzy to give his speech.

Marilyn Manson is an ordained minister of the Church of Satan who was ordained by Anton LaVey. Former President George W. Bush during his time as President one time made a very strange choice about who he was going to honor at the White House dinner ceremony. Of all people he picked Ozzy Osbourne. President Bush often stated to people that his religious belief was born-again Christian, but strangely he was a member of a powerful group called Skull & Bones who are known for doing occult rituals that members are not allowed to talk about. He also stated that he believes that there are many roads to Heaven other than the Way of Jesus which is not what Jesus Christ teaches. In fact, that teaching comes from the New Age faith.

When Bush introduced Ozzy he began to talk about songs that Ozzy did that only hardcore fans of Ozzy would know, and he even stated in a joking way that his mom the former First Lady loved his music. For someone who stated he is a born-again Christian to invite Ozzy, knowing what his music and career promoted made no sense unless you are into satanic themes yourself. Many things were said about President Bush, and a lot of what was said has yet to be proven but one wonders indeed. Many people in both major government parties were very upset that Bush would honor him. Many stated that Bush knew the subject matters regarding him and he still invited him.

When Ozzy Osbourne was doing his reality television show called The Osbournes, former Vice-President Dan Quayle also honored Ozzy and stated that the Osbournes provided good family entertainment, and taught good family morals. The Republican Party often prides itself on promoting Christian morals. So knowing that what was this good family entertainment Quayle spoke on, and people in his party cheered him for saying. According to the tracked ratings about 30 million people a week watched the Osbourne reality show at the height of the show's fame at that time. The show brought in close to 200 million dollars in ads, and merchandise sales of t-shirts, cards, calendars, magazines, snow gloves, posters, and bobble heads. The show had 51 f-words in 15 minutes, and 75 curse words in 30 minutes.

The show featured Kelly and Jack presenting a sexually immoral lifestyle, and a rebellious spirit. The parents taught them no Christian values, and most of the time they let them do what they wanted. Some of the episodes featured the family engaged in acts of vandalism and stalking against their neighbors. When the two kids Kelly and Jack would engage in things the Bible calls sins their parents Ozzy and Sharon's only advice to them was to where a condom and don't get caught.

One wonders what kind of leaders we have in Washington D.C. who think that this is good family morals. There were several other bands that moral groups complained against and two noted ones were Aerosmith and AC/DC.

Aerosmith is a hard rock band who came from the city of Boston. The band was formed by guitarist Joe Perry and bass guitarist Tom Hamilton in the year 1970. These two brought in vocalist and harmonica player Steven Tyler, drummer Joey Kramer, and rhythm guitarist Ray Tabano. The band was nicknamed 'The Bad Boys from Boston'. In 1972 the band was signed to Columbia Records, and for over 40 years they have been one of the greatest Rock n' Roll bands in history. In the 1970's they were a huge multi-platinum selling band. Their biggest albums were Get Your Wings, Toys in the Attic, and Rocks.

They would have had several major hit singles as well, but heavy drug addictions and internal conflicts took their toll on the band which resulted in the band's popular fame to fade and Perry left the group in 1979.

In 1984 Perry returned to the struggling band, and Aerosmith was determined to make a comeback. The comeback happened in 1986 when Aerosmith worked with rap-group Run-D.M.C. on the remake of their song Walk This Way. In 1987 they would release the album Permanent Vacation and the band's popularity they had experienced in the 70's returned once again. The band would go on to release multi-platinum albums such as Pump in 1989, Get a Grip in 1993, and Nine Lives in 1997. This band in combine total albums have sold 150 million albums world-wide.

One of the strange things mentioned about Aerosmith was their famous symbol. There is an actual occult meaning to it but it does not prove Aerosmith knew about it. The famous circle A with the wings represents the serpent biting its own tail, and the A represented the child of the broken cross often called the son of Satan or anti-Christ. This does not prove that Aerosmith knew that their symbol is seen in ancient occult books but it is there in these books.

Moral groups attacked Aerosmith for several reasons. The main one was drug use among the band members and drug use among the fans at the concerts. Often Aerosmith's early concert performances were drug driven where they were often speed-balling at concerts.

To speedball is to use cocaine and heroin mixed together. Their songs often promoted drug use, sexual immorality, macho violent behavior, homosexuality, vandalism, suicide, and general rebellion. It was said that the money value of cocaine the band used could have ended homelessness in three major cities.

The band has stated of themselves that they have long since cleaned up and have quit using cocaine and other hard drugs. Let's hope this is true and it stays that way.

AC/DC is a band that was formed in New South Wales, Australia. They were formed in November of 1973 by Malcolm and Angus Young who are brothers. AC/DC are called one of the major pioneers of Heavy Metal music. Their first lead singer was a man named Bon Scott. AC/DC released their first album called High Voltage in February of 1975, and in 1977 they released a major hit album called Powerage. While recording the album that would be called Back in Black lead singer Bon Scott was found dead in February 1980. Bon Scott was replaced by singer Brian Johnson and soon after they released the album Back in Black.

This album launched the band to new heights of success and became their all-time best-seller where 10,000 copies were sold in just one week. Back in Black would come to sell 50 million copies world-wide. After Back in Black, the band's next album called For Those About to Rock We Salute You would be their first album to go number one on the Billboard charts in the United States of America. After this they began to decline in popularity until they released the album The Razors Edge which produced the hit single Thunderstruck.

It was in 1976 when AC/DC gained international fame when they joined the Lock Up Your Daughters Summer Tour in the United Kingdom. The acts they toured with were Black Sabbath, Aerosmith, Kiss, Styx, UFO, Blue Oyster Cult, and Cheap Trick. The song Highway to Hell is what brought them major popularity fame in the United States.

Highway to Hell came under attack by Church groups for its lyrics regarding Satan. One of the opening lines of the song was 'Hey Satan, paid my dues, playing in a rockin band'. The song was written by Bon Scott who was known to have a love for Satan. Some would wonder how far this love went.

Rumors regarding Bon Scott, and members of the band is that they were members of satanic covens but this has never been proven true. Scott did have a thing for wearing necklaces that had satanic symbols on them. Some said that he sold his soul to the devil to enter into the music industry but this also has not been proven. On February 19, 1980 Bon Scott passed out in a car on his way back to Alistair Kinnear's house. Kinnear stated he was unable to move him, and so he left him in the car until next morning. On that morning Scott was rushed to the hospital and was pronounced dead on arrival. The official cause of death was acute alcohol poisoning but some believed it was even darker than that.

No one could not understand how Kinnear could not tell that Scott was no longer breathing. Some people believe that Scott was not killed in the manner of the report and his body was put in the car along with a bottle of alcohol so that it would look like alcohol poisoning, but there was no evidence to those statements.

In the underground, the meaning of the name AC/DC was to mean Anti-Christ/Devil Children. Church groups and moral groups attacked AC/DC for promoting Satanism, terrorism, revolting on parents and authority figures, sexual immorality, homosexuality, vandalism, violence, murder, drugs, kidnappings, and other vices.

Horrible actions took place at AC/DC concerts. There were several deaths caused by tramplings, stabbings, beatings, and over-doses. Women were attacked and even raped. Drugs were also being sold at many of their concerts by dealers among the crowds.

The Bible tells us that GOD uses Satan to wage a war over the souls of the human race to see who will follow GOD and who will not. Is it so crazy to think that Satan uses music to influence people? It is a known fact that the government used the U.S. Army to set up concert speakers, and to blast AC/DC music at ear splitting volumes as a means of psychological torture to drive Manuel Noriega out of the Vatican. Even the U.S. knows that certain music can cause disturbing emotional states into people, but certain many fans don't seem to care.

Chapter 11

In the 70's a new forms of music was being invented that came to be called new wave. This was music that used new forms of technology that made beats with electro sounds, and electro rhythm samples. These styles of music would be called pop, house, freestyle, mixes, hip-hop and others.

In the late 70's a new craze in music would come forth that was called the music video. A new channel would introduce the world to the music video, and this channel was called MTV. MTV would start what became called the MTV generation. MTV is a basic cable channel which is owned by a company of Viacom Media Networks. The channel's original headquarters was in New York City. MTV was first launched as MTV: The Music Channel on May 5, 1980 and then it was re-launched as MTV: Music Television on August 1, 1981 and it has stayed on the air ever since. Today close to 100 million households have MTV.

MTV was originally started to play music videos guided by television personalities called VJ's. VJ's stood for video jockeys. MTV's main target demographic were pre-teens and teenagers and it still is, although today many young adults watch it. It was said that the Big Booper was the first to make a music video back in the 1950's. From there two groups would be noted for making music videos in the mid-1960's.

The Beatles had started making music videos when they did the movie A Hard Day's Night in 1964. The most noted music video in the film was the song Can't Buy Me Love. A couple of years later from that point a group called the Monkees would debut their television program. They made a great number of music videos for their songs to be shown on their program.

MTV's early history started in 1977 when Warner Cable launched the first two-way interactive cable television system. Among their many specialized channels they wanted to create a music channel. At this time a man named Robert W. Pittman, who was inspired by the Monkees television program, had an idea. Pittman would come to create the original programming format of MTV and pitched his idea to the Warner Cable Company. They decided to first test-drive this idea and so Pittman would host a 15 minute show using this new format on a channel called WNBC located in New York City. The show was called Album Tracks and the cable network liked what they saw.

In 1980 they would release a pilot, and then in 1981 MTV became an official channel. The channel opened with the original MTV theme song with the words, 'Ladies and Gentlemen, Rock and Roll', with a clip of the Apollo 11 footage with the flag featuring MTV's logo changing with various colors, textures, and designs.

Before the show started from late 1978 to 1981 several artists were hired by their record companies to start production on a new format called the music video. The record companies knew that the basic cable network was soon to release their music channel and they wanted these videos on there to promote their artists. The first music video shown on MTV was from a little known early electro-pop group called The Buggles. Their song on the video was called Video Killed the Radio Star. The second video was called You Better Run by Pat Benatar. MTV's effect was immediate, and this channel kicked off what became called the MTV generation do to the look, style, attitude, and fashions of the music videos millions of young people saw.

MTV would also feature artists that radio shows did not play like Bow Wow Wow and Men at Work. After The Buggles and Pat Benatar had their videos shown, the next and new 20 music videos made by music industry artists were She Won't Dance with Me by Rod Stewart, You Better You Bet by The Who, Little Suzi's on the Up by Ph.D, We Don't Talk Anymore by Cliff Richard, Brass in Pocket by The Pretenders, Time Heals by

Todd Rundgren, Take It on the Run by REO Speedwagon, Rockin The Paradise by Styx, When Things Go Wrong by Robin Lane and the Chartbusters, History Never Repeats by Split Enz, Hold On Loosely by .38 Special, Just Between You and Me by April Wine, Sailing by Rod Stewart, Iron Maiden by Iron Maiden, Keep On Loving You by REO Speedwagon, Bluer Than Blue by Michael Johnson, Message of Love by The Pretenders, Mr. Briefcase by Lee Ritenour, Double Life by The Cars, and In the Air Tonight by Phil Collins.

These artists would make music industry history in establishing the sound and look of the MTV generation along with many other artists. Those artists would be Michael Jackson, Madonna, Prince, Duran Duran, Frankie Goes to Hollywood, and scores of others. MTV after its launch would quickly inspire other networks to also create music programs. HBO would air Video Jukebox, SuperStation WTBS would air Night Tracks, NBC launched Friday Night Videos and ABC launched ABC Rocks.

TBS founder Ted Turner started the Cable Music Channel but ended up selling it to MTV who redeveloped the channel into VH1. When MTV first started its only purpose was to play music videos until later when many shows were developed for the channel. Their main creation was the reality show which became a huge craze on almost every major network ten years after the first reality show aired.

MTV was the channel that coined the term VJ or video jockey. When the channel first started they hired fresh faced young men, and women to introduce music videos that were being played. The original first five MTV VJ's were Nina Blackwood, Mark Goodman, Alan Hunter, J.J. Jackson, and Martha Quinn. Throughout the 80's going into the 90's MTV became the voice of the young culture. It would play videos with a wide range of music styles from electro wave, pop, hard rock, soft rock, Heavy Metal, and other forms of music.

They played music videos from artists like Duran Duran, Culture Club, The Cars, Adam Ant, Eurythmics, Blondie, Bon Jovi, Van Halen, Def Leppard, and scores of others. They also played classic rock videos from artists like John Mellencamp, Journey, David Bowie, The Police, Billy Joel, Genesis, David Lee Roth,

Robert Palmer, Linda Ronstadt, The Moody Blues and many others.

MTV videos also helped to push the booming dance wave with artists like Michael Jackson and Madonna who capitalized on dance in their videos with new wave dance moves and break-dancers. Duran Duran even used tribal dance elements with the new wave sound. The most noted was in their video Wild Boys.

MTV also started to get some heat in the press when it was shown they hardly ever showed videos from black artists. They only showed a few black artists in the video line-up. Many African-American groups started to complain and one cable network called BET decided to create their own music show to feature black artists. In fact before 1983 Michael Jackson often struggled getting his videos on MTV. MTV only showed a few black artists like Michael Jackson, Prince, Eddy Grant, Donna Summer, and a very few others. MTV came under fire several times for racism or favoring white artists throughout the 80's. It became so noted that one time in 1983 David Bowie, while doing an interview with VJ Mark Goodman one time asked Goodman why is there not a lack of black artists in the video line-up.

This bad PR regarding racism on MTV did not end until 1988 when MTV debuted the show Yo! MTV Raps. Up-scale African-Americans found it to be an offence that the first show on MTV to feature mostly black artists would be a rap show. They felt this way because they believed rappers promoted the evils that plagued black neighborhoods while hip-hop defenders stated that they were only telling people the truth of what is going on.

Many strange rumors were often said about MTV's founder Robert Pittman. Some said that he was a Mason and that the day he came up with the idea of MTV he was in a masonic temple in Canada, but this has never been proven.

Masons often come under fire for the strange rituals they hold in their lodges. Much study into them shows that the rituals have connections to rituals that ancient people did in honor of Moloch or Baal and many other gods the people worshipped in the past and even to the present day. There has been no proof that masons have human sacrifice rituals like the people in ancient

Canaan did for Moloch, Baal, the Queen of Heaven and others.

However, there is video evidence of one lodge engaging in an animal sacrifice. There is also testimony of many former masons who came to Christ discussing that masons drink blood from a human skull and do other satanic rites that are kept hidden with the degrees of each masonic member. There is also testimony of masons being killed by lodge members for exposing masonic secrets.

In some of the promotion ads of MTV there are strange references to the Freemasons, and no one knows why it's there. There symbols are even seen in music videos of all forms and styles with no answer for why it's there. MTV ads even have references to Satan like Eve biting the apple, and baphomet worship in a Christmas ad from MTV and several others. There have been so many of these references that people have stated that the people who run MTV are members of occults, but no proof was given to show this. Nevertheless, satanic images are often seen in their ads and music videos. Many masons, in their defense, stated that they are not an occult or a coven, and many of them believe in Jesus Christ. However, it is proven that rituals to other gods do go on at the lodges and for a non-occult group they are sure enough determined to be hidden and to keep their practices a secret.

Jesus stated that people are not to put any gods before him and that he did nothing in secret but taught openly for everyone to see. Jesus himself never wanted to be seen as someone who acts as coven members which are in secret. There has been no real proof that Robert Pittman is a Mason. No masonic lodge has ever claimed him as a member but some said there are members that are to remain a secret but no proof was shown to that statement. In fact there are masons that we admired for taking a brave stand during the Civil Rights movement which had many masons in their numbers. In regards to this many have stated that there is light and dark among masons. That you do have masons who work for the good, and that you have others who work towards evil. It is a strange organization indeed with many that have said they have such powerful members that those members hold key positions in our government and among the global movement. Even most of our Founding Fathers were

Freemasons, including George Washington himself.

Many employees who have worked for MTV buildings, and studios stated that each of these buildings do have a masonic lodge and design to them. In fact I came to learn that it's very hard to get into these buildings and in rooms once you are inside.

One of their headquarters has the words Masonic Temple upon the front of the building in very large letters. Some said regarding it that the building used to be a masonic lodge until it was sold to MTV. The question is why didn't MTV remove the letters? Some ex-employees stated that the real meaning of MTV is not music television but mason television. This has never been proven. When someone asked Robert Pittman how he came up with the format for MTV he stated that it was based on his two-point plan. Pittman stated that MTV was aimed at young people, and to get them he would use point one which was to get their emotions going and then use point two which was to make them forget their logic. He believed that if this was done right that MTV would not just be shooting for 14 year olds they would own them.

I found this as a Christian to be disturbing because of what emotions and logic are and what the Bible says about them. The Bible tells us not to be driven by our emotions because many times we can be deceived by them. Emotions tend to fix attention on objects or occurrences which have excited them. So in many instances emotions are succeeded by desires to obtain possession of the objects or events that have awaken them. Emotions can become passions and many times it can become a powerful and even permanent spring of action. Emotions are awakened through the medium of the intellect and can be modified or varied by whatever conception we form of the objects or events. Emotions will manifest their existence and it's character by sensible effects upon the brain and body. Emotions lead to a quiescence and a contemplation, and will combine with springs of action rather it is good or shameful will only be determined by what is the sensation that is comprehended by the expression of countenance, attitude, or manner. If something is ridiculous but the image and sound tells you its sublime that is what your emotions will believe. If something is lustful, hateful, or wrong but the image and sound says it's not that is what your emotions will believe. You actually need your logic in order not to be deceived by emotions.

Logic is the discovering of truth, and using rightful reason, and deductive thinking. Jesus' parables actually took people to discover and use deductive thinking to understand its true meaning. Using reason and thought is very important to grow and learn, and to not sway into something foolish or harmful.

Pittman's statements regarding the idea of MTV should give Christians or anyone pause indeed. Many people spoke about the brainwashing effects many music videos seem to have. Most music videos have a lot of sexual images especially today. Women are often seen as sexual objects were they are seen as stripping on poles, naked in beds with only sheets to cover them, looking for a sexual encounter, throwing their bodies toward the artist or artists in the video. Female artists are often dressed in a fashion of seduction with a style to entice the lust of its watchers. Images like these often lead young men and even women astray from moral grounds, and will cause men to see women only for how they look, and even to use them as sexual objects. Women will feel that this will give them empowerment over men and will seek to act, and dress as the women in the video.

This is not just a Christian understanding it is even an understanding found in secular studies. A high amount of rebellion is often seen in the videos of kids and teenagers rebelling on their parents, and seeking a depraved course in life. Money and material objects are often seen as if they are worshipped rather than a use. Looks are often seen to be more important than a person's inner character, and if a person does not have looks, money, and material objects they are seen as being worthless. Of course it takes education and hard work to get money, and objects but yet education and working hard is also seen in many videos as a downer.

Many hard rock and Heavy Metal videos had themes of the occult and satanic worship. There were images of dark ceremonial settings, and images of witchcraft, Satanism, and altars relating to black masses. Artists in the videos spoke about offering girls to Satan, and even murdering them, and encouraged young people to serve occult interest. There were videos about blind rage, violence, drugs, and even stalking.

Rap videos often came under fire even though rap or hip-hop was originally used to speak on social issues. Many rap stars whose videos came under fire would say their messages are still about social issues. Many Church groups and moral groups stated that rap videos have praised gang violence, and even enticed young people to join or hang out with dangerous gang-members. They stated they have glorified the use of drugs and young people killing other people. That they have glorified criminal actions to rob and hurt people, and rape women. That women in their videos are seen as nothing but whores and toys to be discarded, and used when the need arises. That they speak about killing police officers and government agents, and selling drugs as a means of escape from poverty.

Many rap stars glorify money and power, and domination over others, and today it even shows satanic themes and homosexuality. It shows that some rap is used for knowledge, and awareness, and some rap is just plain twisted, sick, and evil, and no better than a satanic Heavy Metal video.

The two main rap groups that came under fire by Church groups, moral groups, and the media were N.W.A. and Ice-T. Ice-T is often called the father of gangsta rap music. His music was often under attack for promoting violence, drugs, sex, and a criminal lifestyle. In fact, Ice-T was a former pimp, and was part of a crew who would rob jewelry stores. He began to go legit when many of his friends were being locked in prison, and told him not to get caught, and end up there.

After he nearly died from a car accident he decided to stay legit. The two songs that got him into the most trouble were Six in the Morning and Cop Killer. Six in the Morning was about the best hour when a drug dealer could make the most money. Cop Killer was simply about killing cops. Ice T defended his position by stating that what he rapped about in Six in the Morning was not a new kind of thing but it was the truth of what he saw, and knows. Drug dealers do make the best money at early hours in the morning. In fact, I saw that myself, and what he said is true, but one wonders if he is rapping about this to expose it or praise it.

Ice-T defended Cop Killer by stating that cops have shot, and killed young black men who were unarmed, and only suspected of a crime. Much of the case files, and court cases does show a strong truth to this.

Many believe that the reason why cops are so quick to label black men as the bad guys is because of how they were brought up, and how the media has painted many black males as being criminals. Ice-T stated that the song was not about killing cops but about defending yourself against a cop who is trying to kill you by using deadly force upon him. This song caused a nationwide protest from police officers, and government officials who demanded the song to be banned. At first Ice-T was protected under the Federal Law of Freedom of Speech until a young man killed a cop after listening to Cop Killer. From there the song was taken off the album, and only sold as a single, and was banned from several record shops who refused to sell the single.

N.W.A. came under attack for songs about killing cops, murdering people in gang violence, selling drugs, abuse against women, Satanism, and for presenting an evil image for black youths. N.W.A. defended their position by also stating that what they rapped about was not stuff they made up but about what actually goes on in the streets. They stated that gang-members have been killing each other before they started doing records, and cops, because of their abuse toward black men, have been at odds with people in the black community before they even rapped about it. They stated that there are girls out there who are nothing but mean 'hoes' you have to check before they check you, and also you have ladies that are not 'hoes'. N.W.A. was also a group that government officials who even worked with black Church groups tried to ban but they too were protected under Freedom of Speech laws.

I do believe in Freedom of Speech, and telling the truth, but some strange things were said about gangsta rap groups as well. Several people who spoke about why the music industry got into the gangsta rap market stated that it was to help fill the prisons that were being built up at the time and they hoped this music would encourage people to commit crimes and get locked up. But no proof was ever shown to this. Another had to do with satanic worship going on with some of the rap stars like Eazy E. saying the Lord's Prayer backwards which is a well-known practice in the Church of Satan of how Satanists pray to Satan. However, no proof was shown that Eazy E. was really a devil-worshipper.

Hip-hop music and culture was formed during the 1970's at block parties that became increasingly popular in the Bronx area of New York City. These block and basement parties incorporated DJ's to mix sounds of funk and soul music by isolating them into percussive breaks and would use two turntables to do this. The person who is called the real father of rap or hip-hop music was a DJ named DJ Kool Herc.

Herc had originally came from the Island of Jamaica, came to the United States as a small boy, and grew up in the South Bronx. In fact, many early DJ mixers had come from Jamaica, Puerto Rico, or elsewhere among the Caribbean Islands. DJ Kool Herc was said to be the first to start rapping rhymes over the beats he developed.

Rapping is a vocal style where an artist speaks lyrically in the fashion of a poet to rhyme and verse to an instrumental or synthesized beat. Beats came in 4/4 time signature which can be sampled by sequencing portions. Thus, an artist can incorporate synthesizers, drum machines, and even live hard rock bands. Hip-hop's music was developed when turntables were used with sampling technology and drum machines.

These DJ's like Kool Herc learned how to use the turntables and this new music technology to their advantage. The first type of rhymes from Kool Herc and others in hip-hop's infancy was rhymes about dancing and having style. Very soon the rhymes started to verse on social, economic, and political realities of the lives of young African-Americans, and other poor groups of cultures. One of the prime rappers who brought the voice of social awareness to rap was a rapper, and many say the first MC meaning he started out rapping, and not as a DJ, was Afrika Bambaataa.

Afrika was a very feared man who was a former gang-leader of one of the largest gangs in New York City. He was already a natural poet before hip-hop music was developed. He started attending the disco club scene, and block parties, and began hearing DJ's rap. This impulse led him to form a crew, and he began to rap, and he learned how to mix. He became famous in that scene for his fashion sense which was a wild-funk African look. He also was called the best rapper of that time, and came to define the voice of rap music as an outlet that speaks on the disenfranchised youth of low-economic areas. During this time, Afrika, after a friend of his was killed, began to distance himself from the gang he was in and he formed the Universal Zulu Nation whose members were mostly blacks and Puerto Ricans.

Hip-hop music started to become big in the disco club scene as the sound was taken from the streets, and into the clubs. As hip-hop grew, new dance styles were developed with it and one noted dance style was called pop and lock which later became called break-dancing in the 1980's.

Early hip-hop rappers began to also define the sound through shows that were rap battles where rappers out-rhyme and out-style the other. This created different styles of rapping. The early forerunners were DJ Hollywood, Kool Moe Dee, Lovebug Starski, Keith Cowboy, and many others.

In the late 70's a funk group called The Sugar Hill Gang watched Keith Cowboy perform his rhymes. This inspired the group to add hip-hop into their music. The Sugar Hill Gang would then write, and perform a song called Rapper's Delight. The song was then recorded in a studio by The Sugar Hill Gang and it became a hit single on the Billboard charts as it entered the top 20. This song introduced rap music to the music industry. Soon after new rap groups were formed in the 1980's.

The most noted were Run-D.M.C., The Fat Boys, Slick Rick, KRS-One, LL Cool J, Beastie Boys, DJ Jazzy Jeff and the Fresh Prince, and many others. Run-D.M.C is the group that brought rap into the mainstream market. They opened the doors for the kind of money that rap groups can make, and they even appeared in movies like Tougher Than Leather. They were the first group to have rap songs enter the top 10 Billboard charts, and the first to have their albums go platinum.

In August of 1988, MTV debuted the 2 hour show called Yo! MTV Raps. The show was hosted by Ed Lover, Fab 5 Freddy, and Doctor Dre who is not to be confused with Dr. Dre of N.W.A. The first video to appear on the show was from Eric B. and Rakim with the song called Follow the Leader. From there they played videos from Run-D.M.C, DJ Jazzy Jeff and the Fresh Prince, Shinehead, Ice-T, and others. In fact almost every hip-hop artist in the music industry from 1988 to 1995 had their music videos played on the program. This program would be the major vehicle that introduced a vast white audience to rap music. The program did come under fire several times for some of the videos they played. This started when Public Enemy's video called By The Time I Get to Arizona was pulled from the show for being too violent. The program was almost shut-down completely when they played the video from Cypress Hill called How I Could Just Kill a Man.

In 1995 the show would come off the air and it was replaced with a show called Yo!. Since then rap has become a major form of mainstream music and it often has been used in pop and rock songs. New forms of dance moves were also becoming very popular. They were part of the new wave style of dance that was on the rise. These styles were used in pop and hip-hop music.

Pop music had a style of dance that was often scene in funk music, and then new moves came about where the focus was more on feet, legs, and hip movements. This style would develop more when mixes became huge in the club, and then a new style of dance called house was born. Another very popular form especially in the 1980's was called originally pop and lock, and later it was called breakdancing.

Breakdancing started on the streets of New York City among African-American and Puerto Rican youths in the early 1970's. It was moved into the clubs, and the breakers danced to early electro-pop, hip-hop, and funk beats. It soon gained fame through the club scenes, and it spread to other cities all across the United States. In Los Angeles in the late 70's to early 1980's a multi-cultural hip-hop club opened called Radiotron which was based out of Macarthur Park. Breakdancing became huge there, and people who came from other parts of the world would then go to their native countries and they would spread breakdancing in their clubs. This caused breakdancing to be seen around the world. The nightclub scene of Radiotron inspired a German film crew to do a documentary on it called Breakin and Enterin. The documentary featured two people that many said were the best breakers in the world. One was called by the nickname Boogaloo Shrimp who was an African-American who's real name was Michael Chambers. In fact, Michael Jackson learned the moonwalk from Boogaloo Shrimp. The other was nicknamed Shabba Doo who was from Chicago, and he was of Puerto Rican heritage. His real name was Adolfo Quinones.

When these two appeared in the documentary this inspired Cannon Films, whose parent company was MGM, to make a film called Breakin which came out in 1984. Boogaloo and Shabba used to be rivals at Radiotron but they forged a friendship while making the movie. In the movie Boogaloo was called Turbo and Shabba was called Ozone.

Breakin brought the pop and lock culture even further to a world-wide audience, and it was a box-office hit. This movie would be followed by a sequel called Breakin 2: Electric Boogaloo. Ice-T also played a part in Radiotron's club scene.

Ice-T was also a skilled break-dancer and he hung out at Radiotron, and even appeared breakdancing in the documentary. Ice-T first put forth his rap skills at Radiotron, and he made songs for the Breakin 1 & 2 soundtracks. The soundtracks to both films were very successful and they both went platinum, and featured early pop songs, hip-hop songs, and mixes. But in regards to Ice-T, if you ever mention this period in his life and what it was like to appear in Breakin 2 he would tell you that this whole period in his life was 'wack'.

When Breakin was first being made many people in the scene felt it was not true to life, and so they wanted to make a film that would be more real. So in the same year of 1984 a film called Beat Street was released. Beat Street, unlike Breakin, was a drama film that featured the culture of the early 1980's New York City hip-hop culture. The film showed the struggles of the culture of rap, breakdancing, DJing, and graffiti. The film was set in the South Bronx where hip-hop was born, and it was a more real to life film then Breakin. In 1984 MTV aired their first music video awards show called the VMA's.

Ever since the first show, and all the way up to our time there has been strange events, and controversy surrounding the awards show. Many people have said that this is due to the satanic elements working within MTV. Although there is no proof to that but nevertheless some of these occurrences are rather strange, and according to the Bible it would even be called satanic. Let's us take a look at a couple of these shows.

At the 2003 VMA show, the most talked about performance was the one given by Madonna, Britney Spears, and Christina Aguilera when they performed together as a trio. The theme of the show was a homosexual wedding. It even had a message at the end of the performance when the three artists sang that they were tried of the concept of right and wrong.

The way this performance plays out is that the set features a wedding chapel with a white pyramid like shape on top with a staircase leading up to it. The song that begins to play was a song that brought controversy to Madonna back in the 1980's called Like a Virgin. Britney begins to sing the opening lyrics of the song, and then Christina comes out to sing the chorus. While they are singing together soon Madonna makes her entrance when she appears at the top of the staircase dressed in a black tuxedo with a top hat.

Back in the 20's and 30's gay female performers would wear black tuxedos as a sign that they were into same sex practices. When Madonna appears she begins to sing a song called Hollywood, and she starts to descend down the staircase. She then encounters Britney and Christina who are both wearing white wedding dresses. Keep in mind that MTV still aims the show at pre-teens and teenagers. When they are dancing together, and singing this song Madonna does an odd thing. She puts her top hat on top of Britney's head almost as if she is picking her for something. From there the performance goes on, and when it's about to be over Madonna lustfully kisses Britney first, and then she does the same to Christina. From there they declare they are bored with the concept of right and wrong. They did not yell for gay-rights or something specific but only they were bored with right or wrong. Industry insiders stated that the concert was about the feud between Britney and Christina to see who would take the place of Madonna, and when Madonna put her hat on Britney it was a sign that she was picking her. No one really knows if this is true, but there was a feud between the two young pop stars, and there was this talk about which one would take the place of Madonna. Of course I always thought that the one who takes the place should be based on talent, and who the fans pick, and not on who Madonna favors. Some stated that Madonna has the kind of power to make or break other people's careers. One can only wonder.

It is known that Britney and Christina are members of the Kabbalah temple that Madonna is a member of. In fact Madonna is a proud member of it, and she has even expressed that she loves Satan himself. Some stated she is even a high-priestess of some kind but the Kabbalah center refuses to acknowledge this. The Bible would call the Kabbalah an occult because occults are defined in Christian teachings to be any congregation that does not worship the One True GOD. Other people say that people have the right to whatever faith they want to believe in, but of course most of those people have no idea that Freedom of Religion was about different Christian denominations and that the Founding Fathers believe that the GOD of the Bible should be the only authority governing the spirit of the people because humans often rule with tyranny.

Of course I don't think they teach this in school. Their statements about being bored with the concept of right and wrong is also very disturbing. What if people got up and said I am bored with respecting other people's lives, and now I want to kill, destroy, and rape other people? Of course to kill, destroy, and rape other people is wrong but according to statements like that why should you care if it's wrong? Many said that they made the statements as an attack on Christian values who say that homosexual lifestyles are wrong. Well the Bible does say it's wrong, and even science can show you more ways that it's wrong, and even the mental conditions that develop after people turn gay can tell you it's wrong, but that side of the story never gets told in the media. Also you should know that the Laws of the United States were built on Christian values. If those values are discarded then you should wonder what kind of country it will be. I can tell you this, it won't be a better one but it will be what the Revolutionary soldiers fought to get rid of. For a kids show there is some twisted stuff on MTV.

At the 2009 VMA show there was also strange things happening there. The show would open with Madonna doing a tribute speech to Michael Jackson even though it is known that Jackson did not care much for Madonna. When Madonna did the speech she even stated that she hardly knew him even though they have crossed paths many times, and they even went on a date together. Many believed it was Madonna's way of saying that she could care less about him, and Michael Jackson even stated that Madonna was always jealous of him. Either way they could have brought someone in to give the tribute that actually cared about Michael Jackson when you consider the tribute is for someone who has died, and millions of fans loved and respected him.

When Taylor Swift won the award for Best Female Video and went to receive it she was interrupted by rapper Kanye West. West would shame her by telling her that Beyonce had one of the best videos of all time. This would then tell Taylor without saying it that you don't deserve the award but Beyonce does. Taylor seems to handle this well, and she is called back out by Beyonce to be allowed to have her moment without interruption. When Taylor does she has oddly changed her dress from a white dress to a red dress matching Beyonce's red dress. No one seemed to understand why she needed to change her dress. People who know the scene stated that it had to do with a test of character to see if Taylor was really strong enough to be among the A-list of music stars, that what they will do is shame the star somehow to see how they would act, and if they handle it well they are accepted.

Taylor changing her dress to red was supposed to be a sign that she was accepted that she is strong enough to stand in their presence. No one knows if this is really true, but they stated in basic terms that what West did was staged to enact this matter with Taylor Swift. While some have said that there was nothing to it but Kanye West being an evil jerk, but of course there was no answer to why the MTV staff allowed Kanye to do that. During a segment with Jack Black, Black told the audience to put their devil horns in the air, and he then said a prayer to Satan. It seemed on the surface he was kidding but he does finish the prayer with a certain feeling of he did his job. One wonders who he did this job for. Was it really to Satan or is he kidding? Black often invokes Satan in his performances so it does leave one to wonder why he does that so much. Also there were people among his peers who had their horns up praying with him.

Later on Lady Gaga would give a performance that sparked controversy while others said it was brilliant. On stage was a background of ancient pagan settings. While performing she pours fake blood on herself, and pretends like she has been stabbed, and seems to pose as if she is offering the blood. Her dancers then tie her arm to a rope, and she is then lifted up into the air with a pose as if she is dead. A heavy light shines through the background, and her dancers lift their arms in praise of the light. A lot of people found this to be really strange, but what I saw I read about before, and it regards people in Egypt when they would worship the sun-god.

Many times at certain events they would offer a human sacrifice to the sun by stabbing the victim with a blade. They would wait till sunrise, and then hang the victim from a rope, and wait till the sun rays beam upon the victim to offer the victim's blood to Ra their god of the sun. There is no real proof that Lady Gaga did this in honor of Ra but there is no doubt that the manner she did the performance in was the manner these ancient Egyptians offered their victims.

Chapter 12

Pop music is believed to be a term that comes from the word popular, but others have stated in regards to that is that the word pop in terms of pop music is deriving from the term rock and roll. Rock and roll was an underground term for sex and pop was an underground term of the sound that is made when one is having sex. The term pop was used to describe a certain genre of Rock n' Roll music.

In the 1960's hard rock music was on the rise so the style of the Beatles, and others became pop-rock music. Since this style of music was so popular thanks to the Beatles people always just thought that pop came from the word popular. As a genre pop music borrows elements from other styles like urban, dance, rock, funk, Latin, country, and hip-hop. The core elements that define pop music are it's short to medium length of songs as well as the employment of repeated choruses, melodic tunes, and catchy hooks. In the 70's pop music became fused with electric beats, electric drums, and electric bass. Pop music is the genre that has a wide open commercial market that is larger than any form of music in America. The reason for this is because pop-music is pleasurable to listen to even if certain songs do not have artistic depth.

Pop music appeals to the desires of a mass audience especially the young. The two main artists that gave the standard of pop music today were Michael Jackson, called the King of Pop, and Madonna who is called the Queen of Pop.

Michael Jackson was born on August 29, 1958. He is the 8th of 10 children. His mother's name was Katherine Esther Scruse, and his father was a man named Joe Jackson. Katherine was raised in a Jehovah Witness household, and his father did not seem to be a religious man. Joe had spent sometime in the military, and afterward he got into performing music. He would join an African-American R&B band called the Falcons.

The Falcons mainly played in night-clubs, bar lodges, and barn parties. The Falcons sought to make it big one day in the music industry but this never happened. It was a disappointment that drove Joe to be very bitter about it. Joe met and married Katherine during this time in his life. He would move his wife to Gary, Indiana where there he raised his children. Gary, Indiana was an industrial city near Chicago. The Jacksons stayed in a small 3-room house. Michael Jackson had five brothers named Jackie, Tito, Jermaine, Marlon, and Randy. He would have had six brothers but Brandon Marlon's twin died shortly after birth. Michael Jackson also had three sisters named Rebbie, LaToya, and Janet.

Joe often demanded that his children not call him father but were to call him only Joe. He began to train them at an early age to perform music. He wanted his children to become what he was unable to become which is famous. When Joe started the rehearsals they became a form of strict discipline. The rehearsals became incessant, and the Jackson brothers were physically and emotionally abused. Joe, seeing Michael's talent early, drove Michael even harder and he would regularly whip Michael with belts and tree sticks.

He would often verbally abuse him telling him he had a fat nose, and that he was too weak. Michael often cried from loneliness and abuse, and he would vomit after school knowing he had to face his father. Michael during his childhood and into his pre-teen years would develop a deep dissatisfaction with his appearance. He would have horrible nightmares and chronic sleep problems. The abuse caused Michael to remain childlike throughout his adult life due to maltreatment he endured as a young child.

1964 was the year the Jackson Five was formed. Michael was only eight years old at the time. Michael was known to share lead vocals with Jermaine, and he would dance, and play the congas, and tambourine. The Jackson Five toured the Mid-West extensively from 1966 to 1968 as they performed at a string of black clubs known as the 'chitlin circuit'. These clubs often had striptease acts, and other adult acts while the band played.

In 1966 the group would win a major local talent show singing Motown hit songs, and a song from James Brown called I Got You (I Feel Good) as the group's vocals were led by Michael. A record label called Steeltown signed them in 1967, and they would release the song Big Boy. In 1968 Motown Records then signed the Jackson Five to their label. After signing with Motown Records their first album would produce four major hit singles called I Want You Back, ABC, The Love You Save, and I'll Be There. I'll Be There became a number one hit single on the Billboard 100 singles chart.

Soon Rolling Stone magazine began to describe the young Michael Jackson as a prodigy with overwhelming musical gifts. They stated that Michael, and not his brothers was the main draw and lead singer. This made his brothers angry and jealous of young Michael, but the Jackson Five who in the 70's changed the name to the Jacksons stayed a group until 1984. The brothers would even have three more major hit singles called Shake Your Body (Down to the Ground), This Place Hotel, and Can You Feel It.

In the 70's Michael was close to his brothers, but after the media hype, and the Rolling Stone article done on young Michael the brothers began to fight among themselves. Joe at first took the side of Michael because Michael had the most talent, but then Michael started to have enough of Joe telling him what to do all the time. This resulted in Joe then taking the side of Michael's brothers against Michael Jackson.

Michael's fame resulted in solo albums in the 70's. Michael would make 4 solo albums from 1972 to 1975. During this time it was a bad time for Michael due to the fighting in his family. These albums were not the pop-music sound Michael became known for but they did sell well. At this time Michael became good friends with Diana Ross. Diana hearing the problems Michael had at home offered him a place at her home. Michael gladly took it and he started to have a better time in his life. Michael began to party a lot at the night-clubs all across the United States, and especially in New York City, Detroit, and Los Angeles. At that point new forms of music were being played along with new dance moves. Hip-hop, electric-pop, and new wave sounds flooded the clubs along with breakdancing, and new dance styles.

Michael began to learn all the new dance moves, and started to learn about the new beats, and new styles of music. Because he could not sleep, he spent a lot of his time at the nightclubs, and was in the thick and middle of this scene. In the late 70's Michael and his brothers left Motown Records, and signed on at Epic Records, whose parent company was Sony.

Michael began to have a new vision for his next solo album, and he now had the new wave sound that would go with it, but Michael wanted a producer, and a team he could trust that was outside of his father and brothers. In 1978 Michael was working with Diana Ross on the musical film The Wiz which was an urban remake of the Wizard of Oz. Michael would play the scarecrow. While doing the film Michael had a meeting with Quincy Jones. During the meeting Michael told Quincy about his new vision, and sound for his next album, and he asked Quincy if he, and his people would produce it. Quincy agreed and they soon went to work on the album.

In 1979 the album was released, and it was called Off The Wall. This album was the first mainstream nationwide album that established the music that became today the standard of pop-music. The album was a huge success, and it sold 20 million copies. It produced some smash hit singles like Rock With You and Don't Stop Till You Get Enough. In 1980 Don't Stop Till You Get Enough won a Grammy Award and in that year Michael would win 3 American Music Awards. By 1981 he was the highest paid entertainer in the music industry. He broke away from all control that his father had, and bought his own home. He began to soar into new heights in his career. Michael Jackson's next album would be a music industry, and world-wide history making album.

In 1982 Michael would release the album called Thriller. Thriller would sell 65 million copies in the United States, and in total it sold 100 million copies world-wide. No artist in the music industry's history has ever done this from one album. Thriller would enter world record books as the largest selling single album of all-time. The album had 7 smash hit singles that entered the Billboard singles at the top 10. The four most noted singles were Beat It, Billie Jean, Thriller, and Wanna Be Startin' Something. The music video for Thriller made music video history for being the most expensive, and most watched music video of that time. The format for the music video was new at that time, and it combined a horror film story with jaw-dropping dance moves and special effects. Billie Jean was the first music video to debut on MTV from an African-American artist. The song Beat It featured the skills of guitarist Eddie Van Halen, and mixed with brilliant electric beats, and the video featured amazing dance moves from Michael and a fleet of real street dancers.

In 1983 Michael Jackson won a record of 8 Grammy Awards a record that stood until the year 2000 when it was broken by Carlos Santana. Michael would also win 8 American Music Awards in that same year. In March of 1983 Michael Jackson and his brothers appeared on the Motown 25th Anniversary television special. With 47 million net-viewers watching which comes to about 60 million viewers, Michael Jackson appeared in a distinctive black sequin jacket, and a white glove on one hand that was covered with silver rhinestones. Michael would perform the song Billie Jean, and he introduced his signature dance move that he learned from a break dancer called Boogaloo Shrimp called the moonwalk. Michael's moonwalk was far better than Boogaloo's because it had better timing, and it made Michael look like he was floating backwards. At this point Michael wanted to start giving back to society, and he got involved with charity works. He would soon write the song called We Are The World. Michael envisioned to make the song working with all the greatest artists of that time.

While the song was being put together it is believed that this is when people in up-scale powerful positions in government, and banking started to have caution regarding him. The story is that Michael wanted to give all the money made from this big-project single to starving families in the U.S. and Africa, but other unsavory powerful greedy people did not want to see that happen.

Around the time he was working on the project the media started to release nutty stories about him to hit him with controversy. It was said that these hidden power players put the media up to doing that. No one knows if this is really true or not, but also no one knows where these stories about Michael Jackson were coming from. Some of them were so nutty that it was clear they were made up.

On January 27, 1984 The Pepsi Company hired Michael Jackson to film a commercial for them which he did on that day. It would be one of the worst days of Michael's life. The commercial featured a concert setting where Michael would be walking down the staircase to take the stage while pyro-effects would be firing in the back of him, and above him. When Michael was on the top of the staircase, as the filming began, a pyro-effect went off too close to the top of his head. The flash lit the chemicals Michael had in his hair on fire. Michael, thinking quickly dropped to the ground and covered his face so that the fire would not burn his face up. When Michael dropped he began to roll down the metal steps, and people ran toward him trying to put the fire out. Michael's head was completely covered with 2nd degree burns and had to have plastic surgery to cover-up the brutal burn scars. This left Michael to have to halt working on the We Are The World project. Many said that this was done to Michael Jackson on purpose to frighten him off the project to get him to do it their way. but there is no proof to this, and if this is true it did not work. After the recovery Michael went back to work, and got the song recorded.

In 1985 the song We Are The World was released, and it became the largest selling single in history as it sold 30 million copies. Michael would then fight tooth and nail with the record company to make sure every dime went to the families it was promised to. The more Michael was fighting with them at the time oddly the more nasty stories the media released on him. Michael's charity works brought Michael Jackson as a dinner guest at the White House when Ronald Reagan was President. Sometime after this Michael began making plans to build Never Land Ranch. He envisioned a place where poor kids can come and share the privileges that only rich kids could enjoy. The ranch would become a fantasy land of amusement parks, zoo animals, luxury dinners, in-door entertainment, and more.

Around this time he started to have problems with the managers, and people who handled his career. They would do things like turn away invited guests, and cutting off his phone lines or refusing to let him know about phone calls from certain people. It was even said they played mind-games with him to make him feel afraid of going outside. No one really knows why this was going on, but some said that it had to do with Michael's plans for Never Land Ranch. The story is that certain powerful people did not feel it was right that poor kids share the privileges of rich kids, and so they made efforts to keep certain contacts of people away from Michael so that he did not invite these poor children. No one knows if this is true but oddly the media attacks became even stronger when Never Land Ranch was being built. During this time Michael had checked himself in to have another nose job and the media was all over the story.

Back in 1979 Michael had broken his nose. He had only one nose job to fix it, but a strange story was told at the time when Michael was having problems with his management team in the

80's. The story was Michael had a heated argument with a bodyguard of his for turning away some guests he wanted to talk to. During the argument the bodyguard punched Michael in his nose and his nose broke again. No one knows how true this is but it is said that this resulted in Michael going to the hospitable again for another nose job. In fact, after this he would have several due to damage in his nose.

Around this time Michael started to have strange white patches appearing upon his skin. They would appear on his face, chest, and arms. Michael at first used make-up to cover it up until it became more of a problem. Michael then decided to try a treatment that would help his skin to blend into the condition he was having, but instead this made the problem worse, and Michael had to keep coming back for skin treatments that kept making his skin whiter and whiter, and the condition even effected his nose to the point he had to get a fake one. No one was ever sure what the disease was. Some said that the same powerful people who plotted against him where the same people that found a way to do this to him but there is no proof to those statements.

When the media found out he had his skin whiten they ran wild with the story. They would say that Michael hated the fact he was black, and he was trying to look white. This story was not true and even stupid as well. They stated Michael was a strange man who slept in an oxygen chamber and had a strange friendship with his pet monkey Bubbles, but these also were untrue and stupid stories.

On August 31, 1987 Michael Jackson released his next album called Bad. While recording and filming music videos for Bad, Michael also made a film to promote the album called Moonwalker. The company called Industrial Light and Magic made the special effects for the film. Bad became one of the highest selling albums of all time as it sold millions world-wide. In the United States it sold 30 million copies.

Bad would produce five number one hit singles on the Billboard 100 chart. Those songs were I Just Can't Stop Loving You, Bad, The Way You Make Me Feel, Man in the Mirror, and Dirty Diana. The song Smooth Criminal would feature it's music video in the film Moonwalker, and the song would also enter the top 10 Billboard charts. The tour for Bad would be a record breaking event. It saw 123 shows with audience numbers from 200,000 to 500,000 at these shows. To understand, in only 7 shows Michael performed in front of over 4 million people. There has been nothing like this in the history of the music industry.

In 1988 Michael's Never Land Ranch project was finished. True to his word Michael began to open his doors to poor children, and children dying of cancer, and AIDS. At that time the media still continued their attacks on him but Michael's stellar fame overshadowed them. In 1989 at the Soul Train television show the people at Soul Train wanted to give an award to Michael Jackson called the Heritage Award. They would pick legendary actress Elizabeth Taylor, who was a long-time friend of Michael Jackson, to present the award to him. On that night when Elizabeth was doing her speech to present the award she declared that Michael Jackson was the 'King of Pop, Rock, and Soul'. On that night and forever the title of King of Pop was given to Michael Jackson.

Michael Jackson also gave a remembered performance in honor of Sammy Davis Jr. upon the Sammy Davis Jr. 60th Birthday television special. Michael sang a tribute song to him called You Were There in honor of the battle of racism that Sammy fought as a performer in the music industry.

Sometime after this Epic's parent company named Sony was bought up, and taken over by Sony where the company was now called Sony Records. Sony renewed Michael Jackson's contract for a record 65 million dollars plus royalties. In that time Michael would step-up his efforts in helping poor families around the world when he started his own charity called the Heal The World Foundation. When Michael did this it was said that those elite families who had a problem with him, and caused trouble for him would now want at any cost to destroy Michael Jackson's career. There was no proof to this but something very ugly would come Michael's way, and it almost did destroy his career.

On November 26, 1991 Michael Jackson would release the album called Dangerous. The album would produce several top ten Billboard hit singles, and the number one hit single called

Black or White. Michael in the video for Black or White would attack the racism, and prejudice he felt was being done against him. The media, instead of reporting on Michael's defense against ugly statements made against him, decided to report on Michael's crotch grabbing in the video. Michael one time when he did an interview with Oprah Winfrey told her the reason why he grabs his crotch during performances.

He stated that he did not mean to do it but that something inside him takes him over when the beats of the music are playing. When Michael said this oddly a fire-alarm in his house went off. The media's attack on him however did not work, and Michael Jackson's Dangerous album would go on to also become one of the highest selling albums in history. It would sell 32 million copies in the U.S. alone. In 1992 the Heal The World Foundation was bringing in millions of dollars that were helping many families to be pulled out of poverty, and Never Land Ranch was making the dreams of many poor children to come true. Michael was back on top of the music industry, and his music videos were the most watched of that time, but his fame would come to a crashing halt.

Michael Jackson was accused of child-molestation when a child who stayed at Never Land Ranch accused Michael of molesting him. Many people from the start of the accusations believed that Michael Jackson was being set-up. Soon after the child working with a fleet of lawyers, and his parents had sent the police to raid Never Land Ranch. In the process of the raid Michael's animals were harmed, and everything in his home was overturned. Michael was forced in his own living room to a 25 minute strip-search where the police it was said of them needlessly touched Michael in areas they didn't need to. At the end of it Michael Jackson stated that he was molested by the police. The police were looking for evidence in the descriptions that the child gave of Michael's private parts, but it turned out that the descriptions the child gave did not match what the police saw. So after the raid Michael was not placed under arrest due to no evidence.

The parents of this child however, under the advice of the lawyers wanted to still go ahead with a civil-suit. Michael, not wanting to drag this out any further because his career and his foundation was on the line, managed to pay the parents in an out of court settlement so they would leave him alone. The media stated that this made Michael look guilty to settle out of court but in truth it made the parents look suspect.

Most parents who believed that their child had been raped would not in any terms settle out of court. They would want this person locked up for it. In fact, many people who came to know this child later in life stated that he showed no signs of ever being molested.

This event caused many Michael Jackson fans to turn away from him but millions still stayed loyal, and Michael still left his doors open for children to come to Never Land Ranch and helping poor families through the foundation.

Many of the fans turned away because they also stated that no grown man should be sleeping in the same bed with children. But they fail to understand that Michael, due to his own abuse, still had a child-like mind. In his mind it was not sleeping with children but he felt like an equal with these children and wanted to join in with the sleep-over, and have fun with the children.

Some people refused to believe that while at the same time other people knew where Michael was coming from, and that he would never molest a child. Overall Michael was never seen the same way again as he was before the scandal. Around this time Michael became very close to his friend Lisa Marie Presley, the daughter of the King of Rock n' Roll, Elvis Presley. They would soon start to date each other, and then in May of 1994 they were married.

The media soon surrounded this union in controversy. They stated that the marriage was a smoke screen to hide the scandal, and to hide that Michael Jackson was gay. The media provided no evidence to these stories, and these stories also were stupid as well. Michael Jackson, it is well known, stopped being a virgin when he was a pre-teen. Michael also was not gay.

It was well known that Michael dated many famous women throughout his career. Michael has always been a gentlemen about it, and he didn't feel the need to brag about it. Michael also was in a sexual relationship with Lisa Marie before, and after they were married.

Due to the media attacks Michael and Lisa divorced after two years of marriage and remained friends. On June 16, 1995 Michael Jackson released a double-album called HIStory Past, Present, and Future. Regardless of the media attacks HIStory would go on to become one of the largest selling albums in history. It would sell millions world-wide, and it sold 20 million copies in the U.S. alone. Since it was a double album the gross sale would equal an album that has sold 40 million copies in the U.S. The album featured a very expensive promotion commercial that was originally supposed to be seen in the movie theaters but due to media attacks it was shown on T.V. commercials. The double album featured one album that was his greatest hits, and another album that had brand new songs on it. The album had two smash hit singles called Scream which was a duet he did with his sister who is also a famous artist named Janet Jackson. The other hit single was a song called You Are Not Alone which went number one on the Billboard charts.

Michael came under fire for appearing naked in the music video with a naked Lisa Marie, but the reason why Michael did the video that way was in response to the media who stated that Michael and Lisa were not in a sexual relationship. The success of the double album called HIStory would be the last time Michael Jackson was on top in the music industry.

In 1997 Michael Jackson would release an album called Blood on the Dance Floor. The album was a remix album of many Michael Jackson songs. The album had a dark theme to it of drug addiction, evil women, and paranoia. The album would receive minimal promotion due to media attacks, and it's only known single was Blood on the Dance Floor. The album would sell 6 million copies world-wide. Many believed the album would have been more successful if not for the people taking an interest in tabloid stories and Michael Jackson's personal life over his musical career. The album was however the largest selling remix album of all time.

On October 31, 2001 Michael Jackson would release a new

album called Invincible. Invincible would feature brand new songs by Michael Jackson. The album would have three noted singles called You Rock My World, Cry, and Butterflies. These three singles would enter the U.S. Billboard charts in the top 20, and the song You Rock My World was number one in other countries of the world but not in the United States. The album itself would hit number one in eleven countries world-wide but not in the United States. The album was more successful in the United Kingdom, Australia, France, and Switzerland. The album would sell 13 million copies, and most of those sales happened in those four countries. At this time Michael Jackson was in a heated battle over a number of issues with executives of Sony Records. There have been many stories surrounding it. The heated battles would result in Sony refusing to promote the album any further. Some of the stories goes like this.

It was said that Michael got tired of the way Sony was handling his money and his career. Michael believed he was being ripped off by Sony and even stranger story was that Michael was being abused somehow by people Sony was connected to.

Some believed that Michael Jackson was a mind-control victim, and he was revolting on his handlers, but there is no proof to those statements. There was a strange statement Michael Jackson made when asked about this subject. He stated that the only thing he would say is that it's dangerous to talk about it, and Quincy Jones knew more about it, and that he, meaning Michael, won't say anything else about it. When the interviewer tried to push the question Michael said, 'I am done talking about it'. Michael seemed afraid to talk about this subject, and only hinted that Quincy Jones knew more about it.

In 2002 Michael Jackson would win an American Music Award for Artist of the Century. He also was wanting to have children. Michael tried to have a normal marriage but the media constantly attacked it. So Michael would seek out a friend of his who one time worked as his housekeeper.

Michael would ask her if she would become pregnant with his seed through artificial means. She agreed. This woman would become the mother of two of Michael Jackson's kids who were a boy and a girl. Michael was so proud of the birth of his son that while staying in a hotel in Berlin Michael became to overzealous, and while standing on a balcony he lowered his son down so that the fans could see him. The media soon attacked him for this act that many said was child endangerment. The railing was four floors above ground so this was not a smart move on Michael's part but Michael would tell his fans he was sorry for it.

Soon another nightmare would come into Michael's life. Michael once again would be accused of child-molestation.
When this happened Michael's plans to record another album was stopped at that time. Michael also had to hide the faces of his children in public so the media would not know what they look like at the time so that they could not stalk them.

It was believed that Michael for this second-time being charged was also being set-up again to stop poor children from going to Never Land Ranch, and to drain the funds of his foundation to prevent it from helping kids, but no one knows how true that is. The main evidence for the case was from a hidden camera that showed Michael talking to children about bed arrangements. It was already known that Michael would sleep next to the children but he did not molest them, and the kids wanted him there. The media would attack him with venom even outright telling Michael in an interview that he was guilty, and that he should admit it. Even though it's innocence before proven guilty the media was doing things in reverse. At the end of this most expensive trial the evidence against Michael was shown to be no real evidence at all. There was no real and clear proof of any molestation going on.

The jury also found it strange that the one using the camera was one of the kids, and he did so without Michael even knowing it. It was believed that the parents of the kid was setting up Michael Jackson. In the end, Michael Jackson was found not guilty.

Sadly though in 2006 Never Land Ranch had to be closed due to lack of funds. This made Michael angry, and he would quickly get to work on another album to start making money again. But Sony Records once again started to give him problems. This resulted in Michael Jackson coming forward to tell people what he believed is the truth of what is going on.

Michael would hold a press conference where this time the media would not run wild with it. Many said it was because Michael was telling too much truth, and the media really does not like the kind of truth that makes them look bad. Michael would call the CEO of Sony Records a devil, and he compared him to Satan himself. Michael stated that the record company, the media, and certain elite families conspired against him. Michael stated the reasons was the same old reasons that he was a successful black man, and a positive role-model, and they wanted to see positive images of black men destroyed by using slander. Michael would set the record straight that he was proud of being a black man, and that he never sought to look like a white man, and that the media lied about that, and lied about a lot of things regarding him. Michael would state that he only had one album, and one box-set to do for Sony, and after that he was leaving them for good. Michael stated that what they did to him was in the manner they have hurt other African-American artists throughout history like Sammy Davis, Jr., James Brown, and Marvin Gaye.

After this Michael Jackson would soon start to record the album called This Is It along with a documentary to go with it. Michael was also suffering from a lot of pain in his knees and hips, and his sickness was taking a toll on his muscle tissue. Michael had to start taking injections of propofol and benzodiazepine, and other steroids. To promote the album Michael only agreed to do 10 shows which was all he felt he could do at the time. But Sony stated that they would pull the funding for the album unless he did 50 shows. 50 shows was risking Michael's life but he chose to bear it, and was determined to do it so that the album could be sold, and the quicker he could leave Sony. Soon Michael would film a new music video for the song They Don't Really Care About Us. The song was about the injustices of the American system, and how Michael felt like he was in prison working for the music industry.

In June of 2009 Michael Jackson would receive a visit from his personal doctor named Dr. Conrad Murray. Murray would inject Michael with high-doses of propofol and benzodiazepine which is taken for extreme pain, but it turns out that Murray injected such high doses into Michael Jackson that it was enough to kill a man four times over.

Michael Jackson would die on his bed in his rented mansion in Holmby Hills of Los Angeles on June 25, 2009. Michael Jackson's death was ruled as a homicide by the Los Angeles County Coroner. Conrad Murray was convicted of involuntary manslaughter, and oddly was not charged with murder. LaToya Jackson, the sister of Michael Jackson, began to speak out concerning Michael's death. She stated that Murray was only a fall guy, and that Michael constantly feared for his life. She stated that the people Michael spoke against were the people who had him killed.

One day after Michael's death Michael's father Joe Jackson showed up to Michael home in Never Land Ranch with a huge moving truck. He began to move all of Michael's most expensive belongings, and items that he collected over the years. When he was interviewed he showed no remorse for his son's death, and he appeared as if he could care less. Instead of talking about Michael he wanted to take the time to promote another artist he was working with. He also spoke to other people there who were helping to take all of Michael's belongings that he was going to get a lot of money from these items.

Sometime ago a woman by the name of Brice Taylor wrote a book stating she was a mind-control victim who was a white slave used by powerful people working in the Federal government, and in the entertainment industry. She stated that she was a sex-slave to many powerful people in the government, and many famous people in Hollywood. Brice claimed that she managed to escape the hold they had on her after a car accident caused her to start remembering suppressed memories. She would write a book based on these memories called Thanks For The Memories. She stated that she was handled by two powerful people named Bob Hope and Henry Kissinger. She stated that she recalled many famous people who worked in the entertainment industry were being also mind-controlled, and sexually abused.

She recalled a memory she had involving Michael Jackson and the Jackson 5. She stated that she was there the day Joe Jackson introduced the group to Bob Hope. She said that Hope then promised Joe that he would get them on the Ed Sullivan show if he did a few favors for him. She stated that Joe allowed his kids to be victims of certain mind-control programming sessions. She stated that afterward when the Jackson 5 went to the Ed Sullivan show that before they went on they were brought inside a room with heavy lights above them. She said each of the boys were forced to drop their pants, and then turn around and line up. She said then a large man who was there then painfully raped each of the boys in a line-up while Joe watched.

Brice does not have any evidence that could bring charges on anyone, and her book is for the people to decide if they believe her or not. One of Michael's brothers named Jermaine Jackson also spoke about abuse he believed that his father Joe was doing to Michael Jackson. He stated that while Joe was trying to get a record deal for the Jackson 5 he would take young Michael to late-night meetings. He stated that every time Michael came back from them he would be sick with fevers for days, and would vomit a lot when he came back home.

Jermaine stated that he began to wonder if Joe was passing around Michael to be sexually abused. In the early 1990's LaToya Jackson would reveal to the world that Joe Jackson had been sexually abusing her for years and it started as a pre-teen. She stated that Joe had a strange way of making her forget every time he raped her, and that she only started to remember the abuse when she got older. She recalled how she could not date other boys because her father would get jealous of them, and he often tried to control every part of her life. She stated that she married a man he did not approve of, and posed for Playboy as a way of breaking free of him. After LaToya stated her testimony the media began to attack her and called her crazy, but LaToya has shown no signs of being crazy she has only stated what she believes happened to her and usually such a case is taken more seriously. But according to the media, who also have no evidence to their claims, LaToya is crazy and Michael is guilty. One wonders if the media really is controlled by people of a very evil nature.

There were also statements that Michael struggled with demonic possession. This strange story came from the fact that Michael had in his home a large room that was filled with mirrors all around him. Michael stated himself that a ghost named Lee would come forth from the mirrors and speak to him. When Michael would wake-up from these dark encounters he would have songs come to him in his head. Michael even stated that this spirit named Lee helped him to bring forth some of his biggest hit singles.

The Bible calls ghosts familiar spirits. They are demonic spirits who pose as someone else, and stay attached to the person they appear to often haunting their homes. Michael's presence on stage was often even defined as supernatural at times. People stated that the feeling that came from him would be electric, and it would energize people to such a point they would faint. Some said that Michael was just that talented that it caused overwhelming emotions into people while some said there was more to it than that.

Michael as an artist did leave us with some very social awareness songs, and songs that invoked great compassion for the needs of others. Songs like Man in the Mirror, Heal the Earth, Will You Be There, Earth Song, Gone Too Soon, and others really inspired people to do good for other people.

Michael Jackson, within his music industry legacy, is recognized as the most successful entertainer of all time by the Guinness Book of World Records. His music videos and songs like Beat It, Billie Jean, Thriller, and others broke down racial barriers, and transformed the medium of pop-music, and music videos into a world-wide market. His album called Thriller is still the best-selling single album of all-time, and its numbers are a feat not likely to be broken anytime soon, and maybe even never. His other albums like Off The Wall, Bad, Dangerous, and HIStory are ranked among the world's best-selling albums.

Michael Jackson has won a total of 13 Grammy Awards and 26 American Music Awards. He has won a Lifetime Achievement Award at the Grammys, and won Artist of the Century at the American Music Awards. He has also won hundreds of other rewards making him the most awarded artist of all-time. He has had 13 number one hit singles on the Billboard charts. He has personally supported 39 charities, and is called the greatest humanitarian of the music industry. After his death he would make history again. His music documentary called This Is It became the highest grossing documentary of all time with earnings of more than 260 million dollars world-wide.

The artist called Madonna was born on August 16, 1958 in Bay City, Michigan. Her mother's name was Madonna Louise who was of French heritage, and her father's name was Silvio Anthony Ciccone, and his family is from Pacentro, Italy. Madonna's real name is Louise Ciccone, and she did not start calling herself Madonna until she entered the music industry. In honor of her mother she took the stage name of Madonna.

Madonna comes from a large family of siblings. The names of her siblings are Martin, Anthony, Paula, Christopher, and Melanie. Her family was a traditional Catholic family where her father worked for a couple of car companies, one of them being General Motors where he was a design engineer.

Madonna as a little girl was very close to her mother and had an estranged relationship with her father. In 1963 Madonna's mother would die of an undisclosed sickness. Her death left painful emotional scars on Madonna. After her death Madonna would sleep in the same bed as her father. No one really knows why. Some think there may have been sexual abuse going on but there is no proof or confirmation by Madonna regarding it. Her father would remarry, and the person he married was his kids' babysitter. This action it is believed caused anger in Madonna to be distanced from her father. Madonna would not acknowledge the new wife as any kind of mother to her.

Madonna as a child to a pre-teen attended St. Fredericks and St. Andrew's Catholic Elementary Schools, and then she attended West Middle School. She was known for having a high grade point average, and I.Q. She was also known for some unconventional behavior where certain teachers believed she had a behavioral disorder. She would express athletic gifts rather oddly. She would perform cartwheels, and handstands in the hallways between classes. She would dangle by her knees from the monkey bars during recess. She would also do a disturbing action as well that almost got her expelled from school a few times.

She used to pull up her skirt during class so that all the boys could see her underwear. After middle school Madonna went to high-school at Rochester Adams High School. She was a straight A-student, and also very athletic, and she wanted to express that by joining the cheerleading squad. She began dancing in high-school, and she was very gifted at it. In fact she was so gifted at it she won a scholarship to the University of Michigan to major in dance.

Madonna on the outside was on the right track, but there was an underline fear or some say darkness to her on the inside. Some say that Madonna got into some coven practices during college where people are known to experiment with certain things. Some say that there was some satanic things going on already in her house. No one knows what the story really is, but something happened to Madonna while she was in college in the year 1978. Whatever it was it drove Madonna to drop out of college, and she ran away to New York City with only 35 dollars in her pocket, and no connections.

The only goal that Madonna seemed to have was to find a job as a dancer. If she finished school this would have been put into her lap in a much easier way but instead she decided for some strange reason to engage in a manner that was uncertain and dangerous. Most single young girls often do not make it in New York City. Many of these runaways are often found raped, and murdered. Before they are, they usually live a drug-addicted life, and many resort to selling their bodies to survive. No one really knows why Madonna would put herself out there for a life like this.

While trying to find a job as a dancer she would run out of the money she had. For a time she lived on the streets and would eat out of trash cans. She would attend nightclubs, and often try to make friends with other dancers. They would often ignore her until she started to show her moves on the floor, and then they started to slowly open up to her, but she was still homeless for a time with no money, and only had the clothes she carried.

A strange event would happen to Madonna during this time. No one knows how true this story is, but Madonna during this time would meet a pimp. This pimp helped Madonna to make some money by selling Madonna's body to a few men. He even helped her find a place to stay. One of the men he sold

Madonna to knew someone who worked at a dance club that could hire her to dance there. During this time the pimp became angry with a trick when he enjoyed himself on one of the girls without paying. A couple of thugs who worked with the pimp began to beat this man bloody. The cops were called in, and Madonna watched the attack from across the street. One of the cops noticed her and questioned her. At first Madonna refused to talk but the cop threaten to bust her for prostitution unless she rolled on the pimp. Madonna out of fear did so. The pimp threaten to kill Madonna or Louise as she was known at the time, but the man that promised to help get Madonna a job decided to take her in and protect her.

He eventually kept his word, and introduce Madonna to this club owner who needed girls to dance for a disco artist named Patrick Hernandez who was French. Madonna would show the owner what she could do, and she got the job on the spot. It is believed that from this point Madonna needed to get her own place fast but she needed extra money. The owner of the club knew some people who took photos of naked women, and sold them to certain magazines like Penthouse and Playboy. The photographers often paid top dollar to pretty girls who would be willing to show off their bodies.

Madonna then went to their studio, and took nude photographs. She used the money to get her own place and she managed to get a hold of her brother Christopher asking him if he would move in with her. Madonna needed someone to make her feel safe. Her brother was disowned by her father for being gay, and so he had nowhere to go, and was glad to move in. He too also worked as a dancer.

During this time in 1979 Madonna was working as a back-up dancer not just for Hernandez but also for several established artists and she became more and more drawn in to the inner workings of the night-club scene. Many of the girls it was said were into occult and homosexual practices, and Madonna it was said became friends with these girls. It was believed that the girls were into voodoo magic practices.

While working as a back-up dancer one night Madonna was returning home from a rehearsal where she was going to compete for a spot to join Patrick Hernandez's world tour, to become one of his main dancers where this spot would push Madonna further into the doors of the industry. When she was only blocks away from home two men grab her at knifepoint, and forced her into an alleyway. The story is regarding this which also is not proven had to do with the pimp she rolled on. The men were sent there by the pimp to cut her face up and kill her, but Madonna talked her way out of it by offering to give the two men a blow job. She then did so, and they took her money, and then let her go.

Soon Madonna got the spot on Patrick Hernandez's world tour, and she became one of his official girls. The French disco artist would tour to other parts of the world mainly in Europe, and his girls were often seen as sexual witches who could seduce, and inflame lust into people from the way they danced.

Madonna at this time was living with these girls as they lived together. It was said of them that their image was more than an image but they were really into occult voodoo rituals. No one knows how true this is, and what the extent of it really was.

During that time Madonna was offered a part to act in an independent movie called A Certain Sacrifice. There was a very strange story surrounding the making of the movie. The story is that during a scene they were filming Madonna was supposed to pretend that she was getting raped, but what happened was the actor ended up really raping her. As pay back the actor had to pretend that Madonna stabs him in his heart and the story is Madonna really did stab him. His death it was said was caught on tape, and was removed from the film.

It is very hard to believe that Madonna murdered someone. People believe that the story is an urban legend but some have said they have seen the action on snuff films they watched, but no one can clearly say this is true.

After touring with the disco artist Patrick Hernandez, Madonna would meet a man named Dan Gilroy. Gilroy was looking to put together a female rock-pop band. Madonna would show that she also had musical skills. Madonna learned these skills while working in the night-clubs, and she showed a natural talent for singing and playing instruments.

Madonna then became romantically involved with Gilroy who was also a musician. Together they formed the band called the Breakfast Club. Madonna was the lead singer for the band, and she also played drums and guitar, but soon Madonna started to see her old boyfriend from the club scene named Stephen Bray. Bray had an idea for a new rock-pop group called Emmy, and so in late 1980 Madonna left Breakfast Club and joined the band called Emmy.

One day a record producer and DJ named Mark Kammis saw Emmy play. He was very impressed with the music, and he was most impressed with Madonna's vocal and talent. Kammis would tell Sire Records founder named Seymour Stein about Madonna. From there a meeting was arranged between Madonna and Seymour Stein. Stein wanted to turn Madonna into a new wave pop-artist to bring the new club sounds to the mass market for he foresaw that is where the direction of music was heading, and he was right. Seymour signed Madonna to his label, and Madonna recorded two singles

called Everybody which came out in late 1982, and then Burning Up which came out in early 1983. Both singles became huge club hits, and they would film a music video for the song Everybody.

When MTV aired the video Madonna was seen as a hot new pop artist. Madonna began to work on her first album which would be called Madonna. The man who put Madonna's pop sound together was John 'Jellybean' Benitez who also started dating Madonna at that time.

The form of Madonna's sound was an upbeat synthetic new wave sound utilizing the new technology of the music industry like the Linn drum machine, Moog bass, and the OB-X synthesizer. Her first full album came out in 1983, and it was a commercial success. The album produced three hit singles called Lucky Star, Borderline, and the global smash hit Holiday.

At this point Madonna's look, and manner of dressing, her performances, and her music videos influenced young girls, and older women to dress in her style of fashion which became the trend of the 1980's. Her look was created by a designer named Maripol. This look consisted of lace tops, skirts over capri pants, fishnet stockings, jewelry bearing the crucifix, bracelets, and bleached blonde hair.

In November of 1984 Madonna's next album would make her a huge success in the music industry. It would also bring her huge controversy as well. This album was called Like a Virgin. Like a Virgin was an album that topped the charts in several countries, and it was her first album to hit number one on the Billboard 200 albums chart.

The album would cause a huge backlash as it attracted the attention of Church groups, and moral organizations. These groups complained that the song Like a Virgin, and the video promoted premarital sex, and undermined family values. Several of these moralist organizations went so far as to protest for the banning of the song and the video. Madonna in her defense stated that she had pure intentions in the writing, and the singing of the song, but later in her career she contradicted those statements. She would reveal that the song was about a woman being open to her sexual nature.

Madonna has often done this where when you read into her interviews she often says one thing first and then another second. She often seems to catch people off guard with her songs, and videos, and then later she reveals the real reason for it. The reasons in regards to morality and Christianity is to set a trend against those teachings.

The Catholic Church also spoke against Madonna for using the name Madonna which in the Catholic doctrine is the name used for the Virgin Mary, the mother of Jesus Christ, and for also the song Like a Virgin where they believed this was a form of heresy. Madonna actually did not use the name Madonna to mock Mary but it was her mother's name As for mocking religion, Madonna is very guilty of that as you will come to find out or if you already know that. A strange thing I came to learn was the real meaning of the song Like a Virgin. That the song was about the first time a woman has a homosexual relationship. The meaning of the song was that it's about a woman who had all kinds of men, and now she wants something new, and something she never did before which was sex with another woman. Could this really be true? Many on the inside who were around when the song was written said it is, while others say it's about sleeping around. Either way the song was promoting sexual immorality.

Later in Madonna's career, when she started to promote the gay-agenda they asked her the reason for it. She stated that she uses her music and videos to show gay relationships because in her words, 'If people keep seeing it and seeing it then eventually it won't be a big deal.' In science that is called a form of brainwashing people, and that is not an honest way to state the issues regarding it.

At the very first VMA show Madonna came under fire for performing the song Like a Virgin to a mass television audience. Madonna would appear on stage atop a giant wedding cake, wearing a wedding dress and white gloves. The song however it was clear had nothing to do with marriage, and many said it was a way for Madonna to mock the Church groups and moral groups who spoke against her.

The next hit song from the album was a song called Material Girl. This song also came under attack as many said it was a song about a, well in their words, 'a gold-digging whore'. The music video for Material Girl was a mimicry of Marilyn Monroe's performance of a song called Diamonds Are a Girl's Best friend from the 1953 film called Gentlemen Prefer Blondes.

While filming the video for Material Girl Madonna met actor Sean Penn, and she would marry Penn on her birthday in 1985. This marriage was short-lived. The album Like a Virgin would go on to sell 21 million copies, and it was a world-wide success.

In 1984 Madonna would enter into the movie industry. She had a brief appearance as a club singer in a film called Vision Quest. She would record a song for this film called Crazy For You. Crazy For You would hit number one on the Billboard 100 singles chart.

Her major role was in a film called Desperately Seeking Susan that came out in March of 1985. Although she was not the lead actress in the film her role, and profile made the film heavily marketed. Madonna would record a song for this film called Into the Groove which became a huge smash hit single. In 1985 Madonna embarked on what was called The Virgin Tour where the Beastie Boys were her opening act. At that time the songs from the Like a Virgin album called Angel and Dress You Up became huge smash hits. Another backlash would fall on Madonna when Penthouse and Playboy magazines published a number of nude photos Madonna took in New York City in the very late 70's. As you know Madonna took the photos because she needed money at the time. The photos caused a media uproar but Madonna refused to kiss up to anyone about it because those times were a dark period in her life where people do almost anything to survive. Madonna was very unapologetic for it, and during the Live Aid concert she came on the defense, and stated that she would not take off her jacket because the media might hold it against her ten years from now.

The scandal however did not cause fans to turn away from her it only added more to her. In June of 1986 Madonna released her next album called True Blue. This album would produce three number one hit singles called Live to Tell, Papa Don't Preach, and Open Your Heart. It also produce two hit singles that entered the Billboard top 10 called La Isla Bonita and True Blue. Papa Don't Preach was also a song that came under fire for promoting premarital sex and teenage pregnancy. The moral and Church groups also sought to have the song, and the video banned. The album called True Blue would sell 25 million copies, and became her highest selling album in that time.

In 1986 Madonna would appear in two more films called Shanghai Surprise and Who's That Girl. In 1987 Madonna would divorce Sean Penn where the cause of this divorce was centered on cheating on both parts, and abuse done to Madonna by Sean Penn.

There are even stranger stories surrounding it. One part of the story is the abuse that Sean did to Madonna. It was said that their arguments used to be so bad that Penn would slap Madonna around, and Madonna would laugh at him while he did it. One night it got so bad that Penn grabbed Madonna, and threw her on the floor, and locked her in a room. While locked in the room Penn had beat and screamed at her for 9 hours while punching, and kicking her. During the attack Penn would tell her, 'I own you lock, stock, and barrel'. No one knows what he meant by that and Madonna refused to press any charges against him, and then she divorces him as quietly as possible. One story behind this is that both Madonna and Sean Penn were mind-control victims and Penn used to mind-handle Madonna, but no proof was ever shown to those statements.

In 1987 Madonna embarked on the Who's That Girl World Tour. The tour broke several attendance records in several countries like in Paris, France where Madonna performed in front of 130,000 people which was a record in France. After the tour was over Madonna went to work on a new album, and started filming on a movie called Dick Tracy which also starred Warren Betty and Al Pacino. During the filming of the movie she became sexually involved with Warren.

Madonna's next album was believed to have been inspired by a film she saw called The Last Temptation of Christ. Many Church groups and even Christian actors in Hollywood became very angry over this film. They stated that it was a slap in the face to the teachings of Christianity, and showed a huge lack of respect toward Jesus Christ. It happened to be one of Madonna's favorite films where the film showed a love affair between Jesus, and the former prostitute named Mary that Jesus saved, and casted seven demons out of her. In fact it was said that Madonna liked the film so much that she would use this evil and sick theme in her future concerts.

When Madonna finished recording her 4th studio album at the time the Pepsi Company sought Madonna to promote her album so that they could tie in Pepsi soft drinks to her name. Pepsi promised to use their up-coming commercial time where they got a slot for two-minutes to also promote Madonna's new album which featured the song Like a Prayer. Madonna's next album was heavily anticipated, and so Pepsi even gave Madonna a 5 million dollar advancement to her contract.

On March 2, 1989 the Pepsi world-premiere commercial was aired for a record two-minutes in over 40 countries, and shown to millions and millions of people. Madonna's song Like a Prayer was played in bit parts in the commercial where it showed scenes from her new music video. Everyone loved it, and could not wait to see the music video. The next day millions sat in front of the television set, and tuned in to MTV to see the world-premiere video called Like a Prayer. When the entire video was shown the shock reaction from the media regarding the video, and from moral and Church groups was overnight. They stated that Madonna has gone too far, and they could not believe that MTV was allowed to air this video knowing before-hand what was shown in it. The video's theme was an African-American Catholic priest having a sexual affair with a character played by Madonna. They would embrace each other sexually in the middle of the altar in the Church. What made fans angry at her was the scene where Madonna is singing wearing only her bra, and in the background are several burning crosses. The burning cross has several meanings, and none of them are good or Christian. To the KKK it is the symbol of hate toward people of color, and they would burn a cross on the lawns of civil rights leaders to intimidate them. For satanic covens it is the symbol of the light-bearer, the one called Lucifer, who is Satan in the Bible.

The Vatican was outraged over the video because it showed one of their priests engaged in sexual immorality, and they felt this was extremely slanderous to their Church. Many Catholic fans of Madonna turned away from her. CNN would also do a report regarding the song Like a Prayer where they revealed the song had subliminal lyrics. They played the lyrics to their television audience, and the lyrics had four complete words which were, 'Hear our savior Satan'.

The Pepsi Company quickly dropped Madonna from promoting their soft drink, and paid off her contract to get rid of her. Madonna went on the defense several times regarding the video stating it was only an expression of her art-form. Of course by saying that then it leaves one to wonder if she has a sick and lustful view of Jesus Christ and churches.

The next single from the album was called Express Yourself. Despite the uproar over the music video, Madonna clearly still had millions of fans standing by her. The single Like a Prayer would sell 4 million copies, and the album itself also called Like a Prayer would sell 15 million copies.

In April of 1990 Madonna embarked on her Blond Ambition World Tour. The tour would become one of the most notorious for acts of sexual depravity of that time. The tour was met with strong reactions from religious, and moral groups for several actions she did during the performances. In one part of her show, when Madonna would perform the song Like a Virgin, two male dancers would caress her body right before she simulates masturbation.

In another part of the show she simulates sex while sitting on top of a cross. For people to think this is not disrespectful toward Christianity is really not smart at all. The Church of England, The Catholic Church, The Christian Community were all offended and criticized her performances. Pope John even asked Christians everywhere not to attend any of her concerts.

Madonna in a smug way stated that those groups did not have an open mind, and what she was doing does not hurt anyone. Those statements in regards to her defense are ignorant, and not close to true. For so many people to be offended shows they were hurt by it. For her to state that Christians are closed-minded and yet her way is okay shows she herself to be not really of an open mind.

Madonna also does not seem to care that many of her fans are not just adults but she has also fans who are children, pre-teens, and teenagers. As a parent if you came home, and found your 13 year old daughter on top of a cross simulating sex with it how would you feel? If you were a moral parent you would be hurt by it and angry. If you ask your daughter why she did that, and she tells you she saw Madonna do it then how would you feel about Madonna then? You would be angry at her and you would complain. but Madonna shows no concern about this.

In November of 1990 Madonna would release a greatest hits album called The Immaculate Collection. It would become the largest selling compilation album in the history of the music industry as it sold 30 million copies. The album would feature two brand new songs called Rescue Me and the very haunting single called Justify My Love. Justify My Love would hit number one on the Billboard 100 singles chart despite the controversy of the song. When the music video was released for the song it featured scenes of sadomasochism, bondage, same-sex kissing, and brief nudity. The music video would soon be banned from MTV. In response to the banning, Madonna and her record company released a VHS tape soon after of the music video. It became one of the highest selling VHS tapes for a music video in history. The tape was also bought by children, pre-teens, and teenagers, and you can guess where their money came from...their parents.

The ABC program called Nightline would interview Madonna about the video, and they even played the video to a nationwide television audience. An analysis of the song showed some disturbing things. The beats of the song have an intense darkness to it, and is far different from Madonna's common pop sound. Her voice mostly moans through the song she is hardly even singing the lyrics but only speaking in a breath of deep lust. The beats to the song are clearly sensual, and it can arouse carnal emotions especially from young people. The science shows that young people are more influenced by music then adults are. Later on in her career Madonna even did a remix to this song. She called it the Beast Within remix. She would recite full passages from the Book of Revelation into the song. Some may think this is harmless but it is a mockery to the Bible.

The Bible speaks against sexual immorality and Justify My Love promotes sexual immorality. Madonna is not acting in confusion but is showing disrespect towards the Bible's teachings. It is very well known that Madonna is not a Catholic or a Christian she is involved with Eastern mysticism practices and is a member of the Temple of Kabbalah.

In 1992 Madonna signed on to a new record label called Maverick Records who's parent company was Time Warner. They would pay Madonna, and advance of 60 million dollars plus royalties, and it was the second highest contract signing in history where only Michael Jackson had the highest at 65 million.

The contract would also come with a book deal where Madonna was already at work on a coffee table book called Sex. The book had no words just sexual pictures of Madonna and friends, some of them being famous, and her dancers. When the book called Sex came out it was brought under fire by the media. The book consisted of sexually provocative, and explicit images which fueled the negative reaction in the media. In the first week of the release of the book it sold 1.5 million copies at 50 dollars a book. The book would sell out in book stores, and even at places like 7-11 in a matter of hours. People lined the streets so long it went around the corner just to buy this book. Some of the photos were so twisted that it featured Madonna in sexual poses with food and animals.

In that time Madonna also released a documentary called Truth or Dare. The documentary centered on the controversy of the Blond Ambition World Tour. This documentary also came under fire for homosexual kissing, perverted sex games Madonna played with her dancers, and the famous people who were in the film who did not want to be.

Madonna would release her new album in 1992 called Erotica. Most of the songs centered on sexual themes, and the videos featured degenerate sexual content. At that time she would appear in a new film called Body of Evidence which was a highly sexual film that jumped in on the market that a film called Basic Instinct opened. Madonna did scenes in the film of full nudity, and graphic sex scenes, and sex scenes of sadomasochism, sodomy, and bondage. She would appear in another film called Dangerous Game that went straight to video. Madonna performed sex scenes in this film that looked angry, painful, and real where one scene shows her being raped, but according to Madonna what she does hurts no one. It seems that Madonna must have to deny often certain truths about the kind of damaging influences she has done to people in her career. There is nothing romantic or sentimental about sadomasochism, sodomy, bondage, or being raped.

In September of 1993 Madonna embarked on The Girlie Show World Tour where she dressed as a whip-cracking dominatrix. During a performance in the Island of Puerto Rico, Madonna caused many once loyal Puerto Rican fans to turn away from her when she took the Puerto Rican flag, and rubbed it between her legs on stage to simulate she was screwing it. On the David Letterman Show Madonna in an evil manner began saying the F-word over, and over again, and she handed Letterman a pair of her underwear asking him to smell it. Madonna stated that she acted this way toward him because Letterman made her look like a slut when he was introducing her. Of course in truth Madonna was making herself look that way before the David Letterman Show. When Madonna's 6th album called Bedtime Stories was coming out Madonna had to tone down her image. The reason for this was because Madonna was up for the lead role in the film called Evita.

When she got the role the people of Argentina were furious that a person of her character would play their beloved saint, and a hero to the people of Argentina. Many believed that the film Evita saved Madonna's career from being destroyed by the media. Madonna was up for an Academy Award, and the film itself won Academy Awards.

Many people have stated that Madonna is a devil worshipper for several reasons. There is no hard evidence to this but there is some obvious reasons for that statement. One time Madonna was asked to record a song for the Austin Powers movie. The song she made was called Beautiful Stranger. Some people noticed that the song's lyrics had nothing to do with the character in the film or the film itself except in the music video that showed scenes from the film. Some insiders stated that the song was in praise to Lucifer, that the Beautiful Stranger represented Satan himself, but no proof was ever confirmed regarding this song by Madonna.

In a song Madonna did called Intervention Madonna does sing about Satan that she plays Satan's games along a lonely road, and that she will never be the same again. People were also left wondering what she was really singing about. In the music video for a song called What it Feels Like For a Girl, Madonna in the video is staying in a hotel room that is numbered 669 but when she leaves the room the last 9 swings down to form the number 666. Not very long ago Madonna did a video where she is at a Hollywood party, and everybody begins to demonically manifest demons through them as they appear like reptiles. In ancient studies of demons there were some demons who would appear like humanoid reptiles.

The Book of Genesis spoke about one that tricks Eve into eating the forbidden fruit. The only statements Madonna made regarding the video was that it describes her true religion. In the music video for the song Human Nature a strange subliminal scene is shown at 3 minutes, and 35 seconds into the video, for a blink moment it shows Madonna being webbed to the center of a five point pentagram. This symbol is very much used in witchcraft and Satanism.

In the late 90's Madonna would release an album called Ray of Light. She would dedicate the album to her beliefs in Hindu mysticism, and to the teachings that she learned in her studies of the Kabbalah. For anyone that professes Christianity that should raise red flags. The Bible teaches that only the doctrine known to Christians is the true and sole religion from the beginning before the world, and the universe was made. It teaches all other religions that people believed in were false religions, and called pagan religions. The Bible teaches that pagan religions came from Satan in many different forms and ways. Therefore the Bible would teach that all other religions that are not Christianity are in fact of the devil making the followers of those religions to be devil worshippers. Other people will have different views, and that is because they believe in a different doctrine that is not Christian but often found in the New Age religion were many who profess Jesus also agree with the views found in the New Age faith. According to the Bible those who do that are not real Christians. So under a Christian doctrine Madonna would be a devil worshipper but to the rest of the world she is only practicing her faith. In the end we all must decide for ourselves what to believe.

Many stated that the songs Ray of Light and Frozen were songs about Lucifer. Much of these lyrics do seem to suggest it. It seems to show the dark seduction side of Lucifer, and Madonna sings the songs like an ancient siren. At a concert Madonna did in Rome, Italy, Madonna staged a mock crucifixion in front of thousands of Italian fans. Many said that this action was done to express open hostility toward the Christian faith. This resulted in Madonna being asked if she is a devil worshipper, and her response was, 'Well what can I say I just love that guy'. The guy she was talking about was Satan. In fact, during Madonna's Confessions World Tour Madonna often staged a mock crucifixion by lowering a mirrored cross, and putting herself on the cross while wearing a crown of thorns. It is very clear that Madonna was not the one who died for the sins of the world, and there is no reason to do that other then to only mock Jesus Christ.

During the Boy in Oz tour Madonna would open her show with a chant called the 'I don't care if I go to Hell' chant. Sadly thousands agreed with her, but of course when they die their cries will be a different story. But once again it's for the individual to decide to believe in what Jesus says or to believe in what Madonna, and others say. Lately many of Madonna's concerts have her looking like several pagan goddesses, and one such performance at the Super Bowl had her dressed as an ancient pagan high-priestess.

She released her 11th studio album called Hard Candy where she worked with many of the younger pop artists. She was told that the music was good but she was too old to project it look wise because her body, and face has aged a lot over the years. She still has a reputation for sleeping around with other women's husbands, and she has got very deep into Kabbalah.

Chapter 13

In the 80's going into the early 90's Heavy Metal/Hard Rock music was a wide open mainstream market. Several bands would leave their mark of influences on millions of people. Some of their stories, backgrounds, and their art-form had profound effects on their fans. To understand it let us look into some of these bands, and the events they were involved in.

One such band was called Guns N' Roses. At the height of their fame the front-man of the band, and lead singer Axl Rose was called a speaker for this generation. Many said for this to be true showed a huge lack of morals, and knowledge on the part of the people of that time. Axl was born in a small town of the State of Indiana in 1962. His mother, named Sharon Linter, gave birth to Axl when she was only 16 years old. Axl's real father was a man named William Bruce Rose who got Sharon pregnant when he was 20 years old. William did not want to be a father, and he only saw Sharon as a fling. When he found out that Sharon was pregnant he resisted his role as a dad, so when Axl was two years old William abandoned his family.

Axl has no memories of his real father. At that time Sharon was attending Church meetings designed to bring single people together. There she met a man named Stephen Bailey. She would soon marry Bailey, and she quickly changed Axl's last name to Bailey. Originally Axl's birth-name was William Rose but then it became William Bailey. At that point Axl was led to believe by his mother that Stephen was his real father.

The Bailey family on the surface seemed like a nice Christian family who were very involved with the local Church. Sharon would give birth to other children from Mr. Bailey, but some said that this Church group had a dark side that was hidden within the families. Some said that abuse done against the children was encouraged by Church leaders, and even molestation was going on. No one knows how true this is.

Axl was very involved with this Church. He learned how to sing, and learned how to play the piano, and guitar at Church. Axl also had a talented singing voice which was never really heard in full when he sang for Guns N' Roses, but in truth Axl was able to range his voice to several singing styles from tenor to bass to baritone, and soprano. He was so good at different voice ranges that he would often confuse the choir leader during practice just to have fun with him.

Axl first started to develop his musical gifts at age 5. Axl also was a student of the Bible. On Sunday he would teach the Sunday school Bible class. Axl stated that his home-life was anything but Christian. Axl stated that his step-father used to beat him, and his mother telling them that he had to beat the devil out of them. Axl also stated that Mr. Bailey would molest his sister because as Bailey put it, she was evil. Many believed that this abuse that Axl stated is what caused him later in life to have bad relationship problems with women.

When Axl was a teenager attending Jefferson High School in the town of Lafayette, Axel found some papers regarding his birth. Axl found out that Mr. Bailey was not his real father, and a man named William Rose was. When Axl found out his mother lied to him he was deeply angered, and lost all respect for Mr. Bailey who was now this stranger in his life.

In high-school Axl began to rebel in a major way. He stopped going to Church, and wanted to be called W. Rose from now on. He began to drink alcohol, and started to use drugs mostly smoking marijuana. His behavior and his strange demands about his name caused others in the town to make fun of him. This resulted in several fist-fights, and Axl was arrested several times for them. Axl would also get arrested for public intoxication, underage drinking, for breaking curfew laws, and petty possession of marijuana. In total Axl was arrested 20 times in his high-school years, and he began to be seen as a problem in his small town.

When Axl was 16 years old he met a man who would be called Izzy Stradlin. Izzy would become a future guitarist for Guns N' Roses. Axl met Izzy while taking a driver's education class together, and the two of them quickly became close friends. They bonded over their love for rock music, and they often played together.

When Axl was 17 years old his mother and step-father felt he was out of control. One night when Axl came home late his step-father demanded that he cut his hair and get his life in order. This resulted in a pushing fight Axl had with Mr. Bailey. His mother would call the police on her son, and Axl was soon kicked out of the house.

Axl for a time would stay at Izzy's place but then Izzy moved to Los Angeles. From there Axl had to ask friends from time to time if he could stay at their place, but soon he got arrested again, and the local police told Axl to leave the town or else. Axl's public defender told him that his life was in danger, and so Axl left. For a time Axl was homeless, and living on the streets from time to time while wandering through the towns of Indiana. He would play guitar and sing on corner streets for money. From time to time Axl would hook up with old girlfriends in his hometown, and come back there to stay with them. One of his old girlfriends had phone contact with Axl's friend named Izzy.

Izzy at the time was in the nightclub rock music scene trying to make it in a band. He invited Axl, and his girlfriend to come, and stay at his place in Los Angeles. Axl came to L.A. in December of 1982. Izzy, to make extra money, also worked as a manager at Tower Records, and he got Axl a job there as a night-manager. Axl through Izzy soon got hooked up to the Heavy Metal/Hard Rock scene of L.A. and West Hollywood. Axl would play in several bands who were L.A. Guns, Rapid Fire, Hollywood Rose, and others. In one band he played in, Axl, who was still known as W. Rose at the time, changed his stage name to Axl which was the name of that band.

In March of 1985 the management team of the bands L.A. Guns and Hollywood Rose got together to form a new group. They selected Axl for vocals, Slash for lead guitar, Izzy for rhythm guitar, Duff McKagan for bass guitar, and Steven Adler for drums. To name the band they combined the last names of the two bands they came from, and called this band Guns N' Roses.

In June of 1985 after the line-up was finalized the band embarked on a short, disorganized tour of the West Coast leaving from Sacramento, California and to end in Seattle, Washington. The tour was nicknamed the 'Hell Tour', but through their increasing presence on the Hollywood club scene playing at such hard rock nightclubs as The Troubadour and The Roxy, Guns N' Roses drew the attention of major record labels.

They were eventually signed by Geffen Records in March of 1986. They would receive a $75,000 advance. In December of that year Guns N' Roses released a four song EP called Live Like a Suicide which contained three noted songs called Nice Boys, Mama Kin, and Reckless Life. The album would create a label for Guns N' Roses called UZI Suicide.

In July of 1987 Guns N' Roses released their first full studio album. It was called Appetite for Destruction. The first two singles released from the album were Welcome to the Jungle and Sweet Child O' Mine. The album started off very slow at first throughout 1987. But in 1988 the producers of the film The Dead Pool who were still finishing up scenes wanted to use the song Welcome to the Jungle to promote the new Dirty Harry film. The management team of Guns N' Roses agreed to this, and even got the band to do a cameo in the film. This brought world-wide attention to the song. MTV also started to play around the clock rotations of the song Sweet Child O' Mine and Welcome to the Jungle. As a result Appetite for Destruction by the fall of 1988 hit the number one spot on the Billboard 200 albums chart. It would go on to sell 18 million copies in the United States, and 28 million copies in total world-wide.

Guns N' Roses would soon embark on a 16 month long tour called the Appetite for Destruction Tour. Other bands like The Cult, Motley Crue, Alice Cooper, Iron Maiden, and Aerosmith joined them. They would headline in North America, Europe, Japan, and Australia. Guns N' Roses in that time of the late 80's often had uneventful problems during their performances. During a November 1987 show in Atlanta, Axl assaulted a security guard, and was held backstage by the police while his band mates continued playing with a roadie who would step in to sing.

Riots nearly broke out during two shows in August of 1988 in New York State. At England's Monsters of Rock Festival two fans were crushed to death during a Guns N' Roses set by the slam-dancing crowd. In October of 1989 Guns N' Roses were to open for the Rolling Stones at the L.A. Coliseum but Axl threaten to walk out on the band if they did not check their use of Mr. Brownstone. Mr. Brownstone was a nickname for the drug called heroin.

In November of 1988 Guns N' Roses released their second album called G N' R Lies. It would feature the hit single called Patience which hit number 4 on the Billboard 100 singles chart. The album itself would hit number 2 on the Billboard 200 albums chart. When fans heard the song called One in a Million Axl Rose came under fire for accusations of being a racist, and for having homophobia, and hating police officers. It has always been known that Axl had bad run-ins with the law. Axl stated to his defense that he used the word nigger in the song as an insult towards certain black men who tried to rob him. In response to having homophobia Rose stated that he is pro-heterosexual, and he blamed his attitude toward gay people on bad experiences he had with gay men who tried to take advantage of him.

In 1990 Guns N' Roses would enter the studio to record Use Your Illusion 1 & 2. At this time Axl was having a troubled relationship with Erin Everly who was the daughter of Don Everly of the rock-pop group called the Everly Brothers. During this time the story is according to Axl that their manager named Alan Niven was caught by Axl as he was putting the moves on his girlfriend Erin. Axl wanted him fired but his band mates did not want him fired, and they defended Niven. Axl began dating Erin when the band had released their first studio album. Erin even appeared in the video Sweet Child O' Mine, a song Axl wrote for her, but Erin would often break up with Axl due to the abuse Axl would put her through. This abuse was often domestic violence. Every time she broke up with Axl she would end up taking him back after Axl promised he would not do it again. Axl often cheated on her as well.

Axl wanted to marry Erin so badly that one time he showed up to her home in his car, and told her he had a gun, and that he would kill himself if she did not get in the car and come with him to get married. This happened in April of 1990, and Erin ended up marrying him in Las Vegas. Soon the violence and cheating took it's toll on Erin, and she also became pregnant. Due to another fight in October of 1990 Erin suffered a miscarriage, and lost the baby. After this Erin left him for good. Axl tried to get her back by constantly sending her flowers, cards, and even caged birds but nothing worked. One day while Axl was brooding over the problems with Erin, and having lost his child he began to play his music at a very high tone. His neighbor came out and threatened to call the police. Axl took the bottle he was drinking from, and he smashed it across his head. Axl was then arrested for assault with a deadly weapon. Axl and Erin were officially divorced by January 1991.

When Axl's band mates stood by Niven, Axl threaten to discontinue working on the album until Niven was fired. The record company was then forced to fire Niven. This brought even more heat between Axel, and his band mates who already did not like him, and now were starting to hate him. While recording the songs for Use Your Illusion 1 & 2 problems arose also with drummer Steven Adler. When the band was recording the song Civil War Adler was fired because he was unable to perform well. He was struggling with cocaine and heroin addictions which caused the band to do nearly 30 takes of the song Civil War. After he was fired Steven was replaced by a drummer named Matt Sorum who had played before for the band called The Cult.

On September 17, 1991 Guns N' Roses released both albums Use Your Illusion 1 & 2. Both albums would hit the number 1 & 2 spots of the Billboard 200 albums chart. They were the first band in music industry history to have done this feat. Both albums would sell 7 million copies for a combined total of 14 million copies.

Before Guns N' Roses released these two albums they would perform a show at the Riverport Amphitheater in Maryland Heights, Missouri which was a suburb of St. Louis. The concert was called the Riverport Riot. When Guns N' Roses were performing a song called Rocket Queen, Rose discovered that a fan was filming the show with a camera. Rose first told the security to take the camera away from the fan but they refused. Rose then decided to take it himself, and he then jumped into the audience, and he tackled the fan. During the heated confrontation Rose began to physically assault the fan by punching him again and again. The stage crew rushed to pull Axl out of the audience, and Rose took the mic, and said, 'Well, thanks to the lame-ass security, I'm going home!' Rose then threw his microphone to the ground, and stormed off the stage. The angry crowd began to riot, and dozens of people were beaten up and injured. The crowds then began throwing chairs and bottles at the stage to such a degree that thousands of chairs and bottles littered the stage. The crowds were aiming the chairs and bottles at the band and the stage crew. The police were called in and sought to arrest Axl but the band fled before they were able to. The police were not able to arrest Axl for inciting the riot until one year later.

After the two albums were released Gun N' Roses embarked on a world tour. The Use Your Illusion World Tour is called one of the most highest grossing rock tours of all-time, and it's also called one of the most notorious tours of all-time. The success of the tour was overshadowed by riots, late starts, outspoken rants by Rose, drug, and alcohol issues. Axl was often agitated by lax security, sound problems, and unwanted filming by fans.

Axl would also use the in-between time in songs to fire off political statements or retorts against music critics or celebrity rivals.

On November 7, 1991 after a concert in Germany nearly unfolded in a riot, rhythm guitarist Izzy Stradlin quit the band and was replaced by Gilby Clarke. In 1992 Axl was arrested by the police, and received two years' probation for the Riverport Riot. At the second half of the tour the Heavy Metal band called Metallica joined Guns N' Roses, and together they embarked on the Guns N' Rose/Metallica Stadium Tour. Most of the other members of Guns N' Roses got along well with Metallica, but Axl did not for he was jealous of the group after he felt they kept upstaging Guns N' Roses during performances.

On August 8, 1992 at the Montreal Olympic Stadium in Canada one of the worst riots in the history of rock music took place. During the show headlined by Guns N' Roses and Metallica, Metallica was to perform first but during their set front man James Hetfield suffered severe burns after malfunctions with a pyrotechnics blast. Metallica was forced to cancel the second hour of the show.

Guns N' Roses showed up late at the show, and this long delay made the audience very restless. When the band finally showed up, Axl thought that the band would be playing to a pumped up audience but when he heard what happened he was very annoyed. When Guns N' Roses took the stage they put a half-hearted effort into it and played 9 songs for a total of 50 minutes. Axl during the song Double Talkin Jive began interrupting the song to play mind games with the fans by telling them this would be Guns N' Roses' last show. When they did the 9th song which was Civil War they performed the song horribly. To start trouble Axl took the mic at the end of the song and said, 'thank you, your money will be refunded', and he stormed off the stage. When he got backstage members of Metallica, and others asked him what happened, and Axl

took a shot of hard liquor and looked at them coldly and said, 'my throat hurts'. His throat however was not the problem it was in fact his ego. The cancellation of the show led to a huge riot by audience members far worse than Riverport. Rioters beat each other up, and destroyed the insides of the stadium. They took the riot outside on the streets, and began to overturn cars, smash windows, loot local stores, and they set buildings on fire. Local police were barely able to bring the mob under control. When it was over close to about 100 people were injured, and over a million dollars of property was destroyed.

Axl would have other court problems with a woman named Stephaine Seymour. Axl began dating Stephaine in 1991 she would even appear in the music videos for November Rain and Don't Cry. Stephaine in that time was called an A-list model of the modeling industry. Their relationship in 1993 ended due to abuse that was both physical and mental that Stephaine stated Axl did to her and her son. In 1994 Stephaine sought to sue him, and Axl in his defense stated that it was Stephaine who was abusive, and she was lying, but to prove she was not, Stephaine had the courts to bring to testimony Erin Everly. Erin confirmed the abuse she received from Axl, and it was the same kind of abuse Stephaine received. Axl's lawyers encouraged him to settle with Stephaine out of court so he do so, but right after Erin then sued him for abuse after advice she got from Stephaine. Axl then paid her off as well.

During the tour Axl was having major problems with his band mates over copyright issues, and over ego issues. Axl was also coming under fire by the media for wearing Charles Manson t-shirts. Axl even wore a t-shirt of the occult murderer in his music video Estranged. When Guns N' Roses was recording the album called the Spaghetti Incident he had a huge fight with his band mates over recording songs written by Charles Manson. Axl was able to get his way, and the song called Look at Your Game, Girl was recorded, and put on the album but the song was not listed on the jacket of the album nor was it advertised.

In 1994 the band members of Guns N' Roses had a final fall out with Axl when he tried to force Slash and Duff to sign over to him the rights to use the name Guns N' Roses. The two men refused but they were also so sicken by their relationship with Axl that they did not want their careers associated with Axl or the name Guns N' Roses any longer. The final song Guns N' Roses did with Slash on lead guitar, and Duff on bass was the song Sympathy for the Devil which was a remake of a Rolling Stones' song. Guns N' Roses did the song for the soundtrack of Interview with a Vampire.

After 1994 Axl would stop working for a while, and live off his royalties in his mansion in Malibu. Axl mainly lived in recluse making only small appearances here and there. Oddly when he did go out to make these appearances there was times he would still get arrested for violent behavior. Many fans however still wanted to see a Guns N' Roses album, and they would wait and wait. Rumors were it would come out this year, and that year but it never did. Axl stated that the wait was due to him having to bring together new band mates, and they had problems recording new songs once he did so.

After a wait that would take close to 15 years Axl, and this new version of Guns N' Roses released the album called Chinese Democracy. Many said that the songs were good but Axl waited too long to release the album. The album was not a huge success because most of those fans who wanted to see a new album got tired of waiting.

Rumors regarding Axl are that he gave up on Christianity a long time ago. He got into New Age faiths when living, and performing in the Hollywood nightclub scenes. A stranger rumor was that Axl was a mind-control victim, and that he tried to show that in his music video Estranged. No evidence was able to support this.

Metallica is an American Heavy Metal band who were formed in Los Angeles, California. Their sound is noted for fast tempos, instrumentals, aggressive guitar play and drums. Metallica was formed in 1981 when James Hetfield answered an advertisement from drummer Lars Ulrich that was posted in a local newspaper. These two first brought in Dave Mustaine to play lead guitar and Ron McGovney to play bass while Hetfield did rhythm guitar, and vocals with Lars on drums. Lars Ulrich was the one who got Metallica into the music industry when he asked the founder of Metal Blade Records, Brian Slagel, if he could record a song for him if he formed a band. Five months after Ulrich and Hetfield met the band Metallica was formed, and they recorded a song for Slagel called Hit the Lights. After recording Hit the Lights they began to tour the Heavy Metal circuit in Southern California.

Their first live performance was on March 12, 1982 at Radio City in Anaheim, California. One night in the fall of 1982 Ulrich and Hetfield went to a metal show at a West Hollywood nightclub called the Whisky Go Go. There they saw a bass guitarist named Cliff Burton play in a band called Trauma. The two of them soon asked Burton to join the group. At first Burton refused but later in that same year he accepted as long as the group moved to the San Francisco Bay Area. At that point they fired McGovney.

Metallica's first performance with Burton in the group took place at a nightclub called The Stone in March of 1983. In May of 1983 Metallica traveled to Rochester, New York to record their debut album that was originally called Metal Up Your Ass but during the recording sessions the other three members of Metallica got sick, and tired of the violent behavior of Dave Mustaine. Dave had a serious problem with drugs, and alcohol that effected his relationship with the other three members. Dave was soon fired, and Ulrich and Hetfield came to hire Kirk Hammett who used to play for Exodus. Dave Mustaine would go on to form the Heavy Metal group called Megadeth.

After recording their first album the name of the album was changed due to copyright issues, and so the album was called Kill' Em All. The album would be released in 1983. Their first album was not a financial success in fact it did not enter the Billboard 200 chart until three years later in 1986 where it hit the number 120 spot but what the album did do was it gained a growing fan base for Metallica in the underground Heavy Metal scene. In that scene their most popular songs were Whiplash, Seek & Destroy, Hit the Lights, and The Four Horseman. Their songs centered on violence, war, death, and end of days events.

In February of 1984 Metallica supported the band called Venom on the Seven Dates of Hell Tour where Metallica played in front of 7,000 people at the Aardschok Festival in Zwolle, Netherlands. It was their largest crowd to date at that time. In Copenhagen, Denmark Metallica recorded their second studio album called Ride the Lightning. This album came out in August of 1984. This album did much better than their first one as it hit number 100 on the Billboard 200 albums chart. The album was noted for three singles called For Whom the Bell Tolls a song about war, Fade to Black a song that later brought controversy after a young fan killed himself listening to it, and Creeping Death a song about the angel of death that was sent by GOD during the time of Moses to destroy the firstborn of Egypt.

In September of 1984 Elektra Records A&R director named Michael Alago attended a Metallica concert. He was there to scout the group, and he was so impressed with them that he signed them on to Elektra Records. Elektra's people began to heavily promote the band, and released their last two albums under their label. Elektra's management team then put the band on a European tour with the metal band called Tank. Soon on August 17, 1985 Metallica played it's largest show at the Monsters of Rock Festival at Donington Park in England where Bon Jovi, and Ratt also played. Metallica played in front of 70,000 people that day. Soon, at the Day on Green Festival Metallica played in front of 60,000 people in Oakland, California.

In March of 1986 Metallica would release their third studio album called Master of Puppets. This album was the band's first album to be certified gold on November 4, 1986. The album would hit the number 29 spot on the Billboard 200 albums chart. The band would then join Ozzy Osbourne on his United States tour becoming the opening act.

On September 27, 1986 during Metallica's European tour called the Damage, Inc Tour, the members of Metallica drew cards to determine which bunks they would get on the tour bus. Burton won first choice, and chose the top bunk that Kirk wanted. Around dawn near Dorarp, Sweden the bus driver is believed to have fallen asleep at the wheel and he lost control of the bus, and the bus then skidded. This caused the bus to tip off the side of the road, and the bus flipped over several times. Ulrich, Hammett, and Hetfield managed to sustain no serious injuries but Cliff Burton was pinned under the bus when he fell out from the window of the bus. His legs were sticking out from under the bus, and when everyone tried to lift the bus to pull him out they were unable to, and the bus landed back on top of him. Burton did not survive. Hetfield started to yell at the bus driver, and thought the driver was drunk. The driver stated that the bus hit black ice as it was very cold that day. When the driver saw everyone was freezing the driver, with a certain lack of sense, tried to pull the blanket out from under Burton's dead body.

Hetfield began to scream at him, and wanted to kill the bus driver. Hetfield would then walk back down the road to see if there really was black ice. Hetfield saw no black ice, and came back, and told the driver in a very cold fashion that there was no black ice.

After Burton's death Metallica was ready to break up but Burton's family told them that Cliff would have wanted them to carry on, and so they did. At the auditions to choose Metallica's new bass player 40 people tried out. Because Metallica was still in pain over what happened to Cliff all 40 of them were coldly treated. The one who got the spot was Jason Newsted who had played for Flotsam & Jetsam. The three members broke Newsted in by pulling all kinds of pranks on him. One of them was getting him to eat a ball of wasabi.

Newsted's first performance with Metallica was at the Country Club in Reseda, California. Metallica would soon earn a spot as a musical guest on Saturday Night Live in 1987, but Hetfield, who was into skateboarding, broke his wrist a second time while skateboarding. The band was then forced to cancel their appearance on the show.

The band would record their fourth studio album, and their first since Burton's death. The album was called ...And Justice for All. And Justice for All was called one of the best written Heavy Metal albums of all time. The album became a huge commercial success and it hit number six on the Billboard 200 albums chart. The album was released in 1988, and it was certified platinum in nine weeks after its release. In 1989 Metallica received a Grammy nomination for the album. Everyone was expecting them to win including Metallica, but they gave the award to Jethro Tull instead. Tull was even told by his manager not to go to the ceremony because he believed that Metallica would win. It was called one of the 10 greatest upsets in Grammy history.

The most noted single on the album was the song called One. The theme of the song was about a man wounded in war. One is called one of the best Heavy Metal songs of all time, and it's music video was included among the 100 best music videos of

MTV.

In 1990 a producer named Bob Rock who worked with Bon Jovi, Motley Crue, and Aerosmith sought to work with Metallica on their next album to be recorded in North Hollywood. The album they would make was named after the band, but due to the black cover on the album it became known as The Black Album. The recording of the album took a large toll on the band-members. The album had to be recorded three times, and in the process three band members ended their marriages. The Black Album was released in 1991. This album brought Metallica a huge mainstream fan base. It is still their highest selling album as it sold 16 million copies. It had three hit singles called Unforgiven, Wherever I May Roam, and Enter Sandman. There was controversy surrounding the music video of Unforgiven due to a scene of children being thrown into pits by what seems to be their parents. Some said that a few people committed suicide listening to the song but these reports were not confirmed.

Metallica would soon embark on the Wherever We May Roam Tour that lasted for 14 months as they played in the United States, Europe, and Japan. In 1992 they joined Guns N' Roses for the stadium tour. During this tour in Montreal when Metallica was performing the song Fade to Black Hetfield being confused about the pyrotechnic set-up walked into a 12 foot burst of flame. Hetfield suffered second, and third degree burns to his arms, face, hands, and legs. His skin was so heated it was bubbling. Metallica thought Guns N' Roses would save the show but instead they caused a riot. This resulted in Hetfield going on MTV to challenge Axl Rose to a one on one fight. No one knows if they actually fought. Metallica also learned lessons from Guns N' Roses called 'what not to do on tour'. Throughout the early 90's Metallica continued to tour, and they even played Woodstock in 1994. They also did three outdoor shows at the United Kingdom at Donington Park which also featured Slayer, Skid Row, Slash's Snakepit, and a few others.

In 1996 Metallica would release a new album called Load. Load would hit the number one spot on the Billboard 200 album chart, and it would be their second album to hit the number one spot since The Black Album. The cover of the Load album was in a couple of words very sick. The cover was created by Andres

Serrano who pressed a mixture of his own semen and blood between sheets of plexiglass. The band also had a new change in their music sound. They left the Heavy Metal sound, and took on the Alternative/Grunge rock sound. They did this because the Heavy Metal market at the time was crushed by alternative rock. Not only did the band have a new musical direction they even had a new image, and all the band members received haircuts. The haircuts angered other metal bands who once respected Metallica, and even during a concert they did a few of their peers sat in the front row holding signs that said 'friends don't let friends get hair-cuts'. Many of those old metal bands called Metallica sell-outs especially when they headlined the alternative rock festival called Lollapalooza in the summer of 1996.

In 1997 Metallica would release an album called Reload, and in 1998 they released a double album called Garage, Inc. which hit number two on the Billboard 200 chart. In the year 2000 Metallica found out that a song they did called I Disappear which was used on the Mission Impossible 2 film was getting radio airplay without their knowledge. The band would trace the source of the leak, and then they filed a lawsuit against Napster for copyright infringement. The case resulted in Napster to pay millions of dollars to Metallica, and Napster agreed to block users who shared music by artists who did not want their music shared for free. Napster would eventually file Chapter 11 bankruptcy protection due to all the lawsuits against them by other artists. The Napster case turned many college fans against Metallica.

Ulrich tried to make light of it at the 2000 VMA show in a skit with Marlon Wayans where Wayan's character stated he was sharing the music while Ulrich retorted that Marlon's idea of sharing was 'borrowing things that were not yours without asking'. Napster creator Shawn Fanning would appear at the ceremony with a response to Metallica. He wore a Metallica shirt with words on it that said, 'I borrowed this shirt from a friend, maybe If I like it, I'll buy one of my own'. When Ulrich went to introduce the final musical act Blink-182 he was booed on stage.

On January 17, 2001 Jason Newsted left the band after arguments he had with Hetfield and Ulrich over looking to do a solo album. Newsted stated that Hetfield blocked him from having a solo career as punishment for trying to leave Metallica.

In July of 2001 James Hetfield would enter rehab for alcohol and drug addictions. In 2003 Robert Trujillo who used to play for Ozzy Osbourne replaced Jason Newsted as the new bass player for Metallica. In June of 2003 Metallica would release the album St. Anger which would hit number one on the Billboard 200 chart. St. Anger would even win a Grammy Award but it drew mixed reactions from fans.

In 2008 Metallica would release an album called Death Magnetic which brought back a more heavy metal sound, and this album also hit number one on the Billboard 200 albums chart. Their last known album at the time of this writing was called Lulu released in 2011.

There have been rumors regarding Metallica's involvement with Satanism going back to the days they played the Heavy Metal circuits in California. No knows if this is really true. Satanism was in that scene, and other bands did admit they were involved with it, and some said Metallica also was involved with it, but no proof was shown regarding Metallica being involved in it. One song that got pointed out was a song by Metallica called, 'Follow the God that Failed'. The music video, and the song itself mocks Jesus Christ, and the video shows the band members in a possessed state. Another strange occurrence was the backward lyrics on some of their songs. Most of the lyrics stated, 'Our Lord Satan' or 'Our Savior Satan'. It's hard to say that Metallica knew about it or put it there but it is known they are very hands on when it comes to recording their music. In a song they did called Am I Evil that was released on the Garage, Inc. double album the song was from years before that double album, and it was put on the shelf until the release of that double album. The theme of the song was about a man who mocks Jesus Christ, and embraces the spirituality of witchcraft.

Another rock band was the Heavy Metal group called Skid Row. Skid Row was formed in Toms River, New Jersey in late 1986 by bassist Rachel Bolan and guitarist Dave 'The Snake' Sabo. The two of them would bring in Rob Affuso to play drums, and Steve Brotherton to play rhythm guitar. The metal underground scene of New Jersey was largely made up of runaway teens, drug addicts, and prostitutes, hence the name Skid Row.

When the band was formed they were funded by Bon Jovi's manager named Doc McGhee. At the time Jon Bon Jovi had set up a publishing company called the Underground Music Company. Jon was seeking new, and upcoming talent to make money off of through his new company. Jon who grew up in New Jersey was an old friend of Dave Sabo, and he sent his manager Doc McGhee to help him form a new band. Once the band was formed they were looking for a lead vocalist. Doc McGhee saw a Canadian metal magazine called Metalion that did a story on vocalist Sebastian Bach who was singing for a band called Kid Wikkid. McGhee contacted him, and asked him if he would join Skid Row. Bach, seeing a chance to finally break through, and make it big agreed to join the band.

Once the band was formed Skid Row began playing in shows at nightclubs among the underground scene throughout the eastern United States. They quickly built a small fan base, and insiders began to speak about how good their sound was. Jon and Doc would then talk to the people of Atlantic Records, and they secured Skid Row a record deal in 1988. Skid Row would sign a contract with both Atlantic Records and Jon Bon Jovi along with Richie Sambora who also was part owner of the Underground Music Company. The contract with Jon and Richie would prove to be a bad deal. Soon Skid Row was taken to Lake Geneva, Wisconsin to record their first album that was named after the band.

Skid Row was released in January of 1989, and in a short space of time it became a huge success. The album would sell 5 million copies, and produce three smash hit singles called 18 and Life, I Remember You, and Youth Gone Wild. Soon their fame put them on tour with Bon Jovi, and they were featured in rock magazines, t-shirts, and posters. Their royalties were making the band millions of dollars but the problem was they did not see those checks going to them, instead it was going to Jon Bon Jovi and Richie Sambora. The problem was that when Skid Row signed the contract with Jon and Richie they signed away their rights to royalties to them. This resulted in a feud between Skid Row and Bon Jovi that was even profiled on MTV. The feud started to bring bad press to Bon Jovi that this caused

Richie Sambora to give back all the money he made off Skid Row back to them. Jon Bon Jovi refused not to give back not one cent as he put it. As a result Jon Bon Jovi lost his friendship to Sabo, and the rest of Skid Row, and Jon had no regrets about it. After this Skid Row not wanting to tour with Bon Jovi began to tour with Ozzy Osbourne, and then with Aerosmith, but they still kept Doc McGhee as their manager.

Skid Row often had violent encounters at many of their shows a couple of them were well known. On December 27, 1989 Skid Row performed a show with Aerosmith in Springfield, Massachusetts. The show became known as The Bottle Incident. When Skid Row was performing a fan in the front row took a bottle and hurled it at Sebastian Bach hitting him in the head. The bottle did not break and Bach picked up the bottle, and knowing who hit him hurled it back at the fan. The fan quickly grabbed a female, and used her as a shield, and the bottle hit the female in the head, and it smash to pieces on her skull. Pieces of the glass were stuck in the skin of her head.

Bach became enraged, and he jumped off the stage, and attacked the fan, and began to beat the fan up while the massive crowd began to riot. Another strange event took place at a show in 1990. While Skid Row was on stage a fan threw a t-shirt on stage that read 'AIDS Kills Fags Dead'. Bach saw the shirt, and decided to put it on, and play the rest of the set with the shirt on for everyone to read. This caused a media firestorm against the band where they were forced to give a public apology.

In June of 1991 Skid Row released their second album called Slave to the Grind. It was the first pure Heavy Metal album that instead of climbing to the number one spot it debuted at the number one spot on the Billboard 200 chart. The band would then join Guns N' Roses on tour. Their second album was a huge success but throughout the tour the band members were constantly fighting with each other. They began to break down over money issues, ego, jealously, and personal issues with drug addictions. In 1993 they decided to take a break from each other but during that time the Heavy Metal market was crushed by grunge rock.

In 1994 producer Bob Rock worked with them on their third

album called Subhuman Race. Subhuman Race was released in 1995 but it did not achieve the success of their first two albums even though the album had positive reviews. The album took the number 40 spot on the Billboard 200 albums chart and it failed money wise. Soon after, the original band members began to leave the group and Skid Row would fade into nostalgia.

The music influence of Skid Row was one of naked aggression, drugs, sexual immorality, rebellion, and violence. 18 and Life came under fire by Church and moral groups for showing murder done among two teens. Youth Gone Wild was also a song they attacked for encouraging young people to revolt on authority figures. Piece of Me was a song about using women anyway you feel like it and many songs seem to have this message of pushing yourself upon anyone or anything.

Motley Crue is describe as one of the world's most successful and notorious rock bands of all time. They have sold a combine total of their albums 80 million copies world-wide. The band was formed in Los Angeles, California in 1981 by bass guitarist Nikki Sixx and drummer Tommy Lee. They later brought in lead guitarist Mick Mars, and lead singer Vince Neil. Motley Crue is a band noted for their hedonistic, and notorious lifestyles, and their violent persona. All of the original members of the band have had numerous brushes with the law, spent time in prison, and suffered from alcohol, and drug addictions. Their main drug addictions were cocaine and heroin. They had countless escapades with porn stars, and other women. In fact Lee and Neil even made porn videos.

Motley Crue first got started when Nikki Sixx left the band called London in 1981, and he met drummer Tommy Lee. The two of them began rehearsing together, and developed a sound. Soon they decided to put together a band, and they held an auditioned where they brought in Mick Mars, and vocalist Greg Leon. Tommy Lee however did not want Leon for vocals, and he remembered his high-school friend Vince Neil. Lee and Neil used to play together in their high-school days at Charter Oak High School. The two of them used to be members of a garage band where they played the garage circuit.

One night Lee had taken Sixx and Mars to a nightclub called Starwood in Hollywood, California to see a band called Rock Candy where Vince Neil was the lead singer. The three men wanted Neil in the band after they saw the way he commanded the crowd. Neil when offered the spot at first refused until Rock Candy was about to break up, and then Neil contacted Lee, and in April 1981 Leon was fired, and Vince Neil was hired.

When the band was formed they did not have a name yet, and while thinking of one Mars remembered an incident where a band called White Horse were called 'a motley looking crew'. They then took the phrase, and gave it a German spelling they got from a German beer bottle, and called the band Motley Crue. The day they named the band the members were really drunk at the time.

They soon got a manager named Allan Coffman, and then they got a record label called Leathur Records that also had a German spelling due to their love for German beer. The first song they recorded was called Stick to Your Guns/Toast of the Town. They would soon record their debut album called Too Fast for Love on their record label. They managed to sell 20,000 copies of the album.

Motley Crue began to tour the Los Angeles club scene which led to a fan base, and to a negotiation with people from Elektra Records. Elektra Records would sign Motley Crue in the spring of 1982. Motley Crue would then embark on the Cruesing Through Canada Tour in 1982 where many notorious incidents with the band would occur. At the Edmonton International Airport the band showed up at the airport wearing their spiked stage wardrobe, and Neil had a small carry-on bag filled with porn magazines. The band was arrested for dangerous weapons because of the spikes on their wardrobe, and for indecent material due to the porn magazines. While playing at the Scandals Disco in Edmonton Motley Crue's manager had a real not too bright idea to get some attention for the band. He decided to get on the phone, and call the manager of the club, and state their is a bomb hidden in the club, and he wanted to blow up the band. The bomb threat against the band made front page news in the Edmonton Journal. Soon when Tommy Lee was staying at the Sheraton Caravan Hotel Lee threw a television set from the upper story window. From there the band members started to engage in reckless and wild behavior that resulted in the band to be banned from Edmonton, and their tour ended in financial disaster.

Motley Crue then got a new manager named Doc McGhee who was Bon Jovi's manager, and he used to manage Kiss as well. McGhee was the same guy who got arrested for smuggling 40,000 pounds of drugs. Motley Crue through this manager would get to embark on the U.S. Festival Tour that was promoted by MTV.

This tour brought them to international fame. During the tour the band members became notorious for bad behavior and the way they would dress. They engaged in backstage antics, outrageous clothing, extreme high-heeled boots, and heavily applied make-up to such a point that it seemed needless and dirty. There was also their endless abuse of alcohol and drugs.

In the mid-80's they would release three successful albums that MTV also promoted. These albums were Shout at the Devil 1983, Theatre of Pain 1985, and Girls, Girls, Girls 1987. Their songs told the story of their lives where it showcased their love for motorcycles, whiskey, and strip clubs. It told tales of substance abuse, sexual escapades, and general decadence.

In 1984 Neil was driving home drunk from a liquor store when he was in a head-on collision where his passenger Hanoi Rocks was killed. Neil was charged with a DUI, and vehicular manslaughter, and was sentenced to 30 days in jail and a 2 million dollar fine. Neil could have got more time if not for the plea of his lawyers. In 1987 Sixx suffered a heroin overdose, and on his way to the hospital was declared legally dead but the medic revived Sixx by giving him two shots of adrenaline to his heart which brought him back.

The song Kickstart My Heart was about Sixx's two minutes of death. From 1986 to 1987 Sixx even kept a daily diary of his heroin addiction. 1988 was when Doc McGhee was convicted for smuggling 40,000 pounds of marijuana, and as part of his punishment he had to do an anti-drug campaign. Around that same time Motley Crue's drug addictions were so bad that their managers pulled them off the tour in Europe because they were afraid they would come back home in body bags. All the members were then told to undergo drug rehabilitation, and all the members went except Mars.

Mars would clean up on his own. When they got out of rehab the band went to work with producer Bob Rock, and they recorded the album Dr. Feelgood. In October of 1989 Dr. Feelgood was released, and it became the number one album on the Billboard 200 albums chart. It's lead single called Dr. Feelgood was a smash hit. The album is still called their best album, and one of the greatest Heavy Metal/Hard Rock albums of all-time. Motley Crue would become nominated for a Grammy, and the American Music Award, and they would win an American Music Award the following year.

Soon Motley Crue would fire McGhee for favoring Bon Jovi during the slot placements at the Moscow Music Peace Festival. In 1991 Motley Crue would release a greatest hits album called Decade of Decadence which hit number two on the Billboard 200 albums chart.

In the early to mid 90's was the end to Heavy Metal/Hard Rock mass market mainstream, and this mainstream market was replaced by grunge rock music. Neil was eventually fired from the band, and the band broke apart when their new album failed to meet commercial expectations. The band then reunited with the album Generation Swine which hit number four on the Billboard 200 chart but oddly it too was called a commercial failure. This resulted in a fight between the band, and the people at Elektra Records who Motley Crue stated was not supporting them.

The band would then create their own label called Motley Records. In 1999 Lee quit the band due to increasing tensions with front-man Vince Neil. The band members began to go in different directions. On February 14, 2005 in San Juan, Puerto Rico Motley Crue reunited, and began a farewell tour. From 2007 and on they would from time to time play shows together.

The band members still had a way of bringing controversy to themselves. Tommy Lee would get arrested from time to time for fist-fights at nightclubs, and Neil would at times get arrested for drug possession. All the band members had a hard time staying clean, and maintaining long term relationships. In the mid 90's Tommy Lee came under fire by the media for a porn video he did with Pamela Anderson who was a huge television star on a series called Baywatch, and was a former Playboy model. The couple who were married at one time, and then divorced, stated that the sex videos they did were stolen out of their home due to a robbery.

Then someone went, and started to sell them on a VHS tape, and the tape was even in rental stores but it turned out that their story looked more like a lie when large profits from these awful videos went into their pockets.

One of the most remembered festivals of the hey-day of the Heavy Metal/Hard Rock market was The Moscow Music Peace Festival. The festival was put together by Doc McGhee and Stas Namin. It was designed to be a gathering of high-profile rock bands to perform in Moscow when Russia was still the Soviet Union. The festival lasted for two days from August 12-13 of 1989. The festival was to promote world-peace, and to fight the drug war in Russia but the real reason why the festival happened had nothing to do with a concern for peace, and fighting a drug war.

Doc McGhee, after being arrested for smuggling drugs, was ordered by the courts to promote a venue that would promote the fight against drug sales. So McGhee, working with the Make a Difference Foundation along with Stas Namin, and other major players in the Soviet Union and the United States came up with the Moscow Music Peace Festival.

The noted bands that played there were Skid Row, Cinderella, Bon Jovi, Jam, Motley Crue, Gorky Park, Ozzy Osbourne, Scorpions, and a few others. From the very start of the festival there was problems with certain bands that centered around McGhee favoring Bon Jovi. Jon Bon Jovi was a major factor in bringing in funds for the event because he wanted to keep his manager, and friend McGhee out of jail. It has also been believed that the drugs McGhee was smuggling was for the members of Bon Jovi but this has never been proven.

The problem started when Motley Crue asked to use pyrotechnics in their set and McGhee refused but McGhee, unknown to Motley Crue, allowed Bon Jovi to use them. When Bon Jovi finished their set Tommy Lee went looking for McGhee but found Sebastian Bach of Skid Row instead. Bach was drinking a bottle of Russian vodka, and Lee asked him for the whereabouts of McGhee. Bach told him he did not know where he was because McGhee at the time was hiding from Motley Crue. Lee then took the bottle of vodka from Bach, and drank it down, and told Bach, 'Your manager's a fucking asshole'.

Lee however was not done looking for McGhee, and when he finally found him he ran up toward McGhee, and punched him in the face, and fired him. Lee while firing him told McGhee you can go manage The Chipmunks for all he cared. The Chipmunks that he was talking about was Bon Jovi because Motley Crue could not stand the music or the band Bon Jovi.

The festival was held in Moscow's largest stadium called now the Luzhniki Stadium but back in 1989 it was called the Central Lenin Stadium. The festival was designed to be the Woodstock of the USSR. The two day event was the first rock concert held in the stadium where previously it was only used for sporting events. Over 100,000 people attended the festival. Each band was supposed to have a 5 to 6 song set but Bon Jovi was given a longer set for time. The finale to the event was a show featuring Jason Bonham the son of John Bonham on drums with Vince Neil, and Sebastian Bach on vocals where Jason's band called Jam performed the Led Zeppelin hit song Rock and Roll.

Despite the intended anti-drug message of the festival most of the band members, and the people in the crowds were using drugs. In fact Ozzy Osbourne who gave a speech against drugs at the press conference had to be carried back to his dressing room after he performed because of the amount of heroin he used before the performance. Most insiders knew the reasons for the festival was a joke to the rock bands. The only reason the festival was put together was to keep Doc McGhee out of jail. None of these bands really cared about a drug free world. They all loved drugs too much to see it go. Most of the bands also fought with each other over their egos. In fact most of the clashes were all about egos. They argued mostly over who went on before whom.

Ozzy Osbourne wanted the prime middle spot over Bon Jovi but Bon Jovi got it instead, and when Ozzy heard that Motley Crue was going on before him he almost walked out of the festival but Ozzy, having a friendship with Motley Crue decided to stay.

The Heavy Metal concerts still do go on, and one of its biggest shows is called the OzzFest. The OzzFest got started when Sharon Osbourne asked the managers of the Lollapalooza Festival if Ozzy could perform in it. The managers refused to let Ozzy perform because according to them Ozzy was not cool enough, and they stated he was a washed up drug addict. In response to this insult against her husband Sharon created her own festival called OzzFest in 1996.

The first OzzFest was a two-day festival held in Phoenix, Arizona on October 25, 1996, and day two was held in Devore, California the next day. From there it became an annual event. The OzzFest is often seen as a gathering of Heavy Metal bands who can come and perform where people really want to see them.

At the 1997 OzzFest there was large protests outside of the festival where the protest was about cancelling Marilyn Manson's performance. These groups were blaming the music of Marilyn Manson as being one of the causes of the Columbine High School Massacre because the killers Eric and Dylan loved Marilyn Manson's music.

When Marilyn Manson came to the 2001 OzzFest the same groups showed up to protest against him. The band called Iron Maiden also had problems at the OzzFest but it had more to do with Sharon Osbourne. This problem unfolded at the 2005 OzzFest when Iron Maiden came there and they saw the stage crew setting up tele-prompters that had lyrics to songs that were sung by Ozzy Osbourne. Iron Maiden found out that Ozzy needed tele-prompters so that he could read his own lyrics during performances.

When Bruce Dickinson the vocalist for Iron Maiden saw Ozzy he ridiculed Ozzy for this, and for having a reality show. Sharon was not going to let this slide, and so Sharon brought in some fans to sit in the front rows, and she paid them to throw things at the band as soon as they start their first song. When Iron Maiden took the stage, and began performing these fans sent by Sharon bombarded Iron Maiden with eggs, bottle caps, and ice cubes. When order was restored Iron Maiden continued to play but during the three songs that followed next Sharon ordered the stage crew to keep switching off and on the P.A. system, and this was cutting power first to Bruce's microphone, and then she was having this done to all the band members' instruments.

Bruce began yelling at the stage crew that they were deliberately ruining their performance, and he was right. Iron Maiden then walked off the stage. Sharon then got on stage, and told the crowd that she loves Iron Maiden but Bruce Dickinson is a prick.

At another OzzFest in 2007 held in Holmdel, New Jersey at the PNC Bank Arts Center 83 people were arrested at one show for underage drinking and drugs. In addition to this two men had died of drug overdoses, and oddly a third died from not being able to sleep for 4 days after consuming 12 Red Bull cans at an OzzFest show. More, stranger things are the coven members who come to the show who brought dead animals with them to throw on stage. The satanic altar calls the bands like to do still go on. Ozzy, when he reunited with Black Sabbath stated it was only an act but oddly it does not look like that nor does it in anyway feel that way.

Chapter 14

In regards to hip-hop music there was a period in hip-hop music called pop-rap. This period of this style of rap reached its height in the popular market from the late 80's into the early 90's. Many urban fans called this form of rap as being 'happy rap'. It was rap that was not of the social issues that was harming poor neighborhoods nor was it about gang-banging and conflicts with police officers. It was more about rapping about yourself, and praising your ego, and macho nature. It was rap about going to a party, dancing, and embracing all kinds of women. Many called it positive rap. But in a Christian understanding was this kind of rap really all about goodness, and being positive?

Pop-rap was given birth in a period of hip-hop called the Old School. The form of the songs was done in the pop music form but with rap lyrics instead of singing. Let us examine a few artists of this style to understand more about this form of music, and the origins of those who started it up.

The person who is credited for bringing forth pop-rap music to the mainstream market was a rapper named M.C. Hammer who later changed his name to Hammer. His real name is Stanley Burrell, and he was born on March 30, 1962. Hammer was born, and raised in the Oakland Housing Projects in Oakland, California. His father worked as a nightclub manager while his mother was mainly a stay at home mom who took care of the children. Sometimes she too would work odd jobs here, and there for extra money.

Hammer's family was very poor as they lived in a three bedroom project apartment. His parents had a total of six kids, and two of the rooms were used by 3 kids per room. There was also this odd story regarding Hammer's father, and his work in the nightclub, and his connection to the Oakland Police Department. Many said that Hammer's father was a police informant, and he did this work for extra cash. No one knows how true this is, and it would be hard to proof because being a police informant in a criminal area would bring a person a lot of problems.

Hammer's father did not make a lot of money, and it was said that the money he did make he was not always good with it. His father would stay out late, and often come home the next morning. This is common while working at a nightclub as nightclubs don't close until dawn, but there were also rumors that his father cheated on his mom with other women, and sometimes would blow this money on them. This was never proven.

Often Hammer's father would take young Stanley to the nightclubs with him. This is where Hammer's love for hip-hop, dancing, and music in general came from. Hammer learned dance moves, and the latest forms of music at this club. He learned how to have style, and how to dance to such a point he would be able to impress people on the streets.

Hammer was so poor along with his brothers that often they would be hungry and bored. When Hammer was 10 years old a friend of his father gave young Stanley a boom-box stereo. This gift was like a magic box to Hammer, a dream come true.

Hammer also had a smart idea in how to use it to make money. Hammer, along with his brother named Louis, decided to take to the street corners and start street dancing in front of white folks for money that was thrown to them or pitched inside a hat or bowel. This is how Hammer would make money for himself. He went out and earned it. Another idea he had was to go to the Oakland A's parking lot and start to collect baseballs that were hit out of the park or would roam the streets looking for lost baseballs. Hammer would then go to the local ballparks, and sell the baseballs for a cheaper price then at the stores.

When Hammer was 11 years old he, and his brother Louis would dance at the Oakland A's parking lot for money. One day the owner of the team named Charles O' Finley noticed Hammer, and took a liking to his energy, and flair he had about him. Charles was looking for a batboy, and he decided to hire Hammer for the job. This happened in the Spring of 1973. Hammer would work as a batboy every spring through the summer and early fall from 1973 to 1980. Hammer met many famous sports stars through this job. Hammer, who was called Stanley at the time, was not only the batboy but he was also well known for being the clubhouse informant. The nickname Hammer came about through baseball great Reggie Jackson. Jackson nicknamed him Hammer because every time Stanley gave a bad report about one of the ballplayers the 'hammer' of Charles O' Finley would come down on them.

During the off-season Hammer as a young pre-teen to a teenager was having problems making enough money to help support his family, so at that time Hammer, who was already hanging-out with the local young gang-members, decided to become one. Hammer would sell drugs to make money, and help support his family. Hammer was also getting into trouble with the law for street fighting, and for stealing from local stores, and people's homes. It was Hammer's baseball family who helped him to get his life straighten out and to move away from the direction of crime.

After high-school Hammer focused his skills on trying to become a professional baseball player. Through his connections he made as a batboy he got to attend a tryout with the San Francisco Giants but he was cut from the list of players who would be accepted. This was a huge heartbreak for Hammer, and his job as batboy was given to a younger kid. Once again Hammer had no direction in life. He then turned to the club scene, and began dancing there, and he also returned to selling drugs. But soon he got involved with the music scene there, and began rapping as an M.C., and showing off his dance skills that he was very talented at doing. Many people there told Hammer he should become a nightclub entertainer and get a crew going.

In that time of the early 80's he was known in the nightclub scene as M.C. Hammer. Soon M.C. Hammer thought that was a good idea but he needed something to fall back on just in case it didn't work out like his baseball ambitions. Hammer would then join the Navy and he served for 3 years looking for direction. Hammer would even entertain sailors during his time there.

After he was released from the Navy, Hammer returned to the nightclub scene, and decided to push toward a career as an entertainer. He began to have many ideas in how to put together new dance moves, and a new style of fashion. He started to project a look, and style to himself, and started to write down rhymes from songs that he was hearing in his head.

In the nightclub in Oakland he formed a crew of dancers who became famous in the nightclub scene for battle dances as they would crush all other crews who challenged them or those Hammer's crew sought to challenge. Hammer would also rap at the club, and his energy, and style was electric to those who heard it. Hammer called his crew the Oaktown Posse.

Hammer created the style of baggy pants, and steel-tip black shoes and sunglasses. This flashy look would soon become popular with other pop-rap acts like Vanilla Ice and Kid N' Play. After putting together his crew, style, and his rhymes Hammer along with the Oaktown Posse travelled to other nightclubs getting gigs in Dallas, Chicago, New York City, Detroit, and Miami. Everywhere they went they blew the lid off the place, and they would energize the whole crowd, and draw them to themselves.

M.C. Hammer and the Oaktown Posse became an act everyone was talking about in the nightclubs. People praised them for their dance moves and for the rhymes of M.C. Hammer. People stated no one could out dance them or out rap them. This reputation brought Hammer, and his crew to one of the owners of a major Dallas nightclub called City Lights. One of the partners named Tommy Quon, who was the future manager of Vanilla Ice, hired Hammer and his crew to be the main stay act of the club. Hammer, and his crew did so but after working several months there Hammer came to find out that Tommy cheated him out of $15,000. Hammer had many shady dealings with club owners before. It was enough to know that if real success was going to happen for him he had to find a way to get it himself and he would use his name to do it.

One night after praying Hammer got the idea to go to a couple of members of the Oakland A's he knew from his batboy days named Mike Davis and Dwayne Murphy. Hammer wanted to start up his own record label called Bust It Productions but to do that Hammer would need $20,000 a piece from each of them for a total of $40,000. Hammer managed to get them to borrow this money to him, and Hammer used the money to start up the label, and he recorded his first album called Feel My Power.

Hammer then using his van travelled, and got gigs in all the major cities he had been to before, and went to those nightclubs, and performed, and once again blew the lid off of every place he went to. After the show Hammer, who made thousands of tapes of his album, would sell his records out of the back of his van after every show.

He began to market himself non-stop, and posted signs promoting his album, and when he was appearing at certain nightclubs. Hammer also set-up a phone number that went into a basement apartment where there he had thousands of copies of his album. People were able to call the number and place an order for his album where there Hammer hired a woman to answer phones, and ship out the order. As a result Hammer sold 60,000 copies of his own debut album, and got every cent of that money. He paid back the loan to Davis and Murphy with plenty of profits to spare. In short Hammer was making a lot of money on his own without the help of record companies.

As the album began to sell a song from the album called Let's Get It Started began to be heard on the radio station. The song quickly became very popular in the nightclub scene. Lyrics from the song would diss several East Coast rappers which resulted in L.L. Cool J. to diss Hammer in a song. The next song that got radio airwave play from the album was called Ring Em. Ring Em became a huge nightclub hit, and a highly requested song on the radio for a song not released on a major label. This song would increase the sales of Hammer's album, and soon Hammer had 100 people working for his Bust It Productions record label taking orders for his album, and promoting it, and his appearances as well. Hammer would create a nightclub show of a grand design. He would hire for the stage more DJ mixers, dancers, musicians, and singers with him as the center rapper for a jaw-dropping show of mixed entertainment of many styles of music. When the show was put together it was unleashed upon the nightclub scene, and it floored anyone who saw it.

M.C. Hammer and the Oaktown Posse grew very big, and they became mega famous in the nightclub scene before they were famous world-wide. One night a record executive from Capitol Records of Los Angeles came to see a show by M.C. Hammer. Hammer's main nightclub was in the City of Oakland where the executive came to see him perform. The executive heard about Hammer through other scouts who stated that the record company really needed to sign him. When the executive saw him that night he understood why they really needed to sign him. The executive sat down with Hammer after the show to offer him a contract thinking he was making Hammer's dreams come true, but when Hammer read the contract he put it down, and told the executive that he was not the first to offer him a record deal, and that he was turning down his deal because he could make more money then what his company was offering on his own. When the executive understood this he then asks Hammer how much he makes per-album sold. After Hammer tells him and the executive offers him a deal where Hammer could make 3 times that amount per-album, and if the album does really well he could make 6 times more and along with that he would give Hammer an advance check of $1,750,000 right there on the table for signing. Hammer then agreed to sign on for Capitol Records. Capitol Records then took Hammer's first album, and they re-recorded it, and Hammer added new songs on the album. Four of the songs from the album would enter the top 20 Billboard 100 singles chart. These songs were Pump It Up, Turn This Mutha Out, Let's Get It Started, and They Put Me in The Mix.

The album became a mainstream success, and it sold 2 million copies. Capitol Records not only got back the investment but they and Hammer made millions off the album. Soon Hammer was recording a second studio album. He would change his musical direction from house/hip-hop music to another kind of sound that became known as pop-rap.

It should be noted that Hammer is also credited as one of the main dancers who reformed house-music dancing and created a new style for it that was originally a style Hammer formed by fusing together Jazz and Funk dancing. Hammer's signature dance move was called the type-writer.

After Hammer recorded his second album many people were curious to this new sound in rap that Hammer was talking all about. In late 1989 on The Arsenio Hall Show M.C. Hammer debuted his new single from his up-coming album called U Can't Touch This. Hammer performed the song in front of millions of white and black young fans. The single was a wildfire hit as it was released as a single that sold millions, and the song hit number 8 on the Billboard 100 singles chart.

When early 1990 came around M.C. Hammer released the second album called Please Hammer Don't Hurt Em. The album hit the number one spot on the Billboard 200 albums chart. It was the first rap album in history to accomplish that feat. The album would go on to sell an unheard of number for a rap album of over 18 million copies. The album still to this day is the largest selling rap album in history. The album had three major hit singles called U Can't Touch This, Have You Seen Her, and Pray.

At that time Hammer's influence was being felt all over the U.S., and around the world. In 1990 he embarked on a tour in Europe that was promoted by the Pepsi Company But half-way through the tour Hammer came under attack by other rappers who began to call him a commercial sell-out. Rappers like L.L. Cool J., Ice Cube and N.W.A, 3rd Bass, and others were his major vocal critics. But other rappers would defend Hammer like Ice-T who stated that they only attack Hammer because they are jealous of Hammer's success.

When it comes to the music industry there is a lot of truth to Ice-T's statements in defense of Hammer. Hammer would also come under fire for way too many samples he used on his songs, and for way too many commercial deals he signed, and for also having a Saturday morning cartoon show.

At the height of Hammer's fame his image was greatly merchandise on t-shirts, posters, lunch boxes, dolls, and even school products from 1990 to 1991. During that time many artists like Prince, and other funk, and Motown artists wanted to sue Hammer for the use of their music samples on his album's songs but the lawsuits did not fall through due to the fact the record company asked permission to use the samples, and they even gave copyright credit on Hammer's album to the artists the samples originally came from.

Many stated that the only reason why they complained was because of how big the album became, and the amount of money it made, seemed to have made them envious. The attacks on Hammer began to affect how the hip-hop fans viewed him. Many of them would hear about the commercials, and at first they seem to not really care but when the Taco Bell commercials came along many felt this was over the top.

When Hammer's debut of his Saturday morning cartoon came out many hip-hop fans started to wonder if these attacks on Hammer being a sell-out could be true but really in truth what is a sell-out in regards to the music industry.

The aim of every artist in the music industry is far different from what the understanding of sell-out is. Every artist is out for success and money. They will change their style in a heartbeat if the money, and success is there. For instance take Ice Cube. Ice Cube stated that Hammer is a sell-out for appealing to white America, and the mainstream fan base but in truth being a gangsta rapper worked for Ice Cube at the time. That is how he made money. But Ice Cube could not dance nor put together rap songs that appeal to both sides of the coin. Because if he could at the time he would have done so. To understand the proof of this Ice Cube when he began to make movies started to make films that appeal to both white and black America. There were two reasons why he made those films...money and success. In Hammer's time Ice Cube did not have that avenue Hammer did, and he walked through it, and was called a sell-out but when Ice Cube later on got that same avenue he also walked through it so in the understanding of sell-out what does that make Ice Cube? It is always known that artists will hate on other artists who make more money than them in the music industry.

By 1991 the attacks on Hammer were chopping away his famed image in the eyes of the fans. In 1991 M.C. Hammer dropped the M.C. from his name, and officially was called Hammer. He would release his third album that had millions of dollars spent on its promotion. The album was called Too Legit, To Quick. The record company was expecting the album to sell just as many copies as his second album but their gamble did not pay in the end. The album sold 5 million copies. 5 million copies is usually a world-wide success, but not when you're excepting another 10 to 18 million copies. Hammer tried to boost the sales of the album through the Addams Family 2 soundtrack where he even appeared in a cameo in the film. He also tried to boost its sales by hosting an episode of Saturday Night Live where he was also the musical guest. But these efforts failed to raise record sales.

During the time of the album's release Hammer had a very expensive U.S. tour going loaded with dancers, singers, DJs, musicians, and other acts. But lack of sales from the album caused the record company to be unable to fund the tour all the way through. Their next effort was to get the popular Boyz 2 Men R&B group to join Hammer on the tour in 1992 to boost ticket sales but this effort also did not work, and the tour would bring sadness to Boyz 2 Men.

At a concert in Chicago the manager of Boyz 2 Men named Khalil Roundtree was murdered under strange circumstances. The story was he was out trying to score drugs, and was murdered by a drug-dealer who tried to rob him. But the story however has yet to be proven. Because the money that the record company was excepting was not made this brought financial ruin first to Hammer's record label which had scores of artists on it like Oaktown's 3,5,7 who all lost their jobs. Soon lawsuits were filed against Hammer who were mostly charging him with fraud, and not paying them back.

Hammer tried another attempt to make a comeback. Due to the change of taste in fans Hammer changed his image to a more hardcore gangsta image. The album he would release under this change came out in 1994 under the name The Funky Headhunter. Two noted singles were released called It's All Good and Bumps. The video to Bumps featured over 50 half-naked women showing off their breasts and butt to the camera while wearing two-piece swimsuits. Hammer rapped in the mist of them while wearing a one-piece swimsuit which may as well been his underwear. Hammer also filmed this lewd and nasty video in his huge mansion upon his personal swimming pool area. This album also failed, and the domino effect came rolling. In time due to the lawsuits Hammer lost his massive wealth which included his cars, his jewels, his gold, and many other expensive things. He would also lose his massive mansion as well.

Overtime Hammer found a career in another field called the Christian television industry where he preaches sometimes on TBN. Hammer is also an ordain minister. The last known video he made was a video where he was trying to save Jay-Z's soul.

Another rapper of this music style of rap was called by the name Vanilla Ice. Vanilla Ice's real name was Robert Van Winkle, and he was born on Halloween Day in October of 1967 in Dallas, Texas. Robert's dad left his mother when Rob was at an early age. The reason for it was said that Rob's mom had a bad habit of cheating on the men she was in a relationship with.

Rob's mom would marry another man who was a car-salesman.

His last name was Winkle, and so that last name was given to Rob at an early age. Rob's home life was not a functional home. His step-father was constantly fighting with his mother about coming home late with lying excuses, and for strange phone calls she received from other men. This caused Rob to have a troubled childhood, and he often wandered the streets looking for something to do.

As a pre-teen one day Rob wandered his way to a nightclub in Dallas where the scene of hip-hop and breakdancing was going on. At the time it was a new musical movement, and the clubs were the ones promoting it to the mainstream music industry. Rob would sit outside the club listening to the music coming through the walls of the club. He would soon hang out outside the club, and started to get to know the crowds coming in and out of the club. Other young people around his age or twice as old also used to hang out there as well. Rob was usually the only white face there.

Through the crowds and the people who would hang there Rob started to learn the new dance moves, and learned how to break dance. He also learned how to rhyme, and he turned out to be naturally talented at rapping and dancing. Rob was good with words, and how to throw out words to a beat. He was also good at catching on to the timing, steps, and movements in the dance moves he learned. Even though he was the only white face among them he became accepted by the black and Latin crowds because he was able to do what they can do. Rob also took upon himself the street attitude, and slang as it came to him in a natural way for the fact they treated him better then his own family did. To Rob in that time those friends, and that crowd was his family.

Rob spent a few years hanging out there, and soon he found himself going inside the club even though he was underage. What got Rob into the club was that some of his older friends knew people at the doors, and they got him in. Rob would show off his dance skills often in the club, and dress in the style of hip-hop and new wave.

Soon Rob's mother met another man who lived in Miami, Florida, and his mom left his step-father to move into his home. The area was a run-down middle-class suburb of Miami in South Florida. Near this place was downtown Miami, and the famous and also notorious nightclub scene of Miami. The downtown club scene in Miami was a very dangerous place to be at times especially in that time when Rob was very young. Once Rob moved into this man's home things were the same all over again. Rob would witness fights between his mom, and her new boyfriend as she would still come home late, and get strange phone calls from other men.

Rob quickly took to the streets of downtown Miami, and went to a club that played hip-hop, house, and freestyle music. The club he went to was mostly attended by African and Latin American young men and women. Many of them were also gang-bangers and many were not but there for the club scene like Rob was. At first Rob was looked at crossways because he was white showing up at a club that normally did not have any white people in it, but Rob was already schooled in how to talk, and walk the walk of the street culture.

Rob would stand up for himself, and on the dance floor he would show what he could do. Rob also was underage at that time, and he would get into the club using a fake I.D. he got in Dallas before he left. But after a while he did not need the I.D. as everyone came to know him and accepted him as a peer.

Rob was able to dance and rap, and this brought a crowd of friends toward him at the nightclub. Rob also picked up some bad drug habits at the club as well. Many of the crowd goers were into marijuana, cocaine, and a drug that was new at the time called rock-cocaine also known as crack. Rob began using many of these drugs as most of the crowds would.

At this club Rob met a DJ named DJ D-Shay, and the two would become good friends. When D-Shay would mix on the stage he often had Rob to come up, and take the mic and rap to the beats D-Shay would mix on stage. Soon the crowds, because Rob was white, started to call him 'the vanilla rapper'.

Rob at first hated this nickname but D-Shay saw something about the name that it worked as a stage name. Soon Rob started to perform under the name M.C. Vanilla. Rob would find another passion that went on in the Miami streets just outside the club. This passion was motorcycle racing.

After learning from a club friend how to drive and race them Rob wanted to buy his own but did not have the cash to do so. So Rob along with D-Shay sought a job position at the nightclub to be a regular opening act. The owner liked the two of them because they were that good, and gave them the job but this also made other acts very jealous, and Rob without really knowing it made some enemies. During this time when Rob got the job it was said that he also made friends with a drug-dealer he knew from the club. It was said that Rob to make some extra cash would at times sell drugs for him but no one knows how true this is but it is often said regarding his time there.

Soon Rob would get enough money to buy his own motorcycle, and he hit the streets doing drag races on the Miami strip. Rob became very popular in the club scene for his performances and his racing.

Many girls flocked to him, and people respected him, but not everyone liked him. There were also people who hated him. One night after coming out of a club one of these men who hated him challenged Rob to a fist-fight. Rob took him on and beat the man up. When Rob had him down the man being sore about getting beaten up by a white guy took out a knife, and began to stab Rob multiple times in the leg. Rob was rushed to the hospital after losing a lot of blood but he recovered from his injury, and was soon back at the club.

One night while Rob was staying at D-Shay's apartment Rob and D-Shay were looking to get high, and went out to buy some marijuana and cocaine. They drove to the Miami strip and found a guy they usually got drugs from. When Rob and D-Shay saw him they parked the car and got out to buy these drugs from him. Once they bought the drugs they were about to head toward the car when out of nowhere a car came speeding up, and a man pointed an automatic out of the window, and opened fire on the drug-dealers on the strip. Rob and D-Shay quickly threw themselves to the ground as the bullets flew over them hitting the walls. After the drive-by everyone began to scatter as the police were on their way. Rob and D-Shay ran toward the car, and drove out of there quick and went back to D-Shay's apartment. That night Rob and D-Shay were smoking marijuana laced with cocaine wherein if you smoke cocaine it becomes crack.

While Rob was high on these substances he began to have a strange inspiration, and started to write a rap about what he just experienced, and what he was feeling. Rob named the rap-song Ice, Ice, Baby as Ice was the nickname for crack on the streets.

Soon Rob's mother had a nasty falling out with her boyfriend that resulted in Rob's step-father taking his mother back. Rob then had to pack up, and move back to Dallas. Rob once he moved back was quickly back in the club scene in Dallas and began to see old friends. He also started racing his motorcycle where through these drag races he met other motorcycle racers who were connected with the motorcross circuit. They were the ones who brought Rob in to race in the motorcross races.

At that same time Rob was perfecting his breakdancing and dance moves. He soon created a move that became his signature dance move that was called the 'Ice'. Soon Rob was performing his breakdancing skills at the nightclub in Dallas called City Lights. At that time many performers were there wherein many of them later became famous. Performers like M.C Hammer, Public Enemy, N.W.A., and others.

At first Rob would only dance there, and he focused his attention to motorcycle racing. Rob became so good at motorcycling he ended up entering the Grand National Championship. Rob would take first place there to the shock of many. From there Rob would enter the next two Grand National Championships, and he would win also at those races, taking home a total of three Grand National Championship trophies. After that, during a race Rob ended up having an accident, and he broke his ankle. Rob at that point was feeling like racing was not in the cards for him, and he didn't want to end up crippled so he decided to focus his attention on an entertainment career.

After he recovered from the accident, Rob went back to the nightclub at City Lights, and one night the club held an open mic challenge to anyone who could step-up and rap, and command the stage. It should be noted that no white person at the time ever rapped on stage in front of this kind of crowd. The man who brought on the open mic challenge was a DJ named DJ Earthquake who later became Vanilla Ice's main DJ. When Earthquake brought on the challenge one of Rob's friends nicknamed Squirrel dared Rob to go on stage. Rob did so without fear, and grabbed the mic and began to rap to Earthquake's beats. The people in the crowd were shocked that a white rapper could be that good. One of the managers of the club remarked about that night that Rob performed at a level that was just as good as the main acts and that he performed in a way that you saw he belonged on stage, that he performed like a star.

Soon the managers wanted Rob to rap as an opening act if he brought together a crew meaning a DJ, and some dancers. From there Rob called DJ D-Shay from Miami, and told him about the gig, and asked if he would come to Dallas, and stay with him and be his DJ. D-Shay accepted and came to Dallas to be his first DJ. Rob then brought together some dancers from the club who also wanted to be on stage, and they would first practice their moves at malls, and street corners making sure they were fit for the stage.

Once they were brought together Rob called himself Vanilla Ice taking the Ice part of his name from his signature breakdancing move. The crew would call themselves the V.I.P which stood for Vanilla Ice Posse. They were then hired by City Lights to become the opening act of the main acts of the night. Soon

Tommy Quon, one of the owners of City Lights who had connections with the music industry, saw that money could be made off the Vanilla Ice Posse. He knew they could be mainstream stars. Tommy would then go to Rob, and his crew to sign them to a management contract where through it he would be his agent, and get him a record deal. Tommy from the start of becoming Rob's manager seemed to have a strong influence over Rob. Tommy was not only Rob's agent, and manager he was also his boss at City Lights. Whatever Tommy wanted Rob to do Rob would do it or go along with it. Tommy would then put up the money to take Rob, and his crew into the studio to record Rob's debut album called Hooked which was released on an independent label. Tommy would hire several

DJ's to provide beats for Rob's rap songs but Tommy also had a bad reputation for not paying the artists the money they were owned for their work. During the recording of Hooked it was no different as several DJ's were not paid after making beats for Rob's songs. This would bring some major problems for Rob later on.

Once Hooked was recorded Tommy took a page out of Hammer's book, and began to sell the album at nightclub shows the V.I.P would do, and also they sold the album out of the back of a van. They even got several small shopping mall stores to sell the album. Through those efforts the album called Hooked would sell over 48,000 copies which was a nice chunk of cash.

Tommy through his radio connections in Georgia gave the Vanilla Ice single called Play That Funky Music to a couple of DJ's there he knew. When the radio stations first started to play it the song really did not catch on with the people. One night a radio disc jockey in Georgia flipped over the record to play the B-side song of the record which was called Ice, Ice, Baby. Nearly overnight the song became the most requested song on his station. Soon the song caught on with other radio stations, and they started to play it. The song also became the most requested song at those radio stations also.

Soon Tommy Quon put up $8,000 to film a music video for the song Ice, Ice, Baby. They shot the video in Miami, and the video first appeared on a channel called The Box, and then it started to be shown on MTV. Sales for the single started to greatly climb, and it was quickly moving up the Billboard charts.

Around that time Tommy got Vanilla Ice, and his crew to join the last leg of the Stop The Violence Tour which featured other hip-hop acts like Public Enemy, Sir Mix-A-Lot, Ice-T, M.C. Hammer, EPMD, and others. Rob during the tour became good friends with the members of Public Enemy. They sought out Rob as well to come, and join Def Jam Records as they were selling him to Russell Simmons. Rob originally wanted to sign with Def Jam but Tommy wanted Rob to sign with SBK Records stating that SBK was making a better offer. So Rob signed with SBK instead. SBK wanted to re-record the album Hooked to make it better, and Rob would also add new songs to it.

While re-recording his debut album for SBK Rob would make music industry history. The song Ice, Ice, Baby would become the first rap song in history to take the number one spot on the Billboard 100 singles chart. All of America, white, black, Latin, Asian, you name it were listening to this song, and came to know the lyrics by heart.

While the V.I.P was recording the album for SBK Records Tommy wanted to change the image of Vanilla Ice and his crew. He would also change the style of music they did. Vanilla Ice originally was not a pop-rap rapper but he was a hip-hop rapper who also had a more hardcore feel to his lyrics. Ice at the time was rapping about violence, gangs, sex, and drugs. If you understand the lyrics of Ice, Ice, Baby you clearly see that. Tommy however wanted Ice's sound to change, and not his lyrics per-say. Tommy saw the direction Hammer was going in to bring forth pop-rap, and he also knew a lot of money was going to be made from this new style called pop-rap. So Tommy wanted Ice's songs to have the vibe of pop-music, and he wanted Ice to change his style of fashion.

So instead of wearing Adidas' sweat pants, and gym shoes Ice was to wear baggy pants, and steel tip black shoes. Instead of a gold-chain Ice was to wear sunglasses. Instead of a fade Ice was to get lines in his hair. In short, Tommy wanted Vanilla Ice to project the image of M.C. Hammer. Rob really did not like this idea but Tommy demanded this of him. It should be noted that people on the inside at the time remarked that the relationship between Tommy and SBK in how they managed Rob was like a puppet master, and his puppet. Rob was the puppet and they pulled the strings. Soon Rob's debut album was re-released by SBK Records, and the album was called To The Extreme. The album was a smash hit and in 1990 it came to take the number one spot on the Billboard 200 albums chart being the second rap album in history to take that spot.

The album would go on to sell over 11 million copies. Vanilla Ice's fame was at its height from the summer of 1990 throughout 1991. But he soon came under attack by other artists in the music industry. The attack was first started by M.C. Hammer and his people. Hammer stated that Vanilla Ice seized his look and his sound. In truth it was Tommy Quon who did that but Vanilla Ice went along with it.

Also keep in mind that Vanilla Ice's album To The Extreme took over the number one spot on the Billboard 200 albums chart from Hammer's album called Please Hammer Don't Hurt Em. One might think that some jealously issues could have risen on Hammer's part when you consider that Hammer's second album had songs that imitated heavily from other artists.

As a result of the attack Vanilla Ice was to appear on the Arsenio Hall Show. Arsenio Hall was a good friend of Hammer, and helped him to propel his career. When Vanilla Ice was going to come on his show Arsenio had the idea to ambush him, and make him look bad. When Vanilla Ice was on his way there he got word that people were saying bad things about him. They even went so far to call him a racist, and state that the only reason why white people are listening to rap is because they now have a white face on rap. Of course they fail to answer what was the reason all those white fans were listening to Hammer, and buying his t-shirts and posters. The statements being made against Vanilla Ice at that time were in fact lies said out of jealous artists many of them being black, and from the hip-hop, and R&B new jack style who personally did not like Vanilla Ice because he was making more money than them. Vanilla Ice was not a racist, and white fans were not buying rap albums because of him, they were buying them before him, and started to buy them at larger numbers due to Hammer's second album. That was the truth not told on the Arsenio Hall Show that day.

When Ice got on the show he was supported by a friend from Public Enemy named Flava Flav. But Arsenio quickly attacked his friendship with Flav, and he attacked him by saying that Ice said foul statements about Hammer but that was not true at all in fact it was the other way around.

Hall accused the music industry during the interview with Ice for setting up a white face to sell rap albums where people in the audience who were mostly black even booed Hall for saying that. In short Hall wanted to 'punk' Ice because he simply did not like him for being a white rapper. For Rob this was nothing new.

As the fame of Vanilla Ice got bigger due to the record sales the record company made merchandise off the image of Vanilla Ice. Soon several companies began to sell Vanilla Ice's lunch boxes, posters, t-shirts, pencils, dolls, school products, and even a board game, and other products. Ice was also featured in several teen magazines. He would also soon enter into a relationship with pop-singer Madonna but after 11 months of dating each other Rob dumped her when he found out she was putting him in her book called Sex.

The more record sales, and the more fame that Rob was getting the more attacks he received from his hip-hop peers. His main critics were 3rd Bass, N.W.A., Ice-T, and even Kid N' Play, and several others. 3rd Bass even did a music video all about hating on Vanilla Ice called Pop Goes the Weasel. But also one must find it strange that the only time 3rd Bass got a mainstream hit song is when they mentioned Vanilla Ice's name.

Other artists like Kid N' Play, and Marky Mark and the Funky Bunch also mentioned Vanilla Ice in some of their songs, and they also 'dissed' him. In Marky Mark's case one finds it strange that he would diss Vanilla Ice when he being also being a white rapper never would have made it into the market without the door being opened for him by Vanilla Ice. It seems the attacks were just a hater feast on someone else's success.

This is often seen in the music industry but it's usually behind the scenes. Despite these attacks, Rob's career was still going very strong, and his fans in the millions were standing with him. Rob would soon get a part for a movie called Teenage Mutant Ninja Turtles part 2 where he recorded a popular song for the soundtrack called Ninja Rap, and performed it in the movie.

He would also give a show-stopping performance as a musical guest on Saturday Night Live. In 1991 Rob would soon embark on the To The Extreme Tour that would eventually take him around the world. But during the tour the ball so to speak was about to drop. Due to a coming change of taste among fans Tommy Quon wanted to harden up Vanilla Ice's image. He did this by writing a so-called autobiography of Vanilla Ice's life. In this biography Quon over-exaggerated Rob's gang activity in South Florida, and stated other un-truths about Rob's life.

Tommy did this without first speaking to Rob about this but once the biography was put out there Rob once again went along with it. When the media found out about the lies of the biography Vanilla Ice was quickly attacked for it. People in the media, and the music industry started to call him a fraud and a fake. Vanilla Ice would come on the defense, and stated to his peers in the music industry at an awards show that they could kiss his white butt.

By late 1991 due to all the tongue lashing about him in the media, and in the industry Rob's fame as Vanilla Ice was shipwrecked. The evidence to his downfall came in late 1991 when Vanilla Ice was to star in his first full feature film called Cool As Ice. The film was supposed to be a nationwide feature but due to the tongue lashing only MTV promoted the film. The film was also reduced to be shown only in 393 theaters. The film was made for over 2 million dollars, and Rob was paid 1 million dollars to do the film but the film only made $638,000 after it's release in October of 1991.

The career of Vanilla Ice in the U.S. mainstream music industry was now over. From 1992 to 1994 Vanilla Ice was still famous in other parts of the world especially in South America and Russia but no longer famous in the U.S. In late 1991 Rob was indirectly involved with funding the gangsta rap record company called Death Row Records. The story behind this was told by Rob, and other sources, and it is a frightful event indeed.

The story goes back to a DJ mixer who created the beats for Vanilla Ice's hit song called Ice, Ice, Baby. The DJ created the sound while working on the album called Hooked. When looking to get paid Rob's manager Tommy refused to pay him for it, and in short used this DJ for his work. Later on after the fame of the single hit through the roof this same DJ sought help in getting what was owned to him from a man named Suge Knight. Knight was Dr. Dre's partner at the time, and he was a very feared man working as a producer in the rap music industry. Knight is suspected of being a member of the Black Mafia, and police records reveal that Knight has connections with both the Bloods and the Crips in regards to gun-running sales. It was said that Knight has brutal ways of getting what he wants from other artists in the music industry.

Dre and Knight at the time were trying to start up Death Row records but they lacked the funds in doing so. When the DJ came to Knight with this complaint Knight saw a way to get the funds. Knight would get information on where Rob would be at certain times in the day, and even got phone numbers in how to reach him. Knight then began making intimidating phone calls to Rob about the money he owned his 'client'. I say 'client' like this because obviously Knight was not a lawyer, and the people he helped Knight would call them his 'clients'.

Rob at first would ignore the phone calls, and hang up on him. Soon in late 1991 Rob was eating at a L.A. restaurant surrounded by his bodyguards. Suge and his men then entered the restaurant, and Suge's men punched out a couple of Rob's bodyguards, and subdued the rest. Suge and a few of his men sat down at the same table with Rob, and began to further intimidate Rob, and play with his head, and told him he owns them money. One of the managers then threatened to call the police, and then Suge and his men left.

It should be noted that several of Suge's men used to play football for the NFL's Oakland Raiders. Two weeks after this event Rob was staying at the Bel Age Hotel on the 15th floor. While Rob was in his room the door to his room opens up, and Suge and his men come walking into his room uninvited. How they got into the hotel in the first place it was said that someone was working for Suge at the doorway entrance who let Suge and his men in. The man even told Suge what floor, and room Rob was staying in.

When Suge was in the room he asked Rob to come out on the balcony to talk about the problem he had with Rob. Once on the balcony Suge explained to him that he represented a 'client' who worked as a DJ on his single Ice, Ice, Baby, and was not paid any money for it. Suge told Rob that this was an unfair action, and to make it right Suge had some papers for Rob to sign that would sign the rest of the rights of the single over to Suge and the money that would be made from the single from then on would go to his 'client'. In truth it was going to Suge Knight.

Rob told Suge he was not responsible for the man not getting paid. In truth he was not responsible for the man not getting paid, Tommy Quon was responsible for that. When Suge saw that Rob was not going to sign it Suge then put the papers down, and then violently grabbed Rob, and pushed him against the balcony. While Suge was holding him there against the balcony Suge told him that if he did not sign the papers he was going to throw him over the balcony. Rob then signed the papers.

The money that Suge got for Ice, Ice, Baby was used to start up Death Row Records. In 1994 Rob under the name Vanilla Ice released a new album that had a more rasta sound to his rap-style. Rob's comeback album was harder, and darker filled with songs about murder, and hardcore drug use. But hardly anyone bought the album. Rob was still a rich man however, and he still is to this day.

In 1994 Rob was throwing drug parties in his mansion, and fell into a state of depression. One night at a party Rob tried to commit suicide by overdosing on heroin and cocaine together where he tried to speedball himself to death. A friend of his knowing what to do revived Rob, and they then rushed him to a hospital. In time Rob would recover from his depression but he still loves to use drugs. Rob eventually became an underground artist where he does a rap-rock style of music. He also owns a home improvement company.

The music of Hammer and Vanilla Ice may seem tamed in some ways. But under a Christian stand-point, and in the scope of the music there are some influences to it that should be questioned. Their music presented an influence of machoism, suave sexism, and egotism. Along with this you can add a degree of a male supremacist attitude, and sexual immorality. Many songs off of Vanilla Ice's album To The Extreme were often obscene in it's sexual references. When Rob wrote the song Ice, Ice, Baby he was high on marijuana, and cocaine. Such drugs according to the Bible can leave people open to demonic influences when abused. An analysis of the song Ice, Ice, Baby does reveal most shocking things when done in the understanding of what the street slang meanings were, and the state of mind Rob was in when he wrote it.

The chorus of the song is the title of the song called Ice, Ice,

Baby. The word ice back in that time was a street slang for the word krack which is rock-cocaine. So the chorus actually means Krack, Krack, Baby. The opening lyrics to the rap song introduces the listener to a brand new invention. Note that krack was a new form of drug on the streets at that time in the 1980's.

He proceeds to rap about himself as being a vandal which is to mean a destructive person. He then raps about his ego in regards to his dance and rap skills declaring he could take down anyone who challenges him, and he indicates that he does this because he is driven by something evil. He states that he uses his rap ability like a poisonous mushroom that can corrupt a person's thinking like a drug, and that he is always on point, and he does not mess around. Then the chorus comes again with krack, krack, baby. He then raps about the underground culture, and raps about MCs who use rhymes like frying people's brains in a pan, and if an MC is not sharp he burns up.

He then raps about what happened to him regarding the drive-bye he witnessed on the Miami strip and then proceeds to rap about the lifestyle of drug-dealers in downtown Miami. The chorus then repeats again to krack, krack, baby. The last set of lyrics finds him rapping about the Miami music underground scene that housed every form of the new wave music in their clubs. That rappers can influence people like ninja's do to their victims wherein the fan won't see it coming till it influences him or her. Every set of lyrics finishes with the words if there was a problem he would solve it meaning he would violently solve it. The song would finish with the chorus krack, krack, baby.

Keep in mind that this song was a number one song on the Billboard 100 singles chart, and there have been many songs with a subversive meaning from other artists. In the 2000s Rob one time made a You-tube video, and gave an apology for the bad influences his songs caused others, and stated he was only a puppet on a string. Not too many artists ever gave an apology for it.

The two other acts to cover who were popular during this period nicknamed 'happy rap' were the duos of Kid N' Play, and DJ Jazzy Jeff and The Fresh Prince. The styles of these two duos originally was not pop-rap. Pop-rap was not officially born until

Hammer released the album called Please Hammer Don't Hurt Em. The two duos rapped under the form of hip-hop but it was a safe, and commercial form of hip-hop. Meaning it was able to reach a mainstream of whites and blacks, and other up-scale Americans. The duos did not match the image style of pop-rap until after Hammer released his second album.

Kid N' Play was a hip-hop rap, and later comedy duo who came from New York City. The duo is composed of Christopher Reid known as Kid and Christopher Martin known as Play. Their DJ was named DJ Wiz. The height of their fame was in the late 80's to early 1990's. They started off having successful musical careers before branching out into acting. Reid and Martin first started performing in high-school. In the high-school they went to there were many rival hip-hop crews who would perform and battle-rap each other. Sometimes they would fist-fight each other over girls. Reid was part of a crew called The Turnout Brothers and Martin was part of a crew called The Super Lovers. In time Reid and Martin being among the best rappers, and dancers in their crew came to build a respect for each other.

The two of them would join forces, and they formed a crew in 1986 called The Fresh Force Crew. They then began writing rap songs, and soon they made connections with a studio owner. They would manage to raise up some money, and they used it to record two songs in 1986 called She's a Skeezer and Rock Me. In 1987 a record label manager named Hurby 'Luv Bug' Azor who was the manager of Salt-N-Pepper heard their demo tape. Hurby knew these two were future stars, and envisioned an act or image that would make them stars. Hurby brought Reid and Martin in for a meeting to discuss what he had planned, and then later in that same year he got them a record contract. He also would change their names to Kid N' Play. The focus of their style of hip-hop would be positive, and fun lyrics back by pop-instrumental tracks. Later this style was developed into pop-rap.

Kid N' Play would record their first album called 2 Hype in 1988. The image they projected was a teen-friendly image with dance moves that became their trademark moves. Kid's visual trademark was his hi-top fade where at its peak stood ten inches high. Play's visual trademark was his regularly wore eight-ball jackets.

Kid N' Play's most famous dance move was called the Kick-Step. The Kick-Step was pattern after the Funky Charleston which was a dance move during the Jazz Age of the 1920's. In the 1980's was the rise of urban street dancing called by many styles from breakin, house, and new jack swing style. The Kick-Step was different from the Funky Charleston because you needed two people to do it rather than one. The dance move became famous when Kid N' Play did it in their film called House Party in a scene where Kid N' Play dance battle the characters of Tisha Campbell and A.J. Johnson.

The success of the album 2 Hype, and the positive image of the two rap stars made them millions of dollars. Because of this image the duo were offered a movie deal, and at that same time they would record their second album. In 1990 due to the album Please Hammer Don't Hurt Em Kid N' Play would change up their fashion by wearing baggy pants in their music videos.

When they released their second album called Funhouse the album was under the full style of pop-rap music. In 1990 Kid N' Play would star in the movie called House Party. House Party was released by New Line Cinema, and the movie brought in such actors and actresses who were mostly unknown at the time like Martin Lawrence and Tisha Campbell who went on to star in the television sitcom Martin. The film also starred Full Force and Robin Harris. For Robin Harris it was his last film appearance. Harris died of a heart-attack nine days after the film was released.

House Party was a film written and directed by Reginald Hudlin who came from the elite college of Harvard University. It was based on an award-winning student film Reginald did at the film class at Harvard. Reginald originally wrote the feature film version to star DJ Jazzy Jeff and The Fresh Prince, but when New Line Cinema bought the rights to the film they were in the process of suing Jazz and Prince for a song they did called Nightmare on My Street. The people at New Line Cinema then offered the part to Kid N' Play who accepted it.

The film was made for about 2 million dollars, but the film at the box-office would gross 26 million dollars in ticket sales. The film became a huge success in box-office returns. The film would soon come under fire by Church groups and moral groups. They noted that the film was mostly watched by pre-teens and teenagers, and was hardly at all viewed by adults.

The film's characters were seen constantly swearing in every scene they did. The strong language was used throughout the film so much people stated it became its own language, and that it was disgraceful to hear kids use such language because they heard it so much in this film. They also complained about the strong sexual content in the movie. In one scene Kid was shown sneaking into the house of his girlfriend played by Tisha Campbell. When the two characters were in her room they were about to have sex but they stopped because Kid's condom was too old to use. Another scene shows a large over weight man having rough sex with a woman, and when the large man catches the three characters looking in on him he then gets up, gets a gun, and attempts to kill them by shooting at them. Another scene shows Kid being locked up in jail, and he has to rap his way out of being gang-raped by a bunch of men in his prison cell.

Due to the success of the movie their album Funhouse became their most successful album in their career. It produced three hit singles called Energy, Ain't Gonna Hurt Nobody, and Funhouse. The single Ain't Gonna Hurt Nobody hit number one on the Billboard Rap singles chart. The album called Funhouse would hit number one on the Billboard Rap albums' chart.

Soon Kid N' Play went to work in making the sequel to House Party, and they recorded their third album. In 1991 Kid N' Play starred in their second film House Party 2 which was a film that promoted education, and for young African-Americans to attend college. The film also came under fire by Church and moral groups for strong language and sexual content. These attacks would hit hard on them because most of Kid N' Play's fans were children, pre-teens, and teenagers.

The film House Party 2 was made at a higher budget of 5 million dollars, and it grossed at the box-office 19 million dollars making it another box-office gross success. In that same year they released their album called Face the Nation. Their third album failed to reach the success of their second album due to the changing taste of fans. From 1990 to 1991 Kid N' Play's image was made into merchandise as their faces were on t-shirts, posters, lunch boxes, and even dolls. In that time they even had an NBC Saturday Morning cartoon show that lasted for one season.

By 1992 Kid N' Play, instead of making albums, focused their careers on making movies. In that year they would release their third film called Class Act. Kid in the film would lose his trademark hi-top fade. Class Act was an urban retelling of Mark Twain's book called The Prince and the Pauper. The film was made for 5 million dollars, and it would gross at the box office 13 million dollars making it a box office gross success. The duo's film also came under fire for strong language, violence, and sexual content, but the film critics praised them for turning out good performances.

Their fourth film was House Party 3 that featured the debut of Chris Tucker but Tucker refuses to admit he was ever in House Party 3. The film also starred the late Bernie Mac and T.L.C. House Party 3 would be the last film up to now that the duo made together. The film was made for 5 million dollars, and it grossed 19 million dollars making the film also a box-office return success, but the film critics panned the film, and called it a horrible movie.

By 1994 Kid N' Play faded from the popular scene of both the music and movie industry. Currently up until this writing the duo, seeing how the movie industry keeps making one retro film after another are trying to make another House Party film for fans who love nostalgia.

DJ Jazzy Jeff & The Fresh Prince was a rap group who came from the West Side of Philadelphia, Pennsylvania. In the career of this duo they would make history at the Grammy Awards for being the first rap group to win a Grammy for Best Rap Performance for the song Parents Just Don't Understand in 1989.

Rapper Will Smith first met DJ Jazzy Jeff whose real name was Jeff Townes at a house party one night in 1985 that was being held only a few doors down from Smith's residence. Will Smith at that time was trying to make a name for himself in West Philadelphia's local hip-hop scene. When Smith showed up at the party Jazz was already upset that his MC had not showed up yet. Smith asked Jazz if he could fill in, and when he did so there was an instant strong chemistry between the two of them. When the two were rockin' the party Jazz's MC showed up, and Jazz ignored him.

Soon after the party the two of them joined forces along with a beat boxer nicknamed Ready Rock C. The duo, along with Ready Rock C, started playing at many house parties and block parties. At one of the gigs they did the three men caught the attention of a man named Paul Oakenfold who was the A&R man for Jive Records. Jive Records at the time owned Word Up Records which was a label that recorded rap artists. Paul brought Jazz, Prince, and Rock C. there to record some rap singles.

In 1986 the crew recorded their first single called Girls Ain't Nothing But Trouble. The song was the birth of Will Smith's style of rap. The song was about the misadventures Will Smith had with certain girls he dated as the song sampled from the theme song of I Dream of Jeannie.

Smith's style of hip-hop was known for telling light-hearted stories that were free from profanity. The style of DJ Jazzy Jeff & The Fresh Prince was called at the time commercial rap, and later in 1990 they were called pop-rap.

DJ Jazzy Jeff was very well known for his skills as a DJ as he was a master at turntable acrobatics. He is credited for being the inventor of a style of turntable scratching called transforming. One month before Will Smith graduated from high-school the song Girls Ain't Nothing But Trouble became a hit song on the radio. Based on this success Russell Simmons, who was working for Jive Records at the time, signed DJ Jazzy Jeff and The Fresh Prince to Jive Records.

The duo who recorded their first album for Word Up Records would then have to re-record the album for Jive Records to make it better. They also dropped Ready Rock C. from their group, and only used him when they needed him. This caused Ready Rock C. to sue them later on for money that was not paid to him for songs he helped them to do.

In 1987 DJ Jazzy Jeff & The Fresh Prince released their debut album called Rock the House. The album would go gold selling 300,000 copies, and the duo found themselves on a major tour with Run DMC, Public Enemy, and others. In 1988 Jazz and Prince released their second album called He's the DJ, I'm the Rapper. Through this album they released the single called Parents Just Don't Understand. The single was a huge hit, and a music video was made for it, and was constantly played on MTV. This album that was recorded in the U.S. and the U.K. became a multi-platinum seller.

Due to the music video and the success of their single the duo were a household name all across the nation. They would even have a successful 900 number. The duo was launched into mainstream success, and in 1989 they would become the first rap group to win a Grammy at the 1989 Grammy Awards. Their Grammy win however did not sit well with other hip-hop acts who felt that the duo were a commercial group and not a real hip-hop act. The duo's defenders stated that the acts who spoke against them were doing so out of envy.

The next single that was released off their album was called Nightmare on My Street. This single would bring the duo a lawsuit from New Line Cinema for copyright issues. The song was about the duo having a fictional confrontation with the horror film child serial murderer, and dream-demon named Freddy Krueger. The single came out at the time New Line Cinema released the movie Nightmare on Elm Street: The Dream Master in 1988.

The people at New Line Cinema filed several lawsuits against the rap duo for making their star horror film character to look cartoonish, and for making money off the character. Due to the lawsuit by New Line Cinema the movie company refused to allow Jazz and Prince to star in the film House Party. Will Smith, who later spoke about it said that he and Jazz did not care much for starring in House Party, but many said that by not starring in House Party was a career blow to them at the time.

In 1989 the duo released their next album called And in This Corner. The lead single off the song was called I Could Beat Mike Tyson. In the video Will Smith has a fictional fight with Mike Tyson wherein he loses. By 1989 this album would fail to reach the success of their previous one, and in sales it only went gold. The popularity of the group was fading due to the fact that fans got into pop-rap acts like M.C. Hammer, and eventually Vanilla Ice, Kid N' Play, Young MC, and others.

Fans also got into more serious acts like Ice-T, 2 Live Crew, and Public Enemy. Will Smith at the time when the album And in This Corner came out saw the lack of sales of the album started to have self-doubt about his career. He believed it was all over, and fell into a state of depression. He started to have an 'I could care less about life' attitude, and started to recklessly spend his money. In fact at the time he blew 2.8 million dollars buying needless things, and then he drew the attention of the I.R.S. who sought to sue him for back taxes.

Around that same time NBC, who was working with a producer named Quincy Jones, was looking for a rap or urban star to star in a sitcom about a street kid who comes to live with a rich African-American family in Bel-Air. There is a strange and even twisted story in how Will Smith got this part that would eventually make him a world famous actor. It should be noted that the story I am about to tell you has never been proven but said often by insiders in the music industry.

The story is that Quincy has a secret gay lifestyle few people are aware of. When offering Will Smith the part Smith, who was going bankrupted and being sued by the I.R.S, really needed the part. Jones told Smith he could have the part if he allowed him to have gay sex with him. Will Smith, as the story goes, allowed him to, and got the part.

Later on in the career of Tupac Shakur, Tupac said a similar story. Tupac wanted to marry one of Quincy's daughters, and according to Tupac, Quincy would only give him his blessing if he allowed him to have gay sex with Tupac. Tupac refused, and walked out of the house very angry. Overall there is no proof to these stories but they are often said by people in the industry who are well known for telling the truth.

When Smith got the part, the producers named the show The Fresh Prince of Bel-Air. Smith, while filming the first season of the show had most of the sales to his album called And in This Corner going to the I.R.S. The I.R.S. also garnished 25% of Will Smith's first season paychecks. The sitcom became a highly rated show watched by fans of all cultures, and it went on to last several seasons.

In 1991 Will Smith changed his sound of music to pop-rap, and in that year Jazz and Prince would release the album called Homebase. The lead single from the album called Summertime became a huge smash hit. Homebase would become a multi-platinum selling album, and brought the duo back into the mainstream fan-base. The album also produced the hit single called Ring My Bell.

In 1993 the duo released their next album called Code Red. Code Red had a harder rap, and beat sound. The lead single off the album was called Boom! Shake the Room that hit the number one spot on music charts in the U.K. and Australia, but in the U.S. the album only went gold due to a controversy over the samples used on the album.

At that time Will Smith was becoming a movie star. In 1993 Will Smith received movie industry praise for his role in Six Degrees of Separation. Will Smith played the role of a homo-sexual con-artist wherein he did kissing scenes with other male actors along with appearing naked in bed with other men. In 1996 Will Smith starred in the film Independence Day, and the film became a huge block-buster hit. This film cemented Will Smith's place as a major Hollywood box office draw.

Since then he releases records under his real name, and DJ Jazzy Jeff still works with him and creates beats for those records, and for singles he records on his films' soundtrack.

Chapter 15

Another style of music is often heard in the nightclubs across America, and around the world. In the 70's many forms of music that became popular in the mainstream later on were started or made popular in the nightclubs. The history of nightclubs goes back to the City of Paris, France in the late 19th century. It was a place where popular music of that time was played, and featured a show of naked women who danced to it. It was a place where people came to dress in the latest fashion, and came to dance. It was a place where also the criminal element gathered, and drugs and alcohol were used. Not much has changed since then.

In the Roaring 20's is when nightclubs in America became very popular. People came there to drink alcohol which was illegal at that time, and to dance to the latest Jazz moves, and women performed strip shows there. Nightclubs have always housed the latest new forms of music to Jazz, Rhythm & Blues, Rock N' Roll, Pop-Music, and later on Hard Rock/Heavy Metal music, Disco, Hip-Hop, and Electro Music.

Nightclubs in the early 20th century were usually started up by people who had connections to the Mafia or boot-leggers. In fact about 90% of the nightclubs in America were started up with Mob money. Interesting enough the people the Mob used to start their money-making nightclubs had connections or were members of occult groups like the Golden Dawn, Freemasons, OTO, early forms of the Church of Satan, and other groups.

It is often believed that these groups still today own many of the most famous nightclubs in America, and around the world. Nightclubs from the 70's, and up to this present day still have a high use of illegal drugs being used there. Drugs like cocaine, heroin, LSD, and the heroin/LSD pill known as a 'molly', and other forms of drugs are constantly used in nightclubs, and many lives have been taken at nightclubs due to overdoses. Criminal elements like gang-bangers, Mob members, and drug dealers often party or sell drugs at nightclubs, and often violent encounters will take place there. Sexual immorality is a norm at nightclubs, and people have caught many STD's from sexual encounters from people they meet at nightclubs.

Being a Christian, and a nightclub goer to say to live the

nightclub culture, and declare to be a follower of Jesus Christ do not go together. Many of the practices that go on at nightclubs are condemn in the Bible. Many forms of popular music are played at nightclubs, and dancing and music is not a sin. It is simply what you do with dancing and music that can make it sinful or not.

One form of music that was made popular in a nightclub was called House Music. House Music is electronic dance music that originated in Chicago in the late 70's to early 1980's. As it became popularized in Chicago by 1985 House Music fanned out to other major cities across the North, West, and South of the United States. It then came into Europe and Australia, and then soon around the world. By the mid 1980's and up to our time House Music has been infused into mainstream pop, and dance music world-wide. House Music is done by repetitive 4/4 beats, and rhythms mainly provided by drum machines, hi-hat cymbals, and synthesized bass-lines.

House Music was born in the Disco club scene, and has similar characteristics with Disco but it is far more electronic. The rhythm of House Music have core elements like the kick drum on every beat, and ranges the sound to soulful and atmospheric dance beats. In Chicago many DJs who mixed in the style of house reached independent success in the nightclubs to the point they found themselves with their own record labels. Mainstream artists like Madonna, Janet Jackson, Paula Abdul, Britney Spears, Bjork, New Order, and many, many others have also used House Music into their songs.

House Music to this day remains the popular form of music in nightclubs, and it has a strong hold on the underground scene across the globe. The two styles of music called soul and disco were the influences of the sound of House Music. House Music took these two styles, and added mixing, and turntable editing techniques along with using samplers, synthesizers, sequencers, and drum machines.

The DJs who brought House Music to birth were also audio engineers. In the late 70's to the early 1980's these DJs were Walter Gibbons, M&M, Larry Levan, Tom Moulton, Jim Burgess, and the famed Frankie Knuckles. All these DJs got their start in

Chicago nightclubs where they gave birth to House Music.

Frankie Knuckles was the first DJ to open a club that centered it's sound only on House Music. He was also the first to take House Music, and began to produce records, and tapes of pure House Music, because of this he was called the 'godfather of house music'.

In the early 1980's in Chicago House Music began to break into different styles of the new wave scene. These styles were called deep house, acid house, Italo disco, electro funk, and electronic pop. These early DJs who brought these new styles were Kraftwerk, Telex, Yellow Magic Orchestra, and then many others followed.

In 1984 a DJ named Jesse Saunders from Chicago brought forth the House Music track called On and On. It was the first house record to go gold, and it utilized some of the new technology of music mixing like the Roland TB-303 bass synthesizer, and the Roland TR-808 drum machine, and the Kong Poly-61 synthesizer, and used samples from a disco record called Space Invaders. It also featured vocals on the track as well. On and On is often, and mistakenly called the first house record but it is not. There were many before it, but what On and On did do was it became the first house record that brought world-wide attention in the nightclub scene around the world to House Music.

After On and On, and inspired by Jesse's success, many DJs started to mix and record House Music. In the nightclubs of Latin and African-Americans, and even in gay nightclubs House Music began to become a major force for music in the nightclubs. Soon House Music killed disco, funk, and soul music in the club scene by 1985.

In 1985 a DJ named DJ Mr. Fingers created the style of House Music called deep house. His two tracks called Mystery of Love and Can You Feel It brought him success in the nightclubs, and this style became very popular. In 1987 the style of acid house was started by a crew called Phuture who's members were DJ Pierre, DJ Spanky, and DJ Herb J. Their track was called Acid Tracks, and this track made them very popular in the nightclub scene. In Chicago two DJs named Ron Hardy and Lil Louis started to open up local record shops that sold dance music. This is where people were able to buy House Music tracks. These shops eventually became called by the names Importers, State Street Records, Loop Records, and Gramaphone Records.

A radio station in Chicago called B-96 would soon create the popular Hot Mix 5 show that played House Music on the weekend nights from 11:00 p.m. to 5:00 a.m. Soon other cities like New York City and Detroit started to play House Music on their popular radio shows at night on the weekends.

Studio record labels for House Music were created first in Chicago. The first two were called Trax Records and DJ International Records, and others followed. Soon labels started to appear in other cities of the United States, and eventually world-wide. Wider distribution helped to make House Music very popular all over the world.

The origin of the name House Music came from the nightclub that DJ Frankie Knuckles opened in Chicago. This nightclub was called The Warehouse and it first opened in 1977. The Warehouse opened for the purpose of taking House Music which was originally called electro new wave music out of the disco scene and playing it in its own club exclusively. DJ Knuckles was also the exclusive DJ of The Warehouse, and the club became so popular that the music was then called House Music. It was at this club is where DJ Knuckles got the name 'godfather of house'. Due to money problems the club would close in the early 80's while other clubs began to open, and play House Music with DJs they hired.

From the late 1980's throughout the 1990's other DJs rose to fame in the nightclub scene playing and recording House Music, and many of them started, and were from Chicago. A few of these names were Bad Boy Bill, Julian 'Jumpin' Perez, DJ Irene, DJ Richie Humpty, DJ Lynnwood, and others. In the present day House Music carries on through new styles that came about in the late 1990's to the 2000s. Mixers like Daft Punk, Stardust, St. Germain, Cassius, and others carry on the sound of House Music with a new style that came out of the Paris, France nightclub scene. On August 10, 2005 the former Chicago Mayor at the time named Richard M. Daley proclaimed that day as

'House Unity Day' in Chicago to honor the birth place of House Music in Chicago.

Another style House Music gave birth to is, a style called Freestyle. Freestyle music started in the mid-1980's. Its sound came from House Music mixed with Latin, pop and electronic dance and soul music. It's height of popularity was from the late 1980's until the early 1990's when it's popularity began to decline due to a change of taste in music fans.

When Chicago had brought forth House Music it would reach New York City where the Latin-American music scene there began to develop another new wave sound by mixing Latin, hip-hop, soul, and electro-pop with house and dance rhythms. The style became called Freestyle by the Latin-American DJs who created it. Freestyle was born in the Puerto Rican area of East Harlem often called Spanish Harlem. The idea behind it was to create a new form of soul music by bringing vocals to electro mixes and beats. This idea at the time caught on like a wildfire, and it would spread to Miami, Chicago, and other cities in the United States. It would also come to the South American music industry where still to this day the music is still popular.

In the mid-1980's Freestyle's stage was in the nightclubs, and even through its short rise in the music industry it was still based in the nightclub scene while selling records to the mainstream public. When the market opened for Freestyle by the record companies artists who mainly got their start in nightclubs began to be signed by them.

Let us look at some of these artists. Lisa Lisa, and her band called Cult Jam were one of the first Freestyle groups to bring the music to the mainstream public. Lisa Lisa and Cult Jam was the first group to open the market for it in the music industry. The group is made up of three members who were Lisa Velez, Alex Moseley who played guitar and bass, and Mike Hughes who played drums and keyboard. Lisa Velez is of Puerto Rican descent who grew up in an area called Hell's Kitchen which is in lower Manhattan in New York City. She began singing, and dancing at an early age. While attending Julia Richman High School in Manhattan she was discovered by a group called Full Force who sought to put together a group that played Freestyle music so that they could sell the group to a record company.

Full Force would become the creators, and the producer of Lisa Lisa and the Cult Jam. After the group was put together Full Force got them a record contract with Columbia Records. The group would record their first album called Lisa Lisa & Cult Jam with Full Force. The album was released in 1985, and it became the first Freestyle album released by a major record label to the mainstream public. Their first single was a song called I Wonder If I Take You Home. The single would go gold, and the album would hit number 6 on the R&B Billboard chart, and number 34 on the pop-chart in the summer of 1985. Their second single was called Can You Feel the Beat which also went gold, and became a huge nightclub hit. A third single called All Cried Out would also go gold, and by 1986 Lisa Lisa & Cult Jam's debut album would become a platinum selling album.

Soon the group released their second album in 1987 called Spanish Fly. The album had two major hit singles called Head to Toe and Lost in Emotion. Head to Toe went number one on the R&B Billboard chart, and number 5 on the Billboard Pop chart. Lost in Emotion would become the 4th most played video on MTV. Both singles went gold, and the album Spanish Fly went platinum. The group's third album called Straight to the Sky went gold. The group's last hit single was called Let the Beat Hit 'Em that came out on her fourth album called Straight Outta Hell's Kitchen that was released in 1990.

Another group that brought Freestyle to the market was called TKA. The original members were Tony Ortiz, Louis Sharpe who was called Kayel, and Alejandro Escoto who was called Aby but later he was replaced with Angel Vasquez who was called Love. Kayel also called K7 was the lead singer of the group. TKA in the nightclub scene were often called 'the Kings of Freestyle'. The group members are of Puerto Rican descent who came from East Harlem, New York City. The group named themselves originally not after the first letters of their names but after the first letters of their first loves. This is why they mainly sang songs about girls because the songs were based on events that happened in their relationships. TKA was a group who started out singing at nightclubs to Freestyle music. They also would sing at parties, and other social events.

TKA was first discovered when they sang at a sweet sixteen party at a Church in East Harlem in 1984. A record producer named Joey Gardner was at that party to scout TKA after he heard about a performance they did in a nightclub. Joey worked for Tommy Boy Records who were seeking new talent. After TKA performed at the Church Joey sat down with them and then signed them to Tommy Boy Records. The group would record their first single called One Way Love and soon it became a major hit in Latin nightclubs in New York City, Chicago, Miami, Los Angeles, and other cities. This was followed by a second single they recorded called Come Get My Love and this single too also became a major hit in the nightclub scene. They would soon record their third single called Tears May Fall but during the recording of the single Kayel had a falling out with Aby, and then Aby was soon fired. Aby would then be replaced by Angel 'Love' Vasquez. When Tears May Fall was released it became the group's biggest hit, and the single would go gold.

From there the group recorded their first album called Scars of Love. From this album three more club hits would follow called Scars of Love, X-Ray Vision, and Don't Be Afraid. The group's debut album Scars of Love would go gold. In 1989 TKA recorded a song for the Lean on Me film soundtrack called You Are the One. The song would hit the number 91 spot of the Billboard 100 singles chart but the song would become a huge nightclub hit.

In 1990 TKA released their second album called Louder Than Love. The lead single Louder Than Love was a favorite video on MTV for female fans. The album produced three major nightclub hits called Crash (Have Some Fun), I Won't Give Up on You, and Give Your Love to Me. Their album Louder Than Love would also go gold.

Their last nightclub hit was a song called Maria released in 1992 on their greatest hits album.

Another known Freestyle singer was Lisette Melendez who was born in 1967, and was raised in East Harlem, New York City. Lisette Melendez is of Puerto Rican descent who started out singing in a Church choir, and at a community theater. She would pattern her singing style after Barbra Streisand and Bette Midler. In high-school Lisette was a huge fan of Puerto Rican singer Lisa Lisa. Lisette, being inspired by Lisa Lisa's success, sought the nightclubs to do Freestyle music. Lisette, because of her strong voice, was working with DJs and performing at nightclubs at an early age.

In 1988 she got her break when a producer named Carlos Berrios noticed her when he was scouting new talent for Columbia Records. Carlos sat down with her and she then signed a contract to Columbia's record label. Soon she was in the studio to record her first single called Together Forever. When the single was released it became a huge nightclub hit, and soon she recorded her first album. Her first album would go gold.

On her second album she recorded her last nightclub hit in the U.S. called A Day In My Life (Without You), but after recording two more albums that hardly sold in the U.S. she then left the U.S. music industry and became an artist for the South American music industry.

Another Freestyle group were The Cover Girls who were an all-girl Freestyle group from New York City. The group's three original members were Angel Clivilles, the lead singer, Caroline Jackson, and Sunshine Wright. Wright would be later replaced by Margo Urban in 1987.

The Cover Girls started in 1986 as a Freestyle trio who were put together by Andy 'Panda' Tripoli. Andy put them together as an act to play in Sal Abbatiello's nightclub. After the club had success with the group they were soon signed to a record contract. In the process Sunshine was replaced by Margo in late 1987.

The Cover Girls released their debut album called Show Me. Two of their songs called Because of You and Promise Me would enter the top 40 Billboard 100 singles chart. Five of their singles from the album became huge nightclub hits. Their second album called We Can't Go Wrong released in 1989 featured three hit songs that caused the album to increase in sales overtime. The song My Heart Skips a Beat became the group's first top 10 pop hit in early 1990, and this lead to a change in record labels as Epic Records took over their contract and signed them, which led to a bigger promotion of their album.

Their next hit single was a song called Funk Boutique which became a huge radio and nightclub hit. Their next, and last hit single was a song called Wishing on a Star which was a remake of Rose Royce's 1978 song. Wishing on a Star would hit number 9 on the top 10 Billboard Pop charts. From there the group would fade into nostalgia.

Another all-girl Freestyle group was called Expose who were formed by Lewis Martinee who was a Miami disc jockey, and he worked for Pantera Productions. When Pantera was looking for a new group Lewis envisioned an all-girl Freestyle act, and so the talent scouts of Pantera hired Sandra Casanas, Alejandra Lorenzo, and Laurie Miller. The group was named Expose, and soon they recorded their first single called Point of No Return, and it was released in 1985. Point of No Return is the single that is often credited for bringing Freestyle music to a larger audience even though it was not released by a major record label. The song would hit number one on the Billboard Hot Dance Club chart, and the song was a major club hit.

The success of this single led to a record contract with Arista Records when the group was touring nightclubs in major cities. The original group would record their first album for Arista Records called Exposure but problems in the group began to surface. These three women started to have problems with their manager Lewis Martinee who they felt was enforcing unfair demands upon them, and was ripping them off. The arguments became so heated that Lewis wanted to get rid of all of them. Soon Sandra and Alejandra had enough of the problems centered on Lewis, and they both left the group. Lewis then replaced them with Jeanette Jurado and Gioia Bruno. After this Laurie had enough of Lewis, and his demands, and then she left the group, and was replaced by Ann Curless.

All three of the original members of Expose would embark on solo careers, and each of them had nightclub hits as solo artists. That first album called Exposure was pulled by the record company, and the new members of Expose would re-record it, and in 1987 the album Exposure was released with the three new girls on the cover. The lead single on the album was a song called Come Go with Me which hit number 5 on the Billboard 100 singles chart making it a huge hit.

In 1988 Expose would become the first Freestyle group to have a single to hit number one on the Billboard 100 singles chart. The song was called Seasons Change. Seasons Change would also be their last hit before the group faded away.

Another all-girl Freestyle group was called Sweet Sensation. Sweet Sensation was a Puerto Rican female group from East Harlem, New York City. The original members were Betty LeBron who was called Dee, Margie Fernandez, and Mari Fernandez. The group were a nightclub act who ended up getting signed first to Next Plateau Records, but in 1988 Atco Records took over their contract, and brought them to their record label.

The group would record their first album called Take It While It's Hot. The album would hit the number 63 spot on the Billboard 200 albums chart but in the nightclubs the album was a huge smash hit. The album had five hit singles that were all nightclub hits called Hooked on You, Victim of Love, Take It While It's Hot, Never Let You Go and Sincerely Yours. The song Never Let You Go would hit the number one spot on the Billboard Dance chart.

In 1989 Mari left the group, and was replaced by Sheila Vega. In 1990 Sweet Sensation released their second album called Love Child. The lead single off the album called If Wishes Came True hit the number one spot on the Billboard 100 singles chart. They were the second Freestyle group to have a single to hit number one on the Billboard 100 chart. This single would also be their last hit as the group would fade into nostalgia.

Another Freestyle artist was Stevie B. At the height of his career Stevie B. was called the 'King of Freestyle', and many thought he would be the one to break the music to new heights through his career, but this did not happen. Stevie B's real name is Steven Bernard Hill. He was born in Fort Lauderdale, Florida but he grew up in Miami. He was a gifted singer, and songwriter, and skilled at playing the piano. While living in Miami he worked many odd jobs from fast food to washing cars, but at night he became a regular in the Miami nightclub scene in the late 1980's. During that time as he put together his look, and style he became influenced by the Hi-NRG dance scene, and with the music of Latin Freestyle.

He began to sing in the style of Freestyle, and he soon wrote a song called Party Your Body. Soon he would write out, and mix the music for the song working with a club DJ. After this Stevie B got the chance to record the song at LMR Records. In 1987 Party Your Body was released in the Miami nightclub scene, and it quickly became a national club smash hit single.

LMR would record his first album called Party Your Body released in 1988. It would have three top 40 singles on the Billboard 100 singles chart. These songs were I Wanna Be the One, In My Eyes, and Love Me For Life. Each of the songs became huge nightclub hits.

In 1990 RCA Records took over his contract, and released his second album called Love and Emotion. This album became the most successful album in Freestyle history. Through this album he was called the 'King of Freestyle'. The album had four smash hit singles called Spring Love, Love and Emotion, Funky Melody, and Because I Love You (The Postman Song). Because I Love You (The Postman Song) became a number one hit on the Billboard 100 singles chart, and it was the third song from a Freestyle artist to do so. The album Love and Emotion would sell millions, and Stevie B. was being hailed in the music industry, and in the media as one of the next great artists, but soon he seemed to just fade away into nostalgia.

Freestyle music mostly faded away due to the change of taste in fans who wanted harder, darker, and more sexual music at the time. Freestyle is kept alive however by die-hard fans who still love the music. Many of the fans who loved Freestyle were touched in their hearts by the songs or are fans of electric music. Freestyle has major industry life in the South American music industry in places like Brazil, Columbia, Peru, and many countries in South America and the Island Nations. Artists like Stevie B., Lisette Melendez, Expose, The Cover Girls, and many others have continued their careers in South America, and they even draw thousands of fans there. Some shows bring in anywhere from 5,000 to 15,000 fans at a show.

Chapter 16

As the new form of pop-music grew due to the success of Michael Jackson and Madonna other artists would come along who were young female artists, girl groups, or boybands. Many of them would reach super-stardom in the 1980's and 1990's, and even to the present day. Their influences would capture the emotions of millions of fans world-wide. Let us take a look into some of these artists who arose to fame in the 1980's and 1990's.

New Edition is often called the first boyband group who was formed in 1978 in Boston, Massachusetts. Its original members were five young men named Bobby Brown, Ralph Tresvant, Michael Bivins, Ricky Bell, and Ronnie DeVoe. The group first started with three members who were elementary school friends in 1978. These three were Bobby Brown, Michael Bivins, and Ricky Bell who were all living in the Boston area housing projects at Orchard Park when they brought their group together.

These three young men were gifted at singing, dancing, and were inspired by the Jackson Five, and dreamed about becoming them. To make five members they brought in two more friends from the Orchard housing projects named Travis Pettus and Corey Rackley.

The group used to get together, and practice their dance moves, and singing often patterning themselves after the Jackson Five. One day the group entered into a local talent show at the Roxbury to show what they could do. The group's performance would impress a local talent manager, and choreographer named Brooke Payne. Payne took them under his wing, and became their manager who would mold them to become high-level entertainers.
During the intense practice sessions Travis would leave the group, and he was replaced by Brown's close friend Ralph

Tresvant. Soon Corey would leave the group, and he was replaced with Payne's nephew named Ronnie DeVoe.

Brooke Payne, learning that these young men were inspired by the Jackson Five, thought to himself that the group were a 'new edition of the Jackson Five' hence he named the group New Edition. In 1982 Payne entered the group in a talent show called Hollywood Talent Night Show held in the Strand Theatre in Boston. The talent show was brought together by singer and producer Maurice Starr who was looking for new talent. The first place prize award was $500 and a recording contract. New Edition that night won the talent show and the $500. Most importantly, they won the recording contract. No one in the projects ever thought this would actually happen for them...but it did.

Through this contract New Edition would record their debut album called Candy Girl. Their style of pop-music came to be called bubblegum music. It was music aimed at 12 to 16 year old fans. The beats of the music were always soft, un-alarming, and many times hardly had any depth to it. The lyrics were about doing what children do, and oddly falling in love with first loves and girls they dreamed about.

Several psychiatrists and Christian theologians did point out some interesting things about very young artists singing love songs to young children and pre-teens. Children and pre-teens for them to have a more positive upbringing should not be thinking about relationships or getting their little hearts broken according to them. They stated that these young fans being at the tender ages they are cannot have the mental strength to be able to handle it well. In fact adults have a very hard time handling it so image what a child would end up thinking. Relationships they felt should be reserved until they are older, and they stated it is the parents' job to make sure that it is. They felt that this music, no matter how innocent it sounds, could undermine the protection of parents for their children to guard them from having relationships far too early in their young lives, but many other parents disagreed, and saw nothing wrong with this form of music.

One matter I can say was seeing that there were pre-teens at those ages having even sex far too early, and were big fans of this kind of music. Their parents at the time was never around to stop it, some of them didn't even care. The album Candy Girl was recorded on Starr's label called Streetwise Records. The lead single called Candy Girl would hit the number one spot on the Billboard R&B singles chart, and on the R&B U.K. singles chart.

After Candy Girl the group would have three more hit singles called Is This The End, Popcorn Love, and Jealous Girl. They would soon embark on a major concert tour, and the group earned millions of dollars through record sales and ticket sales, but the problem was after the tour was over each of the boys were dropped back off to their homes in the projects with a check for one dollar and 87 cents each for their work. Brown recalled that along with the check he was lucky enough to get a VCR. Brown stated that Starr in Brown's words 'worked at them like negro-slaves, and when we made all that money this is all that we got for our efforts'.

Starr blamed the expenses of the group during the tour as the reason for these horrible checks they got, but in truth the courts revealed that Starr ripped them off. Soon after New Edition got the kind of checks they did their manager Brooke Payne fired Starr, and the group parted company from Streetwise Records. Soon after Starr went off to form another boyband who would be an all-white boyband that later became the New Kids on the Block.

While Starr was in the process of forming his all-white boyband, Payne and New Edition got the law-firm of Steven and Martin Machat to sue Maurice Starr, and Streetwise Records. The law-firm after hearing the story decided to take the case for free to be paid once they won. New Edition won the case, and got back a lot of the money they should have had in the first place.

Soon New Edition was signed by MCA Records but unknown to the group MCA actually signed them to one of the labels they owned called Jump and Shoot Records. This would be a major problem for them later on. The group recorded their second album, and named it after the group by calling it New Edition. The album would have two major hit singles called Mr.

Telephone Man and Cool It Now. The single Cool It Now would hit the number 5 spot on the Billboard 100 singles chart. The album would become a major mainstream success.

New Edition's management team saw that they could make more money if they signed to a long term contract with MCA Records. When they went to do so the problem was MCA executives revealed to them that the group was not fully signed to their label but were signed to the label of Jump and Shoot. Jump and Shoot wanted $500,000 to $100,000 a piece to release each of them from the contract to allow them to sign to MCA.

New Edition were sadden by this because each of them did not have the money, and so MCA offered to borrow it to them to release them from the contract, but this also meant they would be in MCA's debt and most of the money they made from their next album and from the tour would go to MCA.

In 1985 New Edition released their third album called All for Love, and it had three major hits called Count Me Out, A Little Bit of Love, and With You All the Way. New Edition would also appear in the hip-hop and R&B film called Krush Groove in 1985.

In 1985 Bobby Brown was causing major problems, and fights with his other boyband buddies. Brown also at that time developed his awful drug problems. Brown started off smoking marijuana, and then moved up to cocaine, and would lace cocaine with his pot. He also had a hard time controlling his anger, and started to act out having many disturbing episodes of behavioral problems. The other four members began to put pressure on their management team to fire Bobby Brown but MCA Records had the final word if they were going to release Bobby Brown. MCA then allowed the group to make a vote decision to determine if Bobby stays or goes. The vote decision went down in December of 1985.

Michael, Ricky, and Ronnie all voted for Bobby to be kicked out of the group. Only Ralph voted that he should stay. Ralph was always close to Bobby, and grateful to him for bringing him into the group. The vote being three to one against Bobby from there Bobby Brown was kicked out of New Edition, but he was nowhere near done, and he went on to have a successful solo career that was far bigger than the one he had with New Edition. During the year 1986 New Edition performed as a group of four men. At that time a singer named Johnny Gill was trying to get his solo career off the ground. The management of New Edition then sought to bring in Johnny Gill as their new fifth member.

When Johnny Gill was offered he then joined the group in 1987. At first there were tensions between Johnny and Ralph for the fact that Ralph found it hard to accept Johnny because Johnny took the place of his best-friend Bobby Brown, but while recording their new album Ralph warmed up to him.

In 1987 the duo of Jimmy Jam and Terry Lewis who are credited as the music producing team who brought forth the new R&B sound called new jack swing through Janet Jackson's album called Control were hired to produced New Edition's new album. The group would change the musical sound of New Edition, they got rid of the bubblegum sound and gave them a more urban, smoother, and stronger sound.

Their new album would be released in 1988 called Heart Break. Heart Break became their biggest selling album at that time as it sold 4 million copies. The album would have four smash hit songs, and their biggest single was a song called If It Isn't Love.

In 1989 the group members being inspired by Bobby Brown's success would break the group up to pursue solo careers. Ralph Tresvant and Johnny Gill would both release solo records that became multi-platinum sellers.

Ricky Bell, Michael Bivins, and Ronnie DeVoe would form a musical R&B new jack group called Bell Biv Devoe. In 1990 the trio would debut their new album called Poison. Poison became a huge smash hit album, and would sell 3 million copies. The album would have two hit singles called Poison and Do Me. The song Do Me would come under fire by moral groups for the strong sexual nature of the song as the song was promoted to young fans. The message of the song was one of depravity about three men calling out to women to have sex with them at any time of the day.

In 1996 New Edition would reunite, and Bobby Brown came back into the group. Now at six members New Edition recorded a new album called Home Again released in late 1996. Home Again became New Edition's most successful album of all time as it sold 6 million copies. It was also their first album to hit number one on the Billboard 200 albums chart. The 1997 Home Again Tour proved to be disastrous for the group. When they went on tour old rivalries began to surface, and each of them fought struggles with each other over stage dominance, and over the lengths of their solo performances. Throughout the tour Bobby Brown was often high on krack-cocaine, and intoxicated through most of his performances. His old behavior problems would often resurface.

The group finally broke down completely during a concert in Las Cruces, New Mexico. Bobby Brown during his solo set decided to extend it on a whim, and went against what the group agreed on. This made Ricky, Michael, and Ronnie very angry. Ronnie attempted to pull Bobby from the stage but Bobby threw his microphone down, and a fist fight between Bobby and Ronnie broke out on stage. Bobby's bodyguards then rushed to his aid, and at the same time Ricky, Michael, and Ronnie's bodyguards rushed to Ronnie's aid. When the two security forces ran into each other they each pulled guns on each other, and threaten to kill one another. No shots were thankfully fired, and the tour was over. No one knows if New Edition will ever work together again.

Another pop artist named Tiffany was also very popular with young fans. Tiffany's parents had connections with the Country Music Industry as they knew people in Nashville, Tennessee. These connections seems to have been through family relations. When Tiffany was 4 years old her parents discovered that she had a gift for singing and dancing. Her parents had her to start singing all kinds of country songs to develop her voice. The dream of her parents was to one day turn Tiffany into a country music star. In 1980 her parents made contact with one of these country music relatives looking to break their daughter in. They would recommend her parents to a man named Jack Reeves who often performed at the Narods in Chino, California. Around this same time her parents were often fighting and looking to get a divorce. Tiffany's mother brought her to Jack Reeves, and performed for him. Jack was impressed with her, and then made Tiffany his opening act.

By 1981 Tiffany at 10 years old opened for Jack Reeves, and during her first performance she came up with an idea. After the performance Tiffany took her hat, and went into the crowds looking for donations. She would collect $250 on her first night, and after that she made a habit of doing this. Jack took Tiffany under his wing, and Tiffany travelled with Jack, and began to perform at the El Palomino nightclub. At this time Tiffany's parents were divorced.

The El Palomino was a rowdy nightclub filled with drunks, and sometimes bar fights would erupt. Tiffany was exposed to a very sinful adult scene there, and was exposed at times to alcohol even though she was underage. One night during a performance there a couple of country music producers named Hoyt Axton along with his mother Mae Axton noticed her talent. These two, after speaking with Tiffany's mother, brought Tiffany on a tour that would go through several cities in Alaska. Tiffany would join George Jones, and the once famous Jerry Lee Lewis on this tour, and she would become their opening act.

During the tour people were amazed at how talented she was. Jerry Lee was one of those people who were impressed with her and he recommended her to a manager and producer named George Tobin. One night Tobin watched her perform, and wanted to get her a record contract, but first George had to try her out to give the record companies something to sell. George would get her to compete on the television show called Star Search. Tiffany would do very well, and finish in second place.

In fact more people who finished in second place on Star Search got signed to record companies than people who finished in first place. When George was trying to sell Tiffany to record companies MCA was the most interested but they did not want a country music star they wanted a pop-music star. George sat down with Tiffany, and her mother to explain to them that they had to change Tiffany's musical direction, and make her a pop artist. Tiffany then began singing pop songs mostly songs from the Beatles, and other acts. Her singing voice impressed MCA, and they agreed to write out a contract and sign her. The contract that Tiffany would sign was shown later to be a rip-off deal for Tiffany but due to her age she signed it. In short out of

100% of her future earnings 50% would go to George Tobin, and 25% would go to Tiffany's parents.

The last 25% would go to Tiffany who could not touch until she was 18 years old. Soon after Tiffany was in the recording studio to record her debut album.

In 1987 her first album was released called Tiffany. The album at first started off slow in sales, so her management team put together a nationwide shopping mall tour so that Tiffany could be sold to the young fans directly. The tour started from a mall in New Jersey, and it would end in California. During the tour her album's lead single called I Think Were Alone Now became a smash hit single. As it received nationwide radio play her shopping mall tour exploded with thousands of fans rushing to the mall to see her. Her management team decided to make a music video of the song to feature this fan explosion going on during her mall tour. The video was soon released on MTV, and her lead single I Think Were Alone Now became a number one hit single on the Billboard 100 singles chart.

Tiffany's fame would skyrocket to a nationwide level. She became the youngest female artist in history at the time to top the Billboard 100 singles chart. Her second single called Could Have Been would also hit the number one spot on the Billboard 100 singles chart. The single I Think Were Alone Now would sell 2 million copies, and her album called Tiffany would sell 4 million copies. She was known among her fans as the 'Queen Teen'. Her third single called I Saw Him Standing There would hit number 7 on the Billboard 100 singles chart.

In 1988 Tiffany was a huge music industry star. Her face was on millions of posters, and she was on the front cover of teen magazines world-wide. From late 1988 to 1989 Tiffany would embark on a tour that featured for her opening act the New Kids on the Block, but soon the New Kids on the Block would be mega popular with young fans to such a point that the headlines of the tour would change. The managers of the tour, after Tiffany was being booed on stage because the fans wanted to see the New Kids on the Block so badly, decided she would be the opening act and the New Kids on the Block would be the main attraction. Soon, as quick as her popularity rose to fame, so did her declining fame. During that time Tiffany also turned 18, and she would find herself in court-battles trying to get back her money.

The first court-battle came before Tiffany was 18 when she was 17 years old, and found out that her parents were getting very rich off of her, and she was hardly seeing any of her money. Tiffany hired a lawyer, and tried to declare herself as a emancipated minor using the case that her parents were stealing from her. The court rejected the request on the grounds of the contract, and instead made her grandmother her legal guardian. The courts told her she was bound to the contract until she was 18 years old. At 18 Tiffany had a falling out with Tobin over the money he was making off of her that was far more then what her parents were getting. The relationship between Tobin and Tiffany was said by many in the industry to be a kin to one who handles his puppet with Tobin being the handler and Tiffany was the puppet, but Tiffany had enough.

At 18 she sued Tobin for money that she felt was owned to her. The court cases cost Tiffany all the money she earned at the time. Tiffany however would win the case against Tobin but she only received part of the money he made off of her.

In 1989 Tiffany released a second album but due to the fame of the New Kids on the Block, and all the court cases the media reported on, the album failed in sales. Soon Tiffany was put in touch with Maurice Starr's people, and she received two new managers named Dick Scott and Kim Glover who also were part of the management team of the New Kids on the Block.

These two would re-invent Tiffany's image to a more sexual look, and produced her new album under this image, but her third album would fail to grab the attention of the fans due to changing tastes among the fans. Tiffany's last piece of success is when she did a song for the Jetson's movie soundtrack. Tiffany was also hired to play the voice of Judy Jetson which also angered the original voice cast-members.

In time Tiffany tried to kill her bubblegum image in an effort to seek to record another album. She even went so far to pose nude for Playboy magazine. Her young son at the time was subjected to see his mother naked when a friend of his from school had an issue of the magazine and brought it to class.

Another pop-music act that arose to world-wide fame, and huge success were the New Kids on the Block. This group got started, and were founded by Maurice Starr. After Starr broke away from New Edition he realized the success of New Edition as a boyband, and sought to form a new group. This time he wanted the group to be all-white young males because as he put it an all-white boyband would sell far more records.

Starr went to work with his business partner Mary Alford to set up auditions in an Irish-American neighborhood of Boston. The neighborhood he choose was a low Middle-Class to poor white Irish community who were also mixed with other European cultures. Most of these Irish youths were already into the hip-hop/dance culture as many of them would breakdance, rap, and were into R&B music. Many of them also were into the gang-culture as well as there was street gangs there made up of young Irish youths. In fact Donnie and his brother Mark, and other members of the Wahlberg family had police records for certain crimes they committed.

When the auditions were set up over 500 of these Irish-American youths would audition for a chance to join a group, and make an album on a record label. One of those youths who was there was a 15 year old named Donnie Wahlberg. Many strange stories were told of Donnie before he was selected to join this group. Many said that by getting selected it saved him from eventually getting locked up for hard time. Donnie came from a very large family who were called low Middle-Class but they hardly had any money if not no money at all. Money was spent on keeping the house, paying the bills, putting food on the table, putting clothes on their backs, and once all these bills where paid, they had no money left. Donnie and his younger brother Mark, and his other brothers used to run with a local gang there. It is not proven if he and his brothers were actually members but many members were his close friends, and he would even get arrested with them at times.

Donnie's bad boy image that he became known for was in many ways not an image. Donnie's police record shows arrests for petty drug possession which is marijuana, for public drunkenness, and even for vandalism, and street fights. His younger brother Mark Wahlberg who also became famous in the music industry, and went on to become a box-office movie star had a serious offense he was arrested for. Mark was arrested for beating up an Asian teen that the Boston police stated was a hate crime.

During the audition out of over 500 people who auditioned, only Donnie Wahlberg would leave a lasting impression, and was the only one selected to join the group. Starr was impressed with the way Donnie could sing, dance, and rap. Donnie would become the first member of the New Kids on the Block.

Starr then asked Donnie if he knew anyone else who was as talented as he was, and asked him if he could bring them in for an audition. Donnie would bring in his little brother Mark, and his close friends who had talent like he did. These friends were Donnie's best-friend Danny Wood, and the Knight brothers who were Jordan and Jonathan. Each of them would audition, and Starr was impressed with all of them, and selected them as the members of his new group that did not have a name yet. Starr would speak with their parents, and then took them under his wing. He provided an apartment from them to live in along with some spending money and food. The group would have a very rough and tight rehearsal schedule. Starr was their dance drill instructor, and taught the young youths how to sing, dance, and project the image of Hollywood music stars. It would take each of them to develop strong discipline to master this form of high-level entertainment.

The rehearsals were from six to seven days a week at times. Overtime, Mark Wahlberg lacked the discipline to continue to rehearse due to the fact he was sick of projecting an image that was not him. He refused to make those changes, and so he quit and went home. Later on his brother Donnie, after becoming big with the New Kids on the Block, broke Mark into the music industry as a rapper. When Mark went home Donnie called his friend Jamie Kelly to replace him, but in time Jamie too lacked the discipline for the moves and style of entertainment they were training for. Starr would eventually fire him. Soon Starr got the idea to bring in someone very young who can project the image of a young Michael Jackson like singer when he was with the Jackson 5. Mary Alford helped him to look for someone like this, and she made contact with a woman named Katherine McIntyre who was a community theater actress who had a talented young son named Joey McIntyre.

Mary brought Joey to Starr to audition, and Starr was very impressed and hired him. When Joey was brought in he was only 11 years old, and was about to turn 12. The other group members at first hated him because he took the place of their close friend, and also he came from a more up-scale family, but overtime they warmed up to him, and they became close to him like a pack of big brothers.

Once the group was formed and established Starr got a tighter control on them. He would write all their songs' lyrics, music, and would only listen to Donnie for his input now, and again but Starr had final say on all decisions including how much they get paid. And also on where they live, what they ate, what they wear, and who they speak with.

Starr would first name the group Nynuk which was a horrible name, and no one knew what Nynuk was. The group would record a couple of songs, and Starr brought the demo tape and promoted the group to Columbia Records. Columbia Records executives liked what they heard, and the image Starr was selling. They believed this could work, and so they wanted to sign them on one condition. Starr had to change the name of the group.

Starr then thinking about what to name them asked Donnie for his input. Donnie, seeing the demo tape with one of the bubblegum rap songs they recorded for it called New Kids on the Block stated that should be the name of the group. Starr agreed and the group was named New Kids on the Block.

When Starr renamed the group Columbia Records signed them to their label. The group recorded their first album, and in April of 1986 their debut album called New Kids on the Block was released. The songs were mostly bubblegum songs with two noted hits called Be My Girl and Stop It Girl. The group would embark on a short New England tour performing at teen dance clubs, high-schools, and block-parties. The album failed at grabbing nationwide attention, and the money that was spent on it seemed to have been wasted. Columbia Records then put the group on hold, and wondered about what to do with them. Many executives wanted to get rid of the group from their label.

Starr came to realize that it was their sound that was not getting the full attention. Their image also had to be changed to appeal to urban crowds. Starr then went to the studio heads of Columbia Records and begged them for another chance. Starr told them he had a new idea to re-invent their sound and image, and that this would work. Columbia then gave him the go ahead. Starr began working with DJs who did club music like new jack swing, freestyle, and more urban pop-music. Starr learning more about the music would fuse together new jack swing and freestyle into the pop-music form. Once he had the sound he began writing new songs for the New Kids on the Block, and even had them practice new dance moves.

The New Kids on the Block would then record their second album with this new and fresh sound. The album was called Hangin Tough, and it was released in the spring of 1988. The first single from the album was called Please Don't Go Girl. At first the single was not catching on until more radio stations started to play it. Soon fans started to request it more, and more to the point the single became a smash hit. A music video was soon made for it, and the song then increased in sales, and the single hit number 10 on the Billboard 100 singles chart.

By 1989 the group released their second single called You Got The Right Stuff. The song became a nationwide smash hit. The music video for the song became one of the most popular videos on MTV at the time. You Got The Right Stuff would hit number 5 on the Billboard 100 singles chart like a wildfire.

This success would lead the group to perform on the program Showtime at the Apollo, and on Soul Train. People there remarked that for a white group they were highly loved and performed at a level that made black audiences say of them that they are 'white kids born with soul'.

As their success grew the New Kids on the Block were able to reach out to white, black, Spanish, and many cultures of young fans. That is a rare musical act that can do that. During that time for the New Kids to get more tour exposure Starr had them to join Tiffany on her tour to become her opening act. During the tour Jonathan Knight would enter into a romantic relationship with Tiffany that was made public, but what was not made public at the time was the reasons why they broke up. Jonathan was bi-sexual, and he had a habit of seeing other men while with Tiffany. Tiffany would eventually break up with him, and they remained friends.

During the tour the New Kids on the Block released the single I'll Be Loving You Forever. The single was a huge smash hit, and it would take the number one spot on the Billboard 100 singles chart. The album Hangin Tough was greatly rising in sales, and during the tour the fans only wanted to see the New Kids on the Block, and often they ignored the fact Tiffany was there also. This resulted in Tiffany becoming the opening act, and the New Kids on the Block became the headliners.

After this U.S. tour was over Hangin Tough was the number one album on the Billboard 200 albums chart. Two more singles were released called Cover Girl and Hangin Tough, and both singles entered the top 10 Billboard 100 singles chart. Their fame became so great that when fans found out that they had another album out there, which was their first one, they started to buy the first album as well, and then soon the song Didn't I Blow Your Mind off the first album became number 8 on the Billboard 100 singles chart.

New Kids' albums in that time sold like hotcakes right off the pan. By the winter of 1989 the New Kids on the Block released a Christmas album called Merry, Merry, Christmas. The song from the Christmas album called This One's For The Children hit number 10 on the Billboard 100 singles chart. By 1990 the album called Hangin Tough sold 8 million copies, their first album called New Kids on the Block sold 3 million copies, and their Christmas album sold 2 million copies.

By 1990 they were becoming one of the highest paid entertainers in the world. Soon the salaries for their shows would equal the likes of Michael Jackson, Madonna, and Guns

N' Roses. In 1990 the group would release a concert home video that featured a live concert of the group performing their hit songs. This home video at the time would become the largest selling music home video in history. In that year the group would win a Grammy Award for the video and 2 American Music Awards.

The fame of this group was easily compared to the Beatles. Millions and millions of dollars were made on merchandise using the name and image of the group. There were New Kids' lunch boxes, pencils, posters, dolls, school supplies, cups, t-shirts, etc, and etc. The group would even receive their own Saturday Morning cartoon show. Their fan club had an official membership of over 200,000 people which rivalled the fame club of Star Trek. Their 900 number was the highest grossing 900 number in history.

In gross products the New Kids on the Block made more money than Bill Cosby, Michael Jackson, Prince, Madonna, and the leading actors of Hollywood. In the summer of 1990 the New Kids on the Block released their new album called Step By Step. The songs and the music of the album were all written by Maurice Starr. The lead single of the album called Step By Step would hit number one on the Billboard 100 singles chart. Their follow up song called Tonight would take the number 10 spot on the Billboard 100 singles chart.

In 1990 the New Kids on the Block would star in their own pay-per-view special which broke the record for all cable buy rates at the time. In 1990 the New Kids on the Block embarked on The Magic Summer Tour, but during the tour a scandal came their way regarding a few concerts they did. Members of the backstage crew at some of these performances exposed that the New Kids were lip-singing to pre-recorded vocals at these shows. This story came out right at the same time when people were exposing the fact that the New Kids did not write their own songs. Before the scandal could ruin them, the New Kids left the tour to go on the Arsenio Hall Show to address the scandal.

First they would perform live in front of the audience as a way to let the world know they can sing. In fact they could sing but the problem was they did lip-sing at a few of those concerts do to the fact their throats were sore. During the interview with Arsenio the New Kids addressed the issues about their own songs.

Instead of telling the truth that Maurice wrote them they instead said they wrote a lot of their own songs, and did mention Maurice but played down his part in the song-writing. In short the New Kid's lied to their fans to save face. After this scandal had died away a strange thing started to happen to the New Kids on the Block. Their album called Step By Step would sell 4 million copies, and their concert tour would become one of the highest money making tours in history, but the media would state that their album was a failure and their tour lost numbers.

Of course the media failed to explain how 4 million copies sold is a failure, and what numbers are they talking about. The media also started to expose how artists in the industry hated them, and how fans, mostly male, believed they were gay and promoted young men to act like girls.

In truth the artists who spoke against them were indeed jealous of them, and the macho behavior of young men should not have been used as the standard for music criticism. Other attacks would follow that were even more strange. A private investigator one time came out on a media show, and stated that a member of the New Kids on the Block was in a porn film, but he never showed this film to provide evidence he only stated it, and the media was fine with that and reported it.

In time the New Kids were being bashed in the media, and in the industry. This caused the New Kids to harden up their image, and Donnie Wahlberg came on the defense to stick up for the group, and pointed out some of the lies of the media, and that their stories were not making any sense at all. Overtime the media would do this job of destroying the love-fest image of the New Kids on the Block that many fans started turning away from them including female fans.

In late 1990 the New Kids' released a remix album called No More Games. They would have a harder image for the promotion of the album. The lead single No More Games entered the top 20 of the Billboard 100 singles chart with a music video showing a tougher version of the New Kids, but fans on a whole did not buy into it, and soon the fame of the New Kids was over. They later on became a nostalgia act.

Many moral groups seemed to have given the New Kids on the Block a pass in regards to corrupting music. In fact they seemed to like their music, but some Church groups had a different opinion. Many of them said that the New Kids sing innocent but sexual songs to young children and pre-teens. To them this would translate to young children and pre-teens to grow, and think about sex far too early leading them to sexual relationships outside of marriage. Many felt the Church groups were wrong and just out of touch, but in time many former fans of the New Kids were into a lot of sexual entertainment, and were having lots of sex with many partners. It seems those Church groups were right about what they were saying.

Another pop group was the British girl-band called The Spice Girls who were formed in London in 1994. The group's five members were Melanie Brown called Scary Spice, Melanie Chisholm called Sporty Spice, Emma Bunton called Baby Spice, Geri Halliwell called Ginger Spice, and Victoria Beckham called Posh Spice. In the mid-1990's the group would make music industry history when their debut album called Spice would sell 28 million copies world-wide.

The group was formed by a family management team who were Bob Herbert and Chris Herbert, and also Lindsey Casbon who worked for the Herberts. The company that the Herberts owned was called Heart Management. The management team wanted to make money off the pop boy-band market at the time which was dominated in England by groups like Take That and East 17. Their aim instead of a boy-band, they would create a girl-band. Heart Management would place an advertisement in The Stage magazine looking for talented females who looked good, and could sing and dance. The aim was to get these females to audition for the group.

400 women would audition, and then as the months would follow the group of women were broken down to 12, and then out of the 12 five of them were selected to become The Spice Girls. The selection process would take close to 7 months. In July of 1996 The Spice Girls, after recording their first album, released the

lead single Wannabe first in the U.K., and it became a huge hit. When the song came out in the United States it took the number one spot on the Billboard 100 singles chart. Overnight they became very, very famous. When their debut album was released their fame drew comparisons to Beatlemania. The album called Spice would come to sell 28 million copies which was an unheard of feat by an all-girl group on a debut album.

Their second album called Spiceworld would sell 20 million copies in 1997, and produced the smash hit single called Spice Up Your Life. At the height of their career in that time they starred in a movie about their own characters, but this mega huge fame, as quick as it came, would also end quickly as well. The girls soon became a nostalgia act.

Many moral and Church groups pointed out some hard truths about the influences of the Spice Girls. First let us start with stories that were said by insiders who knew the girls before, and after they were famous. Many of these stories had not been proven but they are interesting and strange. Many of them stated that if the Spice Girls did not become famous they would have been great gold-diggers. They stated that they each had a huge love for money, success, and were willing to do anything, and destroy anyone for it.

Some of them stated that the girls posed in nude magazines before they were famous, and afterwards their management team sought out said pictures and destroyed them. Many of them stated that these girls are not sweet and innocent, and they don't have a love for their fans. They stated that the girls were drug users and cursed a whole lot, and often made fun of their very young fans, and were not able to relate to their fans. Many of them also stated that the girls were into homosexual practices, and when Pepsi gave each of the girls one million dollars to do a commercial for them The Spice Girls only agreed to do it if Pepsi would show a homosexual scene in the commercial of two women embracing. Keep in mind their fans were mainly children.

The religious beliefs of The Spice Girls was also said to be nowhere near Christian, and in fact many of their own statements they made public does back this up. Much of their belief falls in line with the New Age faith, and not Christianity. Moral groups and Church groups were often at odds with parent groups over The Spice Girls. The parent groups liked The Spice Girls, and stated that they are empowering young girls to believe in themselves through their 'girl-power' slogan. But the moral and Church groups pointed out the lyrical contents of their songs, and their overly sexual image in their appearances and music videos were not good for young girls or anyone, especially children. The moral and Church groups stated that The Spice Girls are not pre-teens or teenagers but are fully grown women singing about sex to mostly female fans who are from 5 to 15 years old. That many of their songs teach their fans how to use their bodies sexually to feel better about themselves as their lyrics put it, and to even get what they want.

One song they pointed out was a song called Naked. In the music video The Spice Girls are positioned sitting behind chairs while they are naked, and begin to sing the song. Keep in mind children from 5 to 15 are watching this, and at those ages they will want to do what The Spice Girls are doing.

Some of the lyrics of the song goes like this, 'Naked she knows exactly what to do with men like you, she wants to play seek and hide, this child has fallen from grace...she wants to get naked.' If you think there is nothing wrong with singing a song like this to an audience of children then I must say there could be something wrong with you, because let's face it, children are the most easily influenced by music, and pre-teens and teenagers are its most demanding fans, and are always influenced by music. When a group is popular the fans will seek to do things they see the group is doing or singing about. In high-schools and colleges this is seen every single day.

Another song they did was called 2 become 1. The message of\the song was not about marriage but it was about how good The Spice Girls are in bed. The song was to tickle the young fans' ears into understanding that by being good in bed you can control the men you sleep with. Remember that the parent groups who supported The Spice Girls stated that their 'girl-power' slogan was empowering young girls, but how was it empowering them? That question could only be determined by the messages they were sending in their music. The messages were not about Christian morals, nor was it about education, and self-development in future goals to keep one's self on track. The messages were all about sex and depravity done under the guise of innocence.

Take for example the song they did called Do It. The title should tell us all something about where they are going with the song. This song was popular among the age ranges of 5 to 15 year olds. Hear are some of the lyrics to the song, 'Come on and do it, do it, do it, I will not be told, keep your mouth shut, keep your legs shut, go back in your place blameless, shameless, damsel in disgrace, who cares what they say because the rules are for breaking, who made them anyway.'

To understand the core of what The Spice Girls are singing about is actually understood better by young people then their own parents. The rules The Spice Girls are talking about are rules made by GOD, and rules set down by parents with godly morals. The song is about having sex when others like your parents or GOD tell you not to. The song undermines Christian teachings or any parents' teachings who want their kids to wait before they have sex. Understanding this one wonders how could parent groups who support The Spice Girls be so relaxed about them when The Spice Girls' music will even undermine them. It could be that these parents were in the dark about what this music really meant at the time. Sadly today many of them still are, and even dismiss or approve such music.

When The Spice Girls performed on stage their young fans even dressed like them. Keep in mind The Spice Girls dressed in a lewd manner, and so that's what the 5 to 15 year olds are wearing.

The core understanding of their songs were about girls playing with boys like they were toys, girls opening their legs for sex, girls having sex with girls, girls rebelling against the lessons of GOD and their parents. Many parents took their little girls and their pre-teen daughters to these shows, and their daughters knew all the lyrics by heart.

It seems like many of these parent groups who support pop groups like this have become part of the cultural rape of their own children. They seem to forget or not even understand that girls in schools are popular today, and even yesterday by not being smart but by how well they can attract and manipulate boys. This is a problem in schools, and not a norm like so many parents want to believe it is. By believing this is normal is to ignore the problem, and become co-conspirators in the spiritual decay of their own children.

The Bible tells that parents are given the job by GOD himself to raise their children on his values, and to not allow their children to be inspired by sin, but so many parents have other ideas, and so they in their own sins and weaknesses allow their children to run after sexual idols, and put their posters on their walls, and apply the messages of their music into their lives. It reminds me of what Jesus said about what happens when a person truly does become a Christian. That a persons' enemies will be the members of his own household.

Two other pop-groups would also leave a lasting mark on the music industry. These two groups were boy-bands by the names of the Backstreet Boys and 'N Sync. The Backstreet Boys were formed in Orlando, Florida by Lou Pearlman in 1993.

Pearlman in 1992 placed an ad in the Orlando Sentinel looking to compose a boy-band vocal group. A dancer and singer named A.J. McLean was the first to audition for Pearlman where he performed for him in Pearlman's living room. He became the group's first member.

In January of 1993 Pearlman held an open cast call where hundreds of young performers came to audition. Kevin Richardson had come to Orlando, Florida in 1990 to work at Walt Disney World. Richardson would audition for the gig and he was selected. After he was selected for the group he recommended his cousin from Kentucky named Brian Littrell. After a phone call from Richardson, Littrell flew there to audition, and then he was selected. Through the auditions Nick Carter and Howie Dorough were also selected.

Lou Pearlman, after forming the group, began to think about what to name them. He then thought about a teen hang-out called the Orlando Backstreet Market. From there he named the group the Backstreet Boys. Lou Pearlman along with the musicians, and DJs he knew and worked with would write all the songs of the Backstreet Boys. The Backstreet Boys had their first performance at SeaWorld Orlando on May 8, 1993.

Throughout the summer of 1993 they performed at shopping malls, restaurants, and at a charity gala in Fort Launderdale, Florida. Soon they began touring high-schools. Mercury Records was the first label who wanted to sign them, but at the time John Mellencamp who was one of their prime acts threatened to leave the label if they got into the boy-band business. Mellencamp never really gave a reason for this hatred of this style of music. Some said he just simply hated boy-band music, and others think he hated the way producers did business regarding boy-bands.

Soon after in 1994 Jeff Fenster of Jive Records signed the group to the Jive label after seeing them perform at a high-school in Cleveland, Ohio. In June of 1995 the Backstreet Boys flew to Sweden to record their first single called We've Got It Goin' On. The song became a minor success in Europe and America, but soon the song entered the top 5 in Germany, Switzerland, Austria, France, and the Netherlands. They would soon record their first album called Backstreet Boys, and it was released in May of 1996.

Their popularity in Europe grew when the song I'll Never Break Your Heart went gold as a single. Their debut album in Europe would sell 500,000 copies mainly in Germany. When the single called Quit Playing Games with my Heart came out on the radio stations in the U.S. the song took the number two spot on the Billboard 100 singles chart. The song was a huge hit, and their debut album would then sell over 1 million copies in the U.S. at that time.

In August of 1997 the Backstreet Boys released their second album called Backstreet's Back. The album would cement their place in music history as it sold 28 million copies world-wide, and 14 million of those sales were in the United States.

As their fame and success grew, soon Littrell, McLean, Richardson, and Dorough noticed that their paychecks were not up to par with their sales. In short they were being ripped off. Nick Carter also had the same problem but was oddly not vocal about it. The four men then brought a lawsuit against Lou Pearlman for stealing money earnings from the group. Only Nick Carter refused to sue Pearlman. There was no evidence to this but many said it was because Pearlman favored him more than the others, and promised him a solo recording one day.

During the tour to promote the album the Backstreet Boys had many shows cancelled due to open-heart surgery that was done twice to Littrell, and the death of Dorough's sister Caroline. In 1998 while the lawsuit against Pearlman was going the group was still working for him, and Pearlman was still writing their songs. In that year the Backstreet Boys recorded the album Millennium. Millennium was released in May of 1999, and the lead single I Want It That Way hit the number one spot on the Billboard 100 singles chart. Millennium would take the number one spot on the Billboard 200 albums chart, and produced four hit singles. Millennium was an album that also made music history as it sold 30 million copies world-wide with 12 million of those sales in the U.S. The Backstreet Boys became the most successful boy-band in music industry history. Their last major success on an album was in November of 2000 when they released the album Black & Blue. This album sold 10 million copies world-wide, but soon after the Backstreet Boys found themselves dealing with court-cases over money issues.

They also fought with each other over personal issues, and they were struggling with drug, and alcohol issues. McLean became public with his addictions on The Oprah Winfrey Show, and revealed his dealings with drugs and alcohol. The group's fame would soon fade into nostalgia, and later when the New Kids on the Block released a new album after well over 10 years of silence the Backstreet Boys went on a tour with them to entertain fans of nostalgia.

'N Sync was a boy-band also formed in Orlando, Florida. The group consisted of Justin Timberlake, JC Chasez, Chris Kirkpatrick, Joey Fatone, and Lance Bass. This boy-band is the only group who performed at the World Series, the Super Bowl, and the Olympic Games. This group was formed by the same man who formed the Backstreet Boys who was Lou Pearlman.

This got started when Chris Kirkpatrick spoke to Pearlman in 1995 about forming a second boy-band group. Pearlman told him that he would finance the group if Kirkpatrick found other male young singers who could appeal to female fans.

Kirkpatrick was working for Universal Studios in Florida at the time, and he called one of his friends who also worked there named Joey Fatone. Pearlman one day was looking through some old tapes of the Mickey Mouse Club of the late 80's to early 90's, and noticed a former member named Justin Timberlake. Pearlman got in contact with him, and asked him to join and Justin agreed to. While looking for another member Justin recommended a friend of his named JC Chasez, and then JC auditioned and joined the group. While looking for the 5th member Justin called his vocal coach, and he suggested a then 16 year old named Lance Bass from Mississippi.

Bass flew to Orlando and auditioned, and became the 5th member. Pearlman set the five boys up in a house in Orlando where they rehearsed constantly as they learned dance routines and vocal parts. Pearlman and his team of song-writers, and DJs would write all their songs and music. The group would soon record a single called I'll Be Back for More, and the executives at BMG were impressed with it.

During this time Pearlman would name the group 'N Sync by taking letters from each of the names of the group members. When the people at BMG heard the single they asked Pearlman to bring them in so they could see them perform for them. After they performed BMG signed them to work for their label at BMG Ariola Munich in Germany.

Once in Germany the group was sent to Sweden to record their first album called 'N Sync. Their debut album was first released in Germany, and its lead single called I Want You Back was an instant hit, and entered into the top 10 singles chart in Germany. The debut album would soon hit number one in Germany, and soon the album would sell close to one million copies in Europe.

This success resulted in RCA Records to sign them in 1998. In America the single I Want You Back was released, and hit number 13 on the Billboard 100 singles chart, and the album started to slowly increase in sales. When their next single called Tearin' Up My Heart was released it became a huge hit. Even though the single did not hit number one the single became just as big as a number one single due to the music video on MTV that became very popular. This resulted in the sales of the album to greatly increase, and their debut album would sell 10 million copies.

In late 1998 'N Sync would release a holiday album called Home for Christmas which sold 2 million copies. They would also record a song with Gloria Estefan for the soundtrack for her movie called Music of the Heart. The song Music of My Heart hit the number two spot on the Billboard 100 singles chart, but soon after having great success they noticed that Lou Pearlman was ripping them off. The group would file a lawsuit against Lou Pearlman for defrauding them of more than 50% of their earnings, because of the lawsuit and the bitterness they had toward Pearlman the group managed to leave RCA, and signed with Jive Records under new management.

In March of 2000 the group released their second album called No Strings Attached. The lead single called Bye Bye Bye hit the number 5 spot on the Billboard 100 singles chart. The album would go on to sell 10 million copies.

Their last success on an album was their third one called Celebrity, but the group would be torn apart by Justin Timberlake who wanted a solo career, and got one. Many strange stories were told about the members of the Backstreet Boys and 'N Sync along with other artists who have had connections with Disney or Universal Studios. Most of it centers on the stories told about the company called Disney, and the abuse of child stars, and members of the Mickey Mouse Club who worked for them. Mostly all of these stories have not been proven in regards to evidence or court cases, but the stories often come up again and again.

The stories started with a man named Bobby Beausoleil who was a member of the Charles Manson family, and he played Lucifer in Kenneth Anger's film Lucifer Rising. Bobby would be arrested for committing a murder under the orders of Charles Manson. Before Bobby got involved with the Manson family he was a child star, and a former member of the Mickey Mouse Club. The story is Bobby was sexually molested by Walt Disney, and several other executives who worked at Disney, and he was tortured by them as well.

The people who brought this story out stated that Bobby's story is the story of many child stars of Disney past and present. Walt was accused of being a satanic occultist who had a twisted thing for molesting and abusing children that were involved with Disney projects. They stated that the reason that Disney always promoted magic in their films had a lot to do with the religious beliefs of Walt Disney.

One story was even stranger, that the Walt Disney Company was funded by secret agencies in the U.S. government to conduct undercover early mind-control experiments on children. This is very hard to believe for many people but the people who say that it is true stated that people have a hard time believing it only because of the family image of Disney.

Disney pictures do have a lot of occult beliefs, and sexual images of young girls that is a clear fact. Often early Disney pictures even had downright racist images. People who spoke against Walt Disney stated that his image was nothing like the way the man, and the people who ran Disney really were. They stated that Walt was a bi-sexual, and was more gay then straight, and he liked to have immoral relations with children. They also said he beat these children as well. Many said that Disney executives past and present put unfair, and immoral demands upon the parents whose children worked for Disney to use their children anyway they see fit. Often times they were used as sexual slaves. Many even went on to say many of these children were used to test mind-control technology.

Once again no one knows if this is really true, and if it is you can bet the government and Disney will never admit that it's true. Beausoleil's story was exposed by Kenneth Anger's Hollywood Babylon magazine at the time. Hollywood Babylon was a magazine that revealed the dark, and evil lifestyles of Hollywood stars, and famous people in general. Many stated that the stories were made up only to be shown many years later that the stories were true.

Take for instance Jayne Mansfield. Hollywood Babylon was the first magazine to state that Jayne was a Satanist, and a member of Anton's Church of Satan coven in California. No one at the time believed that was true, and said the magazine only told shock stories that were untrue. It turned out the story was true.

In fact, when Anger put a story in the magazine no one in Hollywood wanted to sue him. Many people said it was because Anger could fully prove it, so they left him alone to write, and ignored the story piece while the media called it a trash magazine. Trash or not, people in Hollywood were intimidated by Anger.

Anger began a homosexual affair with Beausoleil, and then Beausoleil exposed the story to Anger of what Walt Disney used to do to him as a child. Other former Mickey Mouse Club members also told similar stories, and the media never even reported on them but ignored it as if it was a subject that could destroy their careers. It makes you wonder how could a company like Walt Disney have this much power if it's only a family fun children's company.

The story with today's pop stars is that many of them who started out with Disney rather as an entertainer or they worked there is that they have been also abused by Disney executives, and their friends. This story has never been proven but often said that many famous pop artists who arose in the 1990s had been sexually molested, and tortured in mind-control experiments. A very strange story indeed, and sadly mind-control abuse is often brought up so many times in the movie and music industry that it's shocking that no police agency investigates it.

When it came to the influences of the Backstreet Boys and 'N Sync, Church groups and moral groups were once again at odds with parent groups. Parent groups made public media statements where they would thank GOD for groups like the Backstreet Boys and 'N Sync because as they put it the two groups focused on good morals, and were pure and good role-models for children, and were a sign of relief from all the gangsta rap music in the industry. There were even young Christians who played their music at Church group functions, but many

Church groups and moral groups pointed out some horrible truths about their influences, and it was not pure, and good, and not a sign of relief.

The lyrics of these two groups are very sexually explicit. The fan base of these two groups are mostly females who range from the ages of 6 to 18 years old. 90% of their fans range from the ages of 6 to 15 years old. The age ranges of the boy-band members are from 20 to 28 years old. If you were a parent or are a parent how would you feel to see a 25 year old man telling your 10 year old daughter that he wants to have sex with her in all kinds of ways, and at all kinds of strange places, and tells your little girl to never tell you about it. You would find this to be evil, and you would get very upset at this 25 year old man.

Yet groups like the Backstreet Boys and 'N Sync can get rich and famous from telling little girls the same thing, and parent groups will even praise them for it. At the height of the Backstreet Boys' fame Nick was 25, Kevin was 28, Howie was 26 and Brian was 25 along with A.J. who was also in his 20's.

The group became famous for singing about sex in all kinds of ways to little girls. If this group went out, and did all those sexual acts they sing about on little girls they would be arrested for sex with a minor and child-molestation. Some of their most popular songs were all about sexual immorality being passed off as good. Like the song If You Want it to be Good (Get Yourself a Bad Boy). This song was very popular with pre-teen girls. The song was about if a young girl wanted to have really 'good' sex she needed to find a depraved rebellious person, and allow this person to do with her anything he wanted to do to her. I wonder where, is the good morals in that son? Or how about the song Lay Down Beside Me where the group sings about getting all up inside a girl, and they are not talking about their feelings either. They are talking about having sex, and then sleeping over her house. What is interesting is that while they sing about getting 'inside' girls they left out the overwhelming rate of transmitted sexual diseases then and now. While young people have been getting 'inside' each other they have been catching at a high rate gonorrhea, syphilis, crabs, NSU, venereal warts, herpes, HIV and AIDS.

The rate that pre-teens, teenagers, and college kids have been catching them is at the same rate that prostitutes, and porn stars catch them. That means that many young people are not having just one or two partners but many of them are having 20 to 50 partners in one year. Many girls even admitted to having sex with a different guy nearly every night out of 365 days a year.

How about the song the Backstreet Boys did called Boys Will Be Boys? How many people even knew that the song promoted date-rape among teenagers? The lyrics of the song are about a guy who could not wait while dating a girl, and he expresses to the girl why he must push himself upon her because he could not control his lust for her. In another song called I Need You Tonight the Backstreet Boys sang that sex should be done regardless if their parents tell them not to. In another song called Get Down the song was about promoting S & M practices which is violent sex.

In a song done by 'N Sync called Space Cowboy the group sings a song about rejecting Biblical prophecies, and calling those beliefs paranoia. They attacked the prophecy regarding Jerusalem, and the end of day's events regarding the ancient city, and tell their young fans that they should embrace sexual fornication instead. In the song they compare their sexual acts to young fans as taking a ride in space. Of course travelling into space is dangerous and not fun. Also their reasons for rejecting Bible prophecies is stupid and perverted. Many people, mostly parent groups and the fans at the time, stated that the Backstreet Boys and 'N Sync concerts were tamed compared to rock concerts.

Let me describe to you one Backstreet Boys' concert that took place in California. What I am about to describe is how many of the Backstreet Boys' concerts went during the height of their fame. When the Backstreet Boys took the stage the mostly female fans would scream their heads off for about 10 minutes. After screaming so loudly many of them would faint or throw up.

Among the massive crowds the management team of the Backstreet Boys had implant people among the crowds holding signs. When the Backstreet Boys started to play a popular song the implant people would hold up the sign. The sign read 'take your clothes off' and 'get naked'. When the signs were held up they were not pointed at the group but pointed at the fans. The fans in the 90% range were 11 to 17 years old.

The girls would get so inspired by it they would reach for their bra and underwear, and throw it on stage in the thousands. Girls as young as 11 years old would do this with or without parent supervision. The fans would also pound the floorboards with such force that it would cause intense vibrations throughout the stage where you can see stage crews running to hold the speakers in place.

At that show a girl about the age of 12 was sitting on a crate near the corner of the stage. Suddenly a 16 year old girl ran upon the stage, and violently kicked the 12 year old off the crate, and took off her shirt, and ripped off her bra to throw it at Nick Carter. Nick was laughing when the 12 year old girl was kicked off the crate.

During interviews with these young fans in regards to their love for the Backstreet Boys they made statements that they would kill other girls to be with them. Some said they would kill themselves if it could save their lives, and so on. Psychiatrists pointed out that girls with this kind of obsession often have a hard time getting along in normal relationships, and often end up in bad relationships due to picking men who look somewhat like their favorite idol, and not picking them based upon if they really respect them.

At a Backstreet Boys' concert in Edmonton, Atlanta this show was stopped due to a trampling that almost killed several young fans. 100 people were trampled who had mostly center row seats, and were injured due to broken ribs, broken noses, broken arms, and legs. The girls that were not injured and caused the trampling said it was the best day of their lives.

At an 'N Sync show in Georgia it was the same scene there. Girls screaming their heads off until they passed out or threw up. Girls would also trample each other as well, and even pull each other's hair out to take someone else's seat to get a closer view of the group. The N' Sync management team also had implant people there among the massive crowds with signs. When N'

Sync sang a popular song they too would hold up signs pointed toward the crowds that read 'drop your panties'.

These girls in the thousands did just that they took off their panties in the thousands, and threw them on stage. The promoters counted over 10,000 panties being removed from the stage after the show, and called it 'a night of 10,000 sexual awakenings'. Many of these panties belonged to girls from 11 to 14 years old.

Chapter 17

In the 1980's R&B music had started to transform its sound by fusing with it new wave beats. Hip-hop, electro funk, and soul were becoming very popular at the nightclubs, and many R&B artists started to jump on board to create what they called the urban sound to R&B music. Many artists would come forth bringing new forms to R&B music using many different musical styles. Let's us take a look at some of them who had left a huge impact or a moment in time impact on the music industry.

Janet Jackson was the youngest of the famed Jackson family. She was born in Gary, Indiana on May 16, 1966. Janet first started her career appearing on The Jackson's variety television series in 1976. Later in the late 70's to early 80's she was a cast member on the television sitcom Good Times. When Janet was a small girl her older brothers Jackie, Tito, Jermaine, Marlon, and Michael were performing in nightclubs as the Jackson 5. When the group was signed to Motown Records they would have huge success, and the Jackson family moved to a mansion in the suburb of Encino outside of Los Angeles in 1971. Janet would develop a love for horses, and would often ride them. She dreamed about becoming a race-horse jockey but her father had other ideas. Her father expected her to go into a career in the music industry. Janet was never asked if she wanted to go into show business it was demanded of her by her father Joe Jackson.

When Janet was growing up she managed to escape a lot of the abuse her brothers got from her father, but what used to bother

her is that her father always demanded that Janet call him Joe and not 'dad'. One time when Janet was 8 years old she called Joe 'dad'. Joe became angry with her, and looked at her coldly, and said to her, 'You will address me as Joe'.

Even though Janet managed to escape Joe's abusive nature she had no close relationship with him as father and daughter. This can be very hard on daughters who often look for this from their father first. Joe was only a manager to her, and he kept it as that. Janet did not start off as a singer but as an actress appearing with her brothers on their CBS variety show.

Soon a producer named Norman Lear casted, her on his television show called Good Times. Janet would play a character named Penny who was an abused child. In 1978 Janet would record her first song singing a duet with her brother Randy called Long Song for Kids. In 1981 Janet joined the cast of Diff'rent Strokes where she played Charlene Duprey. Her character was noted for her fashion as she wore hooped earrings. Soon other young African-American teenage girls also started to wear hooped earrings. This resulted in Janet being seen as a role-model for young black teenage girls.

Janet then would be hired to join the cast of Fame when the show was in its fourth season. This series was filled with cast members Janet could not get along with, and she hated working on the show.

In the early 1980's Janet's father Joe got Janet Jackson a record contract with A&M Records. Janet would record her first album, and in 1982 her debut album was released called Janet Jackson. Joe Jackson oversaw the entire first album, and even though the album took the number 6 spot on the Billboard R&B chart it was not a mainstream success.

In 1984 Janet released her second album called Dream Street where her older brothers now called The Jacksons helped in putting songs together for the album, but this album also was not a mainstream success.

Janet during the early 80's fell in love with nightclub music, and wanted a new musical direction in her next album. She wanted to get out from working with her family, and wanted to do things on her own terms like her brother Michael did. Joe tried to stop Janet from leaving his management control. This resulted in Janet telling Joe she never wanted to work with him again. In short Janet fired Joe Jackson.

Janet went to A&M executive John McClain, and told him about seeking a new musical direction in her album. At that time two record producers, and former DJs named Jimmy Jam and Terry Lewis had developed a new R&B sound. It would later be called new jack swing. New jack swing was a more pop-form of R&B but with urban, and R&B tempos and instrumentals. This new style of R&B was meant to fuse any style into the R&B sound.

John McClain wanted to help Janet to make a better sounding album, and he hired Jimmy Jam and Terry Lewis to work with Janet, and produce her third album. While working on the album in Minneapolis a group of men stalked Janet one night when she was on her way to the studio to work on the album. Janet at first was nervous believing that the men wanted to rape her, but then she became very angry and turned around, and began yelling at them to get them to back down. The men were taken off guard by it, and left her alone. When she went back to the studio the event inspired her to write a song about it. Janet called the song Nasty.

Jimmy and Terry would write most of the songs of the album, and all of the music. When the album was finished it was released in February of 1986. The album was called Control. Control became a huge success, and made Janet Jackson into a mainstream star in the music industry. The album sold 14 million copies world-wide. It produced 5 hit singles called Control, Nasty, What Have You Done for Me Lately, Pleasure Principle, and When I Think of You. Most of her music videos were choreographed by a then unknown Paula Abdul. Control would win 4 American Music Awards, and a Grammy Award in 1987 for Album of the Year. At the American Music Awards Control had 12 nominations which is a record that still stands today. Control was observed as the album that brought the rise of new jack swing to R&B music. The album's songs were a fusion of R&B, rap, funk, and synthesized percussion. In

September of 1989 Janet Jackson released her fourth album called Rhythm Nation 1814. The songs on the album would deliver a socially conscious message, and songs about love and relationships. The songs also spoke about injustice, illiteracy, crime, and drugs. Rhythm Nation 1814 would go on to sell 14 million copies. It is the only album in history to have seven hit singles to enter the top five of the Billboard 100 singles chart. It's main hit singles were Miss You Much, Escapade, Rhythm Nation, Black Cat, and Love Will Never Do (Without You). Janet would win a Grammy Award for her music video Rhythm Nation, and would win a record of 15 Billboard music awards. Janet would soon embark on the Rhythm Nation World Tour, and through the tour she raised 1 and a half million dollars for the United Negro College Fund. During the tour Janet became a fashion icon, and as an entertainer she was on par with her brother Michael Jackson and Madonna. Hoards of teen girls were imitating her distinctive look as they wore black quasi-military long jackets, black tight pants, and big white shirts.

In 1992 she recorded another hit single called The Best Things in Life Are Free with Luther Vandross for the soundtrack of the film Mo' Money. In 1992 Janet also returned to acting when she starred in the film Poetic Justice along-side Tupac Shakur. During the filming of the movie it was said that either Janet or her management team did not want Tupac for her leading male love interest in the film, and they really did not want him to have scenes where he kisses Janet on the mouth. The story is that Janet or her management team were afraid that Tupac may have AIDS due to the amount of women he was known to have been with. So one day while Tupac was in his trailer he got a knock on his door, and it was members of Janet's management team. They told Tupac he could not do kissing scenes with Janet unless he did an AIDS test. Tupac would do the test just to get them off his back, and he passed the test. Tupac also did have a secret crush on Janet Jackson but his experience working with Janet on the film lifted that crush. Tupac did not hate Janet but he hated what he was asked to do simply because he did gangsta rap music.

In May of 1993 Janet Jackson released her fifth album called Janet. This album would debut at the number one spot on the Billboard 200 albums chart. Janet's image for the album along with the songs went in the direction of promoting Janet as a sex-symbol. Most of the songs on the album were about presenting raw sexuality to her fans. Janet would appear on the cover of Rolling Stone magazine topless with her then husband Rene Elizando, Jr covering her breasts with his hands. The album would have four hit singles with the two main single being of which was a song about raw hardcore sex. The other song was That's the Way Love Goes which became a number one hit single on the Billboard 100 singles chart.

The album called Janet became her largest selling album of all-time as it sold 20 million copies. The reasons for such a large scale sell was not so much the music but the sexual image to the music caused a lot of sexually immoral people to buy the record. There is a saying in the movie and music industry that sex sells, and this album was another proof of that.

In the mid-90's Janet would support her brother Michael when he was battling allegations of child sex abuse, but she would turn against her sister LaToya due to the fact she hated LaToya's husband, and thought that what happens in the family should stay in the family.

In 1995 Janet worked with her brother Michael on a song called Scream. In that same year she would release a greatest hits album, but soon she began to suffer from depression and anxiety, and would often have horrible nightmares.

In 1997 she released an album called The Velvet Rope. The songs of the album were darker and more sexual in a whips and chains S&M way. The album would debut at the number one spot on the Billboard 200 albums chart, and sell 10 million copies.

In 1999 Janet would divorce her husband, and in 2000 she starred with Eddie Murphy in the Nutty Professor 2. Her ex-husband would bring trouble into her life over money, and he sued Janet for 25 million dollars. A settlement was reached in 2003.

In April of 2001 Janet released the album called All for You that took the number one spot on the Billboard 200 albums chart.

The album would sell 9 million copies but her concert tour had negative reviews, and critics told her fans she is too old even though she is eight years younger than Madonna. The critics, point of view on it did not make any sense.

In 2004 at the Super Bowl is when Janet Jackson's career would never be the same again. Janet was to perform at Super Bowl 38 along-side with Justin Timberlake who she was dating at the time. In fact, when Justin went solo he was trying to become the next Michael Jackson. A goal that many told Justin was very out of reach for him. At the Super Bowl while performing with Justin, Timberlake while singing the lines 'I bet I can get you naked by the end of this song' Justin tore off a clip on Janet's outfit that ended up exposing her right-breast. Despite what many think this was not planned by Janet but many insiders said it was planned by Timberlake without Janet knowing about it. Her reaction when it happens even shows it when she became embarrassed on television, and did not know what to do. Even though Justin was the one who tore it open, and even had to give an apology for it the media attacked Janet for it instead. The media called it one of the most controversial television events in history. The controversy was so thick that MTV, and many radio stations banned her videos, and music for some years to come after the show. All of her projects were halted, and millions of dollars from investors were lost. Her record company refused to release her new album called Discipline at the time, and when they did they refused to give the album full support.

The Federal Communications Commission had an investigation done against CBS and Janet Jackson. Notice they did not investigate Timberlake who was the one that tore the clip off.

Janet did manage to get another album she recorded called Damita Jo which is her middle name released at the time. Even though the album sold 3 million copies the media trashed the album, and said it was the equivalent of hardcore pornography. Of course they had really no problem with other artists who had a sexual image of hardcore pornography but with Janet it was an all-out assault on her character for the sole purpose of ratings and selling newspapers.

In 2006 Janet released an album called 20Y.O. that sold 2 million copies. In 2007 Janet was still ranked as one of the top 10 richest females in the music industry. In that same year of 07 the album Discipline was finally released with no support from her company. The music critics attacked the album with venom, and her record company said the album was a failure in terms of sales.

In truth they wanted to get rid of Janet, because of this Janet would leave the record label. In 2009 Janet performed Scream at the VMA show as a tribute to her brother Michael Jackson. Janet to this day is still making records, and seeking movie roles but her fame has never been the same since the Super Bowl scandal. Janet's over the top sexual image is often spoken about regarding her career. Ever since she did the album Janet and The Velvet Rope people have wondered why a woman with that much talent needed to go in the direction of smut in her career.

The answer to this had a lot to do with Janet's change in management. One of these changes involved a man named Jermaine Dupri. Dupri was the one who founded the rap group called Kris Kross who had a hit single called Jump in the early 90's. The rap duo were only a couple of kids. This story I am about to tell you has not been proven true, and it is a horrible story. It was believed that Dupri had molested these two boys, and had them passed around to be sexually abused by others. The rap duo was never the same after their fame, and one of them ended up dead due to drug addictions, and the other has a strange form of cancer often caught among people who have had gay encounters.

People wondered how could Janet deal with a man who many said destroyed the lives of two children. Also in time Janet ended up dating him. Most of the over the top sexual images of Janet were put together by Dupri, and his people especially during and after 1997.

Regarding Timberlake who Janet also dated it is often believed that Timberlake set her up at the Super Bowl in an effort to destroy her career and get her out of the way. There has been no proof to this but it's often said by Janet's peers. Timberlake dumped her right after the scandal, and did not stand by her but stood as far away as possible.

Bobby Brown would gain world-wide mainstream success as a solo artist when he was kicked out of New Edition in 1985 for behavior problems. Throughout Brown's life he has always been a troubled young man. Brown grew up in a very poor family in the Boston housing projects. His parents both worked but they had very little money. Brown often would steal from stores, and other friends he knew. As a child to a pre-teen he started to get involved with a local gang, and began to engage in petty theft and robbery. When Bobby was 10 years old he joined the gang he was hanging out with, and during a fight with a rival gang member he was shot in the knee. When Bobby was 11 years old a friend of his was stabbed multiple times at a party. Bobby held his friend in his arms, and watched him die from his wounds. Bobby after this reached a turning point, and joined a Church choir and soon after he became one of the founding members of New Edition.

After leaving New Edition in December of 1985 Brown sought a solo career in 1986. Brown worked with his manager named Steven Machat who got Brown a record deal as a solo act at MCA Records. Bobby's first album was called King of Stage released in 1986. The album produced a number one R&B hit single called Girlfriend that hit the number one spot on the R&B Billboard chart, but the rest of the album did not sell well. On Bobby's next album MCA Records hired top R&B producers and songwriters named L.A. Reid, Teddy Riley, and Babyface. These three wanted to fuse the new jack swing style into Bobby's music. The album they composed together was called Don't Be Cruel released in 1988. This album, along with Janet Jackson's Control album, was also called one of the pioneer albums of the new jack swing style into R&B music.

Bobby's music on his second album was a fusion of hip-hop and soul into R&B. The album Don't Be Cruel would have five hit singles called Don't Be Cruel, My Prerogative, Rock Wit'cha, Every Little Step, and Roni. The album would go on to sell 8 million copies. My Prerogative would hit the number one spot on the Billboard 100 singles chart. Don't Be Cruel was also one of the highest selling albums of 1989.

In 1989 Bobby Brown would appear in the film Ghostbusters 2 playing the mayor's doorman. He would record a song for the soundtrack of the film called On Our Own. On Our Own became a huge hit single, and took the number two spot on the Billboard 100 singles chart. At this time Brown started to use drugs and alcohol very recklessly. He became addicted to cocaine, and then crack, and began to spend a lot of money on it.

Brown would soon venture out on the 120 day world tour called the Don't Be Cruel Project. The tour became a huge success but it would end early in 1990. This was due to Brown getting arrested several times for simulating sexual acts onstage. Many of the girls he danced this way with were underage.

Bobby Brown according stated that he had a sexual affair with Janet Jackson in 1989 when she was still married, but Janet broke up with Bobby because her parents did not approve of him dating their daughter. Bobby stated that this break up is what pushed him further into drugs and alcohol addiction.

At the 1989 Soul Train Music Awards Brown met his future wife the famed Whitney Houston. Whitney was dating film star Eddie Murphy at the time. After Whitney broke up with Eddie she began dating Bobby Brown. Her friends warned her about Bobby's mood problems, and drug addictions, and that he was verbally abusive toward others, but Whitney being a head-strong person herself came to fall in love with Bobby. Bobby was often accused as being the one who got Whitney on drugs. The truth is Whitney was already introduced to drugs before she met Bobby.

Whitney liked to smoke marijuana at the time which was a drug everyone, and their mother did in the music industry. It was said that sometimes she did a line of cocaine at parties. What Bobby did do was made the use of harder drugs a constant habit for Whitney due to the fact it was a constant habit for him. In July of 1992 after a period of courting Brown and Houston got married.

Bobby's next album was released in 1992 called by the name Bobby. The album had two hit singles called Humpin Around and Get Away. The album was not as huge as Don't Be Cruel but it was a success as it sold 2 million copies. After 1992 Brown's career began to fade, and then he became known in the eyes of the media as Whitney's crack addicted bad husband.

Whitney and Bobby had a 14 year marriage which is longer than most marriages in Hollywood culture. The media reported on their frequent drug use as the two of them were addicted to cocaine and crack. Brown was often caught cheating on Whitney, and was often jealous of Whitney's career. There were rumors that Whitney found ways to sabotage Bobby's career so that he would not cheat on her on the road but there is no proof to that.

The couple would have one child together, a daughter by the name of Bobbi Kristina Brown. In 1996 Bobby became involved with running around with gangs again with his brother-in-law. Brown stated that he was trying to get his brother-in-law out of a street gang. One day Brown got the gang his brother-in-law was in to sit down with a rival gang in an attempt to make peace between the two gangs, but during the meeting more gang-bangers came by, and saw the meeting, and shot up the meeting in a drive-by shooting. When his brother-in-law was in the hospital several gang members came in, and shot and killed him in the hospital. Bobby, who was at the hospital that day, narrowly escaped from being shot, and ran from the intruders.

Whitney's family along with Bobby's sister blamed Bobby for the incident. Also in 1996 Florida police tried to pull over Bobby Brown which led to a high-speed chase. In the chase Brown crashed Houston's Mitsubishi car, and when the police tried to arrest him Brown began resisting arrest. Brown began swearing at the officers at the top of his lungs, and when they put him in the backseat of the squad car Brown began to urinate all over the seat.

In 2003 Brown was arrested for battery when he hit Whitney during a heated argument when the two of them were getting high together. In 2004 Brown was arrested in Georgia for a DUI. A few years later Whitney would file for divorce, and by 2007 the couple was officially divorced. In 2012 Brown would be arrested 3 times in one year, and tried to get clean and sober. In that same year Whitney Houston would be found dead. Brown today lives in an Atlanta suburb with his current wife Alicia Etheridge.

Another artist to look into is Paula Abdul. Paula's brand of music was pop-R&B mixed with funk, rock, house, and soul music. Paula was born in a Syrian-Jewish community in San Fernando, California. She was raised in a Jewish home to Jewish parents who were Harry and Lorraine Abdul. Paula was a gifted dancer, and singer. Her talents were shown at an early age. Her parents began taking her to dance lessons in ballet, Jazz, and Tap.

One day Paula saw the film Singin' in the Rain, and she became inspired by Gene Kelly to one day get into show business. While Paula attended Van Nuys High School she became a cheerleader, and a honor student. She was so skilled at dancing that at the age of 15 she received a scholarship to a dance school near Palm Springs. After attending the dance school Paula enrolled at the California State University in Northridge. While there she studied broadcasting, and soon she tried out along with 700 other candidates to join the cheerleading squad of the Los Angeles Lakers. Paula was selected to become a Laker Girl, and in one year she became the squad leader and the head choreographer of the team.

There was also a strange story also regarding her time as a Laker Girl, and the use of drugs. It was said that Paula had an injury during a move she was doing for the Lakers that hurt her back. The pain was so bad that Paula began using cocaine to deal with the pain and work, but this has never been proven.

One day while Paula was working a Los Angeles Laker's game she was noticed for her skills by members of the Jackson family. The Jacksons wanted Paula to do the choreography for their music video called Torture. Paula agreed but was scared to do it for she was only a cheerleader telling the Jacksons what moves to do, but the Jacksons being a kind group of brothers helped her to get through that.

After she did a good job for them she embarked on a career to do choreography for music videos and movies. She was soon hired by Janet Jackson, and her people to do choreography for most of the music videos for Janet's album Control. Paula was also being hired to do choreography for the film The Running Man. She also choreographed the sequences for the giant keyboard scene in the film Big that starred Tom Hanks. She also did the choreography in the film Action Jackson, and in the film Coming to America.

During that time Paula was writing music, and she soon recorded a demo of the song Forever Your Girl. When she finished the demo she soon went to work on the dance sequences for the African dancers in the film Coming to America. It was while working on Coming to America she met television host and producer Arsenio Hall who had connections to many people in the music industry. The story behind Paula and Arsenio is still an unproven story.

In 1987 Paula made a demo tape of the song Forever Your Girl. With this demo she was trying to get a record contract so she could make her own music. Arsenio knew people in the music industry who wanted to be guests on his show. At the time Arsenio's show was the most watched talk show by young fans. The story goes that Arsenio wanted Paula sexually, and so if Paula gave herself to him, he would give the tape to people at Virgin Records, and could even get her signed in return for favors he would do for their artists. No one knows how true this is but it is often said by many insiders at the time.

In 1988 Paula now working for Virgin Records released her debut album called Forever Your Girl. This album became a mind-blowing success for a debut solo female artist. Forever Your Girl would sell 12 million copies, and Paula was hailed as the 'princess of pop'. The album hit the number one spot on the Billboard 200 albums chart.

Paula would have four singles that hit the number one spot from one album and became the second female artist in history to accomplish this feat. The first was Whitney Houston. These singles that hit number one on the Billboard 100 singles chart were Straight Up, Forever Your Girl, Cold Hearted, and Opposites Attract. The video for Opposites Attract was also a milestone for animated special-effects.

The video featured an animated cat named MC Skat Kat who

was Paula's co-star in the video. MC Skat Kat became so popular the character even had an album. The video Opposites Attract would win a Grammy Award in 1990. In 1991 Paula released her second album called Spellbound. Spellbound would sell 7 million copies becoming a major success. Two of the songs from the album would hit the number one spot on the Billboard 100 singles chart. These songs were Promise of a New Day and Rush, Rush. The album would also have three other hit songs called Blowing Kisses in the Wind, Vibeology, and Will You Marry Me?

Paula would soon be paid millions of dollars to appear in Diet Coke commercials where she danced with a digital image of a young Gene Kelly. Paula would embark on the Under My Spell Tour. Many problems would arise for her. The tour was almost cancelled due to an accident Paula suffered during rehearsals. It was said that Paula would deal with the pain with further use of cocaine and pain-pills.

In 1992 she married Emilio Estevez, and then rumors of domestic violence on Emilio's part began to surface. The couple would get a divorce by 1994. In 1992 Paula was in a car accident that almost left her crippled and in extreme pain. She then began to take very high doses of pain killers, and began to use more drugs to deal with the pain. In 1993 Paula was in a plane crash that almost killed her. She would live through her injuries but had to have 15 spinal surgeries to recover. The doctors advised her to retire from dancing. The debilitating pain left her dependent on strong pain medication and cocaine. Many said that since then she has fully recovered, and no longer uses drugs but others state that is not true. It was stated that Paula's injuries were so bad that they still cause her pain today, and she is still addicted to pain killers and cocaine.

In 1995 Paula released a new album called Head over Heels, but her brand of music was not that popular anymore at the time due to a change of tastes by the mainstream fans. Head over Heels was not a failure however it did sell 3 million copies, and had two singles called Crazy Cool and My Love Is For Real enter the top 20 Billboard 100 singles chart. Those two singles also became huge nightclub hits, but due to injuries, personal issues, and lack of fan support Paula stopped making records and started working behind the scenes. She would do choreography for films, T.V. shows, and commercials as well as music videos for up and coming artists.

In 2002 Paula took a job becoming one of three judges for a reality television show that many people say is a pre-planned rigged show called American Idol. Paula worked as a judge on the show for several seasons and left the show in the middle of controversy in 2009. The reasons for the controversy were strange indeed.

In 2004 the producers and executives working on American Idol stated they were having problems with Paula due to her constant use of illegal drugs and her erratic behavior. In that same year Paula was charged by the police for committing a hit and run accident as her car was caught on footage hitting another car and then speeding off.

In 2005 an American Idol contestant named Corey Clark came forward in the media, and said that he had a sexual affair with Paula during the season of 2004. He also stated that Paula came on to him, and stated to him that she would help him to succeed better in the competition for sexual favors. But oddly Corey's statements came right at the time he was bitter about being voted off, and he was trying to get a book deal. Paula never denied the statements, and she refuses to comment on the allegations. Her celebrity peers and her co-workers from American Idol all gave her full support, and trashed Corey's statements as being lies done for publicity.

Paula still works behind the scenes in the music industry. She has also been in and out of rehabs for constant drug use. In regards to Paula's religious beliefs many stated that she was never a Christian and even stopped practicing her Jewish faith a long time ago when she became a Laker Girl. Many insiders stated that Paula was into New Age religions most especially witchcraft, but no proof was ever shown to this. Some also stated that she battles with demon-possession as well but this is not proven either.

Let us look at two acts that left a short but remembered mark on the music industry. C&C Music Factory rose to the heights of fame in the late 1980's to the early 1990's. Their music was a style of R&B new jack swing and house music. C&C Music Factory was formed by Robert Clivilles and David Cole. Robert and David started out in a house music group originally called 2 Puerto Ricans and a Blackman. The group later changed their name to The 28th Street Crew. When they changed their name they began to develop a new musical direction in their sound and started to apply R&B singing, hip-hop, and new jack swing. They would soon add a rapper to their group called MC Freedom. Then they added two female vocalists named Zelma Davis and Martha Wash. The group then recorded their first single called Get Dumb! (Free Your Body). This single became huge in the nightclubs, and it led to a recording contract. When they were signed to the label the executives wanted them to change their name. Robert and David would rename the group to C&C Music Factory taking the two C's from the first letters of their last names.

They would soon record the album called Gonna Make You Sweat. Their first album took the world by a storm. The album would go on to sell 8 million copies. In 1990 the album took the number two spot on the Billboard 200 albums chart. The lead single Gonna Make You Sweat (Everybody Dance Now) hit the number one spot on the Billboard 100 singles chart. Their second single called Here We Go (Let's Rock & Roll) hit the number three spot on the Billboard 100 singles chart. Their next single called Things That Make You Go Hmmm hit number four on the Billboard 100 singles chart. In total they had four singles three of them already mentioned that hit the number one spot on the Billboard Dance Club Party Chart.

From their first album the group would win 5 American Music Awards, 2 VMA's, and a total of 35 music industry awards world-wide, but when they released their second album called Anything Goes in 1994 the tastes of music fans had already changed. Two singles from the album called Do You Wanna Get Funky and Take a Toke were huge nightclub hits but the album failed in mainstream sales. The other group who was famous in the late 80's to early 90's turned out to be a very sad case indeed. This group was an R&B new jack swing duo called Milli Vanilli. This duo came from Munich, Germany. The group was formed by Frank Farian who created the duo's image.

The real singers of Milli Vanilli's songs were Charles Shaw, John Davis, and Brad Howell. The singers who did the female vocals for the songs were a couple of twin sisters named Jodie and Linda Rocco. The idea originally was to get this group of five singers to come together and bring their sound into the music industry, but Frank who was their manager at the time did not think that the looks of this group had a marketable image, only their voices did.

One night at a nightclub Frank saw two men who were Robert Pilatus and Fabrice Morvan. Pilatus and Morvan worked as models, and they were dancers at a Munich nightclub. They also were singers as well but were not good enough singers for the level of the music industry.

Frank was not interested in their singing skills he wanted their looks because through them he can market that image with the voices of Shaw, Davis, and Howell. Frank then came to Pilatus and Morvan who were hungry for success, and had very little money. Frank manipulated the two of them, and gave them an advance of money if they went along with his plan. The plan was he wanted these two to pose as singers, and lip-sync on music videos, and concerts to pre-recorded music. After Frank gave them the advance the two were talked into signing a contract. On the contract Pilatus and Morvan were legal bound to repay the advance.

The contract trapped these two into going along with this awful plan just in case the two men would change their minds because the only way they were able to repay the advance would be through paychecks if the album sold well. In 1989 the album called Girl You Know It's True was released. The album would sell millions of copies, and became a world-wide success. They had four smash hit singles called Don't Forget My Number, Blame it On The Rain, Girl You Know It's

True, and I'm Gonna Miss You.

In 1990 they would win a Grammy Award for Best New Artist, but after the scandal was known the Grammy Award commission withdrew their Grammy win from their records, and ordered the group to return the award. The duo also won 3 American Music Awards but these awards were not withdrawn. The commission of the American Music Awards stated that they did not withdraw the awards because the awards are based on the music consumers, and not on actual talent. That's an eye-opener about the American Music Awards.

The group first got busted for lip-synching during a live performance on MTV at a show held in Bristol, Connecticut. The duo was performing a song called Girl You Know It's True when the record they were lip-synching began to skip over and over again repeating the line 'Girl you know it's' as it skips on the speakers. At first they continue to lip-sync pretending that everything was fine but when the record continued to skip the two of them ran off the stage in panic.

The duo did not get busted in full just yet when that happened due to the fact the fans hardly noticed it. Soon Charles Shaw having enough of the success of his songs being given to impostors disclosed the truth to writer John Leland of the New York Newsday. Frank then paid Shaw $150,000 to retract his statements. Shaw took the money and did so, but the concert, and the newspaper piece began to raise many questions.

The truth became finally known when Morvan and Pilatus managed to pay back the advance and wanted out of the scam, and wanted to sing their own songs. The duo turned on Frank and Frank in return went to Arista record executives with this problem of Pilatus and Morvan wanting to sing their own songs. Arista record executives who were in on the scam told Frank to handle it. So Frank would handle it by giving a confession to reporters on November 12, 1990 that Morvan and Pilatus did not sing the songs on their album.

A firestorm from the media would soon hit them. Record stores in major cities had to refund thousands of copies of the album, and those record stores began to sue the management of Milli Vanilli and Arista Records for the money loss. Frank, to avoid him and the duo from being directly sued, pointed the blame to Arista Records as being the ones who gave Frank the plan to pull off this scam.

In truth the real blame was both Frank Farian and Arista Records, but efforts to avoid lawsuits for him and the duo failed. The lawsuits caused Pilatus and Morvan to lose every cent they earned from the success of that album. A lot of their loyal fans hearts' were broken.

The duo tried to make a comeback by singing the songs from the album themselves but this effort failed. From there every effort of a comeback failed. The duo would eventually find themselves struggling with homelessness and drug addictions. In 1997 Robert Pilatus' drug problems became so bad he turned to a life of crime. He was committing a series of robberies, and ended up serving three months in a jail in California.

When Pilatus got out of jail Frank Farian tried to help him to get sober and wanted Pilatus to fly back to Germany to attend six months of drug rehabilitation. Frank was trying once again to get the duo success by making an international album, but in April of 1998 Pilatus was unable to overcome personal demons. He then took a very large amount of prescription pain killers, and would overdose on them in a Frankfurt hotel room. His body was found dead the next morning by a maid. Morvan managed to find success after a very hard life. He eventually became a DJ at the famed L.A. radio station called KIIS.

Another act was the one often called the 'Queen of R&B' was Whitney Houston. Whitney was born in a middle-class area of Newark, New Jersey on August 9, 1963. Her father was an Army serviceman who became an entertainment executive named Russell Houston, and her mother was a Gospel singer by the name of Cissy Houston. Cissy's cousin is the famed Dionne Warwick who got into promoting psychic reading television ads much later in her career. Cissy was also good friends with Aretha Franklin who became an honorary aunt to Whitney Houston.

Whitney first met Aretha when she was a child of eight years old when her mother took her to a recording studio. Whitney's godmother was Darlene Love who was a famous Gospel and Rhythm & Blues singer. Whitney was raised as a Baptist Christian, and was also exposed to the doctrine of the Pentecostal Church. Her family saw the 1967 Newark Riots that were brutal and bloody. After the riots her family moved to the middle-class area of East Orange, New Jersey. This move took place when Whitney was four years old.

Whitney was born with strong singing gifts, and she started performing as a soloist in the junior Gospel choir at New Hope Baptist Church. When Whitney was a teenager she attended a Catholic all-girls high-school called Mount Saint Dominic Academy in Caldwell, New Jersey. Whitney's taste in music was the styles of Chaka Khan, Gladys Knight, and Roberta Flack. These artists were a heavy influence on her as a singer and entertainer. As a teenager Whitney spent a lot of time with her mom Cissy when she was performing at nightclubs trying to get into the secular side of music. Sometimes her mother would bring Whitney on stage to sing with her.

Soon at the age of 14 a singer named Michael Zager noticed her, and asked Whitney's mother if Whitney could sing background vocals for his band's single called Life's a Party. Cissy allowed her daughter to do so, and from there as a teenager Whitney became a backup singer for the Michael Zager Band. In 1978 when Whitney was 15 Chaka Khan asked Cissy if Whitney could sing background vocals on her single I'm Every Woman. Cissy allowed her to, and the song became a hit single for Chaka Khan. In fact, later in Whitney's career Whitney did a remake of the song for the Bodyguard soundtrack and the song became an even bigger hit single.

Soon, in the late 1970's, Whitney was working as a backup singer on albums for Lou Rawls and Jermaine Jackson. In the early 1980's Whitney started working as a fashion model, and would perform at times at Carnegie Hall. Whitney even became one of the first women of color to grace the cover of Seventeen magazine. Soon Whitney was featured in layouts of Glamour and Cosmopolitan. She also did a soft drink commercial for Canada Dry.

While modeling she continued her recording career, and in 1983 she was signed by Arista Records. She would record a duet single with Teddy Pendergrass called Hold Me that became a top 5 R&B hit. This was Whitney's first taste of success.

In 1985 Whitney released her first album called Whitney Houston. Rolling Stone magazine would give Whitney high praise calling her voice as one of the most exciting new voices of the year. Her album was also hailed as an impressive work from an exceptional vocal talent.

At first her first album was not doing well in sales in the U.S. but in Europe it was selling very well. Whitney would have three hits in Europe during that time called Someone for Me, All at Once, and You Give Good Love. The single You Give Good Love started to rise in sales in the U.S., and was bringing Whitney mainstream attention to her album. The song would soon hit the number three spot on the Billboard 100 singles chart, and it was number one on the R&B chart.

Soon her album started to rise fast in sales. Whitney in that time would go on a nightclub tour to promote the album. She also started to appear as a guest on late-night talk shows at a time very few African-American artists were on late-night talk shows. When the single Saving All My Love was released from the album the song became a smash hit. The song would take the number one spot on the Billboard 100 singles chart in the U.S., and the U.K. MTV who at the time was under fire for not playing enough videos by black artists wanted to film a music video for Whitney's next single.

The next single was a song called How Will I Know. The song became the second single from Whitney Houston's debut album to take the number one spot on the Billboard 100 singles chart. The MTV video for the song received consistent heavy rotation on MTV. Her next single called the Greatest Love of All would also take the number one spot on the Billboard 100 singles chart giving Whitney a total of three number one hits from her debut album. By 1986 Whitney's debut album sold an unheard of for a female artist on a debut record a total of 25 million copies.

In 1986 Whitney would win a Grammy Award, 7 American Music Awards, a VMA, and an Emmy Award for Best Television Performance. In 1987 Whitney Houston released her second album called Whitney. To make her sound to have a more pop-music flavor Whitney brought in Jellybean Benitez, the man who created Madonna's sound, to work on her album with her three main producers. Whitney's second album would also become a huge mainstream success. The album would debut at the number one spot on the Billboard 200 albums chart in the U.S., and the U.K. at the same time.

The album produced four hit singles that all became number one hit songs on the Billboard 100 singles chart. These singles were I Wanna Dance With Somebody, Didn't We Almost Have It All, So Emotional, and Where Do Broken Hearts Go . Whitney was the first female solo artist in history to have four songs take the number one spot on the Billboard 100 singles chart. Her second album would sell 20 million copies.

After the release of the album Whitney embarked on the Moment of Truth World Tour. The tour became one of the highest grossing concert tours in history. In 1988 she won another Grammy Award, 2 American Music Awards, and a Soul Train Music Award. One of her biggest moments was during the European part of her tour when she performed at Wembley Stadium in London.

The concert was to honor the then imprisoned Nelson Mandela's 70th birthday as the show was to promote the fight against apartheid in South Africa at the time. 72,000 people came to the stadium, and over one billion people watched it on television.

In 1988 Whitney recorded a song called One Moment in Time for the 1988 Summer Olympics. The song became a top five hit on the Billboard 100 singles chart. By 1989 Whitney was the third richest African-American in the United States where Bill Cosby, and Eddie Murphy were right above her.

In that year African-American fans started to call her a sell-out but at the 1989 Soul Train Music Awards when Whitney was called on stage in the mist of cheers and jeers Whitney defended herself, and stated that she felt no shame in the way she carried out her career.

In November of 1990 Whitney released her third album called I'm Your Baby Tonight. The album was produced by Babyface and L.A. Reid who applied an urban new jack swing sound to her music. The album was also a huge hit, and sold 12 million copies. It produced two hit singles called I'm Your Baby Tonight and All the Man That I Need, and both singles hit the number one spot on the Billboard 100 singles chart.

At that time Whitney became the spokesperson for the Youth Leadership forum. She would have a private audience with the then President George H.W. Bush in the Oval Office in 1990 to discuss the associated issues. In 1991 Whitney performed a free concert for the soldiers fighting in the

Persian Gulf War where she performed the concert at the Naval Station in Norfolk, Virginia in front of 3,500 military service men and women. HBO aired the concert and it gave HBO it's highest ratings ever at the time.

In 1992, after a period of court-ship, Whitney married R&B new jack singer Bobby Brown. A marriage that many said brought her a slow, down fall into harder drug use. During the 1990's Whitney had many movie offers but she kept turning them down, and she did not feel like working for the movie industry, but her management team came to convince her that it would propel her career further.

She then took her first role in a film called The Bodyguard where she co-starred with Kevin Costner. The Bodyguard was released in 1992, and it became a huge box-office hit. The film took in 121 million dollars at the U.S. box office, and in total the film grossed $410 million in world-wide box office sales. Whitney recorded nearly all the songs on the soundtrack. The soundtrack's lead single called I Will Always Love You hit the number one spot on the Billboard 100 singles chart.

The song was originally written and recorded by Dolly Parton in 1974. The song would become Whitney's signature song, and her most remembered iconic performance. The single alone would sell 12 million copies. The Bodyguard soundtrack album would go on to sell 44 million copies. Whitney would also have two more singles from the album to hit the number one spot on the Billboard 100 singles chart. Those songs were I'm Every Woman and I Have Nothing. The album also produced a smash hit at the nightclubs called Queen of the Night that took the number one spot on the Billboard Dance Club chart. Whitney due to the success of the Bodyguard soundtrack would win 3 Grammy Awards, 8 American Music Awards, 11 Billboard Music Awards, and 3 Soul Train Music Awards. In 1994 she would attend and perform at a state dinner at the White House to honor newly elected South Africa President Nelson Mandela.

At this time Whitney's marriage to Bobby Brown started to get attention in the media for drug use. At first the attention is centered on Bobby, and people told her to get out of the marriage. Before Bobby, Whitney only used soft-core drugs, and that was only at parties like marijuana, but in time Bobby would often lace the marijuana with pieces of rock-cocaine. This caused Whitney to have a full addiction to harder drugs.

Whitney, no matter what people told her at the time, would not leave Bobby because of how much she loved him. In 1995 Whitney would star in the movie Waiting to Exhale alongside Angela Bassett. The movie was about four African-American women struggling with relationships and motherhood. The movie would gross 67 million dollars at the U.S. box-office, and grossed 81 million dollars in total after counting ticket sales world-wide.

Many believe that this movie paved the way for the Tyler Perry movies in the 2000s. The film's soundtrack was produced by Whitney Houston and Babyface. Many R&B female recording artists took part in recording songs for the soundtrack like Brandy, Mary J. Blige, Aretha Franklin, Toni Braxton, and others. The song Whitney recorded for the soundtrack was called Exhale (Shoop Shoop). The song took the number one spot on the Billboard 100 singles chart.

In 1996 Whitney would receive 10 million dollars to star in a movie with Denzel Washington called The Preacher's Wife. This high salary made Whitney one of the highest paid actresses in Hollywood. Many strange stories were said about Whitney during the making of the film. Crew members on the film stated that Whitney was using drugs while making the film. In some of the scenes in the film it was said that Whitney was high on rock-cocaine, but there was no overall proof to it. The film would gross 50 million dollars in the U.S. and Whitney's acting received good reviews. For the soundtrack of the film the album was aimed to be a pure Gospel album.

Whitney recorded several Gospel songs for the soundtrack with the Georgia Mass Choir, and she recorded a duet with Gospel icon Shirley Caesar. One of the reviews noted the power of Whitney's voice. The entire Georgia Mass Choir throughout the recording had a hard time keeping up with Whitney. Whitney's two noted songs on the soundtrack were I Believe in You and Me and Step by Step. This soundtrack would sell 6 million copies, and became the largest selling Gospel album of all time.

In the late 1990's Whitney would do a HBO concert in honor of Dorothy Dandridge who was the first African-American actress nominated for an Oscar. In 1998 Whitney released an album called My Love Is Your Love. The sound direction for the album was far edgier with more urban dance, hip-hop, reggae, with her brand of R&B music which was darker in its sound. The album would have 5 hit singles called Heartbreak Hotel, Its Not Right But It's Okay, My Love is Your Love, I Learned from the Best, and When You Believe. In this album Whitney would work with other artists like Faith Evans, Kelly Price, and Mariah Carey. Her single called My Love is Your Love would sell 3 million copies alone, and the album itself would sell 11 million copies. The single When You Believe was a duet she did with Mariah Carey. The song was featured on the soundtrack for the animated film about Moses called The Prince of Egypt. It marked the first time that Whitney and Mariah worked together as they are regarded as the two best vocalist in the music industry at the time.

When You Believe would end up winning an Academy Award for Best Original Song. In the year 2000 Whitney released a greatest hits album that sold 10 million copies. By 2001 due to the backlash of reports done by the media regarding Bobby Brown, Whitney's drug use became far more exposed. Her good girl image was gone, and a change came over Whitney that was seen more and more as the 2000s rolled on.

Whitney was getting fed up with the media, and started to have problems with Clive Davis the man who signs her checks, and who Whitney oddly calls 'dad' or 'uncle'. Her behavior in the music industry started to become colder, and she was nowhere near happy. Clive Davis also started to turn on her, and many believe it was because Whitney was too addicted to drugs, and she seemed like she was washing out, but others stated that Clive made things hard for her not so much over the drugs but more out of the fact he wanted Whitney out of the way to make room for new and younger talent.

Throughout the 2000s Whitney came to a point where she did not want to work for Davis anymore. Their conflicts would bring about a love and hate relationship until 2012 when the relationship turned to hatred. Through the decade of the 2000s Whitney was constantly revolting on people in the entertainment industry, and also upon her management team, and the record company she worked for. She would often show up hours late for interviews, photo shoots, and rehearsals. She would cancel concerts and talk-show appearances. Her drug addictions were also having horrible effects on her mind.

On January 11, 2000 airport security found marijuana in Whitney and Bobby's luggage at the airport in Hawaii. The two managed to avoid arrest by boarding the plane before the authorities could arrive. The charges were dropped against them due to Clive Davis speaking to certain people on Whitney's behalf, but Whitney still having conflict with Davis refused to show up and perform at the Rock & Roll Hall of Fame when Davis was inducted.

At the Academy Awards Whitney was fired from performing by Burt Bacharach for showing up to the event high on drugs, and then complained she had throat problems while throwing anger issues around at the staff. In August of 2001 it seemed Whitney made up with Davis, and she renewed her contract for 100 million dollars, and was contracted to record six albums, but this amends she made with Davis would not last long at all, and she fell further into the use of drugs.

Whitney would make an appearance at the Michael Jackson 30th Anniversary Special but when she appeared her fans noticed she was extremely thin. This was due to constant drug use. In 2002 Whitney did an interview with Diana Sawyer to promote her upcoming album. Diane began to ask questions about her drug use. Whitney was offended that Diane suggested she was addicted to crack. Whitney would state that crack was cheap, and she, and her husband did not use crack. However she only stated it that way because she felt she was better than an average crack addicted person. Whitney would admit she uses marijuana and cocaine. When cocaine is smoked it hardens into a rock form hence the words rock-cocaine which is crack.

In 2002 Whitney's new album called Just Whitney was released, but Clive Davis refused to help in its promotion, and would not even produce it not even at Whitney's request. This caused their relationship to turn bitter once again. The album would sell 3 million copies but did not do well on the Billboard charts. In June of 2003 Whitney and Bobby took a trip to Israel. The entire trip was exposed by the media, and other insider people for the constant use of drugs, and the constant fights between Whitney and Bobby. When a reporter asked Whitney about the trip Whitney who was high on drugs stated that Israel was like coming home and she felt wonderful.

In late 2003 Whitney would try to mend her differences once again with Clive Davis, and she appeared at the World Music Awards to pay Davis tribute, but it was said that Whitney did so because Davis threaten to destroy her career.

In 2004 Bobby Brown starred in his own reality television program called Being Bobby Brown. Though it was Brown's show Whitney became the prominent figure on the show. The show had high ratings but Whitney came off in the show as a train-wreck waiting to happen. Due to Whitney and Bobby's constant fighting over drugs the show was cancelled.

In 2007 Whitney divorced Brown, and a few days after the divorce was finalized Bobby sued Whitney for custody of their only daughter. Bobby also wanted child and spousal support meaning money from Whitney, but Bobby Brown lost the case and the judge gave full custody to Whitney.

In 2009 Whitney appeared on the Oprah Winfrey Show, and admitted that she, and Bobby used marijuana laced with rock-cocaine throughout her marriage. In 2009 Whitney released a new album called I Look to You. The album would sell one million copies. Her performances during the tour was remarked as being by the words 'weird', 'ungracious', 'horrible', and a 'flop'. It was clear she was still on drugs at that time. It was also clear she had lost much of the power and tones of her singing voice.

On February 9, 2012 Whitney visited two singers named Brandy and Monica together with Clive Davis at a pre-Grammy Awards party at The Beverly Hilton Hotel in Beverly Hills. Whitney would hand Brandy a note and greeted Davis.

To this day Brandy refuses to state what the note said. Whitney's last performance was that same day when she went to Hollywood, California and she took the stage. The last song she sung was Jesus Loves Me.

Two days later on February 11, 2012 Whitney's body was found submerged in a bathtub. She was pronounced dead on the scene. The cause of death at first was said to be unknown, and then later it was ruled as an accident by drowning. The belief is that the coroner's office in Los Angeles County did a toxicology report on her, and found drugs in her system. These drugs were cocaine, Benadryl, Xanax, Flexeril, and marijuana. The report also shows that a large amount of cocaine was used before she went into the tub, and the belief was this large amount of cocaine caused her to pass out in the tub.

Here are some of the problems surrounding her death. An artist named Ray J was suspected of bringing drugs to Whitney being used as a go between of Whitney, and the drug dealer. Ray J was seen leaving Whitney's room in Suite 434 during hours when Whitney was still alive. Ray J is related to the artist named Brandy, and one time made claims he was having an affair with Whitney, but many said that Ray J lied about the affair, and his only connection to Whitney was to bring drugs to her.

During the hours that Whitney was dead in her room Ray J was seen going back to Whitney's room. Ray J was in Whitney's room before and after she dead. Investigators noticed that Whitney's room was swept clean, and they believe the room was being swept clean while Whitney was dead in the bathtub. Ray J was the only person seen going back into the room at an hour when Whitney was dead. To ignore this fact is not smart at all because this makes him suspect of a crime. The belief is that

Ray J came back to the room to bring Whitney more drugs, but instead he finds Whitney dead. The story is that Ray J took all remaining drugs in the room, and cleaned the room to leave no trace to any foul play, but if this is true why would he do that?

There is suggested evidence to the position of Whitney's body in the tub that shows that the body looked to be planted in the tub, meaning she could have died actually in another part of the room, but we will never know for sure because someone swept clean the rooms.

Also cocaine putting someone to sleep is also very suspect as well. Cocaine is not a downer drug it's a very high upper drug that increases the heart-rate, and keeps people awake when just taken. The coroner's office stated that Whitney just took large amounts of cocaine minutes before she entered the tub. The cocaine would have had to be mixed with a harder drug then pills and marijuana to cause her to pass out from it in the manner she did. No such drugs that could have caused it were found in her system. Therefore, due to the amount of cocaine she had in her she would have been awake, and even erratic during those hours where she was said to have fallen asleep and drowned.

These problems in her death are the reasons why people think Whitney was set-up and murdered, but no clear evidence to establish it has not been presented, and when it comes to these types of deaths such evidence usually is not presented, but many say it is buried.

Another strange case is Mariah Carey who was born on Long Island in New York City. Mariah's father was half African-American and half-Venezulan, and her mother was Irish-American. Their names were Alfred and Patricia Roy. Mariah's mother was an opera singer who later became her daughter's vocal coach. Her mother was disowned by her family for marrying a man of color. When Mariah was three years old her mother divorced her father due to a strenuous nature in their marriage. Mariah would go to live with her father after the separation.

Even from a young age Mariah excelled in music. Mariah would write poems and add melodies to them. When she was a pre-teen to a teenager her mother coached her voice as Mariah became a singer and a songwriter. When Mariah was still in high-school she recorded a four song demo tape. She tried several times to pass the tape to record labels but each time her efforts were met with failure. Out of a chance meeting Mariah met pop singer Brenda K. Starr. The two developed a friendship, and Mariah soon became her backup singer.

Starr wanted Mariah to succeed in the music industry, and so one night she arranged a meeting with the CEO of Columbia Records at the time named Tommy Mottola. This meeting took place on a Friday night in December of 1988. The official story is that Tommy heard two songs from the demo tape, and loved it so much he signed her, but others say there was more to the story then that.

Tommy was known even in that time to take sexual advantage of up and coming female artists. The rumor was Tommy took Mariah to bed after hearing the two songs, and then signed her, and he liked her so much that Mariah eventually became his wife. Such events are hardly ever proven much like this story, but the story often comes back to haunt Mariah again and again.

In late 1989 Mariah released her first album called Mariah Carey with a lead single that was released called Someday. The album made her a world-wide success. The album took the number one spot on the Billboard 200 albums chart. It would produce three number one singles on the Billboard 100 singles chart. The album would go on to sell 15 million copies, and Mariah would win 2 Grammy Awards from the album. Her second album called Emotions would sell 8 million copies. While recording her third album, Mariah made the strange choice to marry her own boss Tommy Mottola. Many people stated that Tommy had a strange, and even a sick control on Mariah. No one could understand how Mariah being a strong-willed person could submit to the twisted things Tommy would have her do. Most of these things it was said were sexual acts involving other women and S&M practices.

When Mariah finished her third album it was called Music Box, and it was released in 1993. The album was a huge seller as it sold 32 million copies. In 1995 Mariah released the album called

Daydream, and this album would sell 25 million copies. The lead single from that album called One Sweet Day became the longest running number one single in music industry history. The song was inspired by the death of Mariah's sister Alison who died of AIDS.

In 1997 Mariah divorced Tommy Mottola as stories of abuse and excessive control brought about the divorce. In 1997 Mariah would also release the album called Butterfly. When Butterfly was released it was also a huge seller but Mariah's image changed. She was more sexual and her photos were akin to Playboy shoots. Many felt that along with her strong voice she was selling sex as well, and they were right, but in that time Mariah's mental condition and image began to be compared by many to be expressive of a mind-control victim or a victim of intense abuse and even demonic possession.

People who have studied the symbolism of mind-control often pointed out the heavy uses of the rainbow in Mariah's photos, albums, and upon the clothes she wears. She uses it so often that it seems to have become one of her fashion statements, but people who studied mind-control feel that it's more than just a fashion statement in regards to Mariah, and other artists who use it. They believe it is part of their abuse and the symbol is used as code for a type of control by people who handle Mariah's career. In their research they stated that rainbows are often used as triggers upon the brain of mind-control victims to get them to disassociate from intense abuse that happened to them by switching over to alter-personalities. They stated that the alter-personalities are demonic personalities where demons enter a victim through intense abuse done in program sessions of the victim. When the abuse in the session is done and demons have entered their bodies the victims are given a symbol often a rainbow or a butterfly which causes them not to remember what happened to them, and to be taken over by demonic or alter-personalities.

This is often very hard to believe for many people, especially people who have never studied the research. There has never been any hard proof to show that Mariah was a victim of such abuse but even if she was the people who did this to her would never admit it. Much of the evidence to this is however in the pudding of Mariah's career. One time on MTV Mariah displayed what she called her alter-ego who, was an English character named Bianca. When Mariah first presented this person it was so well done that people thought at first they were looking at two different people in the interview, but later they found out that the Bianca character was Mariah herself.

Many people were stunned by it, and said Mariah must be a better actress then they thought, but later Mariah would state in other interviews that Bianca was an alter-ego she was often haunted by, and she stated that she has another alter-ego she is haunted by named Mimi, and several others. She would also state she was haunted by the ghost of Marilyn Monroe.

The Bible shows us that when Jesus confronted a demon-possessed person the person showed a dual nature of many personalities inside the person. Jesus exposed that the person was possessed by many demons that were also causing this duality within the person.

Often this British alter-ego subject is often seen in many artist suspected of being mind-control victims. Artists like Madonna, Britney Spears, Nicki Minaj, and others have been seen on camera talking in a English accent for no real reason, and they often do it out of nowhere as if something inside them impulses them to become someone else.

Mariah one time spent one million dollars to buy a piano that was owned by Marilyn Monroe. Mariah stated to her close friends that the piano was haunted. Mariah stated to them that when she comes home, and sits down in front of the piano she can hear voices talking to her through the piano, and she often feels that the main voice talking to her was Marilyn Monroe.

The Bible would however call these spirits as being familiar spirits which are demonic spirits familiar with certain human beings who passed away. What Mariah is speaking about to her friends the Bible would call demonic attacks. When Mariah was filming the movie called Glitter she suffered several mental breakdowns. She began to only respond to the cast if they called her Marilyn. Mariah for a time during filming thought she was Marilyn Monroe. Oddly enough many suspected mind-control victims like Anna-Nicole Smith, Madonna, Britney Spears, and others are also noticed for thinking or acting like they are Marilyn Monroe.

Mind-control researchers give an answer for this where they stated that Marilyn was an early mind-control victim, and a former devil-worshiper and girlfriend of Anton LaVey. They stated that Marilyn was put under a mind-control session called sex-kitten programming where victims are forced to do many horrible, and twisted sexual acts and are programmed to use sex as a means to gain wealth and power in the world. Mariah when her image became very sexual she began to take pictures of herself in poses that Marilyn Monroe did before her.

During the filming of Glitter Mariah would also suffer severe headaches and painful stomach problems. The mental breakdown became so bad that Mariah was convinced she was invisible and began taking showers with her clothes on, and was bringing terror to her friends when she was constantly talking to people she could see but they could not. The problem became so bad that when Mariah was about to board an airplane she began screaming out statements that the plane was going to crash. This resulted in Mariah being placed in a psychiatric ward for mental treatment for a couple of months.

In the 2000s Mariah's behavior was still seen as very strange, and she would release an album called The Emancipation of Mimi. Mariah references the title of the album as freeing her alter-ego to the world, but others stated that there was an underline evil to the title, and that Mimi was a demon one among many that lived inside her.

Another symbol Mariah often uses is the butterfly. In fact when she was pregnant she drew a big butterfly on her stomach, and colored the butterfly with the colors of the rainbow. Many close friends and people who knew her found this to be very strange. In mind-control research butterflies represent the feeling of floating in a weightless state where the meaning is the victims become empty-headed after intense abuse is done to them. This program is invoked upon its victims often through electroshock treatment.

Victims are shocked again and again, and are drugged to such a point they feel like they are floating like a butterfly in their minds. Often the victims will draw butterflies as a way to pass along information to themselves of certain things they are supposed to do as a controlled victim. The researchers stated that mind-control victims having children is not a good thing because often the parent or parents will feel that they have to pass down the abuse to their children. They will do this like a command code in their head. If this is really the cause of Mariah's strange and spooky behavior it is truly a sad case indeed.

Chapter 18

In the late 1980's throughout the 1990's, and the 2000s came the rise of a form of rock music called Alternative Rock. Alternative Rock came from the underground scene of independent labels of the 1980's. Alternative Rock's sound is a distinction from mainstream Hard Rock/Heavy Metal music by its distorted guitar sound, transgressive lyrics, and a defiant yet passive bad attitude.

Alternative Rock owns its musical style from the 1970's punk rock sound. Alternative Rock was born from the punk rock nightclubs, and underground scene. In the 1980's Alternative Rock was promoted by regional roots, magazines, word of mouth, and college radio airplay.

The diversity of Alternative Rock are a number of distinct styles such as gothic rock, grunge, noise pop, jangle pop, industrial rock, Britpop, C86, and others. In the 1980's Alternative Rock was limited to independent labels, and it received little mainstream from radio, television, and newspapers, but the break-through of Nirvana changed this, and Alternative Rock entered the popular musical mainstream, and many alternative bands became commercially successful.

The meaning of the name Alternative Rock was corrupted to think it had to do with alternative lifestyles like homosexuality. Though homosexuality was promoted in that underground scene to such a point that it seemed that way but the real definition comes from a variety of sounds outside the mainstream. In the 1980's the punk rock scene started to develop different forms of music that had no name at the time except to call it alternative. The college radio circuit were the ones who brought the different forms of music out to suit the tastes of college students. Soon a market opened up for it, and independent labels started to sell the music to local underground scenes, and to college students.

In the 1980's alternative bands built underground followings by touring constantly, and releasing low-budget albums. This began to create an extensive underground circuit in America and Europe that was filled with different forms of music and lifestyles in various parts of America and Europe mostly in major cities. Soon many Alternative Rock bands started to break forth in the mainstream in the 1980's. These bands were New Order, Public Image Limited, The Sugarcubes, U2, R.E.M, The Feelies, the Violent Femmes and others.

In the United Kingdom British radio disc jockeys promoted Alternative Rock bands far more in the 1980's then those in the United States, because of the U.K. DJs American Alternative Rock bands received greater exposure through British national radio.

When R.E.M. came on the scene in the early 1980's their style of alternative music was jangle pop. Their impact paved the way for other bands to be successful in the music industry. Their debut album was called Murmur released in 1983, and it hit the number 40 spot on the Billboard 200 albums chart. Jangle pop was the popular sound of alternative music before grunge, and it incorporated many sounds of the 60's psychedelic, and folk rock guitar play, and vocal harmonies. The style of jangle pop was believed to have been created by the punk rock group of the late 1970's called The Velvet Underground.

In the 1980's R.E.M. was one of the few alternative bands the mainstream fans liked. Soon another style of alternative music started to get public notice, and this style was called noise pop. The band that brought noise pop to the mainstream fans was a band called Sonic Youth. Another style also got major notice, and it was called industrial rock, and three bands would bring it to the mainstream fans. These three bands were Depeche

Mode, New Order, and Nine Inch Nails.

The style called grunge rock was started in Seattle, Washington. The first two early grunge bands that introduced it to the mainstream public was Soundgarden and Mudhoney. After Nirvana's success Soundgarden would later find major mainstream success with a song called Black Hole Sun.

The style of gothic rock was brought to the mainstream fans by a band called The Cure who came out of the punk rock scene of the late 1970's. Their aim was to take punk rock, and make it darker, and give it an element of deep sadness and a horror vibe.

New Order was different in their industrial rock sound because they experimented with techno, and house music often in their songs. The members of New Order also bought a nightclub in Manchester, England where they brought freestyle, house, and dance & rhythm groups to their club, and signed many of them to their independent label company.

By the late 1980's going into the 1990's R.E.M's success had become the blueprint for alternative bands. In 1991 a group called Pearl Jam whose style was grunge released their debut album called Ten. Ten started out very slow in sales even though the band was well promoted, and music critics hailed them as being a very talented band.

One month after Ten was released an album called Nevermind was released by a grunge style alternative band called Nirvana. Nevermind would take the world of Rock N' Roll music by the horns, and make Alternative Rock as the new standard of rock mainstream music. The success of Nevermind and Nirvana in general became the success of every alternative rock band to come after them including Pearl Jam whose album Ten began to sell in the millions after the album Nevermind did.

The origin of Nirvana starts with a man named Kurt Cobain. Kurt was born on February 20, 1967 in Aberdeen, Washington. His mother named Wendy was a waitress, and his father named Donald Cobain was an automotive mechanic. Cobain's family life was one of a broken home. His parents divorced when Kurt was seven years old. The divorce had a sad effect on Kurt's life, and he developed a certain shame against his parents. Kurt was to live with his father who had remarried to a woman named Jenny Wesleby. Kurt would develop a resentment toward his step-mother.

At times Kurt was sent to live with his mother who began dating a man who was abusive. Many times Kurt watched acts of domestic violence done upon his mother from her boyfriend. One time his mother was hospitalized after her boyfriend broke her arm. In time Kurt started to behave insolently toward adults, and he began bullying another boy at school. This behavior caused Kurt to be sent by his father to a therapist. The therapist was unable to help, and Kurt's behavior which got so bad that on June 28, 1979 Kurt's mother, having enough of Kurt, gave full custody of her son to his father, but soon Kurt rebelled on his father, and his behavior became so overwhelming that when Kurt was a teenager his father kicked him out of the house.

His father had arranged for Kurt to stay with a born-again Christian family who were the Reed family. For a time Kurt was doing better, and became a devout Christian, and regularly attended Church, but Kurt soon changed when he got into high-school. When Kurt got into high-school, one day he renounced Christianity, and began engaging in anti-GOD rants. He then started to embrace the doctrine of Jainism and Buddhist philosophy.

Later he would name his band Nirvana after the Buddhist concept of Heaven. How Kurt lost his Christian faith started when Kurt was a freshman in high-school, and he befriended a homosexual student at school. Kurt at the time was not gay nor bi-sexual yet he simply felt sorry for the young student, and believed, as a Christian, he should befriend him. This friendship resulted in Kurt to suffer bullying from heterosexual students who concluded that Kurt was gay because he makes friends with gay people. The bullying and the name-calling got so bad that it was believed Kurt sought advice from his Church family.

His Church family were little help, and believed Kurt should distance himself from the gay student. This caused Kurt to become very angry, and he then renounced Christianity, and became angry with GOD over a Church group's bad advice. Kurt also was angry at GOD for the way he was being treated at school for making friends with a teenager no one cared about.

Of course this was not Jesus' fault, and Jesus also was attacked for caring about people no one cared about. But Kurt only wanted to listen to his anger, and not to logic or truth. Overtime Kurt's anger turned inward and twisted, and he began to like the fact people thought he was gay because then he did not have to deal with making new friends because he grew to hate people in general.

Later in life Kurt would become a bi-sexual when he got into the music industry. At that time in high-school Kurt began to vent his pain by committing vandalism on Churches. He also started to discover more his musical talent through a family member who was a musician.

Kurt would run around the Aberdeen area with a spray paint can along with his gay friend, and a few other buddies who were also made fun of. They would target pick-up trucks, and other cars parked near Churches or cars belonging to people they knew to be Christians, and they started spray painting 'GOD is gay', or 'Abort Christ', and 'Homosexual sex rules' on their cars. Kurt and his friends also started to target Church buildings themselves, and would spray paint these remarks on their front doors, and on the walls on the side of the buildings.

Kurt would eventually get arrested and caught several times for this kind of vandalism. Kurt began to build up a police record in Aberdeen, and his Christian family began to threaten Kurt if he did not change his ways he would have to leave. Kurt would calm down but only for a little while, and began learning more and more about guitar playing, and began learning how to play rock songs on his guitar. He also started to practice writing music.

Kurt's history with guitar playing started at the age of 14 years old when his uncle gave him a birthday gift. Kurt's uncle used to play in a band, and he knew Kurt had a gift also to play music. Kurt began learning from time to time from his uncle, and eventually he got good enough that throughout high-school Kurt learned to flawlessly play the songs Stairway to Heaven, Louie Louie, Cars and My Best Friend's Girl on the guitar.

During high-school is when Kurt met Chris Novoselic. Novoselic would become the future bass player for Nirvana. Novoselic was bi-sexual, and was also hated in high-school. Kurt and Chris were both skilled in playing music, and so they began playing together and writing songs. Chris also went many times with Kurt on those vandalism runs through Aberdeen. In Kurt's second year in high-school he began going to punk-rock shows in Seattle. He also began to engage in vandalism once again. This got started up again when Kurt and Chris began writing songs, and at times they felt the songs were horrible.

Then they had the evil idea to burn the song lyrics outside the Churches' doors during their Bible meetings and so they took the sheets, and began to target certain Churches, and when their doors were closed, and people were settled inside having Bible class Kurt, Chris, and his other friends would run up to the door and put the sheets very near the door and set it on fire. The Church members would not notice until the smoke was coming into the building, and the door was on fire. Eventually Kurt was caught and arrested for this as well along with his friends.

His Church family wanted to kick him out but Kurt was still underage, and had nowhere to go, so they gave him another chance to get right with himself. His Church family also started to have problems with Kurt going to punk-rock shows. Kurt often came home high on drugs and many times it was noticed by them. They began to restrict him from going to those shows, but Kurt still found ways to go.

Kurt's Church family tried several times to get him to come back to Church. The Church his family went to was on East 2nd Street in Aberdeen. One time and the last time Kurt was forced to go to their Church Kurt, feeling pure hatred that he was there walked up to the Church's wooden notice board, and took it, and smashed it into two pieces. He then took the candles, and the communion trays, and began smashing those items on the floor. As Kurt was destroying other items in the Church people there became afraid. The Church members called the police while Kurt was doing this, and people stated about Kurt's behavior, and his rage was like a person possessed by Satan. Kurt was arrested when the police came, and was never invited back to their Church again.

Soon after Kurt's arrest Kurt was kicked out of the Reed home, and his mother took him back in again. When Kurt was a senior in high-school he had only two weeks to go before his graduation, but Kurt being evil-minded dropped out of Aberdeen High School. His mother was furious, and told Kurt to find a job or leave. Kurt refused to get employment, and soon he found his clothes, and his belongings packed away in boxes, and he was kicked out of his mother's home. Kurt would stay with friends and sometimes he would sneak into his mother's basement to sleep. Often times he would sleep under a bridge over the Wishkah River.

In 1986 Kurt got a job at the Polynesian Coastal Resort that was north of Aberdeen, and he moved into an apartment paying his rent through the checks he got from work. During this time he was traveling frequently to Olympia, Washington to go to rock concerts, and to hang out at the underground scene there. Soon Kurt met a girl named Tracy Marander.

Kurt and Tracy would become a couple. During that time Kurt entered the punk-rock scene, and began learning to play the music. His constant absence caused a strained with financial difficulties in his relationship. Tracy supported the relationship by working at a cafeteria, and often stealing food. Kurt was mostly spending his time on concentrating on trying to play his guitar, and on art-projects. He also spent a lot of his time sleeping and watching television. Soon Tracy told Kurt he needed to get a real job which caused arguments that resulted in Tracy leaving Kurt.

Kurt still managed to maintain his apartment. He often decorated his apartment with baby dolls hanging by their necks with fake blood smeared all over them. He also had books on witchcraft he would often read, and had witchcraft dolls also hanging in his apartment. He had a statue of Mary the mother of Jesus with its head cut off posted in his apartment.

One time during a rock show Kurt went to, he met a woman

named Tobi Vail. Tobi developed a friendship with Kurt, and she brought Kurt inside into the hang-out click of the underground rock scene of North Washington. The main city this click hung around in was Seattle. Tobi was a DIY punk zinester of a punk band called Bikini Kill. Kurt was head over heels for Tobi, and he would even have anxiety problems because of his infatuation with her. Kurt when he was dating her did not know it yet but Tobi's boyfriends were usually fashion accessories. Kurt and Tobi often spent their time discussing political and philosophical issues. Tobi began teaching Kurt how to become a better guitar player, and the two of them collaborated on a musical project called Bathtub is Real.

Soon the two of them begin to record songs on Tobi's father's four-track device. This relationship was making Kurt a real rock musician. One time a friend of Kurt and Tobi named Kathleen Hanna came over Kurt's apartment. Hanna on that day spray-painted the words 'Kurt smells like teen spirit' on Kurt's apartment wall. This is where Kurt came up with the name of a song that would change the mainstream course in rock history.

During that time Tobi broke up with Kurt, and only wanted to be friends. The break up was hard on Kurt but he held in his rage, and kept his peace. Kurt then asked Novoselic to move in with him and form a band with him. Soon the band they put together was called Fecal Matter. The band would tour the garage and club circuit but money problems were something the band often struggled with.

Kurt and the band-mates started to use more drugs and Kurt discovered heroin at this time. Kurt was also opening himself up to homosexuality by practicing it with Novoselic who he often french kissed on stage, and began practicing it with other people he knew from the underground scene. The band were also having problems with being able to draw substantial crowds to them to make a living from it.

Soon Kurt would have a vision about the direction of the music his band was playing. This vision inspired Kurt to rename the band to Nirvana. Kurt at the time would bring in a rhythm guitarist, and a drummer named Chad Channing. The band Nirvana would now start out with four members, and began writing songs, and Kurt was waking up from dreams with new hooks for these songs.

Kurt at this time was in touch with something that he would call 'a divine being' or 'magical'. At that time Kurt began to dive deep into Buddhism, and witchcraft, and was learning about spells that he felt could make him a better song-writer. From there he started to wake up after a night of strange rituals of casting spells with songs in his head.

The Bible would call this a satanic practice, and a form of demonic possession, and dealings with demonic familiar spirits, but Kurt saw it as something that could help him. Near the end of his career these dealings would turn on him. After writing new songs Nirvana began to go through the garage and club circuit tours again. This time they were better, and they began to build a small following.

Nirvana would catch the notice of Jack Endino who worked for an independent label called Sub Pop Records. Jack would bring them to the studio to record the song Love Buzz for the label in late 1988. The single Love Buzz would be released in November of 1988, and it got huge airplay on college radio. This resulted in more fans coming to see Nirvana play. Jack then wanted the group to record an album but there was a lack of funds regarding Sub Pop Records to record a full album for Nirvana. Sub Pop wanted Nirvana to pay one-third of the cost so the album could be made. This resulted in getting more gigs, and giving the money made from them to Sub Pop Records.

The band was struggling very hard at this point. They had drug addictions where their money went to drugs and the studio, and so they barley ate, and were often depended upon friends for food and shelter. Kurt would also sell his body to homosexuals for money and drugs. This activity would bring about a deep coldness in Kurt that resulted in more mental problems. On stage he began wearing female clothes like nightgowns, bras, and panties, and would even wear panty-hoses and high-heel shoes. When Kurt was asked about why he would wear female clothing on stage he stated that he was promoting feminist concepts. In truth his brain was just messed up through the activities he was engaged in.

When the money was put together Nirvana would record the album called Bleach. Bleach was released in June of 1989, and it would sell 40,000 copies. The songs on the album became huge favorites on college radio stations. To promote the album further Nirvana embarked on their first national tour. This tour brought many major problems to the band, and Kurt was often acting out in a wild manner on stage.

One time he climbed the rafters of the stage, and began swinging like a monkey from the electric cords. When he stopped he began to breakdown and cry, and threaten to kill himself. Other times he would get into fights with the secretary guards and fans. The band members would fall deeper and deeper into drugs. After the tour Kurt felt that the music of Nirvana could be better and needed to be better. Kurt would fire the rhythm guitarist, and he got sick and tired of the way Chad played drums. Kurt would soon meet a drummer named Dave Grohl, and after watching him play he asked Dave to join his group. Dave accepted, and then Kurt quickly fired Chad. Now the band was three members, and Kurt would soon write a new song that would later take the world by a storm. Kurt would write a song called Smells Like Teen Spirit. The trio would embark upon a few more shows through the underground circuit, and performed the song Smells Like Teen Spirit for the first time during those first shows when the group was now a trio. The song, and the group caught the notice of the band Sonic Youth who were working for Geffen Records at the time.

Nirvana and Sonic Youth would forge a friendship, and the members of Sonic Youth made repeated recommendations to the executives of Geffen Records. Soon a demo tape was given to Geffen Records by a member of Sonic Youth of the song Smells Like Teen Spirit. The executives loved it, and then bought out the contract Nirvana had with Sub-Pop Records, and the band were now signed to Geffen Records. This signing took place in 1990.

Nirvana began recording their second album called Nevermind that was produced by Butch Vig. Nevermind would be recorded at Sound City Studios in Van Nuys a suburb of Los Angeles. Sound City Studios was a place where a lot of famous bands recorded their biggest albums. It was also a place where a lot of strange events would happen to band members while recording their albums. Nevertheless Nirvana would complete the album, and for the cover of the album the band members made a strange decision to have a baby drowning in a pool with a bill of money.

When Nevermind was released its lead single Smells Like Teen Spirit was also released. The song became a huge smash hit on the radio stations, and when people heard the song they raved over it, and called it the 'best damn rock and roll song of all time'. An MTV video was filmed for the song, and the video was a huge overnight success, and the song became a huge mainstream song. Nirvana now became mainstream famous. Now they had millions of fans seemingly overnight.

Kurt was clearly not ready for this kind of fame, but nevertheless it was put upon the band, and Kurt was being hailed as the voice of Generation X. Smells Like Teen Spirit was the song that crushed the Hard Rock/Heavy Metal market. The market was now taken over by Alternative Rock, and it still holds the market to this day. Smells Like Teen Spirit became almost as if it was omnipresent on the radio stations. No matter how many times a person hears the song they could never get tired of it.

When Nevermind was released it was 1991, and due to the lead single the album sold 400,000 copies in only one week. Nirvana in that time had to go on tour in Europe, and their shows were dangerously oversold, and television crews became a constant presence on stage. Kurt's life was now fully in the spotlight, and he hated the spotlight with venom.

Kurt at the time was also dating his off, and on again girlfriend Courtney Love. Kurt met Love in 1990 in Portland at the Satyricon nightclub. Love began to make advances toward Kurt but Kurt having his heart broken before was evasive toward Love. Kurt kept breaking one date after another, but overtime the two became close especially during Kurt's rise to fame.

The two were also heavy into drugs and homosexual sex. Some people called it a match made in Hell. Later in Kurt's career Love discovered she was pregnant with Kurt's baby, and so Kurt would marry Love in Hawaii. Sadly he also resented having to marry her, and only did it for the sake of the child.

By January of 1992 Nevermind took the number one spot on the Billboard 200 albums chart. Nevermind would sell 30 million copies world-wide, and 10 million of those copies were sold in the United States. Kurt found himself becoming the very reluctant voice of Generation X fans. Kurt really hated fame, and he hated media interviews, and he hated the people who did the interviews.

He would develop a huge discomfort with his fans, and he often expressed hatred to fans, and he expressed even more hatred toward media attention. He often showed up to interviews high on heroin, and wearing dark sunglasses, and sometimes he would wear strange clothes. He would ignore the interviewer while his band-mates did most of the talking, and he would stare at the interviewer like he wanted to kill him or her. When Kurt did speak he promoted gay-rights, and pro-choice, and then later he claimed that he received death threats from anti-abortion groups. No one knows for sure if he actually received such threats but what is clear that in accordance to the Bible Kurt promoted the lifestyles and beliefs that were found in Sodom and Gomorrah.

Many inside people felt that Kurt was so anti-Christian at that point and he would promote anything that was found to be against GOD in the Bible. In September of 1993 Nirvana released their next album called In Utero. In Utero would debut at the number one spot on the Billboard 200 albums chart. During the time after the success of Nevermind Courtney Love would give birth to Kurt's daughter.

A journalist named Lynn Hirschberg had busted Courtney for using cocaine while pregnant with her daughter. The story was exposed in a magazine called Vanity Fair. When Kurt saw the article he flew into a rage. He told his close friends he wanted to kill Lynn, and related his fantasy about killing her dog, and taking the guts' of the dog, and wiping it on her face.

Kurt would also buy a large home at this point, and along with the home he bought a huge collection of guns. He often had the guns displayed around the home ranging from small arms to machine gun rifles and shotguns. During this time a woman accused Kurt of trying to rape her. Her story is that she was hanging out with a couple that were friends with Kurt, and they went into a room together. The girl was a groupie who was a fan of Nirvana. When the couple left the room Kurt started to make-out with the girl. The girl wanted Kurt at first but then according to this girl Kurt grabbed her violently, and pushed her against the wall. While Kurt was being ruff with her he started to growl, and she told him to stop. At that point he laughed at her, and then rammed his hand hard between her legs, and according to her he was going to rape her, but when the couple walked back in Kurt was distracted, and the girl took off running out of the room.

Kurt at the time when he was recording the album In Utero became close friends with William Burroughs and Anton LaVey. Kurt stated that one of the greatest moments in his life was meeting William Burroughs. This is a very strange statement from Kurt indeed. Kurt was a fan of the books written by Aleister Crowley. William had a vast understanding of Crowley's teachings, and became a minister of Crowley's books. William Burroughs was a known satanic worshipper and a child rapist. William stated that he became demon-possessed after killing his wife many years ago from the time he met Kurt.

It is often believed that William was the one who coined the term Heavy Metal to describe the underground music of the dark and satanic hard rock being played in British nightclubs in the mid to late 1960's. William was personal friends with many of those Heavy Metal bands in those days. The interest those bands had in William was his knowledge of Crowley's works. Much of the satanic wisdom William had he shared with Kurt, and Kurt reflected it in certain songs he did for In Utero.

William often bragged about having sex with young boys, and hanging them by their knees. He promoted the use of heroin along with homosexual practices. Kurt also was heavy into heroin at the time, and was bi-sexual at this point. Kurt respected William so much he made sure to give him special thanks on his album In Utero. Kurt also valued his friendship with Anton LaVey. Kurt met LaVey during his success with the album Nevermind. While recording In Utero Kurt asked LaVey to play his cello, and other musical instruments on a few of his songs. Kurt often listened to the teachings of LaVey, and read LaVey's satanic bible.

During an interview that Kurt gave when the interviewer asked Kurt what his aim in his career is Kurt stated, 'My only aim is to get stoned and worship Satan'. The album In Utero would go on to sell 3.5 million copies, and Nirvana was soon on tour. The tour would be marked with riots started by Kurt, and fights between Kurt and Love. Their fights were so bad at times they often turned into fist-fights. Kurt was getting tired of her, and he began to ignore her, and soon he wanted to divorce her.

Love at that time would hire a private investigator to dig up dirt on Kurt so that she could use it in court to get at Kurt's money. The investigator was unable to find anything that could really be used. The only things he found could leave a bad stain on both Kurt and Love and since he was working for Love he knew he could not use what he found. Love became angry about this.

According to this private investigator, Love asked him if he knew people who would be willing to kill Kurt Cobain if someone paid them. The investigator stated that he did not know people like that. He would soon distance himself from Love thinking Love was just hard-up for Kurt's money.

Soon in 1994 Kurt was found dead, and the investigator began to wonder if Love had something to do with it, but there has never been any proof other than the statements of the private investigator that Love did something to Kurt, but many insiders feel and state that she took an active part in destroying Kurt's life in the end.

In November of 1993 Nirvana performed on a show called MTV Unplugged. It was called one of the best performances in the history of the show. The performance would then be turned into an album that sold millions of copies. Before Kurt had to go back on tour he would return to his house. When he got there he noticed that his house was broken into but nothing was missing. Kurt asked his daughter's babysitter Michael Dewitt about the mysterious break-ins but Michael had no answers for them either as they would happen when he went to go take the baby for a stroll.

While at home Kurt was getting strange calls from people who would hang up on him, and calls from people threatening to kill him. Soon Kurt would leave his home to go on tour in Europe in early 1994. On March 1, 1994 in Munich, Germany Kurt would overdose on heroin and pills in his hotel room. Courtney would find Kurt in this state, and he was soon rushed to the hospital. As the news of the overdose was made known to the media Kurt's addiction to heroin then became well known to his millions of fans. During the tour and right up to the time Kurt overdosed Kurt began to fear for his life. The strange break-ins at his home, and the death threat phones calls began to make him very paranoid that people were out to get him.

It was very clear that Kurt never wanted the kind of huge fame, and attention he constantly got after the album Nevermind was released. So at that time in Europe he began to have a change of heart about staying in the music industry to such a point he wanted to retire. When Kurt was in the hospital his band-mates, and friends staged a drug intervention for Kurt and begged Kurt to check into a rehab center. Kurt would do so but then Kurt told close friends that the people in the rehab center were abusing him. As Kurt was less than a week at the rehab center Kurt would climb over a wall of the center and escape. Kurt would board a plane, and fly back to Seattle to his home. He would score some heroin and lock himself in his home.

One week after he returned home he was found dead. The official story of Kurt's death was that he went home, and went inside his private room that was on top of his garage and got high on heroin. It was stated that he then wrote a farewell suicide note to his fans and family and then took a shotgun and killed himself with it. The story is that no one else was in the room when it happened and his body was not found until much later after his death, but there are a lot of problems with the official story. In fact so many problems that it turns out that the evidence that Kurt was murdered was more than the evidence of the official story.

When Kurt's body was discovered one of his credit cards was missing from his wallet. It turned out that someone used the credit card after he already died. If no one else was in the room after he died, and no one else knew that he was dead, then how did his credit card get used while he lie dead and his body was not yet discovered by the babysitter or the police? Video footage also of the person using the card was oddly not released either. The shotgun that was used to kill Kurt was still loaded with three shells after it was used. The most, clear evidence for murder is the fact that all three shells did not have Kurt's fingerprints on it, and also no fingerprints on the weapon itself.

The most shocking evidence was the fact that the trigger of the shotgun also did not have Kurt's fingerprints on it, and it really should have had his fingerprints on it if it was suicide. Evidence showed that the shotgun was wiped clean of fingerprints, and clearly the police were not the ones who covered this evidence so the question is, who did? This evidence was so clear that many investigators who once worked for the police department stated that such evidence proves murder and the case should have been handled as a murder case. The pen that Kurt used to write the suicide note also did not have Kurt's fingerprints on it, and it also appeared to have been wiped clean. The note itself also only has a short footnote of lines at the very bottom of the note that indicates a suicide. The rest of the note was not talking about suicide at all but it was a retirement note address to someone named Boddua. The note in general was explaining why Kurt was leaving the music industry.

Handwriting experts who did an analysis of the note stated that the last footnote lines of the note that contained the message of a suicide did not match the handwriting of the rest of the note. They stated that Kurt did not write those last lines but they believed someone else did.

Kurt also had in his body 225 mgs of heroin in his system when his body was found. This is 3 times the amount that is used even by hardcore heroin addicts. The amount of morphine levels that were in Kurt's blood would have render him incapacitated, and he would have been on his way to overdosing once again. In this state Kurt could not have been able to pick-up a heavy shotgun, load shells and shoot himself. And even if he was able to by some unnatural will he clearly would not have been able to wipe his fingerprints from the shells, the trigger, and the pen he used.

People to this day are often led to believe he died by a suicide when the suicide story does have contradictions in logic, and countless inconsistencies, and plainly much of the story regarding suicide sounds like lies rather than truth when the evidence is compared.

Sadly many Nirvana fans who thought Kurt killed himself ended up killing themselves in honor of their hero Kurt Cobain. One case happened on the night of the vigil of Kurt's death. A fan named Daniel Casper was returning home from the vigil, and got a hold of a gun when he went home. He would go into his room, and put a bullet into his head and kill himself. Another fan who was 16 years old locked herself in a room, and began to listen to Nirvana's music. In honor of Kurt she grabbed a gun that was in her home, and killed herself with it. After Kurt's death there was a sharp rise of suicide deaths by teenagers.

A study into Kurt's music shows that his lyrics were often about his personal life and people he knew, but the way he came up with hooks and music was another story. Kurt often admitted to having dealings with spirits. Kurt would never call them evil spirits but the Bible does call them evil spirits. Evil spirits deceive people into thinking they are good spirits, or ascended masters, or passed away spirits. Kurt named his band Nirvana after having dreams of hearing music and songs in his head. He felt that was the music that would make his band successful.

Throughout Kurt's life he showed deep signs of demonic possession. People who grew up with Kurt often said Kurt was in touch with something they could not see but he could. The source of Kurt's musical inspiration would be shown through Bible teachings to be satanic. He had an uncanny ability for coming up with seductive and transfixing hooks. Kurt would often stumble upon melodies that even he didn't fully understand. Those melodies would be the songs that drove the energy of Nirvana fans. His fans loved Kurt but Kurt it was known, hated his fans.

During shows he used to spit on his fans, and even urinated on them. One time he stated that he felt that 99% of the people in the world should be killed off. It was clear that Kurt rejected

Jesus Christ, and the authority of the Bible over his life. He led millions of people down the road to self-destruction by being the voice of his fans and their generation.

Chapter 19

During the 1990's, and even going up this day rock festivals were still going on at full speed. One of the major rock festivals created in the 1990's is called Lollapalooza. Lollapalooza was created by Perry Farrell the lead singer of Jane's Addiction in 1991. The festival was originally a farewell music festival for his band until, due to its success, it became an annual event. It ran from 1991 to 1997, and then it was revived in 2003, and continues to this day.

The music festival is usually a three day event that hosts over 160,000 people. In 2011 the event was taken overseas for the first time as it was held in Santiago, Chile, and in 2012 it was held in Brazil. In 2013 it was held in Tel-Aviv, Israel at Yarkon Park.

The first Lollapalooza introduced various artists representing different genres. The inaugural line-up featured such acts as Jane's Addiction, Ice-T, Nine Inch Nails, Siouxsie and the Banshees, Jim Rose Circus Side Show, and others. There was also a tent for the display of art-pieces, virtual reality games and information tables for political and environmental non-profit groups promoting counter-culture and political awareness. It was at Lollapalooza where Farrell coined the term 'alternative nation'.

The festivals mainly leaned toward grunge and alternative acts, and featured additional rap acts. The main problem the attendees seem to have are the high prices of food and water. In 1992 when the festival was at the Alpine Valley in East Troy, Wisconsin concert goers ripped up chunks of sod and grass, and threw them at each other, and at the bands that cost tens of thousands of dollars in damages to the venue.

In 1994 Nirvana was scheduled to headline the festival but the band had to be dropped, and at the time no one knew why. Nirvana was dropped before Kurt's body was discovered upon the day the festival began. Nirvana's management gave a cancellation days before they found Kurt's body. The festival's aim has often been to promoted homosexuality and feminist behavior. When Metallica headlined at the event in 1996 fans had a problem with the group being there because they felt they were too macho.

The event often showcased female homosexual acts on stage as women get naked and kiss each other. The event also promoted goddess spirituality. Being a straight man and woman under Christian values is very, hated by the festival's fans, and people who put the events together, but if you love homosexuality and witchcraft then the event accepts such persons.

The Woodstock festivals were also still going on in the 1990's, and even up to the 2000s. Woodstock 94 was another noted event. It was organized to commemorate the 25th anniversary of the 1969 Woodstock Festival. It became a three day event held on August 12 to August 14 of 1994. The event was held on Winston Farm in Saugerties, New York.

Over 350,000 people came to this three day festival. The policy initially restricted the attendees from entering with supplies of food, drink, alcohol, and drugs, but the security staff was unable to handle such a massive crowd, and so thousands got in with these things, and thousands got in for free.

Aside from the injuries people received by the overenthusiastic mud mosh-pits, the event was without total deliberate conflicts and violence. Like the original event it also rained during most of the festival whereby day two the field was one huge mud field. Nearly 70 bands performed at the festival.

The stage was set in two sections called the North Stage and the South Stage where the bands would be organized to where some would play on the north section, and some on the south section. The main headliners were Blues Traveler, Candlebox, Collective Soul, Sheryl Crow, Joe Cocker, Blind Melon, Cypress Hill, Melissa Etheridge, Crosby, Stills, and Nash, Metallica, Nine Inch Nails, Aerosmith, Salt N' Pepa, Arrested Development, Spin

Doctors, Bob Dylan, Red Hot Chilli Peppers, Peter Gabriel, Green Day, Santana, and others.

Some of the noted things of the event were that Nine Inch Nails had the largest crowd density of the event, and before going on stage the band wrestled in the mud and performed completely covered in mud. The Red Hot Chilli Peppers performed in light-bulb costumes, and then later in the set they all dressed up as Jimi Hendrix. Peter Gabriel performed on the North Stage, and closed Woodstock 94. Shannon Hoon of Blind Melon played Woodstock 94 in his girlfriend's dress while tripping on LSD. Bob Dylan who refused to go to the original Woodstock, made up for it by going to this one. Green Day almost caused a riot when they started a mud fight with the crowd and the situation spiraled out of control with fans jumping on stage. This resulted in the security team mistaking bass player Mike Dirnt for a fan, and tackling him that resulted in Mike requiring emergency orthodontia.

This festival like the first one was also filled with every kind of drug you can think of among the fans. People were getting high on marijuana, cocaine, heroin, LSD, pills, and other drugs. The drugs were so extensively used that security gave up on trying to control it. Woodstock 99 however did not go as well as 69 and 94. Instead this four day event that was held in New York State from July 22 to July 25 of 1999 was marred by violence, rape, and fires. These tragic crimes brought the festival to an abrupt end, and brought shame on the Woodstock memory according to many critics. This festival was attended by over 200,000 people, and it was even available on pay-per-view. The festival would feature a two-way stage called the West Stage, and the Emerging Artists Stage.

Nearly 100 bands played for these four days. The main headliners were 3rd Bass, Flipp, Buckcherry, The Roots, Insane Clown Posse, George Clinton & the P.Funk All-Stars, James Brown, Sheryl Crow, Live, DMX, The Offspring, Korn, Bush, Shern Jackson, Bruce Hornsby, Everclear, Ice Cube, Los Lobos, Moby, Fatboy Slim, Kid Rock, Wyclef Jean & the Refugee All-Stars, Counting Crows, Dave Matthews Band, Alanis Morissette, Limp Bizkit, Rage Against the Machine, Metallica, Our Lady Peace, Collective Soul, Godsmack, Megadeth, Willie Nelson,

Jewel, Creed, Red Hot Chilli Peppers, and others.

Security was also a problem at this festival even though 500 New York State Troopers were on hand. Many of the masses of the crowd kept gate-crashing to get in to avoid paying for it. There was some particularly praised performances but they were overshadowed by the deteriorating environment and crowd behavior. The heat at the event was also oppressive as it reached to above 100 degrees, and there was no shade. Food and water was also not sufficient, and at the onsite vendors booths it was over expensive. A slice of pizza was $12 and a bottle of water or soda-can was $4. The number of toilets was not sufficient for the number of attendees, and these facilities were unusable and overflowing.

People stood in mass lines to drink from water fountains, and when frustration took its toll people started to break the water pipes to drink water which caused large mud pits.

The violence started to take place after a performance from Limp Bizkit when Fred Durst told the fans in his lyrics to 'break stuff'. Fred later stated he did not mean it like that but that is hard to believe when you watch the performance, and how he led into it. When Limp Bizkit sang this rap-rock song fans started tearing up the plywood from the walls, and then several women were raped during the performance. Fred stated later that he did not know people were getting hurt but those statements were lies. During the violence Fred stated to the crowd that people are getting hurt, and then he stated to them that he thought they should not mellow out, and now that the negative energy was let out as he stated it, the positive energy should come in according to him.

In short to understand his thinking if someone rapes a girl or beats someone up now that you have committed a crime against them you should help them off the ground, and everyone can be friends again. Fred was never arrested for starting the violence, and really he should have been arrested. The violence would escalate from there during the final hours of the set performed by Red Hot Chilli Peppers.

A peace group called Pax gave out candles to be lit during the song Under the Bridge. This was a really stupid idea. The crowd began to light the candles, and used them to start bonfires as hundreds of empty plastic water bottles were used as fuel for the fires. They also lit the audio tower on fire, and the fire department had to put it out. The Chilli Peppers did not care about the fires but instead they remarked how amazing the fires looked from the stage. People danced in circles around these large bonfires, and when the fires were getting lower the people looked for more fuel. So they began to rip off more panels, and took plywood that was the security perimeter fence to fuel it.

ATM's were also tipped over, and broken into, and trailers of the vendors were forced open, and burgled, and the vendor booths were set on fire. The MTV crew had to flee the scene due to the danger all around them where they called the scene a hateful concentration camp with waves of hatred bouncing all around the place.

The State Troopers, local police, and other law enforcement now had a fight on their hands, and they dressed in their riot gear to stop the rioting. The police also had to investigate the rape cases that took place. One woman who was wearing a body-surfing suit was pulled into the crowd during the Limp Bizkit song, and she was dragged into the mosh-pit and gang-raped. Other women were raped right in the middle of the angry crowds. Most of them were also gang-raped. Only seven men were arrested for it due to the video footage that captured mainly the gang-rape of the woman dragged in the mosh-pit. The others got away with it due to lack of evidence.

Rage Against the Machine would give a strong performance but they also came under fire by the media for burning the American Flag during a song called Killing in the Name. The artists that performed at the festival tried to defend the festival by saying that compared to the numbers at the festival it was only a small group doing the raping, arson, vandalism, robbery, and violence. They would go on to state that most of the over 200,000 people had a good time. But the footage shows a far different story then that.

Interviews with most of those 200,000 people who spoke in large groups only spoke about the fray of twisted acts that happened at the festival. Drug use ran wild at the festival along with open sex done on the fields. Overdose cases were largely overshadowed by the violence. Concerts done by music industry artists have often ended in such ways. Not all of them happen to end on such a horrible note but many of them do.

Going to concerts is often like playing with a six-shooter handgun with only one bullet in the chamber. You go to five concerts, and nothing happens until that one concert where all hell breaks loose. One time an experiment was done at a rock concert using a store bought single egg. The person doing the experiment wanted to compare the effects that the rock sounds coming from the speakers were having on the human brain by seeing what it does to the egg, so he tapes the egg near the speaker so that the egg does not fall or break, and left it there in until the concert was over. Once over he went back to the egg, and to his shock the egg was a fully cooked hard-boiled egg.

The man discovered that the music the rock band was playing was sending sound waves through the speakers that had such agitation, and excitability that it caused a heated bubbling effect inside the egg that ended up cooking the egg. The man saw that if a human person had their head in the spot where he put the egg during the concert it would have fried about half the cells in his brain. The egg was placed only 3 feet away from the first ten rows.

Overall evidence showed that people do lose brain cells, and even lose, of hearing after going to rock concert shows. Another experiment involved positive notes and negative notes. One study showed that most mainstream popular music had depressive notes in its music that could cause several changes in mood and behavior. Most mainstream music did not have a large amount of uplifting notes that were proven to be healthy for moods and behavior. Mostly the music that had a large amount of uplifting tempos was classical music. So, in this experiment, the college students that were running the experiment put a small group into a room for about 6 hours, and this small group were tasked to interact with each other. What the group did not know is that there were hidden speakers throughout the room. The speakers were to play two kinds of music at such low tones that the music could only be heard through their sub-conscience.

At the first session they played classical music at these very low tones for 6 hours while they were in the room. They notice that the group who were a group of strangers got along better, and their moods would improve, and were able to handle being in the room for those long hours. At the second session they played mainstream music at these low tones which was the music with the most depressive notes. They noticed that the group became more negative in their moods, and some arguments arose, and the people became very bitter, and lost patience during the final hours of being in the room.

After the experiment was over the group was told what they did during those two 6 hour sessions when they were in the room. They were shocked because most of them felt that mainstream music made them feel better then classical music, but it turned out it was the other way around.

Uplifting music is clearly not endorsed by the media, and not praised by the media either. Uplifting music does not sell millions of copies nor does it draw in thousands and thousands of people at mega concerts. The real question you got to ask yourself is, why is that? The answer according to some experts is that we as a people have been media brain-washed to think that mainstream music is better for us when many tests have shown it's not.

Chapter 20

Another form of music that became a huge mainstream seller in the late 1980's, and up to this timeframe is a music called Gangsta Rap. Gangsta Rap originally was born from Hip-Hop Rap. When Gangsta Rap first came out it was called hardcore rap because the overtone lyrics of the songs were filled with profanity, murder, images of porn, and violence in all types of forms. The fan-base that Gangsta Rap first had starting out was African-American youths mainly living in urban cities. Soon and very soon the music caught on to white Americans.

The first white American fans who started to buy the music in larger numbers were white female fans. In interviews with them it was revealed that they bought this music because it made their parents angry in all kinds of ways. They stated that their white parents would come into their rooms only to find a cd or a poster of black men or a black man holding a gun wearing street gear, and rapping about killing people, and street issues would make their parents very unsettled. Soon because so many white females liked the music young white males started to buy the music as well.

Interesting enough Rock N' Roll music started out in a similar way. Rock N' Roll was at first music played by black artists, and white young female fans began to show up to underground parties where the music was played, and were the first to start getting a hold on its records.

Then a man named Elvis Presley who grew up, and lived among poor black people began to learn how to play Rock N' Roll music. Elvis became famous from taking songs originally sung by black artists, and he started to sing them. From that point the Rock N' Roll mainstream market was born, and flew wide open for countless of white Rock N' Roll bands. This was the reason why Run-DMC called themselves the kings of Rock N' Roll rather than the kings of Rap because they foresaw that rap music had a similar history with rock music. ʼ

Gangsta Rap music reflects on urban crime, and the violent lifestyles of inner-city gangs. When Ice-T and NWA attracted national attention from the U.S. government, and the media in the late 80's to the early 90's Gangsta Rap became very soon the most commercially, and lucrative style of rap. Gangsta Rap would destroy the Pop-Rap market acts like Hammer, Vanilla Ice, Kid N' Play, Young MC, and others, and it took that market over.

But Gangsta Rap also has much controversy to it, and a strong criminal element behind it. The labels that have produced Gangsta Rap artists, and their records have often been shown again and again to have ties with street gangs, and the Black Mafia. The two main street gangs with ties to these labels were the Bloods and the Crips who have gang sets throughout the West and East coasts of the United States mainly in Los Angeles and New York City.

Police records show that the real violent conflicts between East and West coast acts had a lot to do with the rivalry between Bloods and Crips. This rivalry in the music industry is about money and drugs. The Black Mafia, which was started by Bumpy Johnson in Harlem many years ago and had strong leadership under Frank Lucas who was trained by Johnson, are the ones who became the main suppliers of drugs to these two gangs. They also borrowed money to many of these gangsters who took that money and started record labels with it.

The Black Mafia interest in the music industry, and the Gangsta Rap labels have a lot to do with overseeing their drugs and gun profit sales. Many people working in those labels, mostly behind the scenes, not only helped to produced Gangsta Rap acts they also sold drugs and guns to people in the movie and music industry scene. The people working behind those scenes are usually ex or current gang-members who mainly came from the Bloods or the Crips.

On the streets and even behind the scenes in the gangsta music industry Bloods and Crips kill each other over money and power positions because those positions can bring them more money and protection. This is the world that is often hidden by Gangsta Rap acts, and this is the reason why the police have files on Gangsta Rap acts, and follow them everywhere they go.

Gangsta Rap acts are not all dangerous nor do they have the mind-set to commit crimes everywhere they go. They are mostly artists who came from some dangerous, and violent backgrounds based in poverty and neighborhoods in depraved and horrible states. Many of them used music as a way out of those circumstances. But the police still follow them around because of the kind of people they work for who are far more dangerous than most of these artists.

The controversy surrounding the gangsta rap genre was mostly voiced by religious leaders of the black and white Churches. After them the U.S. government leaders also voiced against them, and the media bull-horned all the statements against these acts. Among the leaders in D.C. the main ones who spoke out against these acts were the White House administrations of both

George H.W. Bush and Bill Clinton. The counter arguments to their concerns were mostly spoken by Ice-T and NWA.

The counter arguments mainly were the administrations lack of actions to end the drug problems, and the gang problems, and race problems in urban cities. The two White House administrations under these former Presidents even at times tried to shift the blame of the chaos happening on the streets upon these acts, but those gangsta acts were not at fault for it because it was going on way before them, and they were products of it. The focus of acts that these two administrations under Bush and Clinton, and even Reagan before them had to handle the street crime problem was to build more jails and lock up as many people as they can. Those acts clearly were not going to fix the problem at all. In fact, no actions came to end the core root of the problem. A core root that it turned out the government itself was involved in.

During Bush's stand on street crime he revealed to the world that a crack dealer was selling crack right across the street from the White House. But the Washington Post busted the Bush administration for lying about it, and it was the CIA who set up the drug dealer to get busted across the street from the White House so that Bush had a reason to increase the building of more jails, and to extend prison sentences for first time offenders.

It also got worse when it turned out that the CIA was helping the Central American drug cartels to sell rock-cocaine to certain dealers in the United States to fund black ops missions against certain governments in South and Central America they deemed as a threat to the U.S.

In fact 'Freeway' Ricky Ross the man who organized the crack-trade throughout the United States by the example of his dealings, got his drugs from a Central American cartel that was protected by our own CIA. Ricky himself didn't even know that the government was helping him to sell drugs to people in his own culture and community. Sadly many gangsta rap acts, and rap acts in general started out making money through crack dealing. Many of them bought their gear, gold-chains, their car, their shoes, and even recorded singles, and started up labels by saving money they made from selling crack to their own people. This is how Eazy-E, a former Crip, started up Ruthless Records.

The complaints against gangsta rap acts by the Churches, and the government leaders were for promoting drug dealing, drug abuse, drive-by shootings, violence, profanity, serial killing, sex addictions, vandalism, racism against whites, rape, disregarding law enforcement, promoting crime, thievery, Satanism, materialism, promoting street gangs, narcissism, abuse of women, and the list does go on.

The counter arguments to the complaints by Church leaders, and government leaders centered on them ignoring the core root of the problem that gives birth to these kinds of lyrics. Gangsta Rap artists stated that they are being unfairly singled out because white politicians, and religious leaders refuse to understand what is going on in communities devastated with poverty, and racism against the people living in those areas. They believe that this form of rap is attacked only because it exposes all the contradictions that white American culture tries to paint to the rest of the world.

They stated that leaders in Washington D.C. voice their complaints only after it was exposed through this music but they represent no political system that intends to deal with, and root out the inner core of the problem. Police and polite society as it is called often label the people as bad guys based on ignorant views, and inner fears within themselves according to many experts. It seems a change has to come upon both sides in order to end the chaos in urban cities.

Many black entertainers have criticized gangsta rap acts for promoting stereotypical characters, and doing so in their words 'by an ignorant manner for the entertainment of the audiences'. The main black artists and leaders who criticized these acts the most were Bill Cosby, Spike Lee, Jesse Jackson, Public Enemy, and many others.

Bill Cosby often spoke against them for using the word 'niggas' or stating of themselves that they were 'niggas'. Bill Cosby knowing that they used this word so often it caused him to tour high-schools made up largely of African-American students to teach young black youths about the evils of this word. Bill would show them pictures of the horrible torture of slaves in the 19th century, and pictures of lynchings done in the 19th, and early 20th century against black people by people who used that word. Bill stated that it was a moral crime that black artists would call themselves under that name knowing what was done to their people by that name.

Gangsta Rap artists would flip the meaning around by stating that the word 'nigga' had a different meaning to them. They stated that it was a word used among them as a sign of their struggle and character on the streets. They also stated that the new meaning of the word to them was 'never ignorant getting goals accomplished'.

Spike Lee and Public Enemy who are rap groups that have spoken against gangsta rap style for promoting to black youths that it is a negative way of handling the struggle. They believed that education, and to better one's self through knowledge was the key in getting out of the urban chaos. Gangsta rap acts would respond to this by quoting Malcom X by teaching his proverb 'by any means necessary' which was a proverb about using violent force to the extent of overcoming one's enemy.

Jesse Jackson would use the religious, and moral aim to show the evils of gangsta rap lyrics but the gangsta rap acts accused black Churches of not being there for the people when the people really needed them. Gangsta Rap artists would overall defend themselves against high-scale black leaders by stating that those leaders and persons of influence are mad because they are saying what those leaders are afraid to say. These gangsta artists would go on to state that they are only telling the truth about the 'hood', and are telling stories about a world that exist in their world outside of the illusions of their perfect world.

Gangsta Rap is believed to have been started in 1986 when Ice-T released a song called Six in the Mornin. Police stated that the song was about the hour dope dealers sell their products, and Ice-T was forced to defend his position, but actually the song as it relates to the streets was about the hour the police will come to bust dope dealers after selling their drugs at 5:00 in the morning.

The police it was said were mad because the song made dope dealers aware of when cops would come for them which is as soon as you are done dealing. Ice-T credited the 1970's pimps for the way he raps because those pimps used a lot of rhymes to get their point across. One pimp especially Ice-T looked up to was Iceberg Slim. Slim used a lot of what became later hardcore rhymes in his raps. Ice-T also credited a rapper named Schoolly D for inspiring him to do an album completely based on hardcore rapping.

In 1987 a rapper named KRS-One recorded an album called Criminal Minded with his group called Boogie Down Productions. Criminal Minded was the first album to have firearms on its cover. A song on the album that fueled controversy was called 9mm Goes Bang. The rap song tells a story of KRS-One killing a crack dealer, and his entire posse in self-defense.

Shortly after the single was released Scott LaRock of BDP who was featured on the album was shot and killed. The inside story is that he was killed to discourage the group from rapping about killing crack dealers because there were certain power players in the music industry who made a lot of money from drug-dealers especially crack dealers. No one knows how true this is but either way BDP decided to stay away from hardcore rap after LaRock's murder.

In 1988 a group that brought a national firestorm upon themselves from the FBI, the media, the government, Church leaders, and others was a gangsta rap group called NWA. NWA was founded by Eazy- E who got a record company started by paying a parent label to support his Ruthless Records. Eazy-E used money he earned on the streets from crack dealing to fund the studio time, and his label. Eazy-E would bring in other talent like Dr.Dre, Ice Cube, MC Ren, and others to form this rap group. NWA was the rap group that smashed the Pop-Rap market, and brought Gangsta Rap to a world-wide mainstream market. The album that started their world-wide fame, and infamy was called Straight Outta Compton. Soon the group would release a single called Fuck Tha Police. The single caused the group to get a letter from FBI Assistant Director Milt Ahlerich who expressed law enforcement's resentment of the song.

The group also came under fire from Church groups, and government and law officials, and the media all at the same time. Church groups would take NWA's first and second albums, and make public demonstrations against them by burning, and smashing their records in front of the media. Law enforcement began to investigate them looking to catch them in some criminal act. The IRS sought to also make them pay. The government wanted to pull the album off the shelves but the group was protected by Freedom of Speech Laws. The efforts from the black Church groups in burning their records, and destroying them did not have them coming off looking good for it. Their actions were compared to the Nazi government under Hitler who burned books that he, and his leaders felt were not acceptable in their vision of Germany at the time. NWA defended their position about the song Fuck Tha Police as a song about police brutality that was sweeping the streets of Los Angeles' urban areas especially among black people. Their defense would prove right in the eyes of the world when Los Angeles Police officers were caught on tape beating up Rodney King, a black man.

They were proven even more right when the officers were found not guilty even though a fellow white officer gave testimony against them. This resulted in the brutal L.A. riots that killed close to 60 people, and left millions of dollars in property damage to be lit in flames.

NWA had did songs predicting this would happen. NWA is also credited for openly bringing out the West and East coast rivalry when they started to take sole credit for hardcore rhymes. The East coast rappers got mad about this because acts like BDP, Eric B. and Rakim, Kool Moe Dee, Big Daddy Kane, and others were ignored for songs they did before NWA which had hardcore rapping upon them.

Many other insiders stated that the rivalry between the groups of East and West was a smokescreen to cover the real issue behind it which was about gangs in Los Angeles and New York City.

The story is that the Crips of Los Angeles helped to fund Ruthless Records due to the fact Eazy-E was a Crip, and they wanted to get in on the action. BDP's record called Criminal Minded was believed to have been funded by the Bloods of New York City's Bronx area. These insiders stated that the hit on LaRock was made to look like it was about crack but there was more to it than that. It was said that the Crips put a hit on LaRock to discourage BDP from getting into the hardcore rap game to leave the market only open to them.

When the Bloods found out the real reason behind LaRock's murder the war between East and West for control of the rap game in the music industry had officially began to turn bloody. Not much proof has been given to show this but if there is any you can be sure it still won't be made public.

In the early 1990's Ice Cube left the group NWA after an argument he had with Eazy-E, and their record label manager. Ice Cube was upset because he was not getting paid for a lot of the hit rap songs he wrote for NWA. One day the record manager offered Ice Cube, and the rest of the group members a check for $75,000. The condition in accepting the check was they had to sign to a very long term contract. Ice Cube felt that the check rightfully belonged to him without him having to sign because they made the money in the first place through his writing, but Eazy-E, and his manager did not agree with Cube. Dre and Ren both took the checks, and signed the contract but Cube being smart because the contract was bad in the long run would quit the group and go solo.

Ice Cube would form a crew called Lynch Mob, and he was able to get a record contract. He began to record rap songs that had a hardcore and socio-political nature to them. He would even go on to star in a movie called Boyz In The Hood. Ice-T would also go on to star in a movie called New Jack City where he played an undercover cop. This was a role he never thought in his lifetime he would see himself playing. The movie reflected the real life crack trade, and street drug lords of that time. Boyz In The Hood was originally supposed to cast the entire NWA group. The movie was directed by John Singleton who was a huge fan of the group NWA. The movie had a very low budget, and it was filmed on the dangerous streets of Compton in Los Angeles.

Due to the beef between Ice Cube, and the rest of NWA John

casted only Ice Cube to appear in the movie. The movie was a very real to life reflection of violent street gangs, and the murders that took place between rival gangs.

Ice Cube after leaving NWA did not think at first there was a problem between him and the other members of NWA. He thought they all understood and respected his choice to leave, but when NWA released their second album they made songs, and music videos where they dissed Ice Cube. They even dissed him in interviews as well.

NWA's second album would make gangsta rap history by becoming the first album to hit number one on the Billboard Pop charts. Along with the usual groups that protested against NWA the gangsta rap group would make another enemy. They were the women's rights groups. The women's rights groups attacked NWA for songs they did on the second album about women giving them blow-jobs, and degrading women to be seen as sex puppets.

The Church groups stated that the songs were about smut porn promoted among young fans. While this was going on Ice Cube would record a single called No Vasoline, and go on the attack against NWA in a very heated way. Many insiders stated that the rap song No Vasoline was Ice Cube revealing behind the scenes secrets about the group that they really did not want people to know about. Ice Cube through the song stated that Eazy-E and Dre had gay sex with their white Jewish manager, and Dre was known to be homosexual during the time he was with NWA.

This would not be the last time people have exposed Dre for being gay. Cube accused them both of being sell-outs, and that neither one of them were not hardcore, and were not living for the hood anymore. The song was said to be so damaging to NWA's image that the group refused to respond to the song, and would not diss Ice Cube at all after he released that song.

Many stated the reason why they did not want to touch on Ice Cube anymore was because he told the raw ugly truth in the song. Soon Dr. Dre had enough of being ripped off by Eazy-E, and his manager, and then he wanted out of his contract. This got started when Dre met Suge Knight. Knight wanted to start up a record label called Death Row Records, and wanted Dre as a partner to help build the company.

Knight is a suspected member of the Black Mafia with ties to the Bloods and the Crips. Police records show that the ties to these two gangs had to do with gun-running sales and drug sales. Dre could not work with Knight due to the contract he signed with Ruthless Records for that $75,000 check. The following story is how Dre got out of the contract with Eazy-E, told by Eazy, and his close friends including his manager, and his wife.

One day Dre called Eazy to meet him at a studio to talk about his contract. Eazy thought he would be meeting Dre all by himself. Eazy came to the studio unarmed, and when he walked through the doors he found Suge Knight, and several of his men standing around Eazy holding baseball bats. Suge told Eazy to sit down, and Eazy did so, Suge then explained to him that he wanted him to sign a release that would cancel the contract between Dre and Ruthless Records. Eazy-E being from the street was not that easy to intimidate, and so he said to Suge to give him the release form, and when Suge did Eazy-E signed the name 'mickey mouse' on the form. Suge then got mad, and man-handled Eazy-E, and slammed his head on a desk to put a gun to his temple, and told him to either sign the release form or he was going to disappear.

Eazy-E, seeing Suge could make good on the threat, signed the release form in his real name. Eazy then went to his manager, and told him that they had a real problem with Suge Knight, and he wanted to call in some Crips to come and kill Knight, but his manager would talk him out of it by telling him that there was too much money to lose by doing that.

Soon Dre would start recording his first album for Death Row Records but Eazy-E did find a way to get back at Dre legally. Though Eazy-E released him from the contract Dre still had to pay a certain portion of any future earnings to repay being released out of the contract at an early time. Therefore a part of the money made from Dre's first album went to Eazy-E, and Ruthless Records.

On the East Coast side of things the East Coast rappers began to battle back as being the ones who really created hardcore rap. They pointed to acts like Slick Rick, Big Daddy Kane, Run DMC, BDP, and others for popularizing hardcore and confrontational styles in hip-hop before the West Coast rappers came along. The question of who really started hardcore rap between East and West is also a beef within itself. Soon hip-hop acts of a hardcore style were now coming out of the urban areas of the South. The first of them was a group from Houston, Texas called Geto Boys.

Geto Boys were inspired by NWA, and they would often go to Dallas to the City Lights nightclub to see NWA perform there. The Geto Boys style of music was a dark, haunting, and mafioso style of gangsta rap. The lead rapper called himself Scarface, and he would go on to have a solo career. This rapper named himself after this nickname due to the love of the movie Scarface that starred Al Pacino. The name 'Scarface' was the original nickname of Al Capone the former Mob boss of Chicago. The rapper called Scarface centered his rhymes on cocaine dealing, and killing rival gang members, and battling inner demons of madness and murder.

The Beastie Boys were often overlooked for their credit to gangsta rhymes. This is because the Beastie Boys were not seen as a true hip-hop group but a rap-rock group who started the style that became later on very popular with groups like Linklin Park, Crazy Town, and Limp Bizkit. Many of the songs from the Beastie Boys from late 1986 to the present were songs that rapped about guns, drugs, and pornographic sex. In their 1989 album called Paul's Boutique the Jewish rap-rock band did songs like Car Thief, Looking Down the Barrel of a Gun, and My Posse.

In 1991 Ice-T released an album called O.G. Original Gangster, and a Rap-Heavy Metal album with his band called Body Count. On the album called Body Count was its lead single called Cop Killer. The song brought a firestorm of controversy on Ice-T. The song enraged government officials, the NRA, and various police groups. Police groups around the nation protested the song, and wanted the song banned. Time Warner Music dropped Ice-T from the label, and prevented his next new album called Home Invasion from being released. Ice-T was also forced to remove the single Cop Killer from the Body Count album, and was forced to sell it as a single.

1992 was the year Dr. Dre released his solo album called The Chronic. The Chronic was a huge selling album, and it went triple platinum in sales. The album also brought funk music to gangsta rap beats, and this fusion was called G-Funk, and it dominated the beats in many Gangsta Rap albums of the 1990's. As The Chronic went on to sell close to 4 million copies Ice Cube's album called The Predator would become a huge selling album. The Predator sold 5 million copies.

Soon after, a new artist called Snoop Doggy Dog would release his debut album, and it would sell over 4 million copies. Ice Cube's album called The Predator would also make Gangsta Rap history as it became the first Gangsta Rap album to hit number one on the Billboard 200 albums chart.

Eazy-E would also find success with his new album, and with a group he signed to Ruthless Records called Bones Thugs N' Harmony who were also selling multi-platinum albums, but Eazy-E after serving a short time in prison would later die of full-blown AIDS.

Gangsta rapper Tupac Shakur's album Me Against the World would sell over 2 million copies while the rapper was in jail. A rapper named Warren G., and the late Nate Dogg would also release a platinum album due to the lead single Regulators.

On the East Coast rap groups like the Wu-Tang Clan, Onyx, Nas, The Notorious B.I.G., Mobb Deep, and others released hardcore rap albums that would also sell in the millions. Gangsta rappers down South also arose to fame through a rapper named Master P who started a company called No Limit Records. No Limit Records produced other southern talented rappers like Mystical and C-Murder. At the height of No Limit Record's fame the company was worth one billion dollars.

By the 2000s this form of macho-headstrong rap began to decline in popularity but still managed to have loyal fans. As a result gangsta rap style began to change into a more flashy, and glamour type of rap that was about the 'bling' meaning showing off jewelry, and about women, and nightclubs. The sounds of the beat became more alternative, and some stated it became even more feminist in many ways.

Gangsta rap artists rap about their looks, their money, how many women they get, how many cars they have, overall their music appeals to the nightclub scene. It no longer appeals to social issues going on in the streets unless they are rapping about buying drugs on the street to take to the nightclubs.

Chapter 21

Many rappers throughout the time of hip-hop have left a mark on the music industry in one form or another, but there has been only one who left this world as a legend. Till this day his death is still not accepted by many of his most loyal fans who believe he is still alive in the same manner devout Elvis' fans believe he is still alive. This rapper's name was Tupac Shakur.

Tupac was born in East Harlem in New York City. He was named after Tupac Amaru who was an 18th century South American revolutionary who was executed while leading an uprising against Spanish rule. The meaning of Tupac's name means 'shining serpent'. Tupac's mother was named Afeni Shakur, and his father's name was Billy Garland. Both of them were active members of the Black Panther party in the late 1960's to early 1970's.

The Black Panther party was a militant group who taught self-improvement among African-Americans through education and self-defense. They also had strong black power views which included the belief in a black revolution, and an over-throw of the current U.S. government to instill a fair communist rule in America to end white oppression of black people. They often did a lot of good for poor black youths by funding food and clothes programs along with education programs. They also had brutal violent confrontations with police officers, and many of them committed serious crimes. Tupac's mother while pregnant with Tupac spent some time in jail when she received 150 charges of conspiracy against the United States government during the New York 'Panther 21' court case. Afeni along with the group were accused of looking to blow-up New York, and government landmarks in the U.S. Afeni would be acquitted of all charges but the case followed her for the rest of her life often leaving her in poverty. Afeni would be denied jobs or would be fired from jobs when it was discovered she was among the group accused. She would often be denied support for housing and support for her children. Afeni would then soon force herself to receive welfare support for housing and food for her two children.

Billy Garland was not in the picture as a father to Tupac throughout Tupac's life. Other men would come into the life of Tupac, and his mother to fill the father role. These men were mostly in the Black Panther party. These men also were convicted of serious criminal offenses, and were mostly imprisoned. Tupac's godfather Geronimo Pratt was a high-ranking Panther but was convicted of murdering a school teacher during a 1968 robbery, but later due to lack of evidence, his sentence was overturned. Tupac's step-father Mutulu was once on the FBI's Ten Most Wanted Fugitives list. Mutulu got on the list after helping his sister Assata Shakur to escape from a New Jersey penitentiary. Assata was imprisoned there for killing a state trooper in 1973.

While Mutulu was wanted, Tupac as a child was often harassed by the FBI while he was in grade school. They would often come into his class, and take the young Tupac aside, and grill him with questions about the whereabouts of his step-father. Because of this other students and teachers were resentful of having Tupac in their school. Mutulu was not captured until 1986 after he robbed the Brinks armored trunk where two police officers, and a guard was killed in a shoot-out.

After Mutulu went to jail Tupac, and his mother and sister moved to Baltimore, Maryland. At the time Tupac moved to Baltimore the urban black communities in the city suffered the most from violence, poverty, and AIDS. Tupac during this time began to develop a strong social conscience regarding the issues effecting the black communities there. He took part in marches and gatherings regarding these issues. Soon Tupac attended the Baltimore School for the Arts where he was trained as an actor, poet, and trained in Jazz and dance. During this time Tupac, who was a huge fan of hip-hop, discovered he was gifted at rapping.

Tupac entered many rap competitions, and won them all. He was called the best rapper in the art school, and became a popular student. He had a more positive character during his time at the art school. Tupac was very different back then compared to the gangsta image of Tupac in the music industry. In those days Tupac was anti-gangs, anti-violence, and his rhymes were about social issues and fantasy rap. He did not believe in using profanity, and he had high respect for girls his age because he was raised to be respectful by a mostly single mother. Tupac was also drug-free and spoke against drugs. He was educated in terms of being a step higher in knowledge then most youths his age.

His first dream was not music but it was one day to become an actor, and he did later enter the movie industry as well. He had a wonderful ability to mix with all cultures of people. He was very well known for his sense of humor, and his high-level rapping skills.

In June of 1988 Tupac's life would change when his mother had to move to the West Coast. This move happened because lack of jobs for Tupac's mother caused more problems for her on the East Coast. She wanted to go somewhere so that she could start all over, and get away from areas who knew who she was. Tupac and his family moved to Marin City in California. The area Tupac moved to was a very poor housing project community dubbed 'the jungle'. Within Tupac's first week of living there Tupac witnessed a woman cut open the throat of her boyfriend with a knife after the boyfriend had spit on her child. Soon Tupac would witness other events like open gang murders, police brutality, racism, women being beaten and raped, overdoses, muggings done for drug money, and gangs ruling the streets. The positive outlets Tupac had at the art school was now gone, and things would get worse at home.

Afeni when she moved into the low-income project apartment in Marin City thought it would be easier than before finding a job, but it was not. Soon she started to go to interviews where her past got discovered all over again, and she would be denied jobs. This caused her to give up on hope, and she started to use crack-cocaine to cope, and soon she was very addicted to it. During that time Tupac made a friend with a neighbor who was also a fellow rapper. The two used to often rap together, and Tupac and his sister became close to his friend's family. In high-school Tupac only had one year and a half to go before he could graduate, but this high-school was brutal at times. The teachers in the high-school did not believe the youths there would amount to anything so they hardly cared to really teach them.

Tupac would often get into fist-fights over protecting girls from abusive boyfriends but this would back-fire on Tupac. The same girls he thought he was helping would only end up with the same abusive boyfriends. They often would end up calling the police on Tupac just for helping them. One time when Tupac was courting a girl that girl broke up with him because she stated of Tupac that he was too nice. Tupac was often lonely, and the guys who disrespected the girls the most would get all the girls while the guys who were nice were mostly alone.

Tupac saw how the guys who hung close to the gangs, and acted in the manner they acted in were respected in the neighborhood, and soon this influence started to change Tupac. Tupac's close friend who he used to rap with showed Tupac what he needed to do to be accepted in the neighborhood. Tupac then started to hang out with the gangs, and began to speak, and act like them in order to avoid trouble, and to have some respect, and some kind of life there.

When Tupac was rude to the girls is when the girls started to notice him, and when Tupac would act wild is when he made more friends. At this time his mother's crack addiction was getting worse and worse. Problems and arguments kept erupting over money, food, and clothes. Tupac soon had to start getting a job but often he found it hard to hold a job due to overbearing bosses or running around with his friends.

Tupac was also part of a program where government study groups did interviews with him about his life from one period at a time. In one interview Tupac had to quit his job at Pizza Hut just to talk with them because his boss told him he could not go.

Tupac losing one job after another brought more fights between him and his mom which resulted in Tupac having to leave his mother's home to stay at the home of his best-friend. Soon Tupac's sister also had problems with her mom, and every now and then when Tupac would return home his mother was so addicted to drugs she began to have very bad anger mood swings and anger management problems. This resulted in Tupac and his sister to have to stay with his friend's family once again.

At this point Tupac was a wild young man. He got into smoking marijuana, and rapping with his friend and chasing girls on the corner. He started to hang out more with the local gang, and he even at times sold marijuana for them. Tupac's friend would rap at a poetry class run by a woman named Leila Steinberg. Tupac's friend introduced him to Leila and Leila wanted to see what Tupac could do on the mic. Tupac would rhyme his poetry to Leila, and she knew at that moment he was not just gifted but he could be a star someday. Leila often opened her doors to other gifted rap, and poetry artists who had bad family problems at home. Tupac fit into that case. Leila offered to take him in, and Tupac would eventually accept due to the fact it was hard for his friend's mom to take care both Tupac and his sister.

Leila's background story has some strange elements to it. Some of it has not been proven but just often said surrounding her. It is known that Leila knows people in the music industry, and she does have connections to them. The rumor is that Leila worked as a scout in the urban areas to seek talented rappers in the hope she can sell them off to the music industry to be used by them. The other rumor is that she is often known to corrupt the religious convictions of the talent that works with her and moves in with her. For instance Tupac's spiritual convictions was Christianity where he believed in a black Jesus type of Christianity but overall he believed that 'black' Jesus was the Son of GOD, but Leila throughout the time Tupac lived with her constantly taught him New Age beliefs, and Tupac would learn about magic, witchcraft doctrines and beliefs more, and more. Leila would try to infuse them into his knowledge of Christian teachings to make it seem that all religious were the same.

The Bible does not teach that at all, and that kind of thinking is called abominable in the Bible. The Bible states that what is holy which is, the Word should never be mixed with what is unholy which is pagan practices and beliefs. But Leila was schooling Tupac into a different kind of teaching. This was changing the way Tupac saw religion and himself. It would lead him to change his spiritual convictions, and get involved with even darker aspects of the music industry.

While Leila was doing this Tupac, and his friend, and other rappers in her home formed a rap group called Strictly Dope. The style of rap of the group was not gangsta, and Tupac was not a gangsta rapper at this point. The group had a hard edge sound with rap that contained social messages of the issues facing black and poor people of America. During the practice sessions Leila lived next door to a neighbor many felt was a covert skinhead. He often played rock-music very loudly, and the police never came to say anything to him. One night while Strictly Dope was practicing for a show this neighbor called the police on Leila, and her friends for loud noises. When the police came Tupac wanted to answer the door because Tupac really hated cops, and was taught by his step-father and mother in how to handle them. But Leila did not want any more problems because often this guy would call the police on her for doing shows in her backyard.

When the cops came to the door Leila promised she would keep it down but Tupac would interfere in the conversation that Leila was having with the cops. Tupac in a nice way would say to the officer that he was going to turn the music off but he wanted to know what volume would be acceptable. So Tupac put in a single on the tape deck from NWA called Fuck Tha Police.

Tupac would press play, and kept it at a low volume just loud enough for the cops to hear it, and then went back to the cops, and said, 'Is this volume okay...officer?' The cops could do nothing but leave in anger.

Leila soon organized a concert promoting Tupac's group called Strictly Dope. The concert was so well received that Atron Gregory the manager of Digital Underground asked Leila to bring Tupac to his office. After the meeting Atron signed Tupac to work as a roadie and backup dancer for Digital Underground's tour for their very successful album called Sex Packets.

During the tour Tupac would have to get the lead rapper of Digital Underground's approval, named Shock G. Tupac did so by rapping, and working hard during the tour, and soon Tupac worked his way to providing Shock G's lines. Soon on the second album Tupac would debut in a song rapping on the hit single called Same Song.

The single Same Song was written for the soundtrack to a movie called Nothing But Trouble. Digital Underground would also get to appear in the movie as Tupac was also in the film with Digital Underground. Same Song was also featured on Digital Underground's second album and it was a success. A music video was filmed for the song that featured Tupac Shakur rapping his part in the video.

Tupac was now in a whole different world called the music industry. This world would come to bring many changes in his character. Tupac at this point was not rich but was working on being rich. His life was wrapped up in the nightclub hip-hop scene that was a world only viewed by those involved in the music industry in one form or another.

Gang members were the prime attendees at those nightclubs as they often worked for producers, and other hip-hop groups. Many of them also came there as drug-dealers, and people who protected other artists. Tupac would become popular at those nightclubs even though he was not a mega star yet.

He would often get just as many girls as the main stars, and this often made him an object of hatred to other crews. Tupac's character, and his looks drew girls to him, and this lifestyle was far removed from the lifestyle of poverty he was living. He became a wild young man, and easily influenced by the scene around him. Tupac became good friends with gang-members who were the Bloods out of the streets of Oakland. These Bloods Tupac knew were high-rollers involved with drug sales, gun sales, and pimping women, and selling drugs to mainstream stars.

It has never been proven if Tupac became a member of the

Bloods during that time but many insiders stated that he did become a Blood. What is very clear is that members of the Bloods became mainstay people in Tupac's crew, and many of them worked for him as bodyguards throughout his career. In those early days Tupac would get his own apartment, and he hung out on the streets of Oakland with Blood gang-members. These friends began to shape his own persona.

The dark aspects that Tupac got involved in was believed to be this aspect of joining a gang, and living the gangsta lifestyle that Tupac would call 'Thug Life'. In the music industry many insiders talked about the Baphomet contract which is controlled by Satanists who control many aspects of the music industry, and can get record contracts for up and coming artists.

It has never been proven that Tupac engaged in a satanic ritual that involved a statement of selling your soul to Satan for a record contract. Many state that Tupac had a limited involvement with it where he was to agree to keep their secrets, and serve their interest, and in return they would give him a solo career, but this overall had never been proven. Either way, Tupac met with some people, and managed to get a record contract to record his first album.

While recording his album Digital Underground especially Shock G. helped Tupac in putting his album together. In fact they helped Tupac with a lot of things like getting his first car, and filling out paperwork for his business ends, and doing a lot of the written work that Tupac did not know how to do. They also noticed the change in Tupac since he started hanging out with the Bloods.

Tupac started several dangerous fights at nightclubs with other gang-members that often outnumbered Digital Underground, and their crew. Tupac had a fearless persona, and in short people stated he was crazy in a lot of ways. Often Tupac would leave his apartment unlocked, and his windows wide open in an area in Oakland where people got robbed doing that.

Shock G. would often come visit Tupac at his place, and there would be times he would find Tupac's place unlocked, and Tupac not there. So Shock G. would lock the place up because

Tupac had some gold records, and other valuable things in his place. Shock G. often warned Tupac to lock the place up but Tupac kept forgetting to do so.

So one day when Shock G. came by, and saw that Tupac forgot once again to lock up Shock G. took all of his things, and made it look like a robbery, and put them all in an empty bedroom in the apartment leaving a note on them. When Tupac came to his place he at first saw all his things missing, and he went nuts, and thought someone rob him. Until he walked into the empty bedroom, and saw all his stuff there with a note from Shock G. that said, 'next time it will be for real'. After that Tupac was more careful about locking his stuff up...but not all the time.

Another visit from Shock G. resulted in Tupac showing off to Shock G. his first AK-47 machine gun rifle he bought off the Bloods. At the time Tupac was bringing in some very young hopeful rappers off the streets who were looking for a chance to make it. Tupac would come to name this group the Outlaws, and many of them were featured on the album called Thug Life. At that time two of the future Outlaws who were very young were sitting on Tupac's couch smoking marijuana while Tupac was trying to show Shock G. how his AK-47 works. While doing so Tupac loaded the AK but the AK had a loose trigger, and when Tupac was trying to set the AK the machine gun went off, and sprayed several rounds into the floor, and the couch where the two young Outlaws were sitting. These two young men came within inches of being shot or killed. Tupac went wild with laughter at the force and power the gun displayed.

Soon Tupac's first album came out called 2Pacalypse Now. At this point Tupac's rhymes were more of the style of gangsta rap but still had social conscience songs like Brenda's Got a Baby, and several others. Tupac's first album was not a hit, and not even close to a success, and he became very bitter about it, but Dan Quayle would change all that.

The former Vice-President was on the Bush bandwagon of blaming rap artists for street violence. During one of his speeches Quayle brought up a case involving a man in Texas who was listening to Tupac's new album. The song the man listened to was called Violent. A Texas defense attorney stated that his client was influenced by the album, and the song caused him to kill a state trooper when the trooper was pulling him over.

Tupac came on the defense after Quayle mentioned him by name, and wanted to pull his album off the music shelves. Tupac stated that he did not record the album to cause anyone to kill police officers. He stated that the album had songs that reflected what he personally seen and been through. Because of the media exposure Tupac's first album would enter the Billboard top 40, and then slowly climb into the top 20. Soon after this Tupac was offered a chance to star in a movie to play a street villain called Bishop in a movie called Juice.

At the time Tupac was going through many changes in his persona. Some said they felt he was possessed by an evil spirit while filming the movie. Whatever the story may be Tupac did have a strong change by the time he went to screen test for the movie. He was wilder, and even colder, and had a strange almost twisted sense of humor. He seemed hungry for success to such a point that many stated he became something else. It was when Tupac played Bishop when his gangsta image was established, and he officially became a gangsta rapper as well.

During the screen test Tupac was to compete with Trench of Naughty by Nature for the part, Tupac was good friends with Trench, and even Trench noticed a change in him. During the reading Trench had to read first, and then when Tupac read for the part he was so energized, and transfixed on his acting that Trench looked at him and told Tupac that he hopes he does gets the part because he no longer wants it anymore.

When Tupac starred in Juice along with Omar Epps he stole the show of the movie. Overnight Tupac's character called Bishop became a street icon, and the movie was a box-office profit hit. Tupac now had doors open to him on both ends in the music and film industry. Tupac was on his way to making more money, and becoming a world-wide success but his new persona was not an image to Tupac but instead it became the reality of his life.

Tupac would record, and release a second album called Strictly 4 My N.I.G.G.A.Z. in 1993. The album would climb fast up the Billboard charts, and became more successful than his first album. The songs were mostly all gangsta rap style songs with hidden social conscience messages. There was only two songs that were not hardcore. One of them was called Keep Ya Head Up a song about inspiring women to get through tough times. The song showed that underneath this hard change in Tupac somewhere the real Tupac was still there. The other single was a song called I Get Around that was a party song with music that Shock G. help to create. During this time Tupac was working with his rap group called The Outlaws in putting together an album called Thug Life.

Having filmed Juice on the East Coast Tupac also befriended up and coming rapper Biggy Smalls, and a DJ named Sean 'Puffy' Combs. Tupac helped Biggy in a lot of ways. He brought Biggy into connections with other beat makers, and producers who started the ball rolling in helping to put together the artist who became the Notorious B.I.G. Tupac also brought Biggy further into the club scene, and would provide room and board for him when he needed it. He also helped Biggy to get girls before he was famous enough to get girls on his own. Overall the plans with Biggy was that Tupac was going to appear on Biggy's first album that would later be called Ready To Die.

Tupac was working very hard at this point. He was writing songs for the album Thug Life, and for his third solo album that would be called Me Against the World. He was also filming another movie with Janet Jackson called Poetic Justice. Tupac would appear on the Arsenio Hall Show, and confirm the rumor that Janet Jackson's management team made Tupac take an AIDS test before doing kissing scenes with her. Tupac never showed it but he was offended by it.

Tupac would also return to Marin City for a homecoming to see his fans and perform there, but a horrible incident would take place. During a radio interview Tupac spoke ill words about the place known as 'the jungle' where he lived and suffered with his mother and sister. Tupac was often known to speak honestly, and very truthfully about certain subject matters even if people don't like what he has to say. On the streets of the jungle the word was Tupac was representing Oakland, and had dissed the jungle being Marin City. When Tupac came there it seemed like all was well, and he performed there as well, but after the show several men, a few of them who had knew Tupac in the days he lived there, stepped up to him to confront him about what he said on the radio station. While Tupac was speaking up for himself one of the men who was a former friend of Tupac during those days told him that he should not have said that, and he punched Tupac in the face. The rest of the men tried to jump him while Tupac using a defensive move he learned from Black Panthers when he was young began kicking at their legs to keep them away from him.

Tupac was not armed, and so his only recourse was to kick out of it, and then he took off running. An entire crowd who got stirred up by the men who tried to jump him chased after him with bottles, and anything they could get their hands on. They began throwing the bottles at him, and Tupac quickly takes cover by throwing himself under a car. The crowd then began throwing bottles under the car to try, and hit him. This went on until the police had to come, and they literally had to rescue Tupac from being beaten to death that day. Tupac decided to stay in Oakland from now on, and while there Tupac got pulled over by Oakland Police officers. When the officers asked for his name Tupac stated it but the officer would not believe his name was actually Tupac, and so an argument broke out, and Tupac was beaten up by two Oakland Police officers.

In another incident Tupac was hanging out in Oakland with his running mates who were Bloods, and then out of nowhere a rival gang began shooting at the spot where Tupac was. Tupac was armed that day, and so Tupac, and a group of Bloods began to fire back, but in the crossfire a little girl named Natasha was killed. The bullet that hit Natasha did not come from Tupac's gun but Tupac lived with the guilt of her death throughout his career.

Tupac's constant troubles with the law began to bring enemies on Tupac that even he did not see coming. Every time Tupac was on the news he also would make public speeches, and would defend himself very well, and began to talk more openly about the real problems on the streets, and in the music industry. This kind of talk did not sit well with others who did not want their business known to the media. Soon Tupac would be charged for rape, and the charge had a lot of holes in it from the start that it looked more like a set-up then an actual charge. The woman that accused Tupac of raping her was a nightclub groupie who was a friend of Tupac's driver, and nightclub running mate who would drive Tupac home when he was too drunk to drive. This driver introduced this woman to Tupac. The girl was seen in the nightclub willingly giving a blow-job to Tupac in front of his friends. She would also go into the bathroom with Tupac where they did cocaine, and she continued giving him a blow-job willingly. She would also give a blow-job to some of Tupac's friends as well. At this point she willingly goes to a hotel room with Tupac, and his crew to engage in sex with them.

Her story is that she only wanted to have sex with Tupac but Tupac forced her to have sex with him and all of this friends. The problem with the story is that there were more women around willing to do what Tupac wanted, and Tupac was very well known to kick women out of the room who did not want to do those things with him. In short Tupac didn't need to force anyone. Insiders stated that the girl willingly had sex with Tupac's friends, and Tupac didn't even touch her in the room he only took off her clothes, and his friends were the ones who had her. Tupac's driver was in the room watching as well.

Very soon after Tupac got a visit from the police, and he was charged with rape based upon only one witness, and with no evidence. The witness was Tupac's driver. Tupac's lawyer discovered that the driver had a long criminal record, and had been extensively involved with court cases where he has accused several people who the government or state government did not like of certain crimes. The lawyer discovered that the driver had committed a series of crimes, and he never served anytime for them, and his cases were always somehow dropped by certain federal agencies.

The pattern in the driver is often seen in government agents working undercover where when they get busted their cases are suddenly dropped to protect them. Tupac's lawyer firmly believed that the driver who was the only witness was an undercover agent. The lawyer also exposed the duality in the so-called rape victim.

In her medical examination there was no evidence of force-able entry, and she had dozens of witnesses against her that gave testimony she was willingly having sex with those men. While there was only one suspect witness who claimed he saw a rape. Also in truth Tupac's charge was reduced to being in cohorts with the men who so-called raped her but yet the media kept on saying it was a rape case when it no longer was. As Tupac paid bail, and the court-date was set Tupac would encounter even more horrible events. Much of Tupac's beat-tracks for the songs he was doing on Me Against the World was at a studio where Tupac was going to work with Biggy on his first album. Around this time it is 1994, and Tupac was offered to come and work to build up the company that would be called Bad Boy Entertainment. Tupac would turn down this offer, and would only agree to help Biggy make his first album. The following story about why Tupac was shot five times the first time has not been proven. It is a story stated by many insiders, and people who were among the scene at the time.

Bad Boy Entertainment is believed to have been built by Black Mafia money. Tupac was still a West Coast rapper at the time, and his success could threaten the success of Bad Boy Entertainment. They first tried to get Tupac to work for their company by using Smalls and Puffy to ask him to join. When Tupac refused to sign the people who put Smalls and Puffy in power were not happy about it, and they wanted him dead.

At the time Tupac was also under constant watch by a police investigation team who also watched other hip-hop artists as well. Later on in the 2000's the group were dubbed the hip-hop police but back then no one knew they existed. It was believed that this police investigation team knew a hit was put on Tupac, and did not tell him about it or even warned him but let him walk right into it, and would come to pick the body up later. The reasons why the cops were willing to let Tupac die had to do with an incident that took place before Tupac was shot. This incident involved Tupac shooting down two cops on the West Coast. What happened that day was actually the fault of the two cops, and not Tupac himself, as the case quickly proved.

On that day two cops were angry at a small time gang-banger who it is believed ripped them off involving some kind of bribe, and false information he gave to the cops. The two cops wanted him dead, and they knew where he hung out at. So they went inside the evidence room, and grab a gun that was used in a different case along with bullets for the gun. The cops planned on murdering the youth with this gun, and even pinning it on someone else. When the cops were officially off duty they then went in plain clothes to their car, and went looking for the guy. The guy was hanging out not too far from another group of people, and Tupac was among that group. Tupac was also armed that day. When the guy left the group it is believed he went walking toward a liquor store when suddenly a car pulled up. Tupac quickly saw what was going down, and raced toward the scene when the two plain clothes officers got out with the gun looking to kill the man they were after, but when they saw Tupac, who also was armed, they swung around to shoot him but Tupac got the drop on them first, and began to open fire on them until they were no longer moving.

Tupac would shoot down two police officers, and saved a man targeted for murder. At first the media was ready to set a firestorm on Tupac when it was found out he shot down two police officers, but when evidence was gathered the case was quickly dropped, and the media barley wanted to speak about it.

Tupac's actions were called self-defense, and the cops were proven to be looking to engage in a murder. Even though Tupac's actions were legal the cops really had it in for him, and wanted to see bad things happen to him in any way they could. Police officers no matter in the wrong or the right have a certain code of honor where they look out for each other. When someone shoots a cop, and can even walk away from it clean and legal, officers will not forget that person no matter what city they are in. The word will spread, and they will seek to bring hell into that person's life. Hence Tupac's so many wild problems with cops from then on.

Now the cops would sit back, and watch Tupac walk into a trap as the story goes. When Tupac was set-up to be killed this took place on November 30, 1994. Tupac and his entourage went to the studio where Smalls, Puffy, and their entourage would be waiting for them. The story is that Smalls and Puffy knew that Tupac was going to be shot, and believed to be killed when entering the studio. But no proof was shown that they knew what was going to happen only their reactions to Tupac being shot would give away they knew something bad was going to happen to him. Tupac entered the studio late because he was waiting for a drug dealer to bring him some marijuana to buy. Once Tupac came to the studio two other men were with him who were Stretch Walker who was from a rap group called Live Squad, and the other was one of Tupac's managers named Freddie Moore. When they walked into the studio there was a man working at the front desk at the entranceway of the office. The man greeted Tupac and his friends, and when they were heading to the elevator the desk worker saw two men coming up behind them toward the door. The man then quickly leaves the desk and seems to go into hiding in the office room behind him. Tupac does not realize that two men are closing in on him because he is distracted by a man called Little Caeser who was on the top floor waiting for Tupac, and he calls down to him while Tupac was heading for the elevator doors. Tupac asked Caeser if Biggy and Puffy are up there, and Caeser tells him that they are.

Once Tupac and his friends are in front of the elevators the two men behind them quickly pull out their guns, and aim them only at Tupac, and began to yell in a rage the words, 'give up the jewelry and get on the floor!' The story behind their statements is that the killers were supposed to make it look like a common robbery so that no trances could be linked back to Bad Boy Entertainment, and their people.

When the men yell these commands Tupac's two friends are frighten out of their minds, and they quickly hit the floor. Tupac however where I must admit he is a brave man. Tupac always had this mind-set not to fear death but rather he fights against it. Tupac does not fall to the floor but he begins yelling back at the two men, and curses them out for being cowards. This action catches the two assassins off guard because that never happened to them before.

When Tupac sees his chance he goes for it, and he quickly tries to jump on one of the men to take his gun away, but the other man grabs Tupac's shoulder, and throws him back, and Tupac hits the ground. The man then proceeds to shoot Tupac five times, and before they leave they shoot Tupac's manager once who also survived. After they shot down Tupac they begin to rip off his jewelry, and they do the same to his two friends. The amount of jewelry they took was worth about $40,000.

When the men took off Moore, the manager who was shot, managed to get up, and he tried to follow them to see the plate on the car they were going to drive off in, but he falls back down in pain unable to see the getaway car. The miracle behind Tupac surviving this shooting was very plain.

The man that shot Tupac did not just shoot him anywhere. He put five well placed shots into him at vital organs on purpose to make sure he bleeds to death. Those five shots were aimed at areas on his body to insure death. The shocking thing is all the bullets instead of ripping apart the organs they all missed his organs, and from the view of the gunman he was unable to tell.

Tupac as he was shot up and bleeding could feel that he still had the strength to move, and he was not passing out from blood-loss or shock. One must say GOD did have mercy on him that night. While Tupac was down like this his other two friends hit the elevator door to open it, and they drag Tupac into the elevator.

The elevator takes them up to the studio floor, and when they get to the studio they help to carry Tupac into the studio lounge. Right across from Tupac is Biggy and Puffy. Tupac was excepting them to be concerned and angry that someone shot him up like this. Instead they are cold and they look confused. Soon they say nothing to him not a word, and they appear to be annoyed that he is not dead. Among those with Biggy and Puffy was Little Shawn who was already crying before Tupac entered the studio room because he heard the gunshots downstairs.

Little Shawn also would not speak to Tupac, and looked ashamed, and had tears in his eyes. The entire room, by their behavior, showed them guilty of knowing what was going to happen to him. None of them would not even pretend to care, they made no movements toward him to help him. When Tupac saw their reaction toward him he knew he was set-up. Tupac was so disgusted with them that he began to look at them coldly, and he tells Walker to roll him a joint. While Walker does so Tupac pulls out his cell-phone, and calls his girlfriend, and tells her to call his mother to explain to her that he has been shot-up. While Tupac is doing this Biggy and Puffy, and the rest are still motionless waiting to see if Tupac will bleed to death. After calling his girlfriend Tupac dials 911 to receive medical help. Walker brings him a joint but Tupac is unable to smoke it. When the medics get there they come in with two officers. They were the same two officers who arrested Tupac for questionable charges of rape. Tupac, seeing their faces made him even angrier, and he knew that they knew about it. The officers were even openly annoyed to find Tupac still alive, and receiving medical attention. To understand the miracle of Tupac still being alive after being shot like that is to understand that two of the shots were well placed shots to his head. The medics would soon bandage Tupac's head, and then Tupac was loaded into the ambulance.

Before he was loaded into the back of the ambulance a photographer took a picture of him, and Tupac would give him the middle finger. It was Tupac's way of letting the media know what he thinks of them. When Tupac gets to the hospital he is treated for his wounds. He would receive much support from many of his Hollywood and music industry peers who called him at the hospital, and made many visits to see him. While in the hospital Tupac starts to strongly feel he is not safe there. So against doctor's orders he checks himself out of the hospital early. The Nation of Islam members would come to the hospital to protect him, and check him out. Tupac had to leave the hospital in a wheelchair as the Nation of Islam members acted as his bodyguards.

The next day after being released from the hospital Tupac had to show up in court for his trial that many felt was a bogus trial. On that first day Tupac had to pay a $25,000 bail to remain free. Many people, including Tupac's lawyer, was telling him that he was going to be railroaded at the trial. Throughout the trial the judge would never look at Tupac's lawyer in the eyes, and he seemed to constantly favor the district attorney's office of lawyers while they presented their case against Tupac.

The evidence against Tupac never showed proof that a rape took place. The witnesses in Tupac's defense were also not respected by the judge, and Tupac's lawyer gave clear evidence that Tupac was innocent but the judge made it hard for Tupac's lawyer while he presented his case. The case would come to concluded that Tupac did not rape the girl.

So the district attorney's office brought the charge of lewd conduct toward Tupac which is a charge of touching the girl in an unwanted fashion. This charge too was also false but Tupac at the end of the trial was found guilty of it. Before Tupac was sentenced he was allowed to address the court. When Tupac went to go do so he noticed that once again the judge would not look at him with respect. When Tupac addressed the court he gave a very moving speech. Some of it went like this, 'Your honor, ever since I have been in your court you have yet to once look my lawyer in the eye while he presented my case. You won't even look me in the eye. You are not treating me or my lawyer like a man, like a human being. I have not received any justice in this courtroom, and no justice is being found in this courtroom. So you go ahead, you give me any kind of sentence you want to give me, because I am not in your hands I am in GOD's hands.' When Tupac said these words the entire courtroom audience was moved, and many of them had tears coming out of their eyes. Even the people working around the courtroom were moved.

The judge would give Tupac the maximum sentence for his crime which was 3 to 5 years in Riker's Island, one of the worst prison's in the world. While Tupac was in jail his crew called the Outlaws finished the album Thug Life for Tupac. The album would go gold in sales. While in jail Tupac had a movie that he starred in before going to jail released called Above the Rim.

Tupac also would have starred in Menace 2 Society directed by the Hughes Brothers but during the early weeks of shooting Tupac had a major argument with one of the Hughes Brothers. This argument resulted in Tupac grabbing a bat, and beating up one of the Hughes Brothers with it.

While in jail Smalls took the beats that were recorded for Tupac's Me Against the World album, and he used them for his debut album Ready To Die. Interscope Records worked out a deal with the courts to allow Tupac a work-release period to be able to record his album Me Against the World.

While in jail Tupac was writing new rap songs for the album, and had to make calls to find DJs he knew who could put together new beats for him after he found out Smalls stole the beats he had at the studio he was shot in. When Tupac was out on work-release he was escorted to the studio to record Me Against the World. Due to legal fees and fines, and other bills, Tupac was in major debt at the time. Me Against the World really needed to be a huge hit. Tupac would not be disappointed. When Me Against the World was released it became Tupac's largest selling album to date. The album would sell 2 million copies, and became a world-wide hit rap album. It is still

regarded to this day as his best album, and one of the greatest albums ever made in the music industry.

The songs were gangsta rap but with strong truth and social conscience messages relating to poverty, injustices, street violence, government neglect, racism, and sentimental issues of family, friends, and urban struggles. It was an album that told the truth, and Tupac would even predict his own death on one of the songs on the album called Death Around the Corner. The most enduring song on the album was a song called Dear Mama. This was a very compassionate song where Tupac raps about his mother, and growing up in hard times.

He presents a great feeling of love and compassion toward his listeners regarding urban family struggles. Tupac would not get to enjoy the successful returns of this 2 million selling album. The money was used to pay for lawyer's fees, doctors fees, court fines, studio time, DJs, and other people who sought money that they believed Tupac owned them. The album did clear him of debt but also he was flat-broke while in jail.

As Tupac's fame grew while in prison Interscope wanted to drop him from the label due to the controversy, and problems surrounding Tupac. The parent company of Death Row Records was Interscope Records, and when Suge Knight heard that Interscope was dropping him from their label he then sought out Tupac Shakur because at the time Tupac was the best rapper in the game, and the most famous as well. Suge saw dollar signs, and a way to get control on a talented artist. While Tupac was in jail he kept on hearing from prison inmates about Smalls and Puffy setting him up to be killed.

Tupac often brooded over this to such a point that he vowed revenge when he got out of jail. Due to good-behavior the courts allowed Tupac an early release time but he had to pay a one million dollar bail fee to be released. Tupac did not have the money. While sitting in jail Tupac would receive a visitor. The visitor was Suge Knight. Knight offered Tupac to pay his bail, and get him out of jail if he signed to a three album contract with Death Row Records. Tupac quickly agreed to this, and signed the contract while in prison. Soon Tupac was released from prison.

Once Tupac got out of jail he had unfinished business with Smalls and Puffy, and the entire camp of Bad Boy Entertainment. The feud between the West and the East Coast rappers was about to blow up even further through the rhymes and statements of Tupac Shakur. Soon as Tupac got back to California he threw himself into working on a double-album that would come to be called All Eyes on Me. Tupac would bring in the Outlaws, and other DJs to work on the album along with Shock G., Dr.Dre, and Snoop Dogg along with others. While working on the album Tupac was also offered movie deals as well, and before his death he would make three more motion pictures. These films were Bullet, Gridlock, and Gang-Related wherein those last two films were released after his death. Tupac would also get into other business ventures as well. He would do modeling shows, and he directed, and helped up and coming rap artists' music videos, and appeared on some of their albums.

Tupac would rent out a studio where he had his own bedroom there to sleep in. He would write about 4 to 5 songs a day, and nearly around the clock he worked with DJs in putting down beats for the songs. Tupac hardly ever slept but was constantly working, and always driven to work. In no time at all Tupac completed two of the three albums regarding his contract for Death Row Records. This was the double-album called All Eyes on Me.

All Eyes on Me would sell 2.5 million copies, and since it was a double album the sales came out to an album that sold 5 million copies. The album was a huge success. The lead single was California Love a song Tupac did with Dr. Dre who did the beats for California Love.

From that point on until his death, Tupac recorded enough songs to fill about 20 albums. A lot of people wonder why Tupac would record so many songs like a madman. Many people who knew him stated that Tupac knew he was going to die young, and he knew it so well that he often talked about it. Tupac wanted to record enough songs to leave a legacy in death that he felt he could not do in a short life.

Tupac would buy a mansion with the money he earned from the double-album, but he hardly ever lived in it. Instead Tupac would find people, and families living on the streets who still had hope in them and he would take them off the streets, and had them brought to live in his mansion until they could get back on their feet. I to this day have never heard of another entertainment star who allowed homeless people, and homeless families to live in their expensive mansions except for Tupac Shakur. Not even leaders in Washington D.C. have ever done that.

While Tupac was enjoying his return success with his double-album he still had not forgotten about Smalls and Puffy. One night during a nightclub industry party Tupac ran into Smalls' wife Faith Evans. Tupac would seduced her, and have sex with her that night. Soon after he attacked Smalls and Puffy in the media, at concerts, during interviews, on his songs, and everywhere he went. He bragged about sleeping with his wife, and soon he would record the most hateful song, and the most evil and twisted beef song ever recorded. The song was called Hit Em' Up. Hit Em' Up was released as a single shortly after the All Eyes on Me double album was released.

In the song Tupac raps about murdering Smalls, Puffy, and every artist on Bad Boy Entertainment's label. He calls out Smalls for setting him up to be murdered, and brags about sleeping with his wife. Soon while Tupac was doing many interviews for various people throughout his time with Death Row

Records, he began to reveal industry secrets about other artists.

From what I studied about this, Tupac was breaking a code in the industry where artists are not to expose events that are still a secret in the eyes of the people. Many insiders stated that the code is much like a code of silence where an artist could be killed or destroyed for exposing things against other artists who have a certain power level in the industry. There has been nothing proven to show the dangers of being killed over exposing inner industry secrets except what is in the pudding.

This got started when Dr. Dre was taking money, and credit for beats he did not write or create on Tupac's album All Eyes on Me. Dr. Dre had only worked on two songs on the album the main song was California Love. Many DJs, and music-mixers who worked on Tupac's previous albums like Thug Life and Me Against the World were the ones who created the beats for the songs on All Eyes on Me. The problem was that they were not getting any checks or credit for the work they did on the double-album from Death Row Records. This made Tupac very angry.

Tupac went to Suge Knight to express his indifference toward Dr. Dre. Knight promised Tupac he would talk to Dre. Later on, when Tupac went to Knight asking about the money Dre owned the DJs who worked on the album, Knight told him that since Dre was the main producer of the album he had a legal right to the money. Tupac was then furious at Dre for he believed he used his position to rip off the people who worked on his double album. Soon Tupac would engage in an interview where he exposes Dr. Dre for being gay. Tupac stated of him that Dre cannot make up his mind if he likes men or women. Tupac also stated that during the time he was recording his double album Dre spent most of his time in his office giving blow-jobs to other men and receiving them from men and women. When Dre found out that Tupac exposed this about him to the public he wanted Tupac fired and discredited, but Knight would not fire him but found ways to suppress the story as best as he could. Knight would then call a meeting to discuss the beef between Tupac and Dre. The meeting would be private where they were to confront their issues against each other. During the meeting Dre defended his right to the money while Tupac stated of him he was a thief and he was gay. Dre took offense to being called gay, and stated that he was not gay because he did not have sex with other men but he only lets other men have sex with him.

Dre stated that there was a difference between a gay man and a bi-sexual. Overall of course Dre was stating according to Knight who spoke about this meeting that he was gay regardless of how he looked at it. At the meeting it was decided that Tupac should not expose secrets about artists connected to Death Row Records but that was not enough for Dre, he wanted Tupac fired but Knight was not going to fire an artist who was making the label millions of dollars.

Instead Dre left Death Row Records, but soon another problem would arise with Tupac exposing industry secrets, and this one had to do with Quincy Jones, and his two daughters. Tupac was dating one of Quincy's daughters while he was also recording songs, and working on his third album for Death Row called Makaveli. He was also filming movies at this time as well.

Quincy's daughters were half-black and half-white, and overtime while dating Quincy's daughter Tupac felt she was not black enough for him because she seemed to act more white then black to him. Tupac then broke up with her, and later made some statements that brought him controversy from up-scale African-Americans.

Tupac spoke against Quincy for being a successful rich black man who married a white-woman. In the statements Tupac stated that there are too many poor black women in need of a strong, and well-off black man, and instead those black men go, and marry a white woman, and have mixed up and spoiled screwed up kids.

These statements angered Quincy, and his entire family. The daughter that Tupac was dating sent a letter in a hip-hop magazine where she disses Tupac, and states that her father meant more to African-Americans then he ever could. Of course she never states just how Quincy meant more other than to diss Tupac, and tell him that he was going to be dead in five years.

Interesting enough even Quincy would admit that Tupac had a larger impact on African-Americans then he did. Tupac's statements angered her a lot but Tupac did feel bad because he did not mean the statements to offend Jones, and his family but to speak on an overall condition that many poor black women need strong black fathers far more then well-off white women need them.

Soon after Tupac was eating at a restaurant when Quincy, and this same daughter comes walking in. Quincy sees him, and decides to be funny, and he sneaks up on Tupac to surprise him. Quincy tells Tupac he needed to speak with him in private, and the two of them have a conversation at the back table of the restaurant. Tupac would give an apology to Quincy for the statements as he tells Quincy he did not mean it like that.

Some weeks after this conversation Tupac thinks he sees the daughter of Quincy he was dating at a nightclub, and he goes to make peace with her, but it turns out to be Quincy's other daughter. Tupac begins to soon date her, and he eventually falls in love with her. Soon Tupac is thinking about marrying the girl, and when his mind is made up he goes to see Quincy at his home to ask for his blessing. What happens next was according to an interview given by Tupac that has been largely suppressed, according to some insiders of Quincy's people but no proof was given to show that Quincy's people are the ones suppressing it.

Tupac stated that after he asked to marry his daughter Quincy said to him that he would agree to the marriage if he would come upstairs with him so that he could have sex with him. According to Tupac he stated to Quincy that he did not get down like that, and he got up, and left the home very angry. Soon after Tupac exposed this secret during an interview.

Many insiders felt that when Tupac told people about this meeting with Quincy that is when people in the music industry wanted to kill him. Some believe his death had more to do with Death Row Records and Suge Knight. In the time leading up to September Tupac was having a lot of emotional, and mental problems with his own persona while working for Death Row Records.

He was not happy, and his violent outbursts on stage, and his personal convictions were constantly a factor in his mood swings. Tupac began to plan to take the over 200 songs he recorded, and make albums for his own record label which was going to be called Amaru Records. After finishing the album called Makaveli Tupac's contract deal with Death Row was completed. Suge wanted him to resign to a new contract with Death Row, but Tupac was stalling him, and would not tell Suge about his plans to leave Death Row at the time.

Tupac no longer felt safe working for Death Row, and the company was far too corrupt for him to stay in it any longer. Tupac was not afraid of Suge in the matter of not telling Suge. Tupac felt a kinship to Suge because Suge gave him a chance when everyone else was happy to leave Tupac in jail. Suge also treated Tupac like a father-figure as well.

To understand, Suge took Tupac to his first NBA game, and to several others as well. He also took Tupac to places of up-scale dining and luxury, and took Tupac to places he had never been to before. Tupac felt bad about having to leave him, but Tupac also felt like he was going insane, and so he knew he had to leave.

12 days before Tupac was killed he hired a lawyer to write out a document explaining that his contract was up, and he was leaving Death Row Records. Tupac wanted all of his studio tapes released from Death Row studios, and since Tupac owned the copyright to the tapes he had a right to take them back. The lawyer would send the document to Suge Knight, and Knight's lawyer David Kenner. Kenner was also Knight's right-hand man.

One day after the document was sent Tupac's business manager named Yaasmyn Fula came to Death Row studios to grab the tapes made by Tupac Shakur, but David Kenner who was there that day stop Fula from getting access to the tapes. This resulted in Tupac confronting Suge. Tupac told Suge that the letter was clear, and that he was leaving, and wanted his tapes back. Suge would act real nice about it while many said he played with his head. He told Tupac that he did not have a problem about him taking the tapes back, but Suge would go on to stay, to allow him a chance to discuss a new, and better deal about resigning to Death Row Records. If he did not like it then he would have no problem with Tupac taking the tapes and letting him go, but many insiders stated that he had a real problem with letting Tupac go because he would lose a lot of money.

The thinking according to these insiders was that Tupac was now worth more money dead than alive. Suge would invite Tupac to come with him to attend the Mike Tyson fight in Las Vegas at the MGM Grand. After the fight Suge would discuss the new contract with him. Tupac would agree to allow Suge the chance. Many private investigators who looked into Tupac's death believed it was a hit put upon Tupac by Knight using connections with street gangs most especially with the Crips. They also stated that certain police officers working undercover also knew about the hit through information they received on the streets, but they never warned Tupac about it.

On the day of the Mike Tyson fight Tupac, Suge, and their entourage arrived at the MGM Grand in Las Vegas. While there, they spotted a man named Orlando Anderson who was a Crip. Among Tupac's entourage was a man named Travan Lane. Lane prior to this event was robbed of his Death Row gold chain at the Lakewood Mall by Orlando Anderson. Lane pointed out Orlando as the man who robbed him. Tupac, who hated robbers, walked up to Orlando, and asked him, 'You from the south'. At that moment Tupac punched him in the face, and then Tupac and the entire entourage began to violently jump Orlando by punching him, and kicking him down in the MGM Grand. After they beat him up they quickly left the scene. The entourage went to their hotel rooms, and got changed for the fight. They stopped by Mike Tyson's locker room to wish him well. The Mike Tyson fight would end very early, and Tupac and the rest of the entourage went back to their rooms to change again. Their plans were to go to one of Suge's homes in Las Vegas, and then to Suge's nightclub called Club 662.

Before leaving the MGM Grand Tupac's bodyguards were waiting for gun permits to be able to carry guns, but the permits oddly never came, and Frank Alexander one of Tupac's bodyguards who was guarding both Tupac and Quincy's daughter who was there following in another limo found it strange that the permits never arrived.

When the entourage headed out Suge and Tupac rode in the lead car as the other cars tailed them. The entourage first went to Suge's home in Las Vegas, and stayed there till after 10:00 p.m. It was believed that is when Suge discussed a new contract with Tupac, hoping he would sign. Tupac had also brought the tape Makaveli for Suge to listen to. Suge did not get a chance to listen to the tape at his home because of the discussion he was having with Tupac.

Tupac, after hearing the new deal, did not resign. After the meeting Suge and Tupac went into Suge's brand new BMW 96 Sedan, and they lead the entourage in the other cars to Club 662.

Suge pops in Tupac's new Makaveli tape to listen to it on the way to the nightclub. At 11:05 p.m. Suge and Tupac are pulled over by the cops due to the loud music coming from Suge's car. Tupac is then annoyed for being pulled over, believing it was done only to harass them. Suge was then given a ticket, and let go. Suge then drove east to Flamingo Road where he stopped at a red light just a half a mile from the Las Vegas Strip. When they stopped a jeep full of girls pulls up to the driver's side window, and they distract both Suge and Tupac who were flirting with them.

It was at that moment is when it happened. A late-model Cadillac quickly pulled up to the passenger side of the BMW where Tupac was sitting. Four men got out of the car. Two of them were armed with a 9mm, and the other two were armed with a .45. All four men open fire directly into the passenger side firing through the window.

The gun-fire was aimed only at Tupac Shakur and none of them aim their guns at Suge Knight who's only injury was a piece of shrapnel that hit his head. When Tupac saw them coming he tried to jump in the back seat but it was too late. Tupac was shot 13 times in the chest, stomach, and legs. After they emptied their rounds through the passenger window the four killers jumped back into the Cadillac, and speed off.

Tupac's killers were never arrested. While Tupac was bleeding to death Suge told him he is going to take him to the hospital but he oddly sped off in the opposite direction of the hospital. Suge, being an ex-football player and a long-time resident of Las Vegas knew where the hospital was.

Soon the Las Vegas Police began chasing Suge's car as it was speeding down the road. The other cars in Tupac's entourage were also following Suge's car. When Suge saw them he did not pull over but went faster. Suge drove over a median and then ran a red light while he popped two tires, and then two more tires popped before running another red light. He crashed the car at Harman Avenue.

The police then held Suge at bay by gunpoint along with Tupac's bodyguards as well. The police called the ambulance to take Tupac to the hospital. Tupac was taken to the University Medical Center. Throughout his time there a vigil by his fans and close friends were held on the streets for him. Everyone in the music industry thought Tupac was going to pull through, and he was going to be even angrier when he woke up. Even his fans thought like this.

When Tupac went into the ER they had to remove his right lung so that he did not die right there and then. After the operation Tupac was placed on a ventilator, and then a respirator, and then on life-support until he fell into a coma. While in the coma his mother Afeni is told Tupac is suffering from brain-damage and the longer he stays in it the more damage he would suffer. This verdict meant he would soon be brain-dead. Afeni no longer wanted him to suffer, so she allowed the doctors to pull the plug.

On September 13, 1996 Tupac Shakur died. After his death Suge and Death Row Records tried to keep Tupac's tapes. Death Row Records would release Tupac's last contract album for them called Makaveli. The album was a huge success with a hit single called Hail Mary. On the cover of the album Tupac wanted a drawing of himself hung on a cross like Jesus Christ. Tupac also wanted statements near the picture stating that the portrait was not done to disrespect Jesus Christ. Tupac felt that he too would one day be unfairly killed in the world, and so that is why the portrait of himself on the cross came out.

Death Row would also manage to release a double album of Tupac's songs but soon Suge was thrown in jail for a time. All of Tupac's songs finally would be released on Tupac's own label which is currently owned by his mother. Every now and again bootleg copies of Tupac's unreleased works would pop up in the underground scene here and there. To this day new Tupac songs are still released which is another reason why people think he is still alive. Investigations that were done regarding Tupac's death reveal who the four main suspects may have been.

Compton undercover police officers, and private investigators reveal that much of the evidence points to four names who were Orlando Anderson, Bobby Finch, Michael Dorrough, and Jerry Stone. The driver of the car was believed to be Jerry's brother Michael Stone. The investigation into them started in late 1996, and ended in 1998 when all five men were killed in strange events. All five of these men were Compton Crips, and each of them had direct or indirect contact with the gangsta rap side of the music industry. The stories of this investigation are like pieces in a puzzle but pull them together and it reveals some shocking things.

On the night of Tupac's death Orlando was in Las Vegas along with Finch, Dorrough, and the Stone Brothers. When Tupac was shot up, and taken to the hospital, according to a Compton undercover police officer, the five men came back to their hoods bragging about that they just killed Tupac Shakur. When the investigations were being done upon them it was revealed that Orlando, who was a rapper, was trying to get a record deal, but he needed studio time to make a record, and that cost a lot of money.

Suddenly after Tupac's death he had a large amount of money to record his songs at a studio. It was said by many of Orlando's friends that people close to Tupac in Death Row Records paid Orlando, and the other four men a lot of money to kill Tupac. The undercover officers thought that maybe it was just street rumors at that time. When the five men went talking about it to other people there was word on the streets that the lives of the five men were in trouble. At first they did not seem to take that word seriously, and for a while nothing happened to them, but soon it was said that the people who put the hit on Tupac came to find out that police investigations were being done on the killers.

If the investigations were successful it could lead back to them. The investigations had received its most critical information by 1998. During that time all five men began receiving death threats, and were shot at, and misleading information was given to them about betrayal among their own gang-brothers. They all became very paranoid that people were after them, and spying on them, and they soon blamed each other for what was happening to them.

Soon a meeting was called between Orlando Anderson and his friend Michael Dorrough. They were to meet Jerry and Michael Stone. Anderson and Dorrough believed that the Stone brothers had betrayed them, and brought the police investigation upon them. The four men were to meet at the intersection of East Alondra in Compton in the parking lot of Cigs Record Store. This meeting took place on May 29, 1998. The four men once engaged in the meeting had a heated confrontation with each other. Witnesses reported hearing Tupac's name come up many times during the argument. The argument would quickly turn to paranoid rage, and the four men pulled guns on each other, and began to shot at each other. When the hail of bullets were unleashed Michael Dorrough was instantly killed. The Stone brothers would also die in the parking lot from bullet wounds.

Orlando, who was also shot up, managed to make it to the car wash before falling down and dying there. When Bobby Finch heard what happened he was planning on leaving the West Coast. Soon after the four men gunned each other down Bobby was walking on South Mayo in Compton when two Bloods came upon him, and shot and killed him. When the two Bloods went running back to the car to get away a strange man came out of nowhere, and gunned down the two Bloods upon those streets. Many thought that the strange man was a fellow Crip but it turned out he was not. Many suspect he may have been a member of the Black Mafia. The thinking was that often the Black Mafia will hire, and use gang-members to do certain killings for them. When they finish the job the killings could bring unwanted attention so they will murder the assassins to silence the information.

Many people state that Tupac Shakur was a prophet. I would not go so far as to say he was a GOD-fearing prophet like Moses or Paul due to the fact he did not live a life that could be fully compared to Moses or Paul. Although they did have some things in common. I do think Tupac had gifts that were gifts that prophets had but were not fully developed due to a short life. For instance Tupac recorded a song called GOD Bless the Dead. The song was about the death of Biggy Smalls. Biggy would die within only months after Tupac died. Tupac knew that not only was he going to die soon he also knew that Biggy was going to die soon as well. Tupac just did not know who was going to die first him or Smalls. So Tupac made a rap song about Smalls' death early just in case he died before he could pay his respects to the once friendship he had with Smalls. That is a person who did see future events because Tupac's prediction came to pass.

The legacy of Tupac Shakur is under the title of greatest rapper to ever live. His lyrics always went deep into the meaning of many political, and social subjects including violence, drug abuse, teenage pregnancy, broken families, and so many deep issues. His life and his art-form was motivated by hard struggles, injustices of American society, and the self-destructions that run like a plague on poor people throughout the United States. His music spoke of the conflicts of why people do the evil things they do while trying to find self- understanding to keep him from falling so far headlong he would not be able to find a way out.

Tupac believed in his own words that the world did not need any more entertainers in the music and movie industry but that it needed more writers, thinkers, and truth speakers. He was very right about that. He was also right about a lot of things he said.

Chapter 22

Among the most wicked images among rock stars would have to be the one promoted by an artist named Marilyn Manson. Marilyn Manson is an artist who hates Jesus Christ. He was trained in Anton LaVey's method of friendly Satanism to make people think he is not that bad but really is evil in a lot of ways. Friendly Satanism is a form of deception to make people think that Satan is not an actual living spiritual being but simply a word for a state of mind.

The Bible does not teach that Satan is merely a state of mind but teaches that Satan is a real living being. In fact even Anton himself knows that Satan is a real living being, and he uses friendly Satanism as a way to deceive people into getting them interested in Satanism in their lives. It is a way to school them in the ways of Satanism through deception so that after they are corrupted they would overtime come to accept the true teachings of Satanism, that the members of the Church of Satan worship Satan as a real being who is a fallen angel.

The life of

Marilyn Manson is best described as a sickness that brings people closer to Hell through a self-destructive life-style. Marilyn Manson, and his band are often called the sickest band that the rock music part of the industry ever promoted. The energy of his music is a high drive of lust, violence, and satanic worship with a higher drive for fleshy and twisted indulgences with no thought of the carnage his influences leave behind on his fans. His music is often called pure demonic music. It often leaves negative reactions on the sub-conscience of the human mind. Many say his music is so demonically potent that it can change a person's thinking sometimes completely over in many twisted ways.

The fans of Marilyn Manson have lived a very sad, and often wasted life. Many of them stated that this wasted life got started when they came to accept Marilyn Manson as a role model. Many of his fans have died due to overdoses, suicide, and murder. Many of them got into homosexuality, vandalism, and coven occult practices.

Many years ago someone like Marilyn Manson would have never been famous, but this is a day and age where serial killers get love letters from women who want to marry them and have their children while Christian minded men are still alone looking for a godly wife.

This is a day and age where evil is called good and good is called evil. It is no wonder then that someone like Marilyn Manson can be famous in a world that is losing sense of what honor is. The music industry is also a world within itself where an artist like Axl Rose can wear a t-shirt of Charles Manson's face on it, and still be leader to millions of lost youth at the height of his career.

Among the inner-circles of Hollywood and music industry stars it would shock people to know how many serial killers these people respected, admired, and were even friends with. The entertainment world in truth is not a lover of Jesus Christ. They mostly hate Christianity while they are famous in a country like the United States that is 85% Christian. Very few entertainment artists in the music industry and in Hollywood are really Christian believers compared to the numbers of them that are not, but most of their fans don't seem to really care or just flat out don't care at all.

It amazes me that a famous artist in America in order to sell millions of copies or to make millions of dollars at the box-office needed money from people with a Christian faith to do that, yet those artists hate Christianity, and yet Christians make them rich and famous. This has a lot to do with the facts.

Fact is most Christian fans have no idea what their favorite artists really believe in. Fact is most artists don't openly reveal they are not Christian. Fact is when Christian fans find out that their favorite artist has admitted he or she is not a Christian that don't seem to care. Fact is when their favorite artist does things that are against the Bible they still don't seem to care. Fact is even when their favorite artist openly speaks against Christianity they are at point now they don't really care. Christians in America generally just want to be entertained. They are content with whoever Hollywood chooses for them to entertain them. Even if those artists think that their religion, and their Church services are stupid.

Fans around the world that have a Christian faith love to listen to music from artists who do not have a Christian faith. Those artists love to tell their young fans to take drugs, and have sex with anyone you want, and wherever you want. Fans around the world with a Christian faith love to go to movies where the hero does not have a Christian faith and kills and lies his way out of trouble. In fact the media, which is another art-form of Hollywood, has been painting Christians as the bad guys lately while promoting homosexuality and New Age spirituality to be what is called the 'in-thing'. They are basically saying in fact plainly saying that Christianity is 'out' and New Age ideas are 'in', and this 85% Christian nation does not want to see the real problem in that.

Marilyn Manson loves to tell his fans that evil is a good thing. In fact many people seem to think that evil is a good thing, but of course when that evil is used upon them then it is no longer a good thing at that point. People will talk and brag about being a wild animal with each other. To use each other. To play mind games with each other. If you can get away with it then it is good. If you can't get away with it then you made a mistake, but these are man-made selfish rules that can easily be changed, and the game flipped over to be played even harder.

Instead of acting like a wild animal with someone people will literally become, in their mind-set, able to do to them what a wild animal does to its prey. Instead of using someone they will enslave and control them. Instead of playing mind-games they will brainwash them, and force them to like the control they are under. There will be no getting away with it because all sense of moral good and evil will be wiped away and only a force of will in its darkest form will be accepted.

That is where things are heading, but people are far too entertained and distracted to care. It seems that the only time they will care is not when their Bible is taken away. It's when their digital television, their cell-phone, their car, their home, their drugs, their porn, and things like that are taken away, that's when they care. They will force themselves to get more evil with people just to get those things back, but the public does not seem to care what the outcome of all this could be. Instead they stick their middle-fingers up at Christians who warned them about it, and many will call themselves Christians while sticking their middle fingers up at other Christians.

Christians are in conflict with other Christians over this issue of Satanism in entertainment. The Bible even speaks about the reality of Satan playing a part in the entertainment of the world but many Christians will refuse to understand that or believe it.

Marilyn Manson is believed to be another pawn of Satan being used as a puppet and a false teacher. He tells his fans that abusing other people is fun but yet he does not want people to touch him or abuse him. Most people who did investigations into Manson know that he is a real Satanist while his fans think it's all just a show.

Many of his fans also profess a Christian faith, and they think Manson is just an entertainment side show, but that is not the full case, and not wise to think it's all just a show with him. Manson preaches that a satanic life will bring freedom to people, but really when you see the end results of a satanic life you find there is no freedom there. It always turns out to be a wasted life. Degeneration has never brought liberation or anything good for that matter.

Manson loves to quote famous philosophical teachers to trick his fans into thinking there is nothing wrong with Satanism, but since most of his fans have never been trained in theology, philosophy, and true Christian teachings, then most of them are going to be opened to being fooled by him. His fans gobble up his lines hook and sinker, and they often find out too late they have been deceived. Lives come crashing down all around the world when lives are thrown away on pleasure and wickedness.

Marilyn Manson described his music as a clever piece of cheese on a rat trap. Have you ever seen what happens to a rat caught in a rat trap? The spine or head is smashed, and broken in pieces. Sometimes it loses its legs or tail. Its body is broken in half.

Manson thinks his fans are rats, and it's his job then to lead them to their destruction by falling for his trap. Manson makes this trap called his image and music by using what Manson describes as 'using magic powers to allure people'. Those are some very interesting statements from Manson because in satanic teachings black magic is taught that it can be a tool to make a person a better musician.

When Manson first came on the scene a lot of people did not know who he was. Some thought he was a child star turned rocker while other ideas came forth about him. What is a fact regarding him is that Manson is an official member of the congregation of the Church of Satan. He was trained as a priest by Anton LaVey. His real name is Brian Warner.

Warner got involved in the gothic scene of the underground rock clubs. He was known to attend Heavy Metal and grunge rock shows. He had a thing for committing homosexual acts, and other twisted acts at rock concerts. One of Warner's aims in his career is to win over fans by declaring that he relates to the lost, but in fact he uses them to get rich off of them.

The Church of Satan is all about preying upon the weak-minded to attain worldly riches. This is what they are actually taught to do. Warner knows very well what he is doing through his art-form. The problem is his millions of fans have no idea. Warner believes that his fans are so ignorant that they allow themselves to be deceived. He takes full advantage of the fact that his fans don't know his real agenda or persona. It is very clear that he is out to push them over the edge.

Manson is a real minister of the Church of Satan and not a fake one. He does do real ministry duties, and rituals for members of the Church of Satan. He is hell-bent on doing as much damage as he can against the teachings of Christianity.

Warner got his stage name Marilyn Manson through the influences of the Church of Satan. There are certain persons in history that the Church of Satan calls inspirations who had spread the works of Satan upon society to a large degree. Among the people they praise are two noted ones who were Marilyn Monroe and Charles Manson. The Church of Satan often hails these two as being great change agents for promoting the anti-Christ religion often known as the New Age faith.

Brian idolized these two so much that he was inspired to call himself after these two individuals by naming himself Marilyn Manson. His band mates would come to follow his example by renaming themselves Daisy Berkowitz, Twiggy Ramirez, Madonna Wayne Gacy, Sara Lee Lucas, and such. His band mates are also members of the Church of Satan.

Our world in its view on things is often removed from truth. The world is desensitized to evil to such a point that often when pure evil is smiling at them, and waving their products in front of them the people get out their wallets, purses, and buy them.

The fact that Manson, and his band mates would celebrate serial killers to praise these murderers, and child-rapers, and still be famous around the world and make millions of dollars is a crime within itself. It shows a very disturbing lost spirituality in America and around the world. It is sad that a man like this can be famous in America which is 85% Christian, and yet Christian art-forms are hardly ever put on the shelves. When they are put on the shelves they hardly ever make millions of dollars. The ones that do hardly ever speak on the evils of the entertainment industry.

Many Christians think that Marilyn Manson is no real concern for Christians and their kids. They think it's all an act regarding him. I wish that were true but it's not. These are the words of Manson, 'As a performer I wanted to be the loudest most persistent alarm clock I could be, because there didn't seem like any other way to snap society out of its Christianity'. It amazes me that Manson can say statements like these while Christian parents can sit there, and think that this is not personal against them. Well it may not be personal against them on a whole but it is very much a personal attack against Jesus Christ that Christians are supposed to be standing up for.

The enemy of the human race especially Christians is Satan. Satan is very real, and always on the hunt. Satan seeks to corrupt us and work against us from finding salvation in Jesus Christ. Entertainment is a word meaning to detain someone's attention. Entertainment is muse meaning also to inspire the mind and emotions of human beings. It is a fact that the Bible tells us that Satan was created with a high-ability to entertain. He is a musical being who was once used by GOD to bring praise to his Name. It amazes me that people think that Satan would not use his art-form gifts to deceive people under the radar when the Bible states that is what he does.

In fact, people in the Church of Satan know that is what Satan is doing to win people away from Christianity and Manson understands that as well. When Manson was a child he already began his hatred toward Christ, and began to find ways to embrace Satanism. As a pre-teen he got a hold of the copy of the Satanic Bible written by LaVey, and began to read it. He soon got a hold of books written by Aleister Crowley, and he came to be deeply inspired by Crowley's book called The Book of the Law. The mind of Brian Warner was shaped by the works of Crowley and LaVey.

Warner came into contact with members of the Church of Satan through the rock underground scene. In time they brought him to Anton LaVey who through a demonic influence Satan told LaVey that Warner one day would serve Satan in a huge way. From that point on LaVey was the spiritual teacher of Warner until his death in 1997. Warner came to see LaVey as his father-figure, mentor, and called him the 'doctor'. Manson would make it a point to drop whatever it was he was doing to go, and see Anton whenever Anton called for him. Anton trained Warner in how to deceive the masses through misleading teachings of Satanism.

Warner became such a prized student that Anton certified him as a minister in the Church of Satan. He gave Warner his certification card called the crimson card. On the day of the ceremony when Warner got this card Anton put a human bone of a finger upon the shoulder of Warner. Warner recalls his body going cold when Anton did this. Anton told him, 'you're gonna make a big dent, you're going to make an impression on the world'. Anton said this to him knowing that Manson would indeed influence the young minds to get them to admire Satan through Manson's art-form. In fact, at the height of Manson's fame there was a sharp rise in the sales for the Satanic Bible written by LaVey. There was also a sharp rise at the same time regarding teenage suicide deaths, homosexuality, teenage murders, an interest in the Church of Satan, teenage runaways, teenagers turning against their parents, and teenage and pre-teen drug use. Marilyn Manson is often called one of the prime reasons for this sharp rise because his music and his concert shows openly promote all of these activities.

Manson often uses against the minds of his fans a tactic called purposeful deception. This tactic is used by Satanists to deceive others in an attempt to win new recruits. The tactic is to water-down or tell fairy tales about Satanism. They will say things like Satan is not real but a symbol of force, and they do that to make new recruits comfortable with serving Satan until they feel those recruits could handle the full truth.

The full truth is the same truth found in the Bible, that Satan is a real living person who was a fallen angel who fell from Heaven. Of course then they sell them on the lies that they have been deceived with like Hell is one big party for a Satanist and so on. They will slowly, if new recruits could handle it, get them in touch with demons for demonic-possession so that evil spirits could use them for whatever agenda they are planning.

Satanic covens often have something called hidden knowledge. Many of them will often know about political and terrorists actions before the rest of the world knows about them. Many of them often target Christian families to see if they can corrupt the heads of those families or their children. Many of them will even pose as Christians, and attend Churches to see what kind of sabotage they could commit against the congregation. Satanists often prey upon the lusts, ignorance, pride, and fear of others. They often spy and stalk their victims, and many of them even kidnap children for satanic rituals. Oddly enough often their crimes are hardly ever reported on in the media.

When Brian Warner was very young he often had a deep need to get in touch with Satan. As a child he often would curse rather oddly alone in his room at night. He would be seemingly cursing at himself as if he was talking to himself. His mom caught him doing this several times, and found this to be disturbing. Manson one time explained that he did this to find a way to tap into a hidden power of darkness within himself.

His mom would tell him to stop doing that but he refused to stop. So his mom in order to frighten him into stopping it told him if he continued to do that the devil would come to him and get him. Instead of frightening him this made young Brian very excited. He would go into his room, and curse even more hoping the devil would come to him. He would want the devil to come to him so badly it became an obsession. When he got older he wanted to experience every sin there was, and so he quickly got into Heavy Metal music.

He was reading about Satanism, and he wanted to learn how to join an occult. He began learning more about the fallen angel Lucifer. The more he learned the more he wanted to be like him. He often dreamed about being worshiped as a rock star god, and he would fill his head with dark imaginations. When he was a teenager his mother noticed the dark interests her son was often into.

She would then send Brian to Heritage Christian School in Canton, Ohio. She thought that the school would teach him Christian values but she was wrong. The students were not as Christian as she thought they were but were formal, meaning Christian on the outside but inside they did not practice what they believed in. The students there would appear to be nice Christians in Church, and with their parents, but they had a hidden world, and they would also desire ways to indulge in sex, drugs, wild music, and they emulated the idols of the world. Brian would come to hate them for the way they often did not include him in their little groups of hidden lusts. Soon his parents would move to a town near Fort Lauderdale, Florida.

Brian was transferred to a public school. There at this public school everything he wanted to do came full speed after him. Brian would soon get a girlfriend who would introduce him to drugs. He befriended a group of friends who were into drugs and occult practices. Many of them were very familiar with the underground rock scene, and that scene became a home for Brian.

Overtime, Brian would leave home and live among his friends in this scene which eventually led him to the Church of Satan. One of the promises the Church of Satan offered him was a chance to become a rock star. Brian was not musically gifted. He cannot sing, he cannot play instruments, he cannot write songs, in short he was not a musical artist, but the people in the Church of Satan who knew people in the music industry knew also that Brian did not have to be talented. They only needed to create an image regarding him, and their people would take care of the rest.

One of those people who helped in putting Marilyn Manson together was the front man for Nine Inch Nails named Trent Reznor. The story regarding this is still not fully proven but it goes like this. Manson met Reznor through a Nine Inch Nails concert. Trent it is believed also had ties to the Church of Satan, and often invited coven members backstage for some sex and drugs. Manson had a homosexual relationship with Trent before Manson was famous.

Trent would take such a liking to him that he would write mostly all of the songs for Manson's first two albums, and he created Marilyn Manson's sound. Manson band mates also were handpicked by members of the Church of Satan who had connections or many of them worked in the music industry. Insiders also said that Manson's voice was a form of screaming out the demons within hinting to demonic possession. Many said that Manson is a poser and fraud regarding his music and image. His music was written by other people, and his image was created by other people. The only real thing about Manson is that he is a real hardcore Satanist.

At the public school Brian attended is when he began to learn about satanic rituals. In that school Brian got involved with a witchcraft coven. In that time he would bully other students weaker then him. He was very clever at manipulating other people. While hanging out with this gothic coven, Brian watched a friend cut himself open to draw blood as a satanic offering to Satan. His friend cut himself in several places, and collected the blood in a cup to pour it on a satanic altar.

When Brian learned from his friend how to do this he began to do this many times, and in fact he still does. Drawing his blood and even drinking it became an addiction for Brian. Brian would get into black magic, and the use of Ouija boards to get in touch with evil spirits.

When Brian was 18 years old is when he left home, many said his mother kicked him out. Brian lived among his coven family along with his girlfriend at the time. Brian wanted to offer Satan a human sacrifice, and would find a legal way to do it called abortion. Brian would purposefully get his girlfriend pregnant, and then convince her to have an abortion. Brian took her to the clinic, and while the doctor was killing his child Brian entertained thoughts about coming up with a good enough excuse for requesting the unborn body of his child. He was unable to come up with a good enough excuse but instead prayed to Satan to offer the action of killing his child to him.

Brian also had an obsession with finding out who the anti-Christ was. He often wondered who it could be to such a point he began to think it could be him. Brian would often wish it was him. He was disappointed when he found out it was not him. Brian's love for Charles Manson did not just start in the Church of Satan but it started in high-school. One time Brian got an illegal copy of a Charles Manson record called Lie. Brian would fall in love with the record, and he would play it over and over again.

Charles Manson was a notorious serial killer, child-rapist, who wanted to start a race war for Satan. During the murders that took place regarding Sharon Tate the Manson family tried to frame the black power groups for the murders. Marilyn Manson views Charles Manson as one of his heroes. It amazes me that Marilyn Manson in this time and age can openly say that, and still be accepted by the mainstream public.

It amazes me that Manson can support the views of Charles Manson and Hitler, and even African-American rap artists would work with him and allow him to appear on their albums. It amazes me that after seeing the horrors from the thousands of pictures and film of the holocaust of World War 2, no one really gets bothered that Manson performs, and goes on tours wearing the symbol of the swastika flag on his clothes. He also had a drapery of it on stage. Overtime it brought him so much controversy that he had to change the symbol but still kept the red, white, and black colors of the Nazi flag, and made the new symbol in the same formation of the swastika.

Marilyn Manson also spoke about the strange demonic occurrences regarding the recording of some of his albums. When Manson was recording his first album called Portrait of An

American Family he was at the home of Trent Reznor. At that time Trent was living in the same mansion that was once owned by Roman Polanski and Sharon Tate. It was the same mansion where Sharon Tate, and several others were killed by the Manson occult family.

Trent had a built in studio in his mansion where him and Marilyn Manson were in Trent's studio where Trent was coming up with hooks for Manson's songs. When Trent came up with a hook for a Manson song something happens there that shocks the two of them.

Samples from a Charles Manson song called My Monkey mysteriously appears on the mix recorded by Trent for one of Marilyn Manson's songs. When Trent and Manson saw and heard this the two of them become deeply afraid. They tried to find a logical reason why it happened but they could not find the reason. The two decided to call it quits for the night, and they quickly left the studio.

Manson would reveal later that this was not the first time this happened regarding his songs. Often backward messages of a disturbing nature often appear in Marilyn Manson songs. Susan Atkins was once a devout member of Charles Manson's occult family. She recalls how Charles Manson use to brainwash her by taking his songs especially the song Cease to Exist which was re-recorded by the Beach Boys, and play it over and over again until she received the hidden messages in the song. She recalled how she was able to let go of compassion and guilt regarding killing and sex every time Charles Manson brainwashed her with these songs. Susan was among the group of killers who murdered Sharon Tate and her friends in her home.

Susan converted to Christianity while in prison. She had been very open about the Charles Manson's family dealings with the Church of Satan, and the 60's Hollywood stars and stars of the music industry. Charles Tex Watson was also among the killers that entered Sharon Tate's home, and was once Charles Manson's right hand man. Before Watson's death in prison he too converted to Christianity, and spoke about how Charles Manson used to brainwash him using his music.

Watson warned the public by stating openly that Marilyn Manson's music was fueled by the demonic forces that fueled Charles Manson's music. That the madness of Charles Manson music is within the music of Marilyn Manson. These statements by Watson were made before the sharp rise of suicides, overdoses, and damaged youthful lives that took place among Marilyn Manson fans. Watson believed that the same brainwashing effects that were in Charles Manson's songs were also in Marilyn Manson's songs.

One time when parent groups confronted Marilyn Manson for the strange deaths, and horrible events that took place in the lives of his fans, Manson only response to them was, 'Raise your kids better or I will be raising them for you'. It's sad because Manson was telling these parents their part in this by letting them know that these kids bought his album using their money.

These parents also don't realize the full scope of the problem. The music industry is controlled by people who don't care about their kids or them. Yet they still make millions of dollars off fans they don't care about. One of the most twisted stage acts of Marilyn Manson is when he got a pregnant woman to come on stage to pretend she was having an abortion on stage. Manson then had a bloody baby doll, and wrapped in a Nazi flag to present it to the television audience as a human sacrifice to Satan.

Manson often promotes the works of Aleister Crowley throughout his interviews and stage shows. During the promotion of his tour called Antichrist Superstar, Manson performed the song called Misery Machine. The song was about Crowley's Abbey of Thelema where Crowley performed sex-magic rituals on children, and had them eat their own waste. According to Italian police he was suspected of kidnapping, and murdering children at the Abbey of Thelema which was in Sicily.

Manson's promotion of a guy like Aleister Crowley is nothing new in the music industry, but it still is a twisted, sick, and disturbing nature that someone who would clearly know these facts about Crowley, and still promote him shows a deep evil nature about that person indeed.

In a song Manson did called Smells Like Children the songs bears reference to molesting and harming children. These are the influences of Manson's music, to promote molestation, satanic worship, Nazi doctrine, Charles Manson, drugs, immoral sexual depravity, murder, suicide, and the list goes on.

Manson's most successful album was called Antichrist Superstar. Manson stated that he heard many of the songs on the album in dreams before they were recorded on the album. The album was made as a tribute to the future anti-Christ.

Many stated that Manson is demonically possessed, and he really does not even try to hide it. On stage he often goes into trances and cut himself bloody to release demonic energy on the crowds he is performing in front of. Manson aimed this album as a message to the youth to forego Christianity, and a relationship with their parents to embrace Satanism, and the coming of the anti-Christ. He wants his fans to relate to serial killers, child rapists, kidnappers, satanic teachers, drug promoters, Nazis, and twisted criminals in general.

Manson's goal is really then to allow Satan to use his body and art-form to destroy the faith of Christianity in the minds of his young fans and fans in general. Manson calls his fans 'the satanic army'. He makes millions of dollars in t-shirt sales selling t-shirts of Nazi symbolism, satanic messages, and other dark themes. He encourages his fans to take drugs at his concerts by having them chant the word drugs over and over again.

Many Christian ministers have often been called in to counsel, and intervene in the lives of young Marilyn Manson fans. These ministers would get calls from parents about their son or daughter being caught in homosexual relationships, hardcore drug use, violent crimes, satanic worship, and other disturbing acts.

Many of the ministers called in were not even aware of the influences of Marilyn Manson until they got to the bottom of the problem and found out that for many of these kids the trouble started for them when they bought a CD of Marilyn Manson's music. Many of these ministers did not think that any artist in the music industry would be the core root of these problems, but they found out different that sometimes their music and influence can be the core of the problem.

Chapter 23

In this chapter you will learn about some of the extraneous, and mysterious strange events in the lives of several music industry stars. These events regarding them are often sad, violent, unusual, outlandish, and even downright satanic.

Sid Vicious was a punk artist who was born in South East London in the mid-1960's. His mother named Anne had married a guardsman who worked at Buckingham Palace named John Ritchie. John was also a semi-professional trombone player who worked among the local London Jazz scene at night. Anne would give birth to John's son who would be the future Sid Vicious. When Sid was born he was given his father's name. John Sr. would soon leave Anne, and refuse to support Anne and his son financially.

Anne would later re-marry a man named Christopher Beverley. Within six months of the marriage Christopher would die of cancer. Anne and her young son John Jr. were then living in a rented flat in Turnbridge Wells in 1968. Anne supported herself by becoming a heroin dealer.

When John Jr. was 17 years old he began hanging around the punk-rock scene of London. His favorite hang-out was at a clothing store called SEX. At that clothing store John and his friends would often steal the clothes to wear the latest punk fashions.

One day at the clothing store John met Chrissie Hynde before she formed the group called the Pretenders. Chrissie tried to get John to marry her so she could get a work permit but John refused. Soon John was squatting with John Lydon, and two other punk rock artists who all had the same first name of John. The four men living in this apartment were called the four Johns.

John got the nickname Sid Vicious when Lydon's pet hamster named Sid had bitten John when he was trying to play with it. John had said after he got bit that 'Sid is really vicious', and the name stuck ever since. The four Johns would form a band, and they used to play Alice Cooper songs on the corners of streets for money. They were so terrible that people paid them to stop them from playing.

Sid often had his mother Anne hanging out with his friends because she often supplied his friends drugs. Sid at this point was not into heroin yet but his friends were. Sid gained fame in the punk-rock nightclubs for his wild and violent behavior during the mid to late 1970's. He would often slam-dance into people to start fist-fights with people. He mostly lost his fist-fights but he loved pain, and being busted open to show the girls his blood and his scars.

He would take broken pieces of glass to cut himself with it, and let the blood run down his chest. His most noted assault was when he attacked NME journalist Nick Kent with a motorcycle chain while his friend Jah Wobble was holding Kent down. Soon Sid's punk charisma and reputation brought him to the stage where he played bass guitar, and drums for several bands before he was brought into the Sex Pistols.

Sid played his first gig with the Sex Pistols on April 3, 1977 at The Screen On The Green nightclub in London. He began recording songs with the Sex Pistols at the studio in the same year. In 1977 Sid met Freddie Mercury of Queen who was working at the same studio. Sid would insult Freddie at the studio wherein many said the insult was over Freddie being gay. This resulted in Freddie grabbing Sid by the lapels, and pushing him out of the studio booth where a fist-fight almost went down before it was broken up. Sid was not a good musician but he made up for it in unmatched punk charisma. He would hurl insults at the crowd, and wear Nazi swastika t-shirts. He would take broken pieces of bottles and slash himself open with them.

Soon the group went on a U.S. American tour where in January of 1978 the Sex Pistols performed in Dallas, Texas at the Longhorn Ballroom. There Sid appeared on stage with the words 'Gimme a Fix' written on his chest. He began to spit on the crowd while mocking, and taunting the Texas audience.

Before the tour in March of 1977 Sid met Nancy Spungen who was a groupie that had a strong addiction to heroin. Sid was introduced to heroin by Nancy, and began using heroin with her. This resulted in a terrible addiction for Sid. Nancy would soon get a mental control on Sid. She became a bad influence which is saying a lot when you consider the people around Sid. Nancy would act as Sid's so-called manager.

During the U.S. tour Sid's relationship with the Sex Pistols deteriorated. The Sex Pistols were not getting along as a group. After their concert in San Francisco at the Winterland Ballroom the group broke-up in 1978. After the break up Sid would embark on a solo career, and was looking to form a new band but it was not to be.

On the night of October 11, 1978 at the Hotel Chelsea in Manhattan, New York City Nancy Spungen was stabbed in her abdomen during a night when Sid and Nancy were getting high on heroin together. The knife that was used to stab Nancy belonged to Sid who bought it on 42nd Street.

The next morning on October 12, 1978 Sid woke up from a drugged stupor to find Nancy dead on the bathroom floor having bled to death throughout the night. The NYPD had questioned Sid who stated that he recalls the knife being in his hand but he did not mean to stab her. He stated that the two of them were having an argument but he does not recall what happened next. He then stated that he believed Nancy may have fell into his knife. The police were looking to charge him with murder after they questioned him.

Ten days after Nancy's death Sid took a light bulb, and smashed it while trying to attempt suicide by slitting his wrist with the broken sharp piece of the bulb. His life was saved after being hospitalized at Bellevue Hospital. Many insiders believed that the reason Sid did not recall killing Nancy was because he suffered from a split-persona.

Sid often believed other people lived inside of him. What he is describing would be called demon-possession in the Bible.

Other people who were close friends of Sid and Nancy believed that Sid did not kill Nancy. They believed that the drug-dealer who they bought the heroin from had returned to the house after Sid passed out. He encountered Nancy still awake where the dealer stabbed her and rob her, or another friend of Sid and Nancy had committed the murder to rob Nancy of the drugs she had on her. Of course their case has far too many holes in it while the police evidence is more solid.

On December 9, 1978 Sid was arrested for the murder of Nancy Spungen after police investigations gathered enough evidence to show that Sid had murdered Nancy during a drug induced fight. Sid was sent to Riker's Island with a bail set for $50,000. Before he was bailed out Sid served 55 days in jail. It would be the worst 55 days of his life. The black prison inmates took a huge offense to a guy who wore a Nazi swastika t-shirt as a fashion statement on stage, and used the word 'nigger' openly as well. Sid was brutally beaten several times by prison inmates. One of the beatings was so bad he was left for dead.

The prison inmates who hated Sid also raped Sid in the shower a couple of times. They were also looking to do more damage to him if he stayed longer. The manager of the Sex Pistols named Malcolm McLaren was trying to raise money for a lawyer for Sid, and money to cover the bond. Soon Mick Jagger of the Rolling Stones stepped in and paid for the lawyers for Sid. He also gave executives at Virgin Records the bond money to get Sid out of jail. Sid was released on bail on February 1, 1979. Mick Jagger wanted no publicity for helping Sid.

On the evening of Sid's release a party was going to be held for Sid at a New York City apartment belonging to Sid's new girlfriend Michele Robinson, a woman Sid hooked up with before he went to prison. Before the party Sid wanted to get high on heroin. When Sid was released he was met by his best-friend, and his mother Anne. Anne had some heroin on her as a gift to her son Sid. They then went to a hotel room where his mother was staying. Sid would shoot-up the heroin his mother bought for him, but after getting high on it Sid got very mad because the heroin was too weak for him to enjoy it. He then talked his best friend into getting him some high-grade heroin. His friend promised to bring it to him at Sid's party.

During the party Sid's friend arrived late, and they went into Michele's bedroom where Sid shot-up the heroin his friend got him. His friend warned Sid that the heroin was very strong and to be careful of how much he shoots up, but Sid did not listen, and shot up more than he should have.

After he shot it up within 15 minutes Sid almost suffers an overdose. His best friend managed to revive him but this frightens everyone at the party, and they all decide to leave. Sid's friend gives the rest of the heroin to Sid's mother with instructions not to give Sid anymore heroin until the next day.

That night Sid has sex with Michele in her bedroom, and afterwards he asked Michele to get some heroin from his mom and shoot him up. Michele did not want to shoot him up, and she goes to Sid's mom to explain the problem. Sid's mom being tired of watching, and knowing her son is suffering decides to do something unthinkable. She walks into the room and tells Sid she will shoot him up.

Instead of giving Sid a normal and small dose she purposely administered a fatal dose of heroin into her own son. Sid was killed within minutes. For a longtime fans of Sid Vicious thought that Sid killed himself on an overdose of heroin. The truth was not known until the mid-1990's when Anne confessed to journalist Alan Parker that she murdered her own son as what she called a mercy-kill.

Another strange controversy surrounded an R&B dance-pop group called B2K. B2K were made up of four members who were Lil' Fizz, J-Boog, Raz-B, and Omarion. The group was officially formed in 1999. Their first major hit single was a song called Uh Huh that led to the group releasing their first album called B2K. B2K was released in March of 2002. The songs were driven by a more edger sound of the new hip-hop beats of the 2000s that set them apart from other boy bands. Their debut album would manage to go gold in sales. They were soon getting nationwide attention by working with other acts like Bow Wow, TG4, IMx, and Puffy Combs. Bad Boy Records executive P. Diddy also known as Puffy Combs, would take over their contract. B2K would record a second album called

Pandemonium! The second album was released in late 2002 in the month of December. The lead single for the second album called Bump, Bump, Bump, hit number one on the Billboard 100 singles chart. The album itself would hit number two on the Billboard 200 albums chart. It would sell millions of copies.

In 2003 the members of B2K would star in an urban dance movie called You Got Served. The movie became a box office hit with urban fans, and the nightclub dance scene, but around the time the movie was released a major scandal fell upon B2K's manager Chris Stokes and the management team who worked with Bad Boy Records.

Three members of B2K named Lil' Fizz, J-Boog, and Raz-B came forward in the press to state they were sexually molested by their management team, and people involved with the film You Got Served. They stated they were victims of what is known in the movie and music industry as the casting couch.

The casting couch is as old as the golden age period in Hollywood where sexual and even homo-sexual favors are done against artists to ensure parts in movies or record contracts. The three members of B2K stated that they were threaten and intimidated to be subjected to allow homosexual men in the industry including their manager Chris Stokes to sodomize them for the movie role, and to record another album. Only Omarion refused to join them in speaking out on what happened but the other three members stated they had raped him also.

The three members decided to come forward because they were disgusted by what happened to them. They no longer wanted to be under their control. They stated that ever since that night they have had terrible nightmares, and struggle with sexual confusion, and having normal straight relationships with other women. The media, who was promoting what is called the gay agenda at the time regarding gay marriage barley exposed the story. As soon as the three men came forward was just as soon as the story was buried. It was said by insiders that Omarion, since he refused to speak against his management team, he was allowed to stay on contract while the other three men were fired. Omarion would go solo, and since then he recorded three more albums but none of them ever reached the success he had with

B2K's second album. Omarion would also work as a judge for a reality dance television show. Omarion would later explain that the music industry was a lot like a gang initiation, and that events in the music industry rather good or bad stayed in the music industry. He would say that it was not always like this but when it is a person could lose their soul.

Gangs it is known that in their initiations people are jumped and beaten. In gay-gangs new members are beaten and sodomized. For Omarion to use the words 'gang-initiation' to describe the inner core of the entertainment industry is very strange and revealing indeed. Most especially the part about losing one's soul.

Another subject is an artist named Ricky Martin who was born in San Juan, Puerto Rico in 1971. At the age of 12 Ricky Martin became a member of the Puerto Rican boy band pop Latin group called Menudo in the early 1980's. Since going solo, and up to this time he has sold a combined total of albums over 70 million records world-wide. He is called the most successful artist in the Latin Music Industry. He has had 95 records to go platinum in sales. He has had 11 number one hit singles most of them in South America. He has had 6 albums to go number one on the Billboard charts mainly in South America. He was won 6 Grammy Awards, 8 World Music Awards, and 10 Billboard Music Awards. His tours bring him to over 60 countries world-wide.

His fame in the United States came with his first English-language album called Ricky Martin. Its first single called Cup of Life brought his album to the fore-front of the U.S. music scene. His second single called Livin' la Vida Loca which means living a crazy woman's life became a number one hit single on the Billboard 100 singles chart. The single became one of the best-selling singles of all time, and the song itself sold 8 million copies. Ricky's English album called Ricky Martin would sell 22 million copies. This makes him the most successful transition artist in the history of the mainstream music industry.

Martin grew up in a middle-class family in San Juan, Puerto Rico. His parents were known to be strict devout Roman Catholics. Martin as a little child served as an altar-boy for the Catholic Church his parents attended in San Juan. Martin began singing and acting at age 6.

By 9 years old he began making Spanish language television commercials. By the time he joined with Menudo he had appeared in 11 commercials that brought him small fame throughout South America and Puerto Rico. When Martin joined Menudo it was often said that the group members of Menudo were often victims of child abuse by the management team of Menudo. The discipline in Menudo was compared to mental and physical abuse. The members were often chastised and even beaten for small mistakes. The members were told that if they didn't like it then they could quit. They were told to do things the managers wanted them to do without question. If they did question it or had a problem with it then they were told they would not be part of the group. The price for fame was a heavy price even in a small island commonwealth like Puerto Rico.

Martin stated that his experience, and time with Menudo cost him his childhood. Other insiders stated that the members of Menudo were even used for sexual abuse as well. These statements have yet to be proven but they are statements made against the management team of Menudo more than once.

The members of Menudo started out at ages from 12 to 15 years old. They were from the start promoted as sex symbols. Martin recalls that he lost his virginity at 13 years old to a full grown woman twice his age. The other members also would be with women far older than them. As Martin grew older it was said that due to the abuse he experienced in Menudo he became confused about his sexuality. He also, overtime, when he became an adult renounced Jesus Christ and got into Buddhism. Many insiders stated he also got into black magic, and New Age spirituality. The song Livin 'la Vida Loca was said to be based upon real events in Martin's life.

After leaving Menudo Martin went solo, and he promised his parents he would use the money he earned from Menudo to get a college education. Martin's money was controlled by his parents until he was 18 years old. Martin would move to New York City to attend Tisch School of the Arts at NYU. During that time he would meet a Mexican woman who was into a South American form of witchcraft. These strange and dark influences would lead Martin to drop out of school just within weeks before classes would start, and he moved with this woman to Mexico City. There Martin who was famous in Mexico used his influence to perform in theaters in Mexico City. His first play was called Mama Ama el Rock which means Mom Loves Rock.

Soon he would record albums for a Latin-American music industry label. He has been doing this work of being a recording artist ever since. Livin 'la Vida Loca is a song that glorifies sexual immorality, sexual addictions, and also black magic. If you really listen to the song or read the lyrics you will come to understand this truth about the song.

The song talks about a woman who loves superstitions, blackcats, and voodoo dolls. These references are based in witchcraft and paganism. Superstitions are based in irrationality and folk lore. Blackcats are often victims of ritual animal killings in voodoo practices. He sings in the lyrics about having premonitions that the girl will make him fall. Premonitions are foreboding emotions centered on fear and paranoia.

The Bible tells us that often these feelings would be caused against people involved with evil spirits. In the song he mentions having 'new kicks in the candlelight'. Satanists and witches often have sex in ritual settings that involve a heavy use of candles all around the room. The song also sings about the power this woman has over him. He compares her kisses to the devil, and that she can push and pull him down as if he is a puppet on a string under her control. This song when it came out was adored by millions of people in the United States, and all across the world, but did people even know what the song really was about? Most likely not, while coven members would clearly admire the song because it glorifies their beliefs.

Ricky Martin had another song called Love You For a Day. The song was about having sex with someone on the Day of Judgment which was a reference to the second coming of Jesus Christ, but the song is even more twisted then having a one night stand when Jesus arrives. Many insiders stated that the song was about having a homosexual affair on the day of the second coming of Jesus Christ. For years this statement was a rumor until the truth became clear.

For many years Ricky Martin hid the fact he was a bi-sexual. It was not until 2010 is when Ricky came forward and admitted that he was gay. In fact today he is more gay then straight, and he is promoting the same-sex marriage movement in the media.

So here we have a sad case of a child abuse victim who became a Satanist/witch, and a new ager and gave up on Christianity. He now supports a movement that within history always was the first sign of a downfall of a nation. The history of the Roman Empire could tell you all about that fact.

Another sad artist in the music industry was GG Allin. GG Allin is an artist most of the mainstream has most likely never even heard of unless they are devout fans of hardcore punk-rock music. His birth name was and I joke with you not, was Jesus Christ Allin. His name was later changed to Kevin Michael Allin. GG Allin is best remembered in the music industry for being the most extreme punk rock star in history. His notorious live performances were filled with acts of self-mutilation, and attacking audience members with extreme violence. His songs were for the most part written by him, and they were filled with blasphemy against Jesus Christ. He would even tell people he was Satan and Jesus all rolled into one.

He promoted pedophilia, homosexuality, and racism. Due to his extreme politically incorrect lyrics he was given limited distribution by his record company, but he still managed to maintain a cult following throughout his career. On stage he would bust himself open with beer bottles, and cut himself so deeply he would be covered in his own blood. He would even shoot-up heroin on stage. He even promised his fans who entertained this thought that he was the second coming of Christ. He also promised them that he would kill himself on stage.

His father was a strange and sick man who gave his son the name Jesus Christ Allin because he stated that Jesus Christ visited him and told him that his son would be a new Messiah to the people. No one knows if his father made this up because he was sick in his mind or if Satan pretending to be Jesus Christ gave him the idea to name his son Jesus Christ to represent a New Age artist. His mother would soon file for divorce from his father because his mental sickness became worse. By 1962 she changed Allin's name to Kevin.

Allin became inspired to do rock music when he got into the music of Alice Cooper in the 1970's. In his mid-teens he formed a band called Little Sister's Date, and began performing cover songs of Alice Cooper, Kiss, Aerosmith, and other Hard Rock bands. In the late 70's throughout the 1980's Allin became part of the underground punk-rock scene. He would perform with bands called The Cedar Street Sluts, The Scumfucs, The Texas Nazis, and several others. The main band he performed with were the Jabbers where he played drums and did vocals.

His debut album with the Jabbers was a record called Always Was Is and Always Shall Be. In the 1980's the Jabbers would break-up due to Allin's extreme uncontrollable, uncompromising, and vicious behavior. In the 1980's Allin had a strong addiction to heroin and alcohol. He would use any drug given to him. Many said he struggled with demon possession as he often heard voices in his head speaking to him, and was often seen talking to invisible people. Along with his violent stage acts Allin began adding defecation to his stage acts by eating and drinking large amounts of laxatives before his performances.

Allin never had a steady job, and he supported himself by selling his own records. Allin also worshiped serial killers. He became a regular pen-pal to John Wayne Gacy, and he even visited Gacy in prison several times. Gacy one time painted a portrait of Allin that was used on the cover of one of Allin's albums. Throughout Allin's career he was arrested a little over 48 times. These arrests were for assault, assault with a deadly weapon, lewdness, disturbing acts of physical abuse toward others, robbery, vandalism, cruel acts towards animals, attempted rape, drug possession, and other crimes which included setting stages on fire. One time during a concert someone threw a dead cat on stage. Allin took out his male-member, and tried to have sex with it.

Allin's performances were the main source of his many arrests. He would cause a large amount of damage to venues and sound equipment. He would get arrested on stage for exposing himself, and for assault and battery many times. His non-stop touring often came to a stop due to jail time. Many times he had to stay for weeks in hospitals for blood poisoning, broken bones, and other trauma injuries.

Allin's threats of committing suicide on stage first came in 1989 when he declared he would kill himself on stage on Halloween Day, but the police locked him up the day before so that he could not make good on the threat. So afterwards he continued his threats each following year stating he would kill himself on Halloween Day, but for those following years he would be imprisoned a day before Halloween.

In late 1989 Allin was arrested for attempted murder of a female he knew in Ann Arbor, Michigan. Allin was having sex with this woman when during sex he cut her open, and began drinking her blood. He then began burning the woman with hot-metal goads, and then he set the woman on fire. The charge was dropped against him when the judge found substantial inconsistencies in the woman's account of the events. It turned out that she was a willing participant in these satanic sexual activities before it became too much for her.

When the charge was dropped Allin was still found guilty of a lesser felonious assault. He would be imprisoned from December 25, 1989 to March 26, 1991. Allin would write a book in prison called The GG Allin Manifesto. After prison Allin appeared on the television news media show called Geraldo to talk about his controversial book. Allin declared on the show that his body was the temple of Rock N' Roll, and that he drew blood and bodily fluids from his flesh as communion to his fans. Allin would compare himself to Jesus Christ on the show, and stated that if he was not a performer he would probably be a mass-murderer. Allin also appeared on the Jerry Springer Show and The Jane Whitney Show in the early 1990's.

Allin's last show took place on June 27, 1993 at a small punk rock nightclub called The Gas Station in Manhattan. When Allin was singing his second song during the set the power at the nightclub went out. In response Allin trashed the venue, and left the darken nightclub by walking out entirely naked. He then walked across the street covered in blood and feces. A fan would give him a pair of shorts to wear, and Allin walked down the neighborhood street followed by a large group of fans. After Allin and this group walked the streets for an hour they went to the apartment of John Handley to have a party.

During the party Allin ingested very large amounts of heroin. Around 2:00 a.m. Allin would pose with fans for photos while the party was about to end. Around 3:00 a.m. Allin fell into an unconscious state, and while in that state he had respiratory failure. The next morning on June 28, 1993 the people there could not wake up Allin as his body was motionless. The ambulance was called in, and Allin was pronounced dead at the scene.

Some strange events involved an artist named Sinead O'Connor. Sinead O'Connor is an Irish singer and talented song-writer who arose to world-wide fame in 1990 with a song called Nothing Compares 2 U that was a song written by Prince. Her career would be surrounded with controversy for her statements, and strongly expressed views on the Roman Catholic Church, and other organized religious groups regarding women's rights and child abuse.

Sinead was a victim of child abuse at the hands of her mother Marie O'Connor after she divorced her father Sean O'Connor. The effects of her abuse left deep mental wounds on the persona of Sinead. At 15 years old she managed to get away from her abusive mother to live with her father, but the effects of her abuse left her a troubled teenager where she was often shoplifting and showing up late for school if not showing up at all. She was then sent to the Magdalene Asylum which was run by a group of nuns who were members of the Sisters of Our Lady charity. Her time there helped her thrive to become a developed singer and writer of music, but the discipline there was often tough on Sinead where she would experience pure panic and terror over anything she did.

After her education that finished at another strict religious school called the Newtown School that was a Quaker boarding school she formed a band with a few other members and embarked on a career in music. After working with several bands and writing songs for several groups in the music industry in the 1980's she found her world-wide fame after releasing her second album called I Do Not Want What I Haven't Got. The album featured the lead single Nothing Compares 2 U which became a number one hit single on the Billboard 100 singles chart.

Sinead's image was vastly different from other top female artists in the industry. She had good looks but a bald head. Sinead stated that she shaved her head as a protest against how the media portrays women as being sex symbols. Sinead from the on-start of her career was very outspoken about the things she believed in. Some said she was a godly person but her homosexual relationships with women would say otherwise according to the Bible.

She was very sensitive about matters of child abuse and religious abuse. She also was not interested in being a total sell out for riches and fame. This does make her a rare artist, and why she is often seen as a one hit wonder. Sinead started to bring controversy toward her when in 1990 she refused to perform the United States national anthem at one of her concerts. Some said that her reasons for this had to do with the poverty in the U.S. that the leaders of the richest nation on earth refused to resolve. Others said it had to do with crimes committed by the United States regarding then President Bush's global policies. Whatever the case was this refusal of Sinead incited anger from a lot of her peers in the music industry.

When music and rat pack legend Frank Sinatra heard she did this he went to the media and threaten to in his words, 'kick her ass'. Sinead was soon nominated for 4 Grammy Awards but she brought more controversy to her by telling the Grammy board members to withdraw her name from consideration. Her reasons for this withdraw was she believed that the Grammys did not honor all artists in general but only artists the industry and the media political system favored.

Around this time is when more exposure regarding priests working for the Roman Catholic Church was being told about their child sexual abuse crimes. No one in Hollywood was doing any protesting about it, not even Madonna who only cares to talk bad about the Catholic Church when they tell her to stop molesting the image of the cross, and stop selling her body to her young fans. Everyone in the entertainment industry was ignoring it. This could be because of the child abuse crimes that go on in the entertainment industry that was exposed by Gary Coleman, Todd Bridges, Corey Fieldman, and others, but Sinead was not going to ignore it.

What brought the famous career of Sinead O'Connor to a full stop happened on October 3, 1992 during a live performance on Saturday Night Live. During the performance Sinead sang a version of the Bob Marley song called War. Sinead sang the song as a protest against sexual abuse among the priests in the Catholic Church. She then presented a photo of Pope John Paul 2nd to the camera, and while singing the word 'evil' she tore the photo into pieces. She then stated 'fight the real enemy', and threw the pieces towards the camera.

Lorne Michaels, and the rest of the staff of Saturday Night Live had no idea what Sinead was going to do. When NBC Vice-President of Late Night Rick Ludwin saw it he fell out of his chair. The audience there in the studio was in shock. They were completely silent with no one booing or giving applause. NBC network received 4,400 calls in one week where all but seven calls were criticizing Sinead. The New York Daily News cover called Sinead a 'holy terror'. Interesting enough there are people who came from Jesuit schools who work for The New York Daily News.

Two weeks after the Saturday Night Live performance Sinead was to perform at the Bob Dylan tribute concert. When she was about to take the stage the crowds started booing. Kris Kristofferson would tell her 'don't let the bastards get you down!' Sinead took the stage, and the noise eventually became so loud Sinead saw no point in trying to continue to perform. She screamed over the audience a rendition of the song War, and walked off the stage as Kris comforted her.

After the Saturday Night Live performance she was often blacklisted in the music industry. She would make several television appearances in the U.S. since that event but she was never famous the way she was before that event. Her career still goes on in Europe where she tours but she rarely records for major studio labels.

Another strange artist is Jennifer Lopez who was born in the Bronx of New York City to Puerto Rican parents Guadalupe and David Lopez. At the age of 5 years old she began taking singing and dancing lessons. In high-school she did not do well academically but she excelled athletically in gymnastics, track, and softball. In her final year of high-school, and against her parents' wishes, Jennifer got into acting.

It started when she won a role for a low-budget film called My Little Girl in 1986. After the film Jennifer stated to her parents that she wanted to be a famous movie star but her parents told her it was a stupid idea especially for a Latin-American. Due to differences of opinions Jennifer moved out of her parents' home, and moved into the apartment of her boyfriend in Manhattan.

During this time Jennifer was seen as a wild girl, and very ambitious to be successful. She made contacts with people working in theater, and soon she performed in productions of theater musicals of Jesus Christ, Superstar! and Oklahoma. She would then go to Europe for five months to do the musical Golden Musicals of Broadway. She experienced discrimination for her Puerto Rican heritage when she was the only member of the chorus to not have a solo. She was in a deep depression, and hated life for those five months.

She would later, after her work in Europe, get a job on a show in Japan called Synchronicity. She worked as a dancer, singer, and a choreographer on the show. During this time Jennifer was making connections with people in the movie and music industries. It first started when she was hired as a backup dancer for the New Kids on the Block in 1991. She would perform with them on live television when the New Kids performed the song Games at the American Music Awards. This led to an audition for a high-profile job to become a Fly Girl dancer for a television show called In Living Color. 2,000 female dancers would audition. After the girls were chosen, wherein insiders stated by questionable means, meaning a couple of them did sexual favors to get the gig, Jennifer was a runner-up to the last girl chosen.

Now here is where things get strange. The unproven rumor was that Jennifer Lopez got into black-magic, and spells during the time when she was working on musicals and entering the scene in Hollywood. The insiders who spoke about this stated that it started for her while living with her boyfriend in Manhattan at the time she was working theater productions.

The story is that Jennifer got in touch with evil spirits, and she cast a spell against the girl who beat her out to make her so sick that she would be unable to appear on the show. Later on the girl who beat her out for the gig would become sick and unable to accept the job.

Jennifer then got the call, and received the role as a Fly Girl on In Living Color. While dancing on the show the show itself would become a huge ratings hit. Around that time Jennifer would seek to get into the movie industry. Other people who were close to her, and knew her like Rosie Perez who was Jennifer's choreographer on In Living Color, and also an actress, stated that Jennifer was a backstabber. She would do anything for a part. She was seen as a woman who would have sex with anyone who helped her to get movie roles.

In Hollywood she was known as a gold-digger, and a money and fame loving harlot. Also witchcraft practices kept coming up regarding the rumors surrounding her. Of course in Hollywood regarding that kind of behavior she would fit right on in with so many of the rest.

Her first two major roles were the films My Family and Money Train. It was stated that she got the part for Money Train because she was willing to do nude sex scenes with Wesley Snipes. It was also said she was willing to sleep with the producer of the film. When Jennifer got the part for Blood and Wine it was stated by rumor that she had sex with Jack Nicholson for the part.

Jennifer became an A-list movie star after starring in the lead role in the movie Selena. Many Mexicans and Mexican-American fans were not too happy that Jennifer Lopez got that part but were happy a film was made about their icon who was murdered by the head of her fan club. Jennifer Lopez, after making the movie Selena, became the first Latin-American movie star to be paid one million dollars per movie role. She would go on to star in many more films.

In the late 1990's Jennifer started dating Sean 'Puffy' Combs. By the time she dated him she already had two divorces and several break-ups. These divorces, and break-ups according to people who knew her stated that they were men who helped her in her career. Once their purpose was served Jennifer would get rid of them.

Puffy Combs helped Jennifer to get a record contract. Jennifer's first album was called On the 6. The meaning of the title according to many insiders was a reference to the number of Satan in Revelation which is 666. Her lead single called If You Had My Love would hit number one on the Billboard 100 singles chart. The album would make Jennifer both a star in music along with being a movie star.

Jennifer Lopez throughout her career was promoted as a sex-symbol. Her image was not about her acting and singing but mostly about her looks like her legs, and especially her butt was often promoted in the media and in photos.

She broke-up with Combs after a shooting at a nightclub nearly killed the two of them. She then used and toyed with an actor named Ben Affleck, and divorced him as soon as she married him. She then married Mark Antony and that marriage does not look to be going too well, and many insiders stated it is also heading for divorce.

The stories of black-magic practices and spells involving Jennifer Lopez still comes up again and again. Many insiders state that she would cast spells on men she had sex with to bring curses in their lives to give them problems in their careers. They also stated that Jennifer is demon-possessed as well, but this has yet to be proven.

What is clear is that Jennifer's views on GOD are not the Christian views on GOD but are the New Age views. She believes that GOD is not a person nor Jesus Christ but is someone who lives in people's hearts, and that your heart and not the Bible is the sole authority for right and wrong. So in that understanding you tell yourself what is sin, and what is not and you give no heed to the Bible according to this belief. So in that understanding if someone has sex with a small child but tells themselves from their heart it was not a sin then we should think that is okay. In that understanding you can do whatever you want, and decide from your heart if it's right or wrong. In fact that is what Aleister Crowley a black-magic Satanist believed in. It looks like there could be something to those rumors of Jennifer Lopez and black magic.

One strange and cold-blooded story surrounded singer and actress Jennifer Hudson. Hudson, who is from Chicago, arose to fame as a finalist on American Idol. She would soon make her film debut in a movie called Dreamgirls released in 2006. The role would make her a star as she won an Academy Award for Best Supporting Actress. Her first album called Jennifer Hudson would sell 1 million copies world-wide, and her second album called I Remember Me would go gold in sales in the U.S.

In 2009 she became yet another Hollywood friend of President Barack Obama. Obama invited her to a fundraiser in Beverly Hills, and she also performed at the White House. In 2013 she oddly received a star on the Hollywood Walk of Fame while many felt she had not accomplish enough to receive that honor. Those same critics also felt she was given that honor by judicious favor.

The strange event involving Jennifer Hudson happened in Chicago in October of 2008. In that month and year Jennifer's 57 year old mother named Darnell, and her 29 year old brother Jason were found shot to death inside the home of Darnell. When the bodies were found an AMBER Alert was issued for Jennifer's 7 year old nephew Julian who was living in the home of Darnell, and was kidnapped after the two were shot to death.

Three days later the FBI found the body of 7 year old Julian who was killed by multiple gunshot wounds, and his body was dumped on the West Side of Chicago. The official story is that the estranged husband of Jennifer's sister Julia had broken into the home, and killed Darnell and Jason. He then kidnapped little Julian, and then drove with him in a car that he stole and went to an area on the West Side of Chicago, and murdered him. The man was convicted of the crime, and sentenced to 120 years in prison without the possibility of parole.

Now here is the other side of the story. Gregory Hill is believed to be the real father of little Julian. When the murders happened Jennifer Hudson was put out of the media spotlight for three months, and was sealed off to law enforcement and media until the story died down, but Gregory wanted Jennifer questioned and gave a testimony about what he feels really happened. Gregory stated that Jennifer became a Freemason, and was involved with devil-worshippers who were connected to Hollywood, and had a lot of power. He believed, along with others, that this group working in Hollywood got her the part in Dreamgirls and a record contract after she lost on American Idol.

This group, who were also believed to be members of masonic lodges, according to Gregory and Professor Griff, former member of the rap group Public Enemy, were a satanic group involved with Moloch ritual human sacrifices for fame. The belief was that these Masons would not help her career nor get her a contract unless Jennifer gave them permission to kill her 7 year old nephew. Moloch was a pagan demon idol where Moloch followers sacrificed children to it. This may sound crazy, and very hard to believe but insiders often speak about the baphomet/Moloch ritual again, and again regarding many artists.

Gregory's story is not proven but he stated that Jennifer allowed a ritual hit to be put on her own family. He would go on to state that whatever is done in the dark will come to the light. To give some light to Gregory's story there is some strange things about what happened regarding the murders. Evidence shows that there could have been more than just one killer in the house, but this evidence was ignored and not reported in the media. The supposed killers, according to this evidence, entered the home in silence while Darnell and Jason were sleeping. This evidence shows that the supposed persons in the house had their sights set not on Darnell and Jason but on little Julian, and their attentions were focused on getting into his bedroom.

During this Darnell and Jason were awoken by hearing people in their home. It is believed by investigating this evidence that Darnell and Jason confronted the supposed killers while they were in the process of kidnapping Julian, and that is when they were shot to death. Julian's body looked to have been abused before he was shot multiple times. The way he was shot up, and the position of how the body was found is common in satanic ritual murders that are on the police and FBI files.

The people in the area, and the word or rumors on the streets regarding people connected to Jennifer Hudson's family also believe this was a satanic ritual hit involving Jennifer Hudson, but none of this has yet to be fully proven.

In the career of Cher she has often promoted New Age themes. Cher is nicknamed the Goddess of Pop due to her string of hit songs throughout her career. She started her career in the music industry as one half of the folk-rock duo Sonny & Cher who's most successful lead single was a song called I Got You Babe.

From the mid 1960's to the 1970's she established herself as a successful solo artist with songs like Bang Bang (My Baby Shot Me Down), Gypsys, Tramps & Thieves, Half-Breed, Dark Lady, and others. In the 1970's she would star along with Sonny in a very popular television show called The Sonny & Cher Comedy Hour. In the 1980's she would become a movie star.

She acted in a film called Silkwood that earned her a nomination at the Academy Awards for Best Supporting Actress in 1983. She would star in other hit films like Mask, The Witches of Eastwick, and Moonstruck. For the film Moonstruck Cher won the Academy Award for Best Actress in 1988. Throughout the 1980's she would record platinum selling albums that had such smash hit singles like I Found Someone and If I Could Turn Back Time. She is among a rare list of artists who have won all three major awards among the fields of art in the United States having won an Oscar Award, a Grammy Award, and a Emmy Award.

Her records throughout her career have sold a combine total of 140 million copies world-wide. She is the only artist in the music industry's history to have had a number one Billboard hit song in the period of six decades which was the 1960's, 1970's, 1980's, 1990's, 2000s, and 2010s.

Cher's relationship with Sonny broke-up due to the many affairs

Cher had with other men in the music industry. Cher at the time was heavy into the drugs, and sex movement but she often kept this hidden and in the closet. The divorce from Sonny came when Cher was caught having sex with David Geffen. Sonny felt betrayed by Cher when Cher used David Geffen to free her from her business arrangements with Sonny. She also exposed Sonny's heroin addiction to the press.

Geffen would then secure a 2.5 million dollar deal for Cher with Warner Bros. Records. Cher after the divorce would carry on a sexual relationship with David Geffen for the next two years. Cher stated that she did this to Sonny because of Sonny's heroin and liquor problems, and his constant control over her, but Cher also battled with drugs and liquor during the time she was with Sonny.

Many believe regarding it is that Cher did not leave Sonny over his drug problems but she left him to make more money and be more successful as a solo artist. In the inner scene of the movie and music industry Cher was heavy into the New Age movement. She also had numerous affairs with actors, actresses, producers, and executives. In the early 1990's Cher began doing television spots promoting psychic hot-lines, and would openly promote New Age beliefs. It was clear that Cher stopped being a Christian a long time ago. What was also clear she had no problem promoting a hot-line that is known to deceive millions of people and take their money.

In the 1990's Cher began promoting the works of her personal guru James Van Praagh. James Van Praagh claims that he is a psychic who can talk to the spirits of the dead. He promotes sorcery, and preaches New Age spiritualism. The Bible calls James Van Praagh's faith to be demonic, and one having dealings with demonic spirits, but his followers, like Cher, think otherwise, and they believe they will find their answers to matters regarding life after death not in Jesus Christ but in people like James Van Praagh.

In the 1990's Sonny would die in a strange skiing accident. Cher spoke openly about missing Sonny after he died, and she spoke about getting in touch with Sonny in the afterlife. Her method of doing this was to go to James Van Praagh wherein he would hold a séance, and call up the spirit of Sonny. Some odd things are seen here as well. Cher openly stated she had nothing to be sorry for regarding Sonny and how she left him, yet many friends who were at the séance were stating that Cher was seeking confirmation that Sonny would forgive her for something she did to him.

It seems that the real reason Cher wanted the séance was not because she missed him in that way but because she was superstitious, and she believed that Sonny could haunt her for a wrong she committed against him. Cher was hoping that James Van Praagh would help her get in touch with Sonny. The story is that he called up Sonny, and Sonny spoke through James and forgave Cher for the offense she was concerned about, making Cher feel all better, and everything then was okay. Of course it was all a con, and Cher was hustled out of thousands of dollars. She was willing to give up thousands of dollars just for peace of mind. No matter how deluded it is.

Another artist named Tori Amos is believed to be a devout witch and satanic worshipper. At the height of her fame she was regarded as one of the best female rock artist in the last 30 years, but at the height of her career she made some shocking and sick statements about Jesus Christ and Christians in general.

One of Tori's hit songs was a song called Spark. In the song she mocks Jesus Christ and the Divine Master Plan by stating that she would rather follow the ways of Jesus' betrayer Judas then to believe in the perfection of GOD's Master Plan. One of Tori's most demonic songs was a song called Father Lucifer. In the video for the song Tori presents herself as a witch singing in front of a candle to represent that she is singing to Satan who was once called the light-bearer. She then covers herself in rats to represent a hatred for humanity, and a love for darkness. The lyrics of the song openly mock Jesus Christ.

During several interviews Tori did she spoke perverted blasphemies against Jesus Christ and Christians. She taught her fans that Satan also called Lucifer was not a bad guy. In regards to Satan Tori stated, 'I wanted to marry Lucifer, I don't consider Lucifer an evil force. I feel his presence with his music.

I feel like he comes and sits on my piano.' Notice how she states that Satan comes to her while she is playing music, and that the music was not her music but Satan's music. Also notice that she is sexually drawn to Satan. In regards to Jesus, Tori Amos stated that she believes that Jesus and Mary Magdalene were having sex, and that she used to feel guilty about wanting to have sex with Jesus. Later on when someone asked her if she was putting a black-eye on Christian beliefs by saying things like this she stated, 'Why don't people want to hear about GOD getting a blow-job? I thought those born again Christians would love that.'

You know what is even more shocking? At the height of her fame Tori's biggest money making fans were Christians. Many of them did not even know she made statements like this, and when the few of them by the numbers did find out she made those statements a lot of those few still bought her album. Her fans at that time simply ignored statements like these. They thought she was talented, and cute even when Tori shows them an evil and anti-Christ nature within her. One of Tori's alarming statements was when she said that one of her mission's in life was to take Christianity over to the dark-side. This means corruption, seduction, and deceiving people about true Christianity for her own selfish and greedy purpose.

Another artist named Amy Grant is often seen as a contradiction artist. In the 1980's Amy Grant gained world-wide fame in the Christian music industry. The story of this Christian artist is often said to be the sad story of many Christian artists. The story is that many of them are not as Christian as people think they are.

In the 1980's Amy Grant had several smash hit Christian singles such as Father's Eyes, El Shaddai, Angels, Thy Word, and others. Thy Word is still a Christian worship song to this day. Her songs were clearly pure and caused people to draw close to GOD, but the artist herself was a lot different than her songs which were usually written by someone else. Amy Grant made history in the Christian music industry. She had the first Christian album ever to go platinum in sales.

Her duet with Peter Cetera called The Next Time I Fall became a number one hit song on the Billboard 100 singles chart. At the height of her career she was nicknamed the Queen of Christian Pop. In June of 1982 Amy Grant married fellow Christian artist Gary Chapman. They would have three children. This couple divorced in 1999 after a long period of an estranged relationship that started in 1990.

The story behind this came from insiders regarding the Christian music industry. It was said that Grant was often cheating on Chapman, and Chapman was not any better. Sexual immorality was the main problem in their marriage. The two of them just could not keep their hands off of other people.

Instead of ministering the Word of GOD off stage they often acted like they forgot they were supposed to be Christians when the camera was off of them. Amy by the late 1980's, after she scored a number one hit on the Billboard charts, wanted to get into the mainstream music industry. She began making contacts with producers and executives from that scene. She would attend many parties among them where the story is she got into New Age practices especially witchcraft and drugs. It was said she often hid these influences from others. It was not known just how deep she was into these practices but many elements of witchcraft are shown in many videos she has done.

In 1991 Amy Grant released her first mainstream rock-pop album called Heart in Motion. The album would become a huge success selling 5 million copies, and it still is Amy's most successful album to date. The lead single Baby, Baby became a number one hit song on the Billboard 100 singles chart. Despite what her loyal Christian fans thought, and despite the lies Amy Grant told them, none of the songs on the album had anything to do with Christianity or Christian values.

Take the song Baby, Baby. This song according to Amy Grant was supposed to be about Grant's newborn daughter at the time named Millie, but the lyrics and the music video of the song told a very different story. The music video and the song itself was sexual in its art-form. She is not singing about a newborn baby but about a boyfriend who makes her feel good. The hook of the song was clearly in relation to a man who makes her moan the words 'baby, baby'. All the songs on the album had premarital sexual influences. They were about premarital encounters, but despite the truth of this her Christian fans who were blind and loyal had bought the album to such a point it even became a number one album on the Billboard Contemporary Christian Chart. This was the first mainstream album to be number one on the Christian chart.

The Bible tells us that GOD does not work in confusion, and confusion is the work of Satan. There was a lot of confusion regarding Amy Grant among Christian music producers and executives at the time. At that time Amy was estranged from her husband Chapman, but in the eyes of the media she, and her management team made it look like they were a happy blessed family. Insiders, however, knew they were not.

Amy Grant at the time was dating, and having sex with other men. Her life was the life of most artists in the music industry. It was filled with drugs, sex, and New Age beliefs behind closed doors, and at nightclubs and parties. Because of the large amount of Christian leaders in the Christian music industry, they often had to shield the truth about her, and prevent many of their artists from being exposed. Amy was often shielded by them, but soon her sinful ways became a problem for them especially when she kept refusing to work things out with her husband.

This then began to generate controversy for Grant by the Christian community who once protected her when people began making complaints that she was too worldly, and too sexy for the Christian fans. At that point her career halted after the success of Heart in Motion. She tried to work things out with her husband, but their differences became too much for them, and they finally divorce in 1999.

Grant at that point tried to restart her mainstream career but all her once millions of fans were now into more sexual and darker artists. Grant then sought to re-enter the Christian music scene, but she got into trouble once again. It was discovered that Grant was having an adulterous affair with country music star Vince Gill when he was still married at the time. Gill then divorce his wife Janis Oliver. In March of 2000 Amy married Vince Gill in the midst of a barrage of condemnation from people in the Christian community, and people in the Christian music industry. Despite this, they still let her return to record albums for them. Amy would state Christian values are important to her in the media but yet she hangs out with music industry rock and pop stars. She attends their parties, and has no problem with what they do behind the scenes.

By 2001 Amy divorced Vince Gill due to affairs on both sides. To this day Amy is in the Christian music industry where her ways are right now not that much of a big deal to current younger Christians in that industry. This is because the spiritual lessons of the Bible is not high in their minds or hearts. They have lost sight of the truth, and replaced it with their own values and beliefs. Instead of the Christian industry being GOD-centered it has become man-centered.

Another artist is rapper 50 Cent who was born Curtis Jackson. He was raised in New York City in the poverty stricken area of South Jamaica in Queens. 50 Cent was raised by his mother named Sabrina who was a lesbian, and worked as a cocaine dealer. His mother would die under questionable rumors.

50 Cent and others believed that his mother was murdered by men she was connected to through the drug-trade. It was said that they poisoned his mother with a drugged drink that knocked her unconscious, and then they turned the gas on in the house. They closed all the windows shut and then left. Later her family members found her died.

When 50 Cent was a teenager he joined a gang, and began selling narcotics. He also at this same time started taking boxing lessons at a local gym. He gained a reputation for being ruthless on the streets where he sold crack on the strip. He would break people's jaws who owed him money or were rival gang-members.

His grandmother found out he was selling drugs after being caught by metal detectors at Andrew Jackson High School. 50 Cent had the crack he was selling in small metal vials, and so he was arrested by the police at school. After getting out of jail he was nicknamed 50 Cent after a street legend who was a Brooklyn robber who lived life by providing for himself by any means.

At 21 years old 50 Cent began to change direction in life, and started to use his gifts to become a rapper. He would rap at basement parties, and soon he made a demo tape. A friend of 50 Cent would introduce him to Jam Master Jay of Run DMC.

Jay saw talent in him, and then he trained 50 Cent in how to create a record by teaching him how to write choruses and structure songs. Afterwards 50 Cent was signed to Jay's new label called Jam Master Jay Records. 50 Cent recorded his first album under Jay's label but a private beef erupted between the two when 50 Cent questioned the career direction that Jay was leading him to. As a result Jay shelved his album, and it was never released. The two however would part ways with respect for one another.

In 1999, after parting ways with Jay, 50 Cent was signed to Columbia Records. There he recorded a single that became an underground hit called How to Rob. In the single 50 Cent rap's about robbing, and smacking such artists as Jay-Z, Kurupt, Big Pun, DMX, Sticky Fingaz, Wyclef Jean, and the Wu-Tang Clan. This made 50 Cent a target of hatred by these rappers in the industry.

Nas however loved the single, and took 50 Cent on to join him on his tour to promote his new album. On May 24, 2000 50 Cent was driven to his grandmother's house so he could pick up some jewelry. After leaving the home and saying good-bye to his grandmother who was in the front-yard he returned to the back-seat of the car. While seated another car pulls up, and an assailant jumps out of the car. He goes up to the car where 50 Cent was seated, and with a 9mm handgun he fires nine shots at close range into the car at 50 Cent. All nine shots hit 50 Cent.

He was shot in his left cheek which resulted in a permanent small slur in his voice today. He was also shot in his hip, hand, arm, both legs, and chest. 50 Cent was then driven to the hospital where his friends thought he was going to die. He spent thirteen days there and lived.

The man who shot 50 Cent was suspected of being Darryl 'Hommo' Baum. Baum was a hired thug, and once was a close friend, and bodyguard to Mike Tyson. The unproven rumor was that Darryl was paid by Ja-Rule's people at Murder Inc. to murder 50 Cent. When 50 Cent was released from the hospital he kept hearing the rumors that people at Murder Inc. had him shot. The beef between Ja-Rule and 50 Cent is believed to have started when they were working together at a studio. While 50 Cent was working with Ja-Rule an argument broke out between the two of them. During the confrontation between Ja-Rule and 50 Cent a member of Ja-Rule's crew named Black Child stabbed 50 Cent with a knife. Some weeks later at a nightclub 50 Cent would get into a fist-fight with Ja-Rule, and he beat up Ja-Rule in the nightclub. Sometime after that in May 50 Cent would be shot nine times.

After getting out of the hospital 50 Cent, to vent his anger, did a song called Ghetto Qu'ran which exposed inside secrets on the streets, and the rap industry about the drug trade. 50 Cent would center the song around Murder Inc's dealings with Kenneth 'Supreme' McGriff. 50 Cent was then blacklisted from the rap labels, and no one wanted to sign him. The word on the streets, and in the industry was that 50 Cent was a rat.

In 2002 Jam Master Jay had defied the industry blacklist of 50 Cent, and was seeking to have it lifted and ended. On October 30, 2002 Jam Master Jay was in the studio at Merrick Boulevard in Queens. While there around 7:30 p.m. three gunmen enter the studio, and forced everyone on the ground. One of the gunman, while covered by his associates, would then murder Jam Master Jay execution style in the studio.

The police during investigations warned 50 Cent that his life could be in danger. The survivors of that studio shooting stated that they believed the killers were connected to people at Murder Inc. Certain police officers who spoke on the case believed that Irv and Chris Gotti, who run Murder Inc., were angry that Jam Master Jay was trying to help 50 Cent to get a record contract, so it was believed that they talked to Kenneth 'Supreme' McGriff, who was a known drug dealer to industry artists and had ties to the Black Mafia, and asked him if he would hire some people to kill Jay as a warning to others not to make deals for 50 Cent. The NYPD and the special task force unit who were looking to throw Irv and Chris in jail were unable to make all the charges they had on them stick, and they lost their case in court.

The hip-hop community and industry would sadly mourn the loss of a legendary rap artist. Regardless of Murder Inc.'s supposed efforts of stopping 50 Cent from getting signed to a label 50 Cent would indeed get signed to a label. Rapper Eminem listened to a 50 Cent track called Guess Who's Back? He then went to Dr. Dre begging him to sign 50 Cent. Dre paid for a plane ticket to fly 50 Cent to Los Angeles where 50 Cent would make a deal. He signed to Dre's production label that owned Shady Records. 50 Cent signed for one million dollars.

While 50 Cent was recording his new album Ja-Rule was in the studio recording his new album. While Ja-Rule was in the studio one night the lights in the studio went out leaving the studio in pitch darkness. At that moment several men storm into the studio armed with butcher knives, and they began to wildly attack several members of Murder Inc. These men cleaved a few of them before Ja-Rule, and his crew went running out of the studio in the darkness and the confusion.

The police questioned 50 Cent about the attack but they were unable to prove he tried to have Ja-Rule cleaved in an attempt to kill him. In February of 2003 50 Cent's album called Get Rich or Die Tryin was released. The album would become a world-wide success. The lead single of the album was called In da Club. The single broke a Billboard record for the most listened to song in radio history. The album would hit the number one spot on the Billboard 200 albums chart. Get Rich or Die Tryin would sell 8 million copies. Later a film was made with the same title about 50 Cent's life and starred 50 Cent. Other platinum selling records would follow along with other strange violent events in 50 Cent's life.

In November of 2 003 Ja-Rule released his fifth album called Blood in My Eye. The album was a pure hate and beef album against 50 Cent, Eminem, G-Unit, and Aftermath Records. Because of this album more violence would escalate in the nightclubs and on the streets. The following year in 2004 Minister Louis Farrakhan called for peace between Ja-Rule and 50 Cent which ended the beef.

Chapter 24

Among entertainers, actors, and rappers in the music industry there is one who fits the bill of all three, and yet hits a creepy nerve within the spiritual lost aspects of people today. That person would be Eminem who often goes by his real name Marshall Mathers. At strange times he goes by an alter-ego named Slim Shady.

Eminem comes from the Detroit area known as 8 Mile. 8 Mile is a poverty stricken place made up of blacks and whites living together in trailer communities surrounded by gangs, drug dealers, broken homes, dysfunctional families, drug addicts, prostitutes, satanic occults, and other down trodden to even dangerous people, but people did at times help each other. Eminem was raised by a single mom, and with one sister in the house. His mom would go through a series of abusive boyfriends. Eminem at a young age was very poor, and was raised up in the environment around him. Growing up Eminem was involved with bad behavior, and running with dangerous crowds. They would get into fist-fights, use drugs, rob people, commit vandalism, and steal cards. Later on they would get into the underground rap party scene where they would learn the style of freestyle rap battles.

Overtime Eminem would want to be a rapper, and then he discovered he had talent to rap. His life at that time was a living hell. He could barely keep a job, he was addicted to drugs, he was still committing crimes, he had a girlfriend named Kim who hated him, and a daughter as well, but he would write rap lyrics, and practice to such a point he would engage in a rap battle. According to Eminem he froze up at the sight of the crowd. He would choke and dash off the stage.

Later on something happens to Eminem that gives him the skill, and strength to re-engage the rap battle. He then beats every single person who steps in front of him. He would soon form a group, and write to eventually record demo tapes. He would work at sending out tapes of himself to such a point Dr. Dre heard one, and saw what he could do, and then signed him.

Since then he has been a world-wide platinum recording rapper and artist named Eminem. Eminem will also go down in history as one of the greatest rappers in history, but the history and the events surrounding Eminem, and his life tells a very haunting and spiritually sad story in his life and also reveals the negative influences that came from his art-form and how demonic it actually was. So demonic in fact it was seen as an influence that led to some real murders.

To understand the mind-set of Eminem is to understand that he is not a well person by any means. He is a man who carries around a lot of sick pain in his mind and has strong spiritual problems. One of these many strange events in the life of Eminem tells a revealing story about Eminem being possibly demon-possessed. This demon may have given Eminem skills to rap at the level he does. This story was told by people who knew Eminem, and even by Eminem himself.

The story centers around how Eminem came up with the Slim Shady alter-ego. This event is believed to have happened sometime after Eminem choked at the rap battle, and ran off the stage.

It was said that Eminem was at Kim's apartment one night when he went to Kim's bathroom. When he did so Eminem was looking at a mirror, and then he saw a spirit in the bathroom. The spirit had a horrible clown like face. Eminem would even describe the spirit as a demon what the Bible calls evil spirits. The demon would put a lot of fear into Eminem, and it was said that from there the demon took full possession of him.

Later on Eminem was hearing voices in his head, and he would later state that the voices in his head was the spirit of Slim Shady. He would also hear rap lyrics in his mind, and would be very inspired to rap against all comers. No one can be sure how true the story is, but Eminem often again and again in his music will rap about being demonically possessed.

When Eminem released his first album its lead single was a rap song completely about his alter-ego Slim Shady. The single would be a smash hit, and his first record would sell in the millions. His appeal and the respect people had for him in the rap industry for being a white rapper helped Eminem to bring two demographics of fans together in a much larger way than before.

With white, black, and brown fans Eminem upon entering his success into the 2000s was called the most successful artist of the 21st Century. By the time he released his album called Marshall Mathers the album being released in only one week sold in just seven days 1.76 million copies. It would go on to sell millions more throughout the weeks. Numbers like that put Eminem on a different pay-rate then most rappers in the music industry.

Eminem's influence with his fans is often very similar with Ozzy Osbourne's connection with his fans. Many Eminem fans see him as god-like, and they often find a big-brother or father-figure in him due to the fact they want to be him and they envy him. He is clearly an idol for them and he knows it, and uses it for his advantage in his fame that would always increase record sales.

Eminem seems to carry around a love/hate relationship with his fans. He is often and even hell-bent on influencing them to do terrible, criminal, and even murderous violent things. For instance after the Columbine massacre was still fresh on the minds of the people in the late 1990's Eminem did a rap song called I'm Back. In the song he agrees, and is even sentimental in a twisted way to the feelings of the two killers of Columbine Eric and Dylan. In the song he even praises their actions. These were the following lyrics from the song, 'I take seven kids from Columbine and stand'em all in a line. Add an AK-47, a revolver, a nine, a Mac-11, and this ought to solve this problem of mine. And that's a whole school of bullies shot up all of the time, cause I'm Shady.'

When Eminem was asked about this song, and why he sides with Eric and Dylan's actions he stated, 'Nobody ever looked at it from the fuckin' point of view of the kids who were bullied.' The problems with Eminem's understanding about this are in fact many.

In Columbine Eric and Dylan when they went to that high-school were not the ones getting bullied. Eric and Dylan were known to be members of a high-school click called The Black Trench Coat

Mafia. The group was not an actual mafia but they were suspected of being involved with satanic occults and ritual activity. The group promoted the teachings of the German Nazis when they were led by Hitler. They also promoted beliefs of Satanism. They were also noted for expressing murderous hatred for Christianity, and Christians in their school before they engaged in the massacre. They would even record their beliefs and put them on the internet. These beliefs included them stating they wanted to kill Christians because of what Christians believe in. They even went on to name Christians in their school they wanted to kill and during the actual massacre Eric and Dylan would end up killing those named. This click, before the massacre took place, was often known to bully the Christian kids, and other weaker kids at school.

These are facts not heard in Eminem's song. In Eminem's song he wants you to think that Eric and Dylan were victims who had enough but that was not the truth in the first place. Eric and Dylan were the bullies, and picked on people that had a known Christian faith. They would even make open death threats at them at the time no one really took them seriously until it actually happened. When it did happen, scores of teenage kids were killed. They were gunned down and murdered in their classrooms, the lunchroom, the hallways, and all throughout the school. The many victims were mostly well known Christians, and among the victims were Christian students like Rachel Scott who was named by Eric and Dylan as being one of the people they were going to murder before they did it.

The targets and true victims at Columbine were not Eric and Dylan. The real and true victims were mostly Christian high-school students. This very real fact is often not said in the media. That fact was clearly not even heard in Eminem's song. Instead Eminem and others that are like-minded want you to think that the carnage of death left-behind by Eric and Dylan was somehow heroic and a statement for fighting the bullies. Crazy enough there are people out there that would believe that and did. In Eminem's rap song maybe he gives a message to why people would believe the incorrect and evil messages of his songs. Here are some followings lyrics by Eminem, 'I take each individual degenerate's head and reach into it, just to see if he's influenced by me, if he listens to music, and if he feeds into this shit, he an innocent victim and becomes a puppet on the string.'

Eminem clearly does know that he can influence people, and is trying to influence people. He wants to speak up for people like Eric and Dylan who were a pack of thugs. Never has he spoken out about issues of poverty, homelessness, violent crimes, government corruption, or other matters of real injustices. Instead Eminem is now worth millions of dollars, and has globs of money, jewels, drugs, cars, houses, women, and all the money that can buy pleasure. The man no longer understands real issues he only raps about his own twisted and demonic views on his own life, and life that surrounds him.

When a person like Eminem can go out and tell people that in defense of Eric and Dylan we should have looked at things through their eyes is like people who defend the Nazi party, and say we should have looked at the Holocaust through Hitler's eyes. The common sense is that what we listen to does influence us, and here we have a rapper who is not sorry about how he influences people when mostly all of it is influencing people to be evil. What makes it worse is the fact that young people are by far the most susceptible to the effects of music being heard throughout their brains because of the state of large amounts of neurological development that takes place in the younger years of a person's life. So when someone is doing music to influence people to evil behavior the effects it will have on their victim's sub-conscience part of their brains will come to the surface later on to have negative effects on outcomes from certain choices in life.

When a person hears an Eminem song wherein he is declaring in his music the words, 'I think I was put here to destroy your little 4 year old boy or girl', and everyone is cheering him for that while making him rich as well, then what does it say about people who go along with cheering people for rapping lyrics like this? It says that society has become very un-sensitive about little children being destroyed because the music to the words sounds good to them. It's a sad reality indeed that sins are becoming fun in society and the Way of Jesus Christ is ignored and hated upon each and every day.

Take a song that Eminem did called Guilty Conscience wherein he raps about a series of twisted scenarios while battling with different voices in his head who are alter-egos living inside of him. Each of these persons inside him are fighting within his conscience about what choice of crime Eminem should commit. The choices they give Eminem are robbery, rape, kidnapping, and murder. Later in the song Eminem reveals that the spirit in his mind doing this to him was Slim Shady. Here is another track by Eminem where he relates demonic-possession experiences with his alter-ego Slim Shady, and here is another track that influences people to think that having demonic voices in their heads is somehow cool.

In another song Eminem did called Low, Down, Dirty he once again raps about voices in his head. In the song the voices whisper the words 'redrum' to him over and over again. Redrum is murder spelled backwards. When a person is hearing this song those words are not just playing at Eminem's mind they also become part of the mind of the person who is also listening to it. Know that millions of people heard the song, but Eminem most likely enjoys the fact millions of people have heard it, and that those words could influence them to do horrible things in their lives.

Take the song he did called Role Model, wherein he raps the following lyrics,'You can try this at home, you can be just like me, follow me and do exactly what the song says; smoke weed, take pills, drop out of school, kill people, and drink. Now follow me and do exactly what you see.'

Most of Eminem's fans would find this to be funny. The problem is that the joke is on them. Eminem does like to influence people, and if people are willing to allow him into their minds to do so Eminem is twisted enough to give them more then what they asked for. In fact, he is so twisted that he would give them a rap song where he raps about slitting his wife's throat, and stuffing her body in the trunk of his car while his kid is sitting in the backseat. In the song he drives with his small kid, and uses baby-talk to convince the child to help him dump mommy over the pier. Things like this are not about music but about pure hate and pain.

In a song Eminem did called Stan he raps about a fan who was influenced so much by Eminem that he killed his girlfriend to pay homage to Eminem. These rap songs by Eminem are not about telling stories they are about entertaining people with sick and disturbing actions of murder.

Eminem is also into promoting domestic violence. In a song called Kim, Eminem raps about catching Kim cheating on him. The lyrics then turn into a disturbing and graphic verbal assault on Kim in the song that turns into graphic sound bites of domestic violence being done upon Kim. While Eminem is brutalizing Kim with domestic violence in the song he screams out the following words, 'Sit down Bitch!, you move again I'll beat the shit out of you. Don't make me wake this baby, she don't need to see what I'm about to do to you. Quiet bitch, why you make me shout at you'. There was nothing good about that song. It does not make you feel good at the end, and really it is not supposed to. It is a song that is meant to be twisted enough to get you to think there is something macho, and hardcore about beating up girlfriends who cheat.

One time after recording the song called Kim Eminem played the song to the actual Kim in his car. After hearing it she told him he was sick. It turns out also that real and even criminal problems often happen to Eminem while dealing with Kim. Kim is not the faithful type, and even with Eminem being rich and famous she is still not the faithful type.

A day in Eminem's life can be a dangerous time indeed. Here is a day that Eminem won't forget do to the fact it made him more famous. On this day Eminem wakes up in the morning or more like afternoon hours. He would get dressed, and with a few bodyguards he would get into his car and drive off. Eminem would arrive at a car stereo shop where they fix your car stereo. Eminem pulls up in there because he sees members of the Insane Clown Posse at the same shop. When Eminem does so he grabs his automatic pistol, and jumps out of the car with it. He walks right up to a member of Insane Clown Posse, and points the gun inches from his face. Eminem then threatens to kill him or any member of the Insane Clown Posse if they ever talk bad about him again. Eminem then gets back into his car, and he drives home.

9 hours later Eminem gets back into his car to go pick Kim up at a nightclub. While Kim was there waiting for him a man named Johnny Guerra began to flirt with Kim at the club. Kim thought he was cute, and so she began to flirt back. This resulted in the two of them to French kiss in the club. Now Johnny wanted to take Kim to the backseat of his car to have sex with her. Kim would go along with that idea, and the two of them walk out of the club. They would enter the parking lot heading for Johnny's car. As they were doing so they would get closer to the car but at the same time Eminem has just entered the parking lot. When Johnny was by his car he kisses Kim again, and Eminem now sees them together. Eminem with a burst of speed drives, and pulls over to where Kim and Johnny are. Eminem jumps out of the car armed with an automatic pistol. Eminem would then walk up to Johnny, and put the gun inches from his face. Johnny now believes his life is over because he is frozen in fear. Eminem yells at him for being with his girl, and tells him he is going to kill him in this parking lot. Johnny would start begging for his life, and then Eminem started to pistol whip Johnny over and over again while he is crying.

As the crowds saw it happening many of them when they saw Eminem had a gun went running out of the parking lot yelling 'Gun! Gun!' After Eminem bashed up the face of Johnny blood-red he then let him go.

Soon Johnny went to the police, and Eminem was arrested for a double-felony charge. The first charge was possession of a gun with intent, and the second charge was assault with a deadly weapon. When Eminem got this arrest he would have a trial because of these charges at a time when his critics in the rap industry were putting Eminem down about being not really street hard. This arrest would silence his critics, and sales from his album at the time would double upon the word he was arrested for such a crime. In the rap industry such an arrest does not break your career it makes you even more popular. So popular in fact that it can inspire real danger, and a loyal bond with fans who are involved with criminal or gang activity.

By having fans like this who hold Eminem to be an idol can result in people getting harmed by devout dangerous people who love Eminem, and will harm people who they think are a threat to

Eminem. This reality was shown in the case involving Eminem at Warren City. One time a Warren City Attorney named George Constance was going to charge Eminem with crimes he stated Eminem committed in Warren City. George Constance would then make his intentions public by speaking about it in the media. A gang in Warren City called the South Warren Kids learn about it, and they were furious. They would write a letter to George Constance. In the letter they stated that if Constance went ahead in bringing charges against Eminem that they would in return start fire-bombing all city authorities, employees, and buildings with bottles full of gasoline. They stated that the reason they would do it is because they believed that Eminem was Christ, and they party in Eminem's name. Constance, out of fear, and not wanting to have anyone hurt dropped all charges against Eminem. Welcome to the strange and awful world you live in.

Another strange event of Eminem's life involved him being part of a group named D12 and a rapper named Proof. The story is a strange and unproven rumor that the death of Proof was a ritual satanic hit. The story is that the group known as D12 got involved with inner groups in the industry who are into satanic ritual hits. This hidden group would promise D12 fame, and to help their careers if they would be willing to kill someone for it usually someone in the group who they betray. That person they would pick would be Proof. The story very much comes to light when certain insiders, and other rappers noted a music video D12 did called Toy Soldiers. In the video Eminem raps about a friend of his he sees that gets murdered on the streets. The rapper they selected to play the victim in the music video was Proof. In the scene Proof is seen getting murdered, and dying in a hospital while Eminem looks on. The scene would be followed by a scene where D12 buries the victim at a graveyard.

When the video was made no one thought anything of it, but then several months later rapper Proof is gunned down and murdered. When he was buried people started to remember the video and wondered about it. That is when insiders spoke about the video being connected to a ritual hit.

Another event involving Eminem's music came from the life of Michael Miller. One day a man named Michael Miller came to his home of Glendale, Arizona. Michael was 29 years old with a wife, and two kids. That night Michael said good night to his two kids, and he tucked in his 4 year old son, and said a prayer with him to GOD because his son was having nightmares. When Michael put his kids to sleep his wife turned in early. Michael went to the living room, and there he started listening to music late into the night. One of his favorite artists was Eminem.

The night was now May 30, 2009, and the time was now passing the 2:00 a.m. hour. Into the 3:00 a.m. hour Michael turned up the volume with his headphones on, and began listening to the Eminem song called 3AM. According to Michael he stated that he felt a strange energy, and a dark demonic presence come over him. While in that state Michael states that he felt total blind and murderous rage.

Michael stated that he walked into the kitchen seeing tunnel vision, and he grabbed a kitchen knife. Michael then went to the door where his wife was sleeping, and as soon as he opened the door, instead of seeing his wife, he states he saw a demon in his mind that looked real to him. So real in fact that Michael attacks it but is actually attacking his wife. He goes crazy while stabbing his wife with the knife over and over again until she was not moving anymore. After killing his wife he then goes into his 10 year old daughter's room. His daughter is already awake, and she is in frozen fear. When Michael opens the door he says to his daughter, 'Here comes Satan. I'm the anti-Christ, I'm going to kill you'. Michael then walks up to her, and stabs her over and over again in a crazed state until she was dead. Michael then walks into his 4 year old son's room, and flips the lights on, and proceeded to stab his son 11 times thinking he killed him. The little boy, to the astonishment of many, survived the stabbing.

After killing his family Michael stated he remembers coming out of it. At the time the event to him was not remembered and so Michael wakes up from it like one does who had a blackout. Michael goes to his wife's room, and according to Michael he is in a state of shock to find his wife, and then his kids stabbed in such a way. Michael realizes that his wife and daughter are dead, and he thinks his son is dead as well. He then dials 911 for help and explains to the officers that he knows that he did kill his wife and daughter but he cannot remember doing it.

Michael would remember events later in nightmares while serving a life sentence in jail. The song 3AM is the Eminem song Michael believes caused his demon-possession. Michael was never prone to anything like this before. He was a earner with a good job, and no history with mental problems nor any mental sickness. He states that one night he heard this Eminem song, and the next thing he knows an evil spirit takes possession of him, and causes him to kill his wife and daughter.

3AM is a song that is about evil spirits taking possession of Eminem. In the music video to the song there is even a seen where Eminem is calling upon them. Truly when I think on this it reminds me what Jesus said about the fact that we must walk in the Light of the Lord holding fast to what you have in Christ Jesus.

Chapter 25

By the late 1990's the musical image, and the direction of music had gone darker, violent, rebellious, and very openly sexual. This would be the direction the music industry would lead the fans with into the 2000s. In the late 1990's the music industry would raise up two pop- stars whose careers were noted for their high-volume of sexual music, and for promoting sex among millions of fans as if it was candy given to children. The company that pushed these two pop-stars into superstardom was Disney. Before these two were mega pop-stars they were child-stars on a popular Disney Channel program called The Mickey Mouse Club in the early 1990's.

These two female artists who took over in the late 1990's where Madonna left off were Britney Spears and Christina Aguilera. The saddest story surrounding them involves Disney and The Mickey Mouse Club regarding the people who ran it. For many years there has been stories that came from people who either worked for Disney or were involved with Disney in some way of child ritual abuse that was done upon child stars of The Mickey Mouse Club. These stories go back as early as the years of the first Mickey Mouse Club. Throughout the decades the stories would surface up here, and there about more abuse being done on kids at Disney.

The stories of the abuse centers around child-stars being sexually molested, beaten, tortured, given drugs, and having adult handlers in their careers who control their lives. Another rumor was even darker that involves child-stars who worked for Disney at the time being used in satanic rituals. One stranger story involves secret mind-control programs of the U.S. government being used at underground chambers at Disney theme parks. This story has never been proven but it comes up again and again. The belief is that mind-control experiments went on at Disney areas since the building of Disney in the days when Walt Disney was still in charge.

These experiments were believed to have taken place upon children and pre-teens. Many state that the experiments still go on to this day. The common thinking regarding it is that Walt Disney was not funded by Walt Disney but it was funded by companies owned by the U.S. government.

The government wanted a place they could conduct mind-control experiments without notice so they created a front-company calling it Disney, and put Walt in charge where their aim was to make family and children's cartoon movies. They wanted a place for people where they can come, and bring their children. They would then hatch out ways into getting their hands on these children. Eventually as the story goes they would select certain children throughout the many years the company has been around, and these children would usually come from parents who are willing to sell their kids out for money. These kids would be at times beaten, sexually abused, given drugs, and then experimentations are done upon them involving electro-shock treatment and torture.

Britney Spears was casted into The Mickey Mouse Club in 1992. She joined a cast that was very popular at the time that included Justin Timberlake. In 1993 another cast member would join this group who was Christina Aguilera. Rumors of these same abuses named were also centered around The Mickey Mouse Club cast of 1991 to late 1993. Some of the more sad stories were drug abuse, and sexual abuse done upon child-stars of that cast by adults working at Disney, and adults connected with the management of those child-stars.

The even stranger stories centers on mind-control once again. The cast members like Ryan Gosling, Keri Russell, Britney Spears, Justin Timberlake, Christina Aguilera, and others were subjected to brutal mind-control experiments. It is said that these children get selected for it because their parents will go along with it. Later on, in front of their child, they will act like they don't know about it. These parents go along with it for the promise that they will be rich by their child becoming rich and famous. Some parents in the music industry even in the Disney music scene, are willing to do anything even if it harms their children to be rich.

So now knowing this story let us look into the events, and influences surrounding these two artists Britney Spears and Christina Aguilera. Let us start with Britney Spears who many believed upped the stage of depravity, and controversy as soon as she became a solo female pop-music star.

Britney was born on December 2, 1981 in McComb, Mississippi. As a little girl her mother would move her and her family to Kentwood, Louisiana where Britney was mostly raised. The parents of Britney Spears were Lynne Bridges and James Spears. Her parents would break up when Britney was young. This caused Britney to be raised mainly by her mother.

Britney's mother was very poor who often dated many abusive boyfriends. Nasty fights often erupted between these boyfriends, and Britney's mother as many of the fights resulted in domestic violence. Lynne was often known to be intoxicated on drugs or liquor. She was often hard on young Britney.

Britney's family seemed to have some connections to the entertainment industry regarding Britney's mother's side of the family. Lynne discovered Britney's talent early in her life when Britney was about 3 years old. Britney, even at that age, showed to be naturally athletic, and was able to sing. Lynne would call one of Britney's relatives asking for advice on guiding Britney's career. Soon Britney's other family members got involved with her life to help in supporting Lynne in getting Britney dancing lessons, singing lessons, and gymnastics.

Britney, from the understanding of her life, never had a real childhood. As soon as it was discovered she had talent like this was as soon as she was put to work, and trained in becoming an entertainer. After taking all these lessons her family put a lot of stress on her because they were now investing money and time to see her succeed.

When Britney was 5 years old she did her first stage show performance at a local talent show contest. Due to winning the contest her family members were now able to get her gigs at block parties, festivals, and even at bars. Britney's skills with gymnastics would also bring more attention to her as a young talented prodigy. Throughout Britney's childhood, and into her pre-teen years Britney won many state-level contests in gymnastics. This skill would make her a stronger dancer throughout her career. As Britney's family would promote young Britney's talent to anyone who would listen the story is someone did listen. This woman was Nancy Carson who worked for the Professional Performing Arts School in New York City. The story was that someone in Britney's family who some say a family friend while many others say it was Britney's mother acting on a relative's advice sent a video tape of Britney's skills to Nancy Carson. Carson was very impressed with young Britney because she saw a future star. Carson's connections to the people who help in getting people fame and success were with people wherein it was said would often take advantage of rising child stars. Carson would pay for air-fare, and a place to stay in for Britney and her mother Lynne in order to get them to fly over to Atlanta so she could meet with Britney. This would happen when Britney was 8 years old.

After talking with Britney, Carson wanted Britney to attend the Professional Performing Arts School in New York City. Someone in the Art's school's higher offices gave Nancy Carson the power to offer room and board for Britney and her entire family. They were willing to pay for all costs regarding the fees of attending the school, room and board for her and her family, food, and transportation. It was not fully clear at the time why the school would be so generous to offer this to have someone like Britney in the school. Many wonder about it to this day.

Why certain kids were selected by the school, and the school even paid them for going while all the rest of the students at the school had to pay for it. The mystery behind it is still unproven but it is a sad and criminal story.

These kids it is believed are selected because they have talent, and also they have the kind of parents or parent who would be willing to look the other way if they used their kids for sexual favors with people connected to the entertainment industry. In return those same people would get parts, and gigs for their kids to be on television, or in the movies, or doing music.

The story behind Lynne is similar to a lot of mothers who are poor, and can find no other way to make it out of these conditions along with their children. So many of them will become hard, and bitter about life. Many of them will allow someone to sexually assault their kids if in return they will help those kids become famous, and this would help them to get paid off their kids' work.

It is believed that Lynne was this kind of mother, and Britney went along with it because that is what she was taught to do by her family. To do things that are hard to do to make it in this world for herself, and her family. As soon as Britney got into the school it was not long at all when she was offered an understudy part for an off Broadway musical called Ruthless. The school wanted Britney to be Tina Denmark's understudy but the director was giving them a hard time about it.

The unproven story surrounding this event is that the director had an evil thing for being sexually attracted to children. The director noticed Britney in that horrible way and told Carson he would give her the understudy part for a favor. It was believed that Carson explained it to Lynne, and Lynne made things clear to Britney. Britney was believed to be sexually assaulted by him, and then was given the understudy part. Soon Britney was offered television commercials. Some commercials she got without having to do anything for it, while others she got from doing sexual favors to people her mother, and handlers directed her to.

Britney would soon get a major television appearance by

competing on the show called Star Search that was very popular at the time. Britney would take second-place like most stars who appeared on Star Search who lost only to later on become famous. Soon Carson and others informed Lynne that Britney was chosen to attend an audition for a part on The Mickey Mouse Club. The Mickey Mouse Club was featured on the Disney Channel, and at the time it was highly rated. Thousands of parents would bring their kids for this audition. Most of them, sadly, would be willing to do a lot of twisted things to see their kids on the show.

Disney as you just read was believed to be involved with child-abuse and possible mind-control experiments. After Britney auditioned for The Mickey Mouse Club she would receive the part in late 1992. She then began to be seen by a nationwide audience in front of millions of young people as a member of The Mickey Mouse Club on cable-television in December of 1992. She would work for Disney throughout 1993 and into early 1994. During this time is when things fall back into stories that are still unproven but believed by many.

In order for Britney to continue working on the show she was at times subjected to sexual abuse from people in the industry and working at Disney who were involved with pedophilia. Even stranger, it is also believed that Britney was even used as a subject for mind-control experiments.

In research done upon real and known mind-control victims that were filmed in Canada that research revealed the side effects to victims of mind-control. They would study the effects their mental breakdowns, disorders, and their struggles with their alter-egos had upon their minds and lives. Much of the effects shown in the video mirror the real events regarding Britney's mind-set throughout her career. In fact much of Britney's career has been shown to many psychiatrists who handle child sexual assault and satanic ritual abuse cases. The satanic case files reveal mind-control tactics used by satanic group leaders to cause their followers to commit crimes. When they watch Britney's life they often agree that there is a pattern shown in her life that is the same pattern shown in victims of child-abuse and satanic ritual abuse. For her to have this pattern it must have come from somewhere, and many point that direction to the people who abused her at Disney or under the cover of Disney.

It was believed that success, and abuse were the mainstays in her life while working on The Mickey Mouse Club as were the lives of the other cast-members. By 1994 Disney no longer had any more work for Britney Spears. At this point her mom could not afford the place they were leaving in unless Britney worked.

Since work did not come for Britney, her mom and family members were sent back to their hometowns. Britney achieved stardom in the eyes of her hometown, and was a hometown celebrity by this point. She would eventually attend Parklane Academy that was near the place of her birth. She was regarded as the most popular teen in her school. Britney was still singing and writing music. She would still practice dance moves. She nor her mother gave up on Britney becoming famous. While in high-school, Britney still did performances where she started to sing pop-songs she knew. She created new dance steps to the songs.

Soon Larry Rudolph saw her perform, and a tape was made of it. Larry would seek out to manage Britney's career to help her to become the next great pop-singer. Larry was sure that his vision for her would work, and so Britney and her mother allowed Larry to try. Larry went to three different record labels with a copy of the tape, and would promote Britney Spears as the next new pop artist, but all three of them said to him that the industry did not want another Debbie Gibson or a Tiffany, but Larry was trying to show them that Britney's image would be beyond anyone who came before her.

The reason being is that Britney's image would be more sexual, and daring then anyone who came before her. After being rejected by these three labels Larry got a fourth try at Jive Records who at the time had a strong interest in doing new pop-music. During the meeting Larry sold them on the idea of Britney Spears. The executives liked the idea but were unsure about Britney Spears because she was new to the full mainstream field. They knew that Britney was still only 16 years old going on 17, and they wondered if she could really project talent at a superstardom level. Now here is where things get strange again.

Britney begins to project a more sexual image. She agrees to a photo-shoot with her in her bedroom wearing openly her bra and panties. Her intention was to use the new photos to promote her new look. The look was very sexual and controversial, and it sparks the interest of one of the main executives at Jive Records who wants to meet Britney. It was said that Britney's mother, and Larry told her to do anything he wants, and do it well. She soon would be signed to Jive Records. Britney would then have a private meeting with the executive from Jive Records. The story is she would sexually service him. In return he got her a record deal, and she was soon signed to the label.

Soon Britney was put to work in their studios to record her first album. She would be given among the best pop-songwriters, beat mixers, and DJs working in the business at the time. They would be the real song writers, and beat and music makers of mostly all of Britney's songs from her first album to every album she did. Britney's image was to take her Disney innocent image, and raw hardcore sexuality, and fuse it together to create what the sound of her music would play like. Also she would look like the image, and present it to her fans. She would become a hyper-sexual princess.

While recording the album the recording team went to Cherion Studios in Stockholm, Sweden to finish the album. During this time many people who were working with Britney at the time saw first-hand how strange her behavior was. She would sit down at bars to turn around, and talk to a guy by taking her shirt, and bra off to get his attention. She would also enter bars underage, and no one in the bar seemed to care. She would tell people she was straight but a little gay, and she was looked upon for being shallow and strangely sexual. She also had a quick and angry temper.

When her debut album was released in the United States Britney came from Europe to the United States to engage in a shopping mall tour to promote her album. This early tour show was a three sometime four women show with Britney being the main dancer and singer.

Her shows even in this early and crude state would still generate sexual lusts from her fans as if it was electricity being shot all around the air. The tour would even increase sales of her albums. Soon Britney's lead single from her first album was released. The song was called Hit Me Baby (One More Time). This song would make her a nation and world-wide success in only a matter of weeks of the song being released.

It was also a very spiritually evil song with a real, and awful meaning to the song. It reveals darker things about Britney Spears. Hit Me Baby (One More Time) would become a number one hit song on the Billboard 100 singles chart. The single alone would sell 2 million copies. At the height of the single's success Britney's debut album would sell through those weeks 10 million copies. She released a second single called You Drive Me Crazy. This single would bring more attention to herself, and her album. Her debut album would end up selling 26 million copies, and breaking records for a debut female solo pop-artist.

 Her success was very much centered around the strong sexual messages in her songs, and the sexual image she projected. The title of the song Hit Me Baby (One More Time) is a street slang term. The real meaning of the words of the title is that she wants her boyfriend to have sex with her again. The term is used for couples who are sleeping together, and they usually are not married couples. In the music video for the song the art-form of the song gets even more twisted. Britney is dressed up as a horny Catholic school-girl, and walks down the hallways of the school in the video singing the song as if she was in heat. The video shows her singing the song this way to nuns, school-teachers, and students. She is telling them all that she wants her boyfriend to screw her once again. In fact she wants them all to be just as excited about it as she is. There are scenes in the video where the nuns, and the school-teachers look at Britney in a wanting way. It is a very creepy video, and others said the video promoted pedophilia.

Around this time Britney and her management team, that was now a vast management team, were constantly getting hit with questions about all the sexual contents in her songs and music videos. Britney was not even 20 years old when her success first came to her, and many felt that for a girl her age with fans that young that her image to them was far too overly sexual and dangerous for children. Britney would mostly wipe her mouth with those questions because she really did not care. She would instead tell meaningless stories to the press, and her fans about her boyfriends, her favorite color, what her hobbies were, and other mind-less things that didn't mean anything.

At this time several photos were linked to the press showing Britney at 16 years old taking pictures in sexual poses, and revealing her bra and panties. Many think that the pictures were released on purpose, and it was planned so that more attention would be put on Britney. The more the press reported on her the more famous she became.

The pedophilia image of Britney's photos would provoke the American Family Association to come after her. They wanted Britney's image, her album, and single to be boycotted then banned from stories. They stated that by banning Britney Spears this would send a message to people in the entertainment industry that America will not support pedophilia.

The media, which was willing to report on everything involving Britney Spears at the time, including where she drinks milk-shakes, down-played or hardly ever spoke about the banning the American Family Association had planned for Britney Spears, and the reasons for it. Due to the fact that the American Family Association did not get the support it needed to ban Britney Spears they would fail at stopping her record and image from being sold to millions of young fans.

When Britney was asked about the scandal involving the pictures and the institutions that came after her, Britney mocked them to the press and told her fans she would take those pictures all over again.

On June 28, 1999 Britney began her North America Tour. This tour was noted for the scandals involving Britney's outfits, and for appearing on stage like a hooker in heat ready to inspire hardcore sexuality to the masses.

Her performances were described by many critics to be a combination of Disney's innocence mixed with triple x sexuality. Others called it 'childhood mixed with prostitution'. Religious leaders stated that Britney Spears had zero regard for morals and Christian values. Other Christians ignored it, and allowed their daughters and sons to buy a Britney Spears CD. By the time the tour was over Britney was a world-wide pop star. She had a strong influence over millions of fans who were mostly young female fans.

One of the most twisted things involving her hit single called Hit Me Baby (One More Time) was that the song had backwards lyrics to it. When the song was played backwards the words found backwards were given an analysis. The lyrics were 'Sleep With Me (I'm Not Too Young) which was heard every time the forward lyrics Hit Me Baby (One More Time) was heard. This is a very disturbing fact because millions of people enjoyed listening to that song, and words like that are in their sub-conscience. Note that Britney's attitude about her overly sexual image is that she does not care.

She often hates it when people bring up Jesus, and Christianity to her. Her religious beliefs was often known even in the days before she was famous to be centered on a lot of superstition and witchcraft. Throughout her famous career she would wear fashion that had the number 666 on it, and would become a member of a magic occult group whose members are among some of the most famous people in the world.

In the year 2000 Britney released her second album called Oops I Did It Again. The songs on this album would be loaded with subversive, and overt sexual immoral songs. Her main fan base would be largely pre-teens, and teenagers who were mostly female. This album would sell 20 million copies, and become a world-wide smash hit album. She would embark on a world tour that generated ticket sales of over 40 million dollars. She would bring more controversy to herself for many of her sexually laced performances during the tour. At that time she started dating Justin Timberlake who she worked with as a child on The Mickey Mouse Club. This relationship would also bring headlines to them both for cheating on each other, and the egos between them. It also exposed Britney's drug abuse and gay-relationships, but people at the time loved her too much to care.

Soon Britney broke-up with Justin Timberlake. Britney's drug abuse from that time on would come up again and again. The more it came up the more people started to realize the reality of it in her life. One of her most notorious performances took place on September 7, 2000 at the VMA. When Britney came on stage to perform halfway through the performance she ripped off her black suit to reveal a very immoral flesh-colored bodysuit. This was followed by a very sexually explicit dance routine. In 2001 she would sign an 8 million dollar deal to do Pepsi commercials.

In November of that year she released her third album. The lead single from the album was called I'm a Slave 4 U. The single would become a smash hit leading the album itself called Britney to sell 12 million copies. This album as well was loaded with sexually explicit songs, and no regard to self-control. Britney would give another notorious performance at the 2001 VMA. Britney's performance there was seen as being drenched in witchcraft. In this performance Britney had a caged tiger in the background, and she was wearing an almost see through sexually immoral outfit that had small pagan images on it.

She then took a very large white python snake, and she draped the snake across her shoulders, and began to do a seductive dance with it. Many said that the performance was done to pay honor to the rebellion of Satan during his attack on Adam and Eve in the Garden of Eden. This performance was condemned by parent and religious groups for being far too sexual for children to watch, and for promoting anti-Christian values. Soon after the performance Britney's stage management team got into trouble with animal rights groups when those groups busted the staff for abusing the tiger they had in the cage.

In 2002 Britney would be caught dating Fred Durst who's climb to fame started with a song about anal sex. In that same year Justin would release what many said to be a diss song on Britney Spears called Cry Me A River. In 2003 came the notorious VMA show where Britney and Christina Aguilera perform together with Madonna where Madonna, in an undercover way picks Britney to be her replacement by putting her top hat on her. In the eyes of the fans the performance was about gay-marriage, and promoting anti-Christian values.

In November of 2003 Britney released her fourth album called In The Zone. She was now at this point an open member of the magic occult society known as kabbalah. She would have three hit singles from the album called Toxic, Everytime, and Me Against the Music. She would also, for the first time, contribute to the writing of the music by co-writing those three hit songs.

In The Zone would go on to sell 10 million copies. Britney Spears would make music industry history by being the only artist to have four straight albums to sell 10 or over 10 million copies. By 2004 Britney was all over the media that reported stories of Britney doing mindless, and stupid things wherein the stories really didn't even mean anything if everyone was only watching it just to see what they say about Britney next.

One night when Britney was very high and drunk she decided to go to Las Vegas, and marry her childhood friend Jason Alexander. 55 hours later the marriage was annulled. More of her drug use, and her nightlife episodes would be exposed by the media. The media in all its forms would not leave her alone, and followed her everywhere she went.

Britney at this time would start having sex with Shar Jackson's finance who was also pregnant with her finance's second son. This person Britney was sleeping with was Kevin Federline. When people found out that Kevin dumped Shar for Britney Spears the relationship between Britney and Kevin brought them loads of controversy. Britney, and her management team would jump on the chance to make millions of dollars off the story of this ego-driven couple.

Millions of people wanted to know all about this relationship even though it really did not truly mean anything. Britney would be paid millions of dollars to do a television program special based

on her relationship with Kevin. The special was called Britney and Kevin: Chaotic. Millions of people nationwide, and around the world sat down to watch a television special about an immoral, vain, ego-driven, and heartless couple's views on life.

Soon after this Britney suddenly wanted to become a mother, and wanted kids. Her management team and her handlers, who were often described as being abusive toward Britney, were completely against Britney Spears' choice to want kids. She also wanted to marry Kevin which was something else they were against because Kevin was already known as a male gold-digger in Hollywood.

After telling Britney not to go ahead with this Britney goes out, and gets pregnant by Kevin. With Britney being pregnant her company would lose money due to the time they lost with Britney being at home, and not on stage performing. After getting pregnant Britney told the press she was going to marry Kevin.

This made her company even angrier because the money could get tied up with Kevin. They would tell her to call off the marriage but she refused to do that. In September of 2005 she gave birth to her first child a son named Sean. In October of 2005 she would marry Kevin. In September of 2006 Britney gave birth to her second child a son named Jayden. By November of 2006 Britney just one month, and a half after giving birth to her second child with Kevin, she filed for divorce. The reason for this is often in the space of some of the story being openly shown, and some of the story still unproven.

It is believed that Britney at that point in her career was working for some very powerful people in the music industry who also had a strong control over her life. They told her what to do, and when she refused to listen to them, and began doing the things she wanted they decided to make her life a living hell. Throughout Britney's two pregnancy periods she was constantly gang-stalked by the press, and stalkers with cameras, and strangers always trying to get pictures and quotes from her. This was something she was always dealing with before but now it got worse being uglier, more vicious, and even dangerous. It was believed that the company Britney worked for wanted to use these pack of wolves to set her up and paint her in a bad way. They would follow her every day, and every time she was with her kids, or her husband, or was out shopping, or was shopping for her kids. They would yell insults at her, insults at her husband, and even her kids, they would ask her openly sexual questions, they would jam sidewalks and streets to harass her, and follow her in dozens of cars everywhere she drove.

At times it was causing Britney to have panic attacks in the middle of the street. The media would paint her as a whore for a wife and mother, and they would trash the thought of Britney being a mother and raising children. The attacks on her started to make her cold-hearted, and she began to hate herself, and sometimes the hatred was turned toward her children. Britney started to have more mental problems, and she started to talk to alter-egos in her head. She was even switching personalities right in front of people at clubs, and even during interviews. The media would turn up the attacks by looking for information to show that Britney was an unfit mother.

Rumors regarding this aim was that it was set up by people working for Britney's record company as another effort to get her back. Britney was having a lot of mental breakdowns and periods of coldness at this time. So it did not take long for the stalking press to provoke her, and even take pictures of Britney doing unwise things with her children. When the pictures were released by the media one of them showed Britney driving with her son Sean on her lap instead of being safely put in a seat with a secure seat-belt. Another was video footage of Britney walking out of a car holding her baby child in her arms, and walking toward the sidewalk. When she reaches the sidewalk she trips, and at that moment her baby's head is seen snapping back the moment she trips.

People stated that this happened because Britney did not know how to hold the baby correctly when people are around. Other events would follow released by the media regarding Britney's behavior, and being an unfit mother. Soon Britney would divorce Kevin for being only interested in himself and Britney's money. He was hardly ever there to help Britney. After the divorce the two would battle it out in court for custody rights over their children. At this time is when things got stranger, and it involves Britney possibly revolting on being used as a mind-control victim again.

This story is still an unproven story but it is a story that has some support to it when other mind-control victims' stories are told.

Around this time Britney was being pressured by her handlers, and management team to check herself into a rehab for drug and mental help. She would often refuse to do that. It was said in accordance to this story is that the kind of rehab we would think of is not the kind of rehab they are talking about. It is believed that in the industry often the code-word for being subjected to a mind-control session is called going to rehab. This practice is said to be an insider practice where it only relates to entertainers who have been mind-controlled before. The thinking is that overtime their programming would break down causing the victims to do more melodramatic things in their lives. When this is happening the handlers believe the programming is breaking down, and they need to be re-programmed which involves more secret mind-control sessions.

Of course in accordance to the story most victims of mind-control do not want to be victims again. Many of them would dread going through that again. For Britney Spears it was said they wanted her to attend this kind of rehab that would re-program her in other words straighten her out, but Britney refused to go, and was not going to relive those events again. So the story goes Britney gets away for a while without notice, and drives to an area in Los Angeles. She then parks the car, and walks into a hair salon. At this point she is in an area where everyone knows her so it is not that long before the stalkers and the press is on the scene.

When she walks into the salon she sits down at a booth looking at a mirror. She tells the hair-stylist to shave all her hair off until she is bald, but the stylist, being afraid because he knows who she is refuses to do it and he puts down the clippers.

Britney, becoming angry, grabs the electric clippers that are near the table and she begins to shave her own head until she is bald. The press all watch this sight of Britney doing this, and they cannot believe she just did that. The stalkers with cameras believe she has finally cracked up. After doing this Britney leaves the salon, and goes to get something to eat. When she reaches the front-door of the restaurant a fan comes walking out the door at the same time. She is shocked at seeing Britney bald. She asked Britney why she did this to herself, and Britney tells her a very strange statement 'I am tired of people touching me and sticking things in my head'. Many believed she was speaking about two abuses which was sexual abuse, and mind-control abuse, but at that time no one really understood what she was revolting against.

After she eats at the restaurant she leaves and walks toward her car. As she is doing so the paparazzi, who I call stalkers, with cameras began to harass her as she was on her way to her car. She quickly becomes angry and yells at them to leave her alone. One of them says a twisted insult to Britney that sets Britney off. Britney then took her umbrella, and she instantly attacked the man with her umbrella. The camera-man got so spooked that he runs towards his car while Britney chases him, and he locks himself inside his car. When he does so Britney begins to use her umbrella to bash up his car. She then turns around on the other camera-men there, and threaten to hit them if they do not get away from her. Britney finally goes to her car and she drives home.

Sometime after this event the media would use all these stories to show the world that Britney is a crazy and unfit mother. The courts during the custody battle would agree. On October 1, 2007 Britney lost all custody of her two children over to Kevin and his family. She would be granted visiting rights that would be under supervision by court approved people.

After losing custody of her kids Britney fell into a hard depression. She began to use drugs more, and began to party very hard. During that time Britney's name in the media would often be mentioned with the names of Paris Hilton and Lindsey Lohan.

Paris was some kind of model who was famous for doing a reality television show, and for releasing a porn-tape. She was also famous for her many real sexual escapades with famous men and women in Hollywood. In the nightclub scene of young, famous, and rich people Paris' is known as a drug-addict, and a trouble-maker in that world. She also has got into many cat-fights with other women over Paris sleeping with their husbands or boyfriends, sometimes even girlfriends.

Paris comes from a super-rich American family called the Hiltons. She was raised rich and very spoiled, and very shallow her whole life. The power behind her family is what brought Paris Hilton to fame. She was able to use that power to gain entrance into the media spotlight, and then draw attention to herself by getting involved with controversy over sexual affairs, drugs, and court cases.

Lindsey Lohan was a child-star now turned adult young actress. The story into her background is that she also comes from a rich family with Hollywood roots. She also as a child was trained to be an actress and entertainer. The other sad story about her upbringing is that she never had a real childhood. She was exposed to an adult, sinful scene very early. This scene would be filled with sex and drugs that young Lindsey would be exposed to. Coming into Hollywood she at first showed promise to be one day a young future movie star. By this point in Britney's life Lindsey is seen as only a few good-roles away from becoming a major female movie actress. The problem Lindsey is having is major drug problems. She often gets into legal problems with the police over drunk-driving, speeding, and drug possession. Now the media is reporting on all the rebellious, sinful, and over-all stupid events involving Lindsey, and her nightclub hopping ways.

The three names became fused together in these endless articles in newspapers, and reports on news television about Britney, Lindsey, and Paris going out to a nightclub, and getting filmed drunk and high. The other point-less stories would be the three of them flashing camera-people with their breasts, or asking the photographers if they could pump the gas for their car, or even the violent outbursts, and strange alter-ego episodes Britney would have with the stalkers and other forms of media.

Some of these stories were about pictures revealing that Britney and Lindsey did not wearing underwear when they go out to the nightclubs. In fact everything they did, no matter how stupid or pointless or even criminal, became daily around the clock stories in the media. Their names were mentioned so often that for Lindsey it would ruin her career, for Paris it would make her more famous and for Britney it made her more famous and infamous.

Britney at that time developed a bad drug addiction and became an alcoholic. The drugs that were bringing her down all the time was heroin and liquor. Britney would release a new album called

Blackout.

The album would receive critical praise for being a solid pop-music album. It was called the best album she ever made up to that point. The album would have three hit songs that became major hit songs on the radio and at the nightclubs. These songs were Gimme More, Piece of Me, and Break the Ice. Each of the songs were about lyrically raw sexual desire and energy. The music video to Gimme More features Britney playing a stripper, and dancing on a pole wearing a see-through dress. The videos are dark and laced with raw, and lewd sexual images with a twisted message that life is one big drunken orgy. The video to Break the Ice had to be completed by taking images from her other videos to fill the missing scenes. This was due to Britney not showing up at times to finish the video. Britney's drug problems, and absent minded behavior started to get in the way of doing her job.

Blackout would debut in the top ten Billboard 200 albums chart. It would also debut in the top ten music charts of several nations around the world at the same time the album came out. The album would go on to sell over 3 million copies.

The album was still considered a success but the reasons why the album did not sell more was because Britney was not interested in working as hard as before in promoting it. This caused her company not to be able to promote it more either. Britney was struggling with a lot of mental breakdowns, and drug-addictions at that time that her problem became now more openly seen.

Especially at the 2007 VMA show. Britney was to perform the song Gimme More, and when she showed up late for her performance her stomach was bloated from drinking while she was high on heroin. Even though she was in this state they dressed her up, and let her go out there. Some insiders think she was forced out there by her handlers. When Britney took the stage she moved very slowly. She would forget where to move, when to turn, and it was clear to millions of people watching that she was very high. This performance would go down in VMA history as the worst performance ever given by an A-list artist. Britney's fans were writing her millions of letters telling her to get sober and get help. Now she was being pressured more than ever to check herself into rehab. Many insiders would say that rehab was something she would try to avoid but soon her company handlers found a way using her family. This process would get started when Britney was visiting her children. This strange story would start on January 3, 2008. On that day Britney was with her two sons, and while visiting them she became overcome with a feeling of resentment, and protectiveness over her children. Due to her exasperation she takes her two sons, and goes into a room with them. She then locks herself in with them. While locked in the room with her children she begins to cry. At this point her time with her children is up according to the court ruling, and when representatives of Kevin came to pick up the kids from Britney they would be ignored by Britney when they came to her door. Britney was refusing to let them in, and she did not want them to take her kids. Kevin's people would call the police expressing concern for the children being locked in the home of Britney Spears. They would also call members of Britney's management team as well. Oddly some of them had keys to Britney's many homes. In this case it was believed that this management team acted more like her handler by now then a management team. They would enter the home with the police and subdue Britney Spears, and take her children. They would strap Britney to a stretcher, and then in front of the media would have her driven to the hospital.

The next thing you hear is that Britney is now in rehab making a full recovery as if nothing really happened, but the strange story is that a lot of things did happen. Many insiders believe that Britney was tortured at the rehab center, and was given more mind-control treatments. When she got out of this rehab her handlers or management team got court documents stating she was dangerous to her children. She was to stay away from them until further notice. They also told Britney that her record company feels she is not mentally sound enough to handler her affairs and her money, so they decided to allow Britney's father James Spears to handle all her money affairs, and to report all abuse Britney does with her money in the future.

It was believed that this arrangement was all about spying on Britney, and controlling Britney through her money being used as leverage against her. It was believed she was warned by her handlers to shape up and do her job or else.

In December of 2008 Britney released a new album called Circus that would debut at the number one spot on the Billboard 200 albums chart. It would also debut number one in several nations world-wide at the same time. The album would go on to sell 4 million copies. The album would produce two hit songs called Womanizer and Circus. Both songs were noted for their very sexually explicit music videos, and the immoral messages of the songs. The video to Womanizer featured Britney naked and lying down in a steam room while singing this song. The song appears to be about men's odious habits of looking at naked women, but the vulgarity in the way Britney presents this message does conspire against the thinking that women should not market themselves as sex objects.

The message of the song conveys not the idea that it is wrong to look at a girl as a sex object but rather that men are special because they do look at girls as sex objects. So Britney inspires that girls should look as sexual as possible to get this kind of attention. The song Circus was vain, ego-driven, and also sexual in nature. The song was about a party that turns into a wild orgy where everyone is doing it with Britney. Britney in the video represents the theme of the orgy as being a circus hence the name of the song. The song also was under analysis when the song was played backwards by several people who investigate backward messages in songs. This song also had a message heard backwards when played. The following backward lyrics were heard every time the chorus to the song Circus was heard forward. The lyrics were 'slit your wrist, hurts a little bit'.

Through this album Britney would embark on a tour that would gross 131.8 million dollars. At that time she would release another greatest hits album that produced a song called 3. 3 would become a number one hit song on the Billboard 100 singles chart. In 2011 Britney released an album called Femme Fatale, and other works would be released since 2011. In 2011 the lead single off that album was called Hold It Against Me. Hold It Against Me would become a number one hit single on the Billboard 100. Many insiders stated that the song was really about mind-control abuse being now promoted by the latest artists.

Britney Spears often lives in a dark, and bitter place called the world of fame. In this world she often feels like a slave who cannot break free. The factors that seem to work against her are being a slave to pleasures and fame, and being in contract to the record company executives. She lives in an industry that takes advantage of her, and her fans. It is clear that Britney suffers from mental sicknesses, and even stranger, people have said she suffers demonic possession. There are people who worked for her, and even ended up suing her who stated that they saw strange acts with Britney that led them to believe she was possessed.

Throughout Britney's career she has sold a combine total of albums of about 100 million copies. Such an influence clearly led to millions, and millions of her fans to embrace raw sexual immorality. The Bible calls this a sin that will ruin lives, destroy homes, cause people to murder, and can even send people to Hell. It is a home-wrecking lifestyle full of betrayals, divorces, crimes of passion, STDs, deceptions, and worse. If kids are involved they suffer the most. It is also clear that Britney's influence destroyed many lives, but try telling her that, and she would tell you to 'piss off' and that 'you're stupid'.

In fact, Britney has made it clear to people around her that she feels her fans are stupid. She also makes it clear that she is not sorry for anything she ever did throughout her career that would have influenced her fans for vulgar and bad behavior. Often when her fans meet with Britney Spears they find it strange that Britney at times will talk down to them rather than talk with them. She often comes off as fake to many people. The story behind it relates to Britney hating her fans, and having a very low opinion about them. She will often state that her fans don't understand what she has been through, and when she tells them plainly they still don't get it. Many have often said the problem with her hatred against her fans also falls in the fact she feels that she is better than them. She feels chosen by something spiritual, and her convictions and beliefs which have nothing to do with the Bible is what she will sing about to her fans. Sadly these beliefs are often no better then what a person would encounter at a red light district.

Sadly as well Britney has many Christian fans who are young teens or young adults. That fact is shocking only because you would think that by calling themselves Christians they would have also read the Bible which warns them of such influences, but sadly the Bible today is not being taught correctly, and in accordance with events happening all around the human race. This is sad because the Bible was given to the human race by GOD so they could understand what is happening around them. These Christian fans of Britney do not really understand that Britney herself is not a Christian. They don't understand that Britney does not like but uses the word hate in regards to Christian teachings. Meaning she hates Christian teachings and many times with a passion she has shown hatred for it. She seems to hate GOD at times even though GOD did not make the bad choices of her or her family in regards to events in her life.

Britney is a highly damaged person who lacks concern and compassion for others. In fact she hardly knows how to really show concern and compassion. She has only known the world of the entertainment business with its hard work and no pain, no gain mind-set, and all the abuses that comes with that lifestyle.

She clearly does need Jesus but she is too busy at hating on Jesus, and pleasuring herself. You would think her young Christian fans would know this but they don't or they don't care when they do know it. Britney Spears is a walking contradiction to her fans as well. She presents herself as an innocent Cinderella but by the end of the night she becomes a hyper-sexual demon in disguise. Her image is fake, and lately people do see more the real character of Britney Spears, and not the image she presents.

For a long time Britney got away with selling millions of children out down the road of self-destruction, and sin in the eyes of millions of parents as she did these awful works in front of them. So many of these parents didn't do anything but buy the albums that Britney Spears made for their children. It was obvious to other parents that Britney's music was harmful, and her image is really no better than a porn film at times, but for millions of other parents they allowed Britney into the lives of their children to play her music in their bedrooms to fill their brains up with the messages she was sending through her music. The results helped to greatly add to the problems of STDs, abortions, broken homes, runaway teens, drug abuse, at home violence, and more. But these parents, like her Christian fans, have very creative sayings, and speeches that have convinced themselves they were doing nothing wrong by allowing their children to watch and listen to Britney Spears. Heck they even paid for all those concert tickets Britney made so much money from.

In all their creative sayings, and speeches regarding this always remember this. A snake is a snake. You cannot look at the snake, and think to yourself that it is not a snake when it really is a snake. You cannot look at the snake, and think it's not a snake then go inside its cage thinking that after it strikes you while putting venom in you that nothing is going to happen to you. Because overtime the poison gets you. Many people were looking at a snake, and told themselves it was not a snake while walking right into its cage to get bit. But to this day many of these fans still don't think there was anything wrong with Britney Spears. While the truth showed a lot of things wrong with Britney Spears.

Her music gives you a very good insight into the mind of Britney Spears. Even though Britney did not write most of her songs she still stands by them, and won't do a song unless it speaks to her soul. A soul that has a lot of darkness in it. The music of Britney Spears are songs filled with sexually explicit lyrics that is used to corrupt the imaginations of millions of people who are mostly children, pre-teens, and teenagers. Many of those teenagers have now become young adults.

Britney's message to the world is best heard in songs like Soda Pop. In this song Britney sings the following lyrics, 'I bet you can pop like we've never popped it before. It's cool Britney when we get down on the floor and we go on and on until the break of dawn.' There was actually people who thought when they first heard the song that Britney was singing about drinking soda. Many people clearly know what the song is about. It does not have anything to do with soda even though the title of the song is Soda Pop. Soda Pop is a drink that young people mostly like. It is an image of childhood because people started drinking soda in their childhood. In the sub-conscience then the word would remind you of something innocent, and even un-alarming and cute. So the title is used to draw young people to the song. When they hear the song they hear Britney not singing about childhood memories but singing about a hardcore sexual encounter. Keep in mind Soda Pop is a title that can draw people as young as 9 years old to listen to the song, and this is what those 9 year olds would be listening to, a song about a hardcore sexual encounter.

To understand this better most people know that 'pop' is also a street metaphor or a slang-word for fornication. Britney's song was in fact a perverted message with a title aimed at children. It was a message to embrace a sexual encounter told in a pop-music innocent way but said in an understanding that is known on the streets as having sex with a girl in a hardcore way. Most children won't catch it at first until they reach pre-teen years, and they begin to understand slangs better because their idols say them, and sing about it.

Soon they catch what it means, and worse they begin to like it. In fact when Britney was talking about her album that released the single Soda Pop she stated that the song Soda Pop was her favorite one to date. At the time Britney said this most of her fans were very young. They were mostly children, pre-teens, and teenagers. Because Britney said this they in turn wanted to listen to Soda Pop over and over again, and give the song their full attention because it's Britney Spears' favorite song.

Now millions of very young minds are listening to a song about a girl being screwed like a porn star throughout the entire night. Such a song robs people of the profound wisdom of GOD. It robs people of the beauty and safety of marriage. It robs GOD himself of glory due to people being turned away from GOD by enjoying songs like this. The song clearly is aimed to corrupt young people's morals, and effect their lives with the damages that sexual immorality can bring.

Britney's fans are mostly females as well. Satan used a female namely Eve to seduce Adam into eating the fruit of the Knowledge of Good and Evil wherein they fell from a state of Paradise into a world of blood, sweat, pain, tears, and sadly sin.

To see the aim of Satan in Britney's life is to know that those millions of female fans of Britney Spears will be inspired to live the kind of life Britney sings about. Many of those millions will in turn seek wild sexual immoral relationships, and many of those millions will also end up with serious problems because of it. When they seek out these unrestrained relationships a lot of young men will be seduce by them. They in turn will lose sight of morals, and forget all about GOD. Other young men will take advantage of these young girls by playing on what they want, and what feels good to them. The results are relationships in turbulent conditions, and with rapacious intentions. This is a major goal of Satan because it sets up divide and conquer among young men, and women which will affect them for years to come. This will create unstable relationships which can lead to unstable families. The costs of sexual immorality is often very clear. This is why Jesus tells us to avoid sexual immorality, and pray for self-control and guidance. This world is in the grip of waves as large as oceans when it comes to sexual immorality.

Many people are taught that it's no big deal when the results tell you otherwise. People go to Hell over it because they become so addicted to it that they won't stop, and they speak of GOD in an awful way because they love that sin so much. They love it so much they have no problem with dealing with the problems it causes. Some people end up in jail or killed over the problems. Some people die of horrible STDs and AIDS over the problem. The problem has led to millions of unwanted or un-excepted pregnancies. The problem has led to millions of abortions. The problem has led to millions of deaths world-wide from deadly STDs. The problem has led to millions of divorces. The problem was led to millions of broken homes. The problem has led to millions turning away from GOD. The problem was led to teen runaways. The problem has led to higher rates in school drop-outs, and drug abuse among the youth that often goes hand and glove with sexual immoral scenes.

As the Word of GOD states we reap what we sow, and lately people have been sowing some awful deeds into the roots of the nations of the earth. Britney's bad behavior often inspires people to act just like her. Young girls will also go to nightclubs not wearing any underwear under their dress. Young girls will also drive their car recklessly down the street. Young girls will also score cocaine, and snort it while looking for the nearest guy to screw that night. Young girls will also go out, and pose naked on the internet, and even pose for porn magazines. Young children as young as 8 years old will come to a Britney concert dressed like and dreaming about being her. Erratic and rebellious behavior will be the mainstays of their lives because it is what idols like Britney Spears promotes. Britney is also not for righteous causes either.

Every media story that the media wanted to praise, and every terrible, heartbreaking, and horrible events our government has done or promoted when the media needed idol stars to encourage the people to go along with such events Britney was a go to person for them as well. She would support these awful leaders, and events not because she believes in any of it but because it helps her career to play along with a marching band that is leading our country, and the world to its doom.

Britney's wide ranging message is a message said by many before her. It is a message coming from what the Bible would call an anti-Christ message. Take the song Britney recorded called If U Seek Amy. The true meaning behind this song when the song first came out was better understood by the youth who heard it then their own parents. One day at a grade school a teacher who was watching the children playing on the school's grounds heard a little girl singing the following lyrics, 'Love me, hate me, say what you want about me. All the boys and all the girls are begging to f-u-c-k me.' The teacher became shocked, and took the little girl to the side to tell her to stop singing that song. The teacher would also ask her where she heard a song like that. The little girl replied that it was Britney Spears new song. The song the girl was talking about was If U Seek Amy.

The real meaning of the song was actually being song by the little girl who had to teach the adult teacher what the song really meant. The song's title is actually a play on words to suggest another meaning then just If U Seek Amy. The chorus line is actually sung in a way to deliberately spell out a different meaning. The sounds of the chorus do not come out or even come off as If U Seek Amy, but it comes off as If=F You=U See=C Ka=K My=Me. So shockingly enough the true chorus of the song is 'all the boys and all the girls are begging to f-u-c-k me.' This was a popular song among children, pre-teens, and teenagers. The music video was very sexually explicit, and took on the appearance of a massive orgy going on in a young wife's bedroom. Britney in the video plays an all-American wife by day but inside her home, which would represent the world the character is in others cannot see the young wife is having sex with dozens of men and women, even having sex with them all at once. This was the message sent to the sub-conscience brain to millions of fans who received it so well they were singing the song on schoolyards. By the time this song came out there was hardly an uproar against it. People were by this point used to Britney's shock image and music. They were mostly content with it, and parents did not seek with passion at all to see the song banned from the air or from record stores. People by this point had become use to this art-form, and started to sadly see it as normal.

For the people to get use to an artist whose image was a blend of childhood innocence, and hardcore sexuality shows that Britney may not be the only one among an elite of artists who have been brain-washed and mind-controlled, but the millions and millions of fans often displayed behavior of being brain-washed and mind-controlled as well. It's just that for the people it's a different method done against us. Its main tools are television sets and CDs. The purpose is to brain-wash us to like them, and buy their products, and defend them at the drop of a hat to secure ourselves in the knowledge that we believe in the works of these artists. It really can be just as stupid as that, and we were all guilty of it.

Britney's strange connection to mind-control is also shown in her music. Take the song Hold It Against Me that became a number one hit single. The song comes off as being about a woman who meets a stranger at a nightclub, and wants to have a one night stand with him. As bad enough as the meaning of the song is the music video tells a different story. In the video there isn't guy, no club, and no sex. In the video we see Britney trapped in a giant cylinder with television screens all around where the image is showing a nightmare world under watch. Britney is attached to intravenous lines while wearing a white wedding gown. Many insiders believe that the video is about her mind-control state. The high-tech devices in the video are said to be seen as tools they use to monitor and program Britney to leave her in a mind-controlled prison built around her, and affects her mind.

The scene is also said to be a symbolism of Britney being mind-controlled and watched by people in the music industry. In the video she is closed off to the outside world, and can only see the images that are fed to her which are images her handlers want her to see. The white wedding gown Britney wears many insiders feel that it represents either a ritual sacrifice in the understanding of ancient pagans who killed virgin women making them into human sacrifices, or it could mean the dying of innocence which means to be ripped apart in all kinds of ways.

When Britney sings the chorus in the video she then starts to levitate in a very creepy way. While she is floating in the air strange eyeless evil spirits emerge from her under-gown appearing as soul-less dancers. The scene is believe to be a symbolism of demonic possession. Britney's eye in the video is shown for a half of a second as having two pupils. Many believe it was a hidden message of the alter-egos that live inside the body of Britney Spears. During the breakdown of the song Britney's IV lines start spilling out colored paint upon her rather than blood all over her white dress. Many believed that the paint actually represented blood, and as this scene goes on the monitor shows images of Britney's youth.

Many believed that the meaning was very sick showing the abuse of childhood rape as a means of a sacrifice. The video ends with a dance number showing Britney dressed as an S&M diva engaged in an immoral dance with a group of male dancers. The story of Britney Spears is sad indeed.

The story of Christina Aguilera is also sad, and twisted as well. Christina Aguilera was born in Staten Island, New York on December 18, 1980. Her father was an Ecuadorian, who was a U.S. Army soldier named Fausto Aguilera. Her mother who was Shelly Loraine, was a violinist and pianist. According to Christina, and other people who have looked into her life, Christina's parents were said to be physically and emotionally abusive toward Christina throughout her childhood, and young teenage life. It was believed that Christina was often a victim of child-abuse, and her parents were very controlling of her life. Her parents would divorce when Christina was six years old but they still held full and abusive control on her life.

As a little girl her talent to sing was discovered very early by her parents who sought to develop her talent. Her mother would have her trained, and would move to Rochester, Pennsylvania after her divorce from her husband. In this town Christina's talent became known when her mother signed Christina up for local talent contests. Christina would win many of them, and locally in the town she became known as the 'little girl with the big voice'. At age 8 Christina won a major talent show contest that brought attention to people who worked for the show Star Search. The story regarding this is a little strange, and there are two sides to the story.

One side is that Christina's mother made a video tape of Christina winning the talent show. She sent the tape to people at Star Search who watched it, and sought out Shelly to bring her daughter on the show. The other story is that Christina's father used connections he had in the military to talk with people connected to the entertainment industry. It was believed by some insiders that Fausto was connected to people who worked in mind-control, and using artists to make them stars in order to keep people brain-washed.

The story is that these people were a secret group made up of people working in the CIA and the FBI who work with the military on black ops projects. Fausto it is believed came into their company by offering his daughter to them to help them in their efforts. This would also bring his daughter to riches and fame which would result in him, and Shelly getting rich as well. It is believed that these military connections got Christina her appearance on Star Search, but there is no proof to this story.

When Christina appeared on Star Search it was in 1990. She would lose the competition coming in second place where Christina joins a list of artists who came in second on Star Search, and then later on became famous. Her run on Star Search would grant another gig for Christina. When she returned home she would sing the Star-Spangled Banner at a Pittsburgh Penguins hockey game.

In 1991 Christina attended Marshall Middle School. When she got there her family made the choice to keep Christina's career, and talent a secret from the other kids at school due to the fact the school was noted to have many bullying students who would quickly hate on someone like Christina Aguilera.

That same year when Christina first attended Marshall Middle School her mother Shelly got Christina an audition that she was very serious about. It was an audition to be selected to join the cast of The Mickey Mouse Club on the Disney channel. The other story to this audition once again goes back to Christina's father Fausto.

To understand it better, Disney is very much suspected of being involved with secret government mind-control experiments. Fausto was suspected of giving his daughter over to government mind-control experiments. So when Disney came calling it was believed that it was already planned out that way. Christina would get her chance, and if selected the deal is she would also be used as a mind-control subject. No one knows how true this is but it does often ring many bells in people's heads who look into this subject with the connection with Disney, mind-control, and young artists.

When Christina got the audition she was soon taken to Disney Studios to audition. Usually what happens is that if they see you got the talent and the looks, and they feel it will be better developed a year or two down the road then what they do is they promise to sign the person later. It means the artist will be selected to join the cast in one or two years. If they see you have the goods now the artist is put on the show right away.

When Christina did the audition she was selected to join the cast two years from then due to her very young age. In that time she would graduate from middle-school and enter high-school. When she was in high-school Christina officially joins the cast of The Mickey Mouse Club in 1993. A cast that included Britney Spears, Justin Timberlake, Ryan Gosling, Keri Russell, and others. Her cast-members were so impressed with Christina's charm, and voice they nicknamed her 'the diva'.

It was believed that the abuses that Disney is believed to be involved with like mind-control abuse, and child abuse against their child stars, were abuses that harmed Christina Aguilera as a child star. The story is that Christina's parents often looked the other way, and pretended not to notice or know when people at Disney or who were with Disney were abusing their daughter Christina. Like Britney Spears, Christina Aguilera is also believed to be a victim of mind-control torture, and a victim of sexual assault. The difference between Christina and Britney is that Christina handles her pain better in the eyes of the public. She is much better at keeping her inner demons hidden wherein Britney exposes her demons for everyone to see.

Following her television appearances on The Mickey Mouse Club Christina would return to her high-school where now her high-school peers knew Christina was a Disney television star. Instead of the popular status it brought Britney Spears, for Christina it brought hatred and discrimination toward her from the high-school students. This hatred was brought on by the jealous nature of her high-school peers who would also call her racist names like half-breed, or racist names that are used at people of Latin heritage.

Christina became a constant victim of bullying, and was constantly made fun of while walking down the halls, sitting in the classroom, and going home from school. Soon the bullying would start to turn violent. One day Christina was threaten with violence from other students when coming home from school. This caused her mother to pick up her daughter herself from school.

One day when she went to do so she parked the car, and went to meet Christina by the school's door to safely walk her back to the car, and drive her home. When they got to the car Christina, and her mother saw that some high-school students had slashed the tires of the family car. Very soon after Shelly took her daughter Christina out of that school, and began to home-school her instead.

Sometime later Christina would no longer be working as a cast-member on The Mickey Mouse Club. Her mother, and other people working with Christina would now direct her career at doing music aimed at older crowds. They started to find gigs for Christina by looking into several nightclubs to see if any of them would hire her, but none of them would give her a shot because of her teen age. Then it was believed that Christina's mother was given some advice to try Christina out at homosexual nightclubs. Christina's mother would do so, and soon one of the gay nightclubs hired Christina. Christina's performances would impress the owners of the club to such a point they made Christina a prime act at their club. This took place around 1997, Christina, still a teenager, was a nightclub act at a gay and lesbian nightclub in Pittsburgh called Pegasus Lounge. Christina got the spot when her mother, while listening to that advice, enrolled Christina into the club's talent show wherein she won.

Afterwards the owners being impressed by her gave her a regular spot. It should be noted that the straight nightclubs did not hire Christina due to the fact she was underage and still a teenager. They felt she should not be in a place exposed to an adult scene of drinking, and people looking to have sex that night. They felt she was too young for it. But this gay nightclub had no problem with it. And sadly due to the influences, and friends Christina made at this club she would turn bi-sexual at the club.

At this time Christina's performances were still being sent to Disney as a way to get Christina signed to a record label they own. Disney in fact owns several record labels in the music industry.

Soon a project came up for Christina while Disney was making their animated film called Mulan. It is believed that the people at Disney connected with the music industry had not forgotten about Christina. They still wanted to use her but not for adult music or contemporary music but they wanted another pop-singer. They wanted another talent that would sell sex like a can of coke.

Disney would call up Christina to record a song for the soundtrack of Mulan. The song was called Reflection. The single would become a hit on the Adult Contemporary Chart. Soon executives from RCA Records had a sit down with Christina wherein they express they wanted to sign her, however they did not want a contemporary singer they wanted a female pop-singer.

They wanted to put her in touch with the best DJs, pop-songwriters, and mixers while changing her image to a sexual teenage siren. The people at RCA foresaw the direction of where pop music was going, and they wanted a star who would sing very sexual music that would appeal to where young girls were heading, which was into more of an open lifestyle of sexual sin. Christina didn't see anything wrong with that. She does not believe that a sexual open lifestyle to have sex with all kinds of men, and even members of the same sex is a sin. In fact Christina was a new ager before she was famous. She did not have Christian beliefs at that time. In fact there does seem to be some Christian involvement when she was a child but it was not present with her when she was a child star, and a nightclub entertainer. When she came into her young adult stage she was very removed from Christian beliefs, and eventually throughout her career she comes to show that she hates Christian beliefs.

There is a darker story regarding her being signed to RCA Records. Some insiders believe that there was more than just the record company telling Christina they were going to use her to sell sex in music. These ones who state this story believe that Christina was shown a darker, and satanic aspect of the music industry. They believe she came in contact with a satanic ritual contract of selling one's soul for a record contract, and becoming famous.

Strange enough often the dealings of the music industry involvements with satanic activities come up all too often when stories like this come out. For Christina it was believed she sold her soul during the ritual, and by serving Satan she became demonically possessed, but this story has never been proven. Christina would sign on to RCA Records. The people at RCA would change her image, and their musicians, mixers, and writers would put together the songs for Christina to sing. She would soon record her first album, and in 1999 it would be released under the title Christina Aguilera. The lead single from the album was called Genie in a Bottle. This song became a huge smash hit, and quickly became a number one hit on the Billboard 100 singles chart. The song would make her world famous over-night. From her debut album she would have a total of three hit songs the other two songs being What a Girl Wants and Come On Over Baby (All I Want Is You). The album would go on to sell an astounding 17 million copies.

Christina was now a world-wide A-list pop star. She would go on to project an image of innocent but raw sexuality. Her career was different from Britney Spears but also in many ways their careers were a mirror to each other, and they both would find themselves in the lead in the pop music scene selling sex to millions of young fans all over the world. The song Genie in a Bottle does have a strange, and even hidden meaning to it when you look at a number of studies into the song.

Genie in the Middle East is another word for evil-spirits meaning demonic spirits. Demons are believed to appear as genies who seek souls by granting them sinful pleasures in order to snare their victims. In the Middle East, and even in Asia this is believed as well. The Bible speaks about members of the human race losing their souls for all the pleasures of the world. The world is spoken about in the Bible as being the realm that Satan controls through people who serve him.

The Bible also speaks about people giving up their souls for a wild and depraved world filled with sinful entertainment. This matter about selling one's soul is a matter that the Bible calls real. People who don't know the Bible won't think it's real, and others won't care but for Christians they should know that the matter is real according to the Bible. When you listen to the lyrics of Genie in a Bottle Christina sings of herself as being the genie, and if a boy rubs her the right way, and pays the kind of price she wants him to pay then she will allow that boy to have all kinds of sex with her. This is the open understanding of the song meaning what the song means to the general public which is bad enough.

Horrible enough is to watch 6 to 10 year old girls dressed up, and singing the song in their bedrooms or at Christina's concerts. The hidden meaning as told by some insiders is that the song is actually about Christina's experience of selling her soul for world-wide fame and riches. The thinking was she was singing the song from the viewpoint of Satan offering her all that she really

441 | P a g e

desires which are the lusts of the world. The chorus of the song may seem like it's singing about a sexual act but yet the melody and lyrics of the song talk more about a mind-set rather than a sexual act.

The song seems to combine a highly sexually suggestive message with a hidden darker meaning. Her mind-set in the song battles with what her body wants but her mind keeps telling her to stay away. Her 'body' in the lyric seems to represent her desire for fame and power which are the lusts of the world. Her 'heart' in the lyric which is telling her no, represents her soul. This brings the meaning forth that Christina is singing about someone who has the power to make all her dreams come true but the price for it is her soul.

Most of the album's song were filled with an overload of sexual innuendo and lust. They were songs about sexual passions, and pleasures sung to very young pop music fans. Starting out Christina's music and image would be sexual with a mask of taste. But soon her music and image invoked the kind of feelings into her fans wherein they did not know if they should dance or start masturbating.

Many of her songs, eventually through future albums, would become twisted and very perverted. Her music videos would also become far more explicit and filled with obstinacy. In 2002 after releasing other successful albums, Christina would revamp her image. She would change her hair color to black, and change her look from highly sexual to hardcore sexual. Her appearance in this look would be darker, more lewd, and very depraved.

Her songs and image would become very more overly, sexual then before and pornographic. The album Christina released that came with this more hardcore image was called Stripped. Stripped was released in 2002, and it was Christina's fourth album by then. This album would also sell millions of copies around the world. The songs and image would bring a hailstorm of controversy upon Christina. Many insiders feel it was planned out to bring controversy to Christina.

Christina at times would often be overshadowed by Britney's

sexual and twisted episodes in her life that were often over-exposed by the media. Christina and Britney are also rivals who make their careers in the same field of pop music where they sell their millions of records to the same fan base group. Britney getting all the attention was bad for business regarding Christina Aguilera, so Christina not looking to be undone would do one better. She would upstage Britney in that time, and go completely sick with her songs and image. This was the thinking by many at the time regarding the album Stripped, and the new image. The lead single for the album was a song called Dirrty. Dirrty, a song about a woman who could screw a whole football team of men in one night, and still be up looking to have sex with more men. The music video for the song was even worse than just listening to the song. Nearly every scene in the video was filled with over the top obscenity and smut. It was non-stop depravity. The video was truly akin to pornography to such a point that the video is not shown on internet systems that have porn-blockers. Christina in the video plays a character that is seen as the champion of hardcore sex. In the video she presents herself in a half-naked gothic manner dancing in boxing rings, gym showers, etc, with all kinds of men.

In the lyrics and video she is presenting herself as the champion who can have sex with dozens and dozens of these men in one night, and still be standing. During the controversy many parents who once allowed their daughters to listen to Christina expressed their outrage to her for the song and the music video. Christina would never give any apology, and instead she states to all those parents who complained against her the following words, 'I do what I want, it's not my job to raise your children.' Christina after making these cold statements to show forth what she truly believes in decides to show further to whom she has given her spiritual life to.

Christina's name comes from the word Christian. Christina for a long time never really liked her name. So she decides to re-name herself by calling herself Xtina to drop the word Christ from her name. She becomes at that time more open about her New Age faith, and even starts to pose for pictures for magazines and events involving witchcraft. Christina's new look also came with several new tattoos and piercings wherein some of the tattoos are occult symbols. During the release of this album, and during

The Stripped Tour Christina would generate more controversy over her slutty image, and for her over the top sexually charged shows that often made Madonna look like a backseat cheerleader compared to what she was doing.

Christina was clearly causing a lot of spiritual damage in that time. She was promoting all kinds of sex in all kinds of ways, and openly hated on Christian values and marriage. She would promote homosexuality to fans as young as 7, and she promoted witchcraft as well. She would go on to make open statements about living a sexual lifestyle that is no better then what a prostitute does as being acceptable for all people. She wants her fans to think that such a way of being is not harmful, and she has no problems leading young children down there as well. She appears to, simply just not care about anyone but what she feels is good for her. If she feels that such practices are good for her then she could care less how it effects your sons and daughters.

To understand better; if your son one day watches a video of Christina singing about having rough sex in the shower, and then gets inspires by it to the point that he rapes his girlfriend in the shower, then you should know that Christina couldn't care less. Throughout her career Christina would do more albums, and do more photo-shoots with the same hardcore satanic sexual themes. She would do even more photo-shoots with witchcraft themes to them, and would promote black magic.

Not too long ago Christina released an album called Bionic. When the album was released the title on the front cover was spelled Bi-On-Ic. It turns out that it was spelled that way on purpose because the title was a code-word. The code-worded title is believed to be related to Christina. It is a slang word for some underground gay scenes. The meaning of the code-word is 'bi-sexual on ice'. It refers to a person who likes to go both ways during sex when they are high on crack-cocaine.

The photo-shoots for the album were also strange as well. The photos had many mind-control themes to them. The form of mind-control the photos often related to were believed to be called beta-programming. This type of mind-control program is also called sex-kitten programming. Some insiders state that this program is a common program given to people who mostly star in pornography films or are in the entertainment industry.

Most of the victims of this program are believed to be female. The torments of sex-kitten programming are shown throughout a music video Christina did for the album Bionic. The music video was for the lead single off the album called Not Myself Tonight. The song has explicit lyrics that Christina wanted to share with the world. The lyrics are, 'The old me is gone, I feel brand new and if you don't like it, fuck you!'

The 'brand new' Christina was talking about her new image that came with the album. Christina added to her dark image a more cyborg look added with S&M fashion, and looking more like a red hot demon. Some of her fans accused Christina of copying the cyborg theme from Lady Gaga because Christina as well does the one eye sign with her hand. The one eye sign is an occult symbol I will explain more about later. But many feel that Christina was not copying Lady Gaga but was only continuing the trend of brainwashing their fans by promoting hidden activities in front of them like mind-control.

It is believed that Lady Gaga is also a mind-control victim, and often promotes mind-control knowledge into her songs and videos. Christina was not noted for doing too many mind-control themes but due to the change in the industry a direction has been taken by record company owners to promote hidden and dark themes like this in music. They would never openly say that they are but they also give no answers to why they are there, and why so many artists are doing them.

Christina was simply changing with the new direction and image that music had now become. In many of the scenes of the Not Myself Tonight video Christina in her character in the video is shown throughout many of the scenes being dehumanized and dehumanizing others. There are short, cut away scenes which shows her being tortured and in some cases liking it. In one scene Christina is shown as being hog-tied with her eyes forced open which is a form of mind-control abuse. Victims of this abuse had been hog-tied, had their eyes forced open, and would tape or attach a device to their eye-lids to prevent the victims from being able to shut their eyes. At this point the victims are forced to watch certain videos that would reinforce their programming.

During the process of the programming victims will be physically, and sexually assaulted at times while watching these videos. During this type of torture the victims' minds begin to break which open the stage to create alter-egos in their brains. Soon the development of this brutal process will cause victims to think pain is pleasure and during sexual acts with their handlers they will beg their handler to slap them, whip them, tie them up, beat them, choke them, and other disturbing acts during sex. In Christina's video there are a lot of acts of sexual satanic practice themes.

Many scenes in the video show Christina behaving like a cat which was common among sex-kitten victims, and wearing black leather to represent an S&M lover who uses a leather whip during sex. Sexual torture was very common among mind-control victims, and they were eventually condition to like it. The art-form of the music industry also inspires millions of people around the world to be condition to start thinking that sex and violence mixed together is 'hot', and people should be doing it.

Strange enough the artists they use to condition people to think this way are artists believed to be themselves under a form of mind-control. In the music video Christina is seen passing through doorways leading to higher rooms, and is seen destroying her old clothes in the closet by setting them on fire. The scene is believed to be a symbolism of Christina proclaiming she is no longer the same person, and that she is now schooled in occultism and the industry. It is believed that she is representing herself as an insider working with more knowledge then her other peers about things hidden from the view of others.

The music video would also have a final series of scenes of Christina, and her dancers performing their slutty dance moves inside a Christian Church. As they do so they then do moves to reveal to the viewers that they are having an orgy in the Church. To do a scene like that is to insult the faith of Jesus Christ called Christianity today. She shows a strong willingness in the scene to corrupt people's values and destroy their faith in GOD.

Chapter 26

Lately in the entertainment industry, and largely in the music industry many fans today thanks to artists like Jay-Z, Lady Gaga, Rihanna, and others have been hearing the word Illuminati. Many people have all kinds of views, and discourses to what the Illuminati is.

Some people have given very good teachings, and backing it up with solid historical events, and documents that supports what the true Illuminati is. While others have given some very far-out, and deceptive views on the Illuminati. Others have even supported the Illuminati by liking it in one way or another, and they wish to find a way to join themselves including their families to the Illuminati even though they don't know what it really is. The general thinking about the Illuminati among the fans, and masses of people who have not learned the true face of the Illuminati is that it's a secret order of rich and famous people who are able to buy the world, re-shape government, and life-changing events. Oddly though these same folks who know this but don't do any research into it believe it's generally not real, and that it's more likely a club among famous artists to show off the power and success they enjoy to the entire world.

In truth most people don't know what the Illuminati really is. That is because even when they hear the word Illuminati they don't understand how to research it without running across information on the internet, and other places that would mislead them or confuse them. To really learn about it a person is going to have to take a lot of time researching many subjects about bankers, secret powerful occults, and groups, also events relating to the Bible happening in our world today, history involving government rulers past and present, why wars get fought, why leaders have been killed, and so many other various subjects. By the time they are done they have been awaken to the reality of the world. Afterward a person studies at putting everything he or she learns together along with the history, the events, and then at that point a person has a better understanding of what the Illuminati really is. So let me share some of that understanding with you so that you can better understand that music industry stars like Jay-Z,

Kanye West, Lady Gaga, and others today, and in the past could have never been real, and true inside members of the Illuminati, but what you will come to find is that the business called the music industry, made up of all of its companies and artists, is owned by people who would be the real Illuminati today.

The Illuminati from the proper research into it is an old order that has been here for thousands of years having had many different names throughout those many centuries. What connects the generations, and cultures of high elite people who have been its select core members is a common faith. The faith is believed to be the worship of Lucifer which according to the Bible is the worship of Satan. The Illuminati also believe that Lucifer is a fallen angel that fell from the presence of GOD, but they believe that one day Lucifer will receive the planet earth for good, and defeat the second coming of GOD. The Illuminati holds very firm to this deception.

So next question would be who are the Illuminati, and what is this all about? To understand that is to understand events of today, yesterday, and to understand the true face of power in the world of nations. Usually people who see openly the power structure rather through media, newspapers, and other outlets would come to see that the world's power structure oddly resembles a triangle. That should be noted because pyramids are built from the idea shape of the triangle. This power structure is suppose, to be, mainly what we see openly as governments, corporations, and bankers.

The governments are suppose to be the watch-dogs of the corporations and bankers. The corporations are to report any foul dealings with the banks to the government officials. The bankers are to act in accordance to the laws of the nations the banks are centered at. This three-fold cord are the fields that govern the entire world as you know it today. Without those fields you would see nothing like what you are seeing today. These were fields that even the Bible states that GOD created so that nations would be born and governed. Of course GOD would leave those nations to the hands of men who would in the many not serve GOD but to serve what the Bible would call serving Satan.

Therefore, the reasons for war, poor people, sicknesses, and other horrible events come from the choices of men and women who make very bad choices. GOD has given the human race the power of free-will, and allowed free room for free-will to be played out by the choices of men and women. GOD does not always stop bad things from happening because it would violate the play-room of free-will. Knowing the power structure that is seen openly what people are finding out today is that the current reins of power are no longer in the hands of governments but have fallen into the hands of bankers, and the corporations do the bidding of the bankers.

This is hard to believe for many because they have lost sight of events in the last 200 years that led up to this current state of affairs. They also don't know that these events have been planned out for a long time. It is believed that the bankers who control the Federal Reserve System, and all major and central international banks also own Wall Street. They bought out every corporation, and media outlet all over the world. It is believed they also bought every nation on earth including the United States of America by controlling, holding, and printing the money supply of every nation of earth by using its notorious and corrupt banking system.

It is believed that they did this through causing nations and corporations to go into debt using the stock exchange rates they control. By putting them into debt, these bankers will step in, and loan those nations, and corporations money to get them out of debt. They will also charge interest with the loan that will be high. Those nations and corporations have a debt with the bankers, and this brings much power over to those bankers. Those bankers can now have access into controlling the governments and corporations of the nations of the earth. They can access any secret they want, and use them in any way they want because they control their money, and put them all in their debt.

The problem is this true condition is not shown to the general public because it would cause an uproar and a panic. So the three fields work together by making people think everything is okay while brainwashing them to accept global ideas and a new world order. Why global ideas? Why a one world government?

Because since the bankers own everything, sooner or later they will have to unite everything under one major company which will be the company called one world government with a world leader for a figure-head.

When the Bible talks about the anti-Christ it was talking about such a person who would lead a world empire under a new religion. This religion is worshipped by the order called the Illuminati. So how does the Illuminati fit into all this? The bankers, corporations, and governments all have to work together to bring all the nations under a world system but they also know they have to create a new world religion that would unite people. In order for them to do that they must bring down Christianity, and promote the New Age faith all over the media out-lets.

That is where the entertainment industry comes in. It is believed that it is used by the corporations to promote new age lifestyles and ideas. All three of these massive fields are made up of a lot of people who run these engines that run the world. The Illuminati is believed to be made up of members who are the prime leaders of these fields. They control all three fields by controlling the leaders of all three fields who in turn control others, and then commands go down the line.

The Illuminati's true and core members are mostly bankers who own the corporations. Some of them are also working for certain governments around the world including the United States. The core members of the Illuminati are mostly men made up of the most powerful families on earth. These families that the real Illuminati members come from are made up of 13 families. These members are monarchs, princes, dukes, lords, leaders of industry, and banking.

They have been for thousands of years the rulers of the nations of the earth as there have been many generations before. These families are made up of 13 families, and the most powerful family among them is the Rothschild family. The Rothschild family it should be noted created the Rockefeller family in the United States. The Rothschild family owns the Federal Reserve Bank, and system that prints all the money in the United States. They own mostly all the gold in the world including the gold of the United States. The United States does not own its money or gold but the Rothschild family does.

The Rothschild family is believed to know every secret in the world that the nations keep hidden. They are the major players behind the coming one world government, because through globalization they will own everything in the world. The policies and plans of one world global government is believed to come from the bankers who relate these plans to others working in the political fields. These world leaders throughout the course of time came to create several political groups that are the groups that tell the leaders of the nations of the earth, the leaders of media and entertainment, the leaders of corporations what they should be doing in the next 20 years. The groups that shape world events are The Bilderbergs, Council on Foreign Relations, Trilateral Commission, the New Age Movement Council, Club of Rome, the United Nations, and others. All these groups work toward an ideal goal which is to bring on global government.

Now let us look into some events throughout history, and what was discovered concerning it regarding this reality of the Illuminati along with the banking, and political systems. The religion called Illuminati today had been around since as early as ancient Egypt. Some stated it even goes back to the time of Cain when he was building the first city of earth that many believed was a kingdom meaning a government. It was often called the most secret of secret orders on earth because the members were the most powerful rulers on earth. They were a group made up of kings, rich merchants, religious leaders, and military generals throughout those times.

These individuals were a selected group of men whose members came from many nations, even nations that were known to go to war with each other. Throughout time, and even up till this day their common interest was their faith in Lucifer who had many names throughout those centuries, also, bringing together their nations to set up a global empire wherein they would be the ones ruling it.

Of course their views at times would contradict certain laws in their own kingdoms, and could even start civil wars within kingdoms among ruling parties. This is way this order became a very secret order, and set apart even from the knowledge of other elite orders. Through the study into history we catch their existence, and certain actions they sought to accomplish. In the actions of Alexander the Great and his world empire, and the actions of the Roman Empire with its world system much of the leaders of those movements were connected to the beliefs, and membership of that day and age's version of the Illuminati.

Another time we hear about the Illuminati is in 1575 in Spain. There was a group there being headed by a Jesuit named Ignatius Loyola. They were a group promoting the ideas of the kingdoms of the earth to one day achieve a greater degree of illumination. The group was made up of some of the very richest, and powerful people in different monarchies at the time. The group was known to speak, and teach a party of mystic enthusiasts who were known to work in business and political fields. Ignatius, and his group themselves were not Christians. They were in fact mystics, theosophs, and believed in the ancient pagan rituals.

They would teach this party a new faith called today the New Age religion. Even back then they taught them that one day Christianity will be removed by fusing it with other religions to create a one world religion. They would also teach distorted views on the Bible. Ignatius in that time would write a book about how the new world order would come about. He focused his writing, and his future new Atlantis to come upon the need of building this new empire in the new world which was at the time North and South America. He believed that the kings of Europe should build these new empires there to let them flourish to one day bring them all together under one crown. Strange enough those kings in Europe did build new nations here in North and South America. The nations of those lands like the U.S. are still in debt to powers in Europe.

The next time we hear about the Illuminati was in 1776. In that time there was a professor of canon law who taught at the University of Ingolstadt by the name of Adam Weishaupt. Adam was a teacher of the beliefs of the Illuminati. It was believed he came from their family stock to enter canon law to make connections with people in education, and government to promote the beliefs of the Illuminati. The Illuminati at the time was looking to draw more power figures in Europe at the time to join their efforts that they also had tied up regarding the 13 colonies that would become the United States of America later on.

It was believed at this time they open up a branch in Bavaria in the Kingdom of Germany at the time. This branch was openly scene at the time but you needed special invitation to get it. The true core power of the Illuminati was still hidden, and in fact the Bavaria branch was only used to recruit certain persons into their causes. Soon they would grow in numbers, and they would bond over what would be called today a new age faith. In their meetings they discussed several things they were going to do. They also discuss the movements going on around the world of colonies of people revolting on the kingdoms like the colonies in America were doing to England. Their plan was to now do the same against the kingdom in Germany.

In the mid-1770's Adam Weishaupt was chosen as their speaker to win over members of the elite who worked in government and law. He would appear as a respected college professor by trade, and would seek certain people to come to secret meetings in Bavaria. There they would hear the agenda, and religious aims of the group that the group was promoting.

On May 1, 1776 the group officially became the Order of Perfectibilists, and due to the group's high volume of membership who were free-masons, the order then established it's self under masonic foundations. They became an organization tied in with the Jesuits wherein many Jesuits were also members as well.

During these secret meetings Adam was chosen to do most of the speaking on behalf of the organization. He declared that the aim of the Illuminati was to elevate mankind to the highest possible degree of moral purity, and to lay the foundations for the reformation of the world by organizing an association of the best men to oppose the progress of what they called moral evil. The moral evil was anyone who opposed their so-called righteous cause.

Whispers of these meetings became more known when Adam

became more open about them. Soon Church leaders were hearing about the meetings, and even came to learn the beliefs about it. Once they learned more about it over time many of them came to see the evil tendencies of the group. They began to even declare the group dangerous to the Christian Church.

The Kingdom of Germany at the time seemed ripe for a civil war. The monarchy in Germany often imposed unbearable restraints on the minds of their people. The Bavaria order was stating things like revolutionizing minds and religions. They stated to their followers that in order to substitute reason in its place they would have to depose all civil powers of the monarch, and establish a nominal republican government after his over-throw.

Many felt that the Catholic Church leadership in Germany was not very helpful, and even at times hard on the people. The Bavaria order would draw more controversy to themselves by playing on the feelings of what German people thought of the Catholic Church leadership. They then would drop a total bomb-shell regarding Christianity itself. They stated that in order to oppose the religious and political Roman Catholic Church they would have to seek out an agenda in abolishing Christianity itself. Soon other new speakers of the Bavaria order arose like Baron Adolph von Knigge, and others. These new speakers would continue the agenda of bashing Christianity. They would state that Christianity was not so much popular anymore, and that it had now become a system that no longer works for the people. They then stated that people among the elect of the world should return more to the ways of ancient mystics, mysterious ceremonies, and new religious forms.

Soon the monarch officials of Germany, and the military officers began to suspect the Bavaria order of being involved with a network system of mutual espionage against the Kingdom of Germany. By this time the Bavaria order has 2,000 members, and have opened up branches like them for the inner-core of the Illuminati in France, Belgium, Holland, Denmark, Sweden, Poland, Hungary, and Italy.

By this point in the 1780's the Bavaria order had organized the men, arms, and method they were going to use in overthrowing the monarchy of Germany. At this time they would send runners to several key people they wanted to win over to their side so they would be assured of success. So they sent runners with letters telling the plans of the order, and what they believed in, and the rewards for those who follow them. The runners were sent out on horseback without notice from anyone.

One of the runners who was close to making his delivery was suddenly struck by lightning. The man would die instantly from the lightning-strike. An official who worked in the monarchy was informed that someone found a note on the body of a dead man that was struck by lightning of plans to overthrow the monarchy. The official would read the note, and at once report it. Soon the military of the German monarchy ambushed the headquarters of the Bavaria order. They would close it down, and secure all papers of the order.

All those that were there when the ambush went down were imprisoned, some were fined, and others were sent in exile. This took place in 1785. Those that were not captured had to quickly flee the country, among them was Weishaupht.

Many people thought that this was the end of the Illuminati but they were really wrong on that one. They forgot that the order that was closed down was a front order, and not the real order itself, but what that ambush did do is that it exposed the plans and beliefs of the Illuminati more openly through the letter found on that dead man.

When people thought the Illuminati was no longer around they would soon find out they were wrong. Within only two months after the ambush members who stated they represented the Illuminati wrote letters threatening the German monarchy with revenge. Many people feel that this revenge came against the monarchy at the turn of the 19th century, and into the 20th century.

When the letters were sent the elector of Bavaria published an edict to warn severe punishment to anyone who speaks against the monarchy. Soon the French Revolution takes place, and once again the Illuminati becomes known, and seen as the real planners of the French Revolution.

In America a Christian minister writes a letter to George Washington asking him if the Illuminati came into America through actions he was aware of. Washington stated to him that no one in the country was more aware that they were here in America then him. It turns out that people in the Illuminati used people during the American Revolutionary War to get certain aims accomplished for them. One of those aims was putting a national bank in America which would lead to them controlling our free country through their expensive money.

The family that arose to full power by their wealth among those 13 powerful families in the late 18th throughout the 19th century, and even still rules what many people would say the world today are the Rothschild family. The Rothschild family would gain control of the most powerful fields on earth by gaining control of their money, and the power that gives them power. They would do this by creating banks for the most elite, and richest people on earth, and thereby use the policies of the bank to control their money. They would even use their money in ways that the people who use the bank would never get to see.

They would often use their money to invest in other government officials in other countries, and buy businesses they were not aware of. They would deal for profits, and power. They would constantly use their money behind their backs. This power-game of dealing with other people's money made the Rothschild so rich, and powerful they soon discovered they very much were above the laws, and reach of even monarchs themselves. The Rothschild got power by buying and putting monarchs in their pockets. Such an idea to do these things came from their beliefs that is known today as the religion of the Illuminati.

The Rothschild are believed to be devil-worshippers who worship Lucifer, and the fallen angels, and they are very serious about their faith. They believe it was their job to capture the world, and then give it to Satan who would come in a form the Bible would call the anti-Christ. It is believed that this is what drives them to target nations, and own them through their wealth. They are doing so in accordance to a plan that is bigger than them.

The Rothschild had already bought people over to their side before during, and after the American Revolutionary War. In fact they have been involved in one way or another in starting every American War the United States ever fought in. They were also the masterminds behind the Bavaria order. In fact the Rothschild arose to power in Germany. They were also the masterminds behind the French Revolution, and establishing the Bank of England. Thereby they got control of the British Empire through its wealth as well.

It was believed that the Rothschild started the French Revolution to overthrow the old government, and to open a way for a person they choose to lead France, and then plunge Europe into all-out war. This person they had in mind for was Napoleon. Napoleon was brought to power by the bankers namely the Rothschild family. It is a known fact, regardless if the Rothschild like to deny it, that the Rothschild funded both sides of what became called the Napoleonic Wars.

They actually controlled the most powerful people on both sides of the conflict by being able to control their money and wealth. They used the fear of Napoleon in England by making people think that during the Battle of Waterloo Napoleon defeated England to make people think that now they had to start selling their shares to the bank. This fear-tactic worked so well that the Rothschild family ended up controlling not only all the elite's money but the money of the people as well.

The Rothschild family in Europe supported and funded Napoleon. They gave him the money for his army, his weapons, and the power to take the French government by an iron-fist, and even bring down the Pope himself. They gave him key advice in the weaknesses of his enemy's army, and he would often win his battles by having this inside information.

The Rothschild would often deny any of this in terms of their descendants but their forefathers really didn't care at the time if people knew it because there was nothing they could do about it. By playing both sides of the Napoleonic wars the Rothschild family would achieve their goals of taking over the power structure in all the nations of Europe. They would take over their main resource which is to control the money resource, and thereby control their businesses, and their armies.

By controlling this aspect then no matter who made the nation's laws, as long as they got a hold over their resources of power, they would be able to truly be those nations' rulers. They would rule over them without the peoples of those nations even knowing about it, and sadder if they did know there would be nothing they could do about it. After using Napoleon they would betray him at Waterloo to have him defeated by giving him misinformation that day which caused him to lose.

In America the Rothschild could not feed a Christian loving country with anti-Christ believing leaders and speakers. That would be a process they would start up much later through entertainment. In America's early days the people were very much Christian, and wanted to stay out of problems in Europe.

They also did not agree with a lot of the anti-Christian speeches that were going on there as well. The Rothschild sought out control over America by seeking to control the money, and wealth of America. They sought to use the leaders in America they bought, and funded to make laws, and policies to bring forth an American central bank they would be in complete charge of. Thereby they would control more closely the destiny of America. Because in their view they wanted to see America become an anti-Christian empire.

Battles among American leaders who did not want bankers controlling the United States would be engaged in against the plans of the Rothschild themselves. This battle got started in the early days of America, and by the 20th century the Rothschild eventually got their way.

This is the entire scope of the story with more evidence, and historical facts being available through other outlets of information. Many people today have a hard time or will not believe it for various reasons, but events being played out in history regarding world government, and a society giving up on Christianity shows throughout the years of turmoil much truth in the story, and intentions of the Rothschild family, and the elite occult called Illuminati.

The battle to prevent a private central bank from controlling the money flow of the United States started when the United States was first building its nation after the Revolutionary War. It was believed that the Rothschild during that time had many U.S. politicians, and banking leaders in their pockets who they were using to help create this central bank, but there were other U.S. politicians who knew the evils of a central bank, and knew that powers in Europe would come to control, and even own America if they are allowed to have this bank in their control.

The gun-duel between Aaron Burr and Alexander Hamilton is believed to have started over the issues of the central bank. Hamilton was in full support in establishing a central bank. He used his power, and influence to see that a central bank was indeed established in America. Hamilton came to power through the money, and the funding of these European bankers who were believed to be working for the Rothschild family. Hamilton had a career in the U.S. government because of the bankers that supported him.

Burr knew that the banks were dangerous to the future of America. He believed that Hamilton was a bitter man willing to sell out his country so that he would never be poor again. Burr vowed to stop Hamilton at every turn from making progress in building the central bank. This is how the gun-duel came about. The debates between the two American leaders became so heated that the two started to dish-out some nasty mud-slinging at each other. The two would start to insult each other's character to such a point that offensives like that back in those times were taken in a very serious manner even among people in high social groups. Often such heated words resulted in gun-duels where the two men square off, and walk backwards from each other several paces armed with a single shot pistol. After counting a certain number of paces the two men turn around, face other, and then take aim and fire. At the time of the debates between Burr and Hamilton gun-duels were no longer legal anymore, but regardless of the law it still went on at least a few to several times a year.

Hamilton, having enough of Burr side-stepping him and insulting him, called out Burr to a duel. Burr quickly accepted but in private he was more nervous about the duel then Hamilton was. Hamilton came from a hard and rough background. He was often struggling, and he was very used to duels having already been involved, and survived a few of them in his life-time. Burr was not used to dueling but he did have military training. On the day of the duel which was held in secret at very early morning hours Burr with a single shot had shot and killed Alexander Hamilton.

Many people believed that Hamilton's death was a blow to the Rothschild family's plans at the time, but the Rothschild still had many other leaders in their pockets to do their bidding for them. Another noteworthy leader would also take his stand against them. That leader was forefather Thomas Jefferson. Thomas Jefferson during the time he was President often made public speeches against the bankers of Europe.

He was against the creation of a central bank. He warned Americans that if a central bank was allowed to exist in the United States that one day the future-generations of America would wake up homeless in the country their forefathers fought and died for, but overtime the U.S. leaders did not heed the warnings, and soon the United States opens up their first national bank.

This bank at the time had the powers like the Federal Reserve does today. That bank was able to print our money and held the entire wealth of America. Soon the bankers were having major control over the U.S. government system wherein it became filled with a mass of corruption. This corruption was effecting the American people at the time who were losing their businesses, and their lands to banks connected with the first national bank.

Throughout the years of these awful events in America a U.S. leader, and a future President who was a war-hero in the War of 1812, would come to see the evils of the national bankers, and wanted them removed from power. The person who fought against them, and even won at the time was Andrew Jackson.

Andrew Jackson as a U.S. political leader, and as President of the United States of America, was a very aggressive opponent against the international bankers. Many believe that these international bankers were sent by the Rothschild family. Andrew became upset at the kind of greedy, and corrupt policies the bankers kept doing to the United States government, and the

American people.

He foresaw that if nothing was done about them then the international bankers would get control over all of America including the freedoms of America. Jackson knew they were trying to accomplish this by being in control of the currency, and wealth of America. Andrew did not feel that it was right that leaders of government should be bowing down to bankers when the bankers are suppose, to be working for the government, and its people.

In 1835 Jackson's outspoken speeches against them would now turn into an all-out assault against them through the weapons of government enforcement against the bankers, and a policy to remove the first national bank from the United States. When these intentions were made known Jackson made a public speech against them declaring, 'You are a den of vipers and thieves, I intend to root you out, and by the Eternal GOD, I will rout you out. If the people only understood the rank injustice of our money and banking system, there would be a revolution before morning.'

At this it was believed that the Rothschild family became very alarmed, and threaten by Jackson's words. They knew he was serious, and he had the passion, and military know how in accomplishing the bank's overthrow. It was believed that the Rothschild family would then seek to assassinate President Jackson. The attempt on Jackson's life came through an ambush that many believed was set-up by people working for America's bank at the time. On that day Andrew Jackson was coming out of his carriage when suddenly a man came seeking through the people as they were looking to greet Jackson. The man would come within inches of Jackson, and pull out two pistols, and open-fire on President Jackson, but as he pulled the trigger on both pistols, both of the pistols would misfire and jam. The man was quickly subdued, and Jackson was taken to a safe place.

Once there, Vice-President Martin Van Buren would come to Andrew, and ask him what happened. Andrew Jackson told him the following words, 'The bank Mr. Van Buren is trying to kill me!' After a very long political fight Andrew succeeded in preventing the international bank from controlling U.S. currency and wealth. Jackson also fired and removed in his career hundreds of corrupt officials involved with the bank. Soon that first international bank was completely removed.

Beating the bank was regarded as the greatest career accomplishment, and moment by Andrew Jackson. On his death-bed his dying words were, 'I killed the bank', and in that time he did, but the Rothschild family as it was believed were not done yet, and they set-up another group of international bankers, and they raise up and funded more U.S. political leaders to take powerful seats of government in the United States once again.

Jackson' victory would soon start to be challenged, and a plan was set into motion to bring a controlling bank back that would be in the hands of the Rothschild family. Their efforts to set this up again would take several decades from the time of Jackson's victory, and in their efforts they would plunge America into its most costly and bloody of all wars America fought which was America's own Civil War. The story behind the Rothschild involvement with the Civil War is still a story hard to believe by many, and a story often not told.

What was believed concerning it is that during the American Civil War the Rothschild bankers, and their international bankers were financing both sides of the war. They had many generals of the North and South in their pockets, and the even more controversial side to it is that there were battles fought in the Civil War where generals would lose on purpose under orders from these bankers who were paying them to lose.

Many who state this story believe that the connections the Rothschild bankers had with Freemasonry is that many international bankers, and the Rothschild's themselves were also masons who used this avenue in putting generals on to their plans, and paying them off. They would secure these generals though masonic meetings at their lodges, and through special invites to other lodges to meet with them.

At this time secret meetings like these were how they were gaining political power North and South, and thereby causing uproars and controversy within the government between North and South that was putting them on course for war. The aim of the Rothschild involvement with the Civil War was to cause economic, physical, and spiritual destruction to such a level that it would break all political power against a world bank in America.

They were once again seeking full control over the money currency and political power in America. They were once again seeking to own America. They even gave money to the U.S. government to have the Capitol Building built. It is believed that their involvement with the Civil War was the reason why the war went on for so many years, and why the battles were so ruthless, bloody, and took so many lives.

Over 2 million people would lose their lives due to the Civil War, and most of that 2 million number would be soldiers, and civilians. The rest of the number would be children, and seniors who could not defend themselves. It is still on record as the bloodiest war in American history at an age where the machine gun was not the standard issued weapon.

Abraham Lincoln's involvement with the Rothschild house, and his stand against them is believed to be the real reason for his assassination. The story behind it is that Abraham Lincoln was also funded, and supported by bankers who were connected with the Rothschild family. They were the money power that brought Abraham Lincoln to power, and helped him to become President of the United States. Lincoln knew that a Civil War was coming, and there was nothing to stop it. He also it is believed had more knowledge then others that the war was planned as well, but he did not think it would take so long, and cost so many lives. His knowledge on what his banker supporters were doing behind his back also seemed to be limited as well. Lincoln foolishly at the time believed that the Rothschild were only supporting the North, and the plan was to break the power families in the South to set-up a major profit return in power to the Federal government. He thought that a stronger, and more united Federal government would then bring America to the forefront of the world as a true world power.

Beating the South was supposed to be for him a quick defeat to show forth America's power, but when all the best generals of the U.S. military branches of the time were going over to fight for the South leaving Lincoln with officers not as good as the ones leaving, Lincoln had a bad feeling about it.

He would soon come to find out the horror of the real problem he was facing, that the same bankers, the Rothschild, who supported him were also funding both sides, and giving the South a lot of money and arms so they could continue on the war to great efforts. The aim of supporting both sides of the war was to cripple the political structure of the United States to get full control over its resources and political engines. The Rothschild family really wanted the gold of America in order to fully accomplish their goals. At the time America was rich with gold after the gold-rush explosions that took place in several places in the open west of America especially in California and Arizona.

The amount of gold America received from it made America independently wealthy, and on course to guide their own policies without outside control. So the Rothschild worked very hard at corrupting, and creating one horrible event after another, and using people to full-fill their aims in order to be the bank that would hold America's gold. Thereby, in getting control of it, they can own America.

When the Civil War was not going the way Lincoln thought it would he also came to understand what the Rothschild wanted. Lincoln would devise a plan against them. Lincoln knew that in order for the plan to work in removing the Rothschild from government influence the Union Army must now really win the war. Lincoln also would fire and remove people involved with the bankers in one form or another who could make trouble for Lincoln. Lincoln would also keep a close eye on his most powerful rivals in government because he knew who they worked for as well.

He also began to employ the workings of a new money policy that would secure America's gold and its future. This policy was to make laws to prevent any private owned international bank to be able to control or print America's money. The other phase was to print our own money to be controlled under our own leaders and laws, and the next phase was to make the value of America's dollar based upon silver instead of gold. Silver was far more abundant then gold, and this would have a better effect upon American society because now far more people who did not have the chance before could now have a better chance at making more money.

America maintaining its own gold would only mean in the long-run a more powerful America as the nations around the world are all basing its markets and power on gold. These plans of Lincoln became more obvious to the Rothschild family through the policies, and speeches Lincoln was giving. In the eyes of the Rothschild they no longer had Lincoln in their pocket, and they wanted to stop him at all costs. So now their goal is to make the South win by getting European nations involved to help the South fight the North. Lincoln would also get involved with the tactics of using European nations to help him keep other European nations out of the war. Lincoln in that time was also in the process of firing, and removing Union generals he suspected of being paid off by the bankers or who were won over to the South in some way.

The European nations came into view during the Civil War when certain Southern Confederate leaders believed to be supported by the Rothschild bankers met with representatives of the governments of England and France. Both England and France at the time did not want to see the United States becoming a whole nation and a world super power because that would reduce their own power as a government.

They both had agreed to these Confederate leaders that they would convince the leaders in their governments to join the war on the side of the South. Lincoln thinking ahead, and knowing that this is what the South would try to do, went to Russia seeking a deal there with the government of Russia. Lincoln at the time would win over the Russian czar, and open a trade deal with him. The czar and leaders in Russia at the time really hated the bankers, and were strong enemies against them. This is one of the major reasons why the bankers supported the communist revolutionary war against the czar government in the 20th century.

The Russian czar at the time not only became a friend to Lincoln he also helped the Union Army as well. He would have his people meet with leaders in England and France, and tell them

Russia's opinions about the American Civil War. They stated that Europe should stay out of the war.

Russia at the time was in a different political position from the western nations of Europe. They knew that if England and France join the South in the war and win then in return this would bring both of those governments added power in overthrowing Russia. So Russia threatens both England and France that if they join the South in the war then Russia will declare open war against both England and France.

England and France could not afford a war with both the Union Army, and the Russian Army, so they agree not to enter the war. This tactic of Lincoln in getting help from Russia overturns the plans of the Rothschild bankers. The only help England was able to give the South was to send ships to run through the Union block-cade to give supplies to the South. The Rothschild would soon have a spy close to Lincoln, and this spy was believed to be Salmon P. Chase who was the Treasury Secretary at the time.

Salmon sought through congress to force a bill called the National Banking Act which would give the private bank the Rothschild owned at the time the power to issue U.S. Bank Notes, and then have the power to create U.S. money. Lincoln would quickly see through Salmon, and fight against the act. In a speech he would warn the people with words that are still a warning today. He stated, 'The money power preys upon the nation in time of peace and conspires against it in time of adversity. It is more despotic than monarchy, more insolent than autocracy, more selfish than bureaucracy. I see in the near future a crisis approaching that unnerves me, and causes me to tremble for the safety of our country. Corporations have been enthroned, an era of corruption will follow, and the money power of the country will endeavor to prolong its reign by working upon the prejudices of the people, until the wealth is in a few hands and the republic is destroyed.'

These are words that are haunting America each, and every day, and people hardly even notice it. The motivating factor of Lincoln's assassination was the fact the Union won the Civil War. Now Lincoln was going to flush out the Rothschild bankers, and remove them from power, but sadly however there were too many people in government at the time who were bought off by the bankers in one form or another.

It is believed that Lincoln's assassination was known about by at least if not over 70 people working in the highest offices of government before Lincoln was killed. It was believed that the bankers had direct people working in Lincoln's cabinet, and working as his secret service security in on the plan of killing President Lincoln. The man who killed Lincoln who went by the name John Wilkes Booth was believed to be far more than just an actor.

The secret service often needed people with talents like some actors have to be able to fit into a group, crowd, or social scene, and gather information for them as they use them for spies. Sometimes they are called upon to commit assassinations as well. It is believed John Wilkes Booth was in reality such a person. John Booth came from a talented entertainment family known as the Booth family who many of them are a family of actors. Some of them were even famous on Broadway at the time. It was believed that John was recruited in the secret service to spy on certain people in the South. He also had to kill some of the people he spied on.

John was called upon to kill Lincoln, and was given access to him at a theater where Lincoln was sitting watching a play. John shot Lincoln with a single-shot pistol in a well-aimed spot to the back of Lincoln's head. After shooting Lincoln John ran, and escape Lincoln's security. Afterwards, the secret service claimed that they tracked down John Wilkes Booth, and killed him when Booth tried to shoot at them. Yet, his body was never shown, and he oddly disappears where you don't even hear about a funeral for him by the Booth family. The secret service it was believed was more concerned with Booth's trunk then they were with him. This trunk had Booth's journal in it that had a lot of information on it.

When the journal was turned in for public records 18 pages of the journal were ripped out before it was handed over. Some people who left accounts of that time, and stated they have seen the journal before the pages were ripped also stated that Booth wrote down coded-messages in his journal. Witnesses who knew Booth when questioned often stated he was with a man named Judah P. Benjamin. Judah P. Benjamin was a Southern Civil War campaign manager for the southern government at the time. He also worked directly for the Rothschild family as their U.S. business manager. It was believed that Judah was used to relay hidden coded-messages to Booth. One of those messages was to kill the President.

Another President they were suspected of killing was President James Garfield. James Garfield was another U.S. leader, and President who fought the international bankers. Garfield found out about the evils of the international bankers, and their quest for world domination while working as Chairman of the House Committee on Appropriations. Garfield was also an expert in economic sciences.

When Garfield became U.S. President he quickly went after the bankers, and he forced out two Senators who he believed were agents for the bankers. Soon Garfield began to make public speeches against the international bankers. President Garfield would declare that whoever controls the supply of money would control the business, and even the activities of the people.

Garfield was also showing that the bankers were seeking to control more than just our money. They were also finding ways to brainwash people as well. Overtime and within only months of being President, Garfield became a huge threat to the international bankers. So it was believed that the Rothschild family would have Garfield assassinated who had been President for only a little over 4 months.

So from there, on July 2, 1881 President James Garfield would be shot and killed. He would become another victim of the world bankers, and the plans of the world elite. It is within this world where the real Illuminati dwells as it is the religion of the Rothschild family, and the other elite branch families.

When the 20th century comes into view the plans of the Illuminati families became more, and more enforced. The world was now heading for World War 1. World War 1 was believed to be a war planned by the world bankers, and leaders at the time. Their aims were to destroy old traditional, and remaining monarchy governments, and seek to establish world-government through the creation of the League of Nations that came right after World War 1. They would accomplish their goals but the League of Nations would not last long so another world war came called World War 2.

World War 2 was believed to also have been funded, and started by world bankers, and leaders. Their goals were the same as before, and they would bring forth the United Nations after the war as a way to test-run world government policies. When President Woodrow Wilson was in the White House he passed a law, and made policies to establish the Federal Reserve Bank as the sole bank that would house, and print America's money.

The Federal Reserve Bank is a private owned bank not in the control of the United States but in control by the sole owners. The true owners of the Federal Reserve Bank is the Rothschild family. The international bankers were the power that brought Woodrow Wilson to the White House. He even helped the international bankers, and the global leaders at the time to create the League of Nations. Wilson thought he was doing something good for the overall future of America, but it turned out he made one of the worst mistakes of his life, and it was a mistake that still effects America today. Even Wilson would come to regret his decision, and he even made public addresses about the fear the international bankers, and their power had over the wills of U.S., and other world government leaders.

The Federal Reserve Bank is not part of the American system of government, and yet it is in full control of America's wealth and money supply. Most people in America don't know or did not know for some time that the Federal Reserve Bank was a private owned bank, and it was owned by a powerful European family of bankers overseas who are the Rothschild family.

The headquarters of the Rothschild family is in the city of London. Due to the power the Rothschild family has over many of the earth's most powerful nations they are above all national laws. Today they are more powerful then governments because they own them by owning and controlling their money, and their leaders which is to control their power.

So therefore the Federal Reserve Bank is not an agency of the United States government. The name Federal was set-up by the Rothschild family to fool people into thinking the bank is part of the U.S. government but it is not part of the government. The Federal Reserve Bank functions like any other private corporation. It pays for its own postage, and pays and hires its own employees, and armed-guards. It does not have any part at all in any system of the U.S. government at all. It does not answer to anyone in the U.S. government. It does not answer to the President, nor the CIA, nor Congress, nor any elected official, nor any police authority, nor anyone from Washington D.C., nor anyone from the NSA or FBI. No government official at all is allowed to enter the Federal Reserve Bank unless the owners of the bank give them permission. No one in government has any idea what they are really doing with America's money, and truly like all banks show you, they do indeed use your money without you knowing about it and they get richer and more powerful off of it without your notice.

Not one single employee working in the Federal Reserve Bank is a civil employee or elected official. If American leaders want to print more money they must make a call to the Federal Reserve, and tell them the amount, and ask if this amount is okay to print. Clearly this is not a bank that is controlled by America, it's a bank that is within full control. They even tell American leaders what they are going to do, and not do.

True government property is not held under private deeds with private employees, and with no outside supervision or any watch at all. Instead it has private ownership rights over all the wealth of America, and thereby gaining a private unimaginable fortune for themselves that goes beyond anything anyone in the world could ever have or think to have.

The Rothschild family are in fact worth trillions of dollars. They now manipulate the price of gold to suit their ends, they manipulate the economy, they start wars, they own the world's entertainment fields like Hollywood, the music industry, and they own U.S., and other world leaders. They control these fields through the banks, corporations, and governments they own.

These prime elite families, because the Rothschild family is not the only family among them, they have the most powerful control all the banks, and governments by controlling the world's money supply. By controlling all the bank companies they could control the money of the corporations. This can also cause them to control their businesses as well hence how they control the entertainment business.

By buying out government leaders, and making their banks for these governments, that is how they got control over those governments, and use them to full-fill strange policies that can only be seen as satanic with aims to build a world government they would control. By controlling governments they are able to control all the secrets of those governments. They would know about what so-called aliens really are wherein the Bible would call them fallen Angels, and they would know about all secrets in general because they were involved with a lot of them throughout their history.

They are also believed to be the ones who put forth plans to engage in the mass-brainwashing of the world, and to even seek an end to Christianity. It is believed that the last U.S. President who took a stand against them was John F. Kennedy. The story is that Kennedy's stand against the world bankers, and the global movement got started when he began to have convictions about secret society involvement within the U.S. government. His displeasure with this hidden factor in government came about because of America's involvements with Southeast Asian affairs, and matters relating to the Bays of Pigs invasion that went horribly wrong. Also Kennedy's purpose in going to the moon is believed to have been caused by Kennedy learning more about what people call 'aliens' today.

The story is that Kennedy knew a lot of secrets, and they were secrets he could not control nor have any power over even though he was President. He felt that if bad things were going to end and good things needed to happen for America, and the world then the activities of secret orders, and meetings needed to be fully exposed and brought to an end. That means the Illuminati would be exposed, and it's members would be revealed as being the world bankers including the Rothschild family. Even oddly by exposing secret elite occults it is believed he would have also been exposing his own family as well.

Kennedy would give a famous speech that many said sealed his doom. It has been called the secret society speech. In the speech he exposes that every field, and engine of government works like a machine controlled by leaders through the policies not of the government but by policies not done in court or in open view of the people. He exposes that their policies come by way of secret oaths and meetings. He states that secret groups exist in the most powerful, and critical places in government, and through secret wars, violence, and corruption they have been corrupting the future of the United States government by engaging their plans through our government without notice from other leaders or U.S. citizens.

What Kennedy was exposing was the fact that secret society groups do exist in government, and they hold a lot of power over the policies of government, and even over the minds of the people. Kennedy in that speech would also expose the fact that as long as he continued as President he was now going to work on exposing these groups and stopping them. Kennedy also knew just how to stop them as well. He was going to cut off the Federal Reserve System, and remove its power over it's control of America's money. Kennedy was going to destroy the power the Federal Reserve Bank had over the U.S government. Kennedy was going to make laws to enforce that America will be printing its own money from now on. Many felt that Kennedy's stand if it had went through would have been followed up with exposing the true Illuminati, and what these banking and monarch families have been doing to the world. It is believed that the most powerful people in the U.S. government, and governments around the world regarding their people turned on him for taking this stand. It was believed that the Rothschild, and many of the families including Kennedy's own family felt that Kennedy needed to die.

It was believed that Robert Kennedy was not in on the assassination to kill President Kennedy but his brother's death caused him as well to seek to do good. It was believed, and there is even evidence to it that often gets ignored that Kennedy's true killers were the CIA who also used the Mafia in helping them to assassinate President Kennedy.

Kennedy would seek to exterminate the Federal Reserve System, and their control over U.S. currency by signing Executive Orders EO-11 and EO-110. These orders would then enforce a return power to the American government the control of printing their own money. The assassination of President Kennedy would take place in Dallas, Texas in front of a crowd of people. Much of this information about the other story of the Kennedy assassination is known of aside from the official story. The official story has been shot up with so many holes that it's amazing it's still called the official story. There was evidence, and even testimony that the CIA was used to plan the hit, and they also used Mafia men to shoot over the crowds to get them in a panic. They also would have men placed in areas in front to be close to Kennedy's passing car so they could take shots at him. One of the men was believed to be holding an umbrella over his head when he shot Kennedy. But this man did not deliver the fatal blow.

The man who did that was believed to have been Kennedy's own driver who was a CIA agent. This man's crime is even seen on the video if the driver is watched closely. The man in a quick second aims a gun while the other agent in the side-seat quickly looks back toward Kennedy, and then in an instant the driver crack-shots Kennedy wherein the bullet blows Kennedy's head-apart. The action of the fatal shot was very quick, and within a second. This CIA agent who shot Kennedy even confessed to doing so according to many witnesses of his family on his death-bed.

Deaths by the Rothschild family did not stop at Kennedy nor are they confined to the U.S. but all around the world. Many world leaders whose names people have never even heard of have also been victims of the Illuminati families.

The blood trail left behind by the world bankers and their followers regarding this occult working within banks, corporations, and governments still goes on to this day. Attempts to audit the Federal Reserve continue to be met with failure, and no popular U.S. leader since Kennedy has ever sought for an audit of the Federal Reserve or sought for its end.

Many U.S. leaders since then, and today have often shown in their careers to be funded, and empowered by bankers, and their Wall Street employees. Attempts to check the gold at Fort Knox, and make an account for it has also been met with failure. Many believe that this attempt is often met with failure because the gold is no longer there. T

he world banking systems around the world currently still controls the U.S., and all currency of world nations. They change the supply of money in circulation which influences interest rates which affects the mortgage payments and jobs of millions of families. They cause the financial markets to go up or down or cause it to fall into recession. They manipulate the U.S. monetary policy for their own agenda to further their global political goals often using our military to enforce world global government policies.

The Federal Reserve now has 12 different banks, and they are all private corporations. Their top eight stockholders are Citibank, Chase Manhattan, Morgan Guarantee Trust, Chemical Bank, Manufacturers Hanover Trust, Bankers Trust Company, National Bank of North America, and the Bank of New York. These banks hold the money for the top five international corporations of the U.S., and around the world. These top five corporations are the main parent corporations that own hundreds of other corporations. In total they own all the corporations you see in America, meaning every logo, and commercial you see are from corporations who are owned by those top five who have their money being controlled by those top 8 banks who are controlled by the Federal Reserve Corporation.

The Hollywood entertainment fields of movies and music were started by families who were related to these international banking families or who worked for them. Many of the families who became owners of movie studios, and record companies were by their religious beliefs nowhere near Christian, and also by their political beliefs they were not patriots of America either. Many of them had world government views, and strange ideas in how to bring it about even at the start of the building of the Hollywood entertainment fields. Many of those families were suspected of being in deals with certain U.S. leaders who supported the goals of international government. In fact, it was believed that they worked together, and they used their brands of entertainment to slowly, overtime, brainwash people to the kind of society they would need in order for such a government to be accepted. Often celebrities are raised up to be the poster-children of their views, and even their spirituality. They are also used to influence people to ungodly behavior as well.

Entertainment by them is designed to suspend the mind, and then program it with the kind of inspiration they want people to have. This inspiration is largely anti-Christian, and about the worship of pleasures and greed. The thinking is that the more the people are removed from Christianity the more they leave themselves open to control.

Chapter 27

Today in the music industry we have many artists being seen as poster-stars for the Illuminati. In fact there are fans, and people who think these artists are actually in the Illuminati to such a point that there are even cartoon sitcoms and shows that have even played on this belief from many people. Many people think that the cause of it is the internet. They who believe that tell people that there are crazy people on the internet telling people about the Illuminati, and how Jay-Z and others run the Illuminati. Now sadly there are crazy or misinformed people on the internet talking about the Illuminati. They say things that are not true or just way out there coming from the source of emotional problems or too many drugs.

Some people talk about the Illuminati on the internet just to be strange and different in some way, but others on the internet have talked about and showed what the real Illuminati actually is. They come with documents, historical accounts, and present a solid case. They do so to make people aware, and not to make people go crazy. The course of all this information about the Illuminati does bring year by year more people looking into it. The relation to this in regards to the music industry is that several artists who are current today are in the Illuminati according to some people who state this on the internet or even make fun of it on Hollywood programs

Well in truth having just learned what the Illuminati is in the last chapter, you can see that there is no way current artists are in the Illuminati, but what you do have are artists being used by the occult factors of these bankers, CEOs, and global leaders.

Artists today and yesterday regarding the entertainment industry have been mediators between the elite, and the people. The artists do the kind of art-forms the elite owners want them to use. They use the artists to use their art-form to convey the ideas of the elite holders of the world to the general population. They use the artists to distract them, detain them, brainwash them, and sleep teach them.

The artists do this for the elite by inspiring people with their art-forms rather it be movies or records. The image is something that is very important to them because it shows an idea through the person that people can be drawn toward, and be inspired from. Artists therefore become their work-dogs so to speak, and they bark out the beliefs of the people that sign their paychecks.

Many artists are believed to be sold-out to these people in all kinds of ways. Much of it is compared to events of a person selling their soul to Satan due to the occult nature of their world. It is believed that this control is so bad that artists become victims to government experimentation like mind-control and other abuses. Many of them are sexually assaulted, abused, and told to do art-forms they don't agree with rather morally or career wise. Many of them are controlled through money, drugs, or blackmail by the people who own the companies they work for. Artists are taken advantage of by the people in those corporations who work with others. This is clearly not the case for all artists but yet most artists are not as famous as the ones that are, and those ones are few in number. Those few are the main suspects of being mind-control, and satanic ritual abuse victims. Those few also are constantly today promoting the image, and even the beliefs of the Illuminati.

Take the artist called Jay-Z who is today's current hip-hop star, and one of the richest people in the music industry today. Jay-Z's notice with the name Illuminati came about mostly when he kept on throwing up the 'diamond' hand-sign. The 'diamond' hand-sign was to take your two hands, and form a pyramid shape with them. The shape is suppose, to represent a 'diamond' until oddly Jay-Z started to cover one of his eyes during a session of photo-shoots while doing the hand-sign.

Some people who investigate the subject matters of occult symbolism pointed out that Jay-Z's hand-sign along with the way he had been doing the hand-sign at concerts, and during photo-shoots is oddly also being done by other music industry stars, and stars in movies and sports. There was this huge pattern of stars who kept throwing up this sign. According to occult experts of satanic occult symbols this so-called 'diamond' hand-sign had been around for a long time way before today's star-artists.

The hand-sign was used, and even spoken about by people like Aleister Crowley, Manly P. Hall, and there is even a rare picture of Hitler using it. The hand-sign is often called the hand-sign of the all-seeing eye. This all-seeing eye is to represent Satan who is also called Lucifer. The pyramid shape in the occult understanding is to represent Satan's corrupt version of the form of GOD which is Father, Son, and Holy Spirit. So therefore it represents a triangle with Satan's eye on top. It goes back to that desire of Satan to be worshiped as GOD is so therefore the all-seeing eye represents also his counter-religion of the true faith known as Christianity.

For many people it is hard for them to believe that Christianity holds the knowledge of the true faith that saves people to bring them to Eternal Life, but it is a fact that Satan, and those who worship Satan in whatever form they do, are not threaten by any open religion on earth rather Islam, Buddhism, or Hinduism but they are very much threaten by Christianity. So much so they press hard to seek its true teachings to be watered down or ignored. They work toward a goal in seeing it removed from society. So this all-seeing eye on top of its pyramid shape is to also represent the faith of the new world order which is the belief in a one world religion that comes to worship their brand new Christ who will be the anti-Christ spoken about in the Bible. The powers today seek to make a world government with a one day dream to have a great leader guiding its course. The Bible tells us that Satan will be this great leader.

There is a lot of information regarding this hand-sign but what is strange is why would Jay-Z, and all these artists keep throwing it up. The answer to that question is within the occult beliefs of many of these artists, and the people who own them and control their careers. This is where the real Illuminati comes into the picture. The all-seeing eye is one of the standard symbols of the Illuminati, and it represents their god and his religion.

Artists work in promoting the images, and art-forms of the people they work for. Those people they work for give the artists the ideas or just tells them plainly what image they will project meaning what hand-signs they will use, and what kind of songs they want the artist to do. So the artist will do those kinds of songs, and project the image the record company executives want them to project. Those executives would be working for CEOs, and owners who are the true family members and rarely even members of the Illuminati through a certain elite blood-line they have.

The artists become their puppets, and they pull their strings throughout their careers. The general public is distracted by the artists, and have become far too attached to having them in their lives. This attraction has even in many cases become an unhealthy interest that blinds people from learning about things that really matter.

Jay-Z is very much part of that process in blinding people from what really matters when so many millions of young fans, and hip-hop fans in general seem to be more concerned with what Jay-Z thinks and does rather than being concerned about what is really going on in the world today. Jay-Z was born, and raised in the Marcy Housing Projects in the neighborhood of Brooklyn in New York City. His real name is Shawn Carter, and the name of his mother was Gloria Carter. The real father of Jay-Z is largely unknown, and it is not sure if he abandoned the family at an early stage when Jay-Z was just a baby or if he was simply never there at all for the birth of Jay-Z. The story is not clear enough for me to write about it.

The only thing that could be told is that some strange affairs were going on in Miss Carter's life at the time, and no one knows for sure what the real story is. While growing up Jay-Z would embrace the street culture of gangs, and drug dealings that was going on at the Marcy projects and throughout the streets of Brooklyn.

Marcy projects was at the time truly a horrible place to live in. Every day there was a violent crime committed there. Every day someone was beaten, murdered, shot, raped, kidnapped, robbed, assaulted, or stabbed. Everyday someone would over-dose there, and often over-dose victims would be found in trash cans on the streets. Sometimes even babies were found in those trash cans.

The drug trade was huge there, and many young black youths joined gangs, and began selling drugs as a way to make money. The drug trade would also bring into the projects murders between rival gang-members, and murders done against drug customers who owned them money.

At the age of 12 Jay-Z would join a gang, and he began selling crack-cocaine at a project house in Marcy. The violent and unstable conditions of the Marcy projects was the world Jay-Z knew at the time. Through the sale of the drugs he was selling Jay-Z would make enough money to buy his own jewelry, clothes, and better shoes. He would even support his mother until the day he moved out.

One time Jay-Z's older brother stole some of his jewelry. Jay-Z then got his gun, and he went looking for his brother. When Jay-Z found his older brother he shot him just to teach him a lesson about never stealing his jewelry again. Jay-Z would get his jewelry back while his brother survived the shooting. It was said that Jay-Z as a gang-banger and a drug dealer was a ruthless person. He was unforgiving toward people who owned him money or who disrespected him in some way.

Another strange story is that the drug connections that Jay-Z had was believed to be undercover government drug smugglers, but this has yet to be proven. Jay-Z, from the time he was 12, and going into high-school was known as a drug-dealer, and gang-banger on the streets of Brooklyn.

Jay-Z first discovered his passion for rapping, and for hip-hop when he was in high-school. Jay-Z attended the same high-school of fellow future star rappers Biggy Smalls and Busta Rhymes. The high-school was called George Westinghouse Career and Technical Education High School. The high-school was supposed to be designed for a certain group of students from urban areas who showed promise, and talent in their educational work.

Jay-Z it turns out is not a slow or unlearned person. He had a high I.Q. but at the time he used his gifts to make money through drug dealing. As a drug dealer Jay-Z would be shot on three different occasions.

In high-school Jay-Z discovered his gift for rapping, and became involved in the urban hip-hop scene. He began to develop his skill for rapping. He would do this by free-styling, writing lyrics, and rapping to beats he played on his boom box. Jay-Z worked his way into the local underground entertainment and insider side of the hip-hop scene by becoming the hype man for several popular local artists. He soon began to work as a hype man for much bigger artists at the time like Big Daddy Kane, Big L, Mic Geronimo, and others. He would then work his way to rapping on some of their songs.

Jay-Z as a hype man would then become an artist himself. He started out as one half of a duo working with his rap partner at the time Positive K. Jay-Z and Positive K used to perform freestyle rap as an opening act for shows featuring Big Daddy Kane and Big L. At that early time in Jay-Z's career Jay-Z would find himself working in competition with fellow up, and coming rappers at the time who were DMX and Ja-Rule.

Jay-Z, now out of high-school, and into the hip-hop music scene, was seeking all kinds of ways to become a star in the hip-hop game. This is where the story gets strange again.

The story is that during that time in Jay-Z's career is when Jay-Z became involved with a Freemason lodge, and then he became a member of the Freemasons. Through these connections Jay-Z would be involved with a powerful lodge that was believed to be satanic, and sought for its new members to prove themselves worthy of their help. This help is believed to come by way of certain satanic rituals that leave people demon-possessed once it's over. The belief is that during that time when Jay-Z first joined, another up and coming music producer, and promoter also joined. His name was Damon Dash, and he also was believed had to prove himself before them as well. Through this inner and strange society it is said that this is how Jay-Z and Damon Dash really met. The two would find that they had a lot of things in common at the time. They came to see that by helping each other they could rise to the top.

Through their ways, and many say through their hidden occult society, they came up with a step by step plan in how to put their foot in the door of the music industry. It was done in a way that would make them rich, powerful, and full owners of their own songs and label. These plans were believed to be in motion at a time Jay-Z was selling his own CDs out of his car. Soon the savoy business gifts of Damon Dash led to him to come to Jay-Z with a plan to create their own record company.

The two of them would create Roc-A-Fella Records. Roc-A-Fella Records was born as an independent label in 1995. The story behind the funding of Roc-A-Fella Records is believed to have a lot to do with secret business partners who were also involved with Freemasonry. This belief became stronger when it became clear that the name Roc-A-Fella was taken from the name of the Rockefeller family.

The Rockefeller family were spawned from the Rothschild family, and the Rockefeller family also are one of the most powerful families on earth wherein many of its members are suspected of being blood-lined members of the Illuminati, and many of them are also masons. The question for many regarding this is why would Jay-Z and Damon give their company this name unless there was money behind their company from people who wanted this name for the label?

When Roc-A-Fella Records was first started up Jay-Z was it's one and only main artist. Jay-Z would take care of all the songs and recordings while Damon Dash would be the hard-nosed business man who would get all the deals done for the label.

Dash was a fiery and pushy business man who was able to

secure many deals for the label, and push the label further up the top of the ladder of success. In that early time Damon would secure a distribution deal with Priority Records wherein soon after Jay-Z would release his debut album in 1996 called Reasonable Doubt. The album started out slow in sales but would eventually pick up, and climb up the numbers on the charts, and the album would go platinum in sales.

In 1997, while the first album increased in sales, Damon Dash would secure another distribution deal for Roc-A-Fella Records with Def Jam Records. This resulted in Jay-Z's second album to be released called In My Lifetime Vol.1. The album would also be produced by Sean 'Puffy' Combs who's Bad Boy Entertainment would also do deals with Roc-A-Fella Records.

The second album would become a hit, and sell more than the first album. Jay-Z was now being more promoted in the hip-hop industry. After the success of the second album Damon Dash would secure a deal for distribution for the third album called Vol. 2 Hard Knock Life. The record executives involved with the distribution company hated the lead single to the third album that was called Hard Knock Life (Ghetto Anthem). They would argue with Dash and Jay-Z about removing the single from the album. Dash would not listen to them, and he challenged their decision, and fought to have the song released.

Soon Roc-A-Fella Records would get their way, and the single along with the album was released in 1998. The single would become a smash hit rap single, and enter the top 10 Billboard 100 singles chart. The single would soon be followed by a second single called Can I Get A...which also became a top 10 Billboard hit. The success of these singles would lead to the album selling 5 million copies, and becoming a smash hit record.

The album would make Roc-A-Fella Records very rich, and the company became a major-force for an independent label in the music industry. At this point Damon Dash uses his business smarts to expand the company into other fields of business to bring more money to Roc-A-Fella. He felt that Roc-A-Fella could not be a powerful fortune 500 company someday if all they were going to sell were rap albums.

Damon had an idea to start a street urban gear clothing line. He would bring Jay-Z into a deal to create this clothing line with several clothing distribution companies. This team would create the logos, and styles of the clothes that were going to be aimed at and sold among urban youths. The new clothing company would be called Rocawear. Damon would fight tooth and nail in the company boardrooms with clothing and record distributers to convince them that lots of money would be made from it, and it would not hurt future record sales.

There were many powers in Wall Street, and among bankers that did not want to see Roc-A-Fella branch out and become mega-rich for various reasons. This resulted in the powers that did want to see the company successful to use whatever influence or ability they had to win over powerful investors to invest in their company. The strange story is regarding that is those investors many of them came by way of occult or hidden connections. Some say that this wheeling, and dealing of Dash to create, and maintain Rocawear and Roc-A-Fella Records is what got R&B singer Aaliyah killed after she made the movie Queen of the Damned.

The story regarding it is an unproven story that insiders, and investigators believe to be true. At this time when Roc-A-Fella Records and Rocawear were starting up, and rising up it was believed that many of those silent investors who put money into their company came with a price. They would state that the price was satanic by nature involving a human sacrifice that is done now a days by way of murder and cover-up.

Aaliyah at the time was dating Damon Dash but sometimes she was passed around to Jay-Z. The three of them often went to popular nightclubs together. One day Dash called Aaliyah telling her that she really needed to get on the plane as he had some business regarding her. Aaliyah did not like to fly and she had a bad feeling all day about getting on the plane, but under pressure from Dash she would board the plane. The official story is that the plane crashed down due to overloading. The problem with the story is that the plane was not overloaded. Investigations showed that one of the engines blew up which caused the plane to catch on fire, and then the plane came crashing down, appearing in a hail of fire and smoke while pieces of the plane were shattered about.

Some of those investigators believe that the engine had evidence upon it that it was sabotaged, but their reports fell on deaf ears. Did Dash and Jay-Z know that Aaliyah was going to be killed on that plane and allowed her, while pressuring her to walk right into a set-up ritual death? One can only wonder until it all comes to be exposed to the light.

During that time Rocawear would become a huge multi-million dollar company, and everyone in the inner cities, towns, suburbs, and around the world were buying, and wearing clothes from the Rocawear brand. Soon Roc-A-Fella became a major company on the New York Stock Exchange as it was bringing in millions and millions of dollars. In fact the money from the clothes would bring in far, far, more money than the records.

Oddly enough the logos and symbols on Jay-Z's clothing line are all symbols that can be found in ancient occult schools and Freemason lodges. Jay-Z even has a sweater that has written on it words quoted from Satanist Aleister Crowley. This is rather very strange for the sole fact that these symbols are the most anti-Christian symbols, and they are symbols relating to the belief that people can be their own gods by believing only in themselves.

Around this time Jay-Z was making new friends with top bankers, and fortune 500 CEO's of other corporations. Many of them saw vast potential in the Roc-A-Fella company, and they sought to invest with Jay-Z to branch his company out into areas for a mass urban market that would include professional sports. Dash on the other hand did not want to share ownership of the Roc-A-Fella company with anyone on Wall Street or anywhere else. Dash only wanted to do business with them but keep them also away from having ownership rights because he knew they could use that later to get control of the company.

Jay-Z did not agree with Dash, and he wanted to be partners with these people, and he wanted to be among them in business to take part in their kind of success. Soon Jay-Z's new business friends were giving him ideas into how to remove Dash from ownership and bring the company under his control. Jay-Z at this time became more distant from Damon Dash. He began to use his power of ownership to make his new partners co-partners with him. These power connections managed to reduce Dash's power to such a point they then as a group with Jay-Z sitting with them bought out Dash's ownership rights. Jay-Z would then take over full ownership, and he brought in these bankers, and these CEOs to share ownership along with him. In short Jay-Z was now in bed, and living it up with bankers, CEOs, and even Hollywood stars, and government leaders.

At this point Jay-Z started through his new banker, and business connections Roc Nation Sports which is a company that hires agents to handle sport stars mainly in the NBA and MLB. Jay-Z through his company would then become part owner of the 40/40 club. At this time Jay-Z's net-worth is over 500 million, and his company is worth in the billions. Dash's prediction however, is coming to pass. Jay-Z has lost a lot of his power as owner, and also he has given more and more of the company to be in the control of bankers, and other CEOs.

On the outside he looks like the boss but in reality he doesn't run the business, other people do. Jay-Z just signs the papers, records albums, and receives a paycheck tied with money he is not in full control of. Those billions of dollars are not in his control but in the control of his so-called partners who in reality have a lot of control over Jay-Z. Many even say they have control over the kind of albums he does now.

Much of Jay-Z's rap art-form, and image has been seen as satanic, and openly corporate, and not real hip-hop, yet his latest records since the start of 2000, and on to this time have been multi-million dollar platinum selling records. Hip-hop did indeed change a lot from the days of the 1980s and 1990s. It became more about pleasure, and showing off rich items, and jewelry. It became more about having very expensive things. It became more about image and less about social issues, and being real. Knowledge was replaced with base-less things wherein at the end of the day the rap song spoke on the artist saying, 'look at what I got, and know that you don't have it'. There are no real issues being spoken about in rap anymore like in the days of N.W.A. and Tupac Shakur. Rap truly became commercial, and corporations have clearly taken over the rap industry today. They are giving the people the kind of rap that glorifies the corporate rich lifestyle. It has nothing to do today with real lifestyles of people still living in street urban areas.

Rap has even given into images, and fashion that many would call homosexual and pop-culture oriented. Some artists still do gangsta rap, and such but they also have changed their image a lot as well. A good example is Snoop Doggy Dogg wherein he is no longer called by this name, and his image became very more commercial pop with a rap style that is no longer hardcore but more about using drugs, having sex, and talking about nothing important at all. He even appears in a music video playing an over-age adult high-school student who fails senior year every year so that he can continue to stay in high-school and never grow up. That image seems to say a lot when it comes to rap today.

Rap also has songs that are filled with a lot of political and business meanings as well that are often hidden from public knowledge. Many believe that the record companies are having them to do rap-songs that speak about events in the world that relates to what people would call the global government plans of the Illuminati. It is believed that this method is done as a way of promoting the Illuminati under the noses of people who won't believe in such things that are going on in the world or they don't care.

Some of these rap songs reveal a lot of information that is very strange when looked at from the point of view of understanding occult knowledge and events in the world today. The song becomes its own telling of such horrible things in a way that the artist or artists are proud of it. Artists today are believed to be emulating the beliefs of a much larger global occult power because that power owns them, and signs their paychecks.

Much of Jay-Z's songs speak on things like this especially a song he did called Run This Town. When Run This Town first came out as a single many people could not make heads or tails as to what the song was really about. Many people however did have many ideas about the song. The ideas surrounding the belief that the song had a lot to do with awful political, and national financial events that could lead to a violent break down of society seems to have weight to it. Also the idea that the song, and music video also had hidden satanic meanings also has weight as well.

So let us look into the song and music video of this single called Run This Town. Many people think that the song, and music video are anti-establishment, which was a word that came from people fighting against corruption among government and business leaders, but when you really look into the meaning of the song, and then look at what the music video scenes show, there is a contradiction to the thinking that it's anti-establishment.

It seems to point that the art-form is pro-establishment. The song, and music video does promote a coming new government taking over the old one. In the understanding of the pro-establishment globalist leaders that is what the one world government hopes to do one day. They hope to take it all over, and they will do this through wars, and violent civil unrests that will be caused by events they will create.

When we see Kanye West in the video leading an army of people against a police military state one must understand that such events is what the global leaders want to happen. These are the goals among the elite who are worshippers of Lucifer, and are the goals of the Illuminati. A violent civil unrest in such a case is a losing battle, and would be used as a violent example to suppress such an uprising through bloody force to use it as a warning against everyone else they seek to control, but to one day have a crowd for a violent civil unrest the plan from the elite would be to plant those seeds in the minds of the people.

Hence we have Kanye West America's favorite rapper at that time leading a violent mob of people against the new authority who would represent the new government which would be the new world order government. Soon we see in the video Jay-Z making his appearance, and then Jay-Z and Kanye start to rap about some topics on their minds. The topics are not about world hunger, violent teen crimes, drug abuse, sex abuse, unemployment, cancer, poverty, government corruption, you know all the issues that matter. Instead the topics within their raps are about how rich they are, and how famous they are.

In fact the so-called deep meaning within those verses of the song is to let all their poor or nowhere near as rich fans to know that they are far, far richer than them. They want to demonstrate just how much richer they are of them by being very careful to rap about the details of how expensive their shoes, cars, and drinks are. In fact the entire subject matter is about praising all these expensive luxuries, and bragging about the fact they cost thousands of dollars. They are happy about the fact that they can afford such things, and mostly everyone else can't. In fact this is what the establishment does to us each and every day.

Rihanna is also in the video, and she plays a part in bringing the people who see the video a hidden satanic message. In the video Rihanna is given a lit torch, and oddly stands in a pose holding the torch wherein the scene captures a sense of a ritual aspect. That is because what Rihanna was doing was actually done among devil-worshippers in the past and present.

The lady holding the torch often represented Lucifer the bearer of the light. This female form is to represent in a broad understanding the desires of man. The torch represents Lucifer as a teacher of knowledge wherein it is a corrupted version of the character of Jesus Christ, as knowledge is symbolized in the Bible as being light. So this symbolism Rihanna is doing in the music video does have an even darker meaning.

The symbolism within many occult schools like the Illuminate is called torch of illumination, and there is a belief that is part of this symbolism. This belief got started since the days the Illuminati bankers and other leaders were involved with revolutionary wars in many places of the world, including the colonies that became the United States of America. The belief is the overthrow of the present nations, and the overthrow of religious groups namely Christianity to bring forth a new world government. Another world Rome or another Babylon but this time with a world-wide king on the throne that all may worship, and hearken to who would be what the Bible calls the anti-Christ. In the doctrine of Lucifer they call this belief also 'the coming forth of the conquering light.'

When Rihanna starts to sing her lyrics for the song her words are dark, disturbing, and oddly have a sense of reality to them regarding world events to come. She sings about bombs dropping on people from every direction, and she sees them all running and screaming in a panic. She then oddly declares in her lyrics that if anyone has a problem with it to let her know now where the urban meaning to that is 'you better not say anything to me or else.' It is rather very dark, and evil to say such a statement when thousands of people are getting killed all around you.

Jay-Z then raps his set of lyrics where he raps about people swearing allegiance to him and his friends, and they do this while wearing black robes. The scene that these set of lyrics are showing can be found in satanic occult groups where members swear allegiance to their order and leader. The lyrics even go on to hint that this group represented by Jay-Z, Kanye West, and Rihanna are a secret group where Jay-Z in his lyrics begins to refer to masonic handshakes, and he even refers to masonic concepts taught in the lodges.

Rihanna then sings another set of lyrics, and she calls life an unfair game wherein she breaks all the rules in life. She could care less who it hurts because in her eyes that is what it takes to walk tall in the industry by watching other people being destroyed. Those ideas are what the new world order global policies are all about. It's amazing that Jay-Z, Kanye West, and Rihanna can do a song like this, and instead of being sick to their stomach with themselves they just throw up Satan's all-seeing hand sign and smile, and collect their paycheck. A paycheck that comes from the money made by the fans they hate and can't stand being around. Fans who made them rich are the same fans they want to see have nothing, not even a country to live in.

The negative art-forms of these artists are clearly being shown to have very awful influences on the blessings and the minds of the people. People will draw to this negative energy, and end up influencing others with it. Often such influence brings harm to people, and when people don't start seeing things correctly they become blind by rage and violence.

Another aspect of Jay-Z involves demonic possession. One time during an on the street camera interview Jay-Z was asked about the reason for his success as a rapper. He would make a very strange statement by stating that he calls on spirits to enter him.

He would compare the experience to what the understanding of possession would be. Jay-Z also calls this take-over of the spirits the 'rain man effect'. Often many music industry artists from rappers to R&B singers, and even pop stars have made songs speaking about a rain man.

According to many music industry insiders the rain man is a nickname for Satan. The name is believed to come from the symbolism of Satan as being a musical being. The understanding is that many artists today know they are demon-possessed, and they are in touch with those evil spirits inside them so much so that they have come up with names for them. Artists also have alter-egos as well, and have given them names to go along with them. Many insiders believe that these alter-egos for many artists are the demons speaking through them.

Jay-Z also has an alter-ego, and he named it after GOD's Holy Name in the Book of Exodus but applied the name Jay in front of it. Many say that Jay-Z does have a God complex that he thinks he is GOD, but others also say that the reason Jay-Z thinks this way has a lot to do with new age doctrine, and his private beliefs in what the Bible calls Satanism. This doctrine teaches that man himself is his own God, and that we do not answer to a Christian GOD. However way Jay-Z looks at it such a belief rather personal or as an image is truly satanic.

Kanye West one time made some interesting statements live on stage regarding Satan, and the matter of selling your soul in the music industry. The words he said on stage in front of thousands of people were, 'I sold my soul to the Devil. I know it was a crappy deal. At least it came with a few toys like a happy meal.' The concert footage of Kanye saying these words were never shown in the mainstream media, and most people don't even know that he said these words to a live audience.

The media would rather you pay attention to things that are vain or really don't matter regarding Kanye West, and many artists. They rather you pay attention to what these artists are wearing for today's fashion, or who they are going to marry or which one of them is cheating. The media will do gossip shows, and run programs about subjects regarding artists that really don't mean anything, and have no real merit to anything really important, but subjects like Kanye stating that he sold himself to the Devil are the subjects the media refuses to look into and report on.

This leaves questions in people's minds however as to why Kanye would make such a statement when clearly such a statement could have destroyed his career if realized by the mainstream public. There have been other statements made by Kanye that were also ignored by the media. After the horrible hurricane in New Orleans that took out the homes of thousands and thousands of people who were mostly African-Americans certain Hollywood charity fund raisers were aired on live television to raise money for the victims. One of the programs featured Kanye West. During Kanye's segment that was being shown on live television Kanye was speaking about the horrible conditions of the victims. He then out of nowhere had said something that was not planned or pre-written, and it shocks his famous co-stars when he said it. Kanye would state at the end of his speech, 'Bush doesn't care about black people'.

Kanye was speaking about the fact that President Bush at the time ignored the pressing needs of the victims of the hurricane at the times they needed help the most. These statements were nowhere near the airwaves of the mainstream media, and were also covered up and buried in the vaults of lost television episodes. Kanye's statements in stating that he sold his soul to the Devil, and how he describes his deal is very chilling. From the understanding of the statements, and why he made them points to that Kanye did it for fame but the fame is hard and the industry is filled with pitfalls loaded with thieves, abusers, and dangerous people seeking to take advantage of artists. This is why he states that it is crappy. But also he states through the 'toys in the happy meal statement' that at least he enjoys a rich life being able to buy expensive things. The industry seems to be a very wicked place indeed.

Kanye West grew up in a middle class area in Chicago, Illinois. He came from a family that benefitted from having high paying jobs. His mother was able to afford a good life for young Kanye at the time. Kanye was also raised in a Christian home, and his family went to Church, but later in Kanye's life it would seem he went in a different direction in terms of spiritual faith. Kanye's mother had common dreams for her son to get an education, and then get a good paying job, but Kanye had also different ideas about his career direction in life, and this idea got started when Kanye was in the third grade. At that time Kanye was introduced to hip-hop music, and he fell in love with it ever since.

As a child he would teach himself how to rap, and he soon developed a natural gift for writing and rapping his own songs. By the time Kanye got to high-school he had bought DJ mixers, turntables, and other equipment in order to make his own beats for his songs. During his high-school years Kanye got heavily involved with Chicago's hip-hop scene that was mostly in nightclubs on the South and West Sides of Chicago. These nightclubs could often be dangerous to go to, and a person had to be a certain way to be accepted there meaning they had to truly live a hip-hop culture.

Often the clubs were dangerous due to gang activities in the clubs along with drugs and sexual crimes. The clubs featured the latest up, and coming hip-hop acts trying to make it into the hip-hop music industry. It is not for sure how much of this life did Kanye expose to his mother and family. It seems he was at times at odds with them about his career choices in life regarding his quest for music stardom. His mother did realize he really was gifted for this type of music, and so she would openly support it just to see where it would go. She did not have a real problem with it overall because at the time Kanye was staying in school.

At the Chicago hip-hop nightclubs Kanye West started out as a hype man, and then became a DJ. As a DJ he would show a strong talent for mixing and making beats. Soon he was working with other artists, and he forms a crew. He begins to write rap songs for other artists that were becoming popular in the nightclubs. He worked his way up to producer as he was working with the club owners who also owned or worked for independent labels that were mostly local but sometimes had far reaching airplay.

Kanye was put to work in producing several of their artists by writing songs and making beats for them. By the time Kanye was done with high-school he would enroll at a college art-school, but at this time Kanye had a strong desire to develop his own crew. He wanted to rap himself, and make his own songs.

Kanye West began to develop his own music, and he would soon start to perform it at various hip-hop nightclubs. Kanye was now performing as an artist, DJ, and producer for these clubs, and this caused him to become distracted from school. Kanye could not find the time to balance school with his true-calling as he put it, and so much to his mother's sorrow Kanye drops out of college after only one semester.

At this time Kanye goes hard into work to develop a better sound. Kanye would start to broaden his music influences to incorporate samples from R&B funk or soul songs along with trip hop, electronica, classical music, industrial, arena rock, alternative styles, and a few other forms to fuse with his own drums and instrumentals to create his own brand of hip-hop.

Once Kanye had this set into motion he soon developed a sound and began recording demo tapes. He then worked hard at getting paid performances at clubs and sending out his demo tapes to record companies. He locally promoted his music and sold his own demo tapes. Often times his efforts in securing a deal with record companies came with failure. This was due to the fact that the record companies at the time did not understand his brand of hip-hop, and they did not think it would sell.

One of these record companies that Kanye sent his demo tape to was, Roc-A-Fella Records. The executives and Jay-Z at the time did not think that Kanye was a marketable rapper, but they did know he was a talented DJ and producer. Jay-Z's people would contact Kanye West, and seek to hire him as a beat maker and songwriter for Jay-Z's album.

At the time Jay-Z was recording an album called The Blueprint. Kanye West would work with Jay-Z on the album, and he created several beats for his songs and wrote songs for the album. Kanye's skills became so noticed that he would become co-producer of the album. In 2001 Jay-Z's album The Blueprint was released, and it becomes a multi-million selling album. It was also called Jay-Z's best album at the time, and Kanye West achieved high recognition for the work he did on Jay-Z's album.

Soon Jay-Z would take Kanye under his wing, and Kanye would make other music industry connections from people who represented artists that wanted Kanye to write songs for them. This would lead to Kanye working on hit singles for Alicia Keys, Ludacris, and Janet Jackson.

During that time Kanye's partnership with Jay-Z now became a contract wherein Jay-Z wanted Kanye West to sign to Roc-A-Fella Records to work as their producer. During this deal some many strange things were said regarding it. The belief was that Jay-Z was introducing Kanye West to more of the darker behind the scenes connections and power of the music industry, that Jay-Z was introducing him to New Age doctrines, and to powerful people in the music industry who were heavy into satanic worship, and were also powerful people by their position and wealth. They also happen to be Freemasons as well. It was said that through these influences Kanye's Christian upbringing, and faith was no longer practiced by him, and even before these influences said to be introduced to him by Jay-Z. Therefore Kanye fell into them, and began to learn more about New Age beliefs and Satanism. This story is an unproven story but believed by many, and it also relates to the contract.

It was believed that Kanye had to join an occult that the Bible would call satanic in order to be signed to Roc-A-Fella Records as a star-producer. Within this occult it is believed Kanye also became a Freemason. When Kanye was signed to Roc-A-Fella Records the year was 2002. Kanye was now their star producer but being a producer only was not what Kanye really wanted to do. Kanye wanted to be a rapper, and he still recorded songs and sought for a chance to record an album of his own as an artist. Kanye would still give his tapes to the record executives of Roc-A-Fella but in all of his efforts they would not take him seriously as a rapper because of his, what they would call his 'pop-rap sound'. Kanye would often be offended at them, and he began to harden within himself, but Jay-Z and others would go to bat for him, and soon they allowed Kanye to record his debut album.

The album was called The College Dropout, and was released in 2004. To the shock of many people the album would hit the number two spot on the Billboard 200 albums chart. The first two singles released from the album were Through the Wire and Slow Jamz. Both songs would become smash hit singles, and Slow Jamz became a number one single on the Billboard 100 singles chart. The next single released from the album was a song called Jesus Walks. The record industry executives did not want Kanye to release this song as a single. They felt in their ignorance, and many say hatred for Christianity that such a song containing such blatant declarations of a Christian Faith would never make it to the radio airwaves. They believed that a rap song that deals with the subject matter of Christianity would ruin a rap star's career. They were wrong. When the song was released it would become a huge Billboard and radio hit song. The single Jesus Walks would lead to Kanye's album being critically acclaimed and voted by many major music publications to be ranked as one of the greatest hip-hop albums ever made. But in the eyes of many hardcore, and street traditional hip-hop fans, and artists Kanye's style of hip-hop and his rap-songs were not respected or seen by many of them as being true hip-hop. They saw it as commercial music or a new version of pop-rap music, but there were also many millions of fans of hip-hop, and other forms of music who loudly disagreed with them, and they made Kanye West a world-wide star.

Kanye's debut album would go triple platinum in sales, and Kanye would also win a Grammy for Best Rap Album of that year. In 2005 Kanye would release a second album called Late Registration that also sold in the millions. His fans came to love his music but his critics who were mostly called hardcore fans along with some industry artists like 50 Cent viewed his music as a replacement of true hip-hop. Along this time some strange events would happen in the life of Kanye West that would bring to questions his involvement with occult activities concerning the strange way his own mother would die.

On November 10, 2007 Kanye's mother named Donda West would die under some strange events. Kanye's mother before her death had undergone plastic surgery where she had a liposuction and breast reduction. Soon not too long after the recovery from the operation she would have a heart attack, and then be rushed to the hospital in Marina del Rey, California. When she arrived there she was pronounced dead. The Los Angeles County coroner's office stated that the official cause of death was heart-attack caused by post-operative factors after plastic surgery.

The problem with their official story is that it came nearly two months after she died. When she died her body was not immediately examined for autopsy. In fact the body stayed in a cooler for some time before they decided to give it an examination. Once they had the results they refused to immediately tell members of her family until some weeks later. This is not common procedure from the Los Angeles Police or County offices regarding the matter of dealing with a dead body. It was not clear in the eyes of many why they handle it this way. One very dark tale involved an occult ritual involving Kanye West. This story has never been proven true but it is believed by many who investigate the inner workings of the music industry. The story even very often comes up again and again regarding Kanye's mom. The story was even more fueled by a cell-phone conversation that was recorded that had Kanye on it talking about the death of his mother, and connecting it to the music industry.

Many believe that Kanye's mother was a target for a ritual sacrifice wherein powerful occults will commit a murder, and have the murder covered up to make it look like an accident or something else. These people targeted Kanye's mother according to the story because Kanye was due to offer up someone in his family as a ritual hit to show loyalty to the satanic occult he is in that is within the behind the scenes world of the music industry. According to this story Kanye did not chose his mother but the people he was connected with did. Some insiders would say that Kanye did not think they would choose his mother because her profile was very much known at that point, but if that was the case then he was wrong.

Later on Kanye would have a cell-phone conversation of him recorded where he spoke about the death of his mother. In the conversation he stated that the industry was taking things from him, and that his involvement with the music industry cost him the life of his mother. It was a very strange statement for the sole fact that it was him working in the music industry, and not his mother. It leaves the question what would his mother's death have to do with the place where he works. How did events in the place he works lead to events involving his mother's death?

Kanye does not work in plastic surgery so how could his business which is the music industry business have something to do with the death of his mother? It is a very strange un-answered question. In 2008 Kanye West would release a new album at the time called 808's & Heartbreak. This album would also be a success, and later on he would release two more successful albums. During that time the rap scene in the music industry was changing in a major way. It became a commercial business now being controlled by 48 to 75 year old white men who make all the decisions regarding it. They now own it and decide who is going to the top in the rap game, and who is not. They even make final decisions on the clothes and fashions they wear in hip-hop, and what the cover of their albums will look like and what kind of image they will sell. They have turned the rap scene to be more connected with pop and alternative rock scenes. They have turned rap into a safe and now commercial industry wherein sometimes their artists will bring controversy to themselves but it won't ever effect the way they now sell them.

The gay fashion industry even made deals with the rap CEO's, and owners of major rap labels to enlist their hip-hop artists to dress, and promote their clothing line by having the most popular hip-hop artists today to wear their outfits. Hip-hop artists today even wear fashion that promotes satanic beliefs, and images as well like the goat's head and more. There are also many rumors, and stories floating around all over the music industry about the growing homosexual activities that are going on behind the scenes of the rap music industry among famous hip-hop stars and producers.

Satanism is also being more and more openly spoken about as a problem in the world of the hip-hop scene. Kanye's image as of late seems to promote both the homosexual style, and also Satanism within his fashion, and even within his own songs. Many of Kanye's songs talk about a belief in God but it's also a trick as well. Kanye wants to win over Christian fans, and then give them the new age version of what Christ is to them. The belief regarding them is that they don't believe in Christ as being a living person controlling and running all of creation. They believe that they themselves are Christ that they are Christ-figures on earth. This means they believe that they are gods and goddesses. This is how crazy it can get for them.

Kanye often in his songs will do songs talking about God but it's not the true GOD from the Bible but their version of who GOD is. Many songs from Kanye West also speak on hidden occult knowledge that could only be learned by people who study it. Kanye West clearly studies it, and he clearly from his songs is not against it. Take the song he did called Power. People who have done investigations into occult symbolism in music videos today and yesterday have noticed strong pagan symbolism in the music video, and the song called Power. There are many occult pagan symbols in the music video that each have deep occult meanings in mystery schools of the occult. Many of the hidden meanings in the video are also seen in Freemasonry as well. The music video, and the song seems to show a certain understanding of what power is in the world as it relates to satanic elite groups. The video starts with a very slow close up shot of the camera moving toward the face of Kanye West. As it does Kanye's eyes begins to glow as to show that something spiritual and supernatural lurks inside him. This can also be a reference to demonic possession as well. The supernatural light coming out of Kanye's eyes also bears a hidden meaning that he is lit from within by the knowledge of Illumination wherein the light actually represents Lucifer in that occult understanding.

In the video Kanye is shown like this standing in between a row of endless columns that were filled with the images of various gods that the Bible would call demons. The scene is reminiscent of ancient pagan Egyptian temples that were used as mystery schools to train their temple priests and priestesses. In the understanding of those schools the columns represented wisdom. So therefore seeing massive columns that are pillar sized in massive endless rows like this would symbolize a vast and seemingly endless knowledge of wisdom. This wisdom appears imposing like this to endorse the belief that such wisdom given from their temple brings a man true power in this world to accomplish many things for the gods. The entrance point where Kanye is standing in also represents in that ancient occult understanding a gateway that leads to the true source of power. The gateway is symbolized by the video's representation of the Pillars of Hercules that are shown in the two front towers.

Kanye stands at the mouth of the gateway, and seemingly it would look like he is presenting himself as an enlighten human being, but shockingly enough when you study the core meaning of the video Kanye is not representing himself in that shot at the gateway. He is not even representing anyone human either. Kanye is representing the sun-god in that shot, and the sun-god in that ancient doctrine was believed to be the creator of humans, and the one who gives his light to give might and power to his chosen few. Those few in that understanding would be the rulers, and the establishment powers of those times. This sun-god is actually what the Bible would call Satan, and Satan desires and lusts for worship, and attention from the human race. He also wants to destroy the human race as well.

Kanye in the video is representing Satan as the giver of power through the light of Satan's wisdom. It's a temptation as old as the Garden of Eden where Satan tricks Adam and Eve through his various ways of deception into believing that power comes from his empty promises. Satan only gives this kind of power, and only sometimes to people he wants to use and control for the sole purpose of destroying other people's lives namely the masses of people, and to further his agenda. Once they have served their purpose Satan will seek to get rid of them in all kinds of ways, but Kanye does not present Satan in truth but presents Satan in the form that pleases Satan the most which is the form he most fashions himself as, the god of light and power who is over the destiny of human beings, but really more like a god of mischief and lies.

Kanye's rhymes in the video seems to reflect the desire of people who seek power to accomplish goals wherein Kanye points them to a supernatural occult understanding. Kanye also wears a very interesting chain around his neck of the Egyptian god called Horus. Horus was worshipped as the son of the sun-god, and also he was that time's version of the anti-Christ. In the video you will notice two horned girls whose skin is pure white like a white-wall, and they are holding staffs in their hands at the gateway of the pillars. They would represent the Egyptian goddesses Isis and Hathor of Egyptian pagan teachings. Isis was the goddess of motherhood, nature, and magic. Hathor was the goddess of music, dance, and the fever of sexual lust.

Notice that the creators of the music video Kanye West is doing would use these two goddesses as they represent everything the music industry inspires today. The sword that hangs over Kanye's head does not represent an assassination as some have been led to believe, but what it actually represents is a killing of one's old self to embrace a dark satanic spiritual rebirth. The hanging sword also represents an occult initiation ritual called the Killing of the King.

To pass the ritual is to understand the meaning behind it. The meaning is that the world is filled with dangers that come from several directions at once, and in order to stand tall within the disorder one must stand with an order wherein the order would be your occult masters, and brothers and sisters. This means that in order to pass the ritual one must be willing to cut away from him or her all traces of their old-selves including disconnection from family members, and to give themselves totally over to the occult. To maintain this power is to understand, and know its source, and obey it's every wish, even if that wish is to kill your family members.

This is truly a strange rap song Kanye West recorded, and for what purpose would he want to make a song like this. It is to brag about the fact that this is a real way to power in this world. It would require you to sell your soul to the devil. Truly that is not the source to power but power is solely in the hands of Jesus Christ alone.

Chapter 28

In this chapter we will look at the careers of two of today's biggest R&B stars who are Beyonce and Rihanna. The style of R&B these two artists have today is seen in the music industry as a blend of pop/hip-hop music fused with R&B music. This makes their appeal very far reaching to all cultures of fans being male and female.

Beyonce Knowles was born on September 4, 1981 in Houston, Texas where she was raised. She came from a middle-class home, and her parents were career people connected with the church scene there in Houston. As a child Beyonce went to mostly private Christian schools where in one of them it was discovered she had a strong gifted singing voice. From there Beyonce's father Mathew Knowles would encourage her to develop her voice. He began getting her more training lessons.

Beyonce would start her career as a child. She began singing and dancing in local talent competitions where she would win most of them. When Beyonce became a pre-teen going into her teenage years her father was getting her gigs to perform solo spots at local shows, parties, and clubs. He would also get her gigs working at shows to perform with various up and coming artists. Beyonce's career in that time, and up until the time she went solo was managed by her father Mathew Knowles.

Many strange things were said about this man that have not been proven but should be explored. Insiders who knew the Knowles family at the time they were trying to make Beyonce a star stated that they robbed young Beyonce of a childhood. They would state that the family appeared Christian on the surface but some strange things were going on in their household.

It was believed that her family, mostly her father, was a mason, and he already knew people in the music industry. Seeing that his daughter had talent, and knowing the kind of people he knew he saw early that a lot of money could be made off his daughter. It was said that from that point he did not fully treat her like a daughter but more like a work-horse, and this work even came with physical and mental abuse. He would push his daughter very hard, and put heavy amounts of pressure on her that were far from what a person should do to a young girl. He would harden, and even damage her mind to have a control over it. It was also said that he pimped out his daughter, and the rest of the girls he managed when they became Destiny's Child to record executives to secure a contract.

When Beyonce was eight years old her father had her audition for an all-girl entertainment R&B group. In the audition she would meet for the first time two girls who were also very young looking to be career singers. They were Kelly Rowland and

LaTavia Roberson. During the audition the managers of this all-girl group they were looking to form selected Beyonce, Kelly, LaTavia, and three other girls to form the R&B-rap group called Girl's Tyme. When Girl's Tyme was formed this was the group Beyonce came to perform with throughout her pre-teen/teenage years while also doing solo shows. Girl's Tyme mainly performed around the talent show, and local club circuits in Houston. The group even appeared on national television when they appeared on Star Search.

In 1995 the pressure for Beyonce was about to be very much increased. Beyonce's father Mathew 'foresaw' as he put it to his family that Beyonce, and her group were going to become very successful and famous. He believed it so much that he quit his job to manage Beyonce and the entire group full-time. This choice of his would result in the family's income to be cut in half. Her parents were forced to move from their own middle-class family home, and had to move into small apartments.

Beyonce's father was very serious about making the group famous because his own family was at stake. It was believed by many insiders that at this point Beyonce was in his full control along with the other members of the group. His behavior toward them was seen by others as not the behavior of a manager but the actions of a handler who was at times abusive. It was said that her father's character at this time came also with the plan to sell his daughter, and the girls in any which way he could. His plan also was to sell the girls in whatever way the record companies wanted them just to secure a contract. At this point Mathew cuts the line-up of the group from six to four women. He would revamp their image to appear more sexual, and would keep their music urban to make the group appeal to both young professionals and urban fans. He would have them work very hard, and would deal his way into getting gigs for them.

The group would impress people working in the nightclub scene who were connected to people in the music industry. These connections Mathew made would lead to the group performing as an opening act for various established R&B groups. Through these performances Mathew got himself, and the group through the doors of the music industry. Soon the group was recording demo tapes, and auditioning for major record labels. The labels kept refusing them.

How Mathew finally got his group signed, and the price they would pay for it is also told by insiders as well. After getting many refusals a record company called Elektra decided to sign them, but these executives Elektra sent were twisted. Before they allowed the group to sign the story is they wanted sexual favors from the girls in the group. No one knows how true the story is but the story would finish with Mathew enlisting the girls to perform sexual favors on them for the contract.

After being signed to Elektra Records the company ended up selling the contract to Atlanta Records, and they inform Mathew that is where the girls will be recording, but when Mathew came there with the group, and the group began recording, the executives at Atlanta did not like the musical sound of the group. So just when Mathew, the group, and Beyonce's family thought they made it the company would cut the group from their label. This huge blow brought bad problems between Beyonce's mother and father. Her parents would separate at that time due to these problems.

Mathew however was still not done, and became more harden, and driven about making them famous. Many insiders stated that at this point he was willing to pay any price. Soon Mathew met a man named Dwayne Wiggins. Dwayne worked for Grass Roots Entertainment who officially help up and coming artists. Others say that the entertainment company actually works as a scout company to sell new talent to record companies by giving them artists who are willing to do more than just sign a piece of paper.

It was believed that this entertainment company seeks artists willing to do sexual, and other strange dark favors for a chance to be successful and record an album. Mathew would sign the girls on to the entertainment company in 1996. The company wanted them to change the name of the group so they could be able to sell them much better. Mathew would name the group Destiny's Child and the group's image became more sexual in a high-heel/short skirt way. Their dance moves became very sexual, and often Mathew would have the girls practicing their dance moves using poles that strippers use.

Very soon the entertainment company was able to sell the girls to a record company called Columbia. The story surrounding this is that these executives working for Columbia were involved with people in government black-ops involving mind-control experimentation. They agreed to sign the girls if the girls quietly agree to be used in several mind-control sessions. It was said that Mathew quickly agreed to it being very hungry for success. He would allow his own daughter, and the other girls to be tortured, abused, and raped in mind-control sessions. For many this is very hard to believe but the theme of mind-control torture often comes up regarding Beyonce along with demonic possession to such a point that it seems it's far more than a theme, but more like a real possible occurrence in her life.

When the group was signed to Columbia Records they would soon record their debut album. Destiny's Child would go on to become one of the world's best-selling all-girl R&B group in the history of the music industry.

During the height of their success Mathew now reunited with his wife, Beyonce's mother, had focused most of his attention on Beyonce. Quietly without telling the other girls he sought for Beyonce to go solo after the fame of Destiny's Child runs out. Beyonce was the lead singer at the time for the group, and all the media attention was being thrown in her direction. She was even being offered parts for movie roles as well. It was only a matter of time before she broke from the group and went solo. At that time it was believed that the members of Destiny's Child were involved with satanic voodoo among hidden circles at popular nightclubs. Their influence was one of a strong but yet highly sexual, and greedy where things are based on looks and wealth. They were known to have a very sexual image, and lived an immoral lifestyle off the camera.

By the time the 2000s came Beyonce would go solo. In 2003 Beyonce released her debut album called Dangerously in Love. The album featured for its lead single the song called Crazy in Love that would quickly become a number one Billboard hit single. Beyonce would record the song, and film the music video with rapper Jay-Z. Some years later after the success of this song Beyonce would become more open about her alter-ego, and would even name it Sasha Fierce. She would state regarding this alter-ego that it was a dark, mean, and highly openly sexual alter-ego.

She discovered this alter-ego when she did the music video Crazy in Love. She would also soon start dating Jay-Z after she made the video with him as well. Jay-Z became more involved with her career, and took over as a manager for her which was the job that was previously her father's job. It was believed Jay-Z introduced Beyonce to more of the behind the scenes power of the controllers of the music industry who are connected with corporate and government leaders. This inner scene involved satanic rituals, and a lifestyle of riches, sex, and drugs.

The album Dangerously in Love established Beyonce as a world-wide star. It would sell over 11 million copies. In 2005 after another album with Destiny's Child the group disbanded. In 2006 Beyonce would release her second album called B'Day. This album as well would sell in the millions. At this point Jay-Z was in the driver seat of her career. He would marry Beyonce at this point.

Many stated that their marriage is really as fake as it comes, and it was done for business purposes, and they have an open relationship, meaning they see other people sexually. Jay-Z is often described to be more like a handler toward her rather than her husband who she is only seen with at public events.

Beyonce at this time was called one of the most desired of women on the face of the earth. Her image became highly sexual and alluring, and she comes off many times as a sex siren on stage and in her music videos. It is also believed that she became a full, and inside member of a celebrity satanic occult in the entertainment industry made up mostly of Freemasons. She then opens up more about this spirit within her and names her album after it. Much of what she will describe about it falls with demonic possession, but the way she talks about it she seems to be happy with it. When Beyonce would release this album she already made a few Hollywood films.

In 2008 Beyonce released her third album called I Am...Sasha

Fierce. The album was named after her alter-ego but a lot of fans were confused about it. She would then do an interview on national television explaining who Sasha Fierce is. Beyonce explained that Sasha was a spirit that comes over her body. She states that this spirit would get her to do things on stage that she could never do in her singing and dancing. She states that she is a gifted singer, and dancer but the spirit of Sasha is better and it makes her a better performer. She talks about this spirit as though it is a living person to her that lives inside her. In later interviews she explains that this spirit came to her when she did the music video Crazy in Love. In the interview she states that by nature she is a shy person but the spirit of Sasha is not, and that spirit helps her to be strong in her career. While Beyonce is talking about this she has a happy, and smiling face on as though she just told the world something wonderful.

Her fans really had no idea what she was really talking about, and many of them felt she was only explaining concepts of art in a new character, but really new concepts don't come by a spirit that you regard as a living spirit with its own personality that comes, and enters your body, and makes you a different person. New concepts come from thinking it out and studying. What Beyonce was talking about is spirit possession. When Jesus was confronted by a demon-possessed person living in the tombs of the city Jesus demanded that the spirit within the person reveal its name. The demon speaking in the man stated, 'my name is Legion for we are many.' Jesus allowed the confrontation to show a true aspect of a demon possessed person. The demon was being made by Jesus to expose its true nature. The demon is saying that though the spirit in the man has only one name, the man in fact does not have only one demon inside him. He in fact has thousands of demons inside him, and they were constantly tormenting him.

Beyonce states that this spirit has only one name but the true reality would be she has thousands of spirits within her. These demon-spirits often gave the man supernatural strength to be able to break iron chains and have tolerance for pain. Those spirits were also making him a madman as well. The man even shows before the demon was casted out by Jesus to have a dual personality to him. One personality was himself, and the other was the spirits living in him.

Beyonce states that she becomes fearless when Sasha takes over on stage, and that spirit makes her a better and stronger dancer which means her body also becomes stronger while under this spirit. Beyonce on stage often appears possessed, and her facial expressions to her movements often seem crazed and even wicked. Beyonce while talking about Sasha is also showing she has a dual nature to herself as well. The more you realize the interview, and what Jesus showed in the Bible it comes to light that there is something seriously wrong with Beyonce, and it centers on demonic possession.

Beyonce's third album at the time would also sell in the millions. The lead single off the album was a song called Single Ladies (Put a Ring on It). A lot of people, mostly women, thought that the song was about promoting marriage or lasting relationships, but that was not what the song really was about, and its real meaning is very twisted. In the music video there is nothing in the video about relationships. Instead in the video you get Beyonce, and a group of back-up dancers dressed like playboy bunnies. While they are dressed like high-priced playboy prostitutes they all start dancing like hookers at nightclubs in scenes that have them on the streets or at photo-shoots and other places. While dancing Beyonce is singing the song, and in the video are scenes of other celebrity people who appear in the video chanting the chorus of the song. Everyone seems to like the chorus, and they like lusting after Beyonce and her dancers as well, but there was nothing in the video about anything meaningful. Just a group of half-naked girls telling you to put a ring on them after you had sex with them. Usually the ring is suppose, to come, along with the marriage, before sex, but the song has different ideas, and these ideas are not found in the Bible.

The term 'put a ring on it' that Beyonce is singing about is a nightclub term. It is a term used among girls out in the clubs where they make their boyfriends spend their money until their wallet is empty because of the kind of sex they give their boyfriends for it. The bait set by these girls is to have wild sex with them, and when those men seek to come back for more than those girls make them spend all kinds of money on them before taking them back to bed for more sex. Afterwards the cycle repeats itself with other guys coming into the picture. This is how a lot of girls at the nightclubs enjoy themselves. Not all of them but many of them, and the girls who are known to do this at the nightclubs are the girls who show up in single groups.

The song is really about singing a subject that is seen as a form of prostitution done in a way that is legal but also a sin before GOD, but Beyonce doesn't care about that. She just tells people she comes from a Christian home, and she is a good Christian while she shakes her private parts all over television and sings songs like this, and tells people that spirits enter her body.

Many insiders believe that demonic spirits had been inside the body of Beyonce before she did the video Crazy in Love. They explained that what happened during Crazy in Love is that those spirits inside her gave themselves a name they wanted Beyonce to promote which was Sasha. The video itself has strong occult meanings, and is done from the view point of these demonic spirits in how they are using Beyonce. In order to understand that one must understand the video itself. Most of the scenes in the music video are filled with symbolism and dark meanings. Most people will not catch it especially those not looking for it due to the catchy hook of the song.

In the video Beyonce is walking toward a car that is speeding toward her. The car that is driving full speed at Beyonce has Jay-Z sitting in the backseat. The driver itself is faceless and unknown. He would within the symbolism represent a spirit what the Bible would call a demonic spirit. In that understanding we have in the video Satan driving a car full speed at Beyonce while Jay-Z is sitting in the back of the car. The scene in the video shows the car running over Beyonce in an imagery way. The scene represents a spiritual take-over of Beyonce. Jay-Z sitting in the backseat of the car would represent someone who is already taken over. He seems to act in the video more like a handler of what Beyonce is doing in the video.

After this spiritual take over we see scenes of Beyonce unbinding her hair, and getting up on top of a warehouse platform. She begins to get on all fours like a dog, and she starts dancing like a whore. I hate to put it this way but there was simply no way to put it in the manner that she did it. That scene was not a dance move it was simply a simulation of a sexual act common with animals. It is believed that this quick scene had a representation of a sexual act because it represented a price for fame. Beyonce in that scene would continue to dance in an unrestrained way while the scene then cuts over to a series of short scenes of young girls dressed like Beyonce. They dance around in a wanton way while they dance the same style of impurity that Beyonce is showing. The girls in the scene would represent the fans who want to be Beyonce. They would be the young fans that Beyonce is corrupting.

The final scenes of the video shows Beyonce sitting in a car while Jay-Z set's it on fire. Jay-Z watches while the car gets blown up and Beyonce now disappears. He begins to rap his verse, and while he does so he calls himself, 'Young'. As far as I can tell the word had a reference to a new age teaching of one who is reborn. The kind of rebirth in occult understanding is when one has been introduced to the inner circle of leadership of the occult, and are given knowledge that is hidden from others. The word is used then as a magical word. After the explosion when Jay-Z is still rapping Beyonce re-appears, and she is dressed like a prostitute, and stands to begin moving in a wanton fashion. She appears in the scene as incoherent and bursting with sexual lust. When she appears this way Jay-Z calls her, 'Young B'. This word also had that same occult meaning but the B' part is added to show someone who is newly born. This then in that hidden occult group would mean she is a new comer to that hidden knowledge.

In a music video Beyonce did called Diva, which is a word used in goddess worship, Beyonce shows a scene of being fully aware that she is destroying the lives of many fans. In fact the true core of goddess worship did require its ancient temple members to go out and destroy lives for the goddess. In this scene Beyonce seems to present herself as being possessed by a dark spirit. She walks up to a car that has an open trunk, and the trunk is filled from top to bottom with human-looking dummies. When she is before this car we see scenes of her dancing, and her dance moves would seem to inspire the hooker in heat impression. While dancing she sings about vain worldly things and acts rude while she does it. She seems to think she is doing us a favor by entertaining us. It reminds me of when Beyonce stated that she learned all her values in Sunday-school at church, and now here she is half-naked in a video showing off her private part by using her body to rub it on a pole. It makes you think what kind of church is this or was she really listening because clearly to make such a statement, and do scenes like that shows that she is a good liar.

After Beyonce sings and dances this part in the video, the scene goes back to Beyonce in front of the car that has the trunk full of dummies. Sad to say but the dummies in the car actually represent the fans that listen and mimic Beyonce. In the video Beyonce shows what she really thinks of her fans. She lights the car on fire, and the car blows up in a huge explosion that destroys all the dummies in the car. The scene is very twisted with a real evil message behind it that many of her fans still refuse to believe. Beyonce sees her fans as dummies because they are dumb enough to idolize her when it is her intent as an artist in the music industry to destroy everything good in their lives. Their destruction comes also through her influences, and so for her in order to be powerful, and famous in the world it must come through the destruction of her fans.

Another video that Beyonce made was called Sweet Dreams. The lyrics, and the music video itself does feature some strange supernatural activities along with dark occultism, mind-control, and demonic possession. To understand some of the scenes is to know some of the effects of mind-control. Victims in mind-control will undergo trauma caused by pain that is induced by electro-shock treatments. These treatments also come with mind-altering drugs that are given to the victim. Along with that it is believed that a satanic ritual is being performed during the process to bring demons into the victim.

Most of the knowledge of covert U.S. mind-control experimentation was taught to the U.S. by the Nazis. The Nazis under Hitler were very deep into such rituals and occultism, and they would often blend it with their sciences. The intense pain of electro-shock under these conditions will cause the victim to feel an intense feeling of light-headedness to such a point that the victim will feel like they are floating like a butterfly in the air.

In the video Beyonce starts to sing a creepy song where she

feels lost in a fairytale. She is in a hazy state of mind, and she is asking for a hand to guide her. She sings about a dual condition going on all around her that her mind feels like she could see a sweet dream but a part of her tells her it could also be a beautiful nightmare. The symbolism in the video seem to suggest that the nightmare is the abuse that is around her.

The lyrics follow with the understanding that she takes this abuse because it offers her the guilty pleasure she desires which would be the fame and the money. In the early scenes of the music video we see Beyonce sleeping on a bed to a creepy lullaby tune. A dove would appear to her, and then suddenly Beyonce in a fashion seen in the film called The Exorcist would start to levitate from her bed. As she is levitating from the bed the lullaby tune becomes more menacing where sounds of screaming are added to it. The scene was a representation of demonic possession, and its effects in the way it haunts people.

The video would then show a short series of scenes that relate to mirror programming. Beyonce is in a room of mirrors in these various scenes, and in the mirrors she sees reflections of herself, but the reflections become alive with their own personality. Soon Beyonce realizes that they are trying to take her over. So she fights with them as the mirrors in the scene come crashing down.

As I covered in early chapters the scene does not mean she overcame the demons but that they took her over. The crashing mirrors represents her mind-state which is broken in pieces with demons now running around her head. The song, according to this understanding along with the video speak on darker issues that affects many artists. These issues revolve around mind-control, and demonic possession.

Beyonce is currently a very popular world-wide star. She has a lot of power in the music industry R&B field. Her Super Bowl performance was loaded with satanic imagery, and her television performances are often loaded with globalism themes including martial law. She is a big supporter, and fund-raiser for President Obama along with her husband Jay-Z as well. Her image is still sexually immoral and still dirty. It is loaded with dark and angry sexual themes. Her concerts are also still loaded with satanic themes along with globalism themes.

Rihanna whose real name is Robyn Fenty was born in Saint Michael, Barbados on February 20, 1988. Her mother's name is Monica Braithwaite and she was of African-Guyanese heritage, and worked as an accountant. Her father's name is Ronald Fenty, and he is of Barbadian-Irish heritage who worked as a warehouse supervisor.

Growing up Rihanna lived in a three bedroom bungalow in the city of Bridgetown, Barbados. She grew up with two brothers, and many half-siblings. Her family often struggled for money due to her father's drug problems. The marriage of Rihanna's parents was violent and turbulent. Her household was deeply affected by her father's horrible addiction to crack-cocaine and alcohol.

Her parents would divorce when Rihanna was 14 years old, and she would live from then on with her mother. Rihanna became involved with the Reggae local music scene when she was a pre-teen and going into her teenage years. Her passion for singing started when she was 7 years old were at that age she discovered her singing voice.

As a teenager she would attend Combermere High School. In high-school she would form a musical trio with two of her classmates. They would perform at local shows, school dance halls, local parties, and clubs. In high-school Rihanna was part of a sub-military program that many insiders say could have been a cover to bring in people of interest for mind-control experimentation.

Rihanna was an Army cadet for the program, and her drill sergeant at the time would also become a singer and songwriter in the music industry called Shontelle. Shontelle would later on come to write songs for many music industry artists including Rihanna. It was said that Rihanna may have been a victim to mind-control abuses while in this program at high-school. It was also said she got involved with the voodoo ritual scene that was in the underground culture of Bridgetown.

Rihanna's entrance into the music industry happened while she was still in high-school. In 2003 Rihanna was at a nightclub with her girlfriends in a Barbados nightclub that was a hot spot for local performers. Often young local female performers would flock there at times to meet people connected with the music scene. When Rihanna was there at this club she was with a group of her girlfriends. At that same time she was there, music producer Evan Rogers was vacationing in Barbados. Through some girls he met he would come down to this club right at the time when Rihanna and her friends were there. The girls that were with Evan knew the girls that Rihanna was among, and they were all friends. The group would soon all join together, and Evan it should be noted, was always on the look-out for new talent.

It was believed he came to the club not so much for the girls but to also seek out new talent. Evan knew that new talent was there a kind of talent he could control, and then sell. While the group was joined together Rihanna's friends told Evan that Rihanna was a performer at that club. He heard about how good she was on stage, and how well she could sing. Evan was highly taken in by her looks, and was pleased to hear that he also found the talent he was looking for. Even though Evan was always scouting talent that night he was also looking to have sex with someone as well. Evan would then start coming on to Rihanna, and began talking about representing her to get her a record contract. He then stated that he needed her to come to his hotel room so that he could hear her audition.

Usually that is a red flag because that is how producers have taken advantage of young artists by getting them alone in their hotel rooms or homes. Auditions usually take place at a studio, office, or even a club. Rihanna being offered this was in a club, and even performed there. She could have just performed for him at the club, and under normal settings that is what the producer would have asked her to do. He normally would not ask her to go to his private hotel room to do it. It was believed that this conversation resulted in what many insiders say is a visit to the music industry's form of the casting couch. The artists will perform sexual favors on producers, and even executives, and in return the artist is pushed through the doors of the music industry.

Rihanna would go to his hotel room. According to the official story Rihanna only went there to perform an audition for him, but most people don't believe the official story because of how well they know about those kinds of auditions. After Rihanna's hotel visit with Evan things would become even stranger. Rihanna must have really impressed Evan because Evan would do something for Rihanna that is also nowhere near normally done. Evan would take Rihanna, and her mother from Barbados, and bring them into his own home in Connecticut to live with him. The official story behind this action of Evan was done so that Rihanna could record some demo tapes, but this is also way out of practice. Usually in such cases the producers will set up the family with an apartment. They would not invite them into their own home.

Many believe that the true motive behind Evan doing this was to get full control over Rihanna's life. Rihanna's life from that point was controlled by record company executives. Evan wanted not only this control but control over her body as well. She would easily become his live-in girlfriend, and this can be turned into a form of human slavery but without chains and whips. It's slavery done by blackmail and covert means. While living with Evan Rihanna recorded a four song demo tape, and Evan sent the tapes out to several labels he was connected to. When this took place it was 2004, and one of the demo tapes becomes noticed by Def Jam Records. At that time do to a deal Jay-Z had with Def Jam Records, Jay-Z was the President of Def Jam Records.

It was A&R executive of Def Jam named Jay Brown who first heard the demo tape sent to him by Evan. Brown would play it for Jay-Z, and he soon invited her to audition for the label. Her audition greatly impressed Jay-Z and the executives to such a point that they signed her to a six-album record deal with Def Jam Records. Rihanna at this time spent several months with Jay-Z, and other Def Jam artists.

It was believed that during this time Rihanna became more involved with the inner satanic workings of the music industry. She began to dive into this lifestyle, and eventually became a member of this hidden new age satanic occult. Rihanna would have a vast management team working with her from the start. Many of them would act more like mind-control handlers then managers. From the start they controlled all the aspects in her life.

Rihanna also had a team of music songwriters, beat makers, rappers, DJs, mixers, etc. who would come to write mostly all of her songs. They would also create her image as well. Rihanna's debut album would be released in August of 2005. The album would be called Music of the Sun. Some believed that the title came about as homage to the Egyptian sun-god. The lead single to the album was called Pon de Replay. Pon de Replay would become a smash hit as a single, and would hit the number two spot on the Billboard 100 singles chart. Her debut album would go on to sell 2 million copies.

After this success Rihanna released her second album called A Girl Like Me. This album also would sell in the millions. The lead single from her second album called SOS would hit the number one spot on the Billboard 100 singles chart in 2006. During Rihanna's career regarding her first two albums Rihanna had a more happy but sexual nightclub friendly image. Her image was not dark and satanic during that time, but that would change when Rihanna recorded her third album called Good Girl Gone Bad. When Rihanna released her third album in 2007 she embraced a new, and more darker demonic image along with a new musical direction. She would bring in more hip-hop, electro-pop, and Latin drum play into her R&B sound. The course of her musical direction would be loaded with dark and sexual themes. Many of these themes had some very dark, and hidden meanings of horrible events going on in the world. The album Good Girl Gone Bad would make Rihanna a bigger star then before. The album would sell over 7 million copies. The lead single from the album called Umbrella became the longest-running number one Billboard hit single since 1994's Love Is All Around. The single also was named as one of the best-selling singles of all time as it sold by itself over 6 million copies. Rihanna would also win a Grammy Award for the single as well.

Since then she released more albums that became huge sellers and her image, photo-shoots, and music videos became even more dark and loaded with satanic symbolism. Her songs would come to be inspired with occult demonic themes, and political events of a dark nature.

Take the song she did called Umbrella. At face value the song seems innocent. It seems to be singing about a girl protecting her boyfriend through good times and bad times, but the lyrics, and over all meaning of the song along with the music video shows a much different meaning. It's a hidden meaning also called a deep meaning. Rihanna herself stated that the song had a much deeper and hidden meaning. She never states that the song is about looking out for a lover's protection. What she states is that the song has a complex meaning which can only be sorted out be trying to find the hidden meanings within the lyrics and the art-form of the song. Within the lyrics of the song Rihanna sings the song as if she is two different persons. She even shows this concept in the music video with the black and white duality. It suggests an alter-ego a person at odds with their own persona, and is having a conversation with it. Many insiders who looked into this song and video feels that Rihanna could be playing the role of herself and Satan. The song talks about a strange storm that is coming, and Rihanna sings a verse about offering protection then her tone changes within her lyrics, and suddenly she sings a verse where she is in love with this protection.

The duality there is that she sings the first verse as this unknown powerful person who could be Satan where she is offering protection, and the second verse is sung as herself being thankful of the protection. The strange storm then would represent un-foreseen events in the world that she could not be saved from by her own power. So in the song she is thankful for this protection. Also to be under this protection means that the thing or person protecting you has far more power over you, and can even control you. The hook and the manner of the song makes it sound like this is beautiful or something of that sort, but this type of control is not romantic for it violates people's lives, and controls the way they live their lives. It is an invasion over a person's will to be who they are, and to seek truths in their lives without such disturbance.

Jay-Z also appears in the song and music video wherein he is featured as an artist on Rihanna's album. When Jay-Z raps his verse he starts rapping about some things that are very deep, and not positive news for the general public. Jay-Z starts rapping about the 'storms' and uses other metaphors to describe the downfall of the economy and the financial world. Jay-Z reflects the situation when he raps about the downfall of the Dow Jones. The Dow Jones is the main indicator of the health of the stock market. If it falls that means a horrible mass of jobs in the millions will be lost. That will result in total poverty, misery, and a struggle for survival among millions and millions of people.

That is not a romantic outlook on things, and that is not cute and warm either. That is a total nightmare, and knowing that doesn't make you what to think about relationships. Jay-Z in his rap lyrics goes on to declare the words 'let it rain' and that he 'hydroplanes in the bank'. What Jay-Z is declaring is that he does not care about the flood storms of economic collapse, and total riots that will result from it. For him when the financial meltdown is unleashed in the future he is declaring that he does not have to worry about because he has inside deals that protects his money, or so that is what they like to tell Jay-Z. Most famous celebrities like Jay-Z do feel this way. Many of them among the A-list have convinced themselves that the people who control them will take care of them. That they will always be under their protection for their service to them, but history often shows a different destiny regarding sell-outs and people that were used by higher powers. They always end up betrayed, poor, or killed. It always ends very sad for them. Rihanna in her lyrics continues to sing the song in a duality state. In one set of the lyrics she is singing again as this spiritual entity which is something non-human. In this character she is trying to seduce herself with the riches of being with this invisible being who invites her to live under its protection. As this character the seduction is being done by using fear tactics to win the prey over.

She starts to sing about dark world events to come that could swallow her up unless she comes under the protection. In the music video we see a scene of Rihanna being covered in silver-chrome paint, and Rihanna is shooting the silver liquid in every direction. This scene was very strange to people, and there was an even stranger belief regarding it. Ancient pagan worshippers used to believe that the semen of their gods was a silver liquid. They would teach that their gods would come down from the sky, and seek a human woman to mate with. They would cover the woman with this silver liquid during the encounters the gods had with these women according to the story.

The Bible speaks about fallen angels in the Book of Genesis coming down from the sky, and mating with human women to produce demonic children with them. The Bible also calls the gods of the world to be actually the council of fallen angels spoken about in the Book of Psalms. It's very twisted that Rihanna, and the creators of this music video, would show such an image. Rihanna seems to be showing in that scene that she wants to have sex with what the Bible calls the Devil. This leads back to the belief that Satan is one of the dual characters she represents in the song.

Another series of scenes in the music video shows Rihanna naked, and covered in this silver paint. Rihanna is sitting inside a triangle where she does an odd series of poses that had references to occult practices and demonic images. The rain drops in the video also have a darker meaning as well. Rain man is a code-word for Satan among the hidden famous scene in the music industry. People who have encountered possession have spoken about a wet feeling they would get at times that felt like a drop or drops of rain on them. Many of those who felt this suffered possession from wanton acts of sexual sins. It's strange that the image of the rain drops in the video comes along with Rihanna appearing to be seduced by it. The song as a whole is about selling your soul to Satan. It's done in a way to make the concept appear to be good and romantic. The song promotes Satan in the world, and that through Satan is how one can be saved from the world. Of course that is not the truth. Satan will only seek to control a person, use a person, and then get rid of the person.

In 2008 Rihanna released a song called Disturbia. The lyrics and the music video reveals that the song is about full-blown demonic possession. It reveals the torments of possession, and its mind-control aspects. The hook of the song is loaded with a witchcraft chant to rhyme with the chorus. It is done that way because according to witchcraft doctrine it's meant to put spells on people. Putting spells on people in real witchcraft understanding is simply to call on demons to make trouble for people.

The entire video is loaded with demon-possessed people. Rihanna is also featured as a demon possessed person in the video where she plays a mother-figure to these possessed people in the video. The scenes are filled with horror, rage, and its direction is to show people in dark, and underground settings living in cages and being tormented by demons.

People in the media said this was sensational, and Rihanna was sexy and things of that sort, but really what music video were they watching or did they not watch the video at all but just read what was on the monitor to say something that clearly was not true. Rihanna does not look happy, and fun in the video. She instead looks like she is going to take everyone down to Hell with her.

Often we tend to forget what famous people are a part of. We even tend to forget that their influences have been helping to reshape the world by destroying it. Clearly when GOD created art-forms it was never his intention to use it to destroy the world. Sadly there are people, and spiritual beings of their own free-will who seek to do that in the world. It's a cold world indeed and GOD is often hated in it. It's truly a last days world when sweet innocent looking artists can inspire things in the lives of their fans that could lead them to their deaths. These same entertainers who do this to us even pretend to worship GOD, and they state that they do only to save face in the eyes of fans they are trying to deceive and get rich from. The Bible tells us that Satan, and his people would do things like this in the last days. In these days people's minds, and emotions are played with constantly through images and music, and political events. We tend to forget that Satan was once in charge of music in Heaven. He knows how to influence people through music. Satan is also a walking muse now filled with evil ideas into how to inspire people to follow him.

When Rihanna released the album R-Rated there was high concern from Christian leaders, and even people working in the music industry that people were going to be inspired to kill themselves through the songs on the album. This came about through the lead single of the album called Russian Roulette. The name of the song comes from the name of a game of death that is played by people who are clearly violent and mentally off balance. Within the game people sit around at a table, and a six-shooter hand-gun is put on the table. The gun is loaded with one bullet, and then the chamber of the gun is given a quick hard spin. Once done the bullet is locked in an unknown spot in the chamber. Each person must take the gun, and as a sign of some macho bravery must put the gun to their head and pull the trigger. Sometimes nothing comes out but other times a person blows their head-off. If the game is played long enough, at the end of the night someone will be killed.

This most deadly game was the game Rihanna felt like promoting in the lead single of her album. She did a song that would influence a person to get a strange feeling in their mind to where one day they will be opened to playing a game like that, and end up blowing their head-off. This song is truly one of the most disturbing R&B songs ever played on the airwaves. Shocking enough is that the song was played so many times in fact over and over again on popular airwave stations. The music video also was very strange as well. The video actually tells a much different tale then suicide however. In fact it goes very much into the direction of mind-control abuse. In the early scenes of the video Rihanna is locked inside a padded room. There is a man there dressed in a military uniform who is manipulating her thoughts though high-tech devices. The man in the video who would represent a handler uses the devices to start sending demonic images into the brain of Rihanna. According to what happens in mind-control these images would come like traumatizing events that do torture a victim's mind. The goal of the torture is to cause so much intense pain by trauma that the victim will dissociate from reality. In mind-control the methods that are used to cause this state of mind are electro-shock treatments, sexual abuse, and burning the victims in areas of their bodies. Other methods are even using demons to attack them. The people who do this to them are doing it to cause a split in the personality of their minds. They can use this split to create a condition inside the victims called Multiple Personality Disorder. In research done through unclassified files regarding mind-control, it reveals some shocking things regarding the creation of this condition. The victims start out first deprived of food, water, and then they are forced to sleep in deprivation tanks. Soon they are hypnotized through various drugs, and they have I.V. tubes feeding their bodies. More drugs are given to them to alter certain cerebral functions. This gives them the access to do serious damage to their minds.

In the music video Rihanna is forced to endure brutal scenarios, and she is tormented in her cell as these intense demonic attacks are being driven into her mind. Her cell is filled with red smoke, and Rihanna's movements become in a very creepy way robotic movements. Much of this points to a scene of possession. The handler in the video presses a button, and Rihanna's demonic experiences become worse. In one scene we see Rihanna floating under water. This was a symbolism of what she is feeling regarding mind-control.

During the intense abuse victims will feel weightless like they are floating. During the scenes in the video bullets are being shot into the water while Rihanna is floating in it. All the bullets will miss her body, and many believe the understanding there related to passing through certain mind-control sessions as one does passing a test. In the final scenes of the video we see a friend of Rihanna in the video shooting himself. This brings to point the major suicide element to the song. The photo-shoots, and the imagery of the posters that were promoting the album at the time was loaded with satanic and sexual themes. In these images Rihanna would wear a tight dress sporting devil horns, and in another picture she shows off her breast while her nipples are wrapped in barb-wire.

She is often wearing a one eye patch or showing one eye which bears reference to the all-seeing eye of Lucifer who is Satan.

Another photo shows a group of mannequins wrapped in barb wires, and thrown about the floor as if dumped around like trash. This photo was to be shown to her fans to bring them in to buy the album. The idea behind it was to show the fans as mannequins wrapped around in barb-wires, and dumped on the side. This is how artists like this see their fans. They are not thankful to their fans they live in their own ego-driven twisted worlds.

The themes of the R-Rated album regarding posters and songs are suicide, demonic possession, mind-control, pain, sexual immorality, sexual abuse, torture, and all restriction from true happiness. In short Rihanna's music is like a ticking time bomb to her fans. It promotes a lifestyle of self-destruction, vanity, and Satanism.

In a video Rihanna did called Who's That Chick this video featured a light and a dark version. The light and dark imagery would be explained in the symbolism of the video that captures many witchcraft and masonic elements. The checkerboard pattern floors are very common in masonic lodges. It has many dual meanings like the yin and the yang does. Mostly it represents positive and negative energies, good and evil concepts. The belief that true godhood is to know you can do both be a follower of GOD and Satan in your life. The Bible states a man cannot serve two masters only one can he serve.

The video also features witchcraft symbolism, and promotes the belief of white and black magic. The video uses symbols relating to both white and black magic like skulls, tear drops, and icons. It should be noted that the skulls in the video are human skulls. When you see the art-forms of these artists you begin to understand why millions of people around the world which adds to billions are becoming very far removed from their Savior Jesus Christ. You begin to understand how a problem involving millions of personal breakdowns, and careless evil attitudes can run so rampant over society. How millions can be so sexually immoral, and engage in erratic activities. They see no need to really investigate the results of the kind of lives they lead, and the beliefs that poison their souls.

Chapter 29

Musical gifts are truly meant to be used to inspire. That is the nature of the word music itself. The word music actually comes from the word muse. The meaning of the word muse is to ponder on emotions and thoughts that are inspired to cause a person to meditate or even day-dream upon whatever emotions and thoughts that are inspiring the person. In the Hebrew language there was two different words for what we call music today. One word was 'shir' that meant 'singing', and the other word was 'zemar' that meant 'the striking of musical instruments'.

The two forms used together creates what we call general music. The Hebrews in those ancient times used their music to inspire people to be moved by the Word of GOD. Their songs were about GOD, or the lessons of GOD, or their lives in relation with GOD.

From the beginning the Book of Job tells us that angels were singing praises to GOD when GOD formed all of creation like humans, and the entire universe. Music is called one of the oldest, and also most natural form of fine arts. Styles of music are found in every nation of people GOD created all over the world. The ancient Romans working in the fields of fine arts often combine their pagan mythological teachings into many forms of fine arts. One of them was music. They in fact took the word music from the word muse, and copied the habits of the ancient Greek nations before them. These Romans had a whole system of beliefs regarding the word muse that was short for muses. They would blend those beliefs into the forms of music they performed for Roman people and other visitors.

Many believe that this system of beliefs still preside in the belief system of the famous music industry today. Most record company owners, CEOs, and executives are not believers in Christianity even though most of the fans of music profess Christianity. Among the owners or controllers of the industry it's a different world, and that world centers around many new age beliefs. New Age faith also has a system of beliefs similar to what the Romans had, to combine all religions into one belief that would be ruled by the Roman system. Today it would be a world government system.

The word muses in ancient Roman pagan understanding was a name employed to designate several divinities who were worshiped called Nymphs. Each of these Nymphs were quite distinct from each other. The Romans would ascribe the power of inspiring songs, poets, and musicians to these Nymphs. They would regard the artists in their time as pupils or favorites of these Nymphs. The worship of these Nymphs in ancient times was turned into a sensation by the Thracians. The Thracians created what was called the original seat of the worship of these Nymphs at a place called Olympus.

Since that time the ancient people considered Olympus as the native country of the Nymphs who were now called the Muses. The doctrine teachings of the worship of the Muses had changed over the many years of its worship. In the earliest period of its worship they started off worshipping a single Muse until it turned into three Muses then finally it was turned into the worship of nine Muses. All these Muses or Nymphs were regarded as spirits that look like stunning females who glowed with a certain bright light.

The tales of their origins in regards to the mythological teachings has changed over the many years as well. The most widely spread beliefs about them in those times were the accounts that they were worshiped as the daughters of Zeus. Zeus was considered to be another name, and form Lucifer was worshiped by in ancient times. The legions of fallen angels under Lucifer were also worshiped as gods and goddesses among the people as well under various names that are familiar today.

The Bible tells us that angelic spirits have the power to shape-shift themselves into different forms even forms that are human. The Muses in those times were also worshipped as the goddesses of songs, and the people believed that they lived on the summit of Olympus where Zeus also it was believed was living there as well.

The Muses were also seen as the companions of Apollo. It was believed that they performed with Apollo wherein they would sing while Apollo played the lyre at the banquets of the immortals. The Muses also played musical instruments as well. In the earliest time of their worship when people only worshiped three of them their main instruments were the flute, the lyre, and the barbiton.

By the time of the rise of the Pythian, musical artists who were popular in their day. The religion of the Muses now turned into nine Muses as more musical instruments became more widespread. It was believed that several of these famous Pythian artists were the ones who also came up with the concept of nine Muses.

At the time most of those artists were devout worshippers of the

Muses, and would study their music at the temples of the Muses. These artists believed that the Muses were virgin goddesses where, as before they were not virgins. They would eventually become very inspired by the new teachings on the Muses to such a point that the people believed that the gods were speaking through them.

Many of the events regarding temple priests and leaders having the gods speaking through them shows classical examples of what the Bible calls demonic possession. The Pythian artists would become very creative in that time under this strange inspiration. During their performances they would be clad for the most part in theatrical drapery. They would appear to the people to have a fine intellectual countenance that would be distinguished from one another by expressions, attributes, and attitudes.

You see this today among the performing artists in the music industry. The Bible tells us that there is nothing new under the sun. It teaches that things that are done today have been done before. It also shows us that Satan is not really original. What he does have is a very big bag of tactics he uses to corrupt human beings, and the world we live in. He uses the same tactics but the reason why they seem new to people is because different generations are born. Generations that have not been taught about things that really happened before. So they have no knowledge of certain tactics. So Satan will use some tactics for one generation, and then save them until later on when a future generation comes he re-introduces it but to the people it appears new, and fresh because most of them never learned about it before.

The reason why Satan has to fake being original is because all true source of original inspiration comes from GOD. Satan has been removed from GOD so therefore he has been removed from the Light of GOD that he once used to empower his creative inspirations. Satan can trick human beings however because Satan is still smarter, and more powerful than a human being due to the fact he is still a spirit born from a higher order of existence made by GOD.

Each of these nine Muses would all come to have names, and

each of their names represent a field of inspiration they inspire into people. Calliope was the Muse of epic poetry, and is characterized by a tablet and stylus or rare times by a roll of papers. Clio was the Muse of history, and was represented with an open roll of paper or an open chest of books. Euterpe was the Muse of lyric poetry, and was seen holding either one flute or two. Melpomene was the Muse of tragedy, and was characterized by a tragic mask, the club of Hercules, or sometimes a sword. Her head is surrounded with vine-leaves, and she wears the cothurnus. Terpsichore was the Muse of choral dance and song. This Muse would be seen with a lyre, and the plectrum. Erato was the Muse of erotic poetry and mimic imitation, and is characterized by a lyre. Polymnia was the Muse of sublime hymn, and was represented leaning in a pensive or meditating attitude. Urania was the Muse of astronomy, and she was seen bearing a globe in her hand. Thalia was the Muse of comedy and idyllic poetry, and was characterized by a comic mask, a shepherd's staff, and a wreath of ivy.

Each of their forms have been seen, and represented in the music industry's history through various artists, and through various songs by artists. Various legends have been told about these Muses. One of them was they would take on the Sirens in singing competitions. The Sirens are often called Mermaids today. The image of the Mermaid was made famous, and even friendly by the many movies, and stories of modern media and films. The Disney movie called The Little Mermaid even made them fun for all children. In the past, images of the Sirens would not make people in the millions run up and buy a ticket to see them. In fact, such images would send millions of people in the ancient past running in the opposite direction of the images, and running for their lives. The stories that were told about them are that they were also called sea-demons, and were believed to be spirits sent by the gods. The understanding would be they were the children of those gods that the Bible would call fallen angels.

The Sirens then would be a form of what the Bible calls Nephilim. Nephilim are the offspring of fallen angels. The Sirens became notoriously famous in the past for using their astounding singing voices to lure men in ships to come to them on far away islands or coastal rock areas. The Sirens were known to take the appearance of a beautiful naked woman while singing their seductive songs. The men they would seduce would get into their small life-boats or even swim to them if they could.

Once they were within range of the Sirens the Sirens would show their true form which was a demonic half-female half-fish looking creature. They would attack the men, and drown them in the sea to eat them. The Muses were said to often be victorious in musical competitions with the Sirens. The temple priests of the Muses used to get government approval to have different provinces of the empire to be assigned to certain Muses. They would engage in this assignment by having rituals and sacrifices done in honor of the Muses. The Roman government would even assign certain doctrines of the Muses to be infused with the teachings of different departments of literature, science, and fine arts. The students of these departments along with the teachers often had to make invocations to the Muses, and recite prayers to them.

Inspiring musical artists of those times often took visits to places that were called sacred areas of the Muses. Back then people often believed that they made their appearances there to inspire ideas in people. These places those artists would travel to were the wells of Aganippe, and the wells of Hippocrene that were on Mount Helicon, and the Castalian spring on Mount Parnassus.

Today many artists in the music industry travel to many far places in the world to seek guidance from new age spiritual teachers or encounters with spirits they would call ghosts or ascended masters. This practice is so often documented and even promoted in the media that today thousands of people around the world go out, and do the same kind of lost spiritual trekking around the world. Often times they run a foul of serious harm and danger, and many also end up killed or kidnapped. Many become members of occult groups, and have been murder victims to occult groups as well. The music industry's faith is clearly a corrupt faith with many dark connections that even goes thousands of years back.

Chapter 30

The ancient Hebrews were an eminently musical people. The history of their music is full of illustrations of their national character and life with GOD. Their literature is a monument to GOD himself. A large portion of the Bible is written in poetry conceived in the form of psalmody. The sacred lyrics were put forward to tell of the perfection of GOD's teachings combined with musical science, and art that still to this day no nation has ever attained among them.

It cannot be doubted that the musical progress and attainments that Israel accomplished went well beyond the narrow limits of modern music today. The writers of music in ancient Israel were known to be touched by GOD. They were blessed, and spiritually gifted in understanding music that praises GOD. Like King David, many of Israel's most famous musicians and singers were called prophets as well, and their words spoke, the very Word of GOD.

Ancient Israel takes a very important place in music history. Its history was important to all human life itself in discovering who Christ Jesus was, and who GOD is and His message to the world. Most of the Bible was written by prophets blessed with musical gifts. GOD used these musical gifts namely poetry to speak his very, Word that would be heard for all eternity.

The music of the Hebrews was very special. It was separated from all the forms of music in the world, and different from anything that was heard then, and from anything heard now. In ancient times their music was celebrated all over the world. It was made famous by the tales of it told to rulers and leaders in many parts of the world. No nation since then has ever dedicated their entire culture of music to the glory of GOD. Before there was an ancient Israel we see early examples of music in the very ancient world in the times documented in Genesis. When Jacob was sneaking away from his uncle Laban we see that in the time of Jacob instruments of various kinds were already widely in use. When Laban catches up to Jacob, and confronts him Laban begins to question him on why he is running away in secret. He then tells Jacob that he should have told him he was leaving because then he would have thrown a party for Jacob, and Jacob could have left to the sound of songs, tabret, and the harp.

Jacob's descendants, who would be the Israelites, would be enslaved in Egypt by a series of brutal rulers for a 400 year period. Egypt at that time was the world-power, and the cradle of the arts, and the sciences. Before Israel was enslaved they got the chance for a short-time to enjoy it and learn it. When Israel was delivered by GOD using Moses they celebrated their departure with outbursts of musical poetry and song. In fact Moses himself was trained by the Egyptian elite in all forms of music. In the land Moses lived for 40 years called Midian that is currently today Saudi Arabia the ancient Arabs of that time celebrated with all kinds of musical instruments, and their female singers often accompanied the music with the employment of many exotic songs. Their style of music was an ancient version of eye-candy music and beautiful singers.

In this we see three ancient styles of music in the Hebrew nation. Abraham and his family came from Chaldea, and the music influence that was in his family was Chaldean. This music style was with the family all the way to the time of Jacob and on. Later the Egyptian style of music was known to the Israelites, and through Moses Arabian style of music was also known to the Israelites.

By the time of David and Solomon the music is believed to be a fusion of all three but with a distinct Israelite sound, and purpose given to them by GOD. Moses and Miriam are both on record in the Bible singing a psalm to GOD. In fact Moses also sang other psalms that were called also the Word of GOD, and added to the Book of Psalms. Miriam who was Moses' sister was a gifted singer with prophetic gifts, and a talented dancer who was skilled at playing the tambourine.

By the time of Samuel, David, and Solomon music was a large part of Israel. It played a vital role in the lives of the Israelites. Under David and Solomon the music history of the Israelites would enter it's golden age. During the golden age songs were sung as the message of GOD throughout the nation, and songs were sung to tell the stories of Israel and its rulers, leaders, and its impact on the world at the time.

One such song is well remembered in fact so remembered it led to a civil war between the House of Saul and the House of David. The song was called 'Saul has slain his thousands and David his tens of thousands'. The song was being sung by a large chorus of Israelite women who were singing the song to thank Israel's national champion. David was the darling of Israel at the time, and was winning the wars for Saul. He was making Israel safer and safer the more he engaged GOD's enemies.

The song would provoke the jealously of Saul who later tried to assassinate David. Saul at the time was rejected by GOD, and battling demonic possession. In that time of David Israel had a systematic cultivation of music that was established by the schools of the prophets. Students of music in Israel learned from Israel's prophets, and music was a very essential part of their practice.

David, along with being a feared and a celebrated warrior, was also a musical genius. He was blessed with the Holy Spirit to sing songs that came from GOD himself. David was called Israel's greatest singer and musical composer. David would be the one GOD used to write and perform most of the songs in the Book of Psalms. David's gifts with music was discovered when he was child. As a pre-teen his skills were called upon to smooth the mind of Saul who often suffered demonic attacks.

David's skills were so blessed that the demons themselves would flee Saul when they heard David playing in his presence. That is what music can be and should be. A weapon against evil, sinful passions, and disturbances. When used for GOD ancient Israel showed that music can be a very great tool indeed. In fact, most of the Bible was written by this influence of using music for godly purposes. When David came to the throne he took the musical schools to a whole new level. He trained and turned the nation of Israel to a nation that had thousands of professional musicians employed to sing the Worship of GOD. Their Psalms would utter the wonders and teachings of GOD.

David's son Solomon would take what his father did, and make it even bigger, and more powerful. Solomon built whole stadiums for them to perform in for the nation of Israel. To give an example under Solomon there was 10,000 singing priests,

40,000 psalteries who all played harps of electrum, and 200,000 musicians skilled with trumpets.

All of their clothes were made of the finest linen, and they were clad in purple and gold. Their instruments themselves were also made from gold or white gold. The female singers in that time of Solomon were also famous. They would take part in the Temple choir during Solomon's reign. They were skilled in playing the flute, and other wind instruments, and were noted for their skills with the timbrels.

Israel's use of stringed instruments was extensive, and they used many different types of stringed instruments. One was called the 'kinnor', and it was a favorite instrument used among the sons of the prophets. The priests at that time would even consecrate the instrument to be used for the express purpose of joy and exultation of GOD. The instrument was furnished with ten strings, and played with a plectrum. There are versions of the instrument made out of cypress wood and made out of white gold.

The kinnor was a light, and very portable instrument. It was also called a favorite instrument of David. There is a traditional story that David used to suspend the instrument during the night over his pillow. The instrument looks similar to a harp but not the same. The strings lay across a flat-board called the sounding board, and the strings are placed across that board in a triangular shape. There was about four known kinds of designs of the instrument.

Another stringed instrument they used was called the 'nebel'. The nebel was an instrument that had 12 strings, and the instrument was played with one's hands. It had a distinctive form were a person could play it similar to the way they would hold a guitar or they could play it by putting the instrument upon their shoulder.

The 'sabbeka' was another stringed instrument they played that greatly resembled the guitar. It was held and played in the same manner you would a guitar, and it was a popular instrument of choice among the female singers of Israel. The instrument was more slender then a guitar and had four sometimes six strings, and was shaped in an oblong triangular form.

The Israelites also employed heavy use of wind instruments. They were skilled with various different types of wind instruments. One of them was called 'shophar'. The shophar was a very popular wind instrument among the Israelites. It was made from the horns of various male animals of the cattle breeds. The instrument received it's name shophar because the word means 'bright-clear'. The word is conceived from the sound of the shophar which has a clear shrilling musical tone that awakes the senses. It was an instrument used to wake up warriors in the morning from their tents. It was also used to call Israel for religious or political gatherings. It was also used in worship services as well.

The shophar became a highly regarded instrument by the priests who came to constantly employ it in the service of GOD. It would come to be used in all announcements, and for the calling of the people, and for holy solemnities, and many other great occasions. Though the instrument was used in religious services it was most likely not used during the singing of psalm music due to the peculiar sound wave of the instrument.

Another wind instrument the Israelites used was called the 'chatsotserah'. This instrument was known as the straight trumpet, and it was often made from silver. It used by the priests of the tabernacle. The straight trumpet of this design was often used for announcing to the people the advent of the different feasts, for signaling the journeying of the camps, and for sounding alarms in times of war. The use of the instrument in sacrificial rites as a musical accompaniment was limited to certain occasions like solemn days, the beginnings of their months, and the day of their gladness. Under David and Solomon the instrument would be in heavy use, and was extended in its use to more religious services.

Upon the monuments of the ruins of Egypt and Assyria were many cravings of the Israelites they encountered in those times. Often they craved them holding and using straight silver trumpets.

Another popular wind instrument was called 'halil'. Halil was a word used to mean bored-through, and it denotes a pipe often called a flute. This instrument looked different from flutes we commonly know, for the fact they made the instrument much longer than average pipes. The pipe was also furnished with far more holes as well. This type of pipe was often made from the bones or horns of animals. Sometimes it was even made of wood and ivory tusks. It was made to be a straight tube without any increase at the mouth. When played it was held with both hands, and the holes were so low that the player was obliged to extend his arms to the utmost. This instrument was a favorite at Jewish celebrations, weddings, and dancing occasions. It was consecrated by the priests to be used for joy and pleasure. In Jesus' time things would change among the Jews, and the Jews began using the instrument at funerals. The halil was also a common instrument used by the female singers of Israel.

The Israelites also employed the use of different types of percussion and agitation instruments. One such instrument was called the 'toph' by the ancient Israelites. The ancient Arabs would call it the 'dof'. The modern word would be drum. This type of drum called the toph looks a lot like Latin drums that are held, and used with the hand to play it. The toph was shaped into a narrow circle or hoop of wood. Sometimes the body of the toph was made of metal. The instrument's body at the top would then be covered with a tightened skin and the skin would be struck with the hand to play the instrument. This was a popular instrument during the time of Moses and Joshua among the Israelites. Moses' sister Miriam was also skilled at using it along with many of the females among the Israelites. Miriam and the daughters of Israel used to use the instrument when singing, and dancing to the song of Moses.

By the time of Isaiah it became an instrument of voluptuaries. The Israelites in the time of Isaiah had greatly fallen away from following GOD. The instrument was used in that time for their carnal and sexual parties, and was beaten for worldly meretricious. But later, on due to the wrath of GOD upon them, the instrument was silenced amid wars and desolations.

At the height of Israelite culture the instrument was used for joyful celebrations, and victorious celebrations when Israel defeated her enemies. It was generally played by the female singers of Israel. Pagan nations often used the instrument for warlike transactions and for orgies. Later on Israel would follow this bad example.

There was three kinds of designs to this instrument. One was circular, another was squared, and the third one was two squares separated by a bar. The instrument when in use was often used in accompaniment with harps, and other instruments. The ancient Egyptians were also very fond of this instrument. They called it the 'tomtom', and when they made this instrument they gave it a longer body, and attached cords to it so they could hold it over their shoulders, and carry it with them.

Another percussion instrument they used was called the 'paamon'. The name comes from the words little-bells, and has reference to the small golden appendages attached to the robe of the high-priest. The instrument were bells that were usually attached to the hem of the garments and were separated from each other by golden knobs, shaped like pomegranates. This is how the persons who would use the instrument would wear them. To play the instrument is to produce a tinkling sound by striking against the golden knobs that were appended near them. The use of this instrument was largely used during dancing. Priests were known to dance for the Lord, and sometimes would wear this instrument to produce melodious sounds to their dance moves. Female dancers would at times use this instrument for the same reasons of producing melodious sounds with their dance moves.

The 'tseltselim' was another percussion instrument they used. The word means bells of the horses, and the instrument was similar to what we call cymbals. In ancient times this instrument was used upon war-horses, and camels used for military use. The Hebrews during their military battles also would use the instrument upon their horses. The instrument was in the shape of small cymbal-shaped pieces of metal that was suspended under the necks of the animals. It would strike against each other with the motions of the animals. The reason why these armies used this instrument upon their animals was to create a terrific and fearful effect into the enemies, and civilians they would encounter in nations they were at war with.

When the horses were being rode in ranks and files in the thousands people would have their senses and nerves shaken by the rapid motions of the incoming animals being driven by fearful warriors. Under King David the instrument would come to be used for religious and feast celebrations for Israel. David had the instruments used during the account when the Ark was being carried up to Mount Zion in Jerusalem. David organized a very large musical service for the celebration, and employed the use of thousands of cymbals. The celebration that day is still remembered in the history of the Israelite Kingdom, and recorded in the Bible. The scene was filled with thousands of musicians employing psalteries, harps, and the sound of the cymbals was being conducted by Asaph, who was David's chief musician.

The high-sounding cymbals used on that day was so well remembered for giving glory to GOD that it's account is seen in the Book of Psalms. The appearance of these cymbals were small round plates of metal fastened upon the thumb and middle finger, and struck against each other by a motion of the hand when playing it. The cymbals would produce a clear and sharp sound. This instrument also did not just come as small sized cymbals sometimes they came in the large round plates of metal. This version of the instrument would produce very large resounding sounds when the instrument is struck. The sounds were known to be very powerful, and the large cymbals had to be played with both hands.

The ancient Israelite nation used in fact hundreds of different types of instruments other than the ones named in this chapter. When Jesus completed his mission the temple service was done away with, and the Christian Church, called the Church from the beginning in the Bible, was established as GOD's true Church according to the Bible. Christian Churches since then, and all the way to our time have had debates with other Church groups over the use of musical instruments in the Church. Many Churches allow it while some do not, and this is a controversy that is still going on for various reasons. In today's time, most Churches use musical instruments while a few compared to the numbers don't.

In the early A.D. periods, and going into the Middle Ages, most

Churches did not use musical instruments for the worship of GOD while only a few compared to the numbers did use them. There was a shift of majority belief regarding the use of musical instruments by the time of the mid-18th century. In that time, instruments were becoming more and more favored to be in use during Church worship service.

By the time of the 19th, and 20th centuries it became in use in almost every Church in America, and eventually around the world. Let's us look into the aspect of this issue. Since the 16th century all religious music was divided into two general musical divisions. One was called choral, and the other was called figurate.

Choral music in its original form is Church singing only. The melody would be either solemnly slow or moved at a sentimental pace. It is devoid of the ornament of musical instruments, and is not always bound to a strict observance of time. Figurate music is the execution of religious pieces with the accompaniment of musical instruments. It combines with choral melodies arranged for four or more voices wherein together they will sing Christian theme hymns, psalms, and passages from the Bible.

Originally musical instruments were not used at the start of the Christian Church in the times of the Apostles. In fact since the start of it, and for the first several hundred years' musical instruments were not seen as being tools to worship GOD with. None of the Apostles in their writing of the New Testament gave any importance at all that musical instruments were needed to worship GOD. From the text of the New Testament it shows that they praised GOD with their voices meaning they engaged in choral music, and the songs they sung were the Psalms. They expressed no lessons to using musical instruments, and in their time musical instruments was in heavy use among pagan worshippers. The reason this is important to understand is because the Christian Church from the start did not want to mimic the ways of the world. They did not want to take part in certain celebrations among the Romans, and other nations at the time because they used such musical accompaniment to celebrate, and honor the beliefs of various gods. Even their fellow Jews at the time were abusing the use of musical instruments. Many of them were falling away from GOD.

For a long time the worship service of GOD in the Church was choral because the choral form was seen by them as the pure way to worship GOD. Over time new cultures are born and new ideas are brought into the Church in the late A.D. periods, and going into the Middle Ages.

Figurate music is believed to have started off when the organ was first introduced into Christian worship services by the Catholic Church. The organ was used to conduct and produce sounds to assist the choral voices in the Church. Over time other priests and music leaders in the Church would add stringed, and wind instruments to produce more sounds to accompany the singing.

This idea to add musical instruments into the choral singing was not a popular one at first. Many priests among the main Churches of the West and East factions who were the Roman and Greek Churches were against the use of musical instruments. These priests often outnumbered the priests who supported musical instruments. They often made trouble for priests who employed musical instruments in their Churches. Members of the congregations were often split on the issue, and would just eventually side with their respective priests on the issue. Many would leave a Church if they used musical instruments, and went to another that did not use them. Some of the people would enjoy the sounds of musical instruments in Church, and would even seek a Church gathering that did use them.

Figurate music in that time was for many decades very unpopular to most of the Church leaders, and the peoples of the congregations. Many Churches that used figurate music were even violently suppressed, and their priests and musicians would be arrested and jailed, sometimes even executed. These executions at times would even make people in the general public have sympathy for those executed seeing that the punishment did not fit the crime.

When the New World was discovered or more like re-discovered the European monarchs started to invest their resources into building colonies in the Americas. This resulted in new

Churches being built up by people who could also have there a different life than the one they were having in Europe. Many of the Church groups who were attacked by the religious political system of the times would leave Europe for the new colonies. There they would eventually settle, and build up Churches without the interruption of the European religious system of that time. This is how figurate music eventually became popular by it being allowed to flourish in certain towns among the colonies.

By 1640 the colonies featured most of the Churches that used figurate music especially the American colonies. The American colony Churches were also a melting pot of people coming from many different European backgrounds. It also had members from other parts of the world which is something most history books don't speak on. These people coming from different cultures added new ideas into the Church service, and community that would become the prime bases of Christian American Churches.

When the American colonies won their freedom they made Freedom of Religion a Federal Law. This law would give Christian Churches the freedom to have figurate music in their services without any crime being held against them. From that point this form of service was becoming more and more popular, but debates in America were still held against it because the Bible never supported the use of figurate music in the New Testament nor gave any permission for it.

The debates reached their fever pitch in the mid to late 19th century but died out by the 20th century. Since that time certain Church groups had decided to separate themselves from Churches that used figurate music, and held the doctrine in their Church to maintain choral music.

Today choral music supporters are now the minority in America regarding the issue while figurate music is highly and overly favored. As mentioned regarding the Bible's teachings of giving no warrant for the use of musical instruments to be used in worshipping GOD, here are some points regarding it. There is no example of its use by Peter, Paul, John, James, and not even the Master Jesus Christ himself in regards to teachings set forth in the New Testament. Musical instruments did not appear in

Churches until what was called the mystery of iniquity sprang forth in the Christian Church when political events introduce different teachings into the Churches, and passed them off as Christian. There is no command in the New Testament to make or to use them. In the New Testament there are no directions for formal or incidental use of musical instruments. Instead what you have in the New Testament is line after line regarding the Apostles worship of GOD that they used singing to do so.

Many people will clearly argue that though it's not in the New Testament it's clearly in the Old Testament regarding its use to worship GOD, and often spoken about in the Book of Psalms. This is the defenders of musical instruments main position on this, and they do have several other positions regarding this, but this position of theirs has some problems as well. Though it is true that the Old Testament priests used musical instruments, and did also members of the congregation who were chosen for this service, what many people don't realize is that it's use was an overall set apart service from the pure solemn service of GOD.

To understand it, in Old Testament Temple worship services you had two parts to it. One part was the gathering of the people, and the celebration of GOD. Celebrating GOD was called praising GOD, and today we see praising as also as a form of worship, but to the ancient Israelites it was not. GOD wanted the Israelites to praise him with all kinds of musical instruments, but the kind of worship GOD wanted was different from the kind of praise he wanted.

GOD wanted humble, and meek hearts, and a solemn worship service which was done during core Temple services, and the reading of the Word. During worship no instruments were used only singing was used, and the form of singing is what is called choral today. When David was bringing the Ark to Jerusalem all kinds of musical instruments were used to praise and celebrate GOD and yes GOD did receive glory from it. In fact GOD wanted that kind of praise. After the praise, when the Ark was set, there was a worship service where no musical instruments were played and only singing was heard. This was the worship GOD wanted, and he also got glory from it as well. This is the understanding that has been largely removed from people. The way the Temple Church was set up back then the musical instruments belonged to the tabernacle, and the Temple.

These instruments were set apart by the priests to be instruments used for the express purpose of praising GOD. They could never be instruments that were used to play any other kind of music, that is to say pagan music. They must be new and reserved instruments, and therefore those instruments belonged to the Temple. The instruments however were never to be used in the worship assemblies of the congregations.

During the time of the Temple, and the synagogues, during Jesus' time the same rules applied regarding instruments, praise, and worship. Musical instruments were also very important for celebrations, and feasts done on certain festivals. They were used for proclamation in going to war, in moving camps, in assembling the congregations as well as in triumphs, coronations, and other extraordinary occasions.

When the Sabbath came about, priests at the Temple, and at synagogues used to blow trumpets six times. The first blast came on a Friday evening, and the men would drop what they were doing and would return home. When the second blast was heard all the offices, shops, and places of business in ancient Israel was closed. At the third blast pots were removed from the fire, and all culinary occupation was suspended. The other three blasts were to designate the line between the common time until the entering of the holy time.

We see that in accordance to what is known about musical instruments they were used to praise GOD under a ceremonial setting, but the pure worship was not to include them but to only use voices. This is the understanding of the Word, and what the Bible teaches. Many people will be for or against the use of musical instruments in Church. Jesus' mission was to indeed end the ceremonial, and corrupt strongholds

that the temple service had become in that time. Jesus wanted also pure worship from the heart.

Jesus also never changed Old Testament laws he only full-filled them. Therefore by the example

Jesus gave, and what he taught to his Apostles regarding worship it was clear that only singing would do. Now this is not to say we should start throwing away musical instruments. This is also not to say you can't use musical instruments to praise GOD. In fact, you still can because GOD made the world to give a platform for such a ceremonial, and honorable act. The problem is most artists refuse or don't praise him. They praise themselves, and Satan instead.

Chapter 31

One pop-artist that came upon the scene to seemingly become famous out of nowhere was Lady Gaga. The influence and music of Lady Gaga right from the start has been filled with sexual immorality, homosexuality, satanic-occult themes and teachings.

Lady Gaga's real name is Stefani Joanne Angelina Germanotta. She was born in New York City to a wealthy Roman Catholic family. Stefani was trained in classical music at a very young age. She was trained to play the piano, and trained to sing. Her parents were of Italian and French heritage. When Stefani was a young girl they encouraged her gifts all throughout her life.

There were rumors that Stefani's parents may have been into other faiths then just the faith of the Catholic Church. The high-rise apartment building that Lady Gaga was raised in is noted for having many wealthy, and successful people living there who practice witchcraft. Stories of strange rituals, hauntings, and accidents have surrounded the history of the building.

Throughout her teenage years Lady Gaga was an honor student and a child of the New York elite who engaged much of her studies in music. In high-school is when she started to have dreams of becoming famous. This would drive her later on when she enters college. After high-school her musical talent would lead her to be enrolled in New York University's Tisch School of the Arts. It was her parents' dream to see her become a classical artist. In college Stefani showed to be also a talented writer. She composed essays, and analytical papers on art, religion, and politics, and these skills helped her to become a better song-writer. While in college those dreams of being famous she had in high-school would resurface. She would express to her parents that she did not want a career in classical music and theater but she wanted a career as an artist in the music industry. She also expressed to her parents that she wanted to drop out of school to achieve this goal.

Her parents were not happy about this, and so Stefani would make a deal with them. She would ask them to give her one year in this pursuit and if nothing comes of it she would return back to school. Her parents agreed to this and set up an apartment for Stefani to live in. They paid the rent for a full year. During that time Stefani formed a band called the SG Band who were made up of students from NYU. This band would perform in bars, nightclubs, and most especially in gay strip clubs throughout New York City. During that time Stefani was looking to call herself by a stage name and was getting many ideas into how to use theater art to shock the audience she was playing for.

One time she was listening to a song by Queen called Radio Gaga. The song would inspire her to call herself Lady Gaga. She would start to write and pattern her music after many influences from Queen, Madonna, Cher, and David Bowie. It was not enough for her just to pattern styles of music from these artists she also wanted to know what they believe in spiritually. This is where early signs of Lady Gaga's anti-Christian faith began to show forth. Even though she was raised as a Catholic she was not a Catholic at heart nor by practice in her life.

She had a wild streak that was about to become even darker. Lady Gaga began to study the New Age religions her favorite artists were into. She began to learn about goddess worship, Satanism, Hinduism, Buddhism, and several others. She began to quote the works she was reading because she started to believe in it. At that time she began to create an art-form in her performances that was combining her music with theater stage acts. She would learn the fashions of the nightclubs, and then take what she learned, and apply it to style her act on stage.

Starting out she was not that good at performing as she was with writing, and thinking it out. There was up and coming artists that were better than her at performing and she knew it. She then developed a deep and dark desire to get better than good, so she threw herself into the nightclub music scene.

She was increasingly fascinated with gay burlesque shows, and she was even go-go dancing at bars dressed in a bikini. She would take bottles of hairspray, and light the spray on fire as part of her act while singing about oral sex. She also had an act where she did bump and grind shows to Black Sabbath songs. She began to engage in a lot of homosexual relationships, and she was often dating more women than men. At that time she developed an extreme addiction to drugs.

Her parents were hardly in the picture during this time in her life. They did not like her open lifestyle of drugs and homosexuality. They continued to support her, and pay her rent even after the one year period because she showed progress in her career efforts by getting nightclub gigs, but also they felt this was not the same person they once knew. In that time Lady Gaga was a heavy user of cocaine, and would use any drug given to her. While doing this she struggled to find a style and format that would put her over the top from the rest.

She was often coming off as a side-show, and the combination of drugs, her lifestyle, and the stress led to Lady Gaga trying to commit suicide. One night she would overdose on cocaine. While in a coma-like state she would have strange experiences with what are called spirits. Soon she would recover, and then very soon, while getting high on cocaine again, a spirit would appear to her.

According to Lady Gaga she stated that it was the spirit of her aunt who died many years ago. She stated that this spirit gave her career direction. It even entered her, and gave her power in controlling her drug addictions. In this testimony from Lady Gaga the Bible would state she was very deceived that day. Demons as covered before like to pose as people who once died to get easy access to enter someone's body. What Lady Gaga just describe would be called demonic possession. After this demonic experience Lady Gaga started to feel more energy within her. More ideas started to come around. She would get back to work with her band, and they would work the nightclubs.

During the performances Lady Gaga would come up with new and more, slutty acts. She still had not found the right persona but she could feel she was closer to it. Many would state that often dealing with the devil comes with a price, and its price was something Lady Gaga was willing to pay. Around this time two events would happen to Lady Gaga that would help her reach her way to the top of the charts. First she would meet an artist named Lina Morgana. Lina had a lot in common with Lady Gaga. They both came from wealthy families, and they both started out around the same time. They both were into the underground gay scene, and they both were into dark themes in their performances. It was also said that they both were also into witchcraft rituals and practices. In fact the name Lina Morgana comes from witchcraft folklore.

Lina was also seen as a rival to Lady Gaga because they both were trying to make it to the business in similar ways. Sometimes they had to compete against each other. When it came to art-forms and style of music and better performances Lina was more talented in that area then Lady Gaga. Lady Gaga however was a better writer then Lina but was not on Lina's level in how to perform the art-form on a level that grabs people's attention. Lina had a look, a voice, and a dark gimmick to her image. She often portrayed the lost and damaged soul in her performances, and early music videos. She would use a lot of dark and witchcraft theme images while singing with a voice of passionate sorrow.

Her look was also creative, and it was a look Lady Gaga wanted. It was believed that Lady Gaga was very jealous of Lina, and had told other people in her circle at the time that if she had that look and image she would be famous. The second event that happened to Lady Gaga was an event that also happened to Lina. Both Lina and Gaga got signed to work with Sony/ATV. Lina would be signed as a new up and coming recording artist. Gaga got signed to work as a songwriter for artists working with Sony. During this time Lady Gaga wrote songs for Britney Spears, the reunited New Kids on the Block, Fergie, The Pussycat Dolls, and a few others. She would even have to write songs for Lina as well.

While the two of them were working in the industry it is believed that they got involved with inner satanic groups working in or with the music industry CEOs and owners. The story behind this is still an unproven story but it is often believed to be the real and hidden reality of the music industry. Both Lina and Gaga wanted to be successful stars. They believed that this occult group would help them to go there. The group would reveal to them that they were not just about satanic rituals, sex, and drugs. They would reveal to them that they were also involved with darker crimes and government mind-control as well. They wanted the two of them to subject themselves to mind-control experiments. In return they would be pushed up the ladder of success.

Lina had more problems with the conditions of subjecting herself to mind-control then Lady Gaga did. Lady Gaga it was said was willing to do anything, and destroy anyone for the chance to be famous. Lina it was said was not willing to cross certain lines. Lina at the time was also deeply suffering from depression and many say demonic attacks. She along with Gaga were both believed to have demons in them that often haunted them. Satanic new age teachings can teach a lot of people to believe in some very sick and twisted things. One of these concepts involves spirits.

In the occult their condition is not called demon-possession but a condition where they believe that angel guides live inside them to help them, and that all souls become ghosts until they find the light-world. Of course that is not what the Bible teaches. When people believe this stuff they can take it even farther especially when they are in a state of life they can get away with certain things. Some new age doctrine will teach especially in Satanism that if a person is killed under an intent as a sacrifice to Satan then the person who did the killing would possess the soul of the person they killed, and take all their gifts into themselves. This belief is clearly crazy but people in occult groups do believe this.

During a study with serial killers, when asked about their experiences when they killed their first victim, about 80% of them relate a spiritual experience that happened to them when they committed their first murder. Many of these now convicts would even express that they feel the experience was demonic, and not soul researching like occultist think it is. They stated in the general base of the story that after they killed the person they would see or feel a spirit either come out of the victim or it would come upon them. They would feel something entering them that would make them go crazy and even scream in agony. They would feel like their brains were on fire, then after the experience they would often talk about the voices that speak in their heads. The Bible would state this is a demonic possession occurrence resulting from a brutal sin.

How this information relates to Lady Gaga and Lina is also an unproven story but believed by many insiders. Because Lina did not want to take part in the darker aspects of the music industry, her group wanted to get rid of her. Gaga was told about this demonic concept of stealing one's soul, and she was willing to do anything for fame. It was believed that Gaga was picked to end the life of Lina, and to offer her death to Satan.

The official cause of Lina's death is believed that she committed suicide by jumping off the balcony of a high-rise building, but at the time she jumped Gaga, and several other so-called friends of Lina were also seen in the building. The questions would remain as to why they did not try to help stop Lina from jumping when they were within range of the incident. The way Lina fell also does not suggest a suicide either even though it was written as a suicide. There were people at the time who stated to the police that they saw someone push her but could not tell who it was.

Of course these statements were not reported in the media who did a very small piece on Lina's death that no one really watched or cared about. The belief is Lady Gaga saw a chance when Lina was standing too close to the balcony with her back turned. At that point it was believed she pushed Lina over the balcony to cause her death, because it was written as a suicide she managed to get away with it. For many people this is very hard to believe that one of their favorite pop-stars is a murderer. It is like I said an unproven story but if it ever became a proven story, unlike the millions of people who would be shocked by that, I won't be.

The music industry along with Hollywood works hand and glove with each other, and since the start of the entertainment industry in America, murders and cover-ups have been constantly going on there. In fact the murders and cover-ups that took place during the golden age of the entertainment industry when they first happened no one believe because it involved their favorite star. Those stories did not get proven to be facts until 20 to even 50 years after it happened.

When Lina died there was a very strange change in Lady Gaga. Lady Gaga was now looking like Lina and would wear her make-up the same way as Lina. Her face seemed to have Lina's face upon her. Many of Lina's family members, and friends believed that Lady Gaga stole Lina's look and image after her death. Some of them even stated that Gaga possesses Lina's soul. Some are even under the conviction that Gaga had something to do with her death to take her soul. Either way, after Lina's death Gaga now took Lina's underground style and image. She fused it with her style and image thus creating the Lady Gaga you see today.

Gaga would also come up with a way to market her image and music. She would win over the executives with this image and music she was now presenting. Gaga was now selling herself to the executives as an artist. It is believed that during this time of creating the Lady Gaga we see today Gaga was also being a test subject for many mind-control experiments. People would notice strange changes in her that came with creepy mood-swings. She would talk with voices in her head. She would also display in her character many alter-personalities.

Soon Chairman, and CEO Jimmy Lovine would be the one to sign Lady Gaga to a record contract with his label. Gaga recorded her first album in Los Angeles called The Fame. The album was released in 2008, and its lead single was a song called Just Dance. Just Dance would catch on as a nightclub hit and soon it became a huge mainstream hit. This single was then followed by a second single called Poker Face. Poker Face would become an even bigger hit then her first single, and the song would make Lady Gaga a household name. Poker Face would become a number one hit single on the Billboard 100 singles chart. The single alone would sell 9 million copies. Her debut album would end up selling 12 million copies. When the music videos to Just Dance and Poker Face debuted on MTV and other music channels people noticed strange and satanic symbolism in her music videos.

A lot of it was plain, and not even hidden but more exposed to even be understood when you study occult beliefs. The song Poker Face also had a hidden and immoral meaning as well. When Lady Gaga was on a radio station, and was asked what the title to her song called Poker Face meant she refused to give an answer. During that time the song was very popular with young fans especially pre-teens and teenagers who bought most of the records. Many of them felt the song had a rebellious female empowerment meaning, but they were wrong.

Most people at the time did not know that Lady Gaga use to write, and sing songs about oral sex during her New York City club days. The true meaning of Poker Face is 'poke her face', and it is an urban nightclub meaning for a guy to take his male member, and poke inside a girl's mouth with it. The song was about a girl giving oral sex to a guy that she does not love. The theme of empty, loveless, premarital sex plays out in her songs over, and over again.

Since 2008 Lady Gaga had released more albums, and had more hit songs. She is currently one of the top pop-stars in the music industry, and she is a heavy hitter in record sales. Since the start of her career Lady Gaga had to compete her album against new albums released by Britney Spears, Christina Aguilera, and Madonna. Lady Gaga's albums would out sell their new albums, and she began to be seen as more hardcore, and sexual then her three top peers. Many say that the shock value of Lady Gaga's image, concerts, and music videos makes what came before look modest in parallel, and that is saying a lot. In fact it was also said for anyone to out-do Lady Gaga would have to be worse than this. To be worse than this is a she-devil coming straight out of Hell. Hence Miley Cyrus' performance in 2013 that stole the thunder from Lady Gaga that night.

In the time of Lady Gaga's career her songs, images, music videos, teachings, and influence have been extremely filled with satanic themes, and dark ritualistic inner-workings of the entertainment industry according to many insiders.

Lady Gaga, after the success of her first album would release her second album called Fame Monster. The lead single to this album was called Bad Romance. On the surface the song seems to be about a girl who falls for a wicked, and murderous man that the girl is lustfully yearning for, but the lyrics, and the music video also carry another theme to the song. A theme that has a hidden message about the industry, and a theme that carries occult teachings.

The music video of the song does not depict Lady Gaga lusting over a man but the theme goes right back to a now familiar theme called mind-control. It appears through the music video that what she is singing about is not love for an abusive man but love for an abusive industry. The meaning of the song is that she is aware of the industry's flaws, and abuse but she still desires to be part of it because she wants fame. She wants fame so badly that if she does not get it she will die or something.

The song also has a strange hook to the chorus, and it comes through Lady Gaga's voice as a chant rather than as a melody. The words are 'Ra, Ra, Roma, mamma'. In occult studies the words have meaning, and it relates to ancient ceremonial ritual chants going as far back as ancient Egypt. This ritual involved the calling up of spirits who they called gods and goddesses. Ra was the name of the Egyptian sun-god, and Roma was the name of the moon-goddess. During the ritual they would chant the names in a manner Lady Gaga was doing to call up these spirits they believed to be their gods and creators. That is where the word 'mamma' had it's meaning in the chant because that word in ancient times was also a word for a mother-goddess. The ancient Egyptian pagan version of the creation of the human race involves Ra and Roma taking the form of the mother-goddess. This is clearly not a normal hook to have for a song, unless you have a motive for putting a hook like that there. The motive could also be the same motive the ancient Egyptian priests and priestesses had for chanting it. This motive would be to conjure demons into the lives of people.

She sings this chorus in step with the lyrics where she is singing about an industry whose love is not real love but dark passions, and it's wrong and sick, but Gaga, knowing that it is, wants in and feels she will learn to like it. The odd thing is that even though millions of her fans do not believe she is singing about the industry or making any reference to satanic worship and mind-control, there is something to consider. They believe she is singing about a bad man, and for this bad man Gaga is willing to learn to love and like to be part of a man who beats her, and does sick and twisted things to her.

Her fans think that this idea is okay but the other idea is not okay. Well really for them to admit that they think the song is about a girl falling in love with a man who beats her, and does twisted things to her, and other people, and love a song like that tells you there is a serious problem in the minds of the people today. Also in truth most of the people who refuse to believe this do so not out of researching it but more out of they love the artist far too much to believe it.

In research however the song reveals a lot of evil things. Lady Gaga in the video shows a series of scenes that once again have nothing to do with a relationship but resembles a lifestyle that is seen in the industry. She emulates a feeling of sadomasochism that tells her fans that she likes to be abused because she is up for it. The song is about submitting to evil.

The song carries a strong mix of twisted horror with hardcore sex references. The music video starts off with Lady Gaga emerging from a sensory deprivation tank. She is deprived of her senses in the scene and is oddly covered. Sensory deprivation is a torture method that was used upon mind-control victims. They use this method in order to break the victim and to facilitate their re-education.

In the video when Gaga comes out of the tank she is roughed up by two women. She tries to fight off the women but they overpower her and then she gives in. This is a practice also seen in mind-control when victims try to fight off their handlers after being tortured.

In the video you see back and forth scenes of Lady Gaga drinking vodka. When MTV got into a little trouble with certain videos that had drugs in it they decided to use 'vodka' in their videos as code for drugs. MTV will deny this but it's often spoken about by insiders among MTV. The idea of Lady Gaga using the vodka was to represent drugs. Drugs also are commonly used upon mind-control victims. The drugs are used to get them into alter-states of conscience to manipulate their minds during certain trauma abuse, and sexual abuse sessions in mind-control practices.

In the video Gaga performs half-naked in front of a group of men who are sitting in chairs wearing masks. Gaga appears to them as a sex-slave in her performance, and she dances to sell herself to them. The scene also had a hidden meaning of sexual favors. Gaga's dance was not about dancing but it was representing sex with each one of the men sitting in the chairs. All the men in the video have something that Gaga wants and that is fame. They are men who can make her famous, and so they would represent record company CEOs. So knowing that the dancing in the video represents sex Gaga in the video while 'dancing' with the men, the men decide to start a bidding war for her. The scene would then show a man who won the bid, and now has won the right to take Lady Gaga all for himself. The scene would then lead to Gaga showing up in the bedroom of the man, but this bedroom has some odd things in it.

On each side of the bed there are satanic goat-heads. This image gave reference to the form of Satan called Baphomet. That is the form Satan is known to go by when people sell their souls to him through certain occult settings. This occult practice with Baphomet is an ancient practice, and was among the ancient Baal worshippers spoken about in the Bible. Often times in this practice a human sacrifice was required for the initiation ceremony of the person seeking to be in Satan's inner circle of family members. Which usually means to be on the inside of things, and it does not mean Lady Gaga is in the Illuminati.

In the music video you will notice the bed catching on fire, and when the fire starts another scene plays simultaneously showing Gaga, and masked dancers dressed in red. This also had a hidden meaning wherein the red in occult understanding was worn by ancient pagans when a human sacrifice was being engaged in. Red in the occult is the color of sacrifice because it's the color of blood. The scene was to show a human sacrifice without actually having to show a real one. What the scene was doing was taking the concepts of human sacrifice and mixing it into the art-form to be used for the entertainment of the masses. It was an art-form promoting murder, and most people were hardly able to see that.

In many new age teachings the sun-god is often worshiped in those teachings since there are many different teachings in new age spirituality the sun-god also has many names. Ra is one of the most ancient names he is known by, and his ritual is thousands of years old.

Gaga in the video seems to really adore Ra as the sun-god. Gaga wears the image of the sun in her razor blade shades, and also wears a golden dress and is surrounded by golden sunlight. Gold is representative of the sun in occultism, and in occultism the sun represents Lucifer. In the video you see Gaga standing in the center of planetary orbs in a position where the sun would be. She represents the sun-god in these scenes, and upon her dress she wears an upside down Christian cross upon her private part. Clearly if you are a Christian you know that is not anywhere near a sign of respect. The scene was aimed to mock Jesus Christ.

Soon in the video we see Gaga battling with inner personal demons that begin to manifest from insider her. Gaga beings to morph, and transform into a demonic creature. The scene was to show demonic possession, and demonic possession is believed to be a main condition in the life of Lady Gaga. These are the themes featured in the video Bad Romance. All of these themes have nothing to do with abusive guy problems. They are about something much bigger than that, and more horrible then that.

Many people who have encountered Lady Gaga state that she is known for being lewd, incoherent, and absent minded. She shows signs to people to the point that when people talk about it they seem to feel that she had some kind of trauma done to her mind. Insiders state that her brain is compartmentalized, and that would make her out of touch with reality, and very much inside a world of her alter-personas. Her lewd, robotic, and degenerate personality does clearly also embody symptoms of mind-control abuse. The name 'gaga' is a term that refers to the meaning of being absent minded, also it is a feeling of being silly and featherbrained. Also added are the feelings of being dizzy along with mental unsoundness like being mad, ill, distraught, moonstruck, manic, unbalanced, unsound, and often wrong about things. The influences of such a term used upon people would result in people being often empty headed about reality. Instead their minds would be open to all types of garbage that Lady Gaga wants her fans to emulate. Their minds would be conditioned to be empty of really important things, and put in a state that would promote another idea for their lives. This idea for them would be to have a mind that says, 'I'm empty-headed, this empty head can be filled with any type of garbage you want.'

Lady Gaga wants people to follow ways that are in line with sexual sins, drug use, and satanic occult influences. Many of her photos also promote satanic influences to her millions of fans. In these pictures of her they also feature her logos and images. One of her logos was a headless female dummy with a bolt of lightning shooting through her and exiting her genitalia. Oddly enough there is an occult meaning behind these images. This bolt of lightning in the occult represents Lucifer the one who fell from Heaven like lightning. The headless dummy represents her conscience thought which is empty and removed. Instead she is charged by the energies of Lucifer that makes her sexual nature to feel electrifying. It is a photo of full sexual idolatry and Satanism.

Her most popular photo is when she does the one eye hand sign. Gaga has several ways of doing this sign, and all of them are occultic in nature. Because Gaga does this hand-sign so often like Jay-Z she is often believed to be a member of the Illuminati, but in truth she is not a member of a banking elite group who buy world leaders like people buy cars. She does not have insider information on the plans, and events that will shape the nations of the world.

All the aspects that the real Illuminati is, and the true core function as an occult group is not the occult group Lady Gaga is part of. Lady Gaga simply promotes the image and beliefs of the Illuminati who own the record company she works for. They own that company through a parent corporation that owns many other corporations that control the music industry. These corporation CEOs are the ones who run things for owners, and high elite bosses who work as bankers. Those bankers would know more about the Illuminati then Lady Gaga ever could.

Sadly many people don't realize the concept of the Illuminati, and so they go on thinking she is in the Illuminati. Most people don't even believe that the Illuminati is real, and therefore do not believe that Lady Gaga is a Satanist in anyway, but Lady Gaga shows in her art-form over and over again, and through youtube videos of her doing witchcraft chants, that she clearly is not a Christian. She very much is what the Bible would call a Satanist, and if those same doubting people ever did real research into the Illuminati, and the Rothschild family they would find out how real it is.

Many of Lady Gaga's photos feature her as demonic creatures. She would often look possessed, and transformed into images that look like ancient demons described in the past. She is often seen throwing up satanic hand-signs like the 666 okay symbol and a few others.

In her music video called Paparazzi the beginning scenes shows Lady Gaga talking in a vapor robotic way about a man who swallowed her brain. During this she is questioned by a man who also talks in a very strange, and hypnotic manner. The scene is very out of place with the song, and upon looking at it becomes hard to understand, but there is something that was done in mind-control that would help to give sense to the scenes. Victims in mind-control were brain washed so badly they would be convinced of things like being pregnant when they were not, or thinking someone swallowed their brain.

The video to Paparazzi is also loaded with satanic symbolism, and mind-control themes. In the video Lady Gaga is fornicating with a strange guy. All around in the rooms of the scenes are masonic checkerboard floors, goat's heads, and other satanic symbols. After the sex scenes the guy in the video starts to act even more strange and in one scene he pushes Lady Gaga off the balcony of a high-rise building. While she is falling down a swirling spiral pattern begins to be seen in the background. The scene was to show hypnotism combined with the trauma of falling off a building. The scene shows trauma with this added hypnotic pattern to give the sense of torture and pain.

In another series of scenes Lady Gaga's clothes are being removed and she is walking around in crutches, but then oddly the scenes change into showing Lady Gaga as a robot who is dressed like Mickey Mouse. As a robot she acts like a complete puppet being pulled on strings. She then is sitting with the guy in the video, and she poisons his drink. Once she sees that she killed him she begins to smile. Many insiders state that the scenes were showing certain kinds of sessions done in mind-control programming.

One of them is called delta programming. It is said to be given to Special Forces, and soldiers of black ops groups. It is also known as killer programming. The victims are forced into intense trauma by being injured to the point of almost being killed. The object of the programming is for them to painfully recover. Then a mission is given to them where they are to kill someone. The Mickey Mouse outfit, and the robot manner Lady Gaga played in the video many insiders stated it had reference to mind-control programs under the cloak of Disney.

Her music videos and images do incorporate a lot of satanic symbolism, and images of mind-control. A lot of the meanings in her videos have very twisted and have horrible deeper meanings. A great deal of Lady Gaga's career centers around satanic symbolism, homosexuality, occultism, occult knowledge, mind-control themes, anti-Christian beliefs, sexual immorality, sexual abuse, and other cold-blooded themes like murder.

Lady Gaga has also done a lot of photos with masonic themes combined with occult symbolism. In one photo she stands between two pillars, and the pillars in masonic lore represent Jachim and Boaz. She wears Hello Kitty shoes in the photo as well. Her eyes are closed but she has wide-open paint on her eyelids. The photo represented one who sees where others don't, meaning it represents that she sees the occult world that is behind the scenes. It's a scene no one can see unless they are invited to go behind the covering. In another photo Gaga is sitting on a masonic throne called the golden seat in Satanism.

The seat is complete with twin pillars, and above her head is the compass of the Freemasons. She is also wearing a lot of Hello Kitty products, and is in a Hello Kitty dress. She appears like a mannequin, and her hands are in a pose that is known in Satanism. The position of her hands come from the iconic arts and images of Satan. Her hands are pointed in one direction being up and another direction being down. This pose is also called the hermetic maxim of Satan, and it means 'as above, so below.' The meaning is that Satan came from above that is Heaven, and fell below to the earth's spiritual realms.

The overwhelming images in the photo of the Hello Kitty products do also have a meaning. The word 'kitty' used as a nightclub or urban slang is a word for the female private part. Loose girls often like to use the symbol of the Hello Kitty. Sadly the Hello Kitty product is a favorite among small female children who learn through their friends in school what the meaning is for certain older girls.

Lady Gaga's fashion sense at award shows and concerts also have mind-control themes to them like the six Alice in Wonderland dresses she worn in one night at the 2009 VMAs, or the robot machine dresses she wears at her concerts with dance moves that look like she is not dancing but being pulled on strings.

Her concerts are also highly sexually immoral featuring Lady Gaga wearing her bra and panties along with her half-naked mostly homosexual dancers. Lady Gaga often comes off as some kind of inspiration to the lost youth. She is seen as a replacement for Jesus Christ in the eyes and minds of many of her fans. Of course Lady Gaga did not love the world to give her life for the ultimate cause of saving souls for a better world. Lady Gaga never rose from the grave. In fact she has been all about herself, and her twisted demonic music. She is what she says she is a 'fame monster'.

For so many people to be out of touch with Jesus Christ, and in touch with an artist who would not enjoy touching them, and lives to corrupt them and harm their souls is a sad world indeed. When Lady Gaga did the song and music video Born This Way many people felt that it was a song expressing homosexual pride. Homosexuals, and other politicians and speakers gave praise to Lady Gaga for the song because according to them the song was about acceptance.

As a Bible believing Christian I do not support the beliefs of homosexuals being 'born this way'. I do agree they should have fair rights in regards to all civil laws and personal freedoms, but I do not agree with gay-marriage. Other people do clearly disagree with me, and state that gay-people are 'born this way', and should enjoy marriage in the sight of even GOD. I am not sure how many Christians know this but one of the aims of the gay-agenda is to have gay-churches and places of worship that accepts gay-marriage, and gay-lifestyles. It's often believed in regards to prophecy, and future events that there will be a society that one day makes this happen for them, but the price for it will be high, and there are no stakes higher then someone's soul.

GOD does not hate gay-people. GOD does hate gay sin. Like all sin GOD hates, GOD died for all these sins to forever place us in Heaven if we believe in GOD, and turn away from sins. Jesus Christ would never beat up or harm a gay person in any way. The issue about Hell comes to this in regards to true Christian teachings on the subject...people send themselves there. They do so because they love sin, and not because they were born to sin but because they came to love sin through various ways. Many times through awful abusive ways. They come to a point in life that they tell themselves, 'I am what I am, and there is nothing wrong with the way I am'. All people, no matter gay or straight who go to Hell have that common ignorant belief. They give up on GOD without really getting to know GOD because they do not want to confront sins in their lives.

Strange enough Lady Gaga's song, though it may seem on the outside to be a song about accepting gay-lifestyles, turns out it has a different, and even sinister meaning. The meaning comes out more in the music video. The music video has strange and occult elements that have nothing to do with gay-rights or gay-pride. The meanings of these elements are occult themes with symbolism that is ancient. Most of her fans who see the video are unaware of it.

Lady Gaga in the video is playing the role of the mother goddess. She declares she is giving birth to a new race. The symbolism in the video would reveal that the giving of this new race would not come from natural birth but it would be artificially done. This new race turns out not to be a representation of gay-people or a new and accepting generation. The process of this birth shown in the video once again relates to monarch mind-control programming. The birth of this 'new race' is actually the birth of a new conscience mind within humanity. It is a programmed mind filled with alter-personas born through the abuses of black magic, trauma, and physical abuse. Born This Way is a video that is a continuation of the mind-control themes shown in her other videos. This video was actually directed by Nick Knight. Nick Knight's videos are often filled with satanic occultism, mind-control themes, rituals, and other pagan symbolism. He is also a popular photographer in the Hollywood scene. Many of his most famous photos have many satanic images. Some of his famous photos include pictures of models missing one-eye with X marks on their foreheads.

Police and FBI files relating to satanic ritual groups who engaged in murder show that the groups would mark an X on their victims' vital areas upon their bodies. They would do this to know where to stab them to cause the most damage and kill them. This director is often seen wearing the official t-shirts of the Church of Satan. Many of the directors Lady Gaga worked with also had this in common as well.

In the video we see an ancient image of a unicorn that is often used in occult lore and symbolism. In Lady Gaga's video the image of the unicorn is inside the shape of an inverted pink triangle. Pink triangles pointing down-words were used by the Nazis who in their occult studies believed in, and worshipped unicorns as well.

The Nazis used the downwards pink triangle symbol to single out, and mark homosexuals in Germany, and other countries they controlled at the time. Those who were singled out and marked were later rounded up along with Jews, and even Christians, and sent to concentration camps. Many homosexuals who had to wear that symbol were killed in gas-chambers and by firing squads. The symbol is an occult symbol as one of the symbols relating to ritual sacrifices. It is a symbol relating to bloodshed of an entire people who, in the video, would be gay-people.

Of course this was not exposed in the media. Most of her fans, and people who saw it never even realized this. This is because history, and true education is lacking in this country and around the world. Why Lady Gaga would also use the symbol of the unicorn also has an occult meaning. The unicorn in occult understanding represents sexual energy and the color of semen. I am sorry if that grossed you out because most normal people don't see the unicorn in that way but occultist do.

The unicorn is also represented as a spirit of enlightenment and fierceness whose sexual energy is one of taking something by force. To understand it better the symbolism is promoting rape. Strange enough that is how a lot of people ended up gay. Many of them were rape beforehand that left many of them later on to be sexually confused.

The unicorn in other ancient occult teachings also represented another form of Lucifer. The horn of the unicorn in those occult teachings was viewed as the union of god and his third eye or all-seeing eye as it's known today. The kind of god they are describing is a god with three eyes, and his third eye is hidden, and within the center of his forehead. The unicorn to them matched the image of their god, and they called him a god of light to mean the being shines very brightly.

The whole concept that is presented in the video was about an offering to Satan to offer him gay-people as victims to feed the blood-lust of Satan. Most people will never believe that but the symbolism's understanding is stating just that. In the video we see Lady Gaga wearing a strange porcelain mask and playing a character.

The character she plays is the god Janus the god of gateways and beginnings. She wears the mask because slaves of the gods and goddesses in ancient times wore masks to honor the gods.

In the music video, when Gaga declared this new race birth that is really a mind-controlled mark of the beast chipped generation she states the following words, 'This is the manifesto of mother monster on G.O.A.T, a government owned alien territory in space, a birth of magnificent, and magical proportions take place.' These lines may sound very strange to people but they do have meaning. The Nazi mind-control doctors used to use certain fun, and strange sounding phrases when telling soldiers they were going to be mind-controlled. They wanted them to see the experience as being fun or magical as it were. A lot of people who speak about Disney being a front for a vast mind-control center also state that the idea for it came from the Nazis. It is believed that Lady Gaga in those words was speaking in code about vast mind-control. When Lady Gaga in a symbolism way gives birth to this 'new race' a swarm of butterflies appear. These butterflies in the video represented this new race of people, but why compare them to butterflies?

The answer to that question seems to be within the understanding of mind-control. Butterflies were often used as a symbol in mind-control upon victims who have completed their mind-control programming. The butterfly is used for them to give the victims an understanding that they have risen from the 'cocoon' which is their brutal programming, and have become reborn into a different person. Of course this new person is more like a thousand people in one, and this new person is a controlled person.

Many also believe that the video was showing aspects about the future relating to what the Bible calls the mark of the beast. Many believe that the mark of the beast is a chip that is used upon people willing to be mind-controlled to be part of the future society that will come under the rule of the anti-Christ. In the music video Lady Gaga portrays her fans as being soulless Gaga-clones with butterflies flying all around them. To further this negative anti-Christian influence in the video the scene also show a semi-hidden skull head made of human bodies. Along with that are scenes of Lady Gaga firing a machine gun while Church bells ring. Shooting off the machine gun, and showing a skull made of human bodies is a celebration of death and not life.

The scenes promote a new society that is engaged in depopulation by killing human beings. In the future, according to prophecy, many Christians will be killed for not accepting the mark of the beast. The governments in that time will become very controlling and oppressive toward the population. The population itself will become more violent and gripped in chaos.

The video wants oppression and mind-control to seem glamorous and attractive. Lady Gaga even states in her lyrics that it does not matter to GOD if you love GOD and sexually love the same members of your own sex. Of course Lady Gaga is very wrong on that. It does matter to GOD, and GOD does not want that kind of behavior from the children He created.

Much of the dualism continues throughout the video with scenes of worldly lives being celebrated by the images of death. The fans and the gay-couples in the video are all shown as being dead zombies. Gaga herself also portrays herself as a zombie in the video appearing inside a triangle with scenes of the symbol of the all-seeing eye being flashed from scene to scene. The video closes with scenes of people being shown as legions of clones.

Like a lot of Lady Gaga's songs and videos, her art-forms are pure evil revealing horrible events and making them to appear glamorous. This mind-numbing repetition of Lady Gaga's works are only the concealment of things going on behind the scenes of powerful companies and governments. Lady Gaga uses in her art-form a contradictory double-ness of thought to conceal the true meanings of her songs by using deceptive titles and song lyrics.

Take the song and music video she did called Alejandro. The song and video had a hidden meaning of a blasphemous, and satanic nature. The music video was directed by Steven Klein who is said to be a Satanist, and a homosexual. Steven Klein is also famous in the fashion industry as a photographer. His most famous photos have exploited many satanic, and homoeroticism themes. The song on the surface has confused a lot of people regarding it's on the surface meaning. Many people think the song is about Lady Gaga cheating on a guy named Alejandro by having sex with a couple of Alejandro's friends.

Some people think the song is about gay-rights or gays being mistreated by Church groups. Others think it's a nightclub song and nothing more, but there is a real understanding to the song and video, and it has nothing to do with those outside understandings believed by her fans. The real understanding of this art-form is also within hidden meaning.

In the video there are scenes of Lady Gaga, and her dancers dressed up as Nazis, and they engage in all kinds of pornographic poses. The images look brutally abusive and not romantic. The video shows representations of orgies and sexual abuse. The symbolism in the video tells a story of spiritual rejection taking place in the midst of an oppressive police state.

Gaga starting out sought her fame during the time of the media terrorist fear campaigns that followed after 911. During that time the whole country was constantly told by the media that America was not safe, and we were on high-alert. Of course next week we were okay and then the following week we were in danger again, and this pattern went on and on. In that time America's armed forces made war on Iraq, a country that did not bomb them, and U.S. armed forces began to police and control Iraq, and other places in the Middle East. Hence America was wrapped up in turning countries into a police state including their own by making laws that were taking away our Bill of Rights.

It was during this time that Lady Gaga officially gave up on GOD according to many insiders. The music video also reflects this as well. The video shows a funeral procession, and Gaga wearing a black veil holding a sacred heart. Gaga was raised as a Catholic Christian so the sacred heart to her is a symbol that represents the heart of Jesus Christ. The sacred heart in Gaga's video however is blacken with a heroin syringe in it. The scene is to show that Jesus Christ is dead inside of her. She killed Christ in her by the vices of her life. The scene was to make a statement that GOD is dead to her.

There are scenes in the video of Lady Gaga wearing a red latex nun suit, and holding a rosary while singing to 'alejandro' to let her go. The word 'alejandro' in the video is actually being used as a metaphor for the word GOD. The concept of 'alejandro' being a boyfriend she cheats on with 'fernando' or 'roberto' is a smoke-screen, and that concept does not have anything to do with the scenes of the music video or the tone of the song.

The video's concept is rejection, and it applies to rejection of GOD. The video also tells the tale of Gaga receiving a new spirituality, and this spirituality is called New Age faith. Gaga in the video is playing the role of a Luciferian priestess. This is why her latex nun suit features many inverted crosses. Inverted crosses are used to mock the faith of Christianity, and it signifies a perverted power found in black magic. The symbol is used for orgies because it is also seen as a phallic symbol in several occult teachings. It is a way to use sex to mock the religion of Christianity.

In the video Gaga swallows the rosary in a slow devouring manner. Gaga also knows that to Catholic Christians the rosary is used by them to make prayers to GOD. By swallowing the rosary Gaga is doing a couple of things. Gaga knows that by doing this it would shock a lot of people and would get her media attention. She is also doing it to mock the power of prayer, and declaring she will do things her own way.

In the video there are scenes with Lady Gaga, and her dancers wherein her dancers begin to violently push her around. After she is abused by her dancers she begins to take off her clothes to engage in a sexual orgy. Throughout the video are scenes of Lady Gaga sexually abusing her dancers and dancing half-naked with them wearing a machine gun bra. From the start of the video to the finish are scenes of Lady Gaga wearing a black dress representing a black magic queen who sees things through one eye.

We see in the background of the video scenes of social unrest, buildings on fire, and a military police state. The scenes are designed to give the viewers a feeling of an intense situation. In some of the scenes the male dancers are shown as puppets on strings, and some of them have guns aimed at their private parts with blank-stare faces as if no one is home in their minds. The scenes show abuse and mind-control to be fused with sexuality to make this oppressive imagery to be desired among people. This is another reason why people today are getting into more S&M practices. In fact one time when Lady Gaga performed this song live on an episode of American Idol she revealed the satanic theme to the song. The stage Lady Gaga was to perform the song on was set up to look like the Garden of Eden.

In the center of the stage was a statue of Lucifer, the one called Satan, who tempted Adam and Eve. Every time Lady Gaga sang the word 'alejandro' fire would come out of the angel's wings. During the performance Gaga is lifted up into the air as a blood-red liquid ooze comes pouring out the statue from the fountain. Another example of satanic worship, and human sacrifice presented by Lady Gaga on live television. When Lady Gaga released the single called Judas certain fans, and people started to slowly wake up to the fact that there is something evil about her. When Judas was released many Church leaders, and speakers of truth called it the most blasphemous pop-song ever recorded.

The song and the music video tells a twisted tale of Judas, and the New Age version of Jesus. The song itself comes off as an ode to Judas the man who betrayed Jesus Christ for 30 silver coins. The amount today would be about 20 dollars. For 20 dollars Judas would seal his fate, and send himself to Hell by committing suicide.

In Lady Gaga's music video Judas comes off as the hero of the story. She promotes the idea of Judas doing the world a favor. Of course this is what makes this song so sick and evil. The song is a continuation of Lady Gaga's anti-Christian beliefs and pro-Satanist themes. Sad enough the song, when released, did not destroy her career nor was there a real media firestorm against her like what happened to Madonna when she released Like A Prayer. Instead the song became a Billboard smash hit, and people were dancing to it at nightclubs. Just one of the reasons why the world is in the shape it is while heading for full scale destruction. Christianity is no longer the main focus of the masses of people. They are becoming more, and more far removed from it. The people, rather they know it or not, are embracing a new kind of spirituality that is actually the same old pagan spirituality.

Mass media entertainment is playing a major role in brain-washing, and reshaping the minds, and emotions of the peoples all over the world. The peoples are being vexed, and hexed by what they love the most which is idolatry. The world idolizes celebrities, and know more about them then the Bible and Jesus Christ. There are even people who profess Christianity, and yet are big fans of Lady Gaga. They have no problem with their daughters or sons listening to her music. The sadness of it all goes back to what Jesus Christ said, 'my people die due to lack of knowledge'. Jesus is really not the bad guy here, but Lady Gaga, and her songs on the other-hand are.

In the music video Lady Gaga portrays Jesus and his Apostles as a modern day motorcycle biker gang. Upon the jackets worn by who are supposed to be Jesus and his Apostles according to Lady Gaga are symbols of skulls, bones, and other satanic symbols. Gaga in the video plays the role of Mary Magdalene, and Mary in the video is suppose, to be Jesus' girlfriend. This is how stupid, and evil this video is, and it gets worse. In New Age teachings gurus teach that Jesus and Mary Magdalene had a child together, got married, and Jesus never went to the cross. This is also the garbage believed by many occult groups in high and low places of society. Lady Gaga also believes these lies about Jesus Christ as well. In fact a lot of young women who are mostly immoral, and think there is nothing wrong with that, started to believe these lies more so around the time several Hollywood films started to promote the idea in the early to mid 2000s.

In the video Lady Gaga is riding on the backseat of Jesus' motorcycle, and as they ride together Lady Gaga begins to yell the name of another man in her so-called boyfriend's ear. That name is Judas. She yells this name in the chorus of the song as the hook, and the way she sings the hook sounds like chanting then singing. The scenes were done to show that Lady Gaga is telling Jesus that she found a new man in her life who is Judas.

The real meaning is hidden, and that meaning is she found a new spirituality, a dark satanic faith that is represented in Judas. In the Bible Judas was taken over by Satan when he betrayed Jesus. Lady Gaga is telling or more like yelling in Jesus' ear that she wants Satan. The song's lyrics begin to tell of Judas seducing Lady Gaga.

In the music video we see scenes of a different version of the events of the Last Supper. Instead of Jesus washing the feet of his Apostles we get scenes of Lady Gaga washing the feet of Jesus and Judas. The scene has a hidden meaning to show Jesus and Judas as being equals to convey the idea that Jesus and Satan are two different equal gods. That is a belief found in occult groups that Jesus and Satan share the same power, and are even brothers. That one represents white magic, and the other black magic. Of course this concept is not what the Bible teaches, and is not the reality of who Jesus is as being One GOD.

In the scene Lady Gaga passes over the washing of Jesus' feet to wash Judas' feet first in an effort to make Jesus jealous. After this comes a series of scenes where Jesus confronts Judas as if they are two guys at a bar going to the back of the alley to fight it out. Lady Gaga in the video pretends to be on Jesus' side, and she pulls a gun on Judas but when she pulls the trigger a stick of lipstick comes out. Gaga uses the lipstick to kiss Judas with it, and she then turns against Jesus to side with Judas. Soon comes the scenes of the gang betraying their leader Jesus. Lady Gaga then takes part in the torture and death of Jesus Christ.

While doing this the song sings lyrics stating 'a king with no crown'. In the scenes with her dancers Lady Gaga is dressed in purple and scarlet to represent the Whore of Babylon, and a few of her dancers are holding a weapon out in the shot. The weapon is called the morning star which was Lucifer's former title name. Some of her dancers are also wearing the official t-shirts of the Church of Satan.

It amazes me that her fans can see this video while hearing this song only to tell themselves it must mean something else. Lady Gaga knows that she is leading people away from Jesus Christ. She knows that her fans are suffering by removing themselves from the Way of Jesus Christ. During a live concert performance Lady Gaga was playing the piano when she all of a sudden decided to stop, and address her fans. She would tell her fans the following words, 'I know that a lot of you are suffering. You are suffering for your love of music...like Jesus did.'

A lot of people did not know what she meant, and most of her fans dismiss it. When suffering happens it comes through evil events being done in the lives of those who suffer. For music to make them suffer this means the music must be evil, and that comes through the evil influence of the music. She added Jesus in there to mock him for dying for a people who rather listen to her music then Him.

These are the times you live in where deceptive ugly events done against the teachings of GOD would run like rivers overflowing. Other events show personal contacts regarding Lady Gaga, and satanic worship, and demonic possession. One event involved Lady Gaga's hair dresser. This story comes from the testimony of the hair dresser. He stated that he had problems with Lady Gaga right from the start as she was often verbally abusive toward him. During a conversation he stated that Lady Gaga began to talk about Jesus Christ, and the hair dresser turned out to be a Christian. The man would defend Jesus Christ, and he stated that when he did that Lady Gaga shot off her seat in a way that looked supernatural to him. He stated that Lady Gaga was looking dead at him with possessed and blank eyes. She began to tell him that his GOD was dead, and she did not want to hear about him. He stated that while this frightening event was occurring what sent him running out of the room is when he noticed that she was levitating off the floor.

Many insiders believe the man's story, and he is not the first ex-employee of Lady Gaga to have strange run-ins with her. Another strange event happened when Lady Gaga was visiting England. Lady Gaga during her visit there, was supposed to visit a masonic lodge in England. Sometimes masonic lodges hire entertainers to perform for them at their lodges, and this is done among lodges with elite members. On the night Lady Gaga went the hotel maid went into her room to clean it up for her. When she went to the bathroom she saw that the tube was filled with blood. The maid would quickly report it, and the story even floated around the news media but was quickly buried. No one knows if the blood was animal or human. Many insiders state that Lady Gaga performed an occult ritual before going to the masonic lodge.

Her latest youtube videos that have millions of followers feature Lady Gaga teaching witchcraft chants to her millions of fans all over the world watching on youtube. Lady Gaga's latest single at the time of this writing was a song called GUY. In the music video Lady Gaga plays Satan where she falls from Heaven. The theme of the story is Satan falls from Heaven so that he could have sex with Jesus Christ. This is the actual theme of the music video that millions of Lady Gaga fans were waiting to see.

Chapter 32

Throughout the history of music, and before there was a modern music industry, there were musicians who became famous for their musical skills. One period in music history was the time of the world-wide fame of classical musical composers. Their rise to fame came about in the Middle Age periods of Europe. Their fame was at the highest during the 16th, 17th, 18th, and 19th centuries. For those four hundred years many famous classical composers came about, and achieved the kind of fame that is compared to the fame in the music industry.

Many people today see these composers as being godly men who did music that would put modern music listeners today to sleep, but this view is far from the truth. To understand it fully is to first know about the times they lived in. Music artists, and popular forms of music were divided into two classes. There were artists, and forms of music for the poor that had many names, and played at theater houses and taverns, and there were artists, and forms of music for the elite and rich that also had many names. Their most popular form of music among the elite in that time is the music we call classical today. For the elite and their families, they were huge fans of this music. They were moved, and inspired by it in the manner music moves people today. So therefore it did not put them to sleep but it was an opposite reaction. They in fact loved this music, and many of them became very extreme fans of the composers who made this music. Most of these composers also did not live godly lives only a few of them did compared to the numbers. For most of them their lives were the lives of rock stars you see today. Women would throw themselves at them, and try to get them alone. Many of these women were married. Many of these composers had drug and liquor problems. Many of them became rich and successful only to end up broke, and dead under strange events. Many of them were abused by their parents, and by the system they worked under. Many of them also had ties to occult secret orders among the aristocracy of the times. The evidence shows a lifestyle among famous classical composers of those times to be filled with certain crimes.

Adultery was a crime back then but it was a crime very often enforced, but this crime often brought violent encounters to classical composers which included pay-offs, cover-ups, and even murder took place surrounding the events. Drugs and strong drink problems were also not to be done in the open. Many composers would make the mistake of doing things in the open that would ruin their careers. Many strange crimes were committed against composers by people looking to steal from them or ruin them. Many composers ended up in serious debts over property, and bad investments that resulted from the over-spending of many of these composers who often spent more than they made. Many of them died questionable deaths with connections to hidden orders that would be called occultic today. Classical composers laid the foundations for popular music today. Because of them many people throughout the ages fell in love with music, and music became an even larger part of education in those times. This would result in thousands, and thousands through the years being able to perform high musical gifts. Such gifts would be passed down through the generations of those families resulting in people of today expressing musical gifts handed down from their family stock.

Among the hundreds of famous classical composers there was only one who was called the greatest among them all. It is even said he was the greatest composer to come in that time in the last 1,000 years before him. During his time his peers marveled at his gifts, and either really loved him or really hated him, but all could not touch him when it came to musical skills, and composing.

Like most of the classical composers he never had a childhood but his whole life was given over to music. This would result for him to grow up to have a child-like complex that would get the better of him at times. His father was also involved with a secret order called the Freemasons, and his family came from the high elite families of wealth. It was said that he was often abused, and pushed to his very limit from the time he was a very small boy to the time he was seen as his own man, but he was so gifted, and so extra-talented that it looked easy when he engaged in music. When he died a hailstorm of rumors and stories came through. Most of them centered around jealous backstabbing peers, members of the monarchy elite he offended, and leaving offenses with social order, and exposing too much of his involvement with the Freemasons which was a secret order and still is. The name of this classical composer was Johannes Chrysostomus Wolfgang Amadeus Mozart.

Mozart was born in Germany in the area of Bavaria before it was transferred to Austria on January 17, 1756. The rumors around his father are that he was an elite merchant who was bred from elite families. His father also had musical gifts, and was able to see early the talent in Mozart. His father is believed to have been a Freemason, and was aware of certain political events that later turned into revolutionary conflicts all over the world. At that time his father's focus was on his business, his music, and his occult interests.

Mozart would be pushed very hard by his father to develop his gifts. Crying or complaining was met with beatings and coldness. His father at the time was an organist for the prince's chapel. So from the earliest age Mozart evinced the strongest predilection for music. When Mozart's father began to see how gifted he was he discontinued the instruction of music to his other students to devote himself to his son's tuition that was also joined with his sister who was four years older than him.

After studying the harpsichord for a full year, the flights of Mozart's genius started to become very rapid. He began to exercise his own inventions of original music composition when he was only five years old. In the classical music scene this was unheard of at the time and still is. When Mozart was six years old he began performing for live audiences among the elite nobility of the times. His performances were so remarkable that his father took him, and his sister who often performed with Mozart, to Munich and Vienna.

Mozart's sister should be noted also possessed similar high

musical gifts, and could have been a great composer in her own right, but at the time the classical music scene was a man's world. Women did perform with them but they were not the main attraction which is to say main composer.

The cities of Munich and Vienna at the time were huge centers for the classical music scene. Many great composers trained in those cities, and got their start there playing for the nobility of those cities. When Mozart's father brought his son and daughter there their reputations came before them. They obtained every kind of engagement, and encouragement from the nobility. They would soon perform for the Elector of Bavaria, and that performance would lead them to perform for Emperor Francis the 1st. Both the Elector, and the Emperor would praise their performances.

In 1763 when Mozart was only seven years old the Mozart family moved to Paris. Paris at the time was seen as one of the capital cities of the classical music scene. During that time the nobility of Paris invited the Mozart family to a social party. During the party they were to meet the nobility members and their guests. They also were not, excepted to perform there. Young Mozart at the age of seven would surprise the party including his father by stepping in with a group of musicians who played as a trio. Mozart would play several stringed instruments with them, and gave the nobility that night a wonderful performance.

During his time in Paris Mozart's fame began to grow along with the popular nature of his performances. He would in that time earn a great reputation as a performer on the organ. One of his most remembered performances is when he performed before the whole court at the Chapelle du Roi as he performed on the organ.

When Mozart was living in Paris as a small child he began to enter upon a career as a musical author. As a small boy he would publish his first two works in Paris. This was also an unheard of feat at the time. From Paris the Mozart family would travel to London in 1764. Mozart as a small child genius would be brought before the royal family. The young boy would exhibit his talents before the royal family.

The royal family would put Mozart under some severe trials where for a child to be subjected to it would be abusive. Mozart would however pass the trials in a most triumphant manner. The English royal family, and the elite nobility of the kingdom were highly impressed with young Mozart. Mozart at that time became what we call today as a child star. His father at the time when asked about how Mozart became this gifted he really did not have an answer for it. His father was an intelligent man, and had a fine education, and a lot of knowledge of the world of his time, but he was unable to describe the astounding progressive improvements of his son during the first stages of his very early life.

His father often regarded it as a miracle an act of GOD being performed upon Mozart, but he was not quick to say that to people which is why he often came off as not knowing how his son got that good. Mozart at the age of eight years old had great knowledge in composition by his writings. His inventions, tastes, modulation, and execution in extemporary playing were such as few professors are possessed of even at 40 years of age. Mozart was now among an adult world, and was seen as a musical gift from Heaven, and the future of music in the world. Around this time Mozart became closer to his father's inner-circle of friends among the elite. It was believed that through the connections with his father, and the England nobility is how Mozart was introduced to Freemasonry.

In that time Mozart was only eight years old, and he was writing symphonies of his own composition while producing them at public concerts in London. London was also a major city of the classical music scene. There in London Mozart composed, and published six sonatas. In 1765 the Mozart family would return to the mainland of Europe. They would pass through Paris, and come to the country of Holland. At the Hague an occasion was going to be held for the Prince of Orange to celebrate his installation. The young Mozart was asked to perform for the Prince of Orange. There Mozart composed a symphony for a full orchestra.

Soon the family would return to Germany, and Mozart began to work for the Orphan House Church in Vienna. There Mozart would gain more fame, and would cause a sensation for his compositions for religious worship services there. This Church in Vienna had for its members an elite group. His performances were so well remarked that Mozart was asked to perform his compositions in the presence of the imperial court. When the Mozarts returned to their home in Salzburg young Mozart began to devote himself most assiduously to the study of his art, and evinced his mastery of the subject.

In 1768 the Emperor Joseph the 2nd at Vienna requested of Mozart to compose an opera for him. Mozart would write the opera called La Finta Semplice. Though the opera was hailed, and approved by all the masters of the period it was never performed. Many believe that this had something to do with the nature of the opera. The opera in the story seems to unveil secrets that goes on behind the scenes of the elite. It was a story based in hardships of that world.

By 1769 Wolfgang Mozart was about 13 years old, and he became nominated to become concert-master to the Archbishop of Salzburg. This was a very envied position at the time. It gained Mozart an independent position, and a salary of his own. Mozart's career at the time was still however very much controlled by his father. His father would come to control the money the pre-teen Mozart was now earning. Through this control his father would hide the real amount of his salary, and only pay Mozart the trifling sum of $5 per annum.

In those years as Mozart was growing into a teenager he became more rebellious to his father. He did not hate his father but he knew his father was stealing from him. So often Mozart would disobey his father, and stray from home to go among the theaters and taverns of the musicians who played for the common people. There Mozart would often get hired by the owners of those places to play, and would earn extra money he kept to himself.

These activities of Mozart could have ruined his career. Mozart was hired by the Church to do religious music, and if caught in a bar playing on instruments, and drinking beer he would be fired from his post and ruined. Due to his appointment Mozart was to travel to Italy where his father went with him. This is where Mozart began to do his side business of playing at the places among the common. When Mozart got to Italy the Italian people most rapturously welcomed him. He was a very famous person there.

His first performance among the elite there was given at Milan. It was met with a huge sensation from the people who adored the young composer and musician. In 1771 Mozart would compose an opera for a grand carnival in Italy, and engaged in performances at Bologna and Florence. He would be praised for these performances, and given a grand reception.

In that time Mozart would come to Rome where he was to take part in the concerts assigned with the Passion Week. In that week on a Wednesday Mozart went to the Sistine Chapel to hear the celebrated work called Miserere. Miserere was one of Italy's national pieces, and by law it was a piece that was prohibited from being copied or published in any manner. Anyone who did so was to be excommunicated from the country. The piece was so good that no one thought anyone could copy it from just simple memory of hearing it, but Mozart was able to.

After hearing it he went home, and made a copy of it. Once he did he realized there was mistakes in it that only he could correct, and he did so. He would take the copy and fold it, and hide it in his hat, and from Wednesday night to Good Friday he would make the correct changes in the piece. When Mozart was to perform on Good Friday he would shock the entire elite crowd by performing the Miserere piece without having to ever see the secret official copy. This circumstance created an immense excitement at Rome.

The peculiarities of the Miserere piece was such that everyone said it was impossible to be expressed by simple musical notation. The masters and the court were stunned that Mozart, in the presence of the Sistine choristers sang the composition, and had the piece performed even though he never acquired it through training. The elite professionals would express their astonishment in unmeasured admiration to Mozart.

Now the fame of Mozart was being spread even wider, and spreading very far. His wonderful musical talents and power of performing on the organ were attributed to an out-going charm he had, and the way he wore his golden ring. Soon the Pope would hear Mozart perform, and he was so impressed with him he conferred upon Mozart the Golden Spur. In Bologna Mozart would receive the honor to be unanimously elected a member of the Philharmonic Society.

To be in the Philharmonic Society at that time was an honor rarely conferred even upon the greatest musicians who were twice his age. By the time Mozart was sixteen years old he was acknowledged as the first clavecinist in the world. He had produced two requiems, and a stabatmater along with numerous offertories, hymns, and motets. He had produced 4 operas, 2 cantatas, 13 symphonies, 24 piano-forte sonatas and an uncountable number of concerts with different instruments, trios, quartets, marches, and other minor pieces.

In 1773 when the American Revolutionary War was about to break out Mozart was producing numerous works including two masses for the chapel of the Elector of Bavaria. By 1775 he was working for the Archduke Maximilian, and he composed a famous piece for him called I Re Pastore. During this time Mozart was now a young man, and his parents still controlled his money especially his father. His father also was at times estranged from his mother do to affairs that were kept quiet.

Mozart would become more exposed to the occult scene of that time among the elite, and many nobles sought to hire him. Mozart was also a teacher to many future great classical composers wherein Mozart took part in their training. One of them was Beethoven who became a great master of music in his own right.

Mozart at this time was becoming more involved with romantic relationships but these relationships never really got off the ground. However he would bed many women who throw themselves at him. He would still often escape to the places of common people to perform for extra-money. He would also do it now as a way to escape the brooding world he was in. In the mid 1770's Mozart's fame was so completely established, and so widely known that he could have made wide choices in his engagements. He could have picked from any capital in Europe to work in, but his father would still have tight control over

Mozart's career choices.

This control, and the fact he wasted, and took Mozart's money would lead to many financial problems for Mozart throughout his career. In that time his father picked Paris as the city Mozart would work in. His parents at the time were having marriage problems, and so his father decided to send away his mother but stay behind himself. He used the excuse that it was for the sake of business. Mozart and his mother would leave for Paris in 1777. Mozart would quickly find work there as a writer of music, and would earn money for his labors with his pen.

Mozart would use this money to support his mother, and the large home they lived in. Mozart did have a much better time, for dealing with his mother was easier, and delightful than dealing with his father, but in 1778 his beloved mother would die. Mozart became heart-broken, and depressed at the loss of his mother. Soon life became insupportable for Mozart in Paris. He was often wasting his money, and was too heart-sick to write as much as before. He began to waste his money on reckless drinking, and nights at the taverns that often accompanied women of the night.

Soon his life was in shambles, and in order to recover he returned to his father at the beginning of the year 1779. In November of 1779 Mozart would settle in the city of Vienna. He began to take up the manners, and habits of the elite people of the city, and became an agreeable neighbor to the people he lived among. His father got Mozart a job to work for the Emperor.

One would think that working for the Emperor would make a person rich, and usually it did but not in Mozart's case. The Emperor paid a modest salary to Mozart that was a lot of money for most people but modest when compared to what other composers were making who were nowhere near as good as Mozart. Mozart's father also still controlled his money, and was still taking money from him.

Mozart throughout his career could never get full control over his money, and was always in need of help in that area. You would think that a family member would be good for that area because they would be honest with you, but in some cases that is not the case. His father saw that his son had talent, and would make lots of money, so he was greedy, and sought a way to be the one who benefits off his son's talent.

When the Emperor had Mozart's salary issued it went to the investors who worked for his father. They would give it to his father. His father would keep most of it, and give what's left over to Mozart. Strange enough this is how executives in the music industry today treat, and have treated many of their star-artists. This is also how child-stars, and celebrities dealing with family problems have also been dealt with in the same like-manner.

Mozart at the time was hardly making any money, and for a guy working for the Emperor he was often broke, and ran into problems with bill-collectors regarding his expenses. In order to make his payments to maintain his rich lifestyle at the time he often hired himself out for outside labors he could make extra money from. He began to make extra money by performing concerts, and musical tours for other elite members in other cities. He also was making extra money for teaching music, and made small profits from the sale of his published works.

Soon Mozart did some extra work for the King of Prussia, and the Prussian king wanted to hire him. The King of Prussia offered a much higher salary then what the Emperor was paying him. When the Emperor learned that Mozart was going to leave him for more money the Emperor was forced to match the King of Prussia's offer, and even raised his salary even higher than the offer. During that time many rulers kept making tempting offers to Mozart that kept forcing the Emperor to do more favors for Mozart, and give him more rewards, because the Emperor would do this he showed to Mozart that he really respected his music. So Mozart began to turn down these many offers on the spot, and stand by his Emperor's side.

Mozart was now making more money but still was not getting all the money he was actually making. His father still was keeping money from him. Mozart's nightlife habits began to slowly creep up in his social life among the elite. He was often getting drunk, and was louder and off-balance at parties. He was known to disappear at a party with a woman or two, and then re-appear along with the women, and their hair, and clothes would be a messed.

Mozart also had a reputation for owing money to such a point that society women did not know if he was really established. His father believed that Mozart could end up ruining his career, and so he decides that the best way to solve this problem is for Mozart to get married. In 1780 Mozart performed his great opera piece called Idomeneo. During the concert performance Mozart's father had arranged for Mozart to meet Mademoiselle Constance Weber, and her entire family. The Weber family were a very rich elite family who were fans of the great composers.

This concert that Mozart gave that night is called one of his greatest performances of all time. The opera he performed that night was listed as one of the great performances in music history. The piece in construction, detail, instrumentation, and every imaginable respect, it was an enormous advance on all of his previous works. The performance re-established his reputation among the masters, and the professionals that he is the greatest composer whom the world had ever seen.

After the performance it was back to a life that was filled with honors but not lucrative, and it often took its toll. The Weber family wanted to arrange this marriage with Mademoiselle and Mozart because it could also elevate their position among the elite in the royal court. Mademoiselle in truth did not want to marry Mozart because she felt that his reputation was one of a loose man and she also did not want to be with someone who was not sufficiently established. Meaning she did not want to be with someone who sleeps around, and does not maintain money well, but her family would not give her any choice, and the same was the case with Mozart. Mozart did not want to marry Mademoiselle but his father stated to him that if he wanted financial security in his life that he must marry her. His father was no longer willing to give him any more money even though it was Wolfgang's money to begin with.

The marriage was arranged so that the Weber family could be seen more in the royal court and in return they would pay for all living expenses of Mozart and Mademoiselle. In short the two become prisoners of other people's devices and intentions.

Soon the two of them would be married, and they would try to live as husband and wife. Mozart's best work would be completed during this time, and he gave very remarkable performances, and was being hailed all over the music world, but still his father would find ways to steal his money, and this would result in Mozart owing money once again to bill collectors. The Weber family also was not happy any longer with the arrangement because it did not produce for them what they were hoping to find. So after paying the bills for the time they did, they eventually decided to stop paying them, and put pressure on Mozart to pay his own bills.

This resulted in an intense situation between Mozart and Mademoiselle because now they both felt they were completely on their own. Mademoiselle's only way out was to leave Mozart and return to her family, but she refused to do that, and did not want to leave him alone. Mozart would turn to the theaters and taverns among the common people seeking to be hired to play for their places of business. In that time they would often hire him, and Mozart was able to keep the wolves from casting him out of his home along with his wife to live upon the streets. In this time it is believed by people who research the aspects of elite occult groups that Mozart had connections with, that Mozart may have been selling occult secrets to other people. It is believed that he did several pieces for unknown clients that were not just pieces of music but had hidden messages about the Freemasons of the time and other occult groups. It is an unproven story but often believed that Mozart sold secrets through his music to afford his home, and support his wife. It is believed that this work of Mozart is what led to his death. It is also believed that it led to the appearance of a mysterious person in his life.

Throughout the 1780's these were the highs and lows of Mozart's life. It was believed that during that time is when he was selling secrets, and possibly even speaking it to others he should not have been. By the time 1790 to 1791 came around Mozart's problems became at its worst. During that time Mozart was working very hard, and was in an intense situation trying to make money and keep the wolf from his door. He was constantly avoiding trouble on account of the many official papers that came to him showing warrants for debt. Mozart was close to coming under full arrest many times.

When arrested for debt what they do is they take everything that you have by force and release you when they feel they have stripped you of enough. These troubles brought on a state of melancholy within him, and it seemed that nothing could be done for it. He would soon come under a state of terror, and began to feel that his end was approaching. One day while sitting at home he was plunged in a state of profound sadness, and soon a stranger was announced at the door. Mozart thought it was another bill collector, and was nervous while approaching the guest. While coming down the stairs he saw that the stranger was of dignified manners, and clearly was not a debt collector. The stranger was an unknown person to Mozart. Mozart had never seen him before, and did not know who he was. The man never even tells Mozart his name. The man stated that he represented an exalted ruler, and that he cannot tell him who this unknown ruler is. The man goes on to state that this ruler wanted to secretly hire him to write a solemn mass for the funeral of the soul. He stated that the one he works for had lost someone he tenderly loved. He wanted a piece of music written for this person to honor the passing.

Mozart was taken back, by the mysterious nature of the man. The whole interview had an air of mystery to it that pervaded the heart of Mozart. He did not understand why this had to be so much a secret, and usually secrets in that world involves someone's death. Mozart was nervous but really in need of money. He did not want to take the job but he had no choice. Mozart would put out a deal of half-now and half-later as a condition to take the job, and he charged the man a lot of money enough to stop the debt collectors, and clear his name. The man oddly does not argue about the price, and he agrees to the terms. Mozart felt that now he can rest easier because he has money to start paying people off.

He promised the stranger that he could finish the solemn mass in one month. He would soon go to work on the project but then all of a sudden he started to have a very bad sinking feeling about the project. Day and night he was trying to work on the project uninterrupted but the progress of the piece was coming along very slowly. The problem was he kept on having gloomy premonitions that this music piece was going to get him killed. He would often express this to his wife who was very worried about him. She would watch him talk to himself about his own impending doom while working on the project.

Some think Mozart was just having a nervous breakdown but why have a nervous breakdown when he can now pay his bills, and do something that is usually easy for him. His wife at that point really did not understand what was wrong. She would question him during one of his mental episodes, and he stated to her, 'Certainly I am composing this requiem for myself...it will serve for my own funeral.'

Mozart was afraid to finish the piece, and instead of constantly working on it he began to suspend the undertaking, but the problem was the money, and he really needed the money. This thought would send him back to work. The work turned out to take longer than a month, and soon the stranger returned at the appointed time. Mozart did not have the piece ready when the stranger arrived, and he stated to him, 'I have found it impossible to keep my word'. The stranger could see that Mozart needed more time, and then he tells Mozart, 'Give yourself no uneasiness. What longer time do you require?' Mozart would tell him that he needs another month. The stranger would pull out some money coins and pay Mozart double then what he was going to pay him. After giving him the money he gave Mozart another month and then left. Mozart did not have a good feeling when he left. He began to entertain thoughts that the angel of death was visiting him. Oddly the next day after he left Mozart had a burst of inspiration and quickly went back to finishing the piece.

Within less than a month about a week before the stranger was to return the piece was finished. It was called the Requiem, and it was Mozart's final piece. One day Mozart, feeling good that the piece was finished and his bills were all paid had been a guest at someone's home. Soon he returned home, and then on December 5, 1791 he was found mysterious dead.

One day later the stranger returns where Mozart's sorrowful widowed wife answers the door. The stranger asks her for the musical piece, and she gives it to him. Many people will say that the Requiem was not played at Mozart's funeral but many other historians and investigators believe otherwise. Many of them state that the Requiem was first played at Mozart's funeral, and that his funeral was arranged to look like a ritual masonic sacrifice.

It is unproven but believed by some that Mozart was poisoned while visiting someone's home. It was believed that he was killed by occult members connected to his employer who was the Emperor. The story is that they were nervous about Mozart telling things to people that could be dangerous for them to know. Mozart was too open and close to the common classes of people, and other elite persons with different political views.

It is believed that they hired someone to go, and request that Mozart write his own mass so that it would be easier to keep a watch on him while they planned to kill him. Such killings are usually ritual in their nature so they will be patient about it. Most people do not believe that this is the way he was really killed, but yet oddly the official story of his death also does not make a whole lot of sense, and it sounds more stranger then the hidden story.

When Mozart died he was only 35 years old. The official story is he died of some strange fast-acting sickness that overtook his body and killed him. Some even said he worked himself to death, and fail to explain how he could do that at 35 years old, and do that as a writer. Also there is more than one version to his official death. Others have said he died of a mental sickness, and he even killed himself. It is clear that the official story is not even a story but more like stories. These stories did not explain the kind of symptoms Mozart's wife described when Mozart was confined to the bed when he was sick.

All the symptoms are shown in people who have been poisoned. Mozart himself even stated to people around him at his death-bed that he was poisoned, and even requested to have pieces of the Requiem played at this side. He even tells people that he wants it played because it was his own funeral song.

Chapter 33

Many people who studied the history of music have often wondered, where did music come from? They have explored the questions of who created music, and who invented musical instruments. These people of education have searched the history of many ancient nations, and ancient cultures looking for that answer. Many of them come up with different answers for those questions, but they hardly ever look toward the Bible's answers to those questions.

The Bible in fact reveals answers to those questions. Since so much study into the history of music is given to secular study, studies that have nothing to do with what the Bible says, I will use this chapter to give the answers that the Bible teaches.

The Book of Job tells us that when GOD created the earth, and the human race there was a race of spiritual beings called angels who lived in Heaven. The Bible states that GOD created the angels, and gave them all their powers. One of the powers GOD gave the angels was the ability to become music. Notice I said become music, and not just sing music. The angels were beings of 'fire' and 'wonders' which means they were supernatural beings who were able to perform feats way beyond the ability of human beings. They were able to transform themselves into different powerful shapes, and designs according to the Book of Ezekiel, and other books of the Bible.

When the angels performed music in Heaven they were able to become music. One angel was able to sound and sing like thousands of musical instruments. Imagine what a whole uncountable chorus of angels would sound like. Knowing this we can see that GOD is the creator of music. The first beings he taught, and empowered to play His gift of music which came in all forms of music were the angels.

In regards to how human beings got the gift of music this gift also came from GOD. GOD created the human race to represent him on earth by giving them his most Holy image upon these children. The first two human beings ever created were Adam and Eve. Adam and Eve use to live in the Garden of Eden, and their first home was Eternal Paradise. They had constant face to face communication with GOD which also means according to the Bible they had constant inter-actions with the angels of Heaven.

Adam and Eve it is also stated worshipped GOD in the Garden of Eden. That means according to the meaning of worship in the Bible Adam and Eve sang the glories of GOD. They in fact were already born with the gift of singing music. Adam and Eve were born also with free-will, they were able to make their own choices in life as a test of their humanity and loyalty to GOD. That loyalty would soon be tested.

Satan who was once called Lucifer was the first angel ever created. He was the most powerful minister of music in Heaven. He was in fact in charge of music in Heaven, but he would rebel against GOD, and start a war in Heaven. A war he lost. He would soon attack the human race, and has been ever since. He first attacked Adam and Eve, and they making a bad choice that led to disobedience before GOD, resulting in them being casted out of the Garden of Eden to live under the hardships of earth.

GOD however had a plan for them, and the entire human race. This plan was seen in Jesus Christ who was also there, and was the Word before anything including angels were there. The Bible states that the Word spoke and life came to be, and this was in fact Jesus speaking on behalf of the Father. Therefore Jesus created the human race, and the angels, and all of Heaven and earth.

When Adam and Eve were casted out overtime they lived under the hardships of earth. Throughout the years they would have many sons and daughters. It is believed that by the nature of Adam and Eve being parents that the Book of Proverbs state that parents raised their children by teaching them right from wrong, and teaching their kids what they know. So Adam and Eve, clearly being in the position they were in needed their children to know everything they knew in order to survive because earth was a hard place in its early development. So naturally singing, and the knowledge of GOD would have come with this teaching while their children would have learned it.

One such child was Cain, Adam and Eve's firstborn son. Cain

turned out to be a wicked man who committed the first murder on earth. He never respected his parent's teachings on spiritual matters. He only took the education to work efforts in glorifying himself. This intent is seen in the Book of Genesis during the sacrifice between Cain and Abel.

Cain and Abel were to give an offering to GOD. This offering was a sign of their faith and belief in GOD. Cain did not believe in GOD, he believed in himself, and showed it through his offering which was rejected. Abel did believe in GOD, and GOD accepted his offering. This made Cain jealous and enraged, and so later he commits the first murder by killing his own brother. GOD would then curse, and banish Cain from the land of his parents.

Cain now having a wife, and in a faraway land that was set apart from the land his parents and his other brothers and sisters where, would raise his own family who would branch out, and descend from him as a nation of people. The people of Cain would create something called the culture of the arts, but this art-form would also not be done for the glory of GOD but it would be done for the glory of their beliefs. The children of Cain did not worship GOD they in fact worshiped Satan.

The understanding is that Adam and Eve were raising their children to obey GOD wherein some of their children listened, and others, like Cain, did not. Cain was raising his children to worship his god who was Satan at this time. From Cain's line a child would be born who would become the inventor of musical instruments. His name was Jubal. To understand more, and to explore the kind of world Jubal was living in will take the teachings of the Bible, and a look into the Christian theological, and ecclesiastical understandings regarding it. We must also look into some of the Jewish oral traditional stories regarding that time period because a lot of it supports Bible concepts about it. When looking at the study under these aspects we will come to find a much larger description of this time period. So to understand it all better the story of Jubal is also the story of his family, his nation, and the negative effects it came to have on the world.

The world of his time was completely brought to an end by the

Flood told in the Book of Genesis. To understand better who Jubal was we must understand better who his father, and family members were. Jubal's father was a man named Lamech. Lamech was the fifth descent from Cain's line, and Lamech was the son of Methusael.

Cain's descendants would come to build nations of their own that would be pattern after the nation of their forefather who was Cain. In Lamech's life-time it was said he was born from a noble family meaning they had rank and money in their kingdom. Lamech was seen as a prince, and a gifted and talented person in the fields of the arts at the time. He also had political ambitions. In Lamech's time the human race lived far longer than they do now. They would live, many of them, for hundreds of years before they died.

When Lamech was coming up in the world Cain was still in rule over his people. Lamech wanted to serve Cain, and sought favor with Cain who was an emperor at this point. I will later explain how Cain became an emperor, and was the human father of pagan-worship. Lamech would go to him, and work his services for Cain. He won him over with his gifts. Lamech was now working in the direct court of Cain. In this court in that early beginning most of the powerful court officials who ran many government affairs were not men. Most of them in Cain's kingdom were women, and all of them were either directly or by descent a blood-line member of Cain. They were called the 'daughters of men.'

This name came from the fact that the belief system among Cain's people was that 'man was a god' and their god who taught men to be little gods was the sun-god. The sun-god according to this doctrine had a human representing him on earth who was Cain at the time. Cain was in fact the first anti-Christ figure in history. The daughters of these men took up the beliefs of their fathers hence that is where the name 'daughters of men' were born from, but these daughters had a different outlook on their god-hood. They believed that they were created by the moon-goddess, and that the moon-goddess was formed by the sun-god who separated his female members to form another god in his image but of the female. The moon would represent this goddess, and she would have even a human representing her who was believed to be the wife of Cain. All of this understanding came from the religion of Cain taught to him by Satan.

These women believed they were goddesses, and how they came to rule was by an event that took place with fallen angels. Cain worshiped fallen angels, and himself, and his children, and his descendants were often visited by them. The fallen angels would be worshiped by Cain, and his people as different gods and goddesses. The fallen angels had a special interest in the women of Cain's family. These women were beautiful and loose with their bodies having the morals of the men they were raised by. Which was really no morals at all.

These women would give themselves to the fallen angels. They even bred children for them that became the various demons of yesterday, and even today according to the Bible. In return Satan assured them a high-place in his human kingdom to even be able to rule over mighty men. Cain in fact served Satan so therefore Cain's kingdom actually belonged to Satan because Cain served Satan.

Satan through his fallen angels would form a pact that became a hidden society for these women. Since they were the wives of the watchers many people in Cain's kingdom worshiped them. These women were seen among them as being god-like themselves from the things they learned from these evil spirits. They were soon also called another name, and today the name is known as witches. Later on even the goddess faith of the past would become known as witchcraft.

In Lamech's time these women were the ones ruling things for Cain from his royal court. Lamech wanted to get in good with these women, and so he began to impress them by his services and his talents. Lamech was also noted for being skilled at chemistry. He was able to make medicines and potions. He was also noted for making powerful chemical libations. Such draughts were very important in those early witchcraft rituals and ceremonies.

Soon Lamech started to take part in their ceremonies which was rare for a man to be invited into their inner circle. Lamech would also start to charm many of these women, and soon two of them fell in love with Lamech at the same time. These two women were Adah and Zillah. Adah and Zillah were believed to be both sisters, and also it was believed they were direct daughters of Cain who were once out-casted by him. These women at the time were said to have a lot of power given to them by Satan himself. This three's company relationship would end up turning into a marriage. This kind of marriage at the time was a direct violation of GOD's orders, and it ranked right up there with gay-marriage.

When Lamech married Adah and Zillah it was also the first official polygamy marriage that took place in Cain's kingdom. This made it possible for many men to start taking the same example, and they did in a most rapid manner. Polygamy would become a problem for centuries after that. It was even overlooked on purpose by GOD regarding his Israelite children until Jesus had to come to show them the Way from the beginning. Lamech was now very close to Cain, and was in a powerful political position himself.

Through his wives he would have some noted children who would create what became called the culture of the arts. One of those children would be Jubal. Lamech, and his wives would raise and train these children. It should be noted that Lamech was also a noted singer in his day, and a gifted poet. He already understood the art of music along with many arts. His wives were also said to be singers, and they were noted for wearing gemstone exotic dresses.

Lamech's first two children came from his wife Adah. They were two boys named Jabal and Jubal. Jabal invented the merchant business wherein he came up with the idea of opening business shops in the form of massive tent markets in other nations. He would do this by taking his herds and goods and travel to distant countries. This enterprise resulted in making him, and his family massively rich, and soon many store owners, and business men followed the same example. This resulted in what you call merchant companies today who sell goods to the people.

Jubal was the inventor of musical instruments, and the one who came to elevate music to another level and style of playing. This style was advance and even heart-stopping, but the musical contents were nowhere near Christian. Lamech's next two children came from his second wife Zillah. These children were a boy and a girl. They were Tubal-Cain, and his sister Naamah. Tubal-Cain, like his father, was skilled in chemistry. He was also skilled in combat and physical arts as well. Tubal-Cain had a strong interest in inventing weapons, and came to have a passion for the blacksmith arts. Through the use of his chemical gifts, and the science of the blacksmith arts at the time he invented a method called forging metals. This is to take two metals, and forge them into a single more powerful metal that a person can create things from. This science resulted for Tubal-Cain to invent new, and more dangerous weapons that his people would go to war with. Tubal-Cain also invented new, and more deadly forms of martial combat with the hands and feet.

Along with being a skilled inventor he was a feared, and very popular warrior. The belief was that he became general of Cain's army. He even had a special sword created for himself that was skillfully pattern after the movements of the snake. It is often believed that the worship of Vulcan was based upon the events in the life of Tubal-Cain. To the people Tubal-Cain was worshipped as a 'fire-god', and he was also called the 'demon-smith'. He was a person who represented to them a supernatural killing machine who was loved, and hated by all at the same time.

Naamah, his sister, is also believed to have been a great contributor to these arts in her own right. Naamah was called an early celebrity if you will. She was famous for her beauty, and for her singing voice, and legendary songs she performed. It was believed that the world called her 'the Mistress of Sounds and Songs'. Her style of music was a form of soul-stirring lamentations, and she is called the greatest human singer to ever live. The entire world lusted after her beauty, and were put in trances by her music. The world would wonder after her especially the descendants of Cain. She had a history where fallen angels were known to lust for her, and would often come to her. It was believed that she even gave birth too many demonic children. Some of this history points to very murderous and demon-possessed actions on her part. It is believed that she use to seduce men by targeting single men who were alone in their homes. She would do this by night where she would get into cold moods, and would sneak off at night. She would search the homes for single young males, and when she found one the man in the home would soon become a victim. It was said that Naamah, in the middle of the night would sing stirring echo songs outside the man's home to lure him out. She would then seduce him, and come to the man's bed. During the sex she would become very possessed, and then proceed to murder the man in cold blood.

As you can see, this is not a stable family. She was also known to have affairs with countless of rich and powerful men from many kingdoms who would give her great riches just for her sexual services. It is also believed that the worship of Venus is based upon events in the life of Naamah. Naamah was worshipped not only as a celebrity but also as a real goddess in the eyes of the people. For all this evil, her performances were famous world-wide but the influence of the music was one of sexual seduction. It is believed that much of her musical accompaniments regarding instruments came from her half-brother Jubal.

When Naamah was born Jubal was already a young man who had discovered his talent to make music out of the resources of the earth. Jubal often spent a lot of time in the forest collecting certain earth elements to use in his early experiments of making sounds come out of them. He was a gifted singer, and he understood the art of crafting, and building very well. He also had a gifted knowledge on using things upon the earth, and also he was skilled as a poet and writing notes. Through his inventions he created the first musical instrument on earth, and today we call it the harp.

His second musical invention would soon follow the harp, and this instrument once created is known today as a pipe-flute. He would master both of these instruments, and gave performances with them in the open-woods, and towns he visited at the time. Everyone would enjoy hearing it, and they were transfixed to it because at the time they never heard anything like it before. Jubal was able to control, and feed their emotions, and thoughts with his instruments.

Overtime he invented more musical instruments that were far more advance, and able to play astounding melodies. Jubal would begin to cultivate music in that time, and he invented new psalteries, and citharas. His performance now had the world, and his kingdom mesmerized. People came from all over to see him, and Jubal also would reach celebrity fame. His performances would hypnotize the audiences who were captivated with instrumental music. They would become moved, and fascinated by the songs and the moods it put them in.

Jubal was also worshipped as a god among the people. His entire life seems to revolve around his music, and his extreme sexual addictions, and drug addictions. It was a lifestyle that many music stars today can relate to, and it's shocking to know that this lifestyle was even a problem for the first person who invented musical instruments. Jubal's music was known to be very moving and engaging. His musical concerts with this style was about lust, bloodshed, revenge, and other dark stories that people were touch by, and moved by, and they even cried over it. Throughout his career he was known to perform with a group of people he trained in understanding musical instruments. Also during that time many people caught on to his inventions, and they too started inventing musical instruments used in their kingdoms.

Naamah his half-sister was known to often perform to Jubal's music. Much of the worship of Apollo and Pan are believed to be based upon events in the life Jubal. Jubal was worshiped as a god. He was often known to have orgy parties in the forests of Nod where his musicians would play his spellbinding music. He had no limits to his sexual immorality or to the use of drugs. He often abused drugs, and always over-did drugs at these sinful celebrations. He was also into homosexuality, and sex with small children, and animals. He was also a servant to satanic occult worship as most of his family members were, but for him it was believed that Satan came to him in a more personal way to use his gift to corrupt the world for the glory of Satan. This would show that Jubal, like Cain, had a pact with Satan, and mostly likely all his brothers and sisters did.

All of Lamech's children all served Cain, and his kingdom and his interests directly. They were all satanic worshippers who later their influences would lead to a massive corrupting of the entire world even upon the children of Adam then Seth.

The man these inventors of the arts served was Cain. Cain's story after he murdered Abel did not get any better as to say he became a man who later found forgiveness, but it shows that the story got worse and darker, and he became a very evil ruling tyrant in the world of his time.

After Cain killed Abel he would flee the land of his parents, travelling with his wife. His wife was also believed to be his sister as well. They would come to Nod that was an eastern land at the time. Overtime they would have many children who in turn had many children. During that time Cain had them, all engaged in the building of a city. He also became their ruler, father, and spiritual leader. Cain became a worshipper of Satan at the time. He employed his gifts and resources, and those of his children and descendants into building an empire for his god Satan. They would soon build the first city in history. Cain would name the city after his firstborn son, and he called it Enoch.

This Enoch is not to be confused with the righteous Enoch of Adam's line. The city was noted for having a twin-tower pyramid palace said to be the place where Cain lived and ruled from. The system of government of the city was one of a monarchy fully under Cain's control. Cain made all the laws to create the system of government of the city. Cain in that time became the first pathfinder of those seeking pagan spirituality. He became not only the ruler but the first occult teacher. He was said to be demon-possessed having been cursed by GOD, and had a deformed mark upon his head.

Many believe that the mark resembled a man having two horns on the top sides of his head. During that time it was believed that Satan spoke to him often about the doctrine of these beliefs, and then Cain would teach it to his people. Once Cain built this city he did not just stop at one. As the population grew he sought to build more cities with them. He had an intense need to control the people, and keep most of the growing population in the cities he would build. This method was done because it was a way for Cain to control entire nations of people, and use them for his own purposes. In every one of these cities he was seen, and even worshiped as their sun-god. Cain was their sole spiritual teacher, and he used his priests and priestesses to endorse his religion in these cities. This resulted in temples of the gods and goddesses being built throughout the cities.

He became the world's first tyrant, and was the first political dictator. He founded a society based in pagan-satanic worship. A New Age faith of a society thousands of years ago. This was not a peace and love, and understanding society. Sometimes they would pose that way but that was not what they were about. The Laws of GOD to that society meant nothing, and they sought a culture that would break all these Laws, and these citizens would be taught to do this as way of reaching a spiritual awakening. Cain often mocked, and engaged in blasphemy against GOD. He mocked all those who would follow GOD, and he mocked anyone who would oppose him.

Since this lifestyle was so new at the time the people simply followed it. They were inspired to do whatever Cain did. Cain and his son, and his household selected family members were the elite nobles of those cities. They lived above the people they governed, and were able to lead by the examples of their actions. They saw themselves as being better, smarter, and more like gods among the people, and they felt that the people were very far below them. They would rule the people like puppet masters pull strings. This elite also had within themselves its own occult.

This group also were selected blood-line family members chosen by their heritage and gifts to rule, and be part of the more so-called inner secrets of Satan. They controlled all the governing, and the businesses, and every aspect of the people's lives from education to religion. They were in short the Illuminati of their time but they did not call the group the Illuminati back then. The group was first called the Order of the Serpent. In this order the real story of Satan, and his causing of Adam and Eve to fall is told but not told as a sad story but told as a moment of victory for Satan. They tell more inner truths but under Satan's still deceiving logic. The group having been founded by Cain where known to wear very white royal clothing with golden trimmings. They often were seen handling very dangerous snakes at public events as a sign of their order. Their leadership was one of total control with Cain leading the charge, and often they led by bloody force, and making murderous examples out of people.

Cain's government started the world's first system of taxation. He, through brutal and clever ways, compelled his citizens to pay taxes to him. Cain managed to do this by first creating the world's first nation that would use a method of coins, meaning money as it's system of economy, and social order. Cain invented the method of money, and after that he invented taxes.

His citizens were taxed for the same reasons people are taxed today. They had to pay taxes for government projects that involved city services, military protection, and government operations. They soon found other ways to tax them. Cain throughout his rule professed himself as being a god. It was a law in his kingdom that people had to worship him as the son of the sun-god. Cain also had propaganda posted and spread about him throughout the cities he ruled. He sought for the people to love him as they would love God. He sought through charming persuasion tactics, and through publicity to keep the people fixed on thinking they needed him for all their support, and spiritual needs. Sadly people did while at the same time Cain's system had people in poverty, and they were starving.

Now for the first time jails were being built, and people were getting arrested and thrown in them. The culture of these cities was a greedy, lustful, and dangerous culture filled with people ready to commit crimes against each other. Cain, during his rule, would develop a God-complex, and he really started to believe his own lies. He was throughout the years becoming mentally unsound, colder and stranger. He would never learn the value of life, and he never turned to GOD. He was filled with pride and vanity, and he believed he was his own god. He would never let anyone walk over him, or anyone insult him in anyway without instantly killing the person on the spot. He was an unforgiving violent man who murdered anyone who got in his way.

When cities tried to make war on Cain by rebelling against his authority, Cain was all-out ruthless toward them. He would kill-off whole sections of people in those cities, even people who did not rebel, just to show the point that he was not to be messed with. He would not give the bodies any burial but use them to create horror scenes in those places for people to see and be afraid.

Cain's empire was a world that became depraved with a violent society that was filled with bloodshed. Demonic occurrences were common there along with demonic possession. Sensual lust ruled the day and night. The system of government, and business was a system of greed, hard competition, and brutal betrayals. Strife and ruthlessness were constant in their lives. Cities were engulfed with fear, and people stayed on their toes, and were watchful for bandits and robbers, as gangs lurked the high-ways, and street-corners. It was a world not that different from major cities today.

Satan's spirit was upon that empire, and in that time that empire is where the throne of the Beast once stood. Wars, homelessness, lawless actions, and greedy evil systems of control were the constant problems among them, but the people were often too brainwashed, and pumped up on drugs, sex, and entertainment to really, and fully understand just how bad they have been had.

Cain's idea to govern the empire by a system of money did not come from Cain himself. It came originally from Satan. Satan knew that was how to really un-bless and curse a people by making their lives centered around making enough coins to survive or be successful. It was a lifestyle that would also distract them, and make them less spiritually aware, and more carnal minded. Cain, like his father Adam, would live for many centuries. It was said that for every century he lived a new illness would overtake him, and add to the sicknesses he already suffered from. By the time he reached 900 years old he went completely mad, and one day it was said he disappeared. This left his throne empty, and so he was quickly replaced by Lamech.

Lamech in that time became the number one ruler of the empire by this point. The story of this period of the empire of Nob involving Lamech is also strange. Lamech, sometime before he took over the throne, was experimenting with a new draught. He decided to test the new draught on himself, and after drinking it he became blind. Through his children and his wives, and his own inventions he was still able to perform his duties but was very bitter, and hateful for the rest of his life when he was blind. Soon Cain would disappear, and Lamech would take over the throne, but then as recorded in the Book of Genesis, we hear about a song Lamech sung in the form of poetry. He seemed to also sing this lament to his two wives as well expressing sorrow for a man he killed.

The oral traditional story around this event told in the Bible is believed that Lamech was at the funeral of both Cain and Tubal-Cain. The belief is that Lamech wrote and sang the lament to express no fault in the killing of Cain and Tubal-Cain that actually came by his own hand. The story is that Cain was out in the fields of Lamech, and was in a state of madness and was acting like a wild animal. He even looked like a wild animal. Lamech and Tubal-Cain heard about the disturbance in the woods, and decided that it was a wild animal. They would find Cain thinking it was a wild animal roaming around in the dark of night in thick bushes. Tubal-Cain was leading his father Lamech, and Tubal-Cain thought that he was seeing a wild animal. He told his father where to point and shoot, and so Lamech did so. Cain would be hit between his eyes, and he would die right there on the spot.

When Tubal-Cain got close to the target he saw to his total horror that they just killed Cain. When he told his father this his father blamed him for telling him to kill Cain. He believed that Tubal-Cain was trying to set him up so that he could take the throne. Lamech then suddenly attacks Tubal-Cain, and he goes for his throat, and chokes him to death. When his wives hear about these events they turn against him, and people begin to plot his assassination. So the lament called Lamech's Song was actually Lamech defending his position about what happened. Also he was threatening his enemies, and anyone who tried to get revenge that he was ready, and if anyone tried it they would be punished far worse than the curse of Cain. Eventually the Flood would have to wipe out this twisted empire, along with many nations who once knew better.

Chapter 34

Around the world fame in the music industry does not revolve around just the U.S. media. There are also many famous people upon the international side of the music industry. Many of these artists also have promoted strange, and satanic themes that are very familiar among U.S. fans. These themes are also familiar among people who study aspects of the occult, and the inside nature of the music industry. The artists who are successful in the international field that have promoted satanic themes are too many to name for just one chapter. So let us look into a few of them.

Let us start with an Eastern European artist named Kerli. Insiders suspect Kerli of being involved with witchcraft, and they suspect her of being a possible mind-control victim. Kerli's music is pop music with a certain gothic sound to it. Her image is also a combination of gothic & pop. When she released her debut album in Europe it became a hit with young European fans. She soon released other albums that also brought her to fame in Europe.

When Kerli recorded the album called Love Is Dead (how romantic), her managers wanted to also release an English version of the album in the United States. They were seeking to make Kerli at the time a cross-over artist. The music of Kerli along with her interviews, and music videos reveal a lot about Kerli's views on GOD. She thinks GOD is dead. She also thinks that everything good, and tender is dead. Well GOD is not dead. Though the business, and the world Kerli is in does not respect love, goodness, compassion, and other virtues does not mean the rest of the people in the world are like that, but according to Kerli's views, and art-form they are.

The sounds of Kerli's music comes off as romantic and sentimental, but the lyrics, and the messages of the songs come off as creepy, cold, twisted, lustful, depressing, painful, and even demonic. Her music videos often have a dark atmosphere to them showing satanic symbolism and themes . Some of her videos even show mind-control themes.

When Kerli's record company wanted to cross-over her album Love Is Dead they approached a man named L.A. Reid. Kerli at the time was already working for Def Jam international, and Reid at that time was an executive for that company. Reid would get the go ahead to have Kerli record an English version of the album.

Def Jam's international company is called Island Def Jam Records. They have many international artists signed to their label, and many of them are famous. Much of the art-forms we see today in America are the same art-forms being seen in international artists all over the world. Many of the artists working for Island Def Jam are also suspected of having been abused, and many are suspected of being mind-control victims.

The man who was instrumental in putting Island Def Jam on the international map of success was L.A. Reid. Reid assembled most of the artists for that label who became famous in Europe. It is said that he is a handler of many of those artists, and that he often steals from these artists as well. Reid, like Babyface, are both suspected of being Masons and very involved with powerful occult groups in the music industry.

Reid was the one who discovered Kerli and brought her into Island Def Jam. She soon became one of their major international artists. Kerli released her first album for Island Def Jam in 2006, and the album Love Is Dead was going to be released in America in late 2008. When the album was released the lead single was a song called Walking on Air. Soon American fans started to see more of the art-form, and image of Kerli. Kerli's album was far more successful in Europe then it was in America, but the album still gained her thousands of American fans. Those fans started to get into her image and art-form, but what were they really getting into as today's imaginations run wild and truth becomes hidden?

Regardless of what could be going on at Island Def Jam there are heavy occult meanings found in Kerli's songs and imagery. There are also connections within her symbolism that leads back to mind-control programming. The song Walking on Air is a clear example of it. The title of the song comes from a phrase found in mind-control. The title comes from a condition that develops during painful trauma sessions that mind-control victims go through. During the painful dehumanizing trauma the victims' brain will break into fragments. The most noted fragmentation of the brain is during the sessions that use electro-shock treatments. During those sessions the pain becomes so unbearable that the victims' mind will shut down causing their bodies to feel like they are floating or walking on air. Hence the title of the song Walking on Air.

Kerli, like most music stars who often dodge these questions or try to laugh it off, also refuses to give more insight into the questions relating to her symbolism, imagery, and themes of her songs and music videos. She only stated that the song was about a broken childhood and lose of her innocence. Her statements are in fact the reality of many mind-control victims, and the reality of many young stars like Kerli with or without mind-control. Although those are sad statements from Kerli, and it is always horrible when people have been abused especially children, but to ignore the themes of mind-control that are also in the song, and the music video called Walking on Air would not be wise either.

Some of the strange aspects of satanic themes in Kerli's life are even seen upon her websites and her promotion photos. Kerli's website at the time contained numerous references to satanic teachings and mind-control. The pictures also show many themes of duality within Kerli as well. These themes center on a person who is embracing two people inside her, but these people don't seem to represent her struggle but more like they represent spirits inside her. The photos are about her embracing those spirits. Many of her photos, like most of the photos of music stars who are suspected of being mind-control victims, feature themes and images of butterflies, and mirrors. These images repeat themselves again, and again within artists who are believed to be under mind-control.

Another constant theme for them are the Alice in Wonderland themes. This theme also comes up in the works and photos of Kerli. In fact Kerli in Europe is seen as an original artist from Estonia, but her works and themes are seen constantly in other famous artists around the world, especially in America.

Kerli also has photos posing in Satan's axiom 'as above, so below' hand-pose, and photos of her promoting witchcraft, and surrounding herself with voodoo dolls. She often does photos as a life-less doll surrounded by voodoo dolls along with photos of herself as a life-less mannequin. In other photos she dresses up as a prostitute who is wearing a one-eye patch while lying in a bed looking to service someone. These satanic photos truly bear a lot of dark and evil meanings.

Kerli also admitted to her fans that she is demonically possessed. Of course she does not see it as possession but her accounts of it the Bible would call it possession. To understand what I mean is to understand the account of these supernatural experiences that Kerli stated she had. Kerli stated that she believes that five people live inside her. She stated that these five people all talk to her inside her head where she could hear them speaking to her. She stated that these voices make her cry a lot.

She often gets confused about what person she is suppose, to be today. She stated that when these voices talk she will often see balls of color wherein spirit investigators call what Kerli saw as being orbs. Kerli stated that the voices often cause her to change her mind within minutes of making a choice. She also stated that the voices often haunt her, and keep her awake. Kerli's personality is described as being cold, and distance with others. She is very distant from her fans, and there is a tight circle of controlling managers, and bodyguards that is always around her. This is the same case for mostly all of the A-list stars in America.

In the music video to Walking on Air the video starts with a series of scenes of a man giving Kerli a strange gift. The gift is a doll that looks just like Kerli. These types of dolls that were presented in the video are also called voodoo dolls. The voodoo doll concept is to create a doll that looks like the person you want to curse or control. In order to cause this cursing or controlling, as this teachings goes, a voodoo priest has to perform a ritual over the doll. Then the person is told to stab the doll in areas you want the person to feel the most pain in. Of course they also tell these people that the injury comes in ways they would not see coming.

So of course when something does eventually happen they think it was voodoo. Sometimes supernatural things will happen in a more sudden unexplained way. That is because when you open up for Satan you get real demons to enter into your life. These dolls are often used in witchcraft ceremonies and rites.

The doll in the music video represents an evil spirit that Kerli will slowly, by the end of the video, be transform into. In the video Kerli will walk into a room that is being watched by a television monitor that is looking at the room with an all-seeing eye. The image is to represent that Satan is always watching her. You will notice the strong black and white duality of the room through the checkerboard black and white floors. The black and white checkerboard floors are a constant, and repeating image and theme in music videos since the start of music videos, it relates to many occult teachings, especially among the Freemasons. It promotes the idea that Jesus and the Devil are equal gods, and that light and dark, and black and white magic must be understood, and worshiped equally. It is a belief system that holds a belief where GOD and Satan are worshiped. This is also called the New Age faith.

The scene would represent the occult that controls Kerli and watches her. In the video while Kerli is in the room her whole world starts spinning around and Kerli begins to fall into a trance. The sensation is representing a condition in mind-control victims when they begin floating due to intense pain. Often drugs play a part in this so the victim will even start to feel they are spinning down a spiral floor. In another series of scenes in the video Kerli is seen stepping out from the room and entering through the wall of another room. The room is an isolated bricked wall room. The room represents the reality of her world, and her life growing up. For Kerli it was a state of imprisonment and isolation. In the scene while Kerli is in this room something magical happens in the room where wind is blowing everywhere and Kerli escapes into a fantasy world. What Kerli was showing here was mental-escapism.

Victims of abuse, isolation, or neglect will often use their minds to escape into a world of their own. Reality for them is painful, and so the mind finds a way to escape from under it. Hence people will chase fantasy created in their minds.

Many Alice in Wonderland themes are also used in this music video from cold ovens to hot fridges, and there are scenes of Kerli lying on a bed dressed as a prostitute wanting to have sex on top of a pile of sharp rocks. These relate to mind-control themes of switching someone's mood or behavior hence the cold and hot theme, and engaging in painful sexual acts. In mind-control pain is called pleasure, and victims will often confuse sex with pain.

In another twisted scene it shows tear drops on Kerli's face that turn into strange little butterflies. To understand the meaning tear-drops are an occult symbol, and even a gang symbol, and it is used as a tattoo to represent a badge of honor to certain occult or gang-members who killed someone for the group. The drops turning into butterflies represent the transformation of when someone crosses a certain line they become possessed with what they call 'power'. In fact it is demon-possession but they call it rebirth. I am not saying at all that Kerli is a murderer. All I am saying is that the images have meaning in the occult and in gangs, and that is its meaning.

The final scenes of the music video shows Kerli looking at a mirror then a person appears in the mirror, and tells Kerli to walk through the mirror. When Kerli steps through the mirror she appears in this dark world, and she also has been transformed into the doll seen earlier in the video. The spirit that told her to walk through the mirror is now controlling Kerli by using her as a puppet on strings. The scene was clear demonic possession, and a sad condition indeed.

Another famous international entertainment industry is the business called Bollywood based in India. Bollywood entertainment is a movie and music industry all fused into one product. It has become a multi-million dollar business in India, and it's art-form is very popular all over Asia, the Middle East, Africa, Europe, and it has a small following in America.

In the East Bollywood has the popular standing that Hollywood does in the West. Also like Hollywood Bollywood it has origins from people who were very deep into Hindusim and New Age occultism. The film style of Bollywood films are musicals set with different art-forms of story-telling like action, drama, comedy, etc.

All the films have huge song and dance numbers throughout the entire film. Most of the stars of Bollywood are not just Indian but they in fact come from many parts of Asia, and the Middle East mostly. The purpose of the Bollywood film and musical industry was in fact to tell the ancient stories of their gods and goddesses of the various temples throughout the East.

The Bible calls this pagan worship but to Eastern people it would be taken as an offense to tell them its pagan worship. In the East pagan worship is taken seriously in many nations especially India. In India much of the cities, and towns are ruled by local temple laws. These temples are the still known temples of the gods and goddesses, and these priests even have the power to legally execute people.

Most of the ticket buying fans of Bollywood come from these very poor, and even dangerous cities and towns. The Bollywood films were not only designed to tell the stories of their gods but to also promote them to the world. Bollywood was built up in the hopes it would spread the messages of these art-forms all over the world. The themes of Bollywood films have promoted just about the same themes you see in Hollywood films just done under an Eastern culture.

In Bollywood films lust, adultery, revenge killings, vanity, greed, sexual immorality, scenes of sexual acts, and pagan worship are all promoted, and laced throughout the films. The Indian government is mostly operated by leaders whose faith are Islam. Many Indian leaders are traditional Muslims who do not like naked women on film or the worship of idols. The people they rule however are mostly Hindu in their religious faith, and they don't share the same kind of morals that Muslims do, but however this is not to say Hindu Indians don't have morals.

Where Hindus and Muslims disagree on is what sin is. Most people in the Bollywood industry like the actors and actresses, directors, writers, etc. are mostly Hindu by faith, and they are a different kind of Hindu. Many of them are what we would call a New Age Hindu, and many of them are also involved with other satanic occults outside of Hinduism. Some of the stars are also Muslim as well, and they too take part in films that promote the Eastern gods who are idols to a Muslim. Also the Indian government has often been very hard on poor Hindu temples, and have greatly reduced their influence over teaching people Hindu, but these Muslim leaders usually turn a blind-eye to Bollywood even though they know it spreads the teachings of the idol gods world-wide.

The reason they turn a blind-eye is because Bollywood stars also have relation to the families of government leaders, and they are all part of the same elite families of India. In those households it seems that Islam is not the only religion being practice there. India also makes millions of dollars off Bollywood. Also Bollywood does not help the very poor Indian people with that money, instead they keep it, and use it to make more films, and buy bigger homes. Hollywood also does that in the West.

Many Bollywood songs are actually songs sung directly to these gods. In the scenes they use the songs to even call on the gods. The Bible would call this the summoning of demons. Also it has become more, and more known that certain Bollywood stars are Masons. Also many Freemasons in the entertainment industry have been coming to Bollywood to invest in film projects there. Since that started happening many Bollywood films have been featuring masonic symbolism to go along with these films. Many of the actors and actresses have also done Eastern porn films, and are part of temples that are deep into occult sex practices.

Stories of demonic worship, and possession have been seen, and told about regarding the behind the scene activities of their world. Christianity is not a subject that you will see promoted in a Bollywood film. In fact what you will often see in Bollywood films are some of the familiar satanic symbolism we see in art-forms in the West. Many Bollywood and international stars are even seen giving or throwing up the sign of the all-seeing eye.

Among the thousands of Hindu gods and goddesses, the people who practice this faith mostly pay honor and worship to the three main gods of this worship. The three main gods are Vishnu, Siva, and Kali or Sakti. Most of the temples and the worship of Hinduism is centered on these three gods.

Bollywood films also represent the doctrine, and beliefs of these three gods in almost every one of their films in one form or another. These films tell the stories of these three gods in various ways. Most of the Indian fans of Bollywood films come from the different sects of the worship of these three gods.

The first largest sect are called the Vaishnavas, and they worship Vishnu who is also called Rama and Krishna. You may be familiar with the word Krishna especially if you live in California. In the cities of San Francisco, and Los Angeles there are church-temples there attended by people who worship Krishna in the United States. There are many famous music and movie industry entertainers who also worship Krishna. There have been many songs from various artists in the music industry from the 60's, 70's, 80's, 90's, and now who have wrote songs expressing their faith in Krishna. The worship of Vishnu is connected with the names of pagan heroes who are seen as the incarnation of this god. The priests of this sect are distinguished generally by an abstinence from animal food, and its worship is seen as less cruel as the other sects. The priests and the followers of this sect are divided into numerous sects by differences in the way they explain the doctrine, but the sect is bonded by the common belief that Vishnu is the supreme god of Hinduism. This whole system of idolatrous worship is mixed with the learning of the Pundits and the doctrines of the Shastra. These doctrines have had a great influence on the minds of the Indian people for thousands of years.

The second largest sect are called the Saivas, and they worship Siva. This sect is very popular among the common Indian people especially among the poor. The followers will often wear a mark on their foreheads that is distinguished by three horizontal lines, and is traditionally drawn upon the forehead using ashes obtained from the hearth where their sacred fire is kept. The difference between the, mark of the Vishnu followers is that the Vishnu followers will use perpendicular lines other than horizontal lines.

A lot of Western Witchcraft is seen in the sect of the Saivas on account that the sect recalls the ancient religion of nature, and the gross dualism of the temples of Phoenicia. This sect is also known for having very cruel ritual rites that it was well documented in Indian history that it was a sect heavy into human ritual killings.

The third largest sect are called the Saktas. This sect worships Sakti who is a god that is both god and goddess at the same time. The power of Sakti is said to be seen when Sakti takes on his female form, and then the active power of his godhood is then felt. Sakti is also considered to be the consort of the abstract attribute. Many sexual orgies and sexual ritual rites are done in honor of this pagan deity.

The images of the Hindu gods are usually of a grotesque kind represented by the heads of animals, superabundant limbs, and other strange disfigured images. The production of these idol images are seen as monstrosities being placed throughout India in innumerable numbers. Most of these images are placed in temples that started out as grottoes but are now built into the shape of a pyramid that is ornamented with columns, statues, and symbolic figures. These temples are usually divided into different courts by colonnades surrounded by high walls, and guarded by the priests. The Veda is the book often read during their temple service, and their worship is accompanied by songs, and dances from the two higher classes of dancing girls. These two classes are called the Devadasis, and the Natakas.

In South Korea and Japan is the now very famous music industry called J or K-Pop. The name represents the Eastern Asian pop-music industry whose stars mostly come from Korea or Japan. This industry has now become a multi-million dollar industry, and these artists have millions of Asian fans who adore them. In Korea and Japan the two main religions are Buddhism and the various forms of sun-worship. Christianity is practiced in Korea and Japan but the followers are small compared to the followers of the other two religions.

Sun-worship, and even anti-Christian themes are often seen mainly in J & K-Pop music videos and songs. Many of the artists are even suspected of being involved with satanic worship, and homosexual practices. Many of them are said to even be undergoing abuse at the hands of their handlers, and are often taken advantage of by the record companies in Asia who are known to have a very tight control on their artists. There are also many masonic elements in many music videos from J & K-Pop artists as well. Artists like the K-Pop group 2NE1 often perform in the backdrop of masonic checkerboard floors, and they even use many satanic images in their art-form.

The Asian international music industry sells the kind of pop-music you hear in America. It has the same format but with a different language, and culture representing it. Many of the famous Asian musical artists pattern their styles, and their dance moves after American art-forms. The pop-fans in Asia have become a huge money-making market base for these Asian record companies who happen to be in business with American record companies. They often work together hand and glove, and many American artists and producers have gone over to Asia to help develop their artists.

Asian pop has the same influence on its fans in Asia as it does upon young American fans. It too has a high influence of sexual immorality and rebellion upon the emotions of these young fans who often are also engaging in sexual practices far too early. They too get caught up with vain subjects and meaningless behavior. Just like Western pop, Christianity is also ignored and seen as a negative in Asian pop art-forms.

Take the K-Pop artist called Narsha who in her music videos shows a lot of satanic, and witchcraft symbolism. Much of Narsha's songs are loaded with messages that promote sexual immorality, homosexuality, vanity, and dark ritual worship. She even mocks Christianity in her songs. Many of her music videos revolve around themes of a ritualistic and spiritual duality. In one video she did called Bbi-Ri-Bop A she even plays Satan himself. In her video she portrays Satan as a being who is desired by both men and women. During the video there are a series of scenes showing Narsha wearing a crown of thorns with a solar-halo around her head. These scenes were not done to honor Christianity but to mock it. The scenes were about showing forth the New Age Christ who the Bible would call the anti-Christ. The solar-halo was used in ancient pagan images to represent the light-god also called in the Bible as Satan.

Satan seeks to be like GOD, and so he wants worship, and often he gets worship by pretending to be Jesus Christ himself. The video goes on to show many scenes relating to Christianity but none of it relates to promoting it. The scenes all relate to core scenes of the artist in the form of Satan showing that the scenes are relating to the anti-Christ faith which is the New Age faith.

Toward the end of the video comes a series of scenes where the artist sings about a ritual sacrifice, and her appearance transforms into a black crow after a scene where she prays. These scenes were about satanic worship. The black crow in satanic symbolism is another form relating to Lucifer. Lucifer is also called the angel of darkness who is represented as having black wings. In her video she takes the appearance of a being with black wings appearing to men she desires. The aim of Lucifer is to seduce men and destroy them.

Another K-Pop group is the boy band called SHINee. The name of the group is in relation to sun-worship, and the members of the group have mostly been given blonde hair to represent the sun. The members of this group are also said to be homosexuals, and very anti-Christian. The group's first album would make them international stars as it sold in the millions in Asia. They became the Backstreet Boys of Korea and Japan. Their second album according to the group members was a tribute album. The title of the album was what they gave tribute to. The second album was called Lucifer.

The lead single from the album was also called Lucifer, and when this single was released it became a smash-hit song in Korea and Japan taking number one on their charts. The group was questioned about the reason why they chose to sing about someone most of the world would know to be Satan. They did not give clear answers for this. In fact they often laughed off the questions. Eventually they stated that the song was about a girl being seduced by Lucifer, but the lyrics, and the music video do not show that or even support that reasoning. The song's lyrics point to the group members themselves being seduced by Lucifer, and not a girl. Even the video shows the same theme. The video also shows the spirit of Lucifer chasing each of the members, and entering them which is a form of possession. SHINee is also a group that performs on stage with many masonic, and satanic symbolism all about them. Also in the song Lucifer there are some strange lyrics relating to being possessed by Lucifer where they describe themselves as puppets trapped in a glass castle.

Chapter 35

In this chapter we will explore some controversial aspects of some various artists in the music industry past and present. Let us start with Bobby Fuller who made his mark in the music industry while playing in his band called The Bobby Fuller Four.

In the mid-1960's Bobby along with his band scored two hit singles called I Fought the Law, and Love's Made a Fool of You. Bobby's start in playing Rock N' Roll music happened when he was 12 years old. At that age Elvis Presley became a world-wide star and Bobby became mesmerized by Rock N' Roll music, and it's underground lifestyle.

Being from West Texas Bobby came to idolize the music and fame of Buddy Holly. Holly became a personal hero to him, and Bobby set out to learn and play the kind of Rock N' Roll style Holly was famous for. When Bobby pursued his own music career he became a vocalist, and guitarist while training as a teenager.

He would soon form a band that starting out often had a change in the line-up. Bobby, and his band started out playing in nightclubs, and bars in El Paso, Texas. This was at the time a ruff, and ready place to perform in. Fist-fights, and even shoot outs were known to take place due to the drinking, and partying that took place there. After some time in performing at the clubs and bars they were soon good enough to record their songs on independent record labels in Texas.

The El Paso local music scene was often filled with drunkenness, and violent encounters even between local music artists. Police often were called in to break up fist-fights, and rumbles that would break out in the western clubs and bars. These activities inspired Bobby to write his future hit song called I Fought the Law.

In 1964 Bobby and his band moved to Los Angeles, and

performed under the name The Bobby Fuller Four. They were soon discovered by a record producer named Bob Keane who worked for Mustang Records. Keane was the man who discovered Ritchie Valens, and produced many of the West Coast surf music groups. When The Bobby Fuller Four were signed the music industry at the time was deep into the British Invasion of pop-rock bands, and deep into folk rock, and acid rock genres.

The Bobby Fuller Four would stick to the 1950's Buddy Holly style of classic Rock N' Roll music. They sought to bring back the music many said was dead since the deaths of Holly, Valens, and the Booper. Bobby wanted to prove that the music was not dead, and he set out to record his first album.

When the band recorded their first album all the songs had influences from Buddy Holly, Elvis Presley, Eddie Cochran, and Little Richard. The group would release their first single from the album called Let Her Dance. The single would break the top 40 but was not a mainstream hit. The group's second single was a song called I Fought the Law. I Fought the Law was released in 1966, and the song became a nation-wide mainstream smash hit. It entered the Billboard's 100 singles chart hitting the number 9 spot. The song would make the band famous seemingly overnight. The group even got to appear in a movie called The Ghost in the Invisible Bikini which starred Nancy Sinatra.

In the movie the band backed up Nancy Sinatra on the song Geronimo, and played during the pool-party scene. At this point The Bobby Fuller Four was bringing back 1950's Rock N' Roll music in a major way. Bobby himself was being called by fans and peers in the music industry as the next Elvis Presley, but in a strange twist of fate, within months after the release of I Fought the Law Bobby Fuller was found dead. His official cause of death like most deaths in the entertainment industry was also strange. The official story did not make much sense.

His body was found in an automobile parked outside his Hollywood apartment. His face, chest, and side was covered in petechial hemorrhages. The medical examiners official report was inconsequential. They stated that the hemorrhages could have been caused by gasoline vapors, and the summer heat, but yet they also stated that they were not sure. The reason they were not sure was because when Bobby was found he looked like he was brutally beaten to death. The examiners made statements that they found no bruises or broken bones on his body, but yet they state they cannot determine what actually killed him.

Other examiners who have looked into the case after Bobby's death have asked how did Bobby get the hemorrhages throughout his body without someone causing him harm? There is also an unproven unofficial story regarding Bobby's death. Some insiders, and people who knew Bobby stated that the Mafia was behind the death of Bobby Fuller. Strange enough the L.A. crime family at the time also had members of the LAPD on their pay roll according to FBI files. The insiders and those who state this story believe that the authorities were paid off to cover up that Bobby Fuller was murdered.

Bobby at the time before his death was sleeping with a girlfriend to a made-man in the L.A. crime family. The people who knew Bobby who believe that Bobby was murdered stated that this sexual relationship was kept a secret until someone from the music industry found out about it, and leaked that information to the Mafia. They not only believe that the Mafia killed Bobby but they also believe that powerful people in the music industry at the time set Bobby up to get rid of him. These insiders believe that Bobby was not killed in the car but placed in the car.

A re-examination into the evidence shows that Bobby did have bruises, and much of the hemorrhages could be traced back to certain poisons that the Mafia, according to FBI files, were known to use.

Bobby's second album would be released after his death under the title of his hit single called I Fought the Law. The songs came from his past recordings under the independent labels he recorded for in Texas. At the time of his death in July of 1966 Bobby was only 23 years of age.

Many people know the musical accomplishments of R&B singer Toni Braxton, but few people know the full scope of it. In the

1980's Toni started out in a singing group along with her four sisters. The group was called The Braxtons. This group was signed to Arista Records in 1989, and recorded the single called Good Life. The single was not a hit song but it would result in the attention of L.A. Reid and Babyface. Reid and Babyface would focus their efforts in signing Toni Braxton as a solo artist. She would soon be signed over to LaFace Records where she began recording her first album.

In 1993 Toni's debut album was released under her real name Toni Braxton. This album would become a smash hit, and would take the number one spot on the Billboard 200 albums chart. The album featured three hit singles called Another Sad Love Song, Breathe Again, and You Mean the World to Me. Another Sad Love Song would take the number two spot on the Billboard 100 singles chart while Breathe Again hit the number five spot.

For this debut album Toni would win 3 Grammy Awards, and 2 American Music Awards. Her debut album would end up selling 10 million copies. Her second album was released in 1996 called Secrets. This album was, and still is her most successful album. The album would sell over 15 million copies. The lead single off the album called You're Makin' Me High took the number one spot on the Billboard 100 singles chart. The album also had two more hits called How Could an Angel Break My Heart and I Don't Want To.

By 1997 Toni Braxton, after only releasing two albums, had already sold over 25 million records. Clearly now she would be getting her financial rewards. She would be buying houses, and gifts for her family members and so on. On the surface she looked very rich and successful, and the media constantly praised her for her music, and her stunning looks, but like the song, this would become another sad story.

After selling over 25 million records Toni Braxton in late 1996 was still waiting for her financial rewards. Her records made the record company she worked for about 200 million dollars. When the check came and Toni opened it, the amount she got was about $5,000. At this point Toni owned over $100,000 to certain bill collectors who the record company refused to pay, and instead stuck Toni with the bills. They would put these bills on her while handing her a check that may as well had been for 5 cents.

She went to Reid and Babyface demanding to know where all that money went. They gave her an account of the money, and what she read sicken her. She was overcharged for all the expense expenditures the record company got while Toni was waiting on her rewards. That is where mostly all of her royalties went according to the record company. The reports Toni read showed that after Reid, Babyface, and all the executives took their overwhelming share, which was more than normal, and after they used Toni's earnings to pay for some of Toni's expenditures they gave her what was left over.

They also stuck her with the rest of the bills from Toni's expenditures. These expenditures were mostly items like her clothes, jewelry, car, etc. Usually record companies would pay for these things themselves if the artist is selling in the millions like Toni was doing, but somewhere along the money trail people who Toni thought she could trust got very greedy for money-gain.

A lawyer of Toni's who came to handle her case compared her ordeal in court to someone being paid slave wages. Toni after reading the account clearly knew she was ripped off, and she wanted her rightful wages returned to her. She would launch a lawsuit against Arista and LaFace Records in 1996. The case would last throughout 1997.

Music industry CEOs, and executives often show how much power they have on media when certain artists combat them. In response to the lawsuit it was believed by certain insiders that the executives began to release stories in the media to attack Toni's character and image. They painted her as a money-loving diva who often wasted all of her money, and caused herself to go broke. Of course they failed to explain in logic how she did that. Most of the things they accused her of buying would have been paid off if she only sold one million copies, and with change to spare. The media would cause a negative public reaction against her at the time. This reaction became worse after Toni did an interview on The Oprah Winfrey Show in Chicago.

Oprah was usually an easy interview for celebrities because Oprah favors them, but Oprah at the time was a friend of Babyface, and the rest of his people. During the interview Oprah attacked Toni on her show, and would demean her in front of millions of people watching at home.

After Toni filed the lawsuit she had to file for bankruptcy to keep herself from becoming homeless. Most of her valued belongings were taken from her to keep the wolves from her door. She also had to sell the Grammy Awards she won just to keep her home. Toni would not win the lawsuit until 1999 when her wages, and possessions, and her Grammy Awards were given back to her. During the period of the lawsuit years Toni began to work for Disney. She became the first African-American woman to have a lead role in a Disney Broadway show. The people at Disney were also said to be very instrumental in helping Toni to win the lawsuit and get her wealth back.

There are insiders who believe that this help came with a price regarding the behind the scenes actions of people at Disney. After winning the lawsuit she went right back to work for the same people who ripped her off in the first place.

Not many people know the strange aspects of the group called The Go-Go's. The Go-Go's were formed in 1978, and they were an all-female rock band. They would make music industry history as the first all-female rock band that wrote their own songs, and performed with their own instruments who became a successful Billboard charting band. Their style of rock at the time came out of the punk-rock underground scene. This style was coined 'new wave rock' because it was seen as a new version of pop-rock.

New wave rock became very big in the 1980's as scores of other bands playing this style of music would come after The Go-Go's. A lot of these bands like The Bangles would be successful in their own right. The Go-Go's got their start by first being everyday common fans of punk-rock music. These young women at the time often partied in the underground punk-rock nightclubs of the L.A. punk community. The original members of this band were Belinda Carlisle who did vocals, Jane Wiedlin who played guitar and background vocals, Margot Olavarria who played bass, and Elissa Bello who played drums. These girls in those nightclubs had a reputation for being fast and loose with their bodies. They also loved to get high on drugs. They were the kind of girls you would find having sex in the bathroom of the club, and using drugs in the parking lot.

All of these girls had a passion for punk-rock music, and would attend most of the concerts in L.A. One night Belinda Carlisle watched Iggy Pop perform live on stage. She became inspired by him to become a rock star. She would soon develop her gift to sing through some very non-traditional ways, like singing punk-rock songs off the stereo or singing them in the shower. Soon she would develop her punk look, and she began to audition for punk underground bands under the stage name Dottie Danger.

The other three girls were also trying to get into a band through non-traditional ways. They too were not trained in music, and were trying to play punk-rock music through listening to it, and then try to copy it. During that time all four girls got to know each other. Belinda would soon be selected to sing for a band called The Germs, but she would come down with mononucleosis, and that resulted in her leaving The Germs before playing a gig with them.

Soon the four girls started to practice together, and they came to find they had a lot of things in common. In 1978 the four girls formed a group, and called themselves after their favorite L.A. club the Whisky Go Go as they called themselves The Go-Go's.

They started getting their first gigs at seminal punk-rock shows at two nightclubs called the Whisky Go Go and The Masque. The group at first was mainly hired because of their looks. As a music band they were not very good at all, and they were hired as a warm-up opening act band. Even though their performances were awful the male fans loved to look at them. This is how they managed to keep getting the opening gig even though they were terrible starting out.

The guys at these punk-rock shows really loved the looks of these girls that came with a strong sexual energy the girls had on stage. These girls were not afraid of these horny male fans, and often they would find ways in pleasure to thank some of these young men. The terrible sound of this band's music would not stay that way for long. In late 1978 the group accepted a new member named Charlotte Caffey. She would become the group's lead guitarist and keyboard player. Unlike the other members of the group Charlotte was a trained musician, and she knew what she was doing. This is why, and how she got into the group because she was going to make the group a better band. Charlotte taught all the band members how to better play their instruments, and how to execute hooks in their songs. She even had to teach them how to better tune their instruments. This was going on from late 1978 into 1979.

Elissa Bello during this period turned out to be a weak member of the group. She was unable to project the sound they were looking for. She would be replaced with a more skilled drummer who was Gina Schock. Under this line-up the group finally discovers their now familiar sound. It was a power-pop sound of punk-rock play.

Soon the girls created several songs, and started to perform them at the L.A. nightclubs. One of those songs was called We Got the Beat. The band went from being seen as a punk band to a now 'new wave' band. In late 1979 the group got enough funds to record a five song demo tape at Gold Star Studios in L.A. They would ship copies of the demo tapes to several record companies.

At this time the management team of the British ska group called Madness would hear a performance of The Go-Go's singing We Got the Beat. Madness at the time was on tour, and they were in Los Angeles at the time. Their next flight was going to take them back to England, and they invited The Go-Go's to join them on their tour to be their opening act.

Stiff Records in England would hear the single We Got the Beat, and they released the single through their company. The single would become a U.K. hit. In 1980 the girls returned home, and now they were in a good position to break through into the industry.

They began to engage in constant rehearsals to develop more songs, but Margot Olavarria, the bass player, was refusing to show up at rehearsals. She was expressing her dissatisfaction that the band had moved away from a punk sound, and into a pop sound. The other band members had enough of her, and so they kicked her out of the band. She was soon replaced by Kathy Valentine who was an experienced guitar player having played for underground bands like Girlschool and Textones.

After The Go-Go's became famous Margot sued the group for throwing her out. The suit was settled in 1984. In April of 1981 it would finally happen for The Go-Go's. They would be signed to I.R.S. Records to record their debut album. In 1982 this album was released under the name Beauty and the Beat. The album would break air-wave barriers at the time, and it paved the way for popular 'new wave' rock. The album itself became a smash hit record seller going triple platinum in sales. The album featured two smash hit singles called We Got the Beat and Our Lips Are Sealed. Both singles became very popular all over North America, and around the world.

In 1982 The Go-Go's were America's favorite rock band, and they gained a massive fan following. They were now rich and successful rock stars, and they truly lived the part. At this time the group's behavior behind the scenes was anything but sweet. Insiders remarked that the girls were highly sexually immoral. They in fact seemed to be overly sexual as if they were in heat all the time. They often had odd, and intense sexual energy coming off of them that people around them would be energized by.

They were known to tape private sex films, and would engage in group sex, and same sex activities. They were also extremely addicted to drugs. The two band members who had the worst problem with drugs were Belinda and Charlotte. Charlotte became very addicted to heroin. Her drug problems would eventually hurt her career, and it started to cause conflicts with the other band members. Belinda became very addicted to cocaine. Her drug problems would follow her even into the successful solo career she had. She would use so much cocaine that she often kept a shoe-box full of cocaine in any room she stayed at. Gina Schock's drug problems would land her with a congenital heart defect that sent her into surgery. Along with this reckless lifestyle the girls were known to secretly receive treatment for certain STD's they would sometimes catch.

Their second album called Vacation would be released in 1983. The album was a hit but did not sell as many units as their first album. The lead single Vacation would become a Billboard hit single, and the group's extreme lifestyle was starting to cause them to turn on each other. Soon the group started to have jealously, and personal issues toward each other.

In 1984 the group released their third album called Talk Show. This album would become a total flop, and did terrible in sales. The personal conflicts, and the differences within the group had the members hating each other. Added to this were the drug problems, and lifestyles the members were living.

Soon, in 1985 the group would disband. Later Belinda Carlisle would have a successful solo career, but it was cut-short due to her drug addictions. The other band members would do other projects, and some of them even got into promoting New Age spirituality. Years later they did come together again, and since that time they do perform every now and again.

Belinda would eventually become a mother after leaving The Go-Go's. When she was in her 40's Belinda decided she wanted to get some very raw attention. She would do that by posing naked in playboy magazine in 2001 for the world to see...including her household family.

Hank Williams, Sr. was an artist who lived a very strange life, and many say a brutal life. Hank was known as an early country-western music star. His styles also included Gospel, Blues, honky-tonk, and folk. In his lifetime career Hank had 35 singles that would rank today in the top 10 Billboard charts. In fact 11 of those singles would have ranked as number one Billboard singles.

Hank was born on September 17, 1923 in the State of Alabama. He would die under strange events on January 1, 1953. He would die at the very young age of only 29 years of age, but if you ever saw pictures of him throughout his career the man did not look, or talk, or even act at all as a man only in his 20's. He had the looks and character of a man in his late 40's to early

50's. His face was very rough, and older looking.

He was also a very tall person. He had scars on his face from the numerous bar-fights he had been in. Many insiders state that the reason for his older appearance was due to a lifetime of intense pain, and dealing with addictions. Hank's real name is actually Hiram King Williams, Sr. Many people might wonder why his parents would give him such a strange name for this part of the world. The reason for that starts with his parents. Hank's father was Elonzo Williams, and Hank's mother was Jessie Lillybelle Williams.

Hank's father was a full, and life-long member of the Freemasons. Hank's mother was a full member of the Order of the Eastern Star which was the branch of Masons that allow females into their group. The Eastern Star has been very largely suspected of being involved with extensive witchcraft.

Hank's real name Hiram was given to him based upon masonic teachings, and lore. Masons tell in their rituals chambers certain doctrines, and legends involving their rituals as they move up the degrees. A popular story they tell among the Masons involves a person named Hiram who is the same Hiram from the Bible.

This Hiram the Masons are speaking about was the King of Tyre. This king was friends with both King David, and King Solomon. In speaking about Hiram the Masons put a different spin on the story from the Bible. Many insiders state that to many Masons in higher degrees Hiram is a figure of worship to them. It was due to these masonic teachings that came the beliefs that led to Hank's parents giving him the name Hiram. Hank's father was a World War 1 veteran who was severely injured. He would work with pain all of his life as an engineer for the railroads' lumber company. His mother was mostly a stay at home mom.

When Hank was born he soon began to live a life of pain. Hank was born with a spinal column disorder. This disorder would give him intense pain throughout his life that only got worse as he grew taller. This pain was the major factor that led Hank to use in an abusive way alcohol, and drugs. His father was in constant pain himself, and due to his job he was hardly ever around. His father would often move his family around to several southern Alabama towns in the late 1920's through the 1930's.

In 1930 when Hank was 7 years old his father began to suffer from facial paralysis. The cause of this condition came from a brain aneurysm he had at work. This resulted in his father being hospitalized for eight years. His mother would now have to carry the weight of the entire family, and young Hank would have to grow up quick.

His family's religious practices at home were anything but Christian. They on the surface looked Christian, and the family even attended Church, but hidden among themselves was Hank's mother's belief, and practices in witchcraft. This type of faith in those times had to be well hidden from people of the towns they lived in. It was a secret faith know only to those who were part of it.

In 1935 the Williams family moved to Garland, Alabama. There Lillie would open a boarding house. The boarding house turned out to fail due to the low number of guests who could not afford a boarding house stay on account of The Great Depression. Soon Lillie had to sell the house to the bank, and move in along with her family to her cousin's house in Georgiana, Alabama. It was said by some insiders that it was through her hidden connections among Masons she managed to find jobs others could not find during The Depression.

She came to work most of the time in a cannery, and she served as a night-shift nurse at a local hospital. Hank's mother would make enough money to buy her family their own home, but their first house would burn down in a strange fire. The family's possessions would also burn up in the fire.

Lillie would start all over again by going back to her cousin's house. There she found work again, and save up to buy another home for her family. This home was on Rose Street, and it had a small garden. She had problems maintaining the bills of the home due to lack of hours at work. She then tries again at seeking to make money by turning her home into a boarding house. For a time this idea would work.

Hank use to make money for the family by growing diverse crops in the garden. Hank and his sister would sell the crops around town. One day a unheard of event would happen in the life of Hank that came from an out of nowhere chance meeting with U.S. Representative J. Lister Hill. On that day Hank was in Georgiana selling his crops while J. Lister Hill was campaigning across Alabama. Hill came to this town on the same day Hank was in town working. When Hank saw him he managed to walk up to him, and speak to him. Hank began to tell Hill about his father's problems with the disability pension, and that his mother needed his help to resolve them. Hill felt sorry for the young man, and would actually look into the problem. Hill would resolve the problem by helping the Williams family by creating a fundraiser campaign to help the families of war veterans. Families throughout Alabama donated money to Hill for this cause, and this work made Hill more popular in Alabama. In turn Hill raised enough money for the Williams family that from then on, and throughout The Great Depression Hank's family was financially well-off.

Hank's passion for music started in the mid to late 1930's in Georgiana. There Hank would meet an African-American man named Rufus Payne who went by the nickname 'Tee-Tot'. Rufus was a guitar playing street performer who played for money tips. He was so good at the guitar that he managed to survive on tips during The Great Depression era. Hank often used to stop what he was doing, and listen to him. Rufus would come to know Hank, and his mother Lillie.

Hank really wanted to take guitar lessons from Rufus, and he often begged his mother to let him do it. His mother finally caved in, and she went to Rufus to hire him to teach Hank how to play the guitar. Rufus would make a deal with his mother wherein he would teach young Hank for a small fee, and a free meal. After Lillie agreed to the deal Rufus began teaching Hank the art of Country-Folk and Rhythm & Blues music. Very soon Lillie would buy Hank's first guitar for him to practice with. Rufus would teach Hank about chords, bass turns, chord progressions. He would even go on to teach Hank the musical style of accompaniment. This style Hank would use throughout his song-writing career.

In 1937 Hank who was suffering from the spine injury he was

born with was asked to do certain exercises by his coach he was unable to do. When the physical education coach was told by his student that he would not be doing those exercises the coach began to push him around. This resulted in a physical fist-fight between Hank and his coach. After the fight Hank's mother wanted the coach fired for punching her son, but the education board refused to fire him. Due to this Lillie felt forced to move again, and she would move her family to Montgomery, Alabama. Hank at that point lost all touch with his musical teacher Rufus after he moved. Hank would never see him again.

In 1939 Rufus would move to Montgomery but he never encountered Hank due to the fact Hank was on the road at that point. It was in Montgomery where Rufus would die a homeless man within only several months of moving there. In 1937 Lillie and her family would use their home in Montgomery to open a boarding house. In July of 1937 Hank up to that point was still called Hiram, a name that often brought kids in school, and later his peers to make fun of him. He would officially change his name in that month to Hank.

That year Hank caught sight of a talent show held at the Empire Theater. He entered into the contest, and went home to write his first song. Hank called the song WPA Blues. When Hank participated in the contest he performed his first original song. Hank took first prize at the talent show, and won $15. He began to take up playing soon after that, and he would play around downtown Montgomery. The other musicians around there were stunned that he could play that good.

All of Hank's compositions throughout his career has been based upon storytelling. At this point Hank worked out a plan to get on the radio. He would use a method that Rufus used in order to eat and survive.

Hank one day after school decided to do a street performance on the sidewalk in front of the WSFA radio station building. He would seek and perform these street performances every day after school, and even on weekends. His street performances were catching the attention of the crowds around him. Soon his performances were catching the attention of the WSFA producers. They went to him and invited him to perform on air.

Soon he became an occasional performer on the radio. The listeners of the radio station called him 'the singing kid'. They soon were making calls, and sending letters to the radio station requesting to hear more of him. Back then in Hank's day entrance into the music industry happened when an artist was accepted by the radio stations, and listeners.

The radio stations at the time worked hand and glove with record companies who, at that time, were starting to grow into nationwide companies. The producers of WSFA then hired Hank to host his own 15-minute show twice a week for a salary of $15 a week. The equivalent amount in our time is that Hank's salary would have been $246 a week in 2014. $15 a week in Hank's day was a very good pay-day. Soon Hank's earnings managed to bring his father back home from the hospital in August of 1938, but his mother by that point had grown distant of him, and his father's stay was not long. Lillie would not allow him to be head of the household because she was not willing to surrender control to anyone.

By September of 1938 Elonzo stayed long enough to celebrate his son's birthday, and he was soon sent back to the medical center in Louisiana. Hank's radio show would become a huge successful show for its time. He soon started to make more money, and to further his music career he would form his own band.

The band would be called The Drifting Cowboys. The original members were Braxton Schuffert (guitarist), Jimmy Porter who was only 13 years old, and he played steel guitar, Freddie Beach (fiddler), Arthur Whiting (guitarist), and the band's comedian was 'Hezzy' Smith Adair. Throughout the years new members would come along, and play for the band. The Drifting Cowboys would tour throughout central, and southern Alabama in the late 1930's performing in nightclubs, bars, and private parties.

In that time Hank dropped out of school to work full-time, and his mother Lillie became the manager of the band. As the manager she would book the band's shows, and she negotiated their pay. The band began taking the tour outside of Alabama, and performed shows in Georgia and Florida. The band soon became popular among honky-tonk nightclubs. In that time The Drifting Cowboys became star performers in the Country-Western scene. It was at this time that Hank developed an addiction to alcohol that became so bad he started to spend a lot of the money the band made off the shows' revenues. This drunken lifestyle of Hank would result in after show fist-fights in bars, and affairs with women.

In between the tour schedules Hank would also return to Montgomery to host his radio show. In 1941 America enters World War 2, and Hank would be drafted into the military along with his band-mates. As Hank's band-mates served in the military, Hank ended up getting a 4-F deferment from military service. The reason why he got the deferment was because Hank took part in a rodeo show where he fell off the bull he was riding on, and further injured himself. This injury resulted in even more pain in Hank's life.

In the 1940's Hank's alcohol problems became even worse. He began to be abusive toward new band members that resulted in many of them leaving the band as soon as they became members of it. He was now constantly showing up for his radio show completely intoxicated. His habitual drunken character resulted in WSFA firing Hank from their radio station.

One time Grand Ole Opry star Roy Acuff, who was a legend in Hank's time, gave Hank some advice. He said to him, 'You've got a million dollar talent son, but a ten-cent brain'. After being fired from the show Hank still continued to have alcohol problems that also resulted in drug-problems as Hank was using too many pills at once.

He was now singing in bars for soldiers on leave from the war. Often times soldiers resented young men in that time who were not in the war, and fighting for their country. They looked down on those men as being weak. Often times Hank would have problems with the soldiers, and combine with alcohol the problems would lead to some brutal fist-fights.

In 1943 Hank met a woman named Audrey Sheppard while attending a medicine show in Banks, Alabama. Audrey at the time had just left her husband, and was in the process of divorcing him. When Audrey met Hank they soon became a couple, and then Audrey would move in with Hank. In that time premarital sex was very much looked down upon. The looks were even worse if you move into a man's home without being married to him, but Hank and Audrey did not care. They clearly did not have strong Christian values.

Even though Hank did Gospel music, and Audrey attended a Church, there seemed to be an underline faith to them that could not be called Christian. When Audrey was living with Hank she became unsettled in the town she was living in. She told Hank that they should move to Montgomery. She also expressed to Hank that she was going to help him start a band, and regain his radio show. Audrey at this point saw that by Hank regaining his show, she would also be in the show.

Hank would marry Audrey in 1944 in a Texaco Station in Alabama. By 1945 Hank was now working again for WSFA in Montgomery. In this time Hank's band The Drifting Cowboys were back from military service, and Audrey was now a full-time member of the band. It was at this time when many of Hank's hit songs that would become classic hit songs in music history were written, and performed by Hank and his band. Hank performed the songs over the radio, and he would weekly write and perform new songs.

His biggest songs at that time were Honkey-Tonkey, My Darling Baby Girl, Mother Is Gone, I Loved No One But You, Let's Turn Back The Years, and many others. Along with being a band-member Audrey also was Hank's manager.

In 1946 Hank auditioned for the Grand Ole Opry but was rejected. His rejection is believed to have come about due to his reputation. It was discovered at that time that Hank's marriage to Audrey was not fully legal. The reason for this was because Audrey during her divorce from her previous husband did not comply with the 60-day trial reconciliation period. She instead moved in with Hank, and married him at a pump-station because most of the Churches could not legally marry them.

Record companies were fast on the rise and record shops were opening all across the nation. Artists knew that this was the future of success in music, and they sought to get signed to record companies. Most major record companies that became the music industry today were actually funded or started by Hollywood film companies. In fact, the film companies were started up by companies that were owned by major international banks and corporations. Hank and Audrey would go to Fred Rose, who was president of a music publishing company called Acuff-Rose Music. Fred had deep connections with Sterling Records, and was known to play ping-pong games at WSM Radio. There Audrey introduces herself to Fred, and asked him if her husband could sing a song for him. When Hank does so this would lead to a six-song record contract with Sterling Records. When these six-songs were recorded they were released in late 1946 to early 1947. Two of the songs called Never Again, and Honky Tonkin became very successful hit records.

After the six-song contract was up MGM Records now wanted to sign Hank Williams. MGM Records would sign Hank Williams in 1947. He would record a song for them called Move It On Over that was released the same year. Move It On Over became a massive hit country song. This success resulted in Hank moving to Shreveport, Louisiana. There he became a performer on the Louisiana Hayride, which was a radio show broadcast that reached living rooms of the entire South-East of the United States.

Hank appeared on this radio program every weekend on a Saturday, and eventually he came to host his own show on KWKH. At this point Hank, and his band started touring across western Louisiana and eastern Texas.

Hank would release more singles that became big radio hits. In 1949 Hank released a song called Lovesick Blues that was a remake of the 1922 version performed by Cliff Friend & Irving Mills. Lovesick Blues would become a huge smash hit, and the song is believed to have been the single to cause an even bigger mainstream cross-over for Country Music. This resulted in Hank gaining a place in the Grand Ole Opry in 1949.

On June 11, 1949 Hank made his debut performance at the Grand Ole Opry. He became the first performer in their long history to receive six encores. Due to this Hank, and his band were now earning $1,000 a show. That is the equivalent today of $10,000 a show.

In 1949 Audrey would give birth to Hank's son who became Hank Williams, Jr. In that same year Hank, and his band joined the European tour of the Grand Ole Opry artists. They performed in military bases in England and Germany. In that time of this great success Hank had seven hit songs released.

By the early 1950's Hank developed huge marketability with his name. He wanted to do some religious-theme music but his managers felt that if he did that he would hurt his marketability, so he began to release these religious-theme songs under the name of what many insiders believe was his alter-ego

called Luke the Drifter. These songs were not considered real Gospel music even though they were meant to be sold as Gospel songs. The songs really didn't talk about the lessons, and life of Jesus Christ. They instead were songs that depicted Luke the Drifter traveling around from place to place, and narrating stories from different characters. He would use a lot of philosophy teachings rather than Bible teachings, and many of the compositions were accompanied by a pipe organ. These songs seemed strange, and dark to people instead of a joyful celebration of GOD.

In the early 1950's Hank would have several more hit songs released but his life was about to become very sorrowful once again. In 1951 Hank went on a hunting trip in Tennessee, and he suffered intense pain after taking a nasty fall. This injury reactivated even more pain in the previous back injury he was born with. Alcohol, and pain killers alone were now not enough to kill the pain in his back. Soon Hank was introduce to heroin, and started to use morphine on a daily bases.

In December of 1951 he would have back-surgery in an effort to get rid of the pain.   After recovering from surgery at his mother's home the pain came back. From there his morphine, and alcohol problems became even worse. His drunk and high problems resulted in Hank being dismissed from the Grand Ole Opry. His once stellar performances were now terrible, and poor performances where he would pass out on stage, and cough through most of the songs. It was at this time that Audrey leaves him, and divorces him.

In October of 1952 while on drugs, and his career is being ruined he marries another woman named Billie Jean Jones. In late 1952 Hank still managed to record hit songs for the record company. His biggest single was a song called Your Cheatin' Heart that came at a very low point in Hank's life.

When Hank met his death this happened at the time he was scheduled to perform in Charleston, West Virginia. Hank had to be driven to the show by a college student named Charles Carr. On that day an ice storm came about that prevented Hank from attending the show, and during a phone call it was decided that Hank should perform at the New Year's Day concert in Canton, Ohio.

When they arrived in Knoxville, Tennessee Hank had to be rushed to a doctor as he overdose on a combination of chloral hydrate, and alcohol. The doctor had to inject two shots of vitamin B12 that contained a quarter grain of morphine just to wake him up. Later on after checking out of the hospital Hank had to be carried back into the car being too weak to walk to the car.

On January 1, 1953 sometime during the midnight hour Hank, and his driver cross the Tennessee state line, and arrive in Bristol, Virginia. Charles stopped at a 24 hour restaurant, and asked Hank if he wanted anything to eat. Hank said he was not hungry, and those would be his last words. After Charles got something to eat he returned to the car to find Hank apparently sleeping, but while driving down the road Charles noticed that Hank was not moving or responding to anything at all. Charles stopped at a gas station, and looked at Hank. At that moment he realized that Hank Williams was dead. In the Cadillac next to his dead-body were empty beer cans and unfinished handwritten lyrics. Some insiders believe that when Charles was eating in the restaurant Hank may have taken another dose of morphine that killed him.

Another artist of interest goes by the name Lil' Kim. Lil' Kim's real name is Kimberly Jones, and she was born in New York City having been raised in Bedford that is a neighborhood of Brooklyn. Her parents were Linwood and Rudy Jones. Kim's father was a hard, and strict man whose character was developed while servicing in the military. He ran his household like a boot-camp where Kim, and her brother even her mother all had assigned work, and curfews. Her father was a good provider money-wise for his family, but when it came to love, and compassion of dealing with a wife and kids his efforts turned out to be very abusive.

Instead of treating his kids like kids he treated them like soldiers under his command. He was also very hard and cruel with his wife. By the time Kim was about 9 years old her mother could not take any more abuse from her husband. She left her husband and she never went back to him. When she left him she took 9 year old Kim with her. Her mother had no place to go, and no home to call her own. Kim, and her mother would stay from time to time with friends. When they could not get a place to stay they would sleep homeless inside the car on many nights. Kim's mother did not want to see her daughter suffer anymore. She decided that until she could make a place for herself Kim should stay with her father.

Kim was then returned to her father, and would live with him up until she became a teenager. Kim's life with her father was hard, and cold. As a pre-teen to a teenager Kim, and her brother found it harder and harder to keep all the detailed rules of their father. Many of these rules were not normal or even wise to impose on young teens. When the rules were broken in any small way for instance if he told you to be at home at 7:00, and you arrive at 7:05 then a beating was coming your way.

The abuse that Kim was suffering at home started to take a toll, and soon Kim, when she entered high-school, began to rebel on her father. Through this rebellion Kim, and her father were often at war with each other. These confrontations resulted in Kim being kicked out of the house as a teenager with no money or support.

The day she was kicked out happened during a fight between her father and her brother. Her brother had come home late and her father was ready to beat him. Kim could not stand to watch the beating anymore so she grabs a knife and attempts to defend her brother by stabbing her father. That is when her father expelled her from the home. Kim was now forced to live on the streets.

She was still enrolled at Sarah J. Hale Vocational High School but was unable to attend classes anymore. When she was kicked out she would stay from home to home sleeping over at her friends' houses. But soon her friends could not always sustain a place for her to sleep. Kim also struggled for money, and food. She began pan-handling for funds. At this point she would try to seek out her mother who she had a tough time trying to find.

Soon men started to notice that Kim was a young good-looking homeless girl. These evil minded men then started to offer Kim money for sex. While struggling for food, and a place to stay, Kim on several occasions would have sex for money. She started to be seen around the neighborhood as a teen prostitute. Before things got even worse, which is saying a lot, Kim's mother would find her. At this point her mother now managed to get a small apartment, and she took Kim in to live with her.

Kim was transferred to Brooklyn College Academy that was a school that sought for its students to be trained for college. This was the same high-school that rappers Nas and Foxy Brown attended. Kim at this point was not interested in going to college. She instead fell in love with the hip-hop culture, and scene. In the two high-schools that Kim attended is where she began to discover her gift for rapping. In these high-schools she was looked upon as a girl who looked good and could rap.

It was clear that she had entertainment gifts, and was often able to project it. At this point she began to dive deep into the hip-hop culture and scene that was made up of mostly men. Her main friends at the time were male friends who were either rappers, gang-bangers, or both. During her time in her second high-school is when she met up, and coming future rap star The Notorious B.I.G. also known as Biggy Smalls.

Biggy at this time had just started working with Sean 'Puffy'

Combs also known as P. Diddy, and the two of them were trying to start up Bad Boy Records. Biggy was working on his first album that later produced the hit single Big Papa that made him famous. When Biggy met Kim he started to flirt with her, and wanted to hook up with her. Kim liked him as well, and began to flirt back at him.

At this time Biggy was also seeing a woman named Faith Evans who was an R&B singer. Biggy would find out that Kim had skills as a rapper, and had the kind of looks that drew men to her. Biggy started a relationship with her that was mutual at first but turned abusive, and controlling on Biggy's part. Biggy then became a key figure in Kim's personal life, and she was even looked at as Biggy's girl more so then Faith, who later became Biggy's wife. Biggy guided Kim into the rap industry, and taught her about the rap business. He showed her how to rap even better, and how to throw hooks into her raps. He would turn her along with several young gifted rappers into true rap industry artists.

Biggy had a long-term goal in mind when he came into the rap industry to record his first album. He wanted to make himself, and his solo album famous and successful. Then he wanted his group he would call Junior M.A.F.I.A. to also hit it big wherein he would be the producer of that group. Therefore Biggy would make money from his own albums, and the albums of Junior M.A.F.I.A.

After Biggy's album became a smash hit along with the lead single Big Papa, Bad Boy Records was now established. Biggy was very popular at the time, and he had a heavy influence on the East Coast rap scene. Biggy would now turn his attention on releasing Junior M.A.F.I.A.'s first album.

For Lil' Kim this would be her first time recording a major studio album with the Brooklyn based group. Lil' Kim was only 19 years old at the time. The recording of the album took place in late 1994, and into early 1995. During that time Biggy was still in a sexual relationship with Kim, and was thinking about marrying Faith Evans.

Biggy had also changed as well. He was not the father-figure type anymore toward the young group he was producing but became more controlling over them. He acted more like an over-bearing boss who would demean them if they messed up in anyway. It was believed that Biggy's fame at the time really went to his head, and he became ego driven. Biggy was always telling Kim what to do, and Kim was getting sick of it. When Biggy told her that he wanted to marry Faith but still wanted Kim as his girl, Kim felt used, and hurt. During the recording sessions Kim would often lash out at Biggy, and refuse to rap a song a certain way. She often treated him with spite at the time. This would result in several combatant confrontations in the studio between Kim and Biggy. Many of them were very ugly resulting in Kim being slapped around. The real issue between them was Kim wanted to be Biggy's wife, and she could not understand why Faith was picked over her.

During the recording of the album Kim found out that she was pregnant. The baby would have belonged to Biggy, but when Biggy found out about it he did not want the problems he said he would have because of it. In truth he didn't want Faith to be upset over it. Biggy would then pressure Kim to get an abortion until she finally did it. Kim was very bitter about the abortion, and she really did not want to do it. The abortion would result in more bad blood between Kim and Biggy.

In August of 1995 Junior M.A.F.I.A. released their first and only major album called Conspiracy. The album did not become the huge mainstream album that Biggy's first album had become, but it did become a successful album among urban, and hip-hop fans.

The album had three singles called Player's Anthem, I Need You Tonight, and Get Money that entered the top ten Billboard Hip-Hop charts. One of the singles called Get Money would go platinum in sales, and the album itself would go gold in sales. Soon after the release of Junior M.A.F.I.A.'s album Lil' Kim would embark on a solo career.

In 1995 Kim would revamp her image to appear more sexual then before. She would go in the direction of presenting herself as a hardcore sexual rapper. Many insiders believe that the idea for this raw sexual image came from Biggy but this has not been proven. What is proven is that both Kim and Biggy put this image for Kim together as they sought to make Lil' Kim's first solo album.

In that time there has never been a solo female rap artist to have their album enter near the top 10 upon the Billboard 200 albums chart. Also in that time solo female rap artists were nowhere near as sexual in their image as Kim's image became. Rap lyrics for solo female rap acts of that time were also not as hardcore sexual as Kim's lyrics became. Lil' Kim was literally going to sell sex along with selling her rap album.

In November of 1996 Lil' Kim's debut album was released called Hard Core. This album would debut at the number 11 spot on the Billboard 200 albums chart. That was the highest debut for a solo female rap artist at that time. The album would sell 78,000 copies in only its first week. Hard Core would eventually go double-platinum in sales. The promotion poster for the album featured Lil' Kim wearing a two-piece bikini while bending down with her legs spread wide-open to focus the picture on her private-part. This notorious photo, and the music of the album itself would quickly cause controversy.

African-American activist C. Delores Tucker became well known and hated in the hip-hop community for speaking against certain rap artists. Tucker had a lot of power backing her up with African-American Church leaders and politicians supporting her. When Lil' Kim's album came out C. Delores quickly attacked Lil' Kim's image and music. She would demand a meeting with the stockholders of Warner Bros. Records who are in fact the true owners of Bad Boy Records.

At that meeting she criticized the company for supporting a label that produces in her own words, 'this filth'. Tucker pointed out the twisted graphic sexual content of Kim's posters, and lyrics. She stated that the album was, 'gangsta porno rap'. Oddly enough during that time Kim also got caught up with a short-lived controversy over a porno tape many said she made. The tape was being sold in underground black-markets before it eventually disappeared. It has never been really clear if that was really Lil' Kim on the tape.

These issues of controversy surrounding Lil Kim's raw hardcore image did not lessen her fame or ruin it. It in fact made her more famous, and her album would go on to also have three hit singles. The two biggest singles were Not Tonight that featured Missy Elliott, Angie Martinez, Da Brat, and Left Eye of T.L.C. The second hit song was called Crush on You that hit number 6 on the Billboard 100 singles chart.

In 1997 Biggy Smalls would be murdered by assassins as he was shot multiple times throughout his body. Investigations into the case would reveal some strange facts. Two crooked police officers who had moonlight jobs working as bodyguards for several rap artists would be suspected of being the real gun-men who killed Biggy. It was also said but not proven that Biggy's murder had more to do with the criminal element that truly ran Bad Boy Records. This element would be the Black Mafia wherein many of its members began starting up hip-hop labels, and clubs according to New York police, and FBI files.

It has often been believe that these men connect themselves to higher international corporations by doing business with them that involves starting up record labels. The inside story is that Biggy used to push cocaine for them by having it sold among the rich artists of the music, and even film industry, but somewhere along the way he did not want to sell for them anymore. Many then would say that this decision resulted in his death, but the story is still unproven.

After Biggy's murder Sean Combs would now manage Lil' Kim's career, and Kim would go on tour with Combs. The No Way Out tour is called one of the highest grossing hip-hop tours of all time. It grossed over 16 million dollars.

In 1998 Roc Management, which was headed by Damion Butler a.k.a. 'D-Roc', took over management for Lil' Kim. They would launch Kim's own record label called Queen Bee Entertainment. Even though she had her own label she was not recording any new album at the time. Instead she was modeling for various fashions shows for companies like Iceberg, Candies, and others. She was also involved with recordings for dozens of remixes, and she made appearances on other artists' records.

In June of 2000, after a four year wait, Lil' Kim finally released an album called The Notorious K.I.M. The album would debut at the number 4 spot on the Billboard 200 albums chart. The album would go platinum in sales despite limited success of the album's lead singles. Many believe that the sales of the album came by way of the long standing beef between Lil' Kim and Foxy Brown.

The feud between these two artists at first started over vain issues, and issues involving the matter of who created the female hardcore image first. The beef would escalate when Lil' Kim talked trash about Foxy Brown on her record. The escalation became so heated that it resulted in nasty violent encounter between the bodyguards of Kim and Brown.

In 2001 Lil' Kim would score a number one hit song on the Billboard 100 singles chart when she teamed with Patti LaBelle, Christina Aguilera, Pink, and Mya to record the remake of the song Lady Marmalade. The song was originally written by the Labelle group about 25 years earlier from that time. The song was not about female power or something like that. It was about a bordello where prostitutes lived, and worked in the voodoo area of New Orleans.

In 2002 Kim was hired by World Wrestling Entertainment to record a new entrance theme song for their Women's Champion who was Trish Stratus at the time. The song entitled Time to Rock N' Roll was used for several years on WWE broadcasts until Trish retired.

Kim's last taste of major success with an album came in March of 2003 when she released the album called La Bella Mafia. This album would debut at the number five spot on the Billboard 200 albums chart. The lead single for the album was a song called Magic Stick. The single was Kim's biggest single of her career. The song featured 50 Cent, and it hit number two on the Billboard 100 singles chart. The song was also the number one song on radio airplay across the nation. Magic Stick was a song about a girl enjoying the pleasures of a man's penis. This was actually the most popular song across the nation among pre-teens, teenagers, and college students. 7 year old girls, and even boys were freely listening, and getting into a song that was all about giving oral sex.

While this song was popular all over the nation, and Kim was recording her fourth album a court case was about to come down upon her. This court case came as a result of an event that took place in 2001 during a heated shoot-out between the bodyguards of Lil' Kim and Foxy Brown. To better understand what the most likely cause of the shoot-out was is to take a better look at events regarding the Lil' Kim, and Foxy Brown beef. This beef goes all the way back when Lil' Kim was in Junior M.A.F.I.A., and Foxy Brown was in The Firm. During that time the two women used to accuse each other of stealing each other's rap style. When their solo albums came out the media outlets began noting similarities between the cover of their albums. Many of Lil' Kim's people at Bad Boy Records, and within her circle of friends accused Brown of trying to sound, and look like Lil' Kim. Brown and her people accused Kim of the same thing.

In 1997 the beef led to the end of their friendship when their respective entourages kept having open conflicts against each other. In 1998 Foxy Brown, and her mother had their home broken into by robbers. Brown, and her mother were both held at gunpoint as the men rob the home.

Kim called Brown after the robbery, and a reconciliation took place, but the peace would not last. Soon the two of them were heard speaking ill words toward each other in the industry. Kim in her 2000 album The Notorious K.I.M. fired the first shot openly at Brown. Kim, and Sean Combs would both diss Brown, and accuse her of copying Lil' Kim. It was believed that Lil' Kim started the feud again when Brown supported Faith Evans in interviews who was Lil' Kim's rival. Kim in that time appeared on Mobb Deep's Quiet Storm (Remix) album, and on one of the songs Lil' Kim disses Brown by calling her a 'bitch', and compared her looks to a pit bull. In return Brown struck back at Lil Kim. She would appear on a track from a rap group called Capone-N-Noreaga, and would push Kim's buttons hard by dissing her failed relationship with Biggy Smalls.

On February 26, 2001 at around 3:00 p.m. Kim, and her entourage were leaving a New York radio station called Hot 97 after Kim gave an interview. As Kim, and her bodyguards were leaving rapper Capone, and his entourage were coming toward the building. As before Kim's people hated Brown's people, and they could not act at all civil toward each other. When the two entourages crossed paths they started mean-mugging each other that led to hostile words between the two entourages. No one is sure who pulled their guns out first but when the guns came out a violent gun fight followed. Many insiders stated that it was Suif Jackson who pulled his gun-out first, and began to open-fire. Jackson would indeed fire 20 rounds at Capone, and his entourage while Lil' Kim was rushed from the scene. Damion Butler also fired several rounds at Capone's entourage. The gun-fight took place between Capone, and his two bodyguards, and Jackson, Butler, and bodyguards of Lil' Kim. During the gun-fight Efrain Ocasio one of the gun-men from Capone's entourage was shot in the back.

When the police investigated the shooting Lil' Kim was asked to testify against Jackson because the police believed he started the gun-fight, but Lil' Kim lived by a street-code where in that code you never inform on your people to the police. Kim would lie to the police, and state that she was never there. Kim would give the same statement she gave to the police to the Federal grand jury, but during the court case police produced video footage placing Lil' Kim at the scene. The video proved she knew what happened.

In July of 2005 Lil' Kim was convicted of three counts of conspiracy, and one count of perjury. She was sentenced to one year in prison, 30 days of home detention upon release from custody, and three years of probation. Kim would serve the full one year term, and was released in July of 2006. Since then she has continued to make albums.

KMFDM is an industrial metal-rock band who have made songs that projected themes of mass-murder, homosexuality, and anti-Christian themes. The band members come from Hamburg, Germany, and they were formed by German multi-instrumentalist Sascha Konietzko. Sascha formed the group in 1984, and since then the band has undergone many line-up changes. The name of the band is often surrounded in a controversial nature. Insiders tell a different story about where the name comes from then the story told by Sascha. Sascha stated that he got the name out of a German newspaper by cutting words out of the paper. When he put the words together he noticed that the words spelled 'Kein Mehrheit Fur Die Mitleid'. In German the words mean, 'No pity for the majority'. That night, according to Sascha, the band had to perform at an opening show, and he introduces the band under the full German meaning of the words. Later on when returning home from the show Sascha while talking with a friend of his and he renamed the band KMFDM, but according to insiders the real meaning of the German phrase is actually what you know as a urban term. In the underground rock scene in Germany the phrase actually means, 'No pity for the masses'. Among the German youths of the underground scene the meaning is the same as telling someone, 'No mercy for the weak'.

The German underground rock scene, and industrial rock scene are filled with a lot of occult groups. The most dangerous group among them are the various neo-Nazi, and new socialist Nazi groups. These groups are made up of mostly young people whose fathers or grandfathers were World War 2 veterans. This means they are the sons, and daughters or grandchildren of former Nazi soldiers, and officers. Many neo-Nazis today carry on the beliefs of the Nazi party even though it is taboo, and shunned in Germany. The neo-Nazis today are seen as an occult-gang like group whose members have committed some violent, and horrible crimes. Their crimes range from assault, rape, murder, blackmail, fraud, rioting, robbery, drug-dealing, kidnapping, and a few others. The phrase that became the initials of the German band was actually started by the neo-Nazi groups. The phrase was in relation to a belief that the neo-Nazis will take revenge on all the enemies of their party. They think that one day they will kill off the masses to purge the world of all 'lower races' as they call it. That is why the phrase is 'no pity for the masses'. It is a phrase that celebrates the hope of a coming genocide.

These twisted groups among the underground rock scene in Germany party with other occult groups in that scene. Many of these groups are also satanic in their beliefs, and ways. Not everyone in that scene is an occult member but that is where many of the German occult groups call home. These groups are into satanic rituals, homosexuality, violent encounters, abusing women, using drugs, engaging in crimes, promoting racist themes, and other foul behavior. The underground scene is where they meet up, and party.

Insiders believe that Sascha, and the various members of KMFDM have been involved with satanic groups. Much of their evidence comes from the scene itself that KMFDM has been part of since the early 1980's. The underground rock scene of Germany does not limit itself to only Germany. The scene itself was started in Paris, France when the first nightclubs opened up in the 19th century. These nightclub owners, many of them, come from elite families that opened up clubs in Germany, England, Denmark, Belgium, Italy, and other nations including the United States. Overtime the taste, and fashions of the underground music scene changes throughout the years, but what does not change are the bad elements of the culture. From the start when nightclubs first opened there were investigations done regarding them that revealed satanic ritual activity being done along with the use of drugs, and other criminal, and moral offenses. Acts of murder, and strange deaths were also reported as well.

The nightclub culture is what created the underground scene that led to the underground musical scenes of today. Today many of the owners of the clubs have been busted or investigated for criminal activity, and some of them even got caught for crimes that would be called satanic.

The inner circle of people that Sascha, and his group deal with are people noted for such crimes. When Sascha officially named his group KMFDM the group performed for the first time under this name in Paris, France. It's original line-up had Sascha singing, and Udo Sturm playing an ARP 2600 synthesizer while Sascha also played vacuum cleaners, and bass guitar. Sascha also had amplifiers spread throughout the building, and to add to their performance that night Sascha had brought to the stage four Polish coal miners to pound on the foundations of the Grand Palais. Sascha met these four Polish miners at a gay-bordello he was visiting. Soon the band got more gigs, and went through its ever changing line-up. At one point the band had 20 people in it. Their stage shows became known for antics such as fire eating, and throwing human waste at their audiences.

From the mid to late 1980's the band released two albums in Europe called Opium, and What Do You Know, Deutschland? The music of the albums glorified racism, murder, homosexuality, drug use, rape, anti-Christian themes, and other negative themes. Soon other albums like this would follow, and the band became very popular in the underground nightclubs of Germany, France, Denmark, and other European nations. The album that made them popular in the underground scene in America was called UAIOE released in 1989.

In 1991, in order to spread their fame further in the underground rock scene of the United States, the band moved to Chicago. In only one year KMFDM became a major rock act of the Chicago industrial rock music scene. They started releasing records through independent labels, and were selling thousands of those records.

In 1994 KMFDM moved to Seattle, and started to have their most successful years. They recorded the album called Nihil that sold 120,000 copies. They would appear on the soundtracks of three films called The Crow, Bad Boys, and Mortal Kombat in the mid 1990's. On the soundtrack for the film Bad Boys was the song called Juke Joint Jezebel. This song would become KMFDM's biggest hit single among mainstream fans. The song took the number 10 spot on the Billboard 100 singles chart, and the single itself sold 1.8 million copies. In Chicago in 1995 their record company seller named Jim Nash who was president of Chicago's Wax Trax would die of AIDS. Seattle would now become their new headquarters.

In 1999 is when the satanic influences of KMFDM became more seen. On April 20, 1999 two young men named Eric and Dylan would take part in what became known as the Columbine High School Massacre. According to the media, and the official story Eric and Dylan planned this attack alone, but according to evidence, witnesses, statements, and even some common sense it shows they did not plan the attack alone. Many people believe that the Columbine Massacre was a false-flag attack. They believe the attack was planned and staged resulting in the real deaths of innocent victims.

The story is still unproven but it does have evidence to support it from people who were there, and saw it happen. Their testimony has often been ignored by the media. Many people commonly find this very hard to believe that the government would ever take part in something like this. Sadly however events in history, and evidence has shown us otherwise. The Native American historians can tell you all about it.

Here is the overview in the evidence regarding the Columbine Massacre being a false flag attack. The entire attack itself was very complex, and too highly laborious to have been executed by only two high-school students alone. Many experts in military engagements, and even in law enforcement have pointed out some things that still have not been explained. To understand the scope of the attack Eric and Dylan needed automatic small-arm machine guns with plenty of rounds to spare. They needed dozens of propane tanks, and had to convert them all into bombs. They also had to quietly, and neatly place all these bombs at certain points in the cafeteria, and simply hope no one saw them. They also had to get bombs that were rigged for cars. They also had to find a way to work, and go unnoticed in front of a school with hundreds of students in rigging all the cars with the bombs. They also had to bring in with them into a school with tight security over 100 explosive devices.

Transporting, and prepositioning the number, and kinds of bombs they used far exceeded what two high-school boys could ever do.

There has never been any clear, and logical answer as to how all those bombs got placed, and brought into the school. The gear, and the machine gun weapons along with the equipment were far too much too be hidden under a trench-coat. They also could not be hidden in a book-bag or brought into the school without someone noticing. There is also another unexplained matter. There was found on the scene different caliber bullets that were used, and did not match the firearms used by Eric and Dylan. The question remains as to who used them. Some of the autopsy reports of the 12 victims were never released when requested. Many believe that the reason they were not released is because it would have shown that they died by different caliber bullets then the ones used by Eric and Dylan, but still this is unproven.

Another matter that I mentioned in a previous chapter is the fact that Eric and Dylan did not just target anyone as the media stated they did. The 12 victims were well known for being Christians, and showing a Christian faith in school. They did not go after bullies they by their own words named some of their victims before they killed them on the internet, and on their web-page. In these video threats they expressed that they wanted to kill them because they hated the fact they stood for Christianity.

Another unexplained matter is the testimony of the witnesses who were the students who survived the shooting. Many of these students stated that they did not just see two shooters but in fact they stated they saw with their own eyes sometimes 3 to 4 shooters at a time. These statements were said over, and over again by these students, and they clearly were not confused about it. Many of them to this day state the same testimony of seeing more than just two shooters.

Another strange matter was how did; the FBI, ATF, CIA, NATO, and the NSA show-up on the scene all at once within five minutes after the shooting was going down? This impossible feat could have only been done if they gathered there way before the shooting was going down. Could they have actually known a shooting massacre like this was going to happen, and then allow it to happen? It seems unthinkable but many insiders believe just that. There has never been any answer as to how they were all there that fast at the same time. The only answer comes from other facts about that day. Did you know that mostly half the students of the school were mostly absent that day?

That day starting off was not a normal day where you have nearly 400 students absent from school on the same day. Strange enough is most of the students who showed up to school that day were the students whose families mostly went to Christian Churches. There has never been any clear answer as to why so many students called off from school that day. The possible answer is within the rumors that were spoken by the students in school. There were students who gave testimony that they received e-mails from some of their friends warning them not to go to school that day because a shooting was going to happen. Many of these students showed it to their parents, and that caused their parents not to send them.

The media often ignores this story, and it is an important fact to know that people in that community knew something was going to happen there, and it is very possible that some of those people would have expressed their concern to law enforcement agencies. That leaves it very possible that those law enforcement agencies who popped up there out of nowhere so quickly knew beforehand that something was going to happen there.

Also there is the fact that Eric and Dylan did post their murderous threats on the web-site for everyone including law enforcement to see. The important question here is why these law enforcement agents didn't stop the massacre from happening? Also there was the police officer who gave a testimony that he was told by his bosses not to try, and rescue any student he sees running for aid, and he was to hold his position if he did. He stated that he found that odd, and when a student jumped out of a window trying to get to safety the officer could not take it anymore, and he ran to help him. According to the officer's testimony he stated that when he tried to do so an ATF agent shot at him. These are the unexplained facts about that day that have led to many unanswered questions about this massacre. So what does this have to do with KMFDM? KMFDM clearly was not involved in the massacre itself, but their music was. One of Eric and Dylan's favorite bands was KMFDM. They often wore the band's t-shirts, and quoted lyrics from the band's music. The underground scene that made KMFDM famous is the same scene that Eric and Dylan were part of. The two teens enjoyed underground European rock bands because of the type of songs many of those bands did. These songs that Eric and Dylan liked so much were songs about committing mass-murder against people.

There is an untold, and unproven story of how Eric and Dylan became killers. The story even points to how it may have been possible that Eric and Dylan were used in some secret black-op that was done against the American people. This story comes from people who did investigations into this aspect of Eric and Dylan being involved with the occult. Much of the investigations shows that Eric and Dylan were deep into occult activities. Their involvement with the occult came by way of the underground rock scene.

Like thousands of young people who get into this scene it begins with a love for this kind of music. Hence a band like KMFDM. Their music does bring in hundreds of new teens, and young adults into the underground scene. Despite what these bands' would say their music when played live on stage does promote Satanism, and even Nazism. The music in general will promote all the things the Bible would be against.

KMFDM would say, and has said that they do not condone Nazism but their fans in the underground scene especially in Europe are into or are full members of various neo-Nazi groups. These groups are the fan-base for many of these bands, and those bands like KMFDM make the kind of music those groups like because those groups buy their albums.

In this underground scene is how Eric and Dylan became members of the Trenchcoat Mafia who were a gothic neo-Nazi group. According to police records in Colorado the Trenchcoat Mafia were suspected of committing several ritual murders before the massacre took place. There is an even stranger, and unproven story regarding Eric Harris, and his father. Eric's father had worked for 20 years for the U.S. Air Force. 4 years before moving to Littleton he worked at the Plattsburgh Air Force Base. This base was suspected of conducting mind-control experiments on Air Force pilots. Eric's father during that time was believed to have been working in the department of intelligence for the Air Force. It was believed that certain mind-control experiments were not just done on soldiers but also on non-military people as well, namely young children, and pre-teens.

The U.S. government, as I mentioned in a previous chapter, did have a mind-control program in Canada wherein the Canadian government had tossed out the U.S. personal for experimenting on children. The question has always been did the government really stop the mind-control experiments? It seems from the case of hundreds of stories that keep popping up about it that the experiments may still be going on.

It is believed that Eric Harris was another victim of it. Eric's father is suspected of handing over his son for such experiments. No one is for sure how true this is but many who knew Eric said he was a very nice kid until he came to Littleton. Many may ask how the government fits into the aspect of occult groups.

During certain law enforcement crack-downs on certain occult groups involved with kidnapping, murder, and drug-dealing the leaders of these groups that got arrested turned out to have some serious connections with the government. It turned out that some of these leaders who were mostly female had husbands who were active agents in the CIA. Some of the leaders themselves were still active agents in the CIA when they got busted. Many of the female leaders who had husbands in the CIA also worked mainly as teachers for elementary and high-schools. Some of the leaders that got arrested were even active in one of the military branches of the United States. Such cases reveal why not enough law-enforcement attention is spent on busting crimes committing by occult groups.

The investigations showed that these underground occult leaders would recruit young teenagers from other underground occult covens, groups, and gangs. They would get a hold on their minds, and brainwash these new recruits. They would control them through certain mental-strongholds they had on them. They would use them to commit murder, kidnapping, and to sell drugs for them.

The underground music scene is where many occult leaders send scouts to recruit certain young people they think they could use. Oddly enough many of the young people they recruit have a history in their family of abuse, and they come from military families. 90 % of the occultist during interviews have stated that they first got into the occult by first being fans of underground music. That music led them to the scene, and that scene led them to the occult.

Eric Harris, when he was only just a few days away from engaging in the massacre, reveals his intentions to kill his fellow students by posting up several web-sites that had hidden meanings about his true murderous intentions. In one of the threating posts he would post up the lyrics to three KMFDM songs. Those songs were Son of a Gun, Stray Bullet, and Waste. All the songs were about murdering people you felt were worthless in your eyes.

In 1999 KMFDM was releasing a new album called Adios. The release of the album coincided with the date of the Columbine Massacre. Some strange things would be reported in the media regarding the album. At the height of the non-stop news reports of the massacre the media reported that Eric posted up his favorite KMFDM songs before the killings. They also busted the rock band for wanting to release their new album on Hitler's birthday which turned out to be the date of the massacre which was April 20th.

In the year 2000 the band would break-up but they came back together in 2002. Since then their works featured themes of world war, and global death…you know all the things the Nazis were into.

Chapter 36

Today the music industry has become a major part of American and world-wide society, having a hold on the minds of billions of people all over the world. It is an industry that holds the life-stories of its many famous artists. Often the story is the same. They achieve great success but they end up falling hard, and often times they lose everything, including their lives. What is to blame for all the bad events, and strange mysteries of their lives? Could there really be something sinister, and hidden about the music industry? As a person who believes in Christ could Christians trust that the music industry's art-forms acted in good faith on behalf of the teachings of the Bible? There seems to be some very hard, and troubling questions about the history, and events of the music industry. There are people who say that if the truth was really known about the music industry it would cause a horde of people to return to Church overnight. Artists themselves have even stated that the music industry is a dangerous industry to be involved with. They have been on record for stating that people lose their morals, and even their souls there. They have also stated that Satan is very real to people there, and that GOD is hated upon in the music industry. Many people would dismiss these statements as being comments made out of stupidity, or drunkenness, but yet events in the lives of artists show forth much proof in their words.

Most fans want to think only good thoughts or good things about the music industry simply based upon the fact they love the kind of music it sells. They usually will quickly refuse to believe anything negative or even spiritual regarding music industry artists. They only want to hear good things or interesting things about them even things that overall mean nothing. Much of the real to life information about these artists is hardly or not at all known to most of these billions of fans around the world. Most fans know the artists' songs, album titles, their fashions, and the stories that the media uses as five minute sound-bites. These fans do not know where these artists come from or how they got into the music industry. That information also seems to frighten them to know as well. It is almost as if they have a certain concept or idea of what these artists are like that suits their own imaginations. When the reality is being told, and it does not fit into their own world they become offended by it. That is within itself a strange mind-set the imagery of the music industry can put inside a person's brain, because like it or not that is what images like that can do to your brain. It can inspire your brain to change the normal way of thinking.

I have noticed that when people do real study into the background information of the lives of these artists, and they are willing to accept what they learn they become changed also. They suddenly do not see the artist in the same way as they did before. The artist suddenly becomes a real person to them now with real problems, and flaws. This seems to bother them, and even depress them for a little while. Some investigators even get really mad at the things they learn. Some have gotten so mad and bothered by it they went home just to throw away all their CDs. Just to learn this information is a life-changing experience within itself. But why is that? Why do people become so shocked about this in the first place? Could it be that maybe our minds were turned off to this information in some way that it caused us to be sleeping to it so to speak? That when we learn something that is outside the fantasy zone our minds get shaken up like one does having water thrown at him early in the morning. This is a strange world we live in. The artists of the music industry today still continue to turn out platinum selling albums and Billboard hit singles. They also have not toned down the carnal, sensual, immoral, and all around degeneracy in the art-forms. In fact the artists have gotten more twisted today.

At the 2013 VMA show the star of this show was an artist named Miley Cyrus. Miley Cyrus is another product of the Disney entertainment machine. She is the daughter of Country Music star Billy Ray Cyrus who in the 1990's had a Billboard hit song called Achy Breaky Heart. Miley became a child star when she starred on a Disney program called Hannah Montana. She would go on to be signed to one of Disney's record companies, and she began to make albums for them. Miley's image, like many of the young female Disney stars, have often brought controversy due to the sexual, and vain images these young female stars seem to present. When Miley became a solo star she was not even 18 years old yet and she was doing sexually suggestive photo-shoots. One of those shoots caused a controversy with her father when Billy Ray posed with his daughter in one of these photo-shoots. People began to question what kind of a father he was to allow his daughter to pose in these kinds of photographs. Billy Ray was also the one who brought Miley into the Disney Corporation. It was said by many insiders that the sexual abuse that is often spoken, and reported about regarding Disney entertainment handlers was being done upon Miley. According to this story that is still an unproven story is that Billy Ray knew what was going on but he kept his mouth shut because they were paying him a lot of money to use his daughter in this way. When Miley began releasing her first set of albums controversy found her again when a series of pictures came out that were shocking to the parents of Miley's fans These pictures featured Miley in sexual poses with other women on the bed, and even in the bathroom, in the tube, and on the toilet.

Soon another set of photographs followed along with a homemade video of Miley smoking a form of crystal meth. When these photos and the video came out, Miley quickly blamed someone for the pictures. According to the report Miley stated that the devil was to blame for those pictures coming out. Many believe that these statements were really done as a copout to hide the fact she was not the innocent, and sweet girl next door that people thought she was. The media however mostly went after Billy Ray Cyrus over this controversy. Billy Ray would blame himself, and he also blamed the Disney Corporation. He stated that the trouble started for Miley when she began working on the Hannah Montana show. He also stated that he should have been a better father, and that he never discipline his daughter or gave her a clear set of guidelines and rules. In short he wants forgiveness for allowing his daughter to do whatever she wants to do. Of course Miley was only a child when she began working for Disney so clearly she could not make all those bad decisions without help from a lot of people who were very greedy.

In 2013 Miley stated that she would be revamping her image. At the 2013 VMA she would outrage, and shock people all over the world when she revealed what this image was going to be. The controversy first started when Miley's new video called We Can't Stop first made its debut in 2013. The video featured Miley's new image, and musical direction. In a word the new look was subversion to an entire generation of new young fans. Miley presents herself as a wild, drug-addicted, bi-sexual, predator in heat. She presents this image under an image of child-hood imagery. She sexually gropes, and dances with teddy bears surrounded by women, and a couple of men she wants to have sex with. In the video she does a series of scenes where she cuts off her toes and fingers. Along with what is called 'cutting', homosexuality, and child-porn Miley's video also promoted cocaine, and ecstasy. In the lyrics of the video she sings about waiting in line in a bathroom to snort more cocaine, and she sings about being high on ecstasy.

Most of Miley's fans range from 7 to 16 years old at the time of the video. When a reporter asked her about the lines in her lyrics if they were really about ecstasy Miley was so bold she would not even lie about it as most artists would.

She told the reporter, 'Of course I am singing about ecstasy you idiots!' Ecstasy is a drug commonly called today as a 'molly'. It has become the new crack as people have become more addicted to it in larger numbers than before. The drug usually comes in a pill form, and it has been around since the late 1970's. In the 1980's, and 1990's the drug became a huge seller at nightclubs, and rave parties. By the 2000's it became more marketed as a street drug especially when more people were suddenly coming out that they were gay all of a sudden.

Ecstasy is a fusion drug that combines heroin, and cocaine which is turned usually into a pill. The drug heightens all sensual senses, and alters brain functions to be very heighten to pleasure that changes the personality of the person. The person will sweat a lot, and will be in a trance like state, and soon will want to start touching things. This is why the drug is used as a sex drug.

At the 2013 VMA Miley would perform the song We Can't Stop on television. Her stage show featured mostly a group of African-American dancers dressed in very tight sweat-pants. The stage also featured a group of dancing teddy-bears. Miley would appear on stage with her hair dressed up as if they were horns, and would come out wearing a two-piece, and sticking her tongue out.

She appeared as a demon who was in heat looking to mate with something. When she came out like this she does not even attempt to dance but simply shakes her butt at the female dancers, and gropes the teddy bear dancers. Miley then starts walking around the stage while singing, and she puts her face in between the butt-cheeks of one of her dancers. While singing she appears as if she is a macho-lady, and while singing an artist named Robin Thick joins her on stage.

Robin is twice her age, and was popular for a pornographic song he did called Blurred Lines. In his video he portrayed women getting hot for animals.

When Robin came up to Miley to sing with her Miley turned around, and bent over to push her butt upon Robin's private part, and she began to rub her butt upon it. Afterwards Miley, while holding the we are number one foam sign, began to take the foam hand-sign, and would mimic masturbation with it on stage.

After the performance a firestorm of media attention came down on Miley. The only thing it did was make Miley more popular who was no where near sorry about it. In fact she was very proud, and happy that her young fans saw it. Fans who range from 7 to 16 years old. Miley's performance would even outrage other music industry artists. One such artist was Sinead O' Connor who was an artist I covered in a previous chapter. Sinead was furious that Miley presented such an image for fans that were not even old enough to attend high-school. Sinead's anger would deepen when Miley stated that her video direction in her new video was inspired by the way Sinead did the video Nothing Compares 2 U. Those statements from Miley were rather confusing because Sinead's video was not all sexual in the way Miley does videos.

It seems that Miley was looking for a way to explain away the reasons for the video direction by misleading people to think it was something other then what the video really was. Sinead most likely knew this, and wanted to set the record straight on how she feels about Miley's new image direction. Sinead would send a letter to Miley, and would send it through the media outlets so that everyone could read it. The letter stated, 'I repeat you have enough talent that you don't need to let the music business make a prostitute of you. You shouldn't let them make a fool of you either. Don't think for a moment that any of them give a flying fuck about you. They're there for the money, we are there for the music. It has always been that way, and it will always be that way. The sooner a young lady gets to know that, the sooner she can be really in control. Whether we like it or not us females in the industry are role models, and as such we have to be extremely careful what messages we send to other women. The message you keep sending is that it's somehow cool, to be prostituted. It's so not cool Miley, it's dangerous. Women are to be valued for so much more than their sexuality, we aren't merely objects of desire. I would be encouraging you to send healthier messages to your peers that they, and you are worth more than what is currently going on in your career. Kindly fire any motherfucker who hasn't expressed alarm because they don't care about you'.

No one is sure what Miley said back to Sinead but what is clear is that the response back was not positive, and it once again angered Sinead. Sinead would send another letter back wherein she stated to Miley, 'It is most unbecoming of you to respond in such a fashion to someone who expressed care for you, and worse that you are such an anti-female tool of the anti-female music industry'.

It amazes me, and saddens me that artists like Miley can be famous while they show that they don't honor any responsibility to what their art-forms can inspire people to do in real life.

At the 2014 Grammy Awards there was more controversy with sexually explicit performances, and even performances that were seen as satanic. Beyonce would perform wearing a nighty dress, with high-heels while sitting on a chair posing as a stripper. The event went on to promote gay-marriage like it was on sale at a mall near you. They would even promote the idea that GOD loves, and agrees with gay marriage while ignoring that the Bible states that GOD feels otherwise. Of course they don't believe in the Bible, and so they make their own views up on what GOD says about the matter. Even so called Christian leaders are back-peddling on their stand against gay-marriage out of fear of what the media would paint them as. Instead of defending the Bible, and having some guts in standing up for the truth they back down, play it off, and pretend that the issue is not there. Of course the gay-leaders realize this, and they take advantage of it all the time, and taking advantage is something gay people know all about according to research done on them by non-Christians.

It seems that the music industry is very interested in seeing people become gay. In fact they are so interested in it that they spend millions of dollars in promoting it. They even show it on their highest rated television event called the Grammys. Of course you got to ask yourself when was the last time we saw Christian lessons given such a stage. It is sad that many people who profess Jesus Christ as GOD and Savior refuse to see how unfair, and clearly hateful that is to not allow the other side of the defense to be openly spoken in the same manner.

At that Grammy event the world got to see a performance done by an artist named Katy Perry. After the performance was over people began to seriously wonder if Katy really is into witchcraft.

The artist herself stated that she stopped being a Christian a while ago. She even stated what impulse her to enter the mainstream music industry.

Katy comes from a well to do Christian home. Her father was a minister, and Katy discovered her gift for music while performing in the Church her father ministered at. According to Katy herself she stated that she tried to enter the Christian Music scene, and she wanted to become the next Amy Grant, but something happened to Katy while trying to make it in that industry that caused her to change her musical direction. According to Katy she had an encounter with Satan, and she sold her soul to him to get entrance into the mainstream music industry. Many people think that Katy was not serious or she meant something, or she was misunderstood, and so on, but Katy never took back her words, and she simply never brought it up again.

Katy Perry reached mainstream fame when she released the single called I Kissed A Girl. The song was done to promote homosexuality among young females. These young females were very young as the song was released to reach girls from 10 to 18 years old. Sadly this song became a smash hit song all across the nation, and became another gay-anthem song for gay females. Katy's father at first supported her daughter when she entered the mainstream music industry, but when her songs were coming out, and he saw the image she was projecting he would have a meeting with his daughter.

No one knows what was said during that talk but whatever it was it induced Katy's father to tell the Church that he thinks his daughter is being used by Satan. Her father did not disown Katy as some might think, and in fact he is still seen visiting his daughter from time to time, but there is something that Katy's father knows about his daughter, and he believes that it is evil.

Katy would score another smash hit single when she teamed up with Kanye West to record a song about a human female having sex with an 'alien'. The video, and lyrics to this song are very disturbing. She sings about a total demonic possessed experience while engaging the 'alien' in a sexual act. According to insiders they believe that she was really singing about Lucifer who is Satan in the Bible. In the song Katy describes the 'alien' as a being that is of supernatural energy which is a very different description then what people usually say about 'aliens'.

The Bible shares such a view about Satan as being a supernatural being made of 'fire' where the term is related to a being of energy. In this case it would be a being of living energy who is vastly more intelligent than human beings. This is how Katy presents the 'alien' in the video. What is sick about it is that she is singing about the pleasures of having sex with it.

More of Katy's music, and videos carry themes that are satanic, lustful, and even themes that can be understood under the teachings about mind-control. In a video she did with rapper Snoop Dogg who is called Snoop Lion now, Katy, along with a fleet of female dancers, present themselves as teen sex slaves who are fed with candy by their handler who is played by Snoop Lion in the video.

Other videos would carry satanic mind-control themes as well. Her recent videos have been promoting the beliefs of witchcraft. In these videos Katy dresses as a witchcraft priestess who is casting spells. The videos shows common witchcraft imagery while telling lore stories. At the 2014 Grammy Awards she would present herself on stage dressed as a witch, and the entire stage theme was loaded with witchcraft imagery and items used in witchcraft rituals.

Another artist named Lil' Wayne who is a rapper made a recent claim that he was the new Tupac Shakur. Of course he fails to explain how he could call himself that. His music, and videos are nowhere near the kind of real truth that Tupac would rap about. His videos, and music are more about some very evil, twisted, satanic, and murderous things.

Take the song he did called Love Me. In this rap song Lil' Wayne portrays dozens of women locked in cages, and made to roll around, and wrestle in blood. He portrays horrible blood-shed, and abuse as being sexual. He raps about these women as if they were nothing but slaves to be tossed about, and discarded. When an interviewer asked him about his opinions of black women in regards to how men should treat them he stated that black women only look good when they are 'red'. The meaning here is that they only looked good to him if they were covered in blood.

Lil' Wayne shows that he does have a very violent, and sick disposition. When Lil' Wayne was a pre-teen he became a member of a street-gang called The Bloods. It is not very clear as to what the extent of his crimes were but his arrest record, and testimonies from people who knew him stated that he is a person who more than likely murdered people.

Lil' Wayne has a few teardrop tattoos on his face just below his eye. It is known among many street gangs like The Bloods, and even other criminal groups that this tattoo means you have killed before for your gang. Lil' Wayne lived mostly with his mother before he became famous. His mother was not a normal mother. She was in full support of his gang activity, and supported it. She even helped him out in it.

When Lil' Wayne was about 13 years old he was raped by an older friend of his family. Lil' Wayne stated that he knew who the person was but he would never report the crime. His reasons for not reporting the crime was because according to Lil' Wayne he enjoyed the experience of being raped. This is not a mentally sound person but a person with some deep seeded evil issues. Many insiders state that Lil' Wayne is gay, and Lil' Wayne does not shy away from those questions. He has made it clear that he is bi-sexual, and it seems he is more into guys than girls. In fact there have been pictures of Lil' Wayne kissing guys, and sleeping naked in bed with them. Lil Wayne also is suspected of being very involved with satanic worship. He often expresses themes of satanic worship in his music, and videos wherein he made one video of having sex with Satan while he was transformed into a woman.

Lil' Wayne is also suspected of being deeply demonically possessed. Many strange stories are told about this. Some of the stories do carry some weight as they are from people who worked for Lil' Wayne. Often they would describe how he would suffer headaches, and talk to invisible people. One time he told his crew that he was really from the planet Mars. On stage he would begin to shake uncontrollably, and the other rappers would get away from him in fear that something took him over.

One time some video evidence came back when Lil' Wayne was on stage at an award show. On the video it showed for about a full second Lil' Wayne's eyes glowing in a strange yellow color. The video would be taken for analysis to see if someone may have tampered with it. The test showed that no one did, and after going through it again, and again no answer could be given for his eyes to glow like that on live television.

Many of the circle of friends Lil' Wayne hangs with are an, who's who of rappers, producers, and dancers wherein many of them are suspected of being gay like rapper Drake. Lil' Wayne not too long ago had went to jail, and when he came out he was more famous than before. A common occurrence in the rap industry. Lil' Wayne would find himself again with controversy when he used the American Flag to wipe the dirt from his shoes during the filming of a new music video he was doing.

Not too long ago we saw the rise of an artist named Kesha in the music industry. Kesha is a white-blonde female rapper who does pop-rap songs with lyrics that are dark, and sexually explicit. Her image and music is all about partying, getting drunk, rebelling on your parents, having all kinds of sex with whomever you want, and even embracing satanic themes.

Kesha's image has also largely portrayed witchcraft, and satanic symbols. She is very much into presenting herself as a lustful, sexual, and bloody occult leader. She seems to play the role of a high-priestess. The song that put Kesha over the top in the music industry was a song called Die Young. This song when it was first released became a major smash hit song across the country, and it was constantly played on the radio. Kesha's fan base by this point were mostly young females ranging from 6 to 18 years old. Even the parents of these young fans openly professed to be Kesha fans, and they openly loved the song Die Young.

When people saw the music video to this song that is when some people started to wonder if there could be some evil message behind the song. Most people also liked the music video, and they never really gave a clear answer for why they like it. They would simply say they liked the video because they like Kesha. Well that is their right but let's us look closer at this video because there is some strange things in it. First look at the title of the song of the video Die Young. The name just about tells you what the song is going to be about. The song is about throwing a non-stop sex party based upon the belief that you may as well party as often as you can because as the song or Kesha would see it, life is pointless, and you are going to die soon anyway. This morbid outlook on young people is clearly not reality, and someone who is as smart as Kesha does clearly know that, but this song that she is doing wants you to think otherwise. The music video makes the meaning of the song even worse. The video features Kesha as an occult leader leading her coven to take over a Mexican Christian Church that is in a small town in Mexico. When she enters the Church with her coven, who are played by Kesha's dancers, a series of scenes follow that shows the coven engaging in ritual sexual acts in the Church while doing dance numbers to the tune of Die Young. Of all the places Kesha could have picked to throw this dirty music video party she picks a Church setting to do these nasty scenes in.

It amazes me that Kesha actually has Christian fans who completely overlook that. In occult understanding to have an orgy in a Christian Church is to defile the place, and disrespect GOD. Kesha uses so many occult references in her songs, videos, and photo-shoots that it would not be wise at all to think she wouldn't know that. She has done television interviews expressing the fact she studies occult knowledge. The music video tells the story of a coven who invades a Church just to throw a sex party in there knowing that when it is over the police would come and gun them all down. That is why they are all singing 'were gonna die young'. Somehow the music video makes them all come off as heroes or something for dying for their right to trespass on Church grounds just to have a sex orgy in there. It amazes me that mom, dad, and kids got together on a live morning news broadcast from New York City square to watch a performance from Kesha who would be singing this song. While singing the song live on morning news television Kesha, in front of all the little children in attendance, would take some time to show these young ones how she enjoys smacking the butts of her male dancers. She would also wear a skin-tight dress with a center design on her body of a upside down cross also called the inverted cross. This symbol in the occult is worn to mock the faith of Jesus Christ, and to declare the death of Christianity. Once again I think Kesha would know that. It was also rather an extreme choice to wear a dress like that, and do a song like that live in front of an audience mostly made up of moms, and their little daughters who appeared in the thousands, and also only looked about 6 to 13 years old. The popularity of this song came down when another school shooting massacre took place at Sandy Hook.

This event has been under constant investigations by many journalists, writers, and investigators for being a false flag event while others believe the event actually happened. Whatever you believe regarding it the event affected the sales of Kesha's single Die Young. The media at that time began to attack the song for a little while as they pushed the Sandy Hook story.

Kesha would release a media statement apologizing for the lyrics of the songs. She even would distance herself from the song at that time by stating that she really did not want to do the song, and that someone else wrote the song, and made her do it, but a previous radio show interview Kesha did revealed that she lied about those statements regarding the song Die Young. Kesha admitted on that show that she indeed wrote that song, and in fact she had to write the song five to six times over again because she really wanted the song to express who she really was. In fact she would add that she works hard on all the writings of her songs because she does not want to be misrepresented. This tells us that Kesha believes in the songs she writes about. She believes that the youth have nothing good to look forward to but for dying young. Of course I think Kesha would not include herself into that mix, she only views this on her fans.

Kesha got her start in the music industry as a song-writer. Kesha's background shows her to be a highly intelligent person having one of the highest I.Q.s among United States citizens. She would use her smarts to get into the music industry with the intentions of becoming an industry artist. The record company first brought her in as a song-writer, and Kesha would write hit songs for Katy Perry, Britney Spears, and a few others.

Kesha even appeared in music videos from Katy Perry, and

Britney Spears before she was famous. After writing hit songs for these artists Kesha would write a single for herself called Tick-Tock. The song was about throwing an end of the world sex party as Kesha rebels against her parents in the video, and leaves their home dressed in a slutty manner to seek out a group of strangers, and attend their sex party. While she does this the end of the world draws near in a series of scenes in the video. This is rather a strange concept for a pop music video but it's a concept she keeps repeating in her songs.

Kesha was also the one who wrote Britney Spear's end of the world song where the concept of that song was also an end of the world sex party held on Judgment Day. The Bible states not to be found sleeping on the day which is an unknown day that Jesus Christ returns to earth. On that day the Bible calls it the true end of the world day. That day is when Jesus takes his true followers and children home to a new world while he destroys this world called earth. The meaning behind 'not to be found sleeping' actually means not to be found in sin, and unbelief on the day Jesus returns, because if you are found that way it will be declared of you that you rejected the grace of GOD. That means you have no forgiveness for your sins, and it also means it will be too late to turn back. That means those people will go to Hell, but Kesha on the other hand seems to really encourage people to set themselves up in life where they could end up going to Hell.

Many insiders believe that Kesha is a Satanist who practices witchcraft, and studies the teachings of Aleister Crowley. This is hard to believe for many devout Kesha fans, and also it has not been proven either. The only evidence given is by the strange art-forms, and statements given by Kesha. At concerts done by Kesha, and her dancers Kesha came up with some really strange ideas that are only seen in the occult. One idea was to take an object that resembles a human heart, and appear on stage with it while drinking what looks like blood from it.

Often times Kesha does the blood drinking act to energize the crowds, and it also energizes herself. In the occult Satanists drink blood because it gives them a strange energy rush, and they even get high on it. Many believe that demonic events happen at such rituals where evil-spirits have been known to appear, and possess people. Why would Kesha choose such an act on stage, and do the act so hauntingly well it even brought her controversy? This controversy started when several very young female fans of Kesha were uploading videos on the internet of cutting themselves, and drinking their own blood. They stated that they were inspired by Kesha. Kesha really had no response to this but largely ignored it. These young fans also uploaded videos of taking their own urine and drinking it. This sick idea was also inspired by Kesha according to the young fans who uploaded the videos. They got this idea from a show Kesha did on MTV where she was keeping a bottle of her own urine in the van she was driving in. While riding down the road while the camera was on her Kesha took the bottle on a dare, and drank her own urine in front of millions of people watching on television.

The idea to drink waste comes also from the occult, and it is done to defile the body to such a point it would summon demons into that body. Of course the occult would call it something else. Aleister Crowley within his teachings stressed to his students the importance of drinking, and eating their own waste for spiritual power.

Within many of Kesha's songs there are lyrics that refer to Crowley's teachings. Kesha also began to promote a condom company for a lot of money. Strangely enough Kesha promised the condom company she would promote their product to her fans. What was strange about it was that many of her fans were not even 12 years old, but that did not stop Kesha from having condoms passed around at her concerts, and telling these young fans that if the condom breaks they have to name their baby after her.

Another strange event is when Kesha requested the baby teeth of her fans because she wanted to make a necklace out of it. Occultist often like to collect teeth for various beliefs based in superstition. Kesha's various photographs from her photo-shoots are also filled with occult symbols ranging from black magic, witchcraft, voodoo, Satanism, and a few others. She even has photos representing Illuminati symbols which is the worship of Lucifer.

In a song she did called Dancing with the Devil, Kesha raps about selling her soul to the devil to get out of the problems she was having in life at that time. Many people felt the song was biographical. One of her most twisted stage acts is called the penis costume. In this act Kesha has someone dressed up in a human-sized costume that is design to be a male penis and they are to dance around in this penis costume. The person who originally wore the penis costume, and so-called entertained the very young crowds with it, was Kesha's own mother. The idea for such a disturbing act could have came also from the occult.

In occult beliefs the male-penis is called a phallic symbol, and it is seen as a symbol of power with lustful energy. Occultist use it often to symbolize what is power to them which is to think with the lower nature. Kesha often does pop-rap songs about thinking with the lower nature. She often raps about meeting guys, and within five minutes of seeing them she raps about them taking off their pants so she can play with their male-member. Most of her songs are about hardcore sex, drug use, parties, and satanic themes. During certain radio interviews Kesha publicly told her fans that she had sex with a 'ghost'.

Kesha stated that she was not kidding about her statements while many of her fans still think she was kidding. What is strange about this is that many insiders believe she was telling the truth under what she believes it was, but to these insiders they think she was recounting an event where she became demonically possessed. Artist of today have continued the same awful themes, and the same sexual depravity as lust, and wealth is glorified to no end while morals decline along with the lessons of Christianity among the people.

The music industry clearly throughout its history has not helped in resolving these problems but rather capitalizes on it, and makes billions of dollars from it. They instead ignore the problems, and continue to promote artists like Nicki Minaj who's name comes from a French sexual term. The term came forth from couples who were swingers, and allowed another woman or man into their bed to have sex with. It means a three-way sexual encounter. Much of Nicki's music is all about satanic themes, twisted acts of murder, and sexual depravity.

The female rapper has even admitted to having problems with certain alter-egos who she believes are living inside of her. In her photo-shoots, and videos she often portrays herself as a mannequin, puppet, or a robot. Along with these mind-control themes are the satanic themes that accompany her image, and music. Much of the mind-control themes are very sexual in nature, and it seems to refer to a sexual sex kitten. Such an image often comes from the hidden world of prostitutes, and sex-slaves, but yet this artist's image is marketed to girls as young as 7 years old.

Nicki often talks about a spirit that lives inside her who she said is, 'an evil boy named Roman'. She states that this spirit was born out of rage, and hates everything in sight. She describes it as a rage filled murderous spirit. During camera interviews Nicki is often seen changing personalities, and her voice is even heard changing in mid-sentence. She will suddenly talk with a British accent, or with a dark manly voice. It became so noticeable it was even made fun of at an awards show. During those interviews Nicki would describe that she had several people living inside of her. One spooky footage showed Nicki's eyes turning into a form of serpent eyes for a split-second. This footage was taken back to be checked because it was so strange, and perhaps something happened in tech-terms that caused such a strange image in her eyes, but nothing was found to show that anything was wrong with the video.

What Nicki describes would be clearly defined under Biblical terms to be demonic-possession. Much of her history shows a lot of disturbing, and chilling events have taken place in her life that may have led her to some occult activity.

Today we have artists that are on the rise, and coming up through the music industry who continue twisted themes. Artists like female rapper Angel Haze whose major debut video was a rap song about kidnapping and murdering little children. In the video she appears as playing the horror film demon Freddy Krueger who became famous on screen for killing children, and teenagers in their sleep, but in her video she leads a band of kidnappers, and takes these children to a warehouse, and ties them up to chairs. Afterwards they present themselves as torturing, and killing these children.

It shocked me that she would use a song, and video like this in an effort to enter into the higher rankings of the music industry artists. I thought that there was going to be an outpouring of complaints done against this artist. I first saw the video on youtube where under every video there is the notorious comment section where anyone could type anything about your video. Even things that are twisted, and sick, but since this video was already twisted and sick I thought I might see some commonsense comments regarding the video. I thought wrong.

The first ten comments were from mostly men who were turned on by the looks of Angel Haze. They stated she was hot, and they were going to buy her album because she was hotter than Kesha, and so on. The next set of comments actually praised the song she did or they did not like the song. Sadly hardly any of them noticed the evils of what she was projecting in the video. Out of hundreds of pointless, stupid, or meaningless comments only a very few of them pointed out the evils of kidnapping, and murdering children.

There is also the artist named Taylor Momsen. Taylor Momsen gained fame among young fans by starring in a television show called Gossip Girl. Soon she revealed that she plays in her own rock band. Lately she has been trying to get serious notice for her band from the music industry record executives. Taylor, and her band regularly play at certain underground clubs that are known to be havens for satanic covens. Taylor herself has often promoted Satanism, and she never fails to wear satanic t-shirts that promote the Church of Satan. During a set of shows Taylor had a satanic t-shirt custom made for her. Along with the five-point star image at the center of her t-shirt she had the words, 'I fuck for Satan' also put upon the t-shirt. She even had herself photographed with the shirt on during a concert for media exposure. Taylor is also good friends with an up and coming artist named Iggy Azalea who is a female rapper. It seems female rappers have also become a trend today. It would be nice if they rap about important issues, but that is not what the music industry gives you anymore. Instead they give you Iggy Azalea who raps about young girls engaging in acts of fornication when most of her fans are still in the 5th and 6th grades. Iggy was actually celebrated by the media for a short time for being a positive role-model to little girls while wearing a dress that was exposing her underwear.

At the Billboard 2014 Awards we saw the performance of up, and coming singer Ariana Grande. Ariana not too long ago shocked the industry when one of her songs hit the number 3 spot on the Billboard 100 singles chart in early 2014. Since then insiders have stated that the artist made powerful friends but all the wrong friends. She soon started to wear Kabbalah jewelry, and she was often seen with Miley Cyrus. At the awards show she would wear her red Kabbalah bracelet along with an outfit that many said represented the black, and white magic belief known in the occult.

In closing upon this final chapter of this book some things should be said by me the writer of this book. This book was not written with the intent to slander, bash, or hurt any of these artists mentioned in anyway. As a Christian, and a writer my job was to simply find this information, and explain it as best as possible. I tried to be as accurate as I could to the information I found but this does not mean all this information is 100% accurate. In truth no information found anywhere could be 100% accurate unless the information was coming from the mouth of GOD himself. What I did was explain in a fair way the information that already existed, and was often not being reported on or even largely studied into. I do believe that there is a lot of strange things out there that cannot be just explained as some crazy theory. There is more to the world we live in that tells us there are hidden things in this world.

As a Christian I believe that one of my duties is to tell the teachings of the Bible in regards to the things in this world. So the viewpoint I often come from is from a Biblical point of view. Many would be offend by that while many would understand. In truth I did not write this to offend anyone but to tell the other story that was not being told, and to allow the people to make up their own mind. I believe in fairness that if a subject comes up that all sides should be told so that all would be known to those who would have to make up their own minds about it.

The problems of the music industry clearly does go way beyond the power of the music industry artists. I do not think that the artists are to blame for these problems. These problems were already there when the artists arrived into the business. Many people will have different views on why these problems are there, and at the same time many will think there are no problems in the music industry. However, the view much of the information in this book are based upon facts that are not positive, and also very disturbing. Clearly rather we like it or not there are some serious problems going on behind the scenes of the entertainment industry that need to be exposed to the light. No one likes to hear bad things about the things they love, but also if these things were not in the field of reality to begin with then clearly it would not be wise at all not to think that bad things could be involved with it.

Either if you may be a Christian or not, one thing is clear that all of us know, within ourselves there is right, and wrong in this world. There are crimes, and victims in this world. It would clearly be a crime not to tell someone that is standing in the middle of the road blind that a truck is coming full speed at them. Information helps people to better understand the world around them, and often this kind of information does not always feel good, and it can be very sad to realize, but life is like that as well regardless of this information. It does not always feel good to know, and do the things we do to get by. Information is part of life because it comes from things going on in life that is not kind because the world rather you believe in GOD or not is filled with evil.

Fame, and success holds all the trappings of that evil because it holds the desires of all men, and women deep down inside them. The desire to be adored, and loved by all. This desire comes with power because the famous person can reach deep down into the soul of a person and can literally change their way of thinking. Power like this we tend to forget is dangerous, and people throughout history have been hurt by power like this in all kinds of horrible ways. Power like this should be used with caution, and with care, and I personally think that the only influence that can guide power like that for the benefit of humankind is through the person, and lessons of Jesus Christ. Others will clearly disagree or take offense to that but when Christianity is truly put into action it has been proven that under accurate teachings it can heal the scars of humanity.

Once again everyone must decide for themselves. My intent is that many will pray for the souls of these artists, the people, and for ourselves, and family.